# THE PRICE OF THORNS

## TIM SUSMAN

The Price of Thorns
Production copyright Argyll Productions © 2023
Text copyright © Tim Susman 2023
Published by Argyll Productions
Dallas, Texas
www.argyllproductions.com

Cover design by James T. Egan of Bookfly Design
Map by Teagan Gavet
Interior design by Argyll Productions

ISBN 978-1-61450-580-8

First Edition Trade Paperback

*For Kobalt*

# CONTENTS

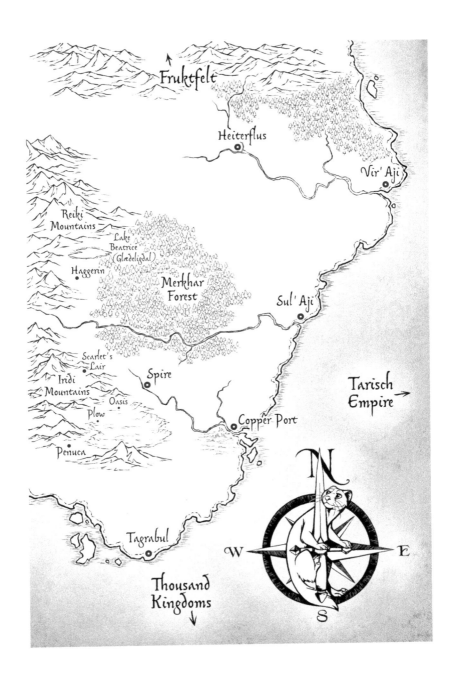

Fruktfelt

Heiterflus

Vir' Aji

Reiki
Mountains

Lake
Beatrice
(Glædeligdal)

Haggerin

Merkhar
Forest

Sul' Aji

Scarlet's
Lair

Iridi
Mountains

Spire

Oasis

Plow

Copper Port

Tarisch
Empire →

Penuca

Tagrabul

N

W          E

S

Thousand
Kingdoms
↓

§ I §

# THE THIEF

## ❧ 1 ❧

# THE WHEEL

The spinning of the great wooden wheel Nivvy was lashed to had become a familiar disorientation, rightways up and upside down blurring together until he couldn't have pointed up even with an unbound hand. He could hear well enough, though. "Give you a penny if you get him in the head," said the slightly darker-skinned boy who'd just spun the wheel, walking back to the slightly lighter-skinned one cupping a tomato in his hand.

"Inira," Nivvy prayed under his breath, "please just send these dirt rats away so's I can finish working at these bonds, and I promise I'll make you proud. I can get out of this. I can—ah, shit."

Even spinning as quickly as he was, he could track the lanky farmer boy's arm as it wound back and then shot forward, releasing its missile. It was going to miss him, no, the wheel was bringing him around to—

The tomato smacked Nivvy on the temple, bursting into juice and seeds that spun into his eyes and hair. "Oy!" he yelled as the boys laughed. "That one wasn't even rotten!"

He'd had food thrown at him in his childhood when he'd ventured out from the Shallows into the city proper, but it had always been rotten (usually fish). Even in the well-to-do parts of Copper Port, fresh fruit and vegetables were expensive. Here in a little farm town on the edge of a desert, where somehow they grew tomatoes and radishes (the other things that had been thrown at him), they should, Nivvy felt, be even more selective about what they threw. With his hands bound, he gave vent to his frustration. "Wasting perfectly good food like that. Y'oughta be ashamed!"

The spinner had just handed a penny to the thrower, and now they both turned to stare at him. The wheel turned in that jerky way it had, speeding up as the rocks tied to his feet descended and slowing as it tried to lift them around the other side. "Reckon he's right," the thrower said to the spinner, and stooped to the ground, rummaging in the dirt.

"No, no I'm not." Nivvy spoke quickly, sideways as the wheel's momentum tried and failed to make one more revolution. He started to spin back the other way slowly, an easier target. "One of my faults, you see, I—hey! You! Uh—farmer boy! Sign says you're not to throw rocks!"

The lighter-skinned boy had straightened up with an egg-sized rock, or, if the gods were smiling, a clump of earth, in his hand. "Don't see nobody here minding the sign," he said.

"When Kingsley comes to set me loose, I'll tell him." Nivvy knew that there were times in his life when it would be better for him to stop talking, but so far, he had not managed to recognize a single one of them before it happened.

"Oh aye? What name will you give?" The boy hefted the rock.

*Clump of earth. Clump of earth.* Nivvy had a strong belief in the power of faith, but it had been sorely tested of late. In this backwards town with one inn and a profusion of young farmer boys with identical dirty faces, huge hands, and simple brains, he had wondered more than once if this experience was a test of his faith or a mockery of it.

He'd settled upright again, barely rocking from side to side as he sorted through the farmers' names he'd heard in his two miserable days here. "Janin's boy."

The boy and his friend exchanged grins. "All the better. He'll get the blame for it. Two filthy birds with one stone." He cocked his arm back, and Nivvy squeezed his eyes shut, not to avoid seeing the stone, but to protect them.

It hit him on the nose, and it was a sharp stone as well as a heavy one. The boys' laughter faded with their footsteps as blood trickled down from both inside and outside Nivvy's nose, mixing with drops of tomato juice. *Faith*, he thought, *must be that Inira is teaching me a lesson here. Perhaps I am not skilled enough to release myself from this wheel.* He had been avoiding this thought, spurred on by the minimal success of having worn through one of the many strands of rope with his finger-nails over the course of an entire day. *Consider it learned, my Goddess! Sometimes I do need help. If you send someone to release me from this wheel, I'll never again think so much of my skills that I underestimate someone's cleverness just because they happen to be riding along Nowhere Road.*

He occupied himself for a few moments with venomous thoughts of revenge against both the merchant's wife who had felt the compulsion to check on her jewelry after a perfectly ordinary burst of lightning, and against Kingsley, the innkeeper and de facto lawman of the town. For a theft in which all the stolen goods had been recovered, banishment was usual in every civilized town Nivvy had known. But the good citizens of Plow had built a wheel like they'd heard of in stories from the long-ago times, the kind of thing nobody in civilized towns had done for hundreds of years, if they ever actually had—stories were just stories, after all—and having built it, they were all very excited to use it, no matter Nivvy's very sensible and logical arguments to the contrary.

The thoughts of revenge helped distract him from the tickling of the blood and the metallic taste of it. It would dry eventually, if the sun remained out, and there was no indication that it would do anything but. His tongue, in fact, was already thick and dry, and licking the blood from his lips just made it sticky and foul-tasting. Blood and tomato juice made a terrible concoction. He sighed and went back to working at the rope binding his hands, because that was better than doing nothing for the remainder of the day.

A shadow fell over him. He flinched instinctively; nobody was supposed to touch him directly, but he'd already experienced how effective the sign was when Kingsley wasn't around.

"So this is what I've been reduced to," a harsh female voice said to his left.

He turned his head until it hurt, enough to see a red velvet dress frayed and mended in several spots, with dirty lace at the collar and cuffs. The neck and chin above it were white as porcelain, but not porcelain that was sitting in someone's cabinet waiting to be liberated from its pristine prison. They were more like porcelain one would find in the back of some peddler's cart, a mismatched set dusty and cracked, not worth the trouble it would take to shout, "Guard coming!" to distract the peddler as you swept the pieces under your cloak. To one side of the neck, Nivvy could see strands of black hair, but the woman's face was hidden in shadow.

This was not the kind of person he expected to see in Plow. Even the nobles he'd been stealing from had been on their way from one better place to another, and though this woman's better days were clearly well behind her, she still dressed and spoke well enough to mark her, like Nivvy, a stranger in this town. "Aye, well, we've both been reduced, then," he said. She wasn't throwing anything at him, and that was a good thing.

"I presumed that your natural state was not being covered in your own piss and blood." Her voice had a haughty tone fractured with notes of uncertainty, and an accent he couldn't place. Northern, maybe. She brought a hand to her nose. "Oh, and you've soiled yourself worse than that."

He couldn't throw back stones at the boys, but when someone lobbed words at him, those he could return. "You get up here for half a day and then an entire night and then half of another day and you see how long you stay pretty and clean. Anyway," he said, "not all that soiling is mine."

"Do you think that makes it better?"

"Depends on whether you're asking after my predicament or my self-control," he said. "And what business have you with either?"

"I'm in the market for a thief. I was brought here to find one, but I wasn't expecting to have to hire a thief who's been caught and humiliated. There must be more to the world than this."

Odd thing to say. "I was only caught," Nivvy said with affected confidence, "on account of a freak lightning strike that panicked a twitchy merchant's wife an' made her run out to check on her precious horse."

He would've gone on, but the woman gave a small sniff and turned. Her footsteps carried her behind the wheel and out of his sight and then stopped. She'd wanted to make a great show of leaving but wasn't sure enough to follow through. Or perhaps it was a test of his abilities. Either way, he stayed quiet until he heard that threadbare dress rustle.

Quickly, then. "I reckon you'll likely head to Penuca then, that being the nearest town with a Thieves' Guild, and there you'll find as many thieves as you might need. But if you had gold to pay a professional thief, I wager you wouldn't be trudging through shit-strewn roads on the edge of the desert looking for one. So you'd likely..." Here he paused for a spate of coughing that did nothing to help his throat. "... walk around seedy back alleys asking after unguilded thieves and end up robbed or with that pretty throat slit."

Nivvy smacked his lips and hoped that had convinced her. He didn't have many words left in him.

Another farmer's boy stormed up, indistinguishable from the rest. "Oi!" he yelled. "You been telling tales 'bout me?"

"Janin's boy?" Nivvy rasped.

"Aye, and what's it to you? I never done nothing to you." Unaware of the irony, the boy stooped to pick up a clump of earth. Definitely just a clump of earth.

"Begone," the lady said. "I am speaking with this wretch."

"No skin off me back," Janin's boy said. "You can speak while I teach him a lesson. He got two ears, ain't he?"

"I said *begone*! May your skin erupt in boils that attract spiders!"

She stepped in front of Nivvy, so he couldn't see her face, but she stood tall and regal. One arm came out as though she were going to throw something at the boy, and then she simply extended it commandingly. Janin's boy, who could see her face, flinched when she cocked her arm, but when no spell or rock came forth, he threw his missile at her.

It struck her on the hip. She dropped her arm and he laughed, at which she picked up the object (it was a rock, definitely a rock) and threw it back at him.

He watched the rock land a good ten feet in front of him and five feet to the left. "Whore," he jeered back at her, and walked off in the direction of the inn.

"That was a good curse," Nivvy said sincerely.

The woman's posture sagged. "It didn't work," she said. "None of them do anymore."

Now, with the hood of the cloak settled back, he had a clearer view of her features. Fine porcelain in disrepair, aye, that described her well. Her jet-black hair would likely be striking when properly coiffed so that the stray hairs didn't frame her face like grasping tendrils; her eyebrows were thicker than was proper for a lady, at least in his experience of ladies dressed in finery. Her pale skin showed red at the top of her high cheekbones where the sun had borne down on her, and a filigree of lines on her brow and at the corners of her mouth marked her as older than Nivvy probably by two decades, if not more. That mouth, thin and severe, parted to reveal teeth that would have been perfect if not for the yellowing. "When are you due to be released?"

"Midday tomorrow," he said. "If Kingsley remembers."

She considered the wheel. "If you accept my commission, I'll release you now and we can be quit of this town before anyone's the wiser."

Since parting ways with the Thieves' Guild a year or so prior, Nivvy had been searching for that one job that would make his reputation anew, one that would let him either return to the Guild triumphant or (in his wild dreams, but such things had been told in stories) found his own. In the course of that search, he had listened to many proposed jobs for an independent thief and found that generally what distinguished them from Guild jobs was that they paid much less. In the few cases where the payment felt sufficient, said thing was guarded by the kinds of large groups of well-armed paid murderers that Nivvy generally preferred to meet in nightmares, because at least then a body could wake up with no more damage than sweaty nightclothes. So by and large, when people asked him to steal something for them, especially people who didn't look like they could pay for his quality of thieving, his response was a polite but firm "take a walk into a wave." However, exceptional circumstances allowed for a rewriting of rules, and besides, this woman had an air about her, something different than the usual unwashed unscrupulous undesirables he'd spent most of his time with over the last year. "What's yer job, then?"

The woman lifted her pointed chin and spoke formally, as though reciting. "My name is Bella and I have need of a good thief. Failing that, I could use a merely competent thief, and—"

Pride overrode the complaints of his throat. "I'll have you know that I am an uncommonly talented thief."

She arched one eyebrow up, which drew his attention to its thickness. "What is uncommon about your talents?"

"No, it's an expression. It just means very talented." Her eyes widened and traveled up from his to the leather bindings that lashed his hands to the wheel. "All right, yes, but look, you know the Tarisch Empire, across the eastern ocean?"

"Yes," she said slowly.

"My second job for the Guild, I stole the jeweled brooch of the emperor's daughter from the topmost tower of the royal palace. Now, the palace itself is in the midst of a compound full of armed guards, and the tower stands two hundred feet off the ground, so I says to myself—"

"I'm not interested in the details of your exploits."

"Well, I stole it, is the point, and they didn't catch me."

"It's conveniently far away," she said. "Which Thieves' Guild could I apply to to find out the truth of that?"

He looked away from her. "It'd be at Copper Port."

"I don't know that place. Is it far from here?"

Her tone was light; she was toying with him. "Go on with what you want, then," he said. "Maybe it's more difficult to nick than Princess Chakali's brooch."

The eyebrows lowered and her feet shuffled. The confidence she'd demonstrated up to that point faltered slightly. "I need you to help me steal a kingdom."

Deference battled with the need to set someone straight, and it was a short, quick battle. "See, the problem with that," Nivvy said, "is that kingdoms are big. People notice when they go missing. And I've never tried to stash a kingdom under my cloak or cross a river with one, let alone sell one in a free town somewhere. I imagine it might be done, but—"

"Funny," she interrupted him. "I knew a fellow once who wagged his tongue like that. He was so proud of it I had it cut out of his mouth and hung from the palace gates where everyone could admire it."

Nivvy shut his mouth quickly. His tongue might be dry and sticky with blood and tomato, but he still very much preferred it remain attached.

Bella went on. "The kingdom is mine by right. It was taken from me a long time ago, but I have recently...found a way to restore myself to the throne. But I need—it will be easier with assistance."

"Speakin' seriously and not tryin' to be funny," Nivvy said, "T'other thing about big things like kingdoms is they tend to be guarded quite well. Steal even the princess's brooch, you might get a flight of crows after you. No great shakes for an accomplished dodger and scarper-mancer such as yours truly. Even got a cantrip or two myself. But the really important royal family things, like crowns and scepters and thrones, they've got end-of-days magic around 'em. Earth splitting; monsters out of stories, like dragons, amassing; entire armies gettin' turned to stone. And not even a stone like marble where you might at least make a nice statue; no, they say when the wizard Gibberfit was defending Ivernia from the invaders, he turned them to sandstone, and they wore down in one generation."

"Gibberfit was an idiot," Bella said. "And anyway, that kind of magic is rare."

Nivvy had not seen any of the aforementioned magic in person, nor known anyone who had, but they showed up often in stories, and he did have some experience with magic. "Aye, that kind of artifact is rare, but that's where you tend to find 'em these days. And any kind of dealing with wizards is dangerous. Mate of mine, Marzin, he tried to steal from a wizard and got turned into a toad."

"How unfortunate," she said in a bored voice.

"You've no idea! I carried him around in a box to make sure he didn't get crunched up or stepped on. Least he could talk, even though after a while he mostly talked about how different bugs tasted."

"You won't get turned into anything," she said.

"I agree, but mostly because right now I don't see as I'd be interested in tryin' to steal a kingdom."

"You haven't heard what I'd pay you."

This was the part where they named their price, which was never as appealing as they thought it would be. He'd been paid three gold crowns for his part in the brooch job and never seen anything that rich again. Not even the ruby crown job had paid that much, though there had been other benefits to that one.

She cleared her throat. "I can offer you one hundred gold crowns."

He couldn't help it; he laughed out loud, hard enough that the wheel listed to one side and then slowly rotated back. His laugh turned into a dry cough that stung his throat. "A hundred!" he said when he recovered his speech. "'Zbells, if you had that kind of coin you'd be wearing a nicer dress, milady."

The unsure expression hardened on her face, and her lips pursed into an even thinner line. "I will pay you from the treasury when the kingdom is mine."

"Ah ha ha, payment on completion," Nivvy said. "That's a refrain I know well. I prefer to hold to the Thieves' Guild requirement of half payment before the job starts."

"If I had fifty gold crowns, do you think I would be standing here in filth talking to an even filthier wretch?"

"I don't know, milady," he said. "It's a problem, it is. And by the way, your feet look very lovely, and you've sidestepped the worst of the filth, I see."

"I'm not certain I have," she snapped.

"All right, even if I did take your word..." He paused to cough again. The bitter tomato taste was getting worse the more it dried out. "We both need to be cleaned up, we'll need food and other supplies, I shouldn't wonder, and where's all that to come from?"

She drew herself up. "I see," she said. "Well, perhaps Penuca will hold a thief willing to take a little risk for the prospect of a great reward." Without waiting for an answer, she turned and strode back behind the wheel again.

A great reward. More than the gold, a thief who helped a queen regain her kingdom would certainly be a figure of stories. The far-off dream of heading his own Thieves' Guild did not seem quite so unattainable to such a figure. Those louts in Copper Port would have to swallow their pride and welcome him back. And oh, he could see his uncles again, head held high.

But...what were the chances that a true queen, deposed and in want of a thief, would find herself in Plow, of all places? She'd go to Copper Port; she'd go to Spire.

Unless she'd been guided by Inira. Unless this was the answer to Nivvy's prayer. What did his uncle Foli always say? "When the tide brings you a silk scarf, grab it, because the tide can take it away again." Even if a kingdom wasn't in his future, she could be the way to a more modest goal of his. Cleaned up, she could get him back into a Thieves Guild, if not the Copper Port one exactly.

"Wait!" Nivvy called out.

"No, I don't think I shall," she said. "You've made your position very clear. I wish you luck in finding a patron who can hold to your guild's rules."

"The thing is," he said, and coughed. "The thing is, I might take immediate release from the wheel in place of some of the coin."

"I couldn't ask you to lower your standards," she said. "I don't want to hire someone who takes work that's beneath him. I want someone worthy of the job."

"How can you know I'm not unless you give me a chance?" he said. "How am I supposed to prove myself bound to this infernal punishment?"

For several seconds he waited, but she neither took a step away nor spoke. With every silent second, Nivvy's bravado retreated. Don't beg, he told himself. Nobody will respect a thief who begs. "I'll do yer job," he said finally, in a soft, husky voice. "If you believe it can be done by a thief, then I believe it can be done by me."

When finally she did speak, she regained her dry, confident tone. "I will trust in the spell that brought me here. I fully believe that within one month, our wheels will have turned, and we shall be in far better circumstances." She walked around to the front of the wheel, gave him a not-altogether-reassuring smile, and reached for the nearest binding.

## 2

# A NEW DESTINATION

"Right," Nivvy said when he was down, "let's scarper before someone notices." No better indication of how pissant this town was than how deserted it was in the heat of the afternoon. Still, another farmer's boy was sure to come along before too long.

"I don't 'scarper,'" Bella said. "And I think the first thing you need is a bath."

"The first thing I need is my horse and pack." He could live with his soiled clothing, but he needed tools and a way to get places he couldn't walk, and besides, Rahila was the closest thing he had to a friend these days and he wasn't going to leave her in the care of dirt-brained tomato-mouthed shitbirds.

Nivvy made for the nearest building, a trading shelter thick with dust. From there he could see the Inn, the only one in town so it didn't even merit a name other than "Inn," behind which sat the stables. He massaged his hands and rocked back and forth on his feet. Being tied up for more than a day hadn't been kind to his extremities, and he needed them in proper working order.

Bella strode up behind him as he was coming up with a plan. "I hired you. That means you listen to me."

Inira save him, she was going to be one of those people. Well, he was no longer tied to a wheel. He was back in charge of his own fate. "Listen, Bella—"

"You may address me as Your Majesty," she said, drawing herself up.

Nivvy leaned against the rough wood of the wall. Already his fingers were recovering their nimble movement. "Funny, my impression was that you weren't Her Majesty yet and that's why you needed my help."

She scowled and tried the staring trick on him, and Nivvy stared right back, no dull-witted farmboy, he. Her frown deepened and then she gave up the staring contest. "Fine. What do I call you, then?"

"My name's Nivali al Tamsin, but most people what know me call me Nivvy, so that's what I answer best to." He pointed at the Inn. "My horse and all I own in this world are over yonder. Where's your horse?"

"Dead," she said.

He stopped his planning to turn back to her. "Not like I ain't heard of riding a horse to death, but seems to me whenever I have, it was to get to a place a sight better than this town."

She sighed. "My horse, my beloved Svartheste, was taken from me when I was sent to my banishment. She must be long in the earth by now even if she did survive the coup. She would allow no other on her back."

"Well," Nivvy said, "I'm right sorry to hear that. So...how did you come to this place? No, no." He stopped himself. "Tell me the story later. Right now we need to get my horse and put this town behind us."

"And get a horse for me," she said.

"You can ride on Rahila's back. She won't mind."

"Mister Nivvy—"

"Just 'Nivvy.'"

"Nivvy." Her lips twisted as though the name were sour without the honorific. "I will have my own horse."

"Aye, yes, you will, I'm just sayin' maybe we get out of here first and then see to other things like a bath, another horse. Because if I get caught here, then I'll be back on the wheel with you tied next to me for the crime of settin' me free."

"They wouldn't dare." Her eyes, steel-grey, looked daggers out at the town.

"Trust me. They would an' they will." He admired that resolve and bearing. Even if the clothes weren't quite regal, she felt like a queen. "Which way we headed from here?"

"The kingdom of Heiterflus lies hundreds of miles to the north, but

I believe we are near one of the last—perhaps indeed the last—person I might consider a friend. We must visit her first."

"Right." Footsteps intruded at the edge of his hearing, not at the square but maybe just beyond it. "Which direction is this friend?"

"There was a place where the earth split and a pillar of fire erupted from a mountain—"

"A volcano, you mean. We're headed for Spire, then, got it." The footsteps stopped, and he knew they'd noticed the empty wheel. He dropped his voice to an urgent whisper. "All right, here's what we do. You're going to go out into the square and tell the people that you saw me runnin' off that way." He pointed the opposite direction from the Inn. "I'll make my way over to the stables. You can't see 'em from here but they're just to the left of that building, you see where I mean?"

She followed his finger. "Yes, I see it."

"There'll be a stable boy there. Distract him, and when you hear my horse ridin' off, walk out to the edge of town and I'll find you."

"Get two horses," she said.

"That'll take longer. We won't have much time."

"I'll make sure you have time." She stared at him.

He felt his will buckle under the weight of her gaze and forced himself to push back. "You're my employer, aye, but I'm the expert in the field an' I know how long it takes to steal a horse, even a horse that's yours to start with."

She lowered her brow. "Get two horses," she said. "If the stable boy interrupts you, you may ride off on your own steed and you needn't come back for me. Take the hours of your life you would have spent this afternoon on that wheel as a gift, and—"

"Fine, yes, fine, two horses it is." A call had just come up from the square as a second set of footsteps joined the first. "Go tell them you saw me run off and I'll see you on the road outside of town that way." He pointed toward Spire.

Her pursed lips and deep frown told him she didn't like being ordered around, but time was of the essence here and she'd have to learn that. She spun and stomped out from behind the building. "I spotted that filthy wretch running off!" she called out. "There!"

Two voices replied in thanks, and the footsteps cleared off in that direction. Nivvy waited a second, then another, but the square remained quiet. Keeping his head lowered, he brushed his black hair down, hiding much of his face. Thus moderately disguised, he reached his left hand over to one of the flat metal shapes that circled his right wrist, bound together with leather.

Thanks be to Inira that the backwards dirt farmers hadn't cut his wristlet off. Probably didn't know what it was or just didn't care. He felt the familiar shape of the cloak under his fingers and murmured, "The Cloak of Shadows, lost by King Amlazar, found in the vault of Khil-Khatoum."

With that, he walked quickly and confidently across the square to the back of the blacksmith's forge. The feeling of being on a job, of being cleverer than the people around him, nimbler on his feet and quicker with his hands, warmed his chest, even though this was a small job compared to what he was capable of. He skipped around loose stones to stay on quieter packed earth, fully aware of how much he could risk with the spell cloaking him and staying in those limits. They were more than enough for him to get the better of this worthless town and get gone.

When he was sure he hadn't been followed, he crept around the Inn to the stables. Bella's voice came to his ear from nearby, stridently demanding something of, presumably, the stable boy. Good; she could follow a simple plan.

She might not have needed to, because his horse, good old Rahila, was tethered up outside. Couldn't be bothered to give her shelter; well, they'd just made it that much easier for him to take her back. And Inira smiled on him for once in the past month: next to his horse was another, a lighter brown than Rahila's lovely sepia, probably a day traveler getting overcooked radishes and tomato stew at the Inn. Not that Nivvy had any intention of taking a second horse, despite what he'd told Bella; trying to ride off while leading a stolen horse was just the kind of thing that got one caught again. But that horse had packs, and those packs probably contained something of value that could ease their travel at least to Spire.

His horse huffed as he got close, but when he put a hand on her withers and said, "Shh, shh, h'san, h'san," she calmed down. Just touching her made him feel whole again. He breathed in the rich, horsey smell and felt comfortable enough to release the Shadow spell.

When he'd left The Shallows, he'd stolen a horse from a stable and had named her Huriya, after a minor goddess of capricious breezes.

Huriya had died a decade ago, and Nivvy hadn't thought he would get another horse, but after a few years he missed the companionship, and so he'd bought Rahila with his Thieves Guild earnings. She'd been barely taller than he was then, and he had spent a good deal of his money keeping her fed, every penny worth it. His comrades at the Guild came and went, some of them retiring, a few killed or turned into a toad, but Rahila had always been with him. And when the rest of the Guild had blamed him for that job gone wrong, Rahila had stayed with him. Until Plow, they hadn't been parted for over a year.

After making sure she hadn't suffered from two days in the care of ignorant farmers, he checked quickly through his packs. They'd taken all his coin, as he'd expected, and his water, the bastards, but they'd left his dagger and his tools, his rope and his blankets, and, thank Inira, the small brass seal that they couldn't possibly have understood the significance of.

The first thing he did was cup his hands in the water trough. Warm and dirty though it was, it was a relief to wipe his face clean and to soothe his parched mouth and throat. After the third drink, he untied Rahila, and the mare stood patiently while he checked the pack on the other horse, his fingers undoing the laces and sliding inside, evaluating what they touched almost without Nivvy having to focus on it. His fingers slid past clothes and blankets to a water skin and a few trinkets of copper and wood—not spell tokens, as far as he could tell—that might fetch a price at a market in another town, and a wooden box that jingled when he moved it. He extracted the water skin, box, and trinkets, slipped them into his bag, then re-laced the other pack.

Though he didn't intend to steal the horse, he did untie her, feeling spiteful toward travelers in general at the moment. She merely blinked amiably as he swung himself up on Rahila and urged her away, past the inn, and out of this gods-cursed town.

"Well," Nivvy said as they rounded a curve in the road and he slowed Rahila down, "they do say that Inira's favor is fickle, so we must be glad she allowed us to find each other again. Those folk might easily have sold you or given you to the nobles as payment. Poor Bella will have to do with your back until we get to Spire. I might say it'd be a lesson in doing without, but I suspect such a lesson is lost on her." He rubbed a hand down Rahila's mane. "Perhaps I should say: Poor you will have to add her weight to mine."

Rahila, unconcerned by all this, tossed her head and trotted on down the road. There were no good places to hide; the brush came up barely to Nivvy's ankles, and the nearest trees looked to be too far off to wait there for Bella. But ten minutes on, behind a stand of scrubby bushes with small, waxy leaves, they found a few tufts of grass. He tied up Rahila to a bush and listened for nearby water, but didn't find any, so he gathered up his robe and sat next to his horse to wait.

It felt so good to sit, even with nothing to lean back against. He stretched his legs out and then folded them under him, and now that he was off the wheel and out of that town, reflected on Bella's job while he devoured a chunk of stale bread from his pack. Since he'd fled Copper Port, he'd wanted nothing more than to prove himself a real thief again. If Bella wasn't delusional and he could really do her job, that would be fantastic luck, but once-in-a-lifetime jobs didn't fall into the laps of disgraced thieves in the middle of nowhere. He wasn't going to build his hopes up only to watch the cold tide of reality wash them away.

If you wanted people to know you were a thief, and a good one, without having to prove it over and over again to them, you had to be a member of the Thieves Guild. Nivvy'd already gone through all that once, only to have it stripped away when his supposed fellows showed more allegiance to a dead comrade than to their living one. Vicho had taught Nivvy—he'd taught them all so much, and yet—well, that was why everyone had blamed Nivvy. That was why he'd blamed himself, at first; that was why a small, hard part of him still did. But to have everyone say it was his fault, well, he wasn't going to be lashed to *that* wheel.

It wasn't so much the people of the Guild that he missed (save for D'Alio, who'd helped him escape). It was the prestige of the Guild itself. There was a saying: "You can't join the Thieves Guild twice." Once you were in, you were in, until you were out, and then you were out forever. But Nivvy had found a loophole: If you were a Guild member from another town, you could join the Guild in a new town with a letter of recommendation from one of your old Guild members —or a contract from your old Guild.

If he could get Bella to clean up just a little, enough to pass for respectable, then she might be able to wheedle a blank contract out of the Thieves Guild in Spire. Nivvy could put his name on that, and the

Guild seal (that, thank Inira, he still had in his pack) would make it look legit. And then he could start over in some other Guild somewhere, Penuca maybe, and even if the Copper Port folks caught up to him, it wouldn't matter. He'd be acknowledged again as the thief he knew he was.

He'd thought of this plan first thing upon leaving Copper Port. The problem was that mostly the people who wanted to hire unguilded thieves were not people a Guild office would trust and issue a contract to. But with Bella's help, he could turn things around regardless of how this job came out.

There was more than a fair chance that she was not right in the head and this dream of a kingdom she wanted him to steal was nothing more than a story she'd told herself so often she believed it. All that talk of spells and being brought places and such? Anyone who had seen more magic than a few cantrips was either rich or dead, in Nivvy's experience. She'd no doubt tell him the rest of the details of the theft soon, but he wasn't worried that it would be beyond him so much as he was worried it would be completely imaginary. And yet, if there was a tiny chance that it wasn't...

Secure in his fallback plan, he let his imagination wander. He pictured himself stealing a royal scepter and presenting it to Queen Bella, standing at her side as she took power, and then riding back to Copper Port to clear his name and prove his worth. If he'd helped a queen regain her kingdom, he must needs be an extraordinary thief, and then that whole nasty business would be the merchant's fault and not his. As it should have been to begin with. Or maybe enough time had passed that everyone could agree that poor Vicho had been the victim of his one weakness.

Maybe when they forgave him, he would recruit the best thieves to join his guild. D'Alio, of course—without D'Alio's help he wouldn't have Rahila and maybe wouldn't even have his life—and maybe some of the others too, if they wanted to come. Marzin, if he were still alive. He could be the Guild mascot.

Nivvy wiped his face as clean as he could and chewed up all the stale bread, planning his path toward this bright future, imagining the shocked faces when he showed up in fine clothes and triumph, and somewhere along the way he slipped into a doze.

The shuffling of footsteps nearby brought him to full alertness.

From behind the bush he watched the road and stood with relief when Bella's red velvet dress swept into view.

He had a long time to observe it as she approached; back in town he'd mostly focused on her pale complexion and then on their plan for escape, which did not hinge on what she was wearing. Now it struck him that even among the many travelers of Copper Port, he hadn't seen a dress in that style: thick velvet fringed with tattered lace and bound with clasps and decorative pins rather than laces or buttons. But perhaps she came from the north, and who knew what the style there was these days? "Ho," he said with a wave.

She stopped a good six feet from him and drew herself up. The lines in her brow deepened as she stared at Rahila. "Is the other horse lying down back there?"

"There's only the one horse," Nivvy said. "I—"

She went on as though he weren't speaking. "I gave explicit instructions to bring two horses. I bought you more than enough time."

"Ay, well, Inira didn't provide. There was another horse, but she wasn't the right temperament."

Bella folded her arms. "If you can't follow instructions, perhaps I should simply find another thief."

He didn't know where she thought she was going to find another thief out here in the middle of nowhere, so he could've told her to suck it up, but he tried to explain. "In my professional opinion as a thief, if I'd tried to take that horse it woulda slowed me down an' then there'd be a crowd of dirty farmers comin' quick behind you down the road. You hired me to be a thief an' that means knowin' how to get the best outcome out of a job an' not"—that wasn't his fault, he reminded himself—"not puttin' myself or others at risk."

Bella's eyes narrowed as she examined Rahila, who did not appear to notice the scrutiny. Her unflappability was one of many things that Nivvy loved about his horse. At last, Bella reached a decision. "I suppose I can ride this one, but it will slow us down considerably to have you walk alongside. Still, it can't be helped."

Nivvy stared at her. "It would slow us down, an' that's why we're not doing that. Rahila can bear the two of us an' hardly slow us at all. Surely you must've shared a horse sometime in your life?"

"I don't object to sharing the horse, if absolutely necessary." Bella waved her slender hand in front of her nose. "I object to being in close quarters with you. You stink."

"Right," Nivvy said, "that's why we're headed for the oasis an' a bath. You think I like smellin' like this?"

"You seem well suited to it," Bella said.

He pursed his lips. "The oasis is a day away. If you walk, it'll be two days. You'll be near the stink either way."

"I'd rather thought that you would walk, since I'm your employer."

Nivvy congratulated himself on the restraint it took not to laugh. "Your thief I might be for the moment, but I won't be put off my own horse, not when you've yet to cross my palm with a single piece of copper, let alone gold."

"I'll buy your horse from you, then."

That almost broke his restraint, but he limited his reaction to a smile. "Even if you'd the gold in your fingers right this moment, Rahila's not for sale. She's the one good thing I've got left to my name and I'm not about to let her go." He untied her, pulled himself up onto her back, and guided her over to stand next to Bella, where he reached a hand down to the former queen. "Come on," he said with a smile. "I cleaned myself up a bit."

"Not nearly enough." Bella took a step back.

"First water we pass, I'll take care of the rest," Nivvy said. He wiggled his fingers. "Walk or ride?"

Somehow she looked down her shapely nose at him from the ground but did not answer. "If it helps," he coaxed, "you can look at the stuff I took off that other horse back there and see what you think it's worth." She wouldn't be as good a judge as he would, he was pretty sure, but at least it would keep her occupied so she didn't spend the whole ride complaining about how Nivvy and his clothes smelled like shit.

She looked away from him and spoke to herself, though not so low that he couldn't hear it clearly. Her hands gestured in front of her as though making a point to an unseen friend. "Won't be the worst I've had to endure, and the end will be worth it." With that she turned her attention back to Nivvy and straightened, her hands smoothing down her dress at her sides. "Part of our agreement," she said frostily, "is that you will never speak to anyone of this." She took a deep breath, grasped his hand in hers, and pulled herself up.

He had to admit that she had a natural way around horses, climbing up easily and settling in behind him as he moved up just behind Rahila's shoulders. She didn't wrap her arms around his waist or even settle them on his hips, not even when Rahila broke into a jerky trot before settling to a canter.

Small burrowing animals ran out of the dusty road as they approached, and crows perched in those waxy-leaved bushes cawed out a warning, but no other horses or men appeared before them. "Where are these items?" Bella asked as they made their way past scrub and sparse grasses. It sounded like she was holding her nose or at least attempting not to breathe through it.

"That pack behind your right leg," Nivvy said. "There's a wooden box and some copper figures."

Now she did put a hand on Nivvy's robe as she reached down and opened the top of the bag, doing it all without losing her balance. She pulled out the box and one of the copper things. "Mediocre craftsmanship," she said. "Just the thing one would expect a mediocre merchant to sell in a mediocre town."

"If you think that town was mediocre," Nivvy said, his spirits considerably heightened by feeling Plow recede in the distance, "then I don't want to know what you may have seen that was worse."

"The people in that town had most of their limbs, as a rule," she said, her voice growing less nasal, "and there didn't appear to be any disease, so yes, mediocre. Hm. This box, though, this shows some small amount of skill. The carvings here were done by a steady, skilled hand."

His opinion of her rose slightly; she'd an eye for craftsmanship. "Like as not that's his personal property and not to be sold. What's inside it?"

There was a click, and then the clink of metal. "Coin."

If Rahila's hooves weren't pounding below him and wind wasn't hissing through his ears, he'd be able to tell what metal from the sound. "Copper or silver?"

"Mostly copper. Three silver."

He reached his hand back. "Let me feel it?"

"Why?"

"I can count it. Let me hold the box."

"I can count," she snapped.

"I mean, I got a spell," Nivvy said shortly.

There was a pause. "You know magic?"

"Ay, well, one or two little helpful things." He waved his hand. "Only takes a second."

She shifted the coins around and then put the box in his hand. His fingers couldn't close all the way around it, but they didn't have to. He focused on the press of the three-coin token against his wrist and in his head recited, "*The three coins of Rezso the Fortunate, who knew each one of his ten times one thousand coins.*" The numbers swam into his head. "You said three silver? Then there's twenty-one copper. Not too bad. Enough to get some lodging and meals." There was no reply, so he shook the box. "I'm done, you can take it back now."

"What other spells do you know?" She lifted the box from his hand.

There were a couple he wasn't going to tell her about. "Shadow, I call it. Makes me kind of invisible, but not really, just makes people not really notice me."

"I see." She slid the box into the saddle bag again and took out the water to take a drink. "Might that not have been useful when you were trying to steal a second horse?"

"I did use it," he said, "only for one thing, it don't mask the sounds you make, and for another, if you're directly interferin' with someone's stuff then they're going to notice you, spell or no."

Her next comment seemed directed at nobody in particular. "Are there not even proper invisibility spells anymore? What has the world become?" She offered the water up to him.

He took it and gulped water, soothing his dusty mouth and throat. "If by that you mean spells what make you completely vanish, then ay, you could maybe learn one of those, but here's the thing about that. First off, holdin' a spell takes some effort. Even Shadow is pretty easy and it's hard for me to do much else when I'm holdin' it. 'Proper' invisibility like you say, I knew a chap took all the time to learn that and he couldn't hold it for more than ten minutes, fifteen at the outside."

"That would have sufficed to steal a horse." She made a clicking noise with her tongue. "I can't believe I'm arguing thievery."

"Second thing," Nivvy went on as he handed the water back to her, "is that 'proper' invisibility isn't some stroll in the orchard. Y'can't see where your feet or hands are, you trip on things an' bump into things, an' it still doesn't hide the sounds you make. You might not know much about thievery," he mocked her tone as he said the word, "but it turns out you do a lot of it with your hands, and it helps if you can see what you're doing."

"I had Unseen Servants who managed quite well," Bella replied haughtily.

Unseen Servants were things out of stories. One more tick in the "not in right mind" column, but you didn't argue with folk like that. "I'm certain you did. I suppose if one was invisible one's whole life, one might very well be used to it. But I," he waved a hand, "live in the visible world and that's where I do my best work."

"Fine," she said. "Any other spells?"

"Nothing related to thievery," he said. The Guild had rules about being honest with your employers up to a point, at least to accurately represent your skills and abilities, and Nivvy appreciated and approved of all those rules. He believed that as you do, so shall you be done by, and while he might liberate the odd piece of property, he tried very hard not to lie.

She didn't say anything for a moment, and then said, "At least we'll be able to buy another horse."

"I'll steal you another horse if you really want," Nivvy said. "We should spend that money on lodging."

"Another horse is more important. We can sleep anywhere."

"Horses and food are easy to steal. Lodging not so much. We should rest up and clean up and we'll steal another horse on our way out of town."

Bella huffed, close enough to the back of his neck that he felt her breath. It had been a long time since another person had been that close to him for longer than a few minutes. The sensation wasn't unpleasant. "Is everything going to be an argument?"

"Listen," Nivvy said. "You hired a thief to steal something. If you could steal it yourself, you would, and since you can't, maybe you should listen to the fellow you hired. I been doing this for fifteen years and I've at least been to Spire before. Have you?"

"No," she admitted.

"Right," he said, filing that piece of information away. "This country's ruled by a Suzerain and each of the cities has a King. Spire itself isn't where the Suzerain sits, but the King of Spire is pretty important and the reason that matters to us is that he has ideas about how thieves are treated. So first thing we gotta do is get a contract, a document that

THE PRICE OF THORNS

says you're hiring me, because that way if I get caught I won't get my hands cut off."

"I would say that if you're such a talented thief, you shouldn't worry about getting caught, but, well."

Nivvy half-turned and then focused on the road ahead. "Well," he said, "if you were such a great queen, you wouldn'ta lost your kingdom, so I guess fair's fair."

He was just congratulating himself on that remark when a blow caught him across the face and nearly sent him toppling off Rahila's back. His balance and riding posture kept him from falling, but only just.

"Are you crazy?" He pulled Rahila to a halt at the side of the road and turned. "You could've knocked me off the horse!"

"You will not speak to me that way." Bella's tone matched the icy, fixed set of her lips and the hard glare of her eyes, now more grey than green. From inches away it was even more intimidating, but Nivvy's blood was up and he'd forgotten about keeping her happy until they could get to Spire.

"All right, we're both in hard times," he said, "but I mean it, if you do something like that one more time, I'm putting you off this horse and you can find yourself another thief."

"I am a queen. You will treat me with respect."

"I was just statin' a fact," he said. "You're not a queen now. You hired me to get you back there. And I'm willin' to do the job, but there's bound to be enough risks along the way without you nearly killing me."

She scoffed. "You wouldn't have died if you'd fallen, and I would've brought the horse back for you."

He stared into her eyes. "Right," he said. "Off."

"What?" Fear cracked the ice of her demeanor.

"Off. I'll make my own way, in Spire or wherever. You can keep the coins from the merchant. Maybe you'll find another thief."

She didn't move. Her eyes remained locked on his, but the defiance was muted now, and the lowering of her shoulders suggested desperation, as it should when someone threatened to put you off a horse in the middle of the desert when you didn't know where you were. Nivvy didn't intend to push her off, but he needed her to know he wasn't joking. "Right now. We're done."

Finally, she spoke, her voice low. "You can't just quit."

"We got no contract, so what are you gonna do, get the Guild after me? Get in line." He shook his head. "If you don't respect me, I don't want to work for you. So."

She straightened. "I shall not strike you again." Though the words were compliant, the tone had regained some of its haughtiness, as though this were a decision she had made on her own.

"Fine." He relaxed.

"As long as you mind your tongue."

Nivvy exhaled. "I'm going to share with you something my uncle Foli told me a good while back. He said, 'Words can only hurt you as far as you let 'em in.' You don't think what I'm sayin' is right and respectful? Prove me wrong. I've been trying to prove I'm a thief to you; prove you're a queen to me."

"That doesn't make any sense. A queen must protect her reputation or else anyone might say anything about her. And," she added, "if people spoke publicly about their disrespect for you as a thief, it would lead to nobody wanting to hire you. So it could hurt you."

"Ay, perhaps, but if I go do good work," Nivvy said, "then people will talk about that instead."

Bella considered this. "Do you really believe that?"

"Well," he said, turning back to the road, "I'm tryin' my best."

As he was about to urge Rahila back onto the road, Bella said, "Actually, I think our first priority should be to find some kind of water, any kind of water." When Nivvy hesitated, she said, "I'm only stating a fact."

"Oh, no, I agree with you," he said. "We should be arriving at the oasis before the sun sets."

"Well before, if it is at all possible," Bella said as they set out.

## ✴ 3 ✴

## OASIS

The dry, dusty terrain did not promise a good deal of water, but after a short time Nivvy spotted a stand of trees and urged Rahila in that direction, off the road. The trees, with ragged bark and dark green waxy leaves, did not stand near water themselves, but from there they could see a depression in the land that shone green in the sun.

As they approached, shapes resolved out of the shimmering dusty haze that surrounded the oasis, carts and horses moving and stopped, small tents of brown and ochre that blended into the dusty landscape. "Not much water along this road, so it attracts people," Nivvy observed. "Even though the edge of the desert is a day that way."

"Obviously," Bella said. "In my day, we would travel with a dowser and wherever we stopped, he would find water and bring it to our camp."

"Heard stories about dowsers," Nivvy said. "Fairy tales."

"They were real wizards. I knew many of them."

"When was 'your day,' exactly?" Nivvy asked. "Come to that, what kingdom is it you've got your eye on? Hiter-something? I'd appreciate a few more particulars of this job before it gets much farther along."

"I'll tell you a little more when you've stopped and bathed." Her voice shifted; she was looking over his shoulder. "Will there be any trouble from the other people there?"

"Nah, not unless we start it. Places like this, there's a truce. We don't fight, we don't steal—unless you've a contract on a person, but even then it's proper to wait until they leave and then waylay them on the road."

"So many rules," Bella muttered.

"It's how we all get along."

"I suppose whatever king rules this oasis is above those rules."

Nivvy laughed. "No king'd bother owning this one. We're two days out of Spire an' you've seen the nearest town. Did that look like a place a king would take an interest in? No, it's just travelers make the rules here."

"How do people know the rules, then?"

"Posted. I'll show you when we get there."

And indeed, as they came up to the edge of the grass, Nivvy directed Rahila around to the wide road so that Bella could see the engraved stone standing there. "You can read that?" she asked.

Another of Nivvy's spells, one he didn't think it necessary to tell her, allowed him to read any language, so after a short recitation in his head (*"The scroll of Maza the Wise, to whom no secrets were hidden."*), he could read all three inscriptions, even the two that weren't in his language. "Ay," he said. "Can you not?"

"I can almost make out the last one." That one was his; the other two were from the Thousand Kingdoms. "But not all the words. I get the sense of it well enough."

"Basically what I said. No stealing, no fighting, no fouling the water."

"How are you going to bathe, then?"

He pointed along the road. "There's tubs. I'll fill one, wash off in it, then dump it on the ground."

"I suppose that will have to suffice."

"As it's our only option, ay, it will," Nivvy said, and urged Rahila along the road into the oasis.

The pond would have taken them maybe twenty minutes to walk a complete circuit around, but they didn't have to go that far. Every half-minute of Rahila's walk brought them to a small cleared area occupied by people, some of whom waved and some of whom ignored the two riders. On the opposite side of the oasis from the road, Nivvy found a space with no travelers on either side. "This looks like a good enough place to spend the night," he said, reining in Rahila.

"Spend the night?" Bella asked as he dismounted. He offered her his hand, but she dismounted without any assistance. "I thought we were merely going to clean you off and then be on our way."

"Have to spend the night somewhere." He pulled the blanket off Rahila and spread it out, then ran his hands over her back, smoothing and scratching where they'd sat on her. She whuffed in pleasure. "Rahila won't run through the night. She needs feeding, and so do we."

As he spoke, the mare lowered her head to crop the grasses. Bella looked around. "Are you going to eat grass as well?"

"If I must. I notice you brought nothing but those fancy clothes. How have you been eating?"

"I'm not hungry."

He squinted at her. "That's not possible. I'm starving, and you haven't eaten since we met either. It's been hours."

"It's not your concern," she said.

"So...will you be hungry, or am I only feedin' myself?"

"I was thirsty." She reached for the waterskin in the pack. "I suppose I will be hungry again in time."

Nivvy leaned against Rahila. A day and a half on the wheel with barely anything to eat had left him rather weak, but he'd endured—well, maybe not worse, exactly, but nearly as bad. "Is this a natural thing, this not needing food? Right now I can't imagine ever being not hungry."

"I suggest you go find food and a bath, then," Bella said. "Don't bother about me."

"Stay with Rahila," he said. "Don't go wandering off."

Bella eyed the mare. "What if she wanders off?"

"Her I trust," Nivvy said with a grin, and made for the oasis.

The baths all stood in the same area, six big wooden tubs. Nivvy found the one set farthest from the others, a learned precaution that had become habit. He thought of it as "the story of Hajimo a'Lorin," a story that, unlike most he knew, had been told to him by its subject. That and its direct relevance to Nivvy gave it a great deal of power in his mind.

Hajimo had been a merchant in Copper Port who sold spices and perfumes. Nivvy, newly apprenticed at the Thieves Guild, had stumbled across his shop with a meager hoard of coins, anxious to wipe the stink of the Shallows from him. The old man, higher-voiced and darker brown than Nivvy, had waved the young thief toward the dull, common oils that could be had for a copper a bag: musk, smoke, spicy citrus, rosemary, lavender.

But when Nivvy'd come to pay for a bag of smoke, a glint of recognition passed between him and Hajimo, a narrow, smooth face staring into a narrow, wrinkled one. The older man had taken his hand, searched his eyes, and then had said, "You's born different."

Only a week before had Nivvy cut his hair and stolen his father's robes. Everyone at the Thieves' Guild had accepted him as a boy without question, but this old man had seen through him? "N-no," he'd stuttered.

Hajimo had smiled. "You made y'self somethin' new, is what I mean." He'd tapped his own chest. "I's born different too. Go put that back, I'll find you somethin' what suits you better."

Nivvy'd followed him through the store, and Hajimo had declaimed as they went. "Copper Port isn't such a bad place to be different. Most everyone leaves you be. But you gotta be sure you're tellin' your story." His crooked finger had stabbed Nivvy in the shoulder. "You tell yer story in all sortsa ways, you do, some you don't know yer doing. You know how I know you's born different?" Nivvy'd shaken his head, and the old man had set a finger aside his nose. "You don't smell like a boy. Yet." His hand had traveled up the small cabinet of more expensive perfumes: sweet myrrh, sandalwood, rose, oudh-based oils. "The oudh is too expensive even for this," he'd chuckled dryly. "But sandalwood, yes, that works. Or the myrrh. Which one smells like you?"

Nivvy wouldn't have been able to afford either, but Hajimo had pressed the choice on him. "I—I like the sandalwood," he'd admitted.

"Fine choice. It's a strong scent, good for a young man."

Nivvy insisted on giving Hajimo what he could, and after accepting his thanks, the old man had fixed Nivvy with an eye. "Remember your perfume," he'd said. "You'll want to tailor that robe, too. I can send you to a woman who'll do it up right. And when you bathe, bathe in private —you know that—an' don't let yer clothes out yer sight."

"Yes, sir," Nivvy had said.

"It's your story," Hajimo had told him. "Tell it well, tell it completely."

The old merchant had died a year later, but Nivvy went to see him often. Knowing there was someone else like him nearby made that first year easier, and Hajimo helped him see the ways in which he could make his story more complete. Nivvy hadn't been able to afford sandalwood for a year, but he'd become adept at finding oils in certain bushes when there weren't any to steal. And he'd never, in more than a decade, bathed in a public place.

Travelers at an oasis weren't interested in other people's bathing. One's companions might be, but Nivvy felt very confident that Bella would not want to see him, so he set about filling the wash tub with an easy mind. Besides that, his clothes would need washing as well, so once he'd filled the tub (which took ten trips with two buckets), he plunged his entire body into the water without undressing. The chill seized him with shivers, but only for a moment. As his body acclimated to the water, he exhaled and leaned his head back to look up at the mauve and gold streaks appearing in the evening sky. Hope felt unusual and welcome after so long. In just a few days, he might have a way to return to the Guild, and perhaps more.

Relaxed as he was, he kept his ears attentive for anyone approaching, aware that every moment brought more chances for someone to intrude. Finally, he left off his pleasant dreaming and began to scrub the worst of the filth from his body and robes. Soon enough the water turned a pale brown, then so murky as to offend his sensibility, driving him to rise and tip the tub over. When it was empty, he brought buckets of water back, knelt in the tub, and emptied the buckets over his head. What he wanted was a good rainstorm, but the clear sky offered no relief on that front.

His robes would not be white again until he had them cleaned, perhaps in Spire, but they at least smelled better than they had, and he felt cleaner by a good bit. So he gathered a few dates from the palms, though they weren't quite ripe yet, and then walked back to where he'd left Bella and Rahila.

Bella was seated, in conversation with a turbaned merchant dressed in brightly colored robes who made a habit of stroking his beard as he talked. This Nivvy took as a very good sign, that a merchant of good station would consent to sit with Bella. It boded well for his plan to have her secure a Guild contract.

She waved at him as he approached, and said to the merchant, "This is my traveling companion, Nivvy. He's not usually this wet."

Nivvy went to stand against Rahila. He steepled his hands together and executed a bow, then spread his arms so his robes would dry more quickly. "Pleasure to meet you," he said. "It's been a long travel and I'd a great need to wash the dust from my body, or else I would join you."

"I am Suleimon al Alasi," the merchant said, pressing his hands together and bowing forward as Nivvy had. He gestured toward a horse just visible at the next clearing over. "I have been telling your lovely companion that I did not expect to find such interesting company on this lonely journey."

"How come you to be on this journey alone?" Nivvy asked.

A smile spread over the merchant's face. "Ah, now, we had just been discussing the possibility of a trade of stories. I have some food that I could share and would be happy to if the stories provided are sufficiently interesting." He turned back to Bella. "You were about to tell me your story."

# ❦ 4 ❦

# THE STORIES AT THE OASIS

"I have many," she said, "but tell me, are you familiar with the tale of Primrose and Just-Rose[1]?"

The merchant sat up straight. "I am not," he said with delight. "Pray, proceed."

So Bella told a story of two sisters, born to a poor woodcutter's family after the woodcutter's wife consulted with a witch who lived in a nearby lake. The fair-haired sister arrived first, and therefore was called Primrose, after the first flowers of spring. The red-haired sister, born second, was called Rose, or Just-Rose, as she came to be known. When the sisters were young women, they met a bear who claimed to be cursed. Primrose believed him, but when she crossed a stream to help him, the bear carried her off. So Just-Rose ventured through the forest to find her sister. On the way she met a hungry fox, a serpent trapped under a rock, and a hawk caught in a bush. She helped all three and in return they showed her the way to the bear's den and told her how to break the curse on him.

This was all familiar to Nivvy, though he hadn't heard this particular story. In old tales, as in the modern world, sometimes people got themselves cursed into animal shapes (and there were magical animals who could talk). In the old tales, though, those curses could be broken and the people returned to human form. In the modern world, people unlucky enough to get turned into animals could talk, but there was no more going back to human.

In the end, Just-Rose found her sister and told her how to break the bear's curse, and when Primrose did, the bear turned into a handsome prince who married her. They always got married in the end. Just-Rose got married too, because luckily the prince had a brother. No mention of their parents, though. Sometimes the hero's families got brought to live in the palace and sometimes they just got forgot.

The quickest way to get to know someone was to see what story they chose to tell, and Nivvy was most struck at how Bella said the line, "Even though Just-Rose had braved the dangers of the forest herself." What he'd thought was a story about two sisters who loved each other enough to risk their lives now took a slight turn; this was Just-Rose's story, mostly, but Primrose married the prince.

When Bella concluded her story, the merchant bowed and stroked his beard quickly. "Where did this story take place?" he asked. "I have never heard of the old witch Adalinda."

"She's dead," Bella said. "This took place to the north, past the great forest and over the Mihilberg mountains."

"The Merkhar Forest I know," Suleimon said, "but I have never heard of the Mihilberg Mountains. Are they beyond the Reiki Mountains?"

Bella didn't seem to know how to answer this, so Nivvy interrupted. "Seems t'me that Rose got the bad end of the deal," he said. "I mean, her sister got carried off by a bear, sure, but Just-Rose had to go through the forest and figure out how to find her and then her sister's the one who gets to marry the prince?"

"She married the prince's brother," Suleimon pointed out.

Bella remained quiet, but Nivvy didn't miss the half-smile she sent his way. "True enough," he said. "Just if I was Primrose an' my sister'd risked so much to rescue me after I got myself kidnapped, I'd let her have first pick of the princes."

"It's but a story," Suleimon said, and sat straighter. "And now it is my turn to return the very great favor you have done. My tale takes place to the south of here."

"Weren't you going to tell us how you come to be traveling alone?" Nivvy asked with a grin.

The merchant's eyes brightened. "I could not possibly dishonor such a romantic story with the pedestrian travails of a simple merchant, his conniving brother-in-law, and the misfortunes of a trading ship. I have a much grander tale in mind. Do you know the Empire of the Isles?"

"Yes," Nivvy said as Bella shook her head. "We call it the Thousand Kingdoms here."

"Indeed, each of the Isles is a kingdom, and a Suzerain rules over them all," Suleimon said. "This story begins on the Isle of Ivory...but does not remain there."

He launched into a story[2] that contained three other stories, a style of storytelling Nivvy was familiar with from Thousand Kingdom travelers that came through Copper Port. Suleimon began by telling of a wise, just king on the Isle of Ivory who every year sought out an unfortunate whose situation he might improve, and this year his servants happened to find three such. The tales contained wondrous sea serpents, magical djinn, entire cities swallowed up in the blink of an eye, and people who had survived all of that.

Nivvy enjoyed getting lost in stories and especially liked the fantastical elements like the great sea serpent and the djinn, powerful creatures he liked to imagine and hoped never to meet. Bella too seemed fascinated by the djinn, leaning forward at that point in the story with a shine in her eyes.

"The King granted his wishes, and all three of the supplicants lived well after that. And when that King passed, his son ruled with the same fairness and justice, and so the Isle of Ivory has been known since that day," Suleimon concluded with a flourish.

Nivvy bowed his head politely, as was the custom after a story, and motioned to Bella to follow his lead. It took him a moment to catch her eye; her mind seemed still lost in the story. "Very enjoyable," he said, "and so artful in the telling."

The merchant beamed. "I chose that one because one of the supplicants was from the North," he said, gesturing to Bella. "I only know a handful of stories that mention the North."

"It was kind of you," she said.

The merchant turned to Nivvy. "Have you a story to share as well?"

Nivvy leaned back to let the breeze and dying sun catch more of his wet robe and searched for a story that wouldn't be too revealing. "Not as elegant nor as artful as yours, but ay, I have one I can share." He cast about the clearing and found three fallen leaves of approximately the same size and shape. On one side of each he scored a mark with his fingernail: a line, a circle, and a triangle.

"Here," he pointed to the triangle, "is the tiger. This is gold," as he indicated the circle, and then his finger moved to the line, "and this the exit." He gathered up the leaves and shuffled them quickly in his hand before laying them out with the symbols face down.

"Now here is the story of Jalil, a thief of great renown, who lived in the great city of Khalbad many years ago. In that city lived a noble who owned a small gold figurine depicting the goddess Inira in her fox form, with emeralds for eyes and diamond dust in her ears and on her tail. The figurine was legendary, and yet few people had ever laid eyes on it, because the noble guarded it jealously.

"So Jalil, who had proven his worth time and time again in lesser challenges, undertook to steal the figurine. Inira, our patron deity, would not want her likeness hidden away, he reasoned. Through bribes of the noble's servants and gossip from the noble's family, he came to know that the prize lay in the lowermost vault of the noble's palace, guarded by a fearsome tiger, but in an unusual way. If a thief were to make his way to the lowermost vault, there he would find a single door that could only be opened by means of three levers, and once one lever was pulled, the other two would be locked in position, and not ten men could thereafter move them.

"One lever would open a hidden panel behind the door and reveal the figurine to the intruder, who would then have to leave the way he had come. One lever would open a door to the outside world so that the intruder would be able to leave safely, though without his prize. And the third lever would open a cage behind the door that contained a fierce tiger, who would immediately fall upon the intruder and devour him.

"Only the noble himself knew which lever controlled which outcome, and Jalil had heard that sometimes the noble would move the mechanisms about so that not even he could say for certain. But Jalil felt that he was favored by Inira and that she would guide his hand to the proper lever for certain.

"On that moonless night, Jalil set out and made his way through the noble's defenses to the bottommost vault, and there, just as had been described, he found the room with three levers." Nivvy nodded to the three leaves in front of him. "Which one did he choose?"

The merchant smiled; he had heard this story before, perhaps. He reached out to one of the leaves but did not touch it. Nivvy nodded, gathered up the other two leaves, and then reached out to the one the merchant had chosen. He turned it over to reveal the triangle.

"Jalil pulled the lever and knew as soon as he heard the metal of the cage that Inira had not smiled on him. Such is the fate of those who trust in the goddess of luck. The door opened, the tiger fell upon him, and for all I know, there his bones lie still."

He discarded all three leaves behind him. "I apologize for the shortness of the tale," he said, but the merchant was already bowing.

"No need," cried Suleimon. "It was a joy to hear and to play the part of the goddess of luck in choosing the ending." He reached behind him and brought out a small cloth, which he unwrapped to reveal oat-cakes and dried meat. "I have not much to share, but what I have is yours."

"We've not much in return," Nivvy said, "but take these figures as our appreciation." He walked over to their pack and retrieved the copper figures he'd stolen from the horse back at the Inn: a horse, a man, and a lion. "These copper figures come from the workshop of the master craftsman Calinha of Khalbad. You can see they didn't come from his hand, but they were cooled in the waters of the pool sacred to Mesic."

The merchant accepted the figures and looked over them. He raised his eyes to Nivvy as the thief sat and said, "So says the follower of Inira."

Nivvy inclined his head. "To the follower of Massi."

At this, Suleimon broke into laughter and stowed the figurines in his pack. "Very good, very good," he said. "Let us eat."

A merchant as well-dressed as Suleimon surely had better food than oat-cakes and dried meat, even if he'd been swindled by his brother, but Nivvy hadn't eaten anything even that good in a week, and he devoured them. It was Suleimon's prerogative to decide what gift to make, after all.

When the shadows had lengthened over the oasis and dissolved into darkness, and the sun had left the sky to the care of the stars, Suleimon returned to his camp with smiles and well-wishes for the both of them.

"You smell a good deal better," was the first thing Bella said to Nivvy when they were alone again. "Though there is still room for improvement."

"Always room for improvement," he said, his mood considerably lightened. "And when we get to Spire, there'll be a proper bath and meal, but that was fine. Almost put that shit town out of my mind completely." He stretched out on the ground, his robes still damp, but not uncomfortably so.

Bella did not lie down but sat with her back against a bush. "What was that 'follower of Inira' exchange you had with him?"

"Ah ha." Nivvy smiled up at the sky. "That was him tellin' me he knew either I hadn't come by the figures honestly, or was making up the story, or both, and me responding that as a guardian of knowledge, the figurines and the story were now his and as true as he wanted to make them."

"Fascinating," Bella murmured. "I don't know anything of your gods here."

"What gods do you worship, then?"

"I don't know that I worship any, not anymore."

Bella's pale face gazed toward the horizon, a faraway look in her eyes. Nivvy turned his head in that direction, but there was nothing but sand and the shadow of the Iridi Mountains to the west. "How's that work?" he asked.

"Well," she said, "what might make you lose your faith?"

Nivvy thought about that. "Catastrophe, I suppose, but like the fellows in that merchant's tale, faith is what's meant to sustain you through tragedy, innit?"

"Meant to, I suppose. But what if it fails to do that?"

He leaned back and stared up at the sky again. "Faith don't seem like a fortress that someone can knock down from outside. Feels more like...a tree, kind of thing what stands until it dies inside, right? But no, I guess a tree can be knocked over too."

"I think a tree is an excellent analogy," Bella said. "If it's battered long enough, it will fall, and whether it dies before or after the fall is immaterial."

"Right, well," Nivvy said, closing his eyes, "Inira's a fickle one anyway, and she smiles most on those who make their own luck. We've full bellies and we've heard good stories, so let's rest, and soon enough we'll be in Spire." He stretched out on the ground, but Bella remained seated, thinking. "If you don't sleep, at least stay quiet, would you?"

THE PRICE OF THORNS

Bella's large dress rustled, and then she said, "I want you to steal something."

Nivvy cracked an eye. "Aye," he said. "That's what we're doin'." If her memory was going...

"From the merchant."

Both eyes flew open, and Nivvy sat up. "The one we just shared stories an' a meal with? What'd he do to offend you?"

"That food he gave us was clearly below his station. It was an insult to our company to give such meager fare."

"He's a right to keep back whatever he wants." Nivvy appreciated that Bella had made the same observation he had. She wasn't completely distant from the world.

"My station is well above his. I should have been given the best he had to offer."

It wasn't worth reminding her yet again that she was not, right now, a queen. "We know his name. You can get yer revenge when we succeed in this job."

Bella gazed levelly at him, sitting very still. "You keep telling me you're a competent thief, or uncommon, or whatever word it is you prefer, and yet the one time I've asked you to steal something you failed."

"Now listen." Nivvy shook a finger at her. "I made a judgment—"

"Yes, yes." Bella waved a hand. "I'm going to need proof that you can actually do this job. It'll be harder than stealing from a merchant at an oasis, so if you fail in this, I'll have to look elsewhere."

"Wait 'til we get to Spire, at least," Nivvy said. "Stealin' is against the code of the oasis, I told you."

"I never agreed to this code." Bella's eyes gleamed at him. "If you don't get caught, you won't have to worry about the consequences of breaking it, will you?"

In the darkness her eyes were unreadable. "It's jus' not done," Nivvy said weakly. Here, unlike out in the desert, Bella held leverage, and she knew it. She could join Suleimon or any of the other travelers on their way to a city and leave him here without a contract, without a future.

"Then if it won't be done by you, I'll find someone who will."

"You won't."

She got to her feet. "I have nothing but time."

The image flashed across his mind of Queen Bella ascending the throne, another thief at her side, Nivvy hearing the tales of it and knowing he could've been there. Where did *he* have to go from here? He'd wasted a year already and this job was the closest he'd come yet to returning to the Guild.

Bella had walked to the edge of their clearing and definitely intended to walk out across the desert. That was somewhat unhinged, but it was a determined sort of unhinged, and Nivvy had to admit that she seemed fully present in reality most of the time. He wouldn't have thought he'd see his friend turned into a toad, but that had happened. "Hsss!" he called after her, a thief's soft call that wouldn't alert their neighbors.

She turned and stared him down. "Fine," he said. "I'll do it. But not the merchant. Anyone else."

Bella put a finger to her cheek and smiled. "No," she said. "I think it must be the merchant."

"Why?" Nivvy wanted to cry out but restrained himself to a whisper.

"He insulted me. Are you loyal to me or not?"

So that was it. He gritted his teeth. The chance that someone from the Thieves Guild would be at the oasis, much less would catch him in the act of theft, was very low (he wasn't worried about the merchant catching him). The chance that Bella would find a new thief in Spire if he didn't go along with her here was measurably higher. "Fine," he said. "Yes."

Giving in to her was the hardest part of the operation. He crept over to Suleimon's camp, stepping on sand where he could and soft grass where he couldn't, proud of how silent his footsteps were, how well he kept his balance. Thieving starts with the feet, his old mentor Polu had told him. Put a foot wrong and the job is ruined before it starts.

So Nivvy made his way to the merchant's saddlebags, undid the clasps with nimble silent fingers, remaining in the shadow of the horse so he'd be less visible from outside the clearing. In the bags his fingers found two packages wrapped in cloth that had the weight and feel of food; the smell of fine cheese wafted out to him. He extracted them, watching the sleeping merchant the whole time. Betraying the merchant's trust gnawed at him, but being able to creep up practically next to a fellow and take his valuables without the fellow even knowing, that was special. Few could do it at all, and fewer still as well as he.

So he returned to Bella with pride and regret warring in him, but all he said as he tossed the packages to her was, "There's yer proof. Hide those in case he comes 'round in the morning."

"I'm not worried about that," she said, but Nivvy walked away without waiting for her to finish.

He lay down and closed his eyes, but even though Bella didn't speak again, it took him a good while to get to sleep.

## ❧ 5 ❧

# SPIRE

When he woke, Bella was still sitting against the same bush, staring into the sky with the sunrise at her back. "Did you sleep?" Nivvy asked as he struggled to sit up.

"As much as I ever do," she said.

He debated for a moment whether to press further on that answer and decided it didn't matter as long as she was allowing him to sleep. "Right," he said, casting an eye toward Suleimon's camp. The merchant did not appear to have woken yet. "With a good day's ride, we should sight Spire today and arrive tomorrow. Let's fill the water skins and see if we can trade coin for food from anyone still here. I don't know what towns there might be between here and Spire. Might be nothing but dirt."

There certainly was a lot of dirt, but the food they'd stolen from the merchant proved to be thick, soft bread and a lovely cheese with a sharp tang to it, which tasted delicious even when Nivvy couldn't quite forget that he'd broken a code to get them. That was the sort of thing that could nullify a contract, so once he had that paper in hand, he'd have to be more careful. The tradeoff, though, would be more than worth it.

The ochre dirt and dull green bushes, broken up by the occasional ghaf tree and the persistent faintly woody smell of the brush made for a monotonous ride and provided no shelter from the sun. Midway through the day, though Bella did not complain, Nivvy took one of his old blankets from the pack and held it back to her. "You can drape this over your head if you like," he said. "Keep you from too much sun."

"It smells of horse," she said. "I don't want it."

"Suit y'self," Nivvy said. "I always seen northerners in Copper Port wearing big hats or cloaks, talk about the curse of the sun turnin' their skin red just like your cheeks is going." She still didn't take the blanket, so he dropped it back into the bag.

"I like the sun," she murmured.

Perhaps her skin hadn't always been that white. Nivvy hadn't seen sun-skin more than a handful of times in his life, so it was possible he'd got it wrong and she'd be fine. In any case, it was her lookout, not his.

A little after midday, when the gentle rolling of the horizon had lifted into real hills, Nivvy stopped at a ghaf tree and tied up Rahila beneath it. "We can rest here for a bit," he said to Bella as he dismounted.

She stayed on the horse. "If you need to rest, you may, but I am anxious to be on our way as soon as possible."

"You don't need to relieve yourself?" Nivvy asked. He walked to a stand of bushes some twenty feet off that would afford him enough privacy.

Bella turned away as he'd thought she would, but as he returned, she dismounted. He hid a grin. "Plus," he said, "take a couple branches an' you can eat the leaves." He reached up and took down a thin branch with rows of narrow leaves on either side of it, stripped the leaves, and stuffed them in his mouth. "Bitter and scratchy like sand, but it'll sustain us for a little."

"I'll wait for Spire," Bella said, walking toward the bushes.

Nivvy went back to Rahila and stared at the horizon. "Ah, you can see it now."

"Don't talk to me," she said. "In fact, go twenty feet down the road."

"Now now, I promise I won't look."

"I know you won't. I don't want you to hear either."

"Tch." But playing with her was only amusing to a point, and her voice was acquiring an edge, so he rubbed Rahila's nose affectionately and walked on down the road. Ahead, just above the hills, a small point protruded into the sky: the spire of Spire.

He stood there looking at it shimmer in the air, judging how far it was. They would have to stop for the night just inside the hills, but the next day they should be able to reach Spire before dark. Riding into a city with a patron normally meant paid meals and lodging, but seeing as how his patron was penniless, more than likely it meant he would have to steal some coin to get them both presentable.

But there, somewhere around that needle on the horizon, was a Thieves Guild that would (with luck) give Bella a contract, which Nivvy could then put his own name on, and after that, he could work on restoring his reputation. Whatever happened with Bella, that was within his reach now. He hadn't felt this hopeful since before that last job, over a year ago. Inira really had provided, and he was going to seize the opportunity.

He sensed movement behind him and turned. Bella was leading Rahila away from the ghaf tree, toward him. "Hey," he said to the mare, "so you'll just go with anyone who unties you, now, is it?"

"She started walking toward you the moment I untied her," Bella said, "so you've no need to fear for her loyalty."

"I don't." As she reached him, Rahila pushed her nose into his chest. He rubbed his hands over the smooth hairs up her forehead and between her ears. "There you are, h'san, you ready to go on our way?"

Once they'd mounted, he told Bella his idea to camp just inside the hills. "Might not find water, but there should be trees and shelter, maybe roots if we're lucky, but we've enough food to get to Spire in any case."

"And where is the mountain of fire from Spire?"

Nivvy frowned. "Day's ride, maybe two, beyond, sort of that way." He pointed to the spire on the horizon and then angled his hand to the left, where the horizon jutted up like teeth. "I think, that is. Don't know anyone who goes that way on the regular 'cept maybe priests and priestesses of Bouli."

"Bouli," Bella repeated. "Which god is that?"

"God of fire," Nivvy said, "and also of anger and of torment, which follows naturally. And by the by, if you see anyone with a pin like a flame-tipped arrow, stay away. They're hired killers. Even the priests— they wear three red triangles set inside one large one—they're not the most pleasant."

"Charming."

"Hang a tic." Nivvy half-turned. "Why you asking about the fire mountain?"

"I told you, that's where my friend is."

"I thought you meant they're in Spire!"

"No," she said. "Spire didn't exist the last time I was here."

Nivvy laughed. "You're havin' me on." But her expression didn't change, and his laughter died down. "Spire's been there for—hundreds of years."

"I don't doubt it."

She might be joking; he had no idea whether she had a sense of humor or what it would look like if she did. He had an idea that he wouldn't be very happy to see her laugh. But if she were telling the truth, then...she was here through magic of some sort. And not charm-on-a-bracelet magic, but proper big kingdom-level magic.

Wasn't necessarily bad, that. She didn't seem to have magic herself, but she could easily be hiding it. So she was the victim of a curse, but if she really had been gone hundreds of years, then whoever'd cursed her was likely gone. Unless it was this friend, but she'd hardly be running toward them, then. She wasn't that crazy. Was she?

He didn't want to accuse her of being crazy, but there was a way to ask that without asking. "So who's this friend, and how are they still around after hundreds of years, and what do you need from them?"

She paused only for a moment. "I hired you to steal something. Does it matter what it is?"

Nivvy choked back his first answer in favor of something that didn't involve cursing. "That's like sayin, 'I brought you something to eat, does it matter what it is?' Of course it matters. Steal a purse from a fellow in the street, easier done than said. Steal a special ring from the King's bedroom of the palace? That's another matter entirely." As should be obvious, he didn't add.

"This friend of mine has a magic artifact that is necessary for me to regain my kingdom, and I'm not sure she will be willing to lend it to me."

"So...you want me to steal from your friend. Not sure what your friendship consists of, but most of my friends wouldn't appreciate me hirin' someone to steal from them."

"I rather think you would do that yourself," she said coolly. "If you really are as good a thief as you claim."

"All right, all right, the point is, friends don't steal from friends. In the Guild they got a rule that nobody in the Guild can steal from somebody else in the Guild. So what's this thing do? Turn people into animals? Make you fly? If it's got to do with killing, you'll have to do a lot more talking to keep me on. Nobody's allowed to have killing artifacts any more, an' all the Kings keep 'em locked up until their stories are forgot. Every now and then one turns up and it always ends bad for the idiot tryin' to use it."

"It's not killing," she said. "At least, it doesn't have to be."

"Not makin' me feel better." Nivvy scratched between Rahila's ears and the mare flicked them against his fingers. When Bella remained silent, he said, "Look, there's no harm telling me what it does. If I don't know the story, I can't use it."

"That's not how magic works."

"Beg pardon," he said, "but it's exactly how magic works. Magic artifact got a story, you know the story, you unlock its power."

"You—" She cut herself off. "You have cast spells," she said, almost to herself. "Strange, that the casting of magic would have changed. One thinks certain things rest on a solid foundation, but even that may shift."

"What's it changed from?"

"Oh," she said, "when I was growing up, if you had magic, you could just cast spells. Some witches looked into the future, some witches turned people into animals, and some just minded their own business until people tried to hunt them down."

"We don't get so much of the future-looking, but people still become animals," Nivvy said, again side-stepping the part where Bella had been alive hundreds of years ago. "My mate Marzin—"

"You've told me his sad tale," Bella said. "The frog, correct?"

"Toad, so at least he didn't have to be wet all the time. Why would people hunt witches if they were minding their business? These days if someone has magic, we all know enough to leave them well alone unless they make a nuisance of themselves."

"Some witches..." Bella's tone grew distasteful. "Some ate people. When a bad witch was discovered, people wanted to put an end to them, and often any other witches they knew about were also hunted at the same time."

*Is that what happened to you?* Nivvy wanted to ask, but their acquain-

THE PRICE OF THORNS

tanceship didn't feel like it had reached that point yet. "How would you prepare a person for eating?" he said. "Never thought about that. Can't imagine as it'd be worth the trouble."

"I wouldn't know," Bella said.

"So what does this magic thing of yours do?"

She paused, then made a small "hmph" noise like she'd lost an argument with herself. "It's a lapis ring that allows me to exchange my likeness with another's so that nobody can tell the difference."

"Oh," Nivvy said brightly. "So your idea is you get this ring, you get an audience with the king of your kingdom, and you switch places. Then you get your kingdom back."

"Crudely speaking, yes."

"So you need me to get you into the palace and make sure nobody sees the switch?" He thought about it. "We'll have to spend a week or so at the palace so's we can observe, but I'm sure I can figure out the best way to do it."

They'd come to the first real rise in the road, and Nivvy slowed Rahila to walk up it. "And you have to steal the ring from Scarlet," Bella reminded him.

"Ay," he said. "You sure you can't just ask for it?"

"Scarlet never gives anything away. There's always price, always a favor of some sort, she has to be invited to a party, or has to have a spiced cake sent to her every day for ten years, or has to have your first-born child, something like that."

Nivvy had been about to say that for the price of a kingdom, those demands didn't seem unreasonable, until Bella had gotten to the last one. That sounded like something a magical spirit out of a story would ask for, which at least explained how this Scarlet might still be around. "Right," he said. "So we're staying with this friend for a few days, time for me to get the lay of the land?"

They reached the top of the hill, and Rahila broke into a jarring trot on the downslope without being urged. When she'd sped to a smoother canter, Bella answered. "I don't know how likely that is. Scarlet loves company but hates guests."

Nivvy's answering sigh must have been audible, because Bella said, "This won't be any trouble, will it? I thought you were an uncommon thief."

The big question was this friend Scarlet's nature and what magic they had, but Nivvy was very confident in his ability to extract a ring from a room, even from someone's finger. The bigger question in his head was whether Bella would demand any more allegiance from him. Already she'd made him break the covenant of the oasis, and while that wouldn't technically anger Inira, it wasn't good form.

But if we were talking about that, how he'd lost his guild membership wasn't good form either. So if he had to break some rules to get it back, well, that he could justify. Especially after the fact. "It makes it harder is all. Not beyond my powers, no."

"Good. There's no problem then."

This, Nivvy thought, was just the sort of thing someone who didn't actually have to do anything would say.

❧

AFTER AN UNDISTURBED NIGHT DURING WHICH HE WAS STILL NOT sure if Bella slept, they set off again in the morning. The great spire for which the city had been named rose before them, tricking them into thinking the city was close until they looked down the road and saw no buildings.

Finally, just after the sun reached its zenith, they crested a high hill and came down the other side into greenery and farmland. No more ghaf trees and scrub brush; lusher, leafier trees spread outward from the hills as though they'd tumbled from the heights and collected in the valley, and here and there were shimmers of streams and ponds.

For the first time they could see the base of the spire. It looked to be at least ten houses wide, and though it narrowed by half at the top, that top was easily fifty houses high, if not higher. From the saucer-like structure at the top of the tower rose a narrow column another two houses high. Now, too, it was possible to make out the darker spirals that circled the column from the top down to the base.

"It's impressive," Bella said as Rahila cantered down the hillside into the cool, green-scented air of the farmlands. "Given the rest of the area. How long ago was it built?"

"Hundreds of years," Nivvy said. "We'll get a guide when we arrive and they'll have the story, so I won't try to tell you the little I know about it. Only been here twice before, an' the spire wasn't exactly the thing I was most interested in." Approaching the city named for it, with the spire the most prominent thing for miles around, Nivvy was aware of the foolishness of that statement, but there it was, the life of a thief.

The sun beat down until mid-afternoon, when clouds muscled in on its sky and shaded the travelers. Good relief, Nivvy thought, hoping they could make it to Spire before the rain set in. He glanced back at Bella and saw that despite two full days of riding uncovered in the sun, her face was no more sun-touched than the day he'd met her. All right, then, that was odd, though he supposed someone claiming to be hundreds of years old might have all manner of magic about them.

Houses became thicker along the road as the wall drew closer, and the road similarly grew more crowded. Scattered raindrops struck Nivvy's face as he had to slow Rahila to a walk to get in the line of people waiting to be passed through the wall. "Looks like we'll be a little wet when we get in," he said cheerfully, the prospect of warm food and a warm bed already raising his spirits.

Bella rested a hand on his arm. "Is it necessary for us to enter the city?"

He turned. "We need to get you a proper contract to secure my services."

"A contract? I thought we had an agreement."

"If I'm to work by the rules of the Guild, I need a contract."

Bella's eyes narrowed. "I thought we had established the priority of rules in this relationship."

"It don't harm you none, an' it protects you if I don't do as you ask."

"I don't need a Guild to protect me in that case."

The iron tone in her voice unwound something in his gut. He hurried on before he could reconsider this whole contract deal. "An' it protects me, in case I get caught doin' yer job, which I don't expect to, but it don't hurt to have it. There's also the matter of a nice bath an' a good meal."

"Your smell is...less objectionable now. If the mountain is another day or two, we could circle the wall and find the road on the other side that leads to it."

"Why don't you want to go into the city?" Here he was, so close to getting the paper that would put him back on the right path, and she wanted to dodge around it. He was good at not letting his alarm show, but it would kill him if she ordered him around the walls and he had to stare at the city the whole time without going in.

She straightened, attempting a haughty look whose power was somewhat diminished by the few inches between them (still, it was a good try). "I am anxious to reach Scarlet as soon as possible," she said, waving a hand toward Spire. "If we enter that city, who knows how long we will be delayed."

"By what? Eating a good meal and sleeping in a bed?"

"This contract you want to have seems to me to be a waste of our time."

"Who's the thief here, you or me?" he demanded. "The contract tells people that if I steal something—"

"You've made its purpose clear," she replied. "But if Scarlet catches you, a contract won't be worth a thing, and in any other case I can protect you."

He nodded toward Spire, keeping his voice low. "What about when I need to steal something to pay for that bed and meal?"

"If we don't go into the city, you don't need to steal anything there."

"I'll need to steal it somewhere."

The rain spattered them as a gust of wind blew her hair and his robes. "We'll find an inn along the way. There are inns along roads, yes?"

"As I told you," he said, "nobody goes to the fire mountain, so not too many inns along that road. Even if there was, you don't piss in your bed." Her confused, annoyed look led him to explain: "You don't steal from the house where you're going to sleep and eat. Too risky. That merchant didn't come after us but he very well might've."

She scoffed. "I'm paying you."

"And I'm tryin' my best to do the job you're paying me for, and part of that is puttin' myself in the best position to do it, and I'm at my best with a full stomach and rested body, and that means finding a place to sleep and that means going in there."

"Fine," Bella said. "Fine. If you're so determined—"

She pushed back from him and slid off Rahila's back. The mare, knowing this wasn't the place to dismount, turned her head as Nivvy did. "Come on," he said, reaching down.

"You go in and do what you have to do, and I'll walk around and meet you on the other side."

If she didn't go into the city, Nivvy wouldn't get his blank contract.

"You'll never find me. And where are you going to sleep? What are you going to eat?"

"Ho, fellow," a robed rider said as he went around them. "Need a hand with your woman?"

"I am not *his woman*," Bella hissed. "Mind your business."

She used that same iron tone she had with Nivvy. The rider laughed, though it was an uneasy laugh, and he urged his horse forward. "Buy her a nice dress, that'll change her mood," he said over his shoulder. "Shame on you for letting her walk around like that."

"We're getting new clothes in Spire," Nivvy shouted after him as the rider walked by, remaining in earshot for far longer than Nivvy would have liked.

"We are not getting me new clothes," Bella said, but they were interrupted at that moment by a hawk that swooped down out of the sky and hovered just over Rahila's head, startling even the usually well-tempered mare into shying backwards.

Nivvy got control of her as the hawk spoke. "Easy, friends," they said. "I'm a guide to Spire and I spotted you from the wall. Looked like you were having an argument and I thought maybe it was about which one of our lovely taverns to visit first, or maybe about where to procure a change of clothes in our tailors' district, or maybe whether anyone's ever attempted to scale our famous spire. I can answer all those questions and more besides, and I'm happy to do it for the price of meals while you're in our city, and since I'm a hawk, why, those meals come cheaper than any other guide's. Now, might I rest on one of your shoulders so my wings don't have to do quite so much work?"

"We don't need a guide," Bella said.

"Let's not be hasty." Nivvy reached into his pack for a blanket and wrapped it around his forearm, then rested that arm on his knee. Transformed animals, unlucky folks that they were, often had a bad go of it, whether it was because folks found them creepy or just assumed they'd done something bad to be cursed. As a result, they were often more helpful for less coin than other resources. Unless they were toads, who had limited usefulness all around.

"Many thanks," the hawk said as they alit on Nivvy's arm, fluffing their wings. A leather cord wrapped around one of their legs was threaded through a hole in a silver coin, Nivvy noticed. "I'm called Zein. How may I address you fine people?"

"I'm called Nivvy, and this is Bella. Bella's not too keen on Spire, I'm just finding out."

"Why's that?" Zein tilted their head and stared down at the former queen.

Nivvy, too, looked down, interested in the answer. Bella stared back at him, not the hawk, and said, "It's none of your concern. I simply don't wish to..." She waved toward the crowd queuing up to enter the city. "I don't wish to."

"But why not?" Zein cried. "Did you know, Spire has more tailors than any other city within a hundred miles? We are renowned for our lovely azure dye, made from a plant that only grows here. Even if I knew which one, I couldn't tell you. The tailors don't tell anyone, and that's why you won't find that color anywhere else in the known world! And I can show you a tavern that makes spiced griddle cakes better than anything you've sampled in the world. Trust me, I've flown over every inch of the city a hundred times and I know which places to go and which places to avoid and where the best food and the cleanest beds are."

"You can see the beds from flying over?" Nivvy asked.

Before Zein could reply, Bella asked, "Can you keep us out of large crowds?"

"Course I can," the hawk said promptly. "I wouldn't send you to the market at midday anyway. You want places out of the way, I can guide you there, too. You members of any guild? There's housing for those."

Bella stared at Nivvy. "Nay," he said. "No guild."

"All good." Zein shifted their weight on Nivvy's arm. "So do you want to hire me? If not, perfectly fine, I understand, I'll be on my way."

"We'll hire you," Bella said.

Nivvy stared. "We will?"

"I'll feel better with someone who knows the city. Since you insist you absolutely must visit it," she said.

"Fantastic!" Zein brightened and fluffed their wings. "You won't regret it. I don't eat much and I know all the places to go. What do you want to do first? Never mind, we've plenty of time for that. Do you know the story of the spire and the founding of the city? That's our First Story and every visitor should hear it, if you haven't already, and even if you have, you haven't heard my version. I know because I only just met you and I haven't told it yet."

Bella ignored Nivvy's outstretched hand and pulled herself back up on Rahila. "That sounds like an excellent way to pass the time."

Nivvy was partial to making plans when plans needed to be made, as they did now, but he had to allow that it couldn't hurt to know more about where they were going. It was hard not to be curious about the great spire in front of them, the great blocks of stone and the saucer at the summit where, now that he stared at it, it looked like something was moving? From this distance, there was no telling whether it was a bird or a man, but it was something for sure.

Zein had drawn themself up and now began with a theatrical flourish. "Now this was a long time ago, before I was born, but I heard it from a river spirit who was there and saw the whole thing. There was a king who had three sons, and the youngest of those was a boy so clever that by the age of five he could solve riddles that baffled grown men, by the age of eight he was holding conversations with the king's ministers, and by the age of twelve, sages across the kingdom would visit him for advice. He was named Joric, but the people knew him as Clever Jorl.

"Now, the king's foremost minister was a nasty fellow, just the worst, and he saw how clever the boy was and he was worried that one day this boy would grow up to be so clever that he'd find out about all the things the minister was doing that he wasn't supposed to be. So the minister went to the temple of Apo, the Sky-God, who incidentally is the god who looks out for people turned into birds, and he's normally a very good god but his priests don't come off so well in this story. Anyway, the minister was good friends with a priest, and he convinced the priest to warn the king that his youngest son was scheming to take the throne for himself, that he would kill first his eldest brother, then his next eldest, and then the king himself.

"The king didn't believe it, of course. Would you? But the minister went and stabbed the eldest prince in the night and lay the blade in the bed of Clever Jorl, where it was discovered in the morning. Now the king believed the false priest, so in order to save his middle son, he ordered Clever Jorl be put to death.

"But Clever Jorl argued that since no man had seen his crime, no man should judge him. He said, 'The gods know the truth, therefore let the gods judge me. Let me go out into the world with only this blade, and if it were my hand that killed my brother, let the blade always turn against me, but if another hand were responsible, let the blade guide me through the world until it finds the guilty party.'

"The evil minister was pretty scared, as you can imagine, so he went to Clever Jorl pretending to be his friend, the louse, and he told him to follow the Kalla River, because he knew that the river led to the country of giants."

The men on horses ahead of them turned, and one said, "Keep that accursed bird quiet."

"I'm a licensed guide," Zein shot back at them, and clacked their beak. "You don't have to listen if you don't want to."

They looked at each other and then one muttered something to the other, and they both laughed and turned forward.

Zein turned their head back and continued as though there'd been no interruption. "So Clever Jorl thought this was good advice, because he didn't know the minister was evil. He traveled along the river and hunted game and had a fine time of it, and—" Here Zein looked to see how close they were to the gate, which was now a matter of only fifty feet or so. "Anyway, he had adventures and you can hear about some of them later. I don't know all the stories but I know a few of them, but anyone can tell you about Clever Jorl and the fairies, or Clever Jorl and the trader's wife. But in the end he came to this town, and the town told him that they were plagued by giants, and the chief promised that if Clever Jorl could make the giants leave them alone, he'd give him his daughter in marriage. And the daughter was beautiful, of course she was, so Clever Jorl said he'd give it a try.

"He walked along the river and found the giants and demanded to speak to their leader, and that was the tallest one, because that's how giants choose their leader, so he came along and wanted to eat Clever Jorl, but Jorl said, you can't eat me because I'm going to prove that I should be your leader. All the giants thought this was hilarious, they laughed and laughed, and Clever Jorl said to the leader, I'll prove it. I bet you can't build a tower that's taller than I am.

"Well, the leader giant said he only needed two stones to do that, so they went to a hill by the river, and he put two stones on top of each other, and lickety-split Clever Jorl went around behind the stones and climbed to the top of them. 'See,' he said, 'I'm still taller.'

"Giants are pretty dumb, so the leader scratched his head and said, 'Wait here,' and he went off to get more stones. While he was doing that, Jorl carved notches in the back of the stones so he could get up and down faster, so he didn't have to just stay on top of the tower forever, you see, and when the leader came back with more stones, Jorl got up quickly to stand on top of them. 'See,' he said, 'I'm still taller.'

"Well, the leader couldn't stand for this. So he got the whole tribe to find stones and keep building this tower, and every time, Clever Jorl climbed up, carved more handholds, and stood atop the new tower. This went on for a year, because giants might be dumb but they're good builders, and at the end of the year they had built a tower that was taller than even the leader, and he couldn't build any more because his arms couldn't reach the top.

"Then Clever Jorl stood on top of it and said, 'Now I am the tallest and I am your leader, and I command that these giants shall walk toward the setting sun until they come to the sea, and they will make their new home there and shall never return to this land.' And the giants grumbled but they had to listen to him because he was the tallest.

"So the giants went off to the west, and eventually they lay down and became stone and that's the Iridi Mountains which you can see from here over on the horizon there where the sun sets, and that's what happened to the giants."

They were almost to the gates. Zein sped up their recitation. "Oh, and by the time the tower was finished there was nothing left of the blade but the handle, so Clever Jorl gave it to the leader of the giants and told him to throw it away, this was before they left for the west and became mountains, obviously, and the giant threw the handle as hard as he could. It sailed through the air all the way back to the original kingdom where the evil old minister happened to be walking out in the garden, and it struck him on the head and killed him, so it found the guilty party at last. And Clever Jorl married the chief's daughter, and they built a big city around the tower and called it Spire, and that's where the city got its name. Phew!"

The moment Zein finished speaking, the horse just ahead of them was waved through the gates and Nivvy urged Rahila forward. "Names and business in Spire?" the guard asked them.

Before Nivvy could say anything, Zein chirped, "Hi, Colli, this is Nivvy and Bella, they come to Spire to admire the tower and I'm going to show them round. We're going to stay at the Giant's Foot and I'm going to take 'em to the tailors' district to get new clothes, you can see they need 'em, don't you? Anyway I vouch for them. Here's my token." They balanced on one leg and held out the other, shaking it so the silver token spun.

Colli stared at the hawk a moment longer and then sighed and looked up at Nivvy. "Did you hire this hawk?"

"We did," Bella said, leaning around.

"All right. Go on through."

They rode on into the town, under the twenty-foot thickness of the wall out into a crowded street. Bella leaned in against Nivvy as Zein called out guidance. "Left, down that street. That baker on the right makes excellent sugar-cakes. There's a good stable here in case the Giant's Foot is full. Now a right turn here."

They turned onto a less crowded street and Bella relaxed back and away from Nivvy, which honestly made him feel better about their prospects in the city. If she was going to be tense the whole time it would make things much harder.

Zein guided them unerringly along streets to a building with a large carved wooden foot out front. "Wait here," the hawk said. "I'll see how full the stables are."

Without waiting for a response, they launched themself from Nivvy's arm into the air, startling a trio of sparrows on the roof. The hawk flapped up, soared in a circle over the building, and came back to land with a satisfied bob of their head. "There's room in the stable. So you can just tie up your horse here and go in and then they'll have someone come out and get her when you've settled for your room. The rooms are reasonable here, but I should have asked you how much you have. They're one silver each if you're with me, plus a silver for the horse, but that includes food for all of you, but not drink, that's extra."

"We have that," Nivvy said, although that would take up much of their remaining money. "Once we get settled here, I'll have you guide Bella to the Thieves' Guild, if you don't mind, and I'll stay here."

"Me?" Bella asked sharply. "You should go to the Guild. I want a bath, anyway."

"You think I don't?" Nivvy said. "I've also got to see to our finances, unless you've an idea for how to do that."

"Wait," Zein said. "Is one of you a thief? You said you weren't with any guild."

"We're looking to hire a thief," Nivvy said quickly, "and since it's Bella's purse, it should be Bella's hand asking for the contract."

"I haven't the experience." Bella's voice was tight.

"Nothin' to it." Nivvy smiled. "You walk in, you say, 'I need a contract for a job,' they ask you who the thief is, you say you haven't decided on one but you want to fill out the contract so it's all ready when you do, they tell you the contract isn't valid without the seal of the Guild, you say, yes, I understand, they give you the contract. Easiest thing in the world."

"It doesn't sound easier than you going to do that," Bella said.

"What are you hiring a thief for?" Zein asked. "I know it's not my business, but I know a couple good ones and maybe they'd be good for what you're looking for."

"I'll let Bella explain it on the way there." Nivvy pulled Rahila up to the front of the inn and slid off her quickly. "Bella, come in and get the room with me. Zein, can you watch Rahila while we're inside? We'll tell the innkeep that you brought us, no fear."

"Of course I can." The hawk fluffed up their feathers and hopped from Nivvy's arm to the saddle, where they perched just like a rider.

"The thing is," Nivvy whispered to Bella as they entered the inn, "I've got to go steal things to make us money, and I'm guessing you can't do that, so you've got to be the one goes to the Guild."

"Why can't you go to the Guild with me and then do your...work... after that?"

"It's already late in the day and merchants have to be open. Guild keeps the same hours." Nivvy hoped this logic would work.

Halfway to the bar where the innkeeper poured ales for the customers, Bella stopped and gripped Nivvy's arm. "I'm not going by myself. I didn't want to come into this city in the first place—"

"Aye, seems you don't like crowds."

"I...it's not that. It's...I prefer to be seen in a better state." Her fingers trembled over the torn lace of her dress. "And I certainly will not run errands for you."

"It's an errand for you," Nivvy hissed, but the woman's face remained set. "I promise you, it won't be any trouble."

"Tell me why you don't want to go." When he looked away, she said, "Now I think it's a big secret and I really won't go unless—"

He strode over to an unoccupied corner, pulling her with him by her grip on his arm. "All right," he said, "fine. Here you go. I'm—not a member of the Guild."

She opened her mouth to say something, so he hurriedly added, "Anymore."

Bella released his arm and leaned back against the wall. "I suspected that when I saw you on a torture wheel and you talked about unguilded thieves there. And earlier, when you told the hawk you weren't a Guild member."

"I wasn't kicked out for being a bad thief," he said. "Someone else made a mistake on a job an' I got blamed for it."

Bella held his eyes. "What happened?"

"All right," Nivvy said, "since we're sharin' secrets and all, how is it you're hundreds of years old? Give as good as you get, eh? Going to explain that one?"

Bella compressed her lips tightly. Nivvy waited.

Finally she said, "What good will this contract do if you're not a Guild member?"

"Ah." He smiled and lowered his voice to a whisper. "I got a way to fake the Guild seal so that way it'll look like I am. More protection for you an' for me."

This confession lightened her brow. "Yes, that makes sense. I assume that since the hawk heard your instructions, she'll be able to help me at the Guild."

"Don't know as Zein is a he or a she," Nivvy said as they headed toward the front. "They ain't exactly said, have they?"

"Wait." Bella grabbed his arm again. "What if you get caught stealing while I'm getting the contract? You won't have it."

"Easy." He grinned at her. "What I got in mind ain't properly stealing, don't worry. Just a way to get a bit of pocket money. Used to play it as a kid all the time, been doing it here and there the last few months. Less you know about it, the better."

She drew in a breath and then let it out in a huff. He fancied he saw respect for his thiefly skills and know-how in her eyes, but the light wasn't good and he could be imagining it. "Fine," she said. "Fine. Let's get a room."

The innkeeper was glad to let them a room, and Nivvy didn't forget to tell him they were here with Zein when he pointed out Rahila out front. "Ah," he said, "good of you to hire Zein. That bird knows this city, but many folk are put off by a talking hawk."

"It's nice to hear praise," Nivvy said. "We haven't regretted our choice yet."

"And you won't." The innkeeper's protective tone shifted to informative. "Supper's a bit before sunset these days, but we serve for an hour. Tonight we've got pork, and there's barley soup and bread from the baker across the way."

"Delicious." Nivvy's stomach rumbled. "And where's the nearest bath?"

"There's a pump out back where you can wash. If you want a proper bath house, Zein can find one for you. Closest one is out that way, around the lamp-post, toward the spire a ways, you'll smell the salts before you see it. Costs a copper or two depending on what services you want."

"Much obliged." Nivvy waited while Bella counted out the three silver. "See you back here for supper, then."

Outside, they handed over Rahila to the care of the stable boy, and Nivvy passed his blanket over to Bella for Zein to perch on her arm. He made sure they were both clear on what to do at the Guild, and then parted from them.

The game he had in mind was one he'd played often as a skinny kid —easier than mucking about for flotsam—and again recently when he'd been removed from the Guild. It was trickier as an adult, but when you couldn't rely on your appearance, he'd discovered, the key lay in the performance.

First you found a merchant, ideally one who sold small, easily concealed goods like fist-sized fruit or bread rolls. Jewelry would be ideal, but jewel-smiths knew how easy it was to palm their merchandise and were alert for it. Leather goods worked sometimes as well, if you had to get creative.

You waited until a customer argued with the merchant. If it didn't happen quickly, you moved on, because you didn't want to linger in the stall or the store or the tent or whatever. If it did, you had to move quickly, and this was the riskiest part: you swiped something and dropped it in the customer's purse or satchel, whatever they were carrying their goods in. Then you went to the merchant, and here was where the performance came in. "Sir," you said, "I don't mean to intrude, but did that customer buy another," apple or roll or whatever it was, "to take on his way out?"

Of course the answer was no, and of course you could show the merchant where it was, and of course the customer was angry. Usually the customer returned the item, which he hadn't wanted to begin with, and sometimes the merchant said, "Don't come back." Once, the guards had been called and the customer taken away shouting; this was when Nivvy had been small and the choice was some inconvenience for a rich man versus his ability to eat in the evening, so he hadn't felt bad about it.

Once the unpleasant part was over, the merchant, if he followed the teachings of Massi, usually rewarded the supposed informant with a copper coin or maybe the stolen item. It wasn't much reward for the trouble it took, but to a desperate child or a thief without prospects, it was enough. The main problem was that if you weren't in a big city, you could only do this for a day or two because you couldn't do it at the same merchant's place twice, and even if you were careful, merchants all talked to each other.

But in a big city, with a need of only a few copper pieces, it was the lowest risk game to play, especially when Nivvy didn't know where anything in the city worth stealing was save for the two targets he'd been here to rob previously, and that outdated information was probably as near useless as made no odds.

After an hour and a half, Nivvy had six copper pieces, a slice of date bread, and a working knowledge of three merchant neighborhoods. Surprisingly, he'd found that playing up a slightly foreign accent helped in the performance. Spire was full of travelers from all over who came to see the legendary tower, and that whiff of not-from-here seemed to disarm even the most suspicious of merchants. At the first attempt, the merchant had asked if Nivvy knew the customer in question, perhaps suspecting a grudge, but once Nivvy had made it clear he wasn't from Spire, the game worked flawlessly.

He passed by the bath house the innkeeper had recommended, and even though sunset was near, he went in and paid two copper for one half hour in a tub of nearly-hot water, perfumed, as promised, with salts. The rooms were satisfactorily private; they didn't have locks on the door, but Nivvy managed to wedge his shut. It wouldn't keep people out forever, but it would give him enough time to get dressed if someone did come in.

When the hourglass set above the door (so it was visible to both sides without allowing anyone outside to see into the room) had almost expired and the bathroom attendant tapped discreetly on the door, Nivvy was already pulling his robes around himself, feeling refreshed and a good deal more like himself than he had in—well, a very long time. With a pleasant scent around him and a bounce in his step, he whistled his way back to the Giant's Foot.

## ✣ 6 ✣

# LEAVING SPIRE

**B**ella wasn't anywhere in the crowded main room of the inn when Nivvy returned. He breathed in the aroma of pork and bread and ale as he walked up to the busy innkeeper amid other patrons waiting for their plates and cups. When it was his turn to be served, he didn't even have to ask for news of Bella. "Your woman's up in your room," the portly man said, preparing Nivvy's plate. "Didn't want to eat down here."

"She's a curious one," Nivvy agreed. "Ale too, if you please." He placed a copper coin on the bar.

The innkeeper took it, then grabbed a large cup to fill. "You'll be getting her some better clothes, I hope. Not much to look at as she is."

"It keeps the other gents away," the thief said lightly. "But she's her own woman and if she wants new clothes, we'll get them."

"Looks like she stepped out of a rag merchant from a hundred years ago," the innkeeper said, setting the full cup next to the plate, and turned his attention to the next person in line.

Nivvy took his plate and ale and headed for the stairs. Upon opening the door to their room, he met the glare of Bella, seated on the floor with a nearly-empty plate beside her.

When he sat next to her, she snapped, "Where have you been?"

"Doin' what I said I was." He took out the three remaining copper coins from his afternoon's work and held them out to her. "Not a lot, but passable."

"It smells like you've been to the baths, too."

"Ay, that I have," he said, "an' I don't regret it at all. I recommend it to you, in fact. For two of those coins you can have a private room for half an hour, and the other one might get you some kind of servicing, if that's what you've a mind for."

"I just need to be clean," Bella said. "A private room sounds quite lovely, but I don't need any...servicing."

"Didn't mean it in a crude way," Nivvy said between mouthfuls of the excellent pork roast, ignoring the look she gave him and the way she said 'private,' clearly referring to the two bedrolls in this room. "Seems like you might be the type who likes being waited on, 'sall."

He'd intended it as a light jab, but she didn't take it that way. "I have been, and I will be again, but I can look after myself until then." She put the coins into a pouch in her dress, one by one. "I suppose I shouldn't ask how you obtained these."

"Not 'less you want to know." The bread, while not as good as the pork, was still better than anything Nivvy'd had in weeks, even Suleimon's cheese.

Bella stared at him and made a face. "Ugh. Must you eat like an animal?"

"Course I mustn't." Nivvy swallowed a mouthful, wiped pork juice from his chin with bread, and grinned. "But I can, so I am. Anyhow, it's an insult to the inn if you don't enjoy their food."

"I'd rather give insult than be seen as a pig at a trough." Bella stood. "The contract you wanted is there." She pointed to a sheet of paper lying on a bedroll. "Zein is off enjoying a dinner of something, I didn't ask what, and I," she walked toward the door, "am going to go take a bath."

"Glad you're takin' my advice," Nivvy said. "Enjoy it."

She stopped at the door. "I'm not doing it because you recommended it. I'm doing it because I want to."

"Ay, of course." He kept the satisfied grin on his face until she was gone and then set to devouring the rest of his meal.

A private room for the two of them was luxurious, even if Bella didn't see it that way, and made him feel more relaxed about the security of their things. Not that they had much, and not that this was the sort of place thieves would wander around in, present company excepted. Thing was, when your room was also someone else's room, they tended to feel like your belongings were at least fair game for looking through.

In any case, Nivvy had more important things to worry about, and having a private room meant he didn't have to look over his shoulder to tend to them. He went back downstairs, begged for a little sealing wax and a candle from the innkeeper, and then returned to the room to meticulously fill out the contract.

With every line his heart leapt. He wrote in the bit about stealing a ring, leaving the details vague, and then added, "stealth mission: get close to target" as the second bit, and "general escort and protection" because he felt generous and Bella needed protecting even if she didn't know it. She hadn't signed it yet, but she could do that later. When he was done, he went back and checked all the parts of the paper again, made sure he'd done everything just as he would have back in Copper Port. He couldn't help picturing the Guild in Penuca examining the contract. Didn't even have to be Penuca; it would pass any inspection once it had the seal on it. He was finally going to be free again to work as a Guild thief.

He was just dripping the sealing wax onto it when a voice said from the window, "I thought I should ask you about that."

Years of experience gave Nivvy the calm and focus to press the seal down into the hot wax before turning. Zein stood perched on the window, watching him with a calm eye. "About the contract?" he asked.

The hawk scanned the room. "Where's Bella?"

"Off having a bath."

"Ah, good." Zein hopped down from the ledge and walked awkwardly over to the contract. "I didn't say anything about it to her, but it seemed strange that you'd be getting a contract before a thief, especially in Spire. I mean, the thieves here are the best in the land."

"Not the best," Nivvy said.

"Ha." Zein looked up from the paper to his face. "So you are a thief. I guess you're not with the Thieves Guild, but she doesn't know any better, so she hired you."

"She knows about the Guild," Nivvy said. "She hired me on account of I was willing to take the job without any coin in hand."

"I don't know how much she does know about the Guild," Zein replied. "They asked her when she got the contract if she wanted to interview some thieves and she said yes, and she talked to three of them."

Nivvy's blood chilled. "What?"

"Let's see, there was a short woman who liked to play with knives, there was a short man who was dressed very fancy, and there was another short man—they were all short, come to think of it, shorter than you even—and he looked shifty. Don't worry, she didn't hire any of them, but that made me wonder if you were lying to me about being a thief, because that is the sort of thing a thief would do, you understand."

"I didn't know how you felt about thieves, so it seemed better not to tell you first thing," Nivvy admitted. "You're sure she didn't hire any of those others?"

"Of course she didn't. I was there the whole time. She asked them about going to the fire mountain, but none of them wanted to do it. I don't mind thieves, you're just doing a job like I am. Nobody thinks to steal from me because I don't really have anything of value. Someone tried to steal me once, but I put a stop to that right away. So why do you need the contract if she's already hired you?"

"In case I get caught stealing something, it'll save me getting thrown into irons, I hope." He studied the contract again, hardly able to believe it was real.

Zein, too, cast a critical eye over the contract. "I'm pretty sure the Guild doesn't let you just use any seal. But that mark does look complicated."

Nivvy held the small metal seal out so Zein could see it. "It's a real Guild seal, just from another city. What happens is the Guild, at least in other places, has a bunch of seals, all a little different, and they change 'em around if they think someone's made a copy or if one gets stolen. So I just nicked one of the spare ones."

"Will the guard here recognize the city it's from?" Zein studied the seal and then the imprint it had left in the wax.

"Don't have to," Nivvy said. "Only has to make the guard think I'm legit, right? By the time they check it out I'll be gone."

"I don't think it works that way," Zein said, "again, I don't know as much as you do, but when guards catch a thief they hold onto him, don't they?"

"Depends." Nivvy set the contract aside for the wax to dry. "Let's just call it insurance of a sort and be done with it, what d'you say? Seeing as how we're leaving soon and I don't expect to be caught here?"

Zein fluffed up their wings. "It's no skin off my nose. Or beak. It's just strange, is all. I know thieves are supposed to be sneaky, but I've never known a thief who was sneaky about being a thief. They swap stories and talk about jobs and things, even with me sometimes."

"I know." Nivvy pushed away memories. "You want stories? I got stories. I'll tell you some of my stories."

"No, I mean, yes I do, but that's not what I'm asking about. I'm a guide and my job is to look after my customers and now Bella's my customer, so if you're planning something against her," Zein gave him a sharp look, "it's my job to stop you."

Nivvy had to grin. "I'm your customer, too, ain't I? Don't worry. She and I walk the same road, and I mean her no harm." He pointed to the contract. "I intend to do everything in that document. It's just that when it's done, I want to be sure I'm set up properly. But look, nothing of this is even happening in Spire, so I don't see as how it falls in your interest anyway."

"Bella talked about keeping me on as a guide if I did a good job." Zein strutted along the floor. "I'd love to go see more places, and to get paid to see them, but I don't know the area, so how could I guide you? I'm a good guide in Spire. I know everyone here and I know I can do a good job and what if something happens to you and I'm a hundred miles from home and nobody knows me?"

"S'pose you'd fly back, hm?"

"I guess you're right." The hawk paced over to the candle, seeming brighter in the darkening room. Brown feathers with black bars shimmered as Zein stretched out their wings. "But how would I find the way? I've never been anywhere else as a hawk. I don't know. Bella gave me the morning to decide, but I can find good work around here so I probably won't."

Nivvy sat on the straw-filled bedroll and leaned back against the wall, running a hand over the rough fabric of his robes. "My uncle told me that the only chains on our spirit are the ones we put there ourselves."

"That doesn't sound right," Zein said. "I didn't ask to be turned into a hawk."

"No, I know. I don't think it's right all the time. People can chain your spirit in the way they treat you, especially if a lot of 'em do it. But I think what he sort of meant was that somewhere at the core of it, under all the things the world an' the gods pile onto you, there's a piece that's just you, and you need to keep hold of it. Don't put chains on it. I dunno, I'm still workin' it out myself."

"So what are you? Under it all?"

Nivvy shot the hawk a look. "Usually I wait 'til I've known someone a whole day before I answer questions about my deep inner spirit."

"All right, well, I'll tell you mine, then. I'm an explorer. I explored this whole city and that's why I know it so well. I love finding new places and learning things. I always have. When I was little, I wandered away from my mother so many times she gave up looking for me after a while, because she knew I'd always come back. Until I didn't, one day."

"Wait," Nivvy said. "How old are you?"

"I was fourteen when I got turned into a hawk, and that was five years ago, I guess. I lost track, but I'm pretty sure I've been to five Peony Festivals as a hawk. Maybe I missed one year. Anyway, even as a hawk it's beautiful. If you're still here you really should see it. So many flowers all over, and it's harvest time so there's food for everyone!"

"All right, all right, I don't plan to be back this way again, but if I am I'll keep it in mind. So if you're an explorer, why not come with us? Not that I'm saying I want you to, mind, but I don't object if Bella wants it."

"That's not a very nice thing to say," Zein said. "But I told you. I don't know the world out there."

"That's why you explore, isn't it?"

Zein paced the floor and turned from Nivvy to stare out the window. "I don't know what the world is like out there for former-humans."

"Former-humans?"

"People who've been turned into animals. If I hadn't found other former-humans, I don't know if I would have survived in Spire. There's a dozen of us and we have meetings sometimes, usually in Terria's stable because it's harder for her to get places. But then sometimes we meet at the river pools because Shanti can't leave the water, so the meetings have to have one or the other but never both. It's sad, really. People don't understand how limiting it is."

"Okay." Nivvy leaned back. "I understand."

"So," Zein said. "What are you?"

"I'm a thief. Even if nobody but me says I'm allowed to be."

"I don't see why you'd ever need anyone's permission to be a thief." Zein glanced at the window, where the sky had darkened from mauve to purple and the stars were out. "But I guess a guild makes it easier."

"They also work with the guard to take care of thieves what don't register with 'em. That's part of the game they play: you want to be a thief anywhere it's worthwhile being a thief, you got to pay their dues and do the jobs they say."

"It doesn't sound very free."

"Free ain't the point." Nivvy thought back to the Guild in Copper Port. "The point is everyone knows yer one of the best. Anyway, easy enough to turn down jobs you don't want. I never wanted to steal from people what couldn't afford it. And I wouldn't steal *for* rich people neither."

"I can't imagine who other than rich people would pay for stealing," Zein mused. "Most of the thieves I know stole things for merchants from other merchants, or stole things from nobles, jobs like that. If they worked for the Guild, I mean. I knew thieves who just stole for themselves or their family, too. I don't think any of them got in trouble with the Guild, but I haven't talked to most of them in a while, so maybe they did, or maybe they joined up."

"Well, ay, that's true." Nivvy stretched his legs out. "I liked working with merchants, people what made their own way, not the spoiled sons of suzerains and kings. Especially when it was stealin' from those spoiled sons. They didn't even miss what I stole some of the time. Though Tolungamon's ruby crown, he missed that for sure."

"Ruby crown!" Zein turned their full attention on Nivvy. "That sounds like a story."

"Oh, it is," he said. He wanted to ask Zein how they'd come to be turned into a hawk, but the talkative hawk hadn't yet volunteered the information, and Nivvy's nerves were still raw from the near-exchange of secrets with Bella that afternoon, so he happily launched into the tale of the theft of the ruby crown.

He told the hawk about Tolungamon, the merchant who had been trying to build the slave trade into Copper Port for years, who had accepted a commission to find a ruby crown for one of the most powerful kings in the Thousand Kingdoms, and about how Tolung-amon had planned to use the proceeds from the crown to flood Copper

Port with slaves. Nivvy had only gotten as far as he and his friend D'Alio sneaking onto the merchant's ship before the door opened and Bella walked back in.

The scent of bath salts wafted in with her, along with the stale smell of her dress. She looked refreshed, even in the same old clothes, and even in the dim candlelight, a smile shone on her face. "Well," she said. "We haven't much coin left, but that was worth it, I should say."

"Good." Nivvy enjoyed seeing her in a good mood. It put him in mind of what things might be like after this job.

"What were you discussing?" She sat on the opposite bedroll.

"Nivvy was telling me the story of a famous crown he stole," Zein said before Nivvy could open his mouth. "But we hadn't even gotten to the crown part yet."

"Don't let me interrupt." Bella lay back on her bedroll, squirming to get comfortable.

"No worry," Nivvy said. "I'll tell it another time, ay?"

"Sure." Zein hopped up to the window. "You're here all day tomorrow?"

"I think we'll leave in the morning," Bella said. "Are you going to guide us to the fire mountain?"

"Ooo, I don't know. There's...nothing really there except a Bouli temple. They do like hawks, but not as much as the Apo priests. You don't really need a guide to get there, either. Just go out the west gate and follow the road for a day and then you'll see the mountain. I wouldn't really be worth bringing along."

"Fine," Bella said.

"But maybe on your way back you can look for me? You said you wanted new clothes, and I know the best tailors. I'll keep an eye out for you at the west gate. Will it take long, what you're doing there?"

"Shouldn't," Nivvy said. "Day at most. But I don't know as we'll be coming back this way, will we? Or will we head directly north?"

He glanced to Bella for confirmation and was surprised to see the glower on her face. She half-sat and said, "That reminds me, Zein, I picked up something extra for you if you'll just come over here."

Nivvy tracked her hand as it reached for her purse, surprised at the sudden generosity, and then he saw the small blade in her hand and leapt for her. He arrived at the same time as the hawk and startled Zein enough that they circled the room and then perched on the edge of the bedroll, watching curiously as Nivvy kept Bella's hand behind her back and pulled a copper coin out of her purse. "Here," he said, tossing the coin to Zein. "For doing such an excellent job guiding us."

The hawk caught the coin deftly in their beak and bobbed their head. "Many thanks," they said around it.

"Now go on with you." He held fast, aided by Bella's reluctance to visibly struggle in front of the hawk. "If we're not back by the west gate within five days, then it was a great pleasure meeting you, and Apo grant our paths will cross again."

"Apo grant it." Zein fluffed their feathers, flew to the window, and then took off.

Nivvy released Bella's hand and sat back on the floor with a huff. The queen turned on him with a glare that would've frozen his blood inside him if she'd had the least amount of magic in her. Relaxed, happy Bella was gone as though she'd never existed. "How dare you?"

"How dare—you were going to kill our guide!"

"Her purpose was served, and I would not have tried to kill her if you hadn't stupidly told her our plans."

"Told them—what?" He racked his brain for what he might have said.

"You told her we were heading north."

Up until this point, Bella had seemed merely eccentric to Nivvy, but this pushed her a little further toward dangerous. He shook his head. "Aye, that I did. You know, presumably, how big the land is and how much is north, eh? Might as well have told them nothing at all."

"I can't risk anyone having any inkling of my plans. If the rulers are put on alert, my only chance will fail."

"They said you asked about bringing them along!"

"But I didn't tell her where. I wouldn't, not until we were on the way and she was hired. If she's not bound to us, she might tell anyone."

He waved an arm. "So buy their silence! That's how we do it now. Where do you come from that you can just kill people to keep secrets?" Not that this practice was entirely unknown to Nivvy, but it felt like more the province of stories: the Emperor of Catharni had commissioned a private palace riddled with secret passages and then killed all the architects so only he would know how to navigate them, the story went (and then he got lost in the passages and starved to death because although his people could hear his cries, nobody could find him, that's how it ended).

"She wasn't a person. She was an animal."

"They were an animal that used to be a person," Nivvy said.

Bella made a "pff" noise. "What's the point of turning someone into an animal, then? The point is, you can kill them if you want to, and nobody will care."

"I don't know as I want to go to this northern kingdom if that's how they view former-humans," Nivvy said, and then remembered the promised hundred crowns, and it occurred to him that someone who killed with impunity might very well be a queen. "I mean, I don't think they do that anymore so maybe you should think about that before you go stabbing hawks who only been nice to us."

She put the knife away, which was a relief because for a moment Nivvy worried she might try to use it on him. "One of my ministers once acted inappropriately toward my daughter. I turned him into a horse and made him work in the fields for a month, and when he was too broken down to work any longer, I had his head cut off and mounted in the third east corridor."

"Ah..." Nivvy tried to think of what to say to that.

"Of course, then he talked to people and helped that one prince, but I didn't find out about that until later."

"Right," he said. "Well. We don't do that no more. If an animal talks, they're to be treated as a person. An' they can't talk with their heads cut off, least as far as I know. Poor blighters, I mean, they get a hard enough time without being murdered for no reason. And Zein was a right useful guide!"

"It wasn't 'no reason.'" She glared at him again.

"I'll keep my counsel better from now on," he promised. Better she be angry at him than at Zein, even though it wasn't likely they'd see the hawk again.

As they prepared to sleep, Bella said, "If she earns enough money, can she be turned back into a human?"

"No," Nivvy said, stretched out on his own bedroll.

"Why not?"

"Ah, there's a whole story there, so I'll save it for tomorrow's ride," he said.

When she didn't respond, he asked, "Why didn't you get a new dress?"

"I'll have one soon enough." Fabric rustled in the dim light.

She remained silent after that, and whether she slept or not Nivvy didn't know. The more he learned about Bella, the more uneasy and intrigued he became, and the battle between those emotions kept him from sleep for a good while. Good people didn't murder—that made him uneasy—but there were two kinds of murderers in his experience: the poor and desperate kind, who murdered for food or coin, and the rich and cruel kind, who murdered when someone looked crosswise at 'em. Bella was surely not the first. So maybe she was all right in the head and had just fallen prey to powerful magic. After all, if people could be turned to animals, why couldn't a queen be kept alive for hundreds of years? If a spell like that was going to be cast, a queen or king would be the one you'd save it for.

She'd taken his counsel, at least, and hadn't insisted on murdering Zein. That boded well for their future relationship. If she had indeed been caught out of time, she would need someone sensible to guide her through the modern world, and why not Nivvy for that job?

❧

THEY STARTED THE DAY AT THE TAVERN ZEIN RECOMMENDED WITH A breakfast of spiced griddle cakes that were indeed as good as the hawk had advertised. Each cake was thick without being dry, full of different spices that complemented each other and didn't overwhelm the savory bready taste of the cake itself. A drizzle of honey took the cakes from merely good to delicious, enough to warrant spending an extra copper for another portion which he and Bella split.

Most marvelous of all, Bella actually showed enjoyment while eating them. After the brief smile following her bath, Nivvy dared to hope this might be a pattern that could continue. "Can you get more money the same way?" she asked as she handed over the copper for the extra portion.

"Not outside Spire," Nivvy said, mindful of the people around them also enjoying breakfast, "but we'll run into a friend with an open purse, or I miss my guess."

"Zein said 'a day' to see the mountain, so another day to get there?"

"P'raps two." Nivvy swallowed the bite of cake and wiped his mouth. "Thought you didn't want anyone t'know our plans."

Bella scowled and looked to her left. They had taken a spot against a wall, but even her glare couldn't stop others from taking a place a foot away from her. Still, those people had their own conversation going on, about fish and the Wet Market, whatever that was. "If someone wants to follow us to the mountain, they are welcome to," she said. "Once there, the situation will be different."

"All right," Nivvy said amiably. "Once we're there, we can beg shelter from the Bouli temple if it don't offend you too much."

"I've no feelings about whatever gods you worship down here one way or the other."

"T'be clear," he said in a low voice, "I don't worship Bouli. But most all temples got space for travelers an' only expect you to say a short prayer of thanks to their god while yer there. Won't always feed you, but shelter's shelter, an' I expect we can live off the land well enough. Until our 'different situation' happens."

Bella smiled at him. "Whatever you think best," she said.

The agreeableness worried Nivvy a little bit, but he put it down to the effects of a bath, a good dinner, and a good breakfast. Perhaps he was right, because the mood persisted through the city, keeping to smaller, less crowded streets at Bella's request, and to the gate where they emerged into a sunny day with a cool breeze that carried the green and earthy smells of forest and farm. Nivvy liked the close smells of the city, all the people and all the food and all the materials packed together; it made him feel safe and at home. But Bella lifted her nose to the fresh air and Rahila also gained some spring in her step as they set off down the road, so Nivvy was pleased that the ladies around him were in good humor.

"So," Bella said once they'd left the walls behind them. "Why can't Zein turn back to human?"

"A story for a story," Nivvy said. "What sort of friend is this we're headed to and why do they live in a volcano?"

It looked like the familiar scowl was trying to make its way back onto her face, but only partly succeeded. "Yes, you should have an idea of what to expect," she said. "I'll share that when you've told your story."

His first instinct was to insist she go first, but her story was a more personal one while his was merely history, so he gave in. The road was wide, straight, and, as Zein had predicted, not very crowded, even though they still rode through farmland and saw a stone barn every ten minutes or so. "Right," he said. "Well, this was round about a hundred years ago, as I heard it. There was all kinds of artifacts to turn people to animals, coz as you pointed out, it was a punishment favored by powerful people against folks that crossed them. There were some could turn animals back human, but not a lot, because the people that turn people into animals don't like for their punishments to be undone, so they'd destroy those artifacts when they got hands on 'em."

"Artifacts again," Bella said. "Does nobody have magic of their own?"

"All magic is in artifacts." Nivvy half-turned.

"You mentioned wizards."

"Aye, wizards have collections of artifacts and know all their stories. Got to keep lots of stories in your head to be a wizard. And not little cantrip stories, but proper long ones."

"It sounds exhausting."

Nivvy turned back to the road ahead. "What is it like having magic? Less exhausting?"

"Not *less*..." Bella thought about it. "But freer. You can cast any spell you like if you can create it, but it takes study to create a good spell, and energy to cast it. We had magic artifacts in my time as well, for people without native magic. I presume that they became more popular as they required neither study nor energy."

"A wee bit of study," Nivvy said.

"You know stories, though. Why is it harder to remember artifacts' stories?"

"Ah, the stories I tell change a bit each time. To make an artifact do the same thing, got to remember the story the same way. Change the story, change the magic, maybe it don't work at all."

"So the stories are like spells. Hmm." Bella shifted, rubbing her chin. "Interesting how things have changed. So you say there were few artifacts to turn animals to humans."

"Aye." Nivvy cast his mind back to remember the story. "The Suzerain Ali Bhai was the one had the bright idea of makin' an army out of animals. He had a small kingdom, not many people, but it bordered a forest full of monkeys and tree squirrels and so on."

"I see where this is going," Bella murmured.

"Well, Ali Bhai was a good sort, and he thought he'd make his kingdom a place where former humans could come be human again. So he collected all the turn-to-human artifacts he could and tried to get that going."

"And then enslaved the humans?"

"What? No. He wanted them to live in his country, and many of them did, but some left, and they were free to go. But he died and his son took over, and..."

"And he enslaved them."

"No. He wanted to grow his lands, but his army was small and weak. So he used the artifacts to turn monkeys and tree squirrels into humans."

"Oh." Bella sat back. "I wouldn't have thought that would work."

"Aye, it didn't, not too well, but well enough. They couldn't converse much, I heard, but they could hold a sword and they could fight, an' he could make more and more of them if he needed to."

"Clever."

"A mite too clever. His army became feared throughout the land, and all his enemies joined together to defeat him. Turned out his new-humans were good with swords but not with boats, so the seafaring nations attacked him with warships and catapults and defeated him in a matter of months."

"Monkey soldiers can't do everything."

"I suppose not, as it turns out. But they, the winning suzerains, that is, declared monkey soldiers an abomination in the eyes of their god, and they destroyed all the artifacts."

"I can't believe they destroyed *all* of them."

"That's what I was told. 'Good intentions make a weak foundation,' that's the lesson."

"I mean," Bella said, "I can't believe that—who was the first one? Ali Bhai? That he gathered all the artifacts in the world. And then that the other suzerains would destroy all of them. Surely one would keep one aside for himself? Even in my day, when we used artifacts more rarely, there were many I kept around because they might be useful one day."

"That's as may be." Nivvy drew a hand down Rahila's mane, encouraging the mare as she cantered along the road. "But that's the story I heard, and I've known a few people turned into animals and none of them ever found a way back. So it don't much matter if it happened the way it says in the story or another way. What matters is there's no way back for Zein."

"What about your friend the toad? What happened to him?"

"Ah." Nivvy set his eyes on the horizon. "Don't rightly know. Had to leave town in a hurry and couldn't take him with me. Hope the others took up his care, otherwise he's likely dead."

"That's what's meant to happen when someone's turned into a toad," Bella said.

"He didn't have to die." He said it more sharply than he intended. "Coulda lived another ten or twenty years with someone takin' care of him."

Bella was quiet a moment. "I only meant that you gave him more life than he should have had."

He swallowed another sharp retort, realizing that she meant it kindly. "Well. We didn't have nothin' like a former-humans meeting group in Copper Port, or maybe Marzin woulda done better."

"Meeting group?"

"Zein was telling me some former-humans know each other and meet on the regular. Sounds like they look out for one another."

They had not passed any inns, just farmhouse and barn after farm-house and barn. "Spire must be rich indeed," Bella observed after a little longer.

"Not so much. I mean, there's rich and there's poor, but I didn't see the kind of rich in Spire I seen in other cities. It's more like a place you stop on the way to richer places."

"But all this farmland." She gestured.

"Lots of mouths to feed. Lots of food to send off t'other places. Copper Port and Tagrabul, an' the Thousand Kingdoms from there. Probably places to the north as well, I shouldn't wonder. Never been farther north than Spire m'self."

"Where are you from, originally?"

He half-turned and grinned. "Ah ah. You owe me. What's the story with your friend what lives in a volcano?"

"Hmph." Her sigh brushed the back of his neck. "Scarlet's a fairy. You know about fairies, right?"

"Believe so. Spirits?"

"Magical beings. I used to have magic of my own, but I also had many magical friends. Now...perhaps only Scarlet remains."

"Rough when yer friends are all gone." Or have turned their backs on you, Nivvy thought, but then they weren't really friends, were they? Except Marzin and D'Alio.

"Many of them were gone before...I left. A few may still be in the north, but Scarlet was the most powerful of those remaining." She gave a half-laugh. "Funny. We always called her the 'southern Fairy,' and here you are never having been farther north than this."

"She'll recognize you after your time away?" Nivvy asked. "Only, magical spirits can be quite fussy in stories."

"She'll know me," Bella said confidently.

"Hope so," Nivvy muttered, and then, louder, "why's she live in a volcano?"

"To discourage visitors, of course."

"Of course," Nivvy echoed. "Tell me, back in your day, did you have signs? Posted notices? 'No trespass' or the like? Cheaper'n living next to a mountain of fire."

Bella snorted. "Scarlet has her eccentricities. But it's worked. She lives just a few days ride from this city, and nobody I talked to had any idea there was anything on the mountain save for a temple to the fire god."

"Bouli, aye. Well." Nivvy scratched his head. "Good on her, I suppose. If she's magical, you s'pose she knows you're coming?"

"Maybe. Her magic wasn't around prescience."

"Presshy-what?"

"Foresight. Seeing the future. Scarlet wasn't an oracle, more of a..." Bella paused. "Creative magic type."

"Creative like..." Nivvy paused, thinking of the kinds of magic he knew. "Like creatin' stone walls out of nothing? Pits of fire maybe?"

"Yes," Bella said slowly. "And...creating creatures. Mythical monsters."

"Ah. Well, that don't scare me at all," Nivvy said. "Mythical monsters were some of me best friends growing up."

"You needn't worry," Bella snapped. "Scarlet won't summon any of her creatures in her own lair."

"Not even against a thief tryin' to rob her?"

"If you're an 'uncommon' thief, she'll never know, will she? I told you she hasn't got foresight."

"That's why I asked." He sighed. "Any idea what sort of defenses she has? Traps, aught like that?"

"She never had any traps that I knew about."

"Course not." Nivvy sighed and set his eyes to the road ahead.

## 7

# THE MOUNTAIN OF FIRE

They spotted the mountain before the sun set, when they crested a hill and the broad, flat cone rose in front of them, closer than Nivvy had expected. Perhaps if the mountaintop had come to a point, as he generally expected mountains to do, it would have been visible from farther away.

Regardless, it was quite forbidding, rising well above the closest peaks, streaked with black and grey at the very top until about halfway down, when it took on an ochre color streaked with darker brown. To the south, along the ridge of what looked like worn-down teeth, two other peaks jutted up above the others, uneven canines in the sky's mouth. But there was no doubt about their destination. The road pointed them straight ahead at the flat-topped mountain and, if that weren't enough, they passed a sign with the three red triangles of the god Bouli on it and an arrow pointing straight ahead.

It took them two more days of riding to reach the temple, seated at the base of the mountain. On the way, Nivvy lightened a few of the packs in the unguarded stables of one inn, one of which even had some coin in it (some people thought themselves tricky, leaving coin in their packs rather than keep it in their room where thieves might expect it). He used that coin and traded some of the pack contents (inns could always use rope and candles) to pay for a room in the next one, and they slept the second night on the road when no inn presented itself. By then they had moved from farmland into a small forest, thick greenery that made Nivvy uneasy about straying too far from the road. In places like this, they were less likely to encounter bandits than be set upon by a bear or forest cat or pack of wolves.

In the event, none of that happened, and they even found some mushrooms that made for both a pleasant supper and breakfast (even accounting for Bella's complaining about the crudeness of the meal). The forest gave way to grassland and then rocky terrain near sunset, as they arrived at the modest stone building with three red triangles above the doorway.

When Nivvy pointed out the temple ahead of them, Bella said, "Very nice," in the distracted tone she'd used whenever he pointed out an interesting tree or flower on the ride, before he stopped doing that.

"Glad we won't have to spend another night on the road," he said.

For a moment she held his gaze, and he could see her gathering herself to command him to go directly to her friend's place. If she did that, he'd likely give in to her and go. But then she looked past him to the temple. "Fine," she said. "I don't know what kind of food Scarlet has, but I wouldn't bet on her having human food."

"Surely she can create some?" Nivvy didn't mean to sound sarcastic, but it rather came out that way.

Bella snorted. "She could. If you want to trust to what she thinks people eat."

"I wager the temple does a better job of that."

"That was my point," she said.

"While we're on the subject of your friend," Nivvy said, "Can you describe this 'lapis ring' more precisely than that? If she's got a whole pile of rings t'sort through, it'd make my job easier if I know exactly what I'm looking for. Also if you know where she keeps it and what might be guardin' it, that would be some help."

"Do you want me to do your job for you?" Bella asked.

"Course not." This was terrain Nivvy was familiar with: the client who thought that a thief could magically navigate any situation. "But you been there and I haven't, and I'll have just a short time to get the lie of the land. The more you can tell me, the better chance we'll get what you want out of it."

Stressing that this whole deal was to her benefit worked, as it usually did. "It's been a long time since I've seen the ring. I recall it having a silver band and mounting, and a blue lapis stone set in it."

"How blue?" Nivvy pointed up at the cloud-dotted sky. "That blue?"

"Darker." She cast about, but nothing else around them was blue. "Like deep water."

"Square stone or round?"

"Square. Not perfectly square. Longer than wide."

He nodded. "What might be guarding it?"

"I don't imagine Scarlet would have anything guarding it except herself. She's very confident in her own power that way."

That could be either a good or bad thing. "If you can keep her out of the room it's in, you s'pose she'd be able to tell if I palmed it?"

Bella exhaled onto the back of his tunic. "I don't think so. She's told me in the past that she's misplaced magical items, so I don't think she can know where they are."

"This ring, is it special to her? Different from the other stuff somehow?"

"No, I don't believe so."

"Right." He rubbed his chin. This was sounding more possible than he would've thought stealing from a magical spirit would be. He hadn't met one before; maybe they were just like wizards but with innate magic rather than stories in their heads. Wizards were protective of their magic items, to be sure, but the Guild had accepted assignments to steal them. Those could still go wrong, as Marzin had learned. But they didn't always, and Nivvy was better than Marzin had been even before he'd been toaded. "You know where she keeps her stuff?"

"She used to keep her rings in a large wooden chest with red and black designs on it. It's magical itself, but only to keep it from rotting and maybe to keep other magical spirits from seeing what's inside. I don't know where the chest will be, but I can show you when we get there."

"Good. And then keep her out of that room. I'll ask to use the necessary or sommat like that, shouldn't take me more than two minutes unless she's got rings for all her fingers and her friends' fingers."

"I can keep her busy for two minutes," Bella said confidently.

"Then you'll have your ring," Nivvy said, and guided Rahila ahead to the stone archway that marked the temple's entrance.

The priests of Bouli did not have a wide range of food that day, but they did have fresh roots and greens from the nearby forest, along with a small amount of meat, and copious amounts of weak wine. There was grass for Rahila, which she ate with some indifference.

Nivvy enjoyed the meat and veg, most of it roasted with aggressively hot spices the like of which he hadn't had since Copper Port. He expected Bella to comment on the spice, but she ate the food as calmly as anything. He wasn't even sure she tasted the spices. The priests ate with them, and over conversation they discovered that there was a holy place two thirds of the way up the volcano but that it was very dangerous, and the priests did not recommend that travelers go near it. Why dangerous, Bella asked, and the oldest of the priests said vaguely that sometimes priests and acolytes didn't come back from travels to it. He remembered one such and waxed eloquent about the devotion of his friend, that Bouli must have thought highly of him to take him so early.

Bella managed to wrangle vague directions to this holy place in between several more warnings and attempts to point them to the more casual path to the top of the volcano, which was a splendid sight. Because Bella couldn't be bothered to respond with the appropriate pleasantries, Nivvy took over the conversation to assure the priest that they would indeed take this safer path and would pay their respects to Bouli at the top of the volcano.

They were shown to separate rooms, Bella's near the female priests and Nivvy's near the male one, and Nivvy was secretly relieved, because for the last two nights he'd been worrying about whether Bella slept or not, and having her in a separate room would allow him to sleep without worrying that she was staring at him all night long.

THE NARROW PATH THAT LED UP TO THE "HOLY PLACE" SEEMED FAR steeper than the casual path, and sharp black pebbles littered it, thick as grass. On the advice of the priests, Nivvy had left Rahila at the temple, so it was entirely up to Nivvy's and Bella's shoes to keep their feet safe, and neither was completely up to the task. Nivvy took to shuffling along so he could kick the sharper stones out of the way, while Bella merely crunched her way up and did not seem to feel any discomfort, even though Nivvy spotted blood on her pale white feet.

The sun beat down, but the farther up they walked, the more the wind bore away that heat. Nivvy's skin felt that curious combination of warm underneath and cool on the surface that he knew well from his childhood by the ocean, so he kept his head turned away from the sun where he could and tried to judge how far up "two-thirds of the way to the top" was from where they were.

"Wish we had Zein here to tell us where this path ends," he muttered.

He was talking mostly to himself, but Bella answered. "I had not thought that talking animals could continue to be useful. Most of the ones I knew were more like your friend the toad."

Nivvy didn't quite like "useful," and didn't appreciate that Marzin, not being so-called useful, would be less worth anyone's time. His friend had plenty of skills, like a gift for accents, but beyond that he was a true and loyal fellow, toad or not. "Moment of rashness, was it, trying to kill them?"

"No," she said. "I don't know what awaits me in the north and I detest being ignorant. I was taking a reasonable precaution. I simply hadn't spared a moment to think about how useful they could be on our return to Spire. Or even," as she stared upward, "on this journey."

"If it's been hundreds of years," Nivvy said, because whether or not it was a delusion, it was best to accept that she believed it, "then surely they won't expect you up in the north. What could one hawk do?"

"My sister had magic," Bella said. "She might have left protections behind, spells that could be awoken with a simple careless word. But you were correct that the hawk was very unlikely to tell anyone. She did say she'd never left Spire."

"Right." This was a new piece of information. "So, takin' the kingdom back from your sister, is it?"

"Her descendants, at any rate." Bella did not seem upset at having let that information slip.

"You're still alive," Nivvy pointed out.

"Not by my choice."

Even for Bella, that seemed an odd statement. Nivvy shied away from it. "So it was your sister took your kingdom from you, then."

"It was." Bella's sigh was long and deep enough to be well distinct from the labored breathing that came to them both from climbing a steep path.

"Must have been a nice kingdom to be wanting it back after all these years."

"Ah, it was lovely." Bella's eyes rose above the path. "So many rose gardens that they sweetened the air for miles around. The loveliest palace, all white marble and gold trim shining into every corner of the city, where elegant stone houses surrounded bustling markets with farmers and merchants from all the neighboring countries come to sell their goods. A kingdom the envy of those around, yet so well-regarded that war never came to us. People came from the world over to seek my counsel."

People in stories were forever going to kings and queens, presuming them wise because they had the favor of one god or another. Nivvy'd never had cause to seek wisdom from anyone more noble than his uncle, but he allowed as how not everyone had wise uncles. "Sounds lovely," Nivvy said. "A sight better than any place I've lived."

"We were a jewel in the north," Bella said. "My people loved me so. And my sister took it all from me and left me with nothing."

"I'm sorry about that." This was easy to say sincerely. And when Bella didn't talk again, Nivvy said, "Didn't have a kingdom m'self but I did have a good job, and this...other fellow went and got himself killed and they made it out to be my fault."

Bella inclined her head toward him, and he took that as encouragement. "It was a simple job, see, an' I did my part an' told him to come away, but he'd spotted some woman and decided he could make time to dip his dowser. So I left, an' turned out he was caught an' they killed him, an' the Thieves Guild pointed the finger at me, said I should've stopped him."

"Ridiculous," Bella said.

"It was!" Nivvy hadn't told the story to anyone since the trial thing, and never mind that he'd fuzzed the details a little (and left out who the other fellow was, because if he said Vicho's name the guilt would surface and swamp the rest of it), the core of the thing was true, and here was Bella taking his side. "I tried to get him to scarper with me, but he wouldn't do it. He was a big fellow, and what was I meant to do, drag him away?"

Bella stared up the mountain. Nivvy followed her gaze to a point where the path appeared to level out and curve around the mountain rather than leading (as it felt) straight up it. Above that point, the rock rose even more steeply and showed no way up except the very end of the more casual path, far to the right. "It would seem my spell chose better than I knew," Bella said.

Because she was looking at the volcano, Nivvy thought at first that she meant the path, and he was going to say that she hadn't cast a spell to choose the path; the priests had pointed it out. Before his quick tongue could form the words, though, he realized that she'd been talking about choosing him. That added to the warmth under his skin as he shuffled his way up the path, and he refused to dispel any of that warmth by asking, *what spell?*

When the path finally leveled out, Nivvy and Bella found themselves facing a shallow alcove in a solid rock wall. Nivvy leaned against the wall, catching his breath while Bella tapped and pressed on the rock inside the alcove and out, and then walked on along the path. At a point some ten feet beyond the alcove, she said, "It's here. There's heat coming through the rock somehow."

"P'raps because it's molten on the other side." Nivvy didn't know much about volcanos, but he knew that they were places where the earth and fire gods melted rock, and sometimes their parties grew violent and explosive.

"No," Bella said. "It's an illusion. Do you have any spells to break illusions?"

"No."

She stared at the wall. "It's all about finding the crack."

For several minutes, Nivvy sat playing with the sharp black stones. Obsidian, they called it, and some people made blades out of it. He wondered if any of the stones around here would be large enough for making one of those. Nice black obsidian dagger would look quite sharp in his hand, wordplay definitely intended, and if Bella couldn't find a way in to her friend it'd be nice to have another keepsake from this journey. Honestly, part of him hoped she wouldn't find a way in. Then he'd be set free with his shiny new contract to go to Penuca, or venture farther north if the itch caught him, and start over with a new Thieves Guild. He could always claim he'd stolen a ring from a magical spirit living in a volcano.

No sooner had he stood up to walk back down the path a little way than Bella said, "Ha. Here it is."

He turned to see her slide her hand into what appeared to be solid rock. "The illusion is anchored here, and if you can get close to the anchor point there's usually a weak link." She stepped into the rock and vanished.

"Ey!" Nivvy called in alarm and hurried over to the rock. Bella's fingers reached out.

"Take my hand," she called. "And probably close your eyes."

He did both of those things. She pulled him forward, which she should not have been able to do, and he should not have been able to take even one step, let alone three, but he did, as a blast of hot air assailed him and the light around him dimmed. Nivvy opened his eyes to see a small tunnel in the rock, lit with a foreboding red glow, and a dead bat stretched out on a wooden pole right in front of him.

He yelled and stumbled back, and stared at the bat from there. Spiderwebs clung to its fur, and its eyes had been ripped away, probably by birds, to judge from the claw holes in the wings. But it didn't smell, and the skin of the wings had an odd iridescent sheen to it in the dim, hellish red light. What was more, from the bat's claws hung a loop of shimmering silver, big enough to be a necklace for one of the giants in Zein's story, and fastened to the thread at regular intervals were teeth. They looked to be human teeth, at least from as close as Nivvy was willing to get to them.

This was Bella's friend's home? This was how she greeted guests? The bad feelings he'd had over Bella trying to kill Zein resurfaced, stronger than before. He'd been able to explain that away to himself as the reflex of someone unsettled in an unfamiliar world, someone who with his guidance could find a better path. But Bella's best friend was someone who spent magic to make this grotesque tableau the first thing visitors would see? Some of those teeth looked not as old as the bat. If this was the company Bella kept...

Not that he hadn't done jobs for unsavory people in his time, but usually the unsavoriness hovered around the level of cheating customers, maybe some bullying, occasionally some truly reprehensible hygiene. One couldn't always be picky about one's clients. But he'd never knowingly worked for a murderer, magical or not, and he was starting to feel like he'd been hired by the latter to steal from the former, which was a worrying situation. Murderers tended to have an easier time murdering than other folks did, just as sailors were better at sailing and so on, and when you crossed one, it was harder to talk your way out of the situation.

Nivvy's nose twitched. "Say," he called to Bella, who had walked on past the bat without a second glance. "What say we give this up for a bad job and go back to Spire to come up with another plan? I could use another round of those griddle cakes."

Bella turned, her black hair glistening with sweat around flushed skin. Her lips looked even redder in the light; her eyes looked almost black. "Don't be ridiculous," she snapped, seizing his wrist and pulling him forward. "We're here and we're going to go in. Are you having second thoughts about your ability?"

"Only I'm pretty sure this is nasty magic sign, here." Nivvy pointed to the bat, ignoring the jab. "Happy fairies with friendly magic don't kill bats and stretch 'em out to greet their guests with."

"It's just her way." Bella smoothed the hair out of her face. "It probably wasn't a former-human, if that's what you're wondering."

Nivvy stared at the bat. "I am now," he said.

Bella pointed forward. "The cave opens out ahead, and from the glow, I think it goes around a lava pit. I believe the entrance is on the other side of it."

"You believe? I thought you knew this fairy."

The queen's lips pursed. "I never had to come in this entrance," she admitted finally. "I was always invited."

"Oh ho, so we're going in the uninvited way. That always makes a fairy well-disposed toward one. It'll be us stretched out on poles as a warning to the next pair, I shouldn't wonder." Nivvy started back down the path, but he'd only gotten two steps before Bella grabbed his arm.

"You can set your superstitions aside. I'm telling you, Scarlet and I have a long friendly history."

Nivvy glared back. "Then why are we sneakin' in the back door?"

"Because I don't know how to get her attention! I had a token, back in the palace, and all I had to do was hold it and think of her and I would be transported to her parlor immediately." Bella's face was, if anything, getting even more red, and Nivvy had already seen that heat didn't produce that effect.

"Why didn't you say so?" Nivvy shook free and marched back to the illusory rock. "We'll just go steal the token. That I can manage."

"Stop!" Bella's shout rang out and did, for the moment, stop Nivvy from walking. "We are here now, and we are going in this way, or you will receive no payment."

Nivvy considered this for a moment, and then a longer moment. The contract sat there in a pocket of his robe, its scant weight pulling him back down the mountain. But as demanding as Bella was now, he couldn't forget the moment on the path up here when he'd felt that they were caught in the same tide. And besides, if he left now, he'd always be wondering what the lair of a magical spirit looked like. Maybe this wasn't Bella's best friend, but—as she'd said, he reminded himself—her only friend. Like if he needed help in Copper Port, and D'Alio and Marzin were gone an' all he had to rely on was Vilo, the big bully. All right. He took a deep breath and calmed himself. "Rather have me own skin than your payment," he muttered as he came back to her, just to show that he was doing this despite his best judgment.

"That's better." Bella eyed the passage, where the reddish glow now waxed, now waned. Even the darkness shimmered with waves of heat that buffeted him constantly. He was used to walking through the desert where the heat was greater than this, but there the heat was merely part of the world, in the air he walked through and the ground he set his feet on. Here it billowed forth like a malevolent guardian—

No. He shook his head. The bat with its necklace of teeth was unnerving him, as it was meant to do. The heat wasn't malevolent here; it was merely heat from molten rock. Stay well clear of the molten rock and you wouldn't get burned or melted. "So how d'we get past this lava?"

"The bat was a warning," Bella mused, "but if she didn't want anyone to pass this way, she would have just closed it off rather than go to the trouble of making an illusion."

"The rock, the bat, the lava." Nivvy ticked off on his fingers. "In stories, the barriers all come in threes. You reckon the lava's the last of them?"

"We'll see when we get past it." She took a step forward and then looked back at him. "Well?"

"How about if you go in, figure it out, then come back. I'll wait here."

"Don't be—" She stopped and gathered her breath. "Wouldn't you rather meet this spirit with someone who's her friend?"

"Who used to be her friend," Nivvy pointed out. "I've friends in Copper Port what I haven't seen in one year and I'd be more cautious if

I went back than you are now. And they've got no more magic than I have."

Bella's face gained a small measure of hope. "You haven't anything that lets you survive intense heat, have you?"

"No."

She sighed. "Never mind, just come along. I'm sure it will be fine."

Her hand tap-tapped at her side. Perhaps it was impatience, but her eyes didn't have the glare he'd come to associate with her "get on with it" mood. It struck him that she might actually be worried about going to see this friend again, and that in her own clumsy way she was tugging on the tenuous bond they'd forged over a few days. "Right," he sighed, and walked forward.

The cave opened out into what must be the heart of the volcano, an enormous cavern with daylight at the top and a hellish red glow from the bottom. Waves of heat blasted them as soon as they stepped out of the shelter of the cave, almost driving Nivvy back. Even the worst days in the desert hadn't subjected him to heat as concentrated and focused as this, the very air rippling and making it hard to discern any details of the walls around him. The grey-black-brown of them seemed to pulse like a living thing, so that after a few steps Nivvy felt he were standing on a ledge around an immense throat.

The ledge, a few feet wide, did nothing to make Nivvy feel better about his situation. It was entirely possible that there was another ledge below it to catch one's fall, one cushioned with soft sand, or it was possible that Bella's friend herself hovered helpfully just out of sight in case someone fell. Many things were possible, but he was not going to know any of them for sure because he did not want to look down and see how rapidly the cliff fell away into a drop that would kill him before the fiery molten rock had a chance to.

Bella, too, hesitated, enough that Nivvy caught up to her in a few steps. She pressed her back to the wall and edged along, and unlike Nivvy, she kept looking down and then jerking her head up.

So Nivvy took her hand, the one closest to him. She pulled away, but not hard enough to break his grasp, and then her arm relaxed and her eyes met his, still defiant. Then she took another step and another, allowing her hand to remain in his grasp.

The ledge was fine, he told himself. It had been here for hundreds of years, at least since the last time Bella had been here. No, wait, maybe not, because she hadn't gone in this way before. She was nervous enough, not the time to ask her about it now, but help, Inira, there are so many questions it's not the time to ask right now.

As if Inira were listening, the answer came to him: you're here because of what you can do, so worry about doing that. You can climb across a ledge even in blistering heat with a fall that would kill you just inches away. You can steal a ring from a magical spirit. Whoever—or whatever—Bella is, she needs you and you need her. If she does get to be queen again—even if she doesn't—you can get back to proper thieving. Just do what you do.

"Right," he said aloud.

"What?" Bella turned.

"Nothing." He gave her a smile that he hoped came off as confident, although in this light who could tell? She looked ghastly in the faint sunlight from above and the red light from below, and if he looked the same, he doubted any expression would instill confidence.

It felt like they'd edged along halfway around the inside of the volcano, but when he looked back, the cave mouth was barely a hundred feet back, and the inside of the mountain ran at least six or eight times that distance, as best he could judge with the rippling heat. Already it was hard to make out the cave, and his eyes watering made it worse.

As hard as it was to see behind them, it was impossible to see what they were edging their way along to. Nivvy squinted, wiped his eyes, and stared ahead, and as far as he could tell the ledge just ended. But Bella slid on with determination, and so he followed along behind.

The next time Nivvy turned to look behind him, the cave they'd come through might have vanished. Certainly his eyes couldn't make it out. Bella still moved forward, one hand clasped in his, the other flat against the wall, and he followed, repeating Inira's message: Do what you can do.

They stopped well short of where the ledge seemed to end, although who could say what was real? The intense heat battered Nivvy, his tunic sticky against his skin, and Bella was the only real thing in this world. He didn't trust the wall he rested against, gritty and warm, nor the ledge below his feet, even though it bore his weight. "Are we there?" he asked Bella.

"Yes. I'm almost sure. It feels...ah. Here." Again she pushed her hand into what seemed like solid rock, and then the rest of her followed. "There's a step," her voice said as her hand pulled him after. "Be careful."

He closed his eyes and kicked ahead carefully. When his foot met solid stone, he stepped up and through the illusory rock.

Cool air caressed his face. When he opened his eyes, the air was crisp and clear, every detail in front of him sharp. This was still definitely a cave in a mountain; the smell of lava persisted in the windowless room, and the weight of the rock felt almost tangible above the domed ceiling. But hung on the smooth rock walls were a dozen or so tapestries depicting what looked like battle scenes, and in front of the tapestries, an odd assortment of furniture was strewn around, as though in the parlor of a merchant who dealt in antiques from no particular age. Two chairs looked to be part of a set: stiff, formal ivory carved roughly with reliefs he couldn't make out from here; a side table's interlocked star patterns in gold inlay reminded Nivvy of similar furniture he'd seen in Copper Port. A wardrobe squatted next to the table, its wood so dark it looked to be the shadow of a wardrobe somewhere else in the room, or maybe in a different room altogether; next to that, a low set of shelves made of hammered metal held various weapons. As Nivvy's eyes lit on it, he saw that not only the weapons but the metal of the shelves itself bore suspiciously brownish-red stains, and that the hammered metal had a sigil on it, like one often saw on armor, and his stomach did a little flip, imagining where those shelves had come from.

Looking up to the tapestries wasn't much relief, because they featured not just battles but bloody, brutal battles: blood-drenched dragon-like monsters killing two and even three armored opponents at a time, arms and heads and legs strewn about the field like boats in a busy harbor on a sea of blood rather than water, and in more than one of the tapestries, a giant head staring down. The head was different in different tapestries: blue-skinned, green-skinned, male, female, reptilian, but in every one its eyes glowed a bright, surreal red.

The rug below his feet was the least disturbing part of the room, and that was clearly the skin of some long-dead giant animal. He could not tell where the light in the room was coming from, but there was enough to see by.

Bella cleared her throat. "Scarlet," she called.

In the instant between her call and the response, Nivvy was seized with a foreboding strong enough that he half-turned to look for the door. Not that he would've run out on a job, Inira, he would not, but the instinct to get out of this situation overwhelmed him for a moment. Could happen to anyone. And anyway, even if he could've figured out which of the tapestries they'd come in through, he wouldn't have made it before Scarlet appeared.

Bella hadn't described Scarlet at all, but Nivvy certainly did not expect a hulking blue warrior with three horns emerging from his head, three necklaces of bones and beads draped down over his bare chest, leather armbands on both arms, and robes draping his lower half.

Nivvy gasped, but before the word "djinn!" could make its way from his brain through his chest to his throat and mouth, the creature turned from Bella to him and fixed its glowing red eyes on him. "Good day," it said in a light, confident woman's voice that felt all the more incongruous for the large, pointed teeth in the mouth from which it issued. "I am Scarlet, a kind fairy. You need fear nothing from me."

As it spoke the words, the air shimmered as it had outside in the volcano, and the form of the djinn blurred and melted. Nivvy rubbed his eyes and blinked, and when he opened them again the djinn had vanished. In its place stood a petite woman with ivory-white skin, a cloud of bright red hair framing her narrow but elegant face, ice-blue eyes, and shining white smile. Her blue gown displayed elegant simplicity, darker blue around the bodice with a sky-blue skirt and beaded trim.

"It's so good to see you again." Bella's voice held raw relief that Nivvy hadn't heard from her in their brief acquaintanceship.

"And lovely to see you, too, *shawka*," the fairy said. Her voice was so smooth and melodious and fit this form so perfectly that the vision of the djinn was driven from Nivvy's mind. "How nice of you to bring me this lovely present."

Bella cleared her throat, so Nivvy held back his own retort. "This is my new assistant," she said. "My new companion. He's going to help me regain my throne."

"How lovely for him," the fairy said. "And how interesting for you." She turned those blue eyes on Nivvy, cold and appraising. "I presume you came to ask my help with something?"

"I know your help comes at a price," Bella said smoothly. "I have been gone a long time and the world has changed. I was only hoping to talk to you for a little. You're the only person still alive that I know."

"A social call." Scarlet smiled, and though the smile was lovely and winning, it was a little too wide, the teeth a little too white, and Nivvy couldn't help but imagine sharp points on them. "How delightful. Why don't you come inside?"

## 8

# THE THEFT

Scarlet glided out of the room through a door that Nivvy hadn't noticed before, which she certainly hadn't entered through, and Bella followed, so he had no choice but to trail after them. He did take one look around to make sure there was no red-and-black inlaid chest.

The next room, a high vaulted cavern whose even higher domed ceiling glowed blue, contained no furniture at all, but taxidermied animals littered the ground, clung to the trees jutting out from the walls, and hung from the ceiling. Many animals Nivvy recognized, and many he did not. Scarlet seemed to float over them as Bella picked a path through the animals and Nivvy followed in the queen's footsteps, avoiding the mice and snakes frozen on the ground. "My menagerie," the fairy said carelessly over her shoulder to Nivvy.

"It's grown quite a bit. They used to be alive, didn't they?" Bella asked.

"It was so messy. This way is less interesting, but if I forget about them for a decade, I don't come back to find shit and corpses all over."

Nivvy shuddered, but Bella merely asked, "Did you have someone prepare them or did you do that?"

"I did it. Come."

They stepped from that cavern into an even larger one, far longer than it was wide, and at this point Nivvy knew that magic had to be at work somehow. Either they were still inside the volcano and made

THE PRICE OF THORNS

much smaller, or they'd been transported into a different, magical space. This cavern far surpassed the greatest armory Nivvy had ever seen in person: every inch of the wall was hung with weapons both familiar and non. There were scimitars and daggers (all kinds of daggers, curved and straight, short and long), there were longswords and swords that looked fit for giants, there were spears and polearms, and then an entire section of different kinds of bows and arrows. Scarlet talked to Bella as they walked. "So tell me where you've been. It's been at least eight hundred years, because that's when Delly was killed, and I remember thinking it was a shame you weren't at the wake. It was a lovely affair."

"I felt it," Bella said.

"You did? I wondered."

"I felt all my friends die. They left me that much magic." The haunted tone in her voice dispelled most of Nivvy's doubts about her age. He put aside whatever feelings that brought up; he was on a job now. "I counted all of them go. You knew Delly, but there were others. Most of them were killed soon after I was imprisoned. That was part of my punishment, to outlive them all and watch my kingdom pass away. How did you escape?"

Scarlet laughed a high, flutey laugh. "Darling, they've been coming after me for centuries. I've no doubt they'll continue to come until one of them succeeds, but until then, I build up my menagerie and my armory." She gestured to the weapons.

Nivvy hung back and let his strides take him closer to the walls so he could see the weapons up close, curious what sort of things someone would bring to hunt a magical spirit. The metal on the blades gleamed, but a few of them still bore bloodstains, as the shelves in the first room had. One drew his eye, a curved sword with an unusual hilt. When he came closer, he saw that the hilt had been crafted out of bronze in the shape of a man's hand. This seemed odd; it did not look like it would be comfortable to grip.

Now was a good time to see if the fairy could sense someone picking up her things. He reached out very carefully and lifted the blade from the wall, watching Scarlet and Bella ahead of him. The fairy didn't turn around. Nivvy wrapped his hand around the hilt and found the way that it fit into his hand. Better than he'd imagined. He gave the blade a swing—

—and he caught sight of a face reflected in the blade, darker than his own, with a full beard and mustache and eerie golden eyes, screaming silently.

Nivvy jumped and looked around, but nobody had materialized behind him. He looked again, and the blade was just a blade. Carefully, silently, he replaced it on the wall and stared at it from different angles.

The face did not reappear no matter how he moved. He hurried to catch up to the others, trying not to think about what he'd just seen, trying not to focus on anything but his job here. He wasn't here to kill Scarlet, just take one of her many, many possessions, a small thing she probably wouldn't even miss, and certainly wouldn't notice if he took. He wouldn't end up trapped in a weapon on her wall.

"...the light was the same twilight all the time," Bella was saying as he rejoined them. "You always felt like there was something just beyond your sight, but then you'd go toward it and it wasn't there. Just the same grey walls, the same four rooms, over and over again."

"It sounds dreadful, darling," Scarlet said. "How did you escape?"

Bella hesitated for a moment. "It took a long time and almost all the magic I had left to craft a counterspell," she said. "But I did it. I broke out and found myself here, in this world where the rules of magic are different somehow, where you're the only one I know."

"Which explains why you have paid me this lovely visit."

"It is good to see a familiar face. And you've lived through the changes to the world. If anyone can warn me what magic I need to be mindful of, or where to get some myself, it would be you."

As Bella said that, the three of them passed a demarcation in the large cavern. Weapons gave way to tiaras and amulets, shirts made of leather, chain mail, and other less identifiable materials. This, Nivvy thought, was more what he'd expected from a fairy's lair: magical items. None of them glowed, or maybe all of them did and he just couldn't tell in the strange light, but the craftsmanship on all the items stood out even more than on the weapons. There was delicate gold filigree and intricate arrangements of stones, one of which he recognized as a constellation in the summer sky over Copper Port, another of which looked like it might be a map of a country he didn't recognize. Bracers decorated with sigils and reliefs of animals; a whole array of wands; gloves with stones on the palm, on the fingers, on the back of the hand; they passed all of these.

And then Nivvy saw the chest, black wood inlaid with red patterns, as long as he was tall. It looked like it would come up to his thigh and was about as deep, and if he couldn't identify the patterns from a casual glance, at least they didn't look as disturbing as some of the other things he'd already seen.

Bella half-turned to Nivvy as they came up to the chest, and he gave her as little a nod as he could manage, somewhat annoyed. She'd described the chest and he'd seen it, so she needed to trust that he could handle the job from there on out. She didn't have to hold his hand every step of the way. In fact, it was more dangerous to do that because she'd risk tipping off the fairy.

"It's all about stories." Scarlet had started talking about magic to Bella, and Nivvy had missed it, distracted with his goal in sight. "So much of the world's magic is stored in objects now and it calcifies, sets, used to one purpose only, and it becomes harder to push it to that purpose. So the spells become more elaborate, more descriptive, more," she waved a hand, "more elegant, in a way." She stopped just opposite the chest, and for a heart-freezing moment Nivvy thought she had divined their plan just from Bella's small tilt of the head. Then she pointed to the wall opposite the chest. "You see this shirt? This is from the last century. The delicate tracery of silver and gold inter-twined, the repeating patterns? Those patterns call back to the work of the Vu Li Empire, which you can see," she walked on a few steps, "here."

The shirt she pointed to now did indeed bear a resemblance to the first one, but the patterns, though similar, did not repeat, and the cloth was dyed rather than set with precious metal. Nivvy could see the resemblance, certainly, but he was only paying just enough attention to be able to respond if Scarlet asked him a question directly about it.

"Patterns become refined and elaborate over time. So does magic. And then sometimes..." Here the fairy's eyes went a bit dreamy, and a smile stretched her bright red lips, "it all comes crashing down and they start over with nothing but scraps of memory to remind them where they've been."

She traced a hand over the pattern in the cloth. Bella cleared her throat. "Has there been a fall since—since I've been gone?"

The smile curved into a pout. "No. Small ones here and there. But the Thousand Kingdoms have proved stable, and the north, well, the north had, I suppose you could call it a stumble, a hundred years after you," she waved a hand, "you know. But they recovered."

"Was it because I was gone?" Bella asked.

The fairy touched her cheek and the smile returned. "Oh, darling," she said. "As much that as anything else."

Nivvy thought this rather a patronizing remark, but Bella smiled back as though it were a great compliment, and they walked on.

At the end of the cavern, three rough archways led out into what looked like smaller rooms, two on either side dimly lit, the middle one brighter. From the rightmost archway came whispers and murmurs, and upon peering closer, Nivvy saw wisps of vapor or smoke floating about in the air, though they didn't dissipate as one might expect well-behaved smoke to do.

"Ideas," Scarlet said.

"What?" He turned to see the fairy looking at him, that faint smile on her lips.

She pointed to the vapors. "Those are ideas."

Bella gave a nod as though she understood. "Ideas you've had that you discarded?"

"A few of those." Scarlet gave no indication that she minded Bella jumping in with the wrong answer, though that would personally drive Nivvy into a temper if he were the one giving the tour and not the one planning to rob the place. "But mostly they're ideas I get from poets and bards. When I'm bored, I reach into their minds and take ideas from them so that only I get to enjoy them. They never make them for anyone else." She hummed softly. "It's more special that way."

Bella's eyes flicked to Nivvy and he thought he saw his horror reflected there, but a moment later the queen's eyes drifted away, and she stared hungrily into the cave. Did she want those ideas? The thought felt wrong to him, but he didn't know what else to think of it.

The darkness in the other archway lay still and silent, and Scarlet gave no explanation for it. She stepped forward to the well-lit exit, and Nivvy, avoiding any glances at the vapors that felt to him even sadder than the menagerie, followed the queen and the fairy into—

—a wallpapered room, a proper room with a roof and floor and corners, with a grand four-poster bed directly facing them, a window next to it looking out onto a night sky (a night sky? Nivvy double-checked and yes, there were the stars and the sliver of a moon, though he was sure the moon had been nearly full the night before), two great chests, one of which had the lid thrown back to reveal satin and silk and the sparkle of gems. Elegant cloth banners hung from the ceiling, and here and there were small cages in which tiny birds flitted and sang. It could very easily have been the bedroom of the Emperor's daughter over in Tarisch, except that that daughter had had a sweets habit and left sticky patches and a cloying aroma of sugar all over everything. The dominant smell here was a pleasant musky wood smell that Nivvy couldn't quite place, like cedar but with a rich undertone to it.

Scarlet paused long enough to watch the reaction of her guests to her room and then three well-stuffed chairs appeared in the middle of the floor. "Shall we sit and discuss what you've come here to learn?" she asked.

"Perhaps you can tell me some of what's happened over the past," Bella glanced at Nivvy, "several hundred years."

There was an art to knowing how to behave in front of someone you intended to rob, and part of it was not taking the first opportunity to go do that. So Nivvy sat in the farthest chair, letting Scarlet and Bella sit closer to one another, and listened attentively while they talked.

Their conversation, about what had happened in countries he'd never heard of (or only heard the names), was interesting enough to listen to; at least, it wasn't as bad as listening to a merchant bloviate on and on about how blessed or skilled they were to have chanced upon the only source of redfruit before anyone else and to have enslaved all the people who lived there.

After some time, Scarlet fixed Bella with a hungry smile. "I am certain that you wished for more than a history lesson to help you regain your throne."

Bella gave a quick nod. Nivvy thought she looked angry, but he could only tell that from a slight crease in her brow; otherwise she hid it well. "I was hoping that you could tell me what kind of magic they have up in the northern kingdoms now. That information, at least, would be valuable to me."

Scarlet considered, one finger with a blood-red painted nail resting on her cheek next to her blood-red lips. "I'll tell you what I know, and what I know is worth, I would say...the true story of what happened to Glædeligdal."

Bella startled, enough to send some strands of hair across her face.

She brushed them back and then looked at Nivvy. "Yes," she said slowly. "I haven't thought about them in...a long time."

The fairy examined her nails. "I rather thought the Gulders were the ones responsible for...you know."

"Oh," Bella said, and then shut her mouth and smiled. "Perhaps they were. But that's another story. We'll see if you have anything else I want to know when we're done with these stories."

The fairy's expression didn't change. "I already know most of it," she said, sounding bored. "But if you are lonely for company, then by all means. Now...Glædeligdal?"

Again Bella's eyes flicked to Nivvy. "Tell me something about the north first. How much magic is there?"

Scarlet sighed and sank back in her chair. "Fine. There are five hundred thirty-one magical artifacts in the kingdoms that lie entirely to the north of here, by my last count. Some may have been destroyed, a few may have been created. Twenty-three of those are powerful enough to cause you great harm. I know the locations of twenty-one of them, as of three years ago."

Bella drank this in as thirstily as she had the water at the oasis. "How many are in Heiterflus?"

Scarlet drew a small circle in the air with her finger: not yet. "Begin your story first."

They stared at each other for several seconds while Nivvy watched, and then, to his surprise, Bella pointed at him. "Not in front of him."

Scarlet turned too, and the full force of the fairy's gaze made Nivvy feel rather like one of the taxidermied animals in her menagerie. "Isn't he your partner in all this?"

"He needs to know the future, not the past," Bella said. "When you hear the story, you'll understand why."

"Very well," Scarlet said. "Shall I take him out of time for a moment?"

"Ah." Nivvy cleared his throat. "If it's all the same, I'll just go use the necessary and not trouble you."

The fairy smiled. "Some of my gentleman callers liked to piss off the cliff down where you came in. Into the lava, you know. I don't mind. Otherwise I don't, you know, so I haven't really got..."

"You don't?" Nivvy stopped himself from following up that interesting line of inquiry. "Right. Mind if I just go back out to the entrance, then?"

The fairy waved a languid hand. "Don't piss inside," she said.

Nivvy laughed. "I wouldn't dare," he replied, and made his way back out into the large hall.

His eyes adjusted to the dimmer cave in a matter of moments. Bella's voice sounded behind him and did not grow fainter as he walked. "First of all," she said, "the reason I didn't ask for your help with Glædeligdal was that you had just had that whole episode with whatever her name was, the fairy from the snow kingdom."

"I remember." Scarlet's voice was matter-of-fact. "I'm not angry with you, *shawka*. It's been a thousand years, and I wasn't even angry then. Cinnabar was a lovely spirit and more than sufficient for your needs, but she was killed right afterwards and then you were trapped or killed, I thought, and I never heard the story and I do so want to."

"It was twenty years for Cinnabar," Bella said, "and five years after that for me."

"Was it the Gulders who did in Cinnabar?"

"I believe so. I never got to ask them, and I doubt they would have told me."

Nivvy walked back past the room of ideas and the silent room, past the patterned armor, where the voices remained clear. Perhaps it was the fairy's magic, a spiteful little gesture to make sure he heard what Bella didn't want him to. It would serve him well, because if they thought they heard something during the theft, their conversation would hitch, and he would hear it.

"I killed two of them for it." A moment of silence, and then Scarlet went on. "But tell me what you and Cinnabar did, and how it came about. The Gulders did not know."

"Nobody did. Nobody except Lars, the idiot."

"The king."

"Yes."

The chest lay ahead of him, black wood with thick red lines in swirls and sigils. Was it protected by spells? Bella hadn't said anything, so Nivvy would have to trust his own instincts.

Bella was going on, her voice still clear. "He wanted his son to marry Roselie and sent envoy after envoy. I let the first one live, and after that

I dealt with them in the usual way." She gave a short laugh. "One of them danced for nearly four hours."

"Yes, yes." Scarlet seemed bored by this. Nivvy had to stop his imagination from picturing what had happened. He focused instead on the chest. Bella was trusting him and paying him, and he wanted to prove that he was worthy of her. What was more, he wanted to prove himself to Inira. This was easily the most interesting and difficult job he'd taken since leaving the Guild, and one of the most difficult of his life.

True, this Bella he was hearing right now sounded cruel, but she might be trying to match the djinn/fairy's casual amorality. Nivvy knew a thing or two about puffing up one's own accomplishments to impress company, and he supposed that if said company was in the habit of imprisoning people in animal forms and swords and whatnot, one might exaggerate in that direction. Djinni weren't people, and they lived by different rules than people did, rules that didn't require them to respect anything but power.

That wasn't a life that appealed to Nivvy, but he could see where it would appeal to Bella. So maybe once they were gone from here, she would settle down back to the person he'd gotten to know. When they were alone, he'd tempered her bad impulses; he could do that again. He just had to get her out of this world of stolen ideas and dead animals and fairies (*djinni*, a voice in the back of his mind whispered) who lived for thousands of years and watched people as though they were fish in a glass bowl.

Bella was still talking. He'd tuned out her words and now paid attention again. "...persisted in his threats. What was I to do? He had that blasted crown—and by the way, I've no doubt he let his son use that on Roselie. She never would have agreed to the marriage otherwise —so any assassins I sent ended up working for him."

"Ah, yes, that crown," the fairy replied. "I was surprised that nobody went to retrieve it. But then again...who would have?"

There was a pause, as Nivvy crept closer to the chest. "Nobody has it?" Bella asked.

"I haven't checked in quite a long time," Scarlet said. "But you know, I kept an eye out for it. It isn't a thing you want just around."

"No," Bella said, "I can see that."

"So what did you and Cinnabar do?"

"I called Cinnabar because, as I said, there was that whole snow kingdom business. Whatever did happen with that?"

"It isn't important. Children going astray as they do. Go on."

"Yes, well, Cinnabar I knew because she'd had some excellent ideas when we had that trouble with the wizard Ktchata. She was delighted to help, and it only cost me sixteen prize bulls."

Nivvy, vaguely aware that Bella was stalling to give him more time, walked to the large chest and stood over it. It did not appear to be locked. "Cinnabar always did love her bulls. Darling, I am not interested in the price you paid or whatever mortal reason you called upon her to ask for her help in your revenge."

"You asked for the story," Bella said as Nivvy slowly slid his fingernails under the lid, and then pressed his fingers to them and lifted. No spell attacked him; nothing impeded him. The lid rose quietly to reveal hundreds of rings, gold and silver and other metals, set with stones in all colors he could imagine. If he'd only wanted to take one, it would have been no problem, but finding a specific one? He hissed softly through his teeth and stored up curses to bestow on Bella after this. "I was protecting my daughter's honor, and King Lars intended to invade my kingdom if I refused to allow the match. He had dealings with spirits himself. If I hadn't done anything, my kingdom would have been lost, my people subjugated by that tyrant."

Scarlet paused, and Nivvy froze, wondering if she'd somehow noticed him opening the chest, but then she said, "I know he did. I dealt with him."

It was Bella's turn to pause. "You did?" she said finally.

Nivvy leaned in close to the rings on the left side of the chest, looking for a square lapis stone among the hundreds of rings glinting in the eerie light of the cavern. Scarlet responded, still giving no indication she knew what Nivvy was doing. "Of course I did, *shawka*, but not with this business with your daughter. You know that I was not yours alone, of course."

"You weren't angry at what I did?"

"If I were, it passed like a storm in summer. I certainly haven't held a grudge for a thousand years. Who would do that? It's exhausting."

"Yes," Bella said, in a tone that Nivvy thought meant that Bella definitely believed Scarlet would hold a grudge for a thousand years.

"What I want to know, my dear," Scarlet purred as Nivvy slid down to the center of the chest, "is how you and Cinnabar went about it. That was a lot of water, and elements have to come from somewhere. Did you make it rain for a month? Did you divert a river? Drop snow on them? I've always wanted to drop snow on a city."

There was a sapphire, it looked like, but not lapis. Fortunately the light and Nivvy's eyes were good enough for him to tell the difference. What if the ring lay at the very bottom of all of these? He shifted to the right side of the chest to get a better angle, and there it was, a silver ring with a rectangular lapis stone in it gleaming at him through the centers of three other rings, buried a small way down. Had to be the one; there was no other lapis that he could see.

"Rain would take too long," Bella said. "We discussed it. Cinnabar said that even if it rained for forty days straight it wouldn't fill the valley, and everyone would have time to escape."

Fill the valley? Nivvy filed those words away as he studied the way the rings lay. In seconds, he had the pattern he needed, and he began removing one ring at a time, silently placing them elsewhere in the chest and moving on to the next one. His fingers worked almost of their own volition once he had figured out the order in which rings needed to be removed.

"And we talked about snow, too," Bella said. "There was something satisfying about it, and Cinnabar did know of a great deal of snow. But we weren't sure whether it would be as immediately effective, you understand. And besides, even though it is the north, it was spring, and you know, snow just didn't feel right."

He'd cleared most of the rings around the lapis one. Don't be in too much of a rush, he told himself, and took one more ring away. Now his target was fully exposed.

"Cinnabar found a sea to the north, frigid and uninhabited. She provided the magic to move it and I guided it. I sealed the valley first, at midnight under a moonless sky. I could still raise earth in those days, enough to block both passes."

Carefully, Nivvy lifted the ring. No sound. He slipped it into the hidden inside pocket of his robe, where it slid down against his contract.

"And Cinnabar dumped the icy water into the valley," Bella said. "In seconds. We watched from one of the mountains. Nobody got out."

Nivvy stopped with his hand on the lid of the chest. Bella had drowned an entire city? The heavy wooden lid weighed down on his fingers. The story must be almost over; he lowered it carefully.

"Very efficient," Scarlet purred. "Thank you for that story. Now tell me, how do you come to be traveling with that companion? Where did you find him?"

"It was a spell," Bella said. "When I broke out of the prison, I cast a spell to find the companion who would help me. The lightning brought me to a small farm town at the edge of the desert, a wretched place, and there was Nivvy in the center of it, tied to a wheel, if you can believe it."

Nivvy let the chest lid close silently and then as he straightened, he thought, *lightning*? The lightning that had gotten him caught?

"Tied to a wheel?" Scarlet sounded amused. "What had he done?"

"He'd stolen—" Bella stopped abruptly. "I don't know, exactly," she said.

Scarlet's voice sharpened. "He's a thief?"

Nivvy turned to see the fairy standing a foot away from him, her bright red lips stretched in a wide smile that showed definitely yellowed, pointed teeth. "So the thief would steal from me," she purred. "You sneaky little weasel."

Bella's voice came to him. "Scarlet?"

"No," he protested, but the words he intended to follow that one snarled up in his throat as he felt himself falling, falling, and landing in muffled darkness among a pile of smelly cloth.

## II

# THE WEASEL

## ❧ 9 ❧

## PLEADING HIS CASE

What sort of sorcery was this? Nivvy struggled, but the cloth around him caught on his claws.

His *claws?*

The darkness around him wasn't absolute. A dim blue light grew brighter, or else his eyes were adjusting. He held up his hands in front of his face.

That was the plan, anyway, but it went wrong from the start. For one thing, his face felt his hands moving too close to it through long whiskers on his cheeks. For another, even if that were possible it shouldn't have been right unless his nose had grown a foot. For a third, apparently, it had. And for a fourth, and most damning, when he finally got his hands clear of the nose that shouldn't be there and away from the whiskers that shouldn't be there and in front of his eyes, it was obvious that they weren't hands at all. They were an animal's paws, with leathery pads on the palms and claws at the tip of each finger, and they were definitely his, because the fingers closed into fists and opened again when he told them to.

He used them to explore his face—pointed muzzle, small roundish ears atop his head—and then the long, furred, sinewy body stretching down from his neck to his stubby legs and his—his *tail*. His claws pinched his tail (there's a thing he'd never thought he'd think) and it hurt, out there in a part of his body he hadn't had a minute ago. "Inira's seven silver bells," he swore aloud, and was a little surprised to hear the words come out. So he could still talk, even though he was now, he supposed, a former-human.

"You'll make a fine addition to my menagerie." Scarlet's voice seemed to be coming from far above him.

Oh no no no. He was not going to be frozen in her collection. He had to get out of here. If he could just get out of his robes, he could dart behind the chest, get away somehow.

But even as he struggled to free himself from the cloth around him, reality closed in. He was a former-human. Just like Marzin, just like Zein. In seconds, his future had been ripped away. Forget the Guild contract and getting a job in a new city; forget the life of a thief. He would have to live off what he could catch (at least weasels didn't eat insects) and what he could beg from strangers. Like Marzin, he'd be left behind by his friends and colleagues to fend for himself in a world that had no more use for him.

This wasn't a future he'd ever pictured for himself. What point was there in moving forward if the only fate ahead of him was dismal?

His despairing thoughts were interrupted as the cloth and Nivvy and everything was scooped up and lifted. "I don't have a weasel in my collection," Scarlet said, and now hands pressed the cloth around his body. He did not like the confinement and squirmed in vain, learning more about how this new body could move.

"What's going on?" Bella's voice, faint and farther.

"Your little thief decided to ply his trade in my gallery," Scarlet said. "So now he will sit in my menagerie."

Bella came closer, her shoes clacking on the floor. Nivvy stilled his struggle to listen, certain she would abandon him. What use was he now?

But: "He's mine," Bella said, igniting a flicker of hope in Nivvy's heart. "You can't just take him."

"He tried to steal from me." Scarlet squeezed as she said the words, setting Nivvy to squirming again. "In my own home."

"Nevertheless." Bella's footsteps stopped some distance away. Nivvy couldn't gauge how far because his frame of reference had been his own body, so what sounded like fifty feet to him was probably now...three? "What have you done with him?"

"I'm in here!" he called before Scarlet could answer. She squeezed again, her long nails pressing in, and this time he squirmed through the folds of cloth and dropped into what had been a sleeve of his robe, judging from the smell (had it always smelled so strong?). Scarlet had both ends of it, so he couldn't fall out, but he did claw at the fabric and make a small hole.

"He is no longer your concern." Scarlet's tone went icy, and Nivvy found himself paralyzed, unable to move. "I suggest you leave before I ask questions about whether you ordered him to steal from me."

"And I suggest," Bella said, definitely trying to match Scarlet's ice and coming up short, "that you return my thief to me before I call on what little magic I have left."

There was a long, long pause. Nivvy imagined the two staring each other down. Fearsome spirit though Scarlet might be, he had trouble seeing her winning a staring contest with Bella. Finally, Scarlet spoke. "You've no magic left. Or you'd be protecting him."

"Or," Bella said, "I have just enough for one...large...stroke." A moment later, a rumble like thunder rolled through the cavern.

Nivvy held his breath until it occurred to him that Bella was defending him because she hoped he'd stolen the ring she wanted, the ring that right now sat in a pocket of his clothes in Scarlet's hands. He strained against the magic holding him paralyzed, to no avail.

"*Shawka*," Scarlet said sweetly, and in that moment the magic holding Nivvy released him. He used his new claws—handy things, it turned out—and scrambled back up the sleeve and around Scarlet's hands, searching for that pocket in his robe where the ring was concealed. He needed to prove to Bella that he was still useful. "I will allow you to leave my cave with your pet only because I have been bored of late, and it will be a diversion to watch your pitiful attempt to become what you were once again."

There: the solid lump of the ring next to the paper of the contract. Scarlet's hands were near, so Nivvy curled his little body around the ring and chewed and tore at the cloth.

"Once again?" Bella said. "I've not changed who I am."

"You value the life of a thief over our friendship?" Scarlet's fingers prodded Nivvy. He protected the ring, and one of the fingers pushed cloth against his eye.

"Ay!" he called. "Leave off and give me back to her!"

The ring jumped in his grip. Perhaps Scarlet was trying to summon it back to her. Nivvy clung tightly to it, but it did not move again.

"Yes," Scarlet said. "Very well. Take it and go, for all the good it will do you."

There was the very disorienting feeling of being flung through the air, and then Nivvy and the clothes were all caught. "This," Scarlet's voice now came from farther away, "will make a passable keepsake of this adventure, trivial though it is."

A small clinking sound, but no indication of what it was. "We will be leaving now," Bella said. "Nivvy, are you there?"

"Ay, I'm here," he answered. He tried to think of a way to tell her that he'd accomplished his mission, but he couldn't think of anything that wouldn't also communicate that to Scarlet, so he just said, "an' more than ready to quit this place."

"Good day, Scarlet," Bella said. "It has been a pleasure seeing you again."

"Farewell, darling," Scarlet replied. "We shall see each other again, I'm certain of it."

Then Nivvy was being jostled in the familiar rhythms of someone walking as fast as they could without running. He continued to work on ripping his tunic enough to get the ring through the hole, keeping hold of it with one paw, terrified that he would lose it. Bella's footsteps echoed in the large room and then were muffled—that must be the menagerie—and then after a short time they emerged into a large space. It took a moment for the sweltering heat of the volcano to make it into the cloth, bringing the smell of rotting eggs along with it.

"We good now?" Nivvy ventured to ask.

"Hush." Bella held him tightly.

He caught her fear through that word and her grip, and quieted. Though she was restricting his movement, it was nothing like being paralyzed by magic. Could Scarlet reach out and paralyze him again? And then, another thought: were those animals in the menagerie paralyzed rather than dead? Trapped in eternal prisons with no change save when Scarlet chose to walk among them? Despite the heat, he shivered and felt cold fear wrap around his heart. Why, why, why had he taken leave of his senses? He ought to've run off as soon as he saw the bat. He'd been completely right about that, and Bella the one who'd talked him into going ahead anyway, and now she was running away on her two human feet and he was a weasel, a former-human condemned to a life of being looked down on literally as well as in every other sense.

But Bella was going to save him. He clung to that thought as tightly as to the ring itself.

Eventually Nivvy perceived that he was being carried down a slope. Bella's footsteps skittered along pebbles, but she didn't loosen her grip. "I want to get back to the temple," she said. "I feel like she's still watching."

Nivvy wanted to say, *If she can see us here, you think she can't see us at the temple?* But he didn't, because he felt it too, and he wanted very badly for Scarlet not to be able to watch them. So he closed his eyes and bore the jostling and bouncing as Bella made her way down the mountain.

To distract himself from his bleak future, he thought back to the conversation he'd overheard. Bella had asked about artifacts, and Scarlet had said there were hundreds of them lying about in the north. And when Nivvy'd told her about former-humans and how they could never be turned back, she'd said that she once had artifacts that might be useful. If Bella got her kingdom back, she might be able to find one of those artifacts—after all, her kingdom was a long way from the Thousand Kingdoms, and maybe an artifact had escaped notice during the Ali Bhai wars. If Nivvy kept on her good side...then she just might be able to turn him back human.

It was the longest of long shots, with "mights" and "maybes" stacked taller than he was (even than he had stood as a human), but a little former-human weasel didn't have any better prospects. All the stories about kings and queens and wizards had them rewarding servants who were faithful to them and punishing those who weren't, and with hardly any other friends in the world right now, and no other way to regain his human form, Nivvy had better stay with Bella as long as he could. She'd almost murdered Zein and had possibly drowned an entire city (Nivvy was still willing to ascribe some of that to Bella wanting to impress Scarlet), so...Nivvy just had to make sure he didn't give her a reason to be mad at him. The ring would be a good start.

He sensed when she'd descended the mountain and had started on the flat path to the temple, then heard her tell the acolyte who greeted her that her companion had unfortunately been lost up on the mountain. Lost? The comment, which he might've passed off as innocuous, felt as though it had punctured his barely-formed hopes, like she was ashamed of him and would get rid of him at the first chance.

She carried him up to her room and then tossed him upside down onto a bed. He'd just righted himself when she picked up the bundle of clothes again and this time shook it out so that Nivvy fell from it onto the bed. This felt like a good fifty-foot drop to him, but he landed safely on straw-packed cloth, on his back holding the ring in both paws.

Bella reached down to take it. "Ahh," she said, grasping it in two fingers, and then paused just as Nivvy let it go, still looking down.

Nivvy did not like having his underbelly exposed, so he flipped himself over. "What d'you mean telling that acolyte I was lost?" he demanded, forgetting for a moment that he wanted to stay on Bella's good side. "They know about former-humans. You could've just told them."

"I—" Bella regained her composure quickly. "I could have told them there was a powerful magic spirit on their mountain, yes. Or else that you'd been changed by their god. Does that seem like the kind of story you want to be a part of?"

"Don't much care," Nivvy said. "I don't intend to hide in corners and packs the rest of my life, if that's what you're askin'."

"It doesn't matter anyway." Bella examined the ring. "They don't need to know what happened. It would only alarm them."

"They oughta be alarmed," Nivvy grumbled. "Livin' down a mountain from a crazy djinn."

"Fairy," Bella corrected absently.

Nivvy was going to say that he'd seen her true form before she'd told him the story about being a fairy, but then decided it didn't matter how she wanted to appear or what she wanted to be called. "Aye, fairy, if you like. But there, I got yer ring for yer."

"So you did, so you did." She kept looking at it.

"It's the one you said. Lapis stone and all. Only lapis stone I saw in there, and there was a lot of rings."

"No, this is the one." Bella put it on. "I feel it."

Nivvy waited, watching Bella. She looked back down, her face wrinkled in concentration. He finally spoke. "Are you s'posed to look different now?"

She frowned. "It might not work on animals."

"Former-humans."

"Whatever." She dismissed him with a wave.

"Did you tell its story?"

"It doesn't need a story."

"Didn't," he said. "But that was a thousand years ago, ay?"

She gave him a look, which he returned as well as he could in his current form. "Didn't you hear her talkin' about how magic changed?"

She tapped the ring. "This hasn't changed."

"But maybe the magic has." He looked toward the window. "That volcano looks the same as a thousand years ago, I wager, but the molten rock inside sure is different."

"Hmph. Don't lecture me on magic," she said.

His reply was forestalled by a knock at the door. Bella looked down at him. "Stay quiet," she said, and threw a sheet over him.

"Why?" he called before he could stop himself.

The only answer was the creak of the door. He listened as an acolyte told Bella that these were all her companions' belongings, and again she was very sorry for Bella's loss. Bella thanked her and dumped Nivvy's belongings on the bed.

"There," she said, and swept out of the room, following the acolyte. The door closed sharply behind them.

"Good riddance," Nivvy said to himself, emerging from the sheets to rummage through his pack. He hadn't brought much up the mountain, but his coin looked to be all accounted for, as were the tools of his trade. He was pleased that his slender lock-picks were light enough that he could still hold any of them in one hand (paw), although he seriously doubted he would be able to muster the force needed to pick any kind of serious lock, even if he swung his whole current body weight up and down.

Maybe with practice, though. The dagger was too heavy for him now, but the fine blade for delicate cuts of cloth and parchment, with its thin wooden handle and metal edge at the end, that would work as a kind of polearm. He tucked it under one arm and swung it out in front of him. It wouldn't do much damage, but enough to deter the average person or animal from doing him harm.

Come to that, he had teeth now too, sharp ones by the feel of them. Biting wasn't a fighting move he'd learned, but in this body, it'd be foolish to waste the best natural weapon he had, so he practiced biting his clothes a few times, feeling foolish at first, and then feeling the power in these jaws that his human form hadn't had. Cataloguing his advantages and possessions showed him a path to possibly surviving his uncertain future.

Lastly, he looked for his charm bracelet, where all his magic resided, but it was nowhere in evidence. He couldn't imagine Bella stealing it—and then he remembered the clink of something falling to the ground, Scarlet claiming it as a souvenir. That would've been his bracelet, all right. So no more magic for him.

It was a blow, and no mistaking. He'd already lost most of the advantage he had in this world, and losing his little spells just made his situation that much more precarious. It was fine, he told himself. He'd been worse off than this—even as he told himself that, he heard it for the lie it was—and he could build his way back up again.

Bella stomped back into the room. Nivvy looked up in time to see her try to slam the heavy door, glare as it ground to a stop a few inches short of closing, and then push it closed. She paced back and forth twice before sitting heavily on the bed beside Nivvy.

"Doesn't work?" he guessed.

She held up the ring and examined it. "I don't know what 'story' it wants to hear."

"Do you know where it came from? Who made it, who used it?"

"No. All I know is that Scarlet took it from someone. I don't know who." Bella took the ring off. "So it's useless now?"

"Ay, that's what happens t'forgotten magic things." Nivvy tried to sound wise and knowledgeable, the kind of fellow you'd want to keep by your side on your quest.

"Can't someone make up a new story? You did with that merchant."

"Those things weren't magic. I heard tell there's a wizard in the Thousand Kingdoms who can, in the court of one of the big Suzerains, probably A'minari."

"The Thousand Kingdoms, that's south of here."

"Aye."

She shook her head. "That's the wrong direction. It would take months."

"Might be someone in the north. I just don't hear those stories." Nivvy cleared his throat. "But there's got to be other magic things you know from all that time ago. Things you know the stories of?"

"There's...oh. You know...now that you mention it, there is one." She rubbed her chin, looking thoughtfully down at the ring in her hand. "I think there is a way that might work."

"Right! There's the spirit. We'll get your kingdom back in no time."

She looked down. "'We'?"

He swallowed against the dryness in his throat and put on a brave tone. "Aye! I know I've completed the job you set for me, but I'm still game to help."

"Oh. No, I don't think so."

"What?" He took a step back, and into his mind flashed a memory of Bella reaching for a dagger to kill Zein. His paw went for his fine blade.

"It will be a hard enough journey without having to keep you safe from predators and being stepped on and whatnot."

"Keep *me* safe?" He brandished the blade. "Keep the predators safe, more like. I can look after m'self."

"I really don't feel that's wise."

With a little effort, Nivvy stood on his hind legs. "I promise you, I'll serve you well," he said. "I can get in small places, I can climb walls, probably. People won't notice me." He tried a laugh. "Imagine if she'd turned me into an antelope." Antelope and gazelle he'd seen in the menagerie.

"Perhaps." Bella rubbed her face. "We can discuss it in the morning."

"Look," Nivvy tried to reason. "You need someone who knows this world. That's me."

Bella's eyes flashed. "I don't *need* you." She stood. "I'll bring you back some food from dinner."

She left the room, and that ended the discussion. Nivvy thought about going after her to apologize for going too far, but he didn't know how the priests of Bouli would take to a former-human weasel running around their temple. Scampering, he thought, and the word seemed so undignified that it sobered him. He would apologize when she came back, and in the meantime he would ponder the many benefits of having a former-human companion so that he could list them for her.

## ❧ 10 ❧

# WINE AND RATS

**U**nsurprisingly, he fell asleep before she returned. It had been a very long, tiring day, and Nivvy's new body burned through energy more quickly than he was used to.

For the same reason, probably, he woke in the middle of the night, stomach aflame with hunger. In front of him on the floor, on a cloth napkin, sat one of the spiced bean cakes he'd had the previous night, next to a bowl almost as wide across as Nivvy was long. Beside the bowl lay a spoon whose head was about the size of Nivvy's head. He picked it up, but though he could lift it, clearly it wasn't going to be any use to him in eating, not even if he managed to scoop some curried goat out of the bowl with it.

He paused. The bowl, though shallow, was high enough that he'd have to get up on his hind feet again to look into it. Thinking about this threatened to bring on a wave of despair and anger at his situation, so he turned to wondering how he knew it contained goat. His nose provided the answer: even under the powerful smell of the curry, he detected the tang of goat, the bitter taste of green peppers, and the earthy smell of parsnips. His new nose could sort through the smells, identify each, and even tell that there were more peppers in the bowl than parsnips.

When he did get himself up and grab the rim of the bowl with his paws, he noted with some satisfaction—the first time he'd felt that in this new body, for sure—that his nose had given him a very accurate picture of the bowl's contents. Learning that he now had an enhanced sense of smell somewhat made up for the new limitations on everything else in his world, including, unexpectedly, his sight. Here in the room he could see everything, but out the window, beyond a few hundred feet, the world blurred into a haze.

But now he could know more things about his immediate environment, and what's more, the room wasn't as dark as he recalled from the previous night. That would be worth exploring too, but first, he had to figure out how to eat this curry.

He was worried that he would have to stick his head in and gnaw at the cubes of meat like an animal, but with some effort, he stood taller, got his front paws into the bowl, and lifted out a large cube of meat. Holding it and eating it felt more civilized than just eating it out of the bowl. Did the former-humans in Spire have tiny eating utensils?

He'd eaten half of the cube, tearing at the tender meat and finding chewing a little difficult (mainly because he didn't have as many flat back teeth as he was used to), before he thought to see whether Bella was awake. She was in the room for sure; he'd smelled her and seen her shape, but his stomach had taken precedence. Now he turned, still holding the meat, and saw the glint of her eyes watching him in the darkness.

She didn't say anything, even when he was looking right at her, and so finally Nivvy said, "Y'know, it gives a fellow the shivers when you just sit there all quiet and watch 'im eat."

"I've just been thinking," Bella said.

"Can't think with the lantern lit?"

"I didn't want to wake you."

He finished his cube of meat and got another, warm and sticky with curry sauce. "Much obliged for the food."

She nodded. "The dinner was adequate."

The fiery complex spice of the curry burned his mouth pleasantly and even set his nose a-tingle. "What's got your mind occupied?"

"I don't see any reason to share that."

"Come on. I got turned into a weasel for you. Want me to tell you what I'm thinkin'?"

She sighed. "Can I stop you?"

He ignored that. "I'm thinkin' that I'm just learning how t'best use this new body. Not that I don't want my old one back—I'm quite attached to it for a number of reasons—but there's advantages to this one. It's got a much better sniffer, I can get into small places, an' people won't expect a little weasel to be a thief even if they do see me."

"It sounds like your career as a thief will hardly be affected." Bella sounded amused.

"That's the spirit!" He finished another cube of goat. "So we'll head out in the morning—you said you had another idea? That's how I like to run my jobs. Run into a problem, whoosh." He was pleased to find that he could still gesture with his front paws as if they were hands, and now he waved them sinuously around an imaginary obstacle. "Go 'round it and find another way." If he said that enough times, he might convince even himself.

"Indeed." She sat still, hands folded in her lap. "This time it will work, I'm sure of it."

Nivvy picked up another piece of goat, but this would likely be his last. They were large, and he might not have eaten the whole bowl even in human form. "So where we off to next? Back to Spire?"

"We can talk about it in the morning." She inclined her head toward him. "Tell me your impressions of Scarlet."

He took a breath. "Seemed a touch brutal. Now, you know, nothing against that, I know those kinds of people too, but generally I tend to stay away from them, you know?"

"Brutal?"

"Aye, you know, the tapestries of blood, the trophies with blood on them still, the, ah," he glanced down at his body, "the animals."

"Interesting," Bella said. "You were struck by the blood more than the power."

"The power?"

"So many trophies, so many battles she's won. Her kind is hunted by people desperate to steal their power, but she's survived for thousands of years. Sometimes the battles are bloody, and she wants to remember how fierce they were, to remind herself of the power that she wields. And to show anyone who might consider coming against her what fate lies in store for them."

"Course, course." Nivvy bobbed his head. "Got to do all that to protect oneself. And I got no quarrel with her turning me," he lied, "because after all, she could've killed me. A thief takes risks and can't say I wasn't fairly warned, like you said. You told me the job was dangerous and I've still got my life." He realized that he was talking too much about his own misfortune. "But she seemed willing to be reasoned with. Could've killed us both, come to that."

"She wouldn't have killed me." Bella sounded far more certain than Nivvy was. "All that at the end was just posturing."

"You know her better'n I do." Nivvy hesitated. "When I first came in...I thought she was a djinn."

Bella didn't say anything for a moment and then asked, "What do you mean?"

"A djinn," he said. "They're great blue-skinned spirit-warriors, and this one had horns and necklaces of bones and beads. All the legends say they're willful spirits an' if you meet one, you've got to be right clever. But the best heroes have captive djinni what work powerful magic for 'em." He sat by the bean cake and ripped off a piece of it to chew on. "Was that what Scarlet was to you?"

"Ha ha!" Bella let out a laugh, but more of a surprised laugh than a real laugh. "Scarlet, a captive? I've heard of captive fairies, I suppose, but no, she appears where she pleases. She and I met a long time ago—even a long time before my imprisonment—and we found that we had many interests in common, so we aided each other from time to time."

The bean cake was pasty and tasted strongly of bean, but it was a nice change after the heat of the curry. "Begging your pardon, but I only know of the one interest of hers, so excuse me if I hope it was another one you shared."

Bella scraped at her dress, the thin sound of fingernail across fabric clear in the quiet room. "My interest was in ruling my kingdom and expanding its lands, and her interest was in watching the creation of an empire."

"She did seem interested in how us humans pass the years. The centuries." Nivvy, not even to the end of his third decade yet, tried to imagine one century, let alone many. If he lived that long, maybe he too would be interested in how patterns on a suit of armor changed.

Bella remained quiet. "We're both interested in power," she said at last. "That's what I hoped to appeal to. There aren't many of us."

"Aren't many who like power?" Nivvy tore off another piece of the bean cake. "Maybe not in your time, but you should go round and meet some folks here. I could introduce you to quite a few. Head of the Copper Port Thieves Guild, for one." He wouldn't be welcome there, much less permitted to make introductions, but he felt sure Bella wouldn't accept that invitation, and he was right.

"Not that kind of power. I mean real power, the kind that's out of the reach of most people. The people you know covet their scraps and lack the imagination or means to pursue the real thing."

"But what do you do with the power?" Nivvy asked. "Scarlet sits in her cave and stares at her trophies and that don't seem like the kind of thing it takes a lot of power to do, unless you're dead set on it and you've got a whole lot of people trying to stop you, which wouldn't be a problem for her if she just didn't have power, but then..." He stopped, going around in circles.

"That's the kind of thing someone asks when they've never had it," Bella said sharply.

He was about to shoot back that that wasn't an answer, but then remembered that he was trying to stay on her good side. "You're right," he mumbled around a mouthful of bean cake. "I don't know what I'd do with it anyway. Rather help you get yours and then take my little reward and go on my way."

"You speak truth," Bella said. "You would not know what to do with it. It is refreshing to hear someone admit it."

"That's me." Nivvy finished up the piece of bean cake. "Speaking of refreshing, I don't suppose there's any ale anywhere abouts, or that fruit wine they had?"

Bella reached down and picked up a plain wooden cup. "I've finished what I had. But if you want to show off your new skills, the wine is in a barrel in the main hall."

Now that he'd eaten, his body thrummed with energy, and he welcomed a chance to use it. This could serve as an audition to continue to serve her. "Easy as pie," he said. "I remember how to get there."

"Go on, then." She sounded amused.

He made it from the bowl under the window to the base of the door in about a second, faster than he would have thought, and paused there, examining it. He didn't want to ask her to open it, because he had to figure this out himself, and it only took another two seconds for him to spot the solution. There to the right, the stone was worn away and the wood of the door warped above it. He'd seen rats squeeze through smaller holes, so he dove at the narrow space and pushed his head through.

He emerged on the other side with his fur ruffled but his spirit soaring. If he could get through that crack, there were very few rooms in the world that would be closed to him now. Could he but go back and forth between his human form and this one, he would be the most celebrated thief in the world before long.

That was a fool's thought, he told himself as he ran the length of the hallway, keeping to the wall. He'd be one or the other, not both. If Bella could change him back, then he'd be human. If not, he'd be a former-human. Although there were some old stories about maidens who put on the skin of an animal and then turned into that animal, weren't there? Those were always curses, though, situations they were freed from by the handsome prince. The handsome prince, the rescuer, he was always human, never half-animal.

The temple was silent; likely the worshippers of a fire god spent the dark night sound asleep in their beds. Out here in the middle of nowhere, there was little need for even a night watch (though if they had any idea what lived halfway up their mountain, they probably would have—well, abandoned the temple, honestly), but Nivvy still kept his ears open for any sounds as he scampered to the stair.

He'd jumped down two steps before it occurred to him to wonder if he could get back up. The steps were not terribly high to a human, but he could barely see over the top of the next one up when he stood on his hind feet, which he was getting better at.

Luckily, his little claws found purchase in the rough stone of the steps, and he swarmed up the side and over the stair with little effort. Thus armed with confidence, he bounced down to the lower floor and found his way to the main hall. None of the doors was completely closed, so he made his way through them all easily, stopping only to check for sounds.

At the dining hall, there were noises: small scrapings and patterings of paws, gnawing and chewing sounds. Keeping to the wall, Nivvy slid along one side toward the large barrels, and that brought him closer to the noises. Now, over the rich smells of food and fruit wine, he detected a rank animal odor that flashed an image of a rat into his mind.

Multiple rats, he thought, sniffing the air again. They'd be about as big as he was, which made them more of a worry. How would they react to him? Should he be prepared to fight? He wished he hadn't left his makeshift blade back in the room. Although how would he have held it? Running on four legs was much faster and more natural, so he would have to build some kind of harness, something like Zein's pouch where they held coin.

Enough light came through the windows from the stars and moon that he could see the furniture in the dining room, as well as the wine barrels, close to him. And when his gaze lingered on the barrels, movement jumped out at him: three rats.

Two of them chewed at something on the floor under the barrels, while the third scurried back and forth from the barrels to the wall. If they'd been on the other side of the room, Nivvy would've left them alone, but he wanted to get a drink from the barrels and they were right there.

When he was a few feet away, they noticed him. All three looked up, eyes shining in the dimness, and froze where they were. Nivvy advanced confidently on them. "Say, fellas," he said, "I just want to get a drink. No need to fight, ay?"

At the sound of his voice, one of the rats sat up on its hind legs. For a moment, Nivvy had the wild notion that they too were former humans and would talk to him, but instead all three of them ran back toward the wall, where they disappeared into a narrow hole.

"Ay, well," Nivvy said. "That was easy. Cowards, rats are."

As well as a weasel could swagger, he did on his way to the barrel, though secretly he was relieved that he hadn't had to fight the rats. He had no doubt that this body with its speed and sharp teeth could do some damage, but he didn't know how he'd fare against three at once, and he wasn't looking forward to the first time he had to kill something with his teeth. Unless he found a way to carry his blade, though, that was going to happen.

He climbed up to where the barrels sat and sniffed at the three of them, then spotted the tap inserted into the side of one. That'd be the one for him. He got himself onto the tap and braced himself against the barrel, then turned the handle, and a moment later was rewarded with a stream of rich-smelling wine. He stuck his head under it and drank a gulp at a time, the sharp alcohol and sweet cactus fruit taste blending in his mouth. It was strong, but he liked the aftertaste and the warmth that blossomed in his stomach when he swallowed it. It made him feel powerful and reminded him of being human.

He took another drink and then another, and then right around the time he was thinking he probably shouldn't have a fourth, the spigot started to wobble and then the room spun with him at the center. He clawed at the wooden handle to keep his balance, and for a few seconds he clung to it successfully, but then it bucked him off and he ended up hanging by his claws, his long body stretching down past the shelf the barrel rested on, his tail dangling a foot above the floor, wine still streaming past him.

Oh.

He was drunk.

He tried to pull himself up, but jumped too hard, overshot the handle, and ended up with his claws in the spigot, hanging down the other side. He tried again, and this time slid around the front so that wine poured down his belly and tail, and at that point he figured there must be enough wine on the ground that he could just drop down and land in a pool of wine, since he was wet anyway, so he let go.

In mid-air, a flash of insight broke through the drunken haze, about the nature of wine and stone floors, but it was too late; he hit with a thud that knocked the wind out of him and made two distinct squeaks, which struck him as odd until he saw the rats running away again. "Ay!" he called after them. "I beat a fairy-djinn! You'd best run!"

Ignoring his soreness, he got up and chased them back to their hole and then, full of bravery and confidence, dove into the hole after them.

From the dim, wine-scented air of the dining room he was plunged into rat-scented darkness. It took him one second to realize his error, and another for shock to clear his head. Out in the dining room, a land that belonged to nobody, the rats had run from him, but here he had invaded their home and threatened the stores of food they'd stored (which he could also smell).

Two of them leapt at him, biting from either side. Nivvy twisted away and bit back out of instinct. Twice his jaws closed on empty air, but with the third attempt he tasted fur and flesh; he bit down harder and heard a squeal as the rich scent of blood filled his muzzle.

At the same time, the other rat, or maybe the same one, landed a gash in his side. The shock of the contact sent Nivvy jumping for the hole before the pain had even registered. He let go of whatever he'd bitten and let instinct send him back the way he'd come in, out into the dining room.

The rats did not follow. Nivvy's momentum took him halfway back to the pool of wine, and then the smell took him the rest of the way. He paused at the edge of the spill—the barrel must have emptied, because the stream of wine had slowed to a drip—and turned to examine the wound in his side.

Blood dripped through his fur and the gash, as long as one of his paws and half as deep, stung. He wouldn't be able to see a healer about it, not even one of the cheap ones around the market who'd sell you colored water for a copper and claim it would cure your limp or your rash. Dressing the wound was out too, unless he wanted to wrap a bandage around his entire midsection. The fragility of this new body struck him like a wave; if he wasn't careful, he'd break or tear something that could never be mended. And the only thing worse than being a former-human was being a wounded former-human, or a dead one.

Before he knew what he was doing, he'd curled his body around so that he could lick the wound. It felt right, his slightly rough tongue cleaning the area around the gash and then smoothing the fur down over it. The motion, over and over, soothed the pain of the wound and calmed his mind. The body had ways to cope with injuries. Of course it did; most animals did.

Bella would be able to help, and she'd be worried about him. He should go back. But if he licked for a little longer, maybe the wound wouldn't seem so bad, and he could play down his foolish charge into the rat-hole. Just a few more licks and then he'd go.

## 11

# THE CAGE

He woke to shuffling and creaks, and then a flare of light. He jumped to his feet and faced a tall silhouette holding a glowing yellow sphere of light in one hand. "Bella?" he croaked.

The shape gave a yell, and the light went out. "Light-Father!" a young male voice called as the shape fled the room. "A rat talked to me!"

The door of the dining hall slammed shut. Now that the glowing light was gone, dawn showed clearly through the windows. Nothing but Nivvy was moving around here.

But that young priest or acolyte was going to bring back people quickly, so Nivvy'd better get back to Bella. He ran to the door and pushed himself through the groove he'd entered by.

The tight squeeze produced a flare of pain from the wound at his side. Once he'd extracted himself, he checked, but the wound wasn't bleeding. Good. Perhaps Inira was smiling on him.

He put that to the test all the way back to Bella's room, keeping near walls and hiding as best he could when footsteps approached. Often this meant dashing under doors or into shadows, both of which were fortunately plentiful in the interior of the temple at this early hour. Most residents were only just rising, and a few were running toward the dining room.

At the stairs, there were few hiding places, but there was no help for it; he had to scramble up them, aware of how exposed he was. Even with his new body's speed, the climb took longer than he'd hoped, and by the time he got to the top, he was panting from the exertion.

He had to hide one more time on the way back to Bella's room when a priest walked down the hall, but finally made it there, got under the door, and emerged inside.

The first sunbeams of the day illuminated drifting motes of dust. Curry smell lingered in the air, as did Bella's scent, but no movement disturbed the silence save for Nivvy's own footsteps (quite silent, he was pleased to note). Her bag was gone, as was any other trace that she had occupied the room. He smelled his robes up on the bed, and the bean cake and curry bowl had been left on the floor. It looked like the rats had been at the bean cake, but Nivvy was hungry again, so he ate the rest of it and then sniffed around the room to see if anything else had been left—a note for him, a token, any kind of indication that he hadn't simply been forgotten and abandoned.

Up on the bed, among his robes, he found a note. He ran over to it and stared down at the paper, but his eyes were so close that he could only read a few words at a time. "Be it known that" seemed like a strange way to start a note, and the writing was crabbed and spidery.

Hope only clouded his memory for those few words before he saw the wax seal at the bottom of the paper and realized what he was reading. This was the contract from the Thieves Guild in Spire, the paper that only a day ago had held so much hope for him. She'd left it behind. She hadn't even signed it.

The door opened. Occupied in this seeming betrayal, his reflexes were delayed by half a second, so the acolyte who'd come in to clean the room had time to exclaim, "Rat!" before Nivvy could leap from the bed.

Hiding place? No good, and there was only one exit. He sprang for the door, darting between the man's feet and out into the hallway before the acolyte could even turn around. He ran for the stairs with no other idea than to get out of the temple, but Inira must be at her afternoon tea or whatever gods did when they couldn't look favorably on their followers, because there were two more priests on the stairs.

Nivvy let his instincts take over, leaping to one side and pressing to the wall as he ran. Behind him, even as he passed the two slow humans, the acolyte from the room called out, "Look out for the rat, Blesseds!"

On the landing of the stair, his wounded pride had time to catch up with his body. He turned around and snapped, "I'm not a rat, I'm a weasel!"

As he fled down the lower half of the stair, voices behind him sounded very satisfactorily impressed. "I told you it could talk!" said the acolyte.

"Was that the rat from the dining room?" a deeper voice called.

"Weasel!" a high-pitched voice called, speaking slowly and distinctly, the way Nivvy might talk to someone who had trouble with their words. "Can you understand us?"

He stopped at the bottom of the stairs and turned. The two priests stood on the landing staring down. "Course I can understand you," he said. "I heard him call me 'rat,' didn't I?"

His fluency did not satisfy the priest, who kept talking as though Nivvy were a beggar in rags struggling to string three words together. "What business have you here in our temple?"

He paused, staring up at them. "I just need to find someone," he said, taking a cautious step backwards.

"We can help with that." The high-voiced priest took a step down. "Why don't you tell us who you're looking for?"

He considered telling them everything, but if he told them about Scarlet, sooner or later someone would go up the mountain looking for her and get themself killed. In the worst case, she might just kill all the priests. So he said, "It was a woman here last night. Might have left this morning or she might still be here."

"Ah, yes, the woman." The priest descended another step and gestured Nivvy to come closer. "She rode out before dawn, I'm afraid. What business did you have with her?"

"That's my concern an' hers," Nivvy said, staying where he was. "If she ain't here then I'll just go."

"Please!" The priest held up a hand and drew a vertical circle in the air with an index finger pointing straight up. "It appears there is a curse on you. Perhaps Bouli can help lift it."

"Not likely," Nivvy snorted. "You lot never heard of former humans?"

In that moment, his world went dark with a loud clunk as something big and wooden came down around him, imprisoning him in the small space. "Ay!" he yelled. "What's this about?" He ran from one side of the bowl—that's what it was, smelling faintly of the bread it had recently held—to the other. Some soft-footed sneak must have come up behind him while the priest distracted him. He'd thought the priest was gesturing to him, but he'd been waving at the person behind, the one Nivvy could've heard or smelled if he'd been paying attention and alert instead of panicked and trying to escape. Stupid, stupid.

Outside the bowl, either they couldn't hear him or they were ignoring him. "What shall we do with it, Blessed?" a young voice asked.

"Keep it and study it. Now, perhaps, more of the priests from the temple in Spire may choose to come out to the Temple of the Sacred Mount to see the talking weasel. That would please the Brightest."

"You don't have to study me!" Nivvy yelled. "You have to let me go!"

They did not listen to him. "Talking animals are not unknown in Spire," the deep-voiced priest said.

"I've never seen one. Have you?"

"No."

"There you are. We will have our very own specimen here at Sacred Mount."

A specimen. He was going to be a specimen, an exhibit here at the temple. They'd lock him up tight, and Bella was somewhere in the vast expanse of territory north of here with his horse (*Rahila, how could you let someone else ride you away?*), having given up on him.

He curled up and didn't answer when the priest told him they were going to move him and he shouldn't try to escape. They lifted the bowl and threw a net onto him, then picked him up and poked at him, asking if he could hear and understand them.

"Perhaps the curse has been lifted and the spirit inside the weasel gone," one of the priests said.

"Or it is simply sulking at its capture," the high-voiced one said. "Let us leave it in the cage and we will see. And give it some food."

Here was the point where Nivvy might say farewell to courtesy and simply tell them that he had been a guest of theirs and had been turned into a weasel by a djinn living in their precious sacred mountain, because he really didn't care now whether they all ran up there to fight or embrace it and got eaten or placed in the menagerie or whatever other cruel fates Scarlet could dream up for trespassing humans over the centuries. Two things prevented him: one, if the whole temple was killed, that wouldn't make him human again, nor even free him from their cage necessarily, and he knew he would feel bad about it later even if he didn't particularly now. Inira did preach self-preservation but also frowned upon putting others in needless danger. And two, these Bouli priests, the ones who'd chosen to sequester themselves days away from the nearest city to be closer to their god, they barely seemed inclined to listen to him at all. Giving them a more plausible explanation for his appearance wouldn't win him his freedom either. The only thing he could do was refuse to talk, because that was the only part of his life he still had control over.

They took him into the library (the smell of parchment and vellum told him that) and after some tinny rattling, threw him onto a pile of cloth. He sprang to his feet reflexively and found himself looking at the priests through metal wires which rose up all around him and then curved gracefully outward before meeting at the top, from which a small perch dangled. The birdcage was decorated with curlicues and spirals, a modest work of art that would be quite lovely if only Nivvy were admiring it from the outside.

As he watched, the priests closed the door, fastened the latch hook into the eye, and then the older priest and the acolyte turned to leave. The younger priest, though, watched Nivvy's eyes, and called the older priest back. "Light-Father," he said. "If the weasel can talk, perhaps it can also understand simple mechanisms."

"Ah." The older priest looked at Nivvy, then at the latch. He lifted his hand, on which he wore a large gold ring inlaid with three red jasper triangles, and placed the ring next to the latch. He mumbled the ring's story under his breath.

For a moment, nothing happened, but then the metal of the latch smoked and melted—not quickly, but oozing like wax. It fused with the metal of the eye, and then the priest lowered his hand and the metal's movement slowed. "There," the older priest said. "Should we need to remove him, we can cut the latch off." His dark brown eyes bored into Nivvy's, and then he turned and left, and this time the younger priest followed.

When they'd left the library, Nivvy let out a few choice curses in their direction. "Think you can keep me in here, hah?" He ran back and forth and then calmed himself. Inira said you had to know a problem before you could solve it, so he set himself to examining his prison.

It hung from the ceiling, swaying with his every movement. Outside the thin metal wires, sunbeams coming through several windows illuminated a room with many other cages, most of which contained birds. Along the walls stood shelves holding a multitude of books, one sleeping cat, and two paintings: one of a black crow sitting on a scrubby little tree, the other a close-up of a reddish-brown bird on a branch. Nivvy hoped the artist was one of the priests, because otherwise it spoke to the terrible taste in art of the priest who'd bought them (or the poor quality of his eyesight, but the pictures weren't that far away).

His side ached, but the pain wasn't as sharp as it had been the night before. He tested it with his paw. While the wound felt messy, it wasn't oozing blood anymore and it didn't smell bad. That was as much as he could hope for in that area.

More troubling was the emptiness of Bella's room. She wouldn't have left without him. She couldn't have. She'd have to have taken Rahila, and you wouldn't just take a fellow's horse.

Maybe you would if you were the sort who hung about with murderous djinni and bragged about drowning your enemies.

Or maybe, Nivvy thought, you would if you wanted to keep her safe for your companion, who had vanished in the night and not returned. But his attempt to make Bella a better person in his head didn't hold up to logic. She'd known he was going to the dining hall, and he'd been passed out there. Surely on her way out she would have at least looked in.

Maybe she had seen him. Passed out drunk on the floor? Nivvy, in her place, would have gone to check and make sure he was well. But either she'd seen him and had left him, or had left without looking for him, because she'd thought him useless.

And he was. He'd gotten drunk and fought rats, so he'd passed out licking his wounds rather than returning to Bella's room. Then he'd allowed himself to be caught, hadn't been paying attention to his new body's senses. As a human he was attuned to people sneaking up on him, but his senses as a weasel were different. Thinking back, he'd definitely felt movement behind him but had put it down to the air currents in the temple. He hadn't focused on them enough to feel that it was a human body disturbing the air, hadn't even reacted when the bowl started to descend, which he should have. He'd been trapped so easily.

He sprawled out on the cloth covering the wire floor beneath him and looked around the room as his cage spun slowly in reaction to his motion. The birds in the library sang only sparingly and forlornly, and Nivvy knew how they felt.

## ❧ 12 ❧

# BREAKING THE CURSE

n the morning, Nivvy woke with renewed purpose. Inira had little patience for people who sat around and moped and pitied themselves; she reminded her followers that she gave them the fortitude to learn to help themselves and she wouldn't do everything for them. There would be a way out of the cage and out of the temple, and even as cursed as he now was, he still had the wits to find it. Remember the story of Tali'a Ma[1], he told himself, the merchant who was turned into a cat by a djinn and who nonetheless bartered and haggled his way to a small fortune, starting only from a fish carcass he'd found in a trash bin. Of course, he'd been able to talk to other animals in the stories, and the birds here were useless. When Vicho had told him the story, he'd said, "No matter how bad your situation, there's always something you can do. Now, you probably won't be turned into a cat..."

Thinking about Vicho made him sad, and sad was not a helpful emotion right now. He needed confidence. Not for an enterprising and accomplished lock-dodger like Nivvy, the cage life. He'd never met a situation he couldn't escape eventually, even with little more than his wits—look at how he convinced Bella to let him loose from that accursed wheel (the further ramifications of that decision he pushed to the side). So he assessed his situation.

Below the cloth lay more wires, close enough that he could stick a leg through, but not much more than that, and his strength wasn't enough to bend the wires below or around him.

He could climb them, though. Their rough surface gave his paws enough traction to climb straight up the sides of the lower half to the bottom of the spherical part, and then along the bottom of the sphere and up the sides. To go farther would mean climbing almost upside down, but, Nivvy reasoned, it wasn't that far to fall, and his paws had got him this far. He'd never know what they could do if he didn't give them a chance. So he kept on going up and up, his lighter weight much easier to climb with, until he was hanging by all four paws from the top of the cage.

He reached outside and grasped the hook that suspended his cage but couldn't get his paw any farther out, and he wasn't sure he'd be able to unhook it even if he could. Right now, there didn't seem to be much point to it unless he wanted to be in a cage on the floor, which he could not see as a dramatic improvement in his situation.

Four bodylengths to the floor of the cage from where he was. He could climb down, but he could also drop that far, especially to cloth, so he let go and fell. When he let his body do what it wanted, it twisted him around in the air so he landed on his feet, and had there been anywhere to run to, Nivvy would've been ready to run there. So along with the very obvious drawbacks of his new body, there were at least a few advantages: climbing, spryness, squeezability, and overall quickness. He listed those things over and over and took some pride in them. Maybe those other former-humans were miserable because they didn't take full advantage of the small blessings they'd gotten in trade for their humanity. Except Zein; they had become a guide and made a good life for themself as a hawk.

Now that he was sure he would make a plan to get out, he told himself, he'd need to make another plan for when he did get out of the temple. He'd never catch Bella without assistance, and he couldn't even tell anyone which direction to go along the road to find her. He'd need someone who could move fast, who could search the landscape the way he could survey the floor of the library from the hanging birdcage. He'd need a bird.

Nivvy looked around at the birds in the cages around him. "Any of you chaps former-human?" he asked.

They turned to him, beady eyes fixing him for a moment. Then, finding him uninteresting when he wasn't talking, they resumed preening or staring at the painting or thinking about whatever birds thought about during the long hours in their cages when they weren't being fed or played with. The cat, too, lifted its head from the shelf where it slept and glanced past him before gazing hungrily at the birds.

No help here. But Inira had put Zein in his path, and now he'd be able to call on them when he needed their special skills. The thought cheered him. So he only had to get from here to Spire, and that wasn't such a difficult task. If he had to, once he got free of the temple, he could run back to Spire. It'd take days, and he'd have to learn how to hunt (the fight with the rats was a somewhat encouraging start), but he could do it.

So he was back to getting out of the cage. Once he knew how they intended to "study" him, he could formulate a better plan. Maybe they would want to talk to him, and he could convince them to let him out, or maybe he could feign illness and they'd take him out to look at him. He could bite a hand, startle someone into dropping him, dash for the door.

In the meantime, he'd better be able to make the best of this body. He'd tested out its athletic abilities, so now he remained still to see what he could learn about his senses. His ears were more sensitive in the direction he was facing, but less sensitive to noises anywhere else. He'd already discovered that he could see better in the dark, but that his sight couldn't reach as far in the light. He slid his paws along the wires of the cage; fortunately he did not seem to have lost much dexterity in his fingers, though of course his whole foreleg was barely the size of one of his human fingers. All the better to do delicate work with, right?

Most intriguing were his whiskers. When he closed his eyes, he noticed how sensitive they were to air currents in the room. They felt a bird ten feet away flapping its wings, and they could even tell when someone passed by the door to the library (if the door was open, not if it was closed). When he wasn't paying close attention, their twitches felt like itching, which his reflex was to ignore. He'd trained himself to be alert to sounds and smells in the course of becoming a thief, so he applied those same lessons to the itching-twitching of his whiskers.

That first day, two priests came into the library, and neither of them tried to talk to him. Nivvy pretended to ignore them while he experimented, keeping his eyes closed and tracking their movements with his ears and whiskers. They took down books from the shelf, sat in the little chairs and read them, and sometimes whistled at the birds. One of them stayed for what felt like hours; the other checked four different books and then found something in the last one and left. None of that seemed useful on the face of it, but Nivvy was of the strong opinion that the more you knew about someone, the better, so he stored it all away in case it would come in handy later.

The next day, the high-voiced priest tried to get him to talk. "Tell me about yourself," he said. "How did you come to be in the temple?"

Nivvy acted as much like a non-former-human weasel as he could, and when, after an hour, the priest said with some exasperation, "You've already spoken to us! Stop pretending you don't understand," Nivvy exulted. He'd won at least that first struggle.

But after that, they gave him only water, no food. "When you ask us for food, you can have food," the priest told him.

This presented another challenge, but Nivvy was game to figure out how long a little weasel could go without food. He wouldn't put it past the priests to starve him to death, so he'd have to be careful.

Later that day, the first possibility of his escape presented itself. The door opened, and he'd got himself all braced to act dumb, turned away from the door and all, when he realized that the person who'd entered didn't sound like a priest or, when the air currents reached him, smell like one.

This traveler wore a dusty hide jacket and trousers, and his close-shaven blond hair and beard definitely marked him as not a priest. Behind him, a golden-robed priest with shaggy brown hair and a beard down to his chest escorted the visitor and told him a few things about the books, and then they picked out some books and sat down together to read through them.

Here was a possibility. Of course all the priests and acolytes would have been told not to let him out, but they might not have cautioned their visitors the same. He pretended to sleep, waiting for his chance.

Another priest came in, refilled his water, and then fed the birds. He exchanged some words with the escorting priest and then left. And then the visitor got up and left the room, and Nivvy felt a flare of panic until he looked down and saw the books still on the table, the escorting priest still sitting there. Probably just using the necessary.

Indeed, the visitor returned a moment later and took his seat again. And a few minutes later, Nivvy's chance came.

The escorting priest rose, stretched, said he'd return in a moment, and then left. The library door remained open, but now there was nobody in the library except for Nivvy and the visitor (and the cat and birds, but nobody else who could carry a conversation).

So Nivvy crept up to the edge of his cage and looked down at the traveler, engrossed in his book. "Hsst," he whispered, keeping his whiskers alert to the open door.

The visitor didn't react, so Nivvy hissed louder. "Hsst!"

Now the man looked up, curious. His eyes skipped past Nivvy at first, and then returned. "Up here," Nivvy said unnecessarily.

"I...beg your pardon?"

Good. He seemed to be familiar with former-humans, at least enough to accept a talking weasel. "I only have a moment," Nivvy said, trying to impart urgency in his tone. "I'm being kept prisoner here. I need your help to escape."

"My help?" The man glanced down at his book. "I'm not—" He looked back up. "If they're keeping you prisoner, you must have done something wrong. What did you do?"

"I didn't do anything! I—they want to find out why I'm a weasel!"

"So tell them. Maybe they'll let you go."

Nivvy was finding out all sorts of things, like the fact that when he was frustrated, his tail lashed back and forth. "You're not listening to me. I need your help to get out."

"Look here," the man said. "I'm only here to work on a map for the Suzerain. I don't need any trouble. I'm not going to cross the priests here."

"All right," Nivvy said. "Suit y'self then."

He sat back crossly and then wondered what might happen if the man told the priest about their conversation. Ears trained on the doorway, he caught the faint tread of footsteps returning. "I just hope you don't end up in one of these cages too," he improvised quickly.

"What? Why would I?"

"Oh, just last week they caught someone talking t'me and turned him into that red bird over there." Nivvy resisted the temptation to sit up again to see the man's expression.

"Just—" The man stopped talking as the priest appeared in the doorway.

Footsteps into the room and then the priest's voice, from very close by Nivvy's cage. "Were you talking to someone?" he asked.

"No," the mapmaker said sharply. "I was—I was sounding out the name of this town marked on the map. It's not one I've seen on the Suzerain's maps, and I wanted to be sure I could speak it properly to him."

Nivvy was more than a little pleased to hear the haste and worry in the mapmaker's quick response. The priest seemed to detect it as well. "If you were talking to someone," he said, coming closer still to Nivvy's cage, "I trust you would be honest beneath Bouli's light."

"Of course I would." Papers rustled. Nivvy held his breath, but the man didn't go on.

"Very well, then." The priest sat down. Nivvy closed his eyes and relaxed.

⁂

He had two days to think of a better strategy before a second opportunity arose. Two days of eating bits of the cloth lining the bottom of his cage, a poor substitute for food but enough to keep him alive. Two days of priests cajoling and threatening, and one instance of a priest intoning what he said was a magic spell channeling the power of Bouli. Nivvy bore it all stoically, especially the spell, which amused him with all of its rigamarole to no effect. He'd firsthand experience of powerful magic now, thank you, and he could tell a bunch of dressed-up fakery from the real thing.

Why didn't he simply talk to them? He considered this in the spaces of night when he woke, his body restless and hungry. He'd tried and they'd captured him and locked him up. As long as he didn't talk to them, he retained some measure of power, the only power he had at this point. What if he told them his story, or a safe version of it that wouldn't send them all up the mountain, and they judged it wanting? Or what if they decided to send him somewhere else? They'd betrayed his trust once, and he wasn't about to give them another chance. Given the choice, he'd wait for another outsider.

He didn't have long, he knew. Without proper food, he slept more, and when he was awake, every movement took more effort as his body tried to preserve what resources it had left. On the third day of his captivity, as he lay sluggishly in his cage, an acolyte nervously suggested to the high-voiced priest that maybe they should feed him before he died, but the priest responded scornfully that if the weasel allowed itself to die from stubbornness, then it was better off dead.

Nivvy considered this possibility as well. At what point would he be too weak to even ask for food? When that time came, he would deal with it, but he hadn't let the Thieves Guild pin Vicho's death on him, and he hadn't let the idiots in Plow keep him on the wheel, not for the whole time, and he wouldn't let these priests keep him in a cage forever. Even if he had to beg them for food, he would never stop planning his escape.

On his fourth day of captivity, another traveler entered the library, and Nivvy roused himself enough to take stock of him. This new arrival looked like he was of a station above the mapmaker who had been too afraid to help Nivvy. He wore not dusty travel clothes, but fine velvet with beaded trim, unstained by the road, which meant that either he'd traveled here in a carriage, or he'd brought these clothes to wear at the temple. If he were already rich and powerful, that might be good, because the rich and powerful always wanted more wealth and power, but it might also be bad because he might be too worried about losing what wealth and power he had. Nivvy would have to tread carefully with this one.

But then the man set a small travel pouch on the table, and Nivvy made out the mark of the Suzerain on it. That put a different complexion on the situation. The light blue velvet color, if the Suzerain's court in Tagrabul followed the same hierarchies as the court in Copper Port, indicated a lower-level functionary, but still one with power. The velvet doublet showed wear at the elbows, and the brocade had been mended in several spots. The man's black hair thinned at the top and his beard bore speckles of grey in it.

This man, on the far side of middle-aged, had likely struggled his whole life to attain this position at the Suzerain's court, and he was still being sent on errands days out of Spire. Perhaps he had an attendant, but likely not. The way he walked assuredly to one of the shelves and pulled out a book without looking at the other titles showed that he'd been to this library before, but he did not smile as he found the book nor as he sat down to turn its pages carefully. Every movement spoke of weary resignation that Nivvy understood as clearly as if the man had said aloud, "Why am I still looking up texts in books out in the mountains at my age?"

Here was something Nivvy could work with. Anyone in court was desperate to improve their station, and a promise of something they could bring to the Suzerain would be irresistible honey to them, especially someone counting the years he had left.

So when this man was left alone in the library, Nivvy crept up to the edge of his cage and peered down. In his weakened state, he did not have to work to put a little quaver into his voice as he said, "Sir? Sir, are you a gentleman of good character and honest spirit?"

The functionary snapped his head up and looked around the room. "Who said that?" he asked, not looking up to see Nivvy.

"Please, sir," Nivvy said, "do not look up, I pray you. It is as much as my life is worth to be seen talking to you."

The man kept his head bowed; good. "But who are you?" he asked.

"I will tell you my story, and possibly you may benefit from it, but you must promise, if it is not to your liking, that you will pretend you never heard my voice."

"How might I benefit?" he asked, suspicious.

"I was cursed in my quest for a diamond-decorated golden music box, which I wanted to bring to the Suzerain, may he live forever."

"May he live forever," the man echoed.

"I thought that if I brought it to the Suzerain, perhaps in his eternal wisdom he would see fit to grant me a station at his court. After all, it belonged to his grandfather's grandfather."

That was a bit of improvisation Nivvy threw in, having just remembered an old story in which a king sought out a charm that had belonged to his grandfather's grandfather. It was far enough back that nobody was likely to remember, but close enough to be relevant and interesting. And indeed, the functionary's head shot up, almost turning toward Nivvy despite the warning. "His grandfather's grandfather? The great Suzerain Rasha al'Aba?"

"The very same." Nivvy committed that name to memory in case he needed to recite it later. Footsteps sounded in the hall outside. "Alas, I was betrayed. Now quiet! The priest returns. But seek me out after sundown and I will tell you more."

"I don't hear—" The man stopped as a shadow fell over the door, and bent back to his book.

Satisfied, Nivvy slunk down into the bottom of his cage and rested there.

The shadows lengthened and the man continued his studies, then left when the smells of dinner wafted into the room. Nivvy got his customary water and a reminder that he could have food if he but asked for it. He remained prone on the floor of his cage, not looking at the priest even though the smells of dinner made his stomach twist and growl like a wild cat.

The library door was closed and locked, the light gone. All the birds slept on their perches, and the noises of the desert outside came through the window in a soothing chorus that Nivvy had gotten used to: scratching and scurrying, squeaking and shuffling. Leaving its bed on the bookshelf, the cat patrolled the floor, watching for rats who might come in eager to nibble on parchment or vellum. The temple, too, had its nighttime sounds, although most of the priests went to bed with the sun. Doors creaked, settling without any human touch, and breezes soared in through the open windows to rustle tapestries, play with dust, and brush along Nivvy's fur.

A scratching woke Nivvy from his doze. He thought at first that the cat was stalking some rats, so he rolled over to see if it would kill one of the little vermin. But the cat sat quietly staring at the window as the scratching got louder. A shadow loomed behind the window, and then the shadow resolved into the functionary.

The man was not graceful, but he clambered through the window and dropped to the floor of the library without falling or knocking anything over, at least. Nivvy refrained from voicing any of the many corrections he could have made, watching instead as the man got up and brushed himself off. He inspected the elbow of his doublet and picked at a hole or a piece of dirt there, as though someone of importance was going to be judging his garb, and then he straightened and looked around the library.

The cat made a low growling noise. "Are you the poor unfortunate?" the man whispered, taking a step forward.

The cat leapt to a higher shelf and regarded the man with luminous angry eyes. The man shook his head and then looked around the room. "Hello?" he whispered.

Nivvy let him say, "Hello," two more times before he responded.

THE PRICE OF THORNS

"Bless you, kind sir, for returning," he said. "If you look up, you will see the pitiful circumstances I find myself in."

The man looked first up at the red bird, sitting on its perch with its head tucked under its wing. He gasped. "You are a lovely bird, I must say."

"I thank you," Nivvy said, "but I am not a bird."

The man turned and stared up at him. As dramatically as he could manage, Nivvy raised himself up and said, "You see me before you, a lowly weasel being starved to death. Such is my punishment for attempting to bring a gift to the Suzerain."

"How can I help you?" The man wrung his hands together.

"May—" He almost said Inira and then switched to Apo, from whom the Suzerain received his right to rule. "Apo bless you for your charity. If nothing else, some food would relieve me a great deal."

"Of course. I have no food with me, but I can bring some later."

"Apo bless you," Nivvy repeated, and threw his mind back to storytellers he'd listened to. He could mimic their speech well enough, he hoped. "I will tell you quickly of my story.

"I learned of this artifact and knew at once that I must procure it. So I traveled to the Tarisch Empire and purchased it for a fair price, knowing that it held much more value for the Suzerain. But my assistant, a cruel and vain man, betrayed me upon our return. He had obtained a magic object that could transform a person into an animal. I had locked up the music box in my apartments in Spire and was settling down to rest, dreaming of the warm reception I would receive upon traveling to the Suzerain's court. But as I slept, this villain crept into my room and turned me into the animal you see here.

"He threw me into a sack before I could come to my senses and sent me here to this temple, away from everyone, with the instructions that the priests should keep me here for the rest of my life. Meanwhile, the music box sits safe in its hiding place."

"Safe?" The man interrupted. "Surely this villain procured it for himself."

"Nay. He thought I had placed it in the chests where we keep all of our most valuable items, but I hid it in a place known only to me, a cunning compartment in my chambers."

"How do you know he did not find it?"

"Because." Here Nivvy lowered his voice. "He came here to this temple not two days ago, furious. Have you seen the sky before a desert storm? So dark was his visage, so thunderous his voice. And yet I did not speak to him. I have not spoken since being put in this cage. That is why the priests do not wish me to talk to anyone: they worry that I will give away his secret and then he will no longer favor them with the gold they love so."

"How villainous," the man breathed.

"I have been waiting for someone true of heart, who can deliver me and allow me to lead him to this treasure. Perhaps the Suzerain, in his mercy, will allow me to live in his palace for the rest of my life, even as a weasel. He is merciful."

"He is merciful." The man stroked his beard, thinking, no doubt, of the reward he would get for the music box. Perhaps he was also thinking about how easy it would be to dispose of a little weasel; Nivvy could not yet tell how good a person he truly was. What mattered was that he would get Nivvy out of the cage and to Spire.

"Can you help me?" Nivvy asked, when the functionary did not follow up that comment.

He knew well the curves of a smile shaped by greed, even though the man tried to conceal it in his tone. "If I release you," he said, "and bring you to Spire, you will show me the location of the box and allow me to bring both it and you to the Suzerain?"

"I will, good sir," Nivvy cried, "for how could I come before the Suzerain alone in this form? How could I even carry the box? You shall be rewarded handsomely for your kindness."

The trick was to make the story familiar enough, like the old stories of cursed people who needed some kind stranger to free them from their plight, and offer a reward they couldn't resist. A jeweled music-box held no particular significance—unless it had belonged to the Suzerain's family.

The man approached the cage. "You know that you cannot be returned to your human form?"

"Alas," Nivvy said, "you speak the saddest of truths." Mix in truth with the lies, make the lie the thing he wants to believe. "But I can be killed easily, and I fear that these priests of fire have many tortures in store for me. And then the Suzerain might never get his music-box." And you, you would never have the chance to present it to him.

The man looked into Nivvy's eyes and then said, "I am Caphram al-Malac. How were you known when you bore a human form?"

"I was called Nivali al Tamsin." Nivvy did not want to have to remember another fake name on top of everything else.

"Very well, Nivali." Caphram looked around the library. "Is there a way to liberate you so that, ah, it might appear that you made your own escape?"

"I admire your discretion," Nivvy said. "If you were able to bend the wires of the cage here, I can effect my escape, and then you can bend them back, leaving the priests with a mystery to ponder. But will they not suspect when you depart in the middle of the night?"

"Ah." Caphram had lifted his hand to the cage and now lowered it again. "I had thought...perhaps...I might conceal you amongst my personal possessions and leave as scheduled in the morning."

"If such a generous and noble soul believes that to be the correct course of action," Nivvy said, his tail lashing, "then I submit to your wisdom."

"Yes." Caphram lifted his hand again. "Yes, that will work. I will keep you in the pocket of my robe and you will not betray me, nor...nor bite me." His fingers twitched.

"I promise I will not bite you," Nivvy said.

Still nervous, Caphram reached up and first tried the door, which remained sealed shut, of course. Only then did he heed Nivvy's advice and test his strength against the wires of the cage nearest the door. Then followed several minutes during which Nivvy watched Caphram's fingers slide off the wires or grip them without leverage so he could not pull them. Twice, he started to say something acerbic about the man's skill and had to change it to a grateful blessing. "Truly," he said, "your fingers are—the most welcome sight I've seen in days." And, "Apo above, man, can you—believe my good fortune that Apo brought you to me?"

Finally, three of the wires had been pulled apart to leave a space that Nivvy could wriggle through, which he proceeded to do with alacrity. He was weaker than he'd expected, so he half-fell down to Caphram's shoulder and caught himself in the fabric of the doublet. The functionary jumped, which would have unseated Nivvy if not for his claws. "Mind the vest," Caphram gasped. "Don't tear it."

"Then don't—" Nivvy stopped himself. "I beg your pardon," he said. "The joy I felt at my release overwhelmed me."

"Understandable." Caphram reached over to his shoulder and those clumsy fingers closed around Nivvy's ribcage.

Nivvy suppressed the urge to run away but could not restrain a small squeak. "I'm simply putting you in my pocket, as we agreed," Caphram said, cautious. "Trust me, I would not endanger you in any way."

"It took me by surprise," Nivvy said, and allowed himself to be carried through the air and dropped into a large, musty pocket. He explored it while Caphram attempted to bend the wires back into place, counting himself fortunate that he didn't have to witness those attempts, nor the final position the functionary would consider good enough. He didn't care if the priests knew he'd had help escaping, except in that if they stopped Caphram, they'd recapture him and would never leave him alone with a visitor again.

◌⚜◌

CAPHRAM WOKE EARLY, DRESSED IN HIS RIDING CLOTHES (ALAS, NO carriage), and after accepting a piece of bread with honey for the journey, hurried out to the stables. Nivvy, eating a large piece of bread Caphram had given him, curled up at the bottom of the man's bag, but could not relax. At any moment a priest might cry out for him to stop, and then rough hands would plunge into the bag and find him, or Caphram might lose his nerve and confess his crime, or the priests might smell the impossibly wonderful fragrance of the bread or hear Nivvy tearing into it and gulping it down.

None of this happened. Minutes later, the familiar bounce of a cantering horse rocked him gently in the bag. Only then did he turn his mind from preparing to dive out of the bag, perhaps biting a hand along the way, to what he would do when they arrived in Spire.

When he'd conceived this plan, he'd figured he would slip away, as that was one of the things he was now very good at doing, and leave this witless functionary. But the telling of the story had created a cage of another sort around him. He'd played the role of the cursed soul rescued in exchange for the promise of treasure, and now he felt an obligation to deliver on that promise. Which was complicated, because there was no diamond-encrusted music box hidden in a house in Spire, or if there was—it was a large city, after all—Nivvy couldn't lead Caphram to it, nor did he have any claim to it.

When all was dark, Inira taught, wait for the dawn. Whatever you might not be able to see right away could be right in front of you if you had but the patience for it to reveal itself. And the bag, though not completely dark (it was a loose fabric weave) was certainly dim. So Nivvy relaxed as best he could while completely at the mercy of someone else and waited for whatever else Inira might reveal to him— apart from the odors that filtered through to him, which revealed that Caphram loved to eat bread at least as much as his body disliked receiving it. Being able to tease food smells out of a person's gas was not a skill Nivvy ever expected to have, nor particularly wanted to culti- vate, but hanging in a bag at Caphram's hip gave him ample opportu- nity to practice.

When they stopped for the night, Caphram took a private room and brought some meat up for Nivvy. He hadn't spoken at all on the ride to the inn, but while Nivvy ate, the man took the opportunity to unburden himself about his life.

As Nivvy had surmised, he was a minor functionary in the court of the Suzerain and had been in that position for a long time. His family had served the Suzerain going back many generations, but his two brothers had risen farther and faster in the court than he had. He complained that they had been blessed with facility of tongue (the eldest) and pleasant features (the middle son), which had enabled their rise, whereas he had been passed over time and again.

From the volume of his complaints and the eagerness with which he explored every detail of them (being sent out to the temple beyond Spire figured greatly in his litany of grievances: "it is the job of a young clerk, not a seasoned one"), Nivvy suspected that they lived perma- nently in his head, and that very few of his friends or family were recep- tive to them these days.

But Nivvy listened patiently, and Caphram had the grace to say, as his catalog neared its end, "I do apologize for troubling you with the details of my sad life. As many misfortunes as life has heaped upon me, I have not been cursed into an animal's form and placed in a cage."

Despite the apology, he did not ask more about Nivvy's life prior to his transformation, but settled back, muttered prayers to Apo, and sank into a deep sleep.

Having slept much of the day in Caphram's bag, Nivvy had too much energy to fall asleep. The rest of the inn beckoned, with sleeping patrons, some of whom might have unguarded valuables and spare coins lying about that they might not immediately miss. He was on a journey to regain his humanity, but until then he was still a thief, and when Inira put an opportunity in front of a thief—like, say, being a sneaky little animal in a place that was not secured against sneaky little animals—it was an insult to the goddess if he did not take it.

The upper hall was deserted, with snoring coming through a few of the six doors. At the end of the hallway, noise and the smell of ale and smoke filtered up from the common room below, and after peering down and seeing only a blurry haze of people and tables, Nivvy retreated to the doors.

The scale of the hallways and doors now did not deter him as it had back in the temple; he saw the long, exposed hallway as dangerous and the large doors as opportunities for his new form to squeeze into what people thought of as well-secured rooms. His nose and ears gave him ample warning if anyone was coming, and his whiskers felt air currents that led him to places to hide, as well as gaps between doors. Most of the doors of the inn were well secured, so tightly closed that even a small weasel couldn't force himself past, but one was badly fit into its frame. Nivvy sniffed at it, and finding it empty of people, squeezed himself through and into the room.

There were two bags there, and in both he found a small cache of silver pieces. He took one from each and fit them with some difficulty into his mouth so that he could run faster. Checking the hall first, he ran across and back into Caphram's room, where he secreted the coins at the bottom of the bag.

There, he thought, and said a short prayer of thanks to Inira.

Nobody missed their coins in the morning, or if they did, they didn't suspect the minor functionary of the Suzerain's court. He rode out with Nivvy in his bag, and Nivvy held the two silver coins as they rode, rubbing them between his paws. The feel of them made him smile even through the rather objectionable smells of the journey. When he reached Bella again, he could tell her how not even Scarlet's curse could keep him from his destiny as a thief. She would be impressed, enough to put him at the head of the Thieves Guild, or maybe keep him with her. When she regained her kingdom, everyone would know her name, and Nivvy would be part of her story, recognized for his true talents.

The next night, at the inn he and Bella had stayed at, he stole another silver coin from a pack. The doors at this inn were not as well-fitted, and Nivvy stealthily explored every room, but only in one did he find enough coins that he judged one would not be missed. Anyway, one was enough for the idea he had formed about how to end his story with Caphram.

On the third day, Caphram broke his riding silence. "We shall arrive at Spire within the hour," he said, startling Nivvy out of a half-doze. "Where shall we proceed once in the city?"

This was the weakest part of Nivvy's plan. He climbed up to the top of the bag and pushed his head out, taking in the other people and horses around them, the walls very close now, and the great tower of Spire beyond them. More days had passed than the five that Zein had said they would be watching for Nivvy and Bella, and the hawk wouldn't be expecting a weasel anyway, so he had to find a way to reach them somehow.

But he didn't have to do that right away. "Take a room at an inn called the Giant's Foot," he said, and dove back down into the bag to wait.

Soon enough, the smells of Spire, as personified by the fifty or so nearest people in various states of perfumed unwashedness, permeated his bag, along with familiar sounds: horses' hooves clopping along stones, snatches of conversation. Nivvy kept an ear perked, but nobody mentioned Zein. In a city this large, he would have been surprised if they had.

The sounds and smells changed when they entered the Giant's Foot: more concentrated talk amid odors of ale and roasted meat. Caphram asked for a private room and sounded put out when told none were available; he took a shared room whose other occupants were currently dining, paid, and walked upstairs, bouncing the bag over his shoulder as he did.

In the room, Caphram set the bag down on the bedroll. "We have arrived," he said. "Where shall we go now?"

Nivvy examined the layout of the room. It was much as he remembered from their stay...he counted back. Nine or ten days ago? He was getting better at adjusting proportions as he saw them now to his human recollection. Most importantly, the window was open. Just a crack, but it would be enough.

He brought the three silver coins out from the bag. Caphram's eyes widened, and his hand went to his purse. "Are those mine?"

"Hear me, Caphram al-Malac," Nivvy intoned. "You have been tested and you shall receive your reward." He set one coin on the bedroll and then took the other two in his mouth and darted to the windowsill.

He needn't have worried; Caphram looked from the coin to Nivvy. "When are we going to get the music-box?" he asked.

No wonder this poor chap hadn't risen far in the court. Nivvy set down the coins. "You are not worthy of the music-box," he said. "I was sent by Apo to judge your worthiness of serving the Suzerain. Here now is my verdict."

Caphram stared at him, enrapt. "You have a good heart and many qualities that will serve the Suzerain well. Yet you are well in need of a lesson. Consider that silver piece. That is my verdict."

"I..." He looked down at the coin. "I am worth one silver piece?"

"Silver," Nivvy said, "has value of itself. Look how it shines. With that piece, you could buy food and clothing, or you could buy entertainment. You could purchase a gift for a loved one. Does the silver care that it is not gold? Does it worry that you love the gold more than you love it? No; the silver has worth and value, and that is enough."

Caphram frowned. "Should I eschew gold for silver? Is that my lesson?"

Nivvy restrained a sigh. "You are the silver piece," he said, hating that he had to spell it out, but with some folk you just had to lead them right up to the bar and pour them the ale. Maybe he should've picked a copper piece—no, that would have been cruel. After all, Caphram did serve the Suzerain. "You have value: intelligence, loyalty, dependability. Why else would the Suzerain allow you to go by yourself to the Bouli temple at the Sacred Mount? Clearly he considers you a trusted servant. And how do you repay him? By lamenting that you are not more trusted, more favored, more beloved. Caphram al-Malac, you are a good man. Keep this silver piece to remind you that you are more than what others see in you."

THE PRICE OF THORNS

"Wait," Caphram said. "So I'm not gold? This is a cruel lesson."

He looked truly pained. Nivvy shook his head. "We are not all of us destined to be gold, but many of us are not even destined to be silver. That piece," he pointed to it with a small paw, "will now hold more meaning for you because it will remind you to trust in yourself. Perhaps, if you believe in your own value, someone else will see your value as well."

The man looked doubtful but bowed his head. "I thank you for the lesson, Nivali."

"Oh," Nivvy said as he grabbed the other two silver pieces, "and it wouldn't hurt to eat less bread." With that, he leapt out the window and left Caphram to ponder his fate and his diet.

## 🦊 13 🦊

# FLIGHT OF THE WEASEL

**N**ot bad, Nivvy thought to himself as he gained the sloped wooden roof. At worst, he'd just paid a man a silver piece to take him from the Bouli temple to Spire. At best, he'd imparted a life lesson that would serve Caphram well at the Suzerain's court, and given him a story to tell. There almost never was a diamond-crusted music-box at the end of any story, and if you believed there was, you deserved to be taught the ways of the world. That very lesson had been a teaching from Inira back when Nivvy was quite young, how you should value your talents and work to improve what you lack rather than coveting what someone else has. "Don't drop your copper to chase a glint of gold," is how Nivvy'd learned it, which had given him the idea to use the silver to teach Caphram that same lesson.

Now there was just the matter of finding Zein. He set the two silver coins out on the roof and then scanned the skies. His eyesight wasn't good enough to see anything more than black dots dancing in front of the clouds, but if the old saying about "eyes like a hawk" was based in fact, he hoped the two silver coins would stand out to a curious hawk.

Course, there was barely half an hour of daylight left, and the chance that Zein might be flying overhead was small enough. Nivvy took his silver pieces and made himself inconspicuous at the base of the inn's chimney, which had the added advantage of being a little warmer than anywhere else.

In the morning, he put the coins out again and watched the skies until he got tired of it, at which point he stretched out and dozed with one eye on his coins, trusting his senses to wake him if anything approached. And just before noon, a shape dropped out of the sky with a rush of air that flattened his whiskers against his body for a moment.

He rolled over and away and then got up to all four feet as a hawk alit a foot away, eyeing the coins curiously. They were huge, and the curved beak and sharp talons drew his attention, making him back up a step. That beak could snap him in half; those talons could shred him like an old rag.

"Are these yours?" the hawk asked, and with a flood of relief he recognized Zein's voice. "Only I've never seen a weasel with silver before, and I don't think there are any former-human weasels in Spire. At least, there weren't any at our last meeting, but you could very well be new in town, in which case, welcome. It's not a perfect place for former-humans, but there are a few of us here and we look after each other. If you want to be part of that sort of thing. If you'd rather just sulk, that's okay. We have a few of those too."

"Zein," he said. "It's me."

They cocked their head. "How do you know my name? Have we met? I feel certain I'd remember having met a weasel before."

"I wasn't a weasel when we met," he said. "I'm Nivvy. You were my guide when I was here last week. With Bella."

"Nivvy? Nivvy the thief Nivvy?" Their manner changed from curious to delighted. "By Apo's wings, I'm so sorry this happened to you, but oh! You have some coin and you're in the right place now. You can join our little group and we'll all look out for you. We'll help you get used to being a former-human. I promise you it's not all bad. Sure, there are problems, but you need to eat a lot less. I mean, a lot, especially you. And you can probably still be a thief if you want. Look at me! People hire me to be a guide."

"I know," he said, cutting off their speech. "Means a lot to me, that does. More'n I can really say. But—not just yet, that life."

Zein tilted their head. "What do you mean, not yet?"

"Here's the thing. I want to hire you."

"Me? To...take you 'round the city? To get you settled? No, I'd do that for free, I just told you." They peered down at him. "Then for what?"

He put one paw down on the nearest coin. "Bella—she left me like this. She ran off and took my horse. I want to find her."

Zein shuffled on the roof. "Her Bella, or her the horse? Because thing is, I'm not sure you'd have much use for a horse right now. And she might not even recognize you. That happens a lot with people, let alone horses. Although I never had a horse, so I don't know. Maybe she might recognize you. The horse, I mean, not Bella. Unless Bella didn't know you're a weasel now?"

"She knows." Nivvy set his teeth. "It happened because of her. I—"

"Oh," Zein interrupted, "since you're a former-human now, there's a couple things you oughta know, and one of them, the big one, really, is that we don't talk about how we were changed. It's kind of a rule we have here that Shanti started because she says if we dwell too much on how we were changed we start thinking about what we've lost and not what we've got, so if there's a danger to someone then we warn them but otherwise we just look at who we are now and what we can do."

"Right," Nivvy said. "I didn't mean offense. I was goin' to say only that it happened cause of her and then she abandoned me an' I ended up in a cage. But, ah, I still got my wits, so I got out of the cage, came back here, an' found you, with silver to boot."

"And you want me to help you get your horse back? Honestly, I know you liked Rahila—that was her name, right?—but it seems like Bella probably has more use for her than you do. Not that a horse isn't useful to get around, but how would you control her?"

They were missing the point. Nivvy ran in a small circle and then sat up again. "No idea," he said, "but that don't matter. She's my horse an' Bella has no right to take 'er."

"Okay," Zein said, "I understand you. There's another big thing you need to know about being a former-human and that's that, ah, you can't have a horse."

"I can an' I do. You saw her."

"Right." The hawk shifted again. "Thing is, though, according to the laws of Spire, she's not your horse anymore. So Bella can just take her."

Nivvy opened his mouth and then shut it again, considering his complaint. He had no reason to doubt what Zein said. Just a few days ago he likely wouldn't have considered that former-humans needed property or anything except a place to sleep and get food. He'd never even spared a thought for where Zein lived or whether they could own anything.

"I get that," he said through the uncomfortable fur-prickle of guilt. "But I'm not askin' the Suzerain to make her give Rahila back. Wouldn't know where to start, for one thing, an' for another, I never exactly had a good eye-to-eye with his men, you know." He paused. "Definitely be even worse now, unless I caught 'em when they were lyin' down so I could get right up on the bed an'..." he mimed staring someone in the eye.

Zein laughed. "Lovely," they said. "It's important to find humor where we can."

"But what I want is to confront her," Nivvy said. "She left me behind on account of she felt I wasn't useful an' I need to show her that I am, and so I can kind of have my horse if I'm workin' for her, Bella, I mean, and she's keeping her, Rahila, I mean. You follow me?"

"You can be useful around here," Zein said. "A little thief who can sneak into places? The Guild would hire you for sure. I know because they asked me once if I'd work for them and I thanked them for it but it wasn't really what I wanted to do. But if I wasn't earning enough as a guide, I'd go back. I could find the fellow I talked to and bring you there. They'd give you a place to stay and plenty to eat."

This, Nivvy had never considered. He could go to the Thieves' Guild. He could give them another name; how would anyone know? This time he could be a better Guild member. This time he wouldn't have a choice but to respect their rules, because he wouldn't have any other way to earn a living. Desperate people might hire a human unguilded thief, but never a former-human one. He'd be in a cage of circumstance, one that was suspended not over a comfortable library floor, but over a bottomless pit.

"Let's say," he said slowly, "I hire you to take me to Bella, an' if that don't work out the way I hope, you bring me back here an' we'll look up your friend."

Zein shifted again and looked over his head, toward the city wall. Clearly the silver wasn't going to be enough to convince them. "Say," Nivvy said, "didn't you say you had a hanker to explore?"

"Oh, yes," Zein said.

"Well? Here's yer chance." He pointed vaguely north. "We go out there a ways, you an' me, and you get to see more of the world, an' when you come back here you get two silver. With or without me."

"It does sound nice." Zein followed his paw. "I just don't want you to be disappointed. I don't think this is going to work the way you think. Do you know exactly where Bella is?"

"No," Nivvy admitted.

"Then first we have to find her, and then, I know she's a very nice person, but if someone already decided not to keep hiring you, it's not usually a good idea to go chasing her and insist she reconsider. I think it might be better for you to spend your two silver getting a little food and maybe a job here. It doesn't have to be with the Thieves Guild. I'd just feel a lot better about you if you did that. If we go out there and don't find her and come back, I'll feel really guilty about taking your money, but I do need to eat too."

Of all the things they'd said, that one pulled at Nivvy the hardest. It had been a long time since someone had turned down money because they thought he needed it more, longer since someone who knew his circumstances cared about what happened to him. He thought about this for a good number of breaths in and out while Zein waited patiently.

"I know," he said finally, "that we're not supposed to talk about this. But...Bella has magic."

The hawk's head drooped. "Oh, no," they murmured.

Nivvy pressed on. "She said that if she's successful in what she wants to do, she might—she might be able to—"

"You're not going to be changed back," Zein said. "That magic is gone."

"You don't know her—"

"If I leave," Zein said, "then you can't give me your money. I'm sorry, Nivvy. I hope you find somewhere to stay. If you want to see me again, come back to this roof. I'll find you." And before he could say anything, they took off.

"Fine!" he yelled at the shrinking shape in the sky. "Fine! I don't need you anyway! I was jus' tryin' to be nice and take you on an adventure! Maybe get you turned back human too!"

Zein didn't come back. Nivvy stomped around the roof as hard as a little weasel could, which was not very hard, but still satisfying. "I'll make m'own way," he growled, baring his teeth. "I got from the Bouli temple to here, I can get from here to there."

In the course of his stomping, he investigated the perimeter of the roof, casting glances back at his silver pieces to make sure some enterprising crow didn't scoop them up. Any great plan starts with a first step, and his first step was to get off the roof.

That was going to take some thinking. He could get down the way he'd come up, climb walls down to the street, but then he'd be a weasel running around the street with two silver pieces in his mouth. Unless he hid the pieces up here and then went to find someone.

Who? Who would be willing to take him north on a journey with no guarantee of finding what they were looking for? Who could outpace Rahila so they could make up for Bella's four-day head start? He had an idea of the place she might be going, but not of where it was, so second thing after getting off the roof and stashing his money, he would have to find someone who knew that, because no guide was going to be hired to take someone to a name if they didn't know where it was. Third thing, find someone to take him. Fourth thing, steal more money, because any guide who'd take him on a horse would need a lot more than two silver to feed guide and horse for however long the trip was going to be.

That was a lot of things for a plan, and the only one he felt confident in was "stealing more money." He returned to the two silver pieces and rolled over on his back, staring up at the sky and leaning against the chimney. To his left, the great tower of Spire rose, so high that with his new eyes he couldn't make out the top, and the birds wheeling around the tower were nothing but smudges. Maybe there was another hawk in Spire, or a raven or an owl or something, who would take him north.

But Zein would be the best option. They already knew and liked him and Bella, and he felt sure that the hawk's good nature would bring them back to check whether Nivvy was still on the roof. Maybe he could trick them with a story the way he'd tricked Caphram? If he'd thought about it, he would have told them that Bella had asked him to meet her somewhere and he needed a ride to get there. Then Zein would have been more likely to take him. Now he couldn't use that excuse because they'd know it was a lie. Moreso, though, the thought of lying to Zein made him feel guilty now, as if they were one of his uncles. Foli in particular he could never lie to.

So...what if he told them more of the truth? What part of his story would they want to join? It was a pretty good story up to now, he thought. This was just the part where he had to figure out how to get back to Bella. Then she would get her kingdom and her magic back, she'd turn him back to human, and all would be right in his world.

ZEIN DIDN'T COME BACK BEFORE NIGHTFALL, AND AFTER NAPPING ON and off, Nivvy woke hungry. Only a faint glow from the moon struggled through the cloud cover, but it was enough to bathe the roof in a shimmering silvery light that made it easy to find his way around. When he moved to the edge and looked down on the street, his eyes were drawn to small movements, and it didn't take him long to see the rats in the shadows, small flitting things from his vantage point with a slender tail following just after them, sometimes curling like a whip and sometimes trailing straight back. The rats, some alone and some in pairs, ran along the darkest part of the street, where the walls of the buildings met the stones, and when they stopped moving, they became essentially invisible, although if Nivvy concentrated and they were close, he could make out the small hump of their furry body and the muted shine of the hairless tail.

For a while he watched, mesmerized by the parade of rats through the streets. A dozen went by in the short time before he stopped counting. Were they a particular problem in Spire? He hadn't noticed them previous nights he'd been here. More likely, his current body was very good at spotting other things his size.

They were teaching him something, too, he realized: where to run on the street and how to move. Dart from shadow to shadow, wait, assess, dart forward. When a person walks by, freeze until they pass. His stomach growled as he watched; he realized that he was thinking about the rats he'd fought in the dining hall of the Bouli temple, how he'd bitten one, how the blood had tasted in his mouth.

No. He didn't want to eat raw rat, not unless he had to. Unless he was mistaken, the kitchen below him had been cooking some kind of fowl, and there would be scraps and maybe more in the kitchen.

When the street below was relatively quiet, or at least free of people, Nivvy made his way down the wall to the stones below. The rats avoided him, which made his way easier as he copied their movements, sticking to the shadows, moving a little bit and then waiting before moving again. Another benefit of this style of movement, he discovered, was that it allowed him to keep track of the shifting, swirling profusion of smells in the air. When he was running, he could follow a scent or react to a particularly strong one, but it was like having blinders on. When he stopped and gave his whole attention to his nose, the world opened up for him.

The kitchen of the Giant's Foot might as well have been glowing like a full moon for as brightly as its odors came to his nose. It was no trouble at all to follow the base of the building around and find the kitchen door. Unfortunately, the kitchen clearly had been raided by rats in the past, if not weasels, and none of the cracks he was expecting to squeeze through were large enough. There was a waste bin, covered, next to the door, and beyond that, several rats whose eyes shone out of the shadows at him.

"You can have the rubbish," he told them. "I'm for what's behind the door."

In his search to find another way in, he passed a small metal door that smelled strongly of meat and roots: probably the storage basement. The wooden frame around the door held the scent of rat as well as an area nibbled away, not big enough for him.

But he had one up on the rats: he knew he could brave busier rooms and reach the kitchen that way. The innkeeper was smart enough not to leave kitchen windows open, but halfway around the building, Nivvy caught the movement of air above him and climbed up to it. This was one of the windows of the main room, and it was only open a crack, but that was enough. He paused to sort out the smells and sounds. It seemed that everyone had gone to bed, so he darted through.

From there, it was short work to get to the kitchen door, much less secure from this side, and then through into a feast. At first Nivvy was drawn to the fat clinging to the stove and the cutting boards, but that sweet appetizer only fed his hunger. His nose led him to a large iron pot, still warm, and when he pushed the cover off, he found a stew with chunks of parsnip, carrot, and various meats swimming in a rich, thick gravy.

The profusion of smells made him as heady as a mouthful of fruit wine would. Not just the meat and vegetables but also the various herbs made his mouth water enough that the fur around it grew damp from how often he licked his lips. Perched on the edge, it wasn't easy to fish out chunks of meat; more than once he worried he'd overbalance and fall in. But he persevered, and after a little while, he'd gorged himself on several large chunks of fowl and pork, his nose full of glorious scents and his mouth slick and warm with fat and broth, and he felt quite pleased with himself. He fished through and found a leg bone with some meat on it, clamped his jaws around it, and hurried back out the way he'd come. Let the innkeeper wonder how the cover'd come off his stew pot. Nivvy chuckled to himself at the thought, hurrying out the window and back up to the roof.

He woke the next day to bright sun and a shadow over him. "Looks like you've made a nice little home for yourself here," Zein said.

Nivvy stretched out to his full length and yawned up at them. "Morning," he said, and pushed the bone toward the hawk. "Want some?"

They eyed it. "Where'd you get it? The rubbish heap? It looks fresh. Did you steal it off a plate?"

"Stew pot." He grinned, rather proud of his own work. "The one down there."

"Well...thank you." They grasped the bone in one talon, then bent down and tore at the meat with their hooked beak. Nivvy watched, fascinated, unable not to imagine that beak tearing through his flesh. Just have to make sure he stayed on Zein's good side.

"Why did you come back?" he asked, though he was pretty sure he knew the answer.

"I wasn't going to leave you all alone in Spire," they said between mouthfuls, confirming his guess. "This is good, by the way. Usually when I get stew it's old and they've set it aside for the animals."

"I wouldn't stand for that." Nivvy watched, fascinated, as they finished the meat and then cracked the bone with very little effort. The splintering snap sent chills along his spine. "Glad you're enjoying it."

"Very much." They picked at the marrow in the bone. "Raw meat is nice because it's so fresh and juicy, but if it's going to be cooked it's nice for it to have seasonings. Thank you for sharing. Anyway. I felt bad leaving you on the roof like this. I can just fly away but I know not everyone can and sometimes I forget that. Especially with you being a new former-human and all. It wasn't nice of me to leave you and I'm sorry about that."

They met his eyes, pausing their eating for a moment. Nivvy cleared his throat. "Oh, well, that's all right," he said. First Zein turned down money for him, now they were apologizing to him? Didn't they know that made it harder for him to talk them into something they didn't want to do? Of course they didn't; they wouldn't be purposefully nice to him for deceitful reasons. They were just nice, and that meant it was going to be more difficult to talk them into taking him, because he was going to have to be honest.

"Listen," he said, "I know you said no to taking me, but hear me out, I just want to tell you more about it, an' then you can make the decision yourself. Just one more time, an' if you still say no, then I promise you can take me to the Thieves Guild here in Spire an' I won't say more about it."

They stared at him and then picked at the bone again. "All right," they said, "I'll listen one more time."

Nivvy drew in a breath. "Bella's not what she seems to be," he started. "She's crazy old an' she pals around with djinn. Or fairies, whatever you like. She's going north to take back a kingdom she used to rule. I was meant to help her, but she left me behind. I just want to see her face to face and have her tell me I'm no use to her. That's proper, that's the way you should do business, isn't it?" Before Zein could reply, he added, "And I do want to tell Rahila good-bye. She was all I had in the world."

The words came out like that, laying it on a little thick but not insincere. Zein shifted again; their expression was hard to read, but they seemed to be thinking it over. "And," Nivvy said, "you could go exploring an' I'd be with you so you wouldn't be alone, right?"

"But," Zein said at last, "what if I take you there and Bella takes you back but doesn't want me?"

Nivvy sat back. "Course she'll want you," he said. "Who wouldn't want a hawk to help 'em out? She told me she thought you were very helpful."

"She didn't want to bring me out to wherever you were going."

"That was a short trip. Who needs a hawk when you're heading for a great damned mountain? We could've used you on the mountain, it turned out."

"She didn't come back to get me afterwards."

"She left me behind too." Nivvy looked up at the hawk's golden, guileless eyes. "I'll tell her the two of us are a team. And if she don't want you," he said, "then I'll say goodbye to her. I'll come back to Spire with you."

He wasn't sure what moved him to make this pronouncement. Had he been standing outside his body listening to himself utter those words, he would have confidently said, "Liar." But as he said them, they didn't feel like a lie.

Zein lifted their head, keeping him fixed in their gaze. "That's very sweet," they said. "You haven't known me as long as you've known her, and we don't have a contract or anything, so I won't hold you to that promise. But it does feel good that you made it."

Nivvy was both relieved and disappointed at that but shook off those confusing emotions. "Like as it won't come to that. Most likely we go out there, I say goodbye to my horse, she tells us to get lost, and we come back here. You get to explore the world to the north an' I get to leave all that in my past and get a start on this new life I got." He held both paws out in front of him. "So what'cha say?"

Zein fluffed their wings. "Where did you have in mind to go?"

That was it, they were on board. "I don't know exactly where she's gone to," Nivvy admitted, "but I heard her talking about a place with... well, listen, here's what happened to us since we saw you last. We went to the Bouli temple, then walked up the mountain, and Bella found hidden in the rock this cave that belonged to a djinn, or a fairy, or something, I dunno, she confused me. Anyway, they talked a while about their past together and then I tried to steal the thing Bella wanted me to steal—"

"She hired you to steal from a fairy?" Zein's feathers fluffed out and then sleeked back down. "I don't know much about fairies but that sounds pretty dangerous to me. Oh—I suppose that—well, it was dangerous, wasn't it?"

"I was lucky not to be killed. Anyway, I overheard them talking about one place from their past, and then after, when we were looking at the thing I stole—"

"You did steal it?"

He fancied he heard a bit more respect in their voice. "Course I did. Just got caught at the last minute, that's all. And lost my charms, but who knows if those would even work for me now. When I'm hired to do a job, I do the job." He wanted very badly to tell them that it was more Bella's fault than his that he'd got caught, but that felt like it would be protesting a little too much.

"Well. I never met someone who met a fairy, let alone stole from one."

"Now you have." He puffed out his chest. "But it didn't work, the magic thing, that is, an' I'd told her it wouldn't, but she didn't listen, so there we were. But then she had another idea about a place to go, an' the only thing I can think was that fairy mentioned a big powerful thing that she said 'you don't just want lyin' around,' so...you know a place called..." He hoped he was pronouncing it right. "Glædeligdal?"

"Glædeligdal." Zein lifted their head to look up at the clouds. "I don't know if I know that place, but I know someone I could ask. Oigal —the storyteller up on Dellane Street—knows all kinds of stories and he'd be able to tell us if anyone could."

"So..." Nivvy waited until the hawk's eyes came down to meet his. "Does that mean you'll do it?"

Zein stretched their wings out. "It sounds like it will take more than two days."

"Maybe. Depends how far this Glædeligdal is."

"Normally I would ask a silver a day."

Nivvy started to say that he could steal more to pay more, but Zein went on. "But...I suppose I could charge you a friend's rate and it would only be two."

"Oh." The word "friend" had an unusual warming effect on him, making him shift his feet. He hadn't had a real friend since D'Alio a year ago, unless you counted Rahila, who was a different kind of companion. If Zein considered him a friend and was willing to help him, that meant that they believed in him, and by association his plan, however complicated and unlikely it was. Belief had been in short supply for Nivvy for a while, and especially since his weasel-fication, it had been completely supplied by him. He had not realized how exhausting that was until this moment, how relieving and uplifting it was to have someone trust him that much. "I suppose that would be fine, if it suits you."

"It does." Zein lifted their leg with the small pouch tied to it, and Nivvy obligingly put the two silver coins into it. "So do you want to hold onto my back or let me hold you in my talons?"

Nivvy stared at the broad, smooth back lined with feathers that likely came out with the merest tug, especially if one were holding on hundreds of feet in the air. Then he looked down at the talons that were almost as long as his arm. "Don't suppose you've got a saddle or sommat?"

"Ha ha!" Zein laughed. "I think you're safest in my talons. I promise not to let go and you can hold onto my leg if you want to. But if you feel daring you can ride on my back and I'll try very hard to fly level so you don't slip off. But don't pull too much on my feathers if you do because that's quite distracting."

"Tell you what." Nivvy swallowed. "You just tell me where this story-teller is an' I'll meet you there."

"That's fine if you want," Zein said, "but it won't work on the way to Glædeligdal, wherever that is, unless it happens to be a place here in the city, which it doesn't sound like it is, so you might as well get used to being carried or riding, whichever."

"No chance you can fly like two feet off the ground, ey?"

Zein clacked their beak. "I'll carry you to Oigal and if you don't like that, you can try riding." They took off, wings beating a strong gust of air down at the roof, and then eight hooked talons dove at Nivvy. He closed his eyes.

## ❧ 14 ❧
# THE STORY OF GLÆDELIGDAL

He did not like being picked up at all, and he did not like the way the points of the hawk's talons pressed into his body, though they did not break the skin. And he did not like the wind rushing past him, not at first. Zein had said he could hold onto their leg, but that would mean twisting around in their grip and that might startle them and make them let him go and then he would be in a decidedly bad situation for a little flightless weasel.

"Almost there!" Zein sang out.

Already? Nivvy's eyes flew open despite himself, and he discovered in that moment that there was something he liked even less than being picked up and carried, less than talons pressing like sword points into vulnerable areas of his body, less than the wind streaming into his eyes and through his fur, and that thing was being so high up that the ground was a mass of brown and red and grey shapes with little blurs moving around the shapes. Most of what he could smell was smoke, with whiffs of other things that went by too quickly for him to process properly, and apart from Zein, he couldn't hear anything, so it was rather like being suspended out of reality altogether.

He shut his eyes again quickly and gasped out, "Good."

The wind changed direction, rushing up against his belly, and with it came the very familiar feeling of falling. That lasted only five seconds, or about sixty beats of his terrified heart, and then Zein let go of him.

The panic that flashed through him had not even had time to register as such before his feet touched the wooden beams of a roof. He lay down flat against its warmth, breathing in its scent and listening to the sounds of Spire moving around him, the world real and solid again.

"I've never carried anyone before. You didn't hold onto my leg so I guess it was okay. Was it okay? I tried not to get too fancy with flying, but I can't just fly like a sparrow; I'm supposed to climb and drop and dart through the air. My body's made for it so that's what I do. Was it okay? Are you all right? I can hear your heartbeat; I know you're still alive."

Nivvy was rethinking his whole plan. Maybe what he should do was go work for the Thieves Guild, save up money for half a year or so, then hire someone who would take him on a horse up to wherever Bella would have by then finished taking over whatever kingdom it was. He'd just ride up and say, hello Queen Bella, remember me? I'm the one who stole the useless ring for you and then got turned into a weasel and then you went ahead and did your whole mission without my help but now that you're a success I'm here to offer my help and service.

He closed his eyes and sank his head to the wood of the roof. "I'm fine," he said.

"Was it scary? It was scary for me the first time I flew because I'd never done it before, but then I found out I can fly. Oh, but you can't fly. Still, don't worry. I won't drop you, and even if I do, I'll catch you. I can catch birds, and you wouldn't even dodge like they do."

Nivvy rolled onto his back and opened his eyes. The hawk's beak hovered unsettlingly close to him, but behind it, the golden eyes were concerned and curious. "I believe you won't drop me," he said. "I just never flew before."

"Now you have. Next time'll be easier, I promise. You can look down at the little people and think about how they have to climb all the way to the top of a great huge tower to be able to have this view while you can have it in just a few seconds. Sometimes I fly to the top of the tower so I can see how tired the people are and how sad they look when they realize they have to walk all the way down. Although they don't always. Twice I saw people jump."

The world felt solid now, the warm wood against his back and the sun on his belly. Nivvy flipped over and shook himself. The action, something he'd learned while in the cage, settled his short fur and gave him a brief sense of calm that he especially appreciated now. "I'll skip the tower for the moment," he said. "Let's go see your friend."

"He's not exactly a friend," Zein said. "Or maybe he is. I bring people to him for stories, and so sometimes he sits and talks to me if there isn't anyone paying. He's told me stories sometimes."

"Oh." Nivvy considered this. "So I should pay him, then, if I'm asking for a story."

"I'll tell him you don't have any money. Since you're a former-human, he might be willing to tell you a story." The hawk tilted their head. "I've never brought a former-human to see him before."

"I'd rather have money to pay him." Nivvy sighed. "Would a silver piece be enough?"

"More than," Zein assured him. "If you want to use one of your two silver, you can find me another silver later."

Nivvy's heart had slowed to a normal pace. "Or you can point me to an inn where people might leave their belongings. I'll steal another one, easy peasy."

Zein turned their head. "There's an inn a little ways down, but I don't know."

"They got rooms above the inn?"

"I'm pretty sure. I don't know the inn all that well, but I guided someone there once. People stay there. They have a stable."

"All right." He took a breath. "Can you take me to their roof?"

This time, it wasn't so bad. Being picked up still wasn't enjoyable at all, and the talons made him tense, but Zein didn't fly as high, and it was over very quickly.

Zein waited while Nivvy poked his head over the roof, looking for an open window, which was difficult because his head was small and the angle steep. After several minutes of this, the hawk grew restless and took off with a great gust of air that startled Nivvy. He tracked them as they dipped, circled the building, and came back. "On the other wall," they said when they landed, "closer to that corner, there's an open window."

"Thanks."

He hurried over there, climbed down the wall to the window, which was indeed open, and made his way into the room. It was empty, but he followed his nose to a more recently occupied room and there found a leather pouch from which he took a silver piece and a copper piece, held them in his mouth, and was back on the roof in a trice.

Not a bad bit of thievery, if he did say so himself. He'd gotten enough to pay for a story, and a little more besides. Being pleased with himself definitely improved the experience of being carried by a hawk, and when Zein deposited him back on the storyteller's roof, he said, "We make a good team, you know?"

Zein fluffed their feathers. "I'm not a thief," they said. "I like my work as a guide."

"All right, I didn't mean nothin' by it. Just appreciated your help."

"You're welcome." Zein did seem mollified by that. "Come on, he leaves a window open around here when the weather's nice."

They led Nivvy to a window and swooped down through it, leaving Nivvy to take the silver piece in his mouth and climb down after.

He emerged into a small, close room packed with parchment and scrolls that smelled strongly of old parchment and of an old man. One ornately carved wooden chair was the only piece of furniture Nivvy could see, unless low tables or chests were buried under the piles of parchment.

"Oigal!" Zein called out.

Nivvy made his way over to the chair and set a silver piece on it, then sat beside it to wait. The wood had been smoothed and polished so much that it was quite pleasant to sit on, and under the odor of the man he presumed to be Oigal, the scent of the chair and the oil used to polish it lingered as well.

Zein waited on the windowsill, and a few minutes later footsteps sounded outside. The door swung open and a stooped, wrinkled man with white hair and a long beard stepped in with surprising energy. He wore an old black robe cinched around his waist and a bright smile. "Zein! It has been such a long time. How lovely to see you—what, who's this?"

"I'm—"

"This is my friend Nivvy," Zein said. "He's a former-human but a new one. To Spire, I mean. Anyway, he wants to hear a story about a place called, what was it?"

Nivvy enunciated as clearly as he could. "Glad-lig-dal." He lifted the silver coin and held it up.

Oigal reached down and took it gently from Nivvy's paws, then slid it into a pocket of his robe. "May I have my chair, Mister Nivvy?"

"It's just Nivvy." Nivvy jumped down to the floor.

"We must retain some measure of respect even if we do not wear the form we prefer," Oigal said. "I would much rather wear the body I had thirty years hence, but alas, the world moves on and the past slides away."

"Thought your whole job was remembering the past." Nivvy curled up on a parchment.

"It is, it is. But the past is a lens through which we look to the future." Oigal shuffled through the papers to a small pile, where he picked up and tossed aside several parchments. "Now, the story of Glædeligdal, let me see." He pronounced it more fluidly than Nivvy had, "glehd" rather than "glad," and a half-breath before the "lig-dal" part. Nivvy took this to mean that he knew the name. Good.

Oigal reached for a sheaf of parchments on a high shelf and blew dust from them. "I know that that is an ancient name for something, but I don't remember quite...is it Galadal? No...ah! Here we are." He picked one out of the sheaf and put the rest back on the shelf. "Glædeligdal is an ancient name for Lake Beatrice. I believe it was one of the kings who named it for his daughter a long time ago. Now how did you come to know the name 'Glædeligdal,' I wonder. I only have it in notes I made from notes my old master took at a library in..." He checked the parchment. "Sul'Aji."

Nivvy tried to think of a believable reason he would know that name. "I heard it from a very old friend of mine," he said finally as Oigal sat back in his chair.

"She must have also heard it from a very old friend," Oigal said. "It's been Lake Beatrice as long as I've known it. But the story of Lake Beatrice is even older than that, so I presume it was first told about Glædeligdal, as it was then known."

"He's really good," Zein chirped up. "You'll see. I haven't even heard the Lake Beatrice story, but it's got to be good."

"I'm afraid I don't tell it often, partly because Lake Beatrice is quite a long way from here, but also because it isn't, in fact, one of the better stories. It mostly explains the existence of the lake. But I will tell the most interesting version of it."

Quite a long way didn't sound like it was going to be easy for Nivvy and Zein to get there, but maybe "a long way" meant something different to people who weren't hawks. "Do you know where it is?" Nivvy asked.

"In a very general sense," Oigal said. "As the story goes, it was a long time ago and a long way away from here, past the Merkhar Forest, in the foothills of the Reiki Mountains. There was a valley, and a kingdom in the valley, and a king who ruled the kingdom.

"For many years, the land was prosperous. Bouli, the god of fire and smithing who lives in the mountains, smiled upon them, and they made obeisance to him. He gathered into this kingdom some of the finest workers of metal and the finest cooks in all the world. It was said that in this kingdom, the poorest beggar's meal was finer than that of a king in any other city."

Nivvy had been about to open his mouth to object, but the mention of Bouli stilled him. He'd paid for the story, so he might as well listen, and maybe he'd learn more about the god of fire whose priests had been keeping him captive.

"With these glories came scribes, of laws and of stories, and Bouli's fire burned in all their works. And with them came great generals and conquerors. The glory of the kingdom grew so great that the last king believed that Bouli intended for their valley to be the center of a great empire. Under his orders, the kingdom amassed a great army and set forth to conquer the rest of the world.

"Their army came to Vir'Aji. You know the place?"

"Heard of it," Zein said, while Nivvy shook his head.

"Vir'Aji is a great port on the Northern Sea, many miles north of Sul'Aji. If I were simply telling this story to someone from Spire, you understand, the army would arrive at Spire and the story would go on. For someone from Copper Port, it would be Copper Port. But the first time I heard it, it was Vir'Aji, and because the goddess Aji is the one to strike back, I believe it makes the most sense to say Vir'Aji. It could also be Sul'Aji, but the notes came from there, so I will cleave to that version. You understand, yes?"

Nivvy got it; the stories were shaped to the listener. There was a time when he would have loved to hear a story of the glory of Copper Port, but those days were fairly far in his past, even the latter days he'd lived in that pit.

"The armies of Vir'Aji were small, but the goddess's spirit flowed strongly in them, and they beat back the king's army. Furious, the king instructed his army to destroy every temple to Aji that they could find, and his men burned a dozen of them. Then he retreated back to his kingdom's valley to gather his strength and plan a new attack."

Oigal leaned forward and lowered his voice. "But the goddess followed them." He paused, and Nivvy's fur prickled with the tension, even though he knew how this story ended. "The mountains that ringed the valley had glorious caps of snow, and Aji walked among them, looking down at the kingdom that had dared defile her temples. While the king sat in his palace, brooding over his failure, Aji gathered the snow from all the mountains. She sent it streaming down at the kingdom, and in an instant, as quickly as you might fill a basin from a well, the valley was gone. In its place was a bright white sheet of snow, sparkling in the sunlight as though thousands of people had not just been killed below it."

Not too far from what Bella had told (apart from the snow), although in this version the kingdom definitely deserved it. You didn't go around defiling temples unless you wanted gods to be mad at you. Maybe this king Bella had been talking about had done some of that and that's why she was able to drown the valley. The thought felt comforting, but in the way a coarse wool blanket might keep you warm: it was nice, but it was too itchy to stay under for long. Thoughts could be itchy too, when he knew they weren't quite right.

"When the people of Vir'Aji sought out the attackers to find out what had happened, they traveled for days and never found a trace of the kingdom, but they found a beautiful lake and their king named it for his daughter Beatrice. And that is what happened to the kingdom that lies beneath Lake Beatrice." He beamed at them. "Or, as you know it, Glædeligdal."

"Thank you!" Zein cried. "That was lovely! Ooh, the image of that valley filling with snow. But I suppose they were wicked people and deserved it."

Nivvy pushed aside the itching from that remark and asked, "People have seen it then? The city under the lake?"

"Oh, yes. Another name for this story is the Tale of the Drowned Kingdom." Oigal nodded vigorously and gave a short laugh. "I have a list of places I would like to see before I die, and Lake Beatrice on a clear day when you can see the buildings below the water is one of them. But the list is longer than the hair on my chin, and I fear my remaining days are as short as the hair on my head."

"We're hoping to go there," Zein said, "and I promise we'll tell you all about it when we come back."

When we come back? Nivvy stared up at the hawk. Did they not believe in him after all? Was this merely a journey they were taking out of pity for his plight? Like he'd done with old Polu, when she started to forget where she was and how old she was. Nivvy and Marzin had taken her to a merchant's stall and paid the merchant for whatever she took, all so she would believe she was still a thief. Yes, he'd told Zein that it was likely they'd come back, but he'd said it the way you'd say, "Like as not the necklace has been locked up an' we won't get past the guards," before you went and stole it. It was just so you could expect the worst. But you didn't believe it, not if your friend had gotten the job for you, and you didn't tell your guild master that you'd be coming back empty-handed.

"You're going to Lake Beatrice, eh?" Oigal beamed. "Oh, to be a hawk with the freedom of the skies! Or," he looked down at Nivvy, "a weasel small enough to be carried by a hawk."

"You're welcome to it," Nivvy said, trying to put aside his uncertainty. "Got a spell to trade places?"

"Ha ha!" Oigal laughed.

"Failing that, you have a map or any such? 'Far away north' leaves a lot of room."

"Ooh, a map, of course, I have maps. You want to see the maps from Daga's Five Voyages? Or my old master Portina's attempt to place all the stories we know on a map of the world?"

"Just a reg'lar map," Nivvy said, "preferably one what shows Spire and Lake Beatrice both."

"Of course, of course. Daga traveled very near to Lake Beatrice, you know. His story 'The Tale of the Frost Giants' takes place in the Reiki Mountains as well." Oigal rose from the chair with a spring in his step and danced unerringly to another cluttered corner of the room. "It's in here," he said, and pulled out three parchments. After a quick look, he discarded two of them and spread out the third in front of Nivvy.

"Here," he said as Zein flew over to perch on the arm of the chair and look down. "Can you still read?"

"Yes." Nivvy squinted at the map. "But it don't matter so much if I can read it cause I'm just the passenger." He looked up at the hawk. "This make sense to you?"

Oigal turned the map so it faced Zein, and they scanned it. "Where's Spire? I don't see Spire."

"Ah, this is an old map, older'n Spire." Oigal pointed to a mark. "This here is the Sacred Mount at the Bouli temple, so Spire would be right about here." He slid his finger over to one side.

Nivvy couldn't help noticing that there was a town where Oigal's finger landed and that it was named "Fort of Sand." But Zein either didn't notice or didn't care, tracking the finger from Fort of Sand across a large forest to the southern end of a mountain range where there was a little drawing of what Nivvy presumed was a Frost Giant; it wasn't half bad, a tall shaggy white-haired man wielding either a very big icicle or a sword made of ice.

"All right," Zein said. "It looks like if we head toward the northern mountains, we should see them in a day or two, and then the lake is just in front of the first bunch of mountains. Unless there are a lot of lakes around there? Are there, Oigal, do you know?"

"I have heard only that Lake Beatrice is remarkable, so I would guess that there are not many other lakes of that size. But if there are, you could wait for a sunny day and fly over each of them. The one with a Drowned Kingdom below the surface will be Lake Beatrice."

It was a funny remark, but Nivvy wasn't in a laughing mood. He kept thinking that Zein believed this was a fool's errand, which made him (in their eyes) a fool. Fine. If Zein didn't believe in him, then maybe he wouldn't come back to Spire, even if Bella never showed up, even if they never found the lake. He asked, "You think you can find it?"

"I think so," they said. "I mean, I know so. As long as it's there when we get to the mountains, we'll find it."

"Good." He bowed his head to Oigal. "Was a pleasure meeting you, sir, and a fine storyteller you are. Thank you for your assistance."

Oigal beamed. "Go find the Drowned Kingdom and then come back and tell me your story."

"Of course we will," Zein said. "It's been lovely to see you again. I'll be back soon, I promise."

They looked at Nivvy and spread their wings, but rather than wait for them to come pick him up, he ran to the window, and climbed up there, through, and up to the roof. There he stood in the sun, enjoying the warmth in his fur and steeling himself for the cold, windy, terrifying experience to come.

Zein soared up and alit beside him. "Wasn't that a good story? And we got a map, too. It's so exciting. We're actually going to do this." Their feathers fluffed all up as they gazed out at the walls of Spire.

Nivvy kept quiet. Once he proved his worth, he wouldn't have to worry about anyone believing in him. Once he was part of a queen's court, he wouldn't have to worry about much at all. He clung to that itchy thought and told himself that he just had to get by until they found Bella.

## 15

# LEARNING TO HUNT

They took the journey in flights of about an hour, with little rests in between each one. Zein hunted for squirrels and grass-rats when they stopped, and offered their kills to Nivvy. He refused at the first break, but as he figured out that Zein didn't intend to stop at any inns or anywhere human food was available, his stomach urged him to give in, and by the time the sun hung low and red in the sky, he'd devoured raw pieces of multiple grass-rats. Once he stopped thinking about eating raw meat, it tasted rather good.

"I've never flown for so long at once," Zein said. "I can't see the mountains yet, but I hope tomorrow we'll be able to. I think I can do one more stretch if I take some rest, and then we can stop for the night. It's already cold. Are you okay? You've got fur but I don't want to assume you're warm enough."

"I'm fine." Zein had dropped him near a large wide tree with low spreading branches, which he'd climbed while they hunted. Now he sat comfortably in the angle of the branch and trunk of the tree, about twelve feet off the ground, while Zein perched a foot or so away from him on the same branch. They held the body of a grass-rat in one talon while they tore at it with their beak, which did not unnerve Nivvy as much as he'd feared it might. Maybe that was because he'd eaten from their kill as well, the body torn in half as casually as human-Nivvy might have broken a piece of bread. While he'd eaten his half, Zein had devoured theirs and then gone hunting for another.

Zein was being as nice as they always were, and Nivvy was trying to respond appropriately, but he remained in a bad mood, and he didn't know what to do about it. Normally he'd have some ale, but there wasn't any ale here, and anyway the memory of getting sick on wine still made his stomach uneasy. He might go out to lose his troubles in other people's, or to lift his spirits with a little petty thieving, but the only thing here he could steal was food, and Zein had just given him as much as he could eat. When he was upset with Marzin, the cure was to go off on his own for a bit and come back, but he couldn't do that either.

So he stayed quiet while Zein chattered about how lovely the forest was and how they hadn't been to a real forest in so long, and he worried about what he would say when they met Bella (he shoved away any doubts; he was *going* to find Bella). Was she even at Lake Beatrice yet? The map had made it look like around twice the distance than the Spire to Copper Port journey, and that was four or five days depending on how big a hurry you were in. It had been eight or nine days since Bella had left, and if she knew where she was going, Rahila might have gotten her there by now. But Rahila needed food and sleep, even if Bella didn't, and Bella probably didn't know where the towns were. If she followed the roads, she might take a bit longer. If there were even roads that went to Lake Beatrice. Nivvy hadn't seen many towns on their flight, although granted he'd kept his eyes shut or staring at Zein's belly for most of the time, and now they were well into the Merkhar Forest, he wasn't likely to see anything but trees.

"Hey, Nivvy," Zein said.

"Aye?"

"Was the flight very bad?"

He shook his head. "It was fine. We're covering the distance right quick."

"Is it the food? I know you haven't been a former-human for very long. It took me a little while to get used to eating raw meat."

"It's fine," he said, and then seized on this to explain his mood. "But a stop at a pub wouldn't be amiss."

"Oh." Zein paused in their dismembering of the grass-rat and turned to Nivvy, a piece of sinew hanging from their beak. "I heard that outside of Spire, people don't always know about former-humans and we should be very careful because 'talking animals' might startle them and they could kill you."

"Or put you in a cage," Nivvy agreed, "but we don't have to talk to people. We can sneak in and steal stew bits and maybe some other food."

"But that's one reason I agreed to come along. We didn't have to talk to any people who don't already know us. Just Bella."

"Spire can't be the only place halfway decent to former-humans." Nivvy settled against the tree. "I've heard so many stories about them. They were...there were some of them around in Copper Port as well."

"Stories are one thing. I've had visitors to the town scream when I talked to them. Not many, but when it happens once you're kind of always scared it's going to happen again."

Something else to worry about. "Grass-rat's fine," Nivvy said, curling up in the crook of the branch. "Thanks for the hunt."

"This whole day has been fun," Zein chattered on. "It was so interesting flying over those hills where there'd been a fire and all those burned trees stood like a beaten army in a wasteland. Or that place with the cliffs where you could see red and yellow in the cliff face, all bright and almost glowing. That was far away, though, and you might not have seen it. Oh, or those rivers coming together, the way one of them snakes back and forth like it's trying to delay joining the other one, and then they come together in this big froth of waves and water. What was your favorite part of the flight?"

"I didn't really look," Nivvy said. He closed his eyes.

Zein scraped along the branch near him. "Are you all right?"

"Fine." He pulled his tail over his face, thin though it was.

They were silent for a moment, then said, "Only you were talking so much about how we were a good team before we went to see Oigal, and then after Oigal you were quiet, and you've been quiet all day. I know I've been doing all the flying, but you did convince me to come out here and I think it's worked well so far, but if I'm doing something wrong I do wish you'd tell me, because there's nothing worse than not being told when you're hurting someone, even if it's just with words."

Telling them wouldn't help anything. He'd say, "You didn't believe in me," and they would say, "Of course I believe we're going to find her," but he'd know they were saying it to make him feel better, not because they meant it. "It's fine," he said without opening his eyes. "I just want to go to sleep."

"All right." Zein shuffled away from him. "But if I did something wrong, then tell me. I won't be mad at you for telling me."

Fatigue blurred his annoyance into guilt at being sulky and then back to annoyance at feeling guilty. "It's nothin'," he said, but he couldn't tell whether or not they heard him.

He woke twice during the night, as he was accustomed to doing now, and the second time, a soft susurration filled his ears, so quiet that he wasn't sure at first whether it was real or part of a dream that had followed him into wakefulness. His nose told him there were no immediate threats, and that Zein remained close by him; a moment later he made out their shape on the branch.

It took him another few seconds to place the soft hissing as rain, although he remained dry. He turned his head and the sound lessened, so the rain was traveling toward them up from the south.

A moment later, the first drops hit the tree they were in, and then a chorus of soft pattering surrounded them. Nivvy leaned against the tree, waiting for the rain to trickle through the leaves and hit him.

The first droplets felt like light tapping on his fur, but after a little while the cold and wet seeped through to his skin. Larger droplets gathered on the leaves above him, then splashed onto his back, his legs, his ears. He curled up even more tightly, trying to shield his ears with his tail, as rain dripped down through the branches and leaves overhead, and what had been a soft hissing sound became a full roar of the heavens opening.

Wet and cold, he didn't think he would get back to sleep, but he didn't account for how tired he was, nor for how easy it was to ignore rain when one was already wet. He stirred, found that the day was considerably lighter, and then lifted his head to find Zein standing over him, partly sheltering him from the rain. "It's raining," they said. "Did you notice? I woke up and my feathers were all soaking wet."

"I noticed." Nivvy stood and judged the branch thick enough that he could shake himself on it, so he went ahead and did that. Zein didn't react, even though he must have sprayed them with water. "What's this mean? Can you fly in the rain?"

"I can fly in the rain," Zein said. "It'll just be a bit more wet. That's the main difference with rain. It's more wet than when there's not rain."

Nivvy frowned up at the hawk, who returned his gaze steadily and then said, "That's meant to be funny. Of course you know rain is wet. That's the whole point of it."

"Oh." He didn't know if this body could smile, but he gave it a try. It felt awkward and toothy.

"I can't tell what that means." Zein stared down at him. "Are you trying to smile? Former-humans can't smile the proper way, but when they try to it sort of looks like that. But you might also just be snarling at me."

"It was a smile," Nivvy said, resolved to show less of his annoyance. "It's funny. Let's go ahead then."

"You won't get so wet," Zein assured him, "being underneath my wings and all."

"I'm already wet, so it won't make any difference."

In the event, Zein was wrong about that. They hadn't taken into account that they would be flying forward much faster than the rain fell, so Nivvy was carried full-force into the drops. He clung to Zein's leg, eyes squeezed shut, every moment they were in the air; he spent most of their resting periods flattened to a tree branch and panting, miserable, trying to remember what it was like to not be a small, wet, helpless creature. Zein would try to cheer him up on these occasions with platitudes: "No matter how wet you get, you'll be dry again when the sun comes out. And it always comes out." He would say something back like, "I know, I know," so that they wouldn't ask him again if he was okay, and he'd press his chin and stomach and hips to the rough bark of the tree and think about how wonderful it was to be on something solid.

And then Zein would chirp, "You ready?" Nivvy would sigh and push himself up so that his fur dripped onto the wet bark, and the hawk's talons would pick him up to drag him through rain for another hour or so.

Toward the end of that day, they escaped the rainstorm, flying out into cool, thick air. Zein gave a short cry and said, "Look, look," and Nivvy, against his better judgment, opened his eyes and twisted around. The horizon, previously a wall of grey, had resolved itself into a jagged jawline pointing up into a purpling sky. "The mountains!" they cried. "We're close!"

"Brilliant." Nivvy squeezed his eyes shut again. "Tonight?"

"No. Maybe midday tomorrow."

"Right. Well. At least we'll be dry by then."

He fell asleep dreaming of that lovely state of being dry again and woke to the rattle of rain in the leaves above him and water splashing into his fur. "Looks like the rain caught up with us," Zein said cheerfully, seeing him awake. "We'll get out ahead of it again tomorrow."

"There's no way we'll see into the lake if it's raining."

"It'll stop eventually, and in the meantime, we can look for Bella if you want." Zein spread their wings and shook the water off them.

*If you want.* Unspoken at the end of that was the sentiment, *if you want to waste your time.* Nivvy curled up again. At least he was getting good at ignoring the rain.

In the morning, he woke still wet but with the smell of hawk strong in his nose. He lifted his head and felt in his whiskers that Zein was right overhead. Behind him on the branch, their talons sank into the wood.

Around him, rain still danced through the leaves, but the hawk's body kept most of it from hitting him. Through the rain, glimmers of pink and orange lit the tree, a soft glow catching some of the drops as they fell. A couple insects made their way over his fur, struggling to get back to the tree bark. He'd had insects crawl on him before, and as long as they didn't bite—which these showed no inclination to—he didn't see any hurry in shaking them off until he was ready to get up. More would just crawl on.

His fur was still wet, but it wasn't getting wetter, and though the dawn air was chilly, he wasn't all that uncomfortable. The hawk's warmth radiated down a little ways, enough to be comforting. Nivvy looked up at the feathers. "Lonely?" he asked.

Zein, still asleep, did not respond nor move. Nivvy exhaled across his own fur. This whole situation was freeing in a way. He had no money to his name, but he could survive by hunting rats if he needed to. He could still thieve. And once he got a chance to show Bella what he could do, he'd have a patron.

In the meantime, he could hope to be human again, but as Zein had sort of pointed out to him, he might as well not complain too much about the rain while waiting for the sun to come out. They could still move forward in the rain. They'd just be wet, and honestly, he'd been wet for a day and a half, and "dry" was only a memory.

He swiveled his ears around, taking in the sounds of the morning.

Above them on the tree, there were scrapes; something else was roosting up there. Other birds tended to be scared away when Zein swooped onto a tree, so maybe it was squirrels in a nest.

The feathers above him shifted and fluffed. "You awake?" he called up.

"Morning," came Zein's cheerful voice. "Look at the sky! It's so pretty with the sun below the clouds there."

Nivvy blinked out at the pink and orange-shaded mist. "It's nice," he said, "for a rainy day."

"There were nice sunrises in Spire, but this is so quiet, just us and the rain."

It was quiet, but now that Zein was up, Nivvy stretched and shook the remaining insects off him. "I would've climbed up to try my luck at hunting whatever's up there—squirrels, you think?—but figured I'd wait for you to get up. You been doing all the hunting so maybe I can do it sometime."

"That would be nice," Zein said. "Want to climb down and see what's around?"

"In a moment." Nivvy stretched again, lazily. "You get lonely in the night? What you end up over here for?"

"Oh." They fluffed their feathers again, sending a spray of water outward. "You looked wet, and I figured if something under me was going to be dry, it might as well be you and not just a bare tree branch that can't even say thank you."

"Ah." Nivvy looked up, but Zein's eyes were hidden by their body. "Well, thank you kindly. Made for a more pleasant night."

"Good." They paused and then, when Nivvy didn't say anything, went on. "I know you don't like being carried, but did you like traveling around when you had another way to do it? I mean, if, say, I could carry a little basket that you could ride in, would you like it better? I'm not offering, mind you. I don't know how to weave a basket. But I know someone who makes things for former-humans and he might be able to make a little basket. You know, if after we get back to Spire, you want to go on trips again."

Zein had been so nice to him, and then they said something like "after we get back to Spire" that pierced Nivvy like a thorn in his paw. All right, he wasn't going back to Spire anyway, so Nivvy said, "Aye, that sounds nice," because his sides did hurt where Zein's talons gripped him.

"I like traveling and it seems like you do too, and it's nicer when there's someone to do it with. We don't have to go all the way up to the mountains every time, but maybe a day to go down to the desert. I was thinking about Oigal and his list of places to see. It might be nice to see them, don't you think?"

"It would be interesting, aye," Nivvy said. He stretched again and now hunger made itself more known, scraping at his insides. "I'll go see how I do on the hunt now, shall I?"

He ran easily down the tree and set off on his first real hunt. His nose identified a number of grass-rats, shrews, and rabbits around, as well as one or two scents he didn't recognize. The rain clearly wasn't keeping them from feeding, or maybe it had been going on long enough that the desperate creatures had no choice. He aimed for the closest grass-rat and soon found it digging through rain-splashed mud puddles in search of worms.

For several beats of his heart, he watched it. Defending himself against the rats in the Bouli temple had been a matter of survival, not hunting and killing. He'd done that back in his human days too, some-times even hunting rats, but it had always been with a knife or a trap, never his jaws.

His stomach growled again, reminding him that this, too, was a matter of survival. He'd eaten grass-rat for the last day, and these were not former-humans; they were only animals. If he waited much longer, it would spot him and then he'd have to find another one. He was only getting wetter and hungrier. He readied his jaws and leapt.

Perhaps he'd been stealthy or perhaps the sound of the rain had covered his approach; the rat was taken by surprise. It fought, but Nivvy tore at it with his teeth and claws, and eventually its struggles weakened and then stopped.

Rain washed the blood around its fur and Nivvy's as the thick coppery smell suffused his nose. He turned to look for his tree, and now it looked a mile away. Well, he'd signed up to hunt, so he had to bring the hunt back.

He dragged the dead grass-rat by its tail, walking backwards through the rain in slick grass and mud. By the time he reached the tree, both he and the meal were much the worse for wear.

"Ho!" he called at the base of the tree. "Zein! Come down, I can't drag this thing up a cursed tree!"

There was a fluttering and then the hawk dropped to the earth, landing in a spray of water. They stared at the grass-rat and then looked at Nivvy. "Did you already eat your half?"

"No." He pushed at the bloody corpse. "It got a bit messy, that's all."

"A bit messy? It looks like it's been turned inside out and then buried and dug up again."

"It was my first hunt." He bristled. "I can't just jump on it and shove great thick claws into its heart."

"You'll get better." Zein reached down and ripped the body in half effortlessly. "My first kill struggled a lot and was messy too. I mean, not this messy, but you're right, I have bigger talons. It's easier to kill little things like rats. You'll get the hang of it."

"I don't want to get better at it," he snapped, hunger and annoyance at Zein's facility with their beak and talons making him more honest than he normally would be. He tore meat from a haunch, chewed it briefly, and swallowed the chunks. "I want to—"

He realized what he was about to say and stopped. Zein tilted their head, fixing him with one golden eye, but then gulped down another piece of rat meat and looked back at it. "It's a good fat one," they said, though the grass-rat's ribs carried barely any fat on them. Winter was not so far gone that its scarcity was forgotten, and surely any creature that didn't need to hunt in this rain would be safe in a den somewhere.

Fat or not, it filled him, and soon enough they were on their way. "When we get to the lake," Zein said as they struggled to take flight under the pelting rain, "you should wash all that mud off. Even your white parts are brown."

"I won't need to," Nivvy called back, closing his eyes against the rain lashing him. "Gonna get a bath just being carried there."

They flew for an hour, rested in the shelter of a thick-leaved tree, then flew for another hour. The sky brightened somewhat as the day approached what Nivvy guessed was noon, but rain drove down constantly and the clouds remained thick, hiding the tops of the mountains. When they rested, Nivvy climbed around the tree to get a better view of the horizon, but could only see a grey wall, which he assumed had gotten closer because they were flying toward it. There was no way to tell: the grey of the clouds and mountains blurred together, and even with superior human sight, he wasn't sure he would have seen more than a hazy wall, a sea of undefined mist that might swallow them up.

In those moments, he wondered why he was so intent on flying into that unknown world. Then he reminded himself: Bella was there, and she would guide him the rest of the way, be it as a weasel or in a return to his humanity.

On their fourth flight, in early afternoon, Zein called out, "I see it!"

Nivvy's eyes flew open, but against the driving rain he could barely see anything, and he didn't dare let go with even one paw to wipe his eyes clear. "Are you sure?"

"It's several miles that way," Zein said as they banked, temporarily shielding Nivvy from the worst of the rain. "We were close. It's a good thing it's such a big lake. It's the only thing that looks like a lake that I can see."

"That sounds like it." His body vibrated with excitement. Bella certainly hadn't expected him to find her when she'd abandoned him at the temple, and now he was going to show up at the lake. She couldn't deny that he was worthy of being her—

Her what? Assistant? Paid help? Hired thief? Didn't matter, whatever it took to get him human again and then he'd deal with whatever came after that.

What if she wasn't even there yet? Well, that'd show her even more, he thought smugly. Leave me behind at the temple and I beat you where you're going, that's the sort of thief you've got when you hire me. Maybe he could even get into the lake (somehow) and get the thing she wanted (without knowing anything about it), have it ready and waiting when she showed up.

(But what if he'd been wrong? What if she'd gone somewhere else entirely?)

Zein banked again. "What is it?" Nivvy called.

"There's a town. I'm just going around it. The lake's on the other side but we can come at it through the mountains. It isn't too far out of the way."

"A town?" Nivvy opened his eyes and looked down, but the grey-green smear below him revealed no details. "No, no, fly over the town and look for Bella!"

Zein straightened out their flight but said, "I don't know if that's a good idea."

"Then fly as close as you can so you can see Rahila if she's tied up somewhere, or maybe Bella."

"Nobody's going to be out in this rain."

"Then there's no reason not to!"

Zein didn't say anything, just banked lightly back and flew straight on. Nivvy squeezed his eyes shut and waited.

A short while later, Zein said, "The town looks deserted. Everyone's inside." Nivvy risked another look and saw brown smears give way to green as they passed the small town and soared over the woods. Zein went on. "At least the rain's not as bad now. Maybe by the time we get to the lake, we'll—"

The hawk's body jerked, and the world spun around Nivvy as though he were back on the wheel in Plow. Grey sky, green ground, grey sky, green ground, and then the ground was coming closer. Zein's talons loosened their grip on him, and though he clung frantically to their leg, it was wet, and his paws were slippery. Next to him now for some reason quivered a slender piece of wood with fletching on the end, and his panicked mind said, *what would an arrow be doing up here*, as the hawk's leg slipped through his fingers and he fell.

## ❧ 16 ❧
# THE GARDEN OF ASKA

His body twisted around so that he was falling feet-first, not through any conscious effort on his part. Nothing was going to matter anyway. Several seconds was long enough to regret all the wrong turns he'd made in his life, most of all talking to Bella while he was on the wheel. If he'd just ignored the crazy woman who wanted him to help her steal a kingdom, the way he should've, the way his parents had raised him to ignore crazy people, then he'd likely be wandering around in a comfortable desert now, perhaps poor, perhaps eating rats, but not soaked to the skin, not falling out of the sky to his death, and definitely, absolutely, under no circumstances would he be in the body of a weasel.

After this rush of thoughts, his mind returned to the arrow he'd seen. Oh. Zein had been shot. That made sense. Sorrow and guilt drove all the other thoughts from his mind, and then he struck the ground.

The impact knocked the breath out of him, splashed water and mud all around him. He lay there stunned for a moment, the world still and at peace, light rain washing the mud from his fur. He wasn't dead. He wasn't even knocked out.

He struggled to his feet, wobbly but upright. Nothing seemed to be broken, although he was going to have a set of bruises on his side to make Inira proud.

His first instinct was to look around and try to spot the fallen hawk, but with his head only three inches above the ground, he couldn't see anything but muddy grass. Right, he remembered, use your nose.

The breeze did not bring any scent of hawk, but it did bring the scent of a man, the tanned hides he wore, and the multiple days, possibly weeks, since he'd bathed. A hunter: that was who was going to find the hawk.

But carried on the breeze was also the unmistakable scent of water, a lot of it. Not too far away, not longer than a whole, healthy weasel could travel in a day, so surely he could reach it easily by tomorrow.

Ah, not this again, he moaned to Inira. Why?

It wasn't the same situation, though. Zein wasn't a more experienced colleague who could be reasonably expected by anyone who knew them to fend for themself, plus Zein was almost certainly hurt and in imminent danger, if not already dead. If they weren't dead...what could Nivvy do? Could he really get to the hawk before the hunter did?

His annoyance at Zein dissolved, leaving him only with guilt and anguish. Fine, he told the goddess of thieves. You want me to learn a different lesson, I've learned it. And he ran as fast as he could toward the scent of the hunter.

The man's great steps thudded through the ground a moment before Nivvy laid eyes on him, a seeming giant walking through the rain with determination. Nivvy paced him easily, even on the muddy ground, and the hunter didn't notice the small weasel racing through the grass behind him.

He must have lost his mind. That man was huge. What could Nivvy do to stop him? He had to try, and he was going to try, because he couldn't very well say that what happened to him while working for Bella was her problem to fix and not own up to the same when someone was hurt working for him. That wasn't how Inira did things. Don't steal from someone who can't afford it; don't hurt someone who didn't hurt you, or a friend of yours, or who wasn't a danger of hurting you in the future; and don't put someone in a bad situation and then skip out.

There was some grey area around that last one but not now. Now Zein was helpless, and this great oaf was coming to probably kill them, and Nivvy was the only person around to help.

Zein had said that people around these parts didn't know former-humans, so maybe he could pull the old "cursed spirit" trick again.

Wasn't good to keep going back to the same well, but he didn't have a lot of other options, did he?

The man he was following stopped, and as Nivvy bounded behind him, he saw the mass of brown and white feathers in the grass in front of him at the same time as Zein's scent hit him. He darted forward, skidding to a stop in front of the body and turning to face the man, who had an arm raised and something glinting in his hand.

"Hey!" Nivvy yelled as loudly as he could. "Leave this hawk alone!"

The man stopped, staring down, and then crouched slowly. His black-bearded face was shielded by a wide-brimmed hat from whose edge rain coursed down, but Nivvy could see that the man's complexion was paler than his own—paler than his own had been, that is. "What's this?"

Nivvy took a breath. "This hawk and I have been cursed. If you will but help us, we may assist you in turn."

The man grunted. "No interest in your stories. All I need is meat." And the hand with the blade in it came down.

He wasn't particularly fast. Nivvy had plenty of time to ask himself what to do now and come to the conclusion that there wasn't much left to him but teeth and claws, to prepare for the hand to get into range, and then to jump and sink his teeth into its fleshy heel much as he had the shoulder of the grass-rat. He bit down hard, tore, and then let go, dropping a full second before the man's other hand would have smacked into him; instead it hit the fresh wound.

The man roared. "I'll kill you, you cursed demonspawn!"

"Have to catch me first," Nivvy taunted him. The man was slow, or else Nivvy's weasel reflexes were fast. He dodged another knife swipe easily and jumped for the wound he'd inflicted, tearing at it and opening it further.

The hunter yelled another curse. Nivvy dropped to the ground and ran around behind the man, who twisted to follow, but too slowly; Nivvy jumped to the back of his leg and climbed up his back to his shoulder, where he sank his teeth into the man's ear.

"Rraaaaah!" The man tried to smack Nivvy away, but again his hand only managed to hit the fresh wound, boxing his own ear as well this time. Nivvy ran around to the other shoulder to bite that ear, this time coming away with a sizable chunk of flesh.

"Demons!" Now the man was running, so Nivvy dropped from his shoulder to the ground. The cries of "Demons!" grew fainter with the heavy footsteps.

He allowed himself one moment of pride and a yell of, "Hah! That's what you get when you don't respect the cursed!" Then he turned back to Zein, who, it came to him, had not moved nor spoken this whole time.

The hawk lay in an untidy pile on the ground, one wing stretched straight out, the other held up artificially by the arrow sticking through it. Nivvy came up closer and rested both paws on Zein's shoulder. "Hey," he said softly. "Hey, Zein. You...okay?"

No response. "Inira's bones," Nivvy swore to himself. "Don't be dead, okay? Wouldn't be fair to me and certainly not to you." He put his head next to Zein's.

There: his whiskers twitched. Had it been a breath or just a trick in between raindrops? No; there was another one. "Zein. Zein."

He shook the hawk's shoulder. "Come on," he said, "I can't even drag a grass-rat very far and that guy will be back soon, come on, you're gonna have to get up."

The rain, light as it was, made it hard for him to tell whether the hunter was coming back or not. The constant background patter, both the sound and the little constant impacts on the grass, combined to make him feel uneasily exposed. He searched for the hawk's ear and couldn't find one. Did hawks even have ears? They could hear well enough. What if their ear was on their feet or something? He put his nose next to Zein's head behind the closed eye and kept talking. "Zein, come on, get up, if he comes back with help I can't protect you." He nudged the hawk. "Come on, we gotta go. Let's go."

After the third "Let's go," the hawk stirred and the eye facing Nivvy cracked open.

"Zein!"

The eye blinked. "Niv? Nivvy?"

"It's me. Come on, you need to get up, let's go, let's get out of here."

"My wing hurts. What—" They lifted their head and tried to look around. "Something hit me in the air."

"You got shot, there's an arrow in your wing, there was a hunter and he's going to come back, so we need to get out of here now."

"I can't fly," Zein complained.

"I know," Nivvy said. "There's cover not too far from here, we can walk there, we have to leave now though."

"I don't know if I can." Zein fixed him with a look and their voice pleaded. "It hurts."

"All right." Nivvy's mind raced. "We can't take the arrow out yet, but, but..." He ran around to the injured wing.

Zein's head swiveled to follow. It looked like the arrow had stuck in the mud, but it wasn't deep. "I can get this," Nivvy said with more confidence than he felt.

"Why can't we take the arrow out?" Zein asked. "It hurts."

Nivvy set his paws to the arrow and tried to break it off, but his strength wasn't up to that task. Desperate, he settled for tugging it free of the mud. It fell flat, bringing the wing with it and a sharp cry from Zein. "Because it might be stopping you from bleeding," Nivvy said. "Learned that in my training. If you get stabbed, don't just pull the knife out. Get to a healer first."

"Is there a healer around?" Zein asked with a hopeful note.

Nivvy gritted his teeth. "One thing at a time. Let's get to cover. Can you walk?"

The hawk struggled and with some effort rose out of the muddy grass. Nivvy tried to steady them, but his little weight didn't help very much. Zein took a step and fell, but before Nivvy could exhort them further, they got up. "I can do this," they said. "Where's the healer?"

"This way." It was shorter not to explain.

The walk with the slow, wounded hawk was nerve-racking. Nivvy held the arrow to keep it from dragging on the ground and catching on anything, and meanwhile had to keep an eye on the hawk to make sure they kept moving forward, another eye on the dark green forest he was guiding them toward, and his nose to the wind for any scent of the hunter returning. Even if he caught wind of the hunter, he didn't know what he could do except urge Zein on faster, and the hawk was going as fast as they could. The only benefit was that the rain eased up to a thin misting.

"How much farther is it?" Zein asked when they were about halfway there.

"Not far," Nivvy said. "Can't you see?"

"I can see the forest. Where are we going inside it?"

"Let's get to the forest first, then we'll figure out the next thing."

So Zein staggered along with Nivvy encouraging them until they finally reached the dark cool embrace of the forest. Nivvy nudged the hawk to go a little ways in until he found a thick bush that would conceal them well. "Let's rest here," he said.

Zein worked their way in through the branches, catching the arrow several times with cries of pain. Nivvy helped them work out of those snags as best he could, but by the time the hawk collapsed on the ground, shielded by branches, their beak was hanging open and they looked as distressed as Nivvy had ever seen an animal, or a former-human. They turned to him and said, "I'm going to die here, aren't I?"

His heart tightened, and for a moment he couldn't form words. "Hush," he said finally. "Nobody's dyin'. I'm gonna go and fetch you something to eat, keep your strength up, replace that blood yer losin'. Then I'm gonna go find Bella by the lake."

"Bella? She's a healer?"

Nivvy licked his lips. "I...I know she's got some magic."

"Healers don't use magic. If she knows healing—"

"I don't know!" Nivvy ran in a circle, frustrated. "But I can't go to town on accounta how I attacked that hunter and that's where he went, sure as the tide, to tell all those townspeople about the cursed hawk and weasel, an' likely bring 'em out in force. Bella's the only one around here I even trust just a little bit and I can't think of any other way to help you 'less you think you can just sit here an' heal y'self."

"Sorry," Zein said meekly. "I know you're doing all you can to help. It just—it hurts a lot. And I feel really sleepy."

"Don't sleep! I'll be right back with some food." Zein's apology made Nivvy feel worse because he was the cause of their injury in the first place.

He made his way through the branches and had just escaped the bush when Zein spoke up again. "You'll come back, won't you?"

"I'll come back."

"I hope you find her."

"I will."

He set off, angry at Zein for thinking he might not come back, mostly because that thought had been itching at him. By the time he found Bella it would be a day or two later and either Zein would have healed or died. And what could Bella do anyway? Zein was right, she wasn't a healer, and Nivvy was as sure as a magic lock that Bella wouldn't walk hours away into a forest to tend to an injured hawk she'd almost killed already.

But what else could he do? Strut into a town full of people he didn't know—except for the one he'd attacked—and ask them to do the same? At least with Bella there was a chance he could find an angle: a hawk would be a useful ally, or he could find something to trade. At any rate, the alternative to doing something hopeless was to do nothing, and Inira rewarded those who tried, that was what he'd learned, first in life and then in lectures. And then again in life several more times, if he was being honest.

First things first, though: get some food. Though the rain had mostly stopped, water still dripped from the leaves in the forest, a pattering background noise loud enough to drown out any scrapings of possible prey. So he lifted his nose and searched for the now-familiar grass-rat scent. A weak scent led him past a dozen trees before he lost the trail; he cast about for another and found one, ran after it, and lost it again. He ran deeper into the forest and found a grass-rat, only to have it dive into its den, where the memory of the rats in the Bouli temple kept him outside (but he marked the den in case there was no other option). Then, as he was chasing another grass-rat, a shift in the wind brought a thick concentration of them. He ran in that direction, thanking Inira for the gift as he did.

After what felt like hours of running and chasing the scent over roots and debris and moist soil, he caught the sounds of many grass-rats running around. Even through the background patter of water dripping, the scratchings along with the scent (thicker in the wet air) were unmistakable.

He crept through the cover as quietly as he could, making his way around trees and bushes, following his nose and the sound, and then stopped. There was another scent, well hidden by the smells of the forest, but the undertone was there: a human scent. Not the thick smell of the hunter, but definitely some kind of human.

He doubled his caution, slowing to a crawl until he stopped just at the edge of a small clearing. There were half a dozen grass-rats lazily browsing the short grass and picking through brush. On the other side of the clearing sat a large rock, and bushes flanked the rock on either side. The entire clearing lay within the range of his sight, and he was sensitive to motion even beyond that distance. Grass-rats dotted the ground, and squirrels danced about in the branches of the walnut trees. Birds flitted about and chirped at each other, and moles dug in the dirt, but nothing larger than a grass-rat moved nearby.

Nivvy tested the air. The human was around, but not visible, and a human in the woods probably wasn't hunting grass-rat, so he shouldn't care if Nivvy ran in and swiped one. Maybe they were bait for something larger the man was lying in wait for, but in that case, too bad. Nivvy needed them more.

Not that this whole situation didn't put him on edge, because it definitely did. Grass-rats and moles didn't usually amble around in big groups like this, incautious and exposed, especially with human scent around. But he wasn't going to have a better chance to get Zein the food they needed.

He crept slowly around the edge of the clearing until he was in range of the closest grass-rat. This one was fatter than the last one he'd killed—in fact, all of these were fat. Maybe they really were bait of some sort.

It was worth a little extra time to scan the clearing for traps. Probably someone using the rats as bait was after a forest cat or another larger animal whose fur would fetch a good price. They wouldn't waste their time on a little weasel. Still, he didn't want to get caught in a trap for something else. He'd end up just as dead even if the trap wasn't meant for him.

Another several minutes of scanning with eyes and nose and whiskers turned up a large wild cat covered in long tawny fur, stretched out on a tree branch, asleep. That was definitely strange. Why wasn't it hunting the prey all around it? As Nivvy watched, a squirrel ran right around the cat, and it didn't so much as twitch its tail.

Something very strange was here. But Inira had placed this before him, and he trusted that she wouldn't throw anything at him that his instincts and reflexes wouldn't be able to handle. Besides, this new body couldn't do a lot of things, but it sure was better at getting out of scrapes. If that cat wanted to wake up and jump at him, he'd just, well, he'd scarper and hide.

No point in waiting any longer. He crouched back, feeling the muscles in his haunches compress and strain, and then he released them and bounded out into the clearing.

This grass-rat seemed slower than the previous one. It ran mere inches ahead of Nivvy, and though it wasn't as fast, it dodged well every time he made up ground. The other grass-rats scattered, and the squirrels shrieked at him from the safety of their branches, but he ignored the noise and focused on his target.

It dove for cover, and that was its mistake; the branches slowed it just enough for Nivvy to get his jaws into its hind leg and tear. It squealed and pulled away, but it couldn't run anymore, and with his next lunge he caught its throat and clamped down, suffocating it even as his teeth ripped through flesh and sinew. Blood gushed into his mouth. He held on as its struggles slowed and finally stopped.

The squirrels kept yelling at him. The wild cat didn't move. He didn't care. He had to get the body, twice as big as his own, back to Zein to keep them fed while he went on his errand.

Something large moved nearby. Nivvy froze, thankful that he was at least partly hidden. The smell came to him a moment later: this was the human, but his scent mingled with the forest smell, somehow. Everyone in Spire smelled like the other people in Spire, at least a bit; the hunter smelled strongly of people too. This human smelled only like himself and the dirt and trees and squirrels around him.

"What's going on out here?" His voice was low and melodious. Nivvy released the body and panted from his exertion. Between the scent and the calm voice, the man felt like less of a threat than Nivvy had feared. "Are you all fighting? Did a snake get into the clearing?"

The squirrels kept chittering, their alarm subsided even though Nivvy hadn't moved. "Oh," the man said. "Something's happened here. Not a snake, though." His steps came closer to the bush where Nivvy was hiding. "It looks like a little meat-eater. A weasel, is it? I haven't seen one of those around here before. Hello, little friend. I have something here you might like more than meat."

"I need the meat," Nivvy snapped back. He was going to add his line about being cursed, but held off until he could see how the man would respond.

There was silence for a moment. "Did you all hear that too?" the man said, his tone unchanged. "I've talked to many of you for years, and you always talk back, but this is the first time you've used words."

"My friend is hurt," Nivvy said. "I need to bring them this meat."

"Those are certainly words." The man crouched down. "How do you come to use words like a man?"

"I used to be one. I was turned into an animal."

"Turned into an animal? My goodness! Such a thing is possible? I thought it only happened in stories."

"I'll tell you a story if you want." Nivvy couldn't see a face through the leaves, but he could see that the brown-skinned man was naked. "But my friend—who also got turned into an animal—they're a hawk and they're hurt, and I need to get them this food. Ay—are you a healer?"

"Oh, I wouldn't say I'm a healer." The man chuckled softly. "The body heals itself. But I know a few plants that can help. Aska teaches us that the whole world is one, and she provides the means for us to tend to our own gardens. Many of us choose to go live among Aska, and some of us choose to extend her blessings to those who live with her as well."

"I've never heard of Aska," Nivvy said. "Is she your teacher or your goddess?"

The man laughed, an easy, contagious laugh that made Nivvy feel more comfortable. "Our goddess. I have traveled rather far toward the rising sun from the places where Aska is well known, and truthfully there are many who do not follow her as devotedly as I do."

"I 'spect you've never heard of Inira then, either, so that makes us even."

"Well said." The man cleared his throat. "Have you a name, Weasel, or had you a name before your transformation?"

"I was called Nivvy an' still am."

"Pleasure to meet you, Nivvy. I'm called Frankh by those who have use of names. Now, as you appear to be a being with a mind, I must ask you to refrain from hunting any further around my home. I know well that life consumes other life and Aska smiles on all of it, but I have made a safe haven here for those who wish it."

"Fair enough," Nivvy said, and refrained from asking how Frankh kept other predators from feeding on the fat grass-rats here. "Since I already killed this fellow, though, mind if I just take 'em back to my friend?"

"Of course not. May I be of assistance?"

"If you can heal an arrow wound then aye," Nivvy said. "That's the kind of assistance we most need."

"An arrow, yes, of course. That happens quite a bit around the edge of the forest." Frankh got to his feet. "The, ah, the one who shot the arrow isn't still looking for it?"

"No. Least, not last time I was there." Nivvy grabbed the grass-rat by its tail and dragged it out of the bush, away from the clearing. Frankh's "yes, of course" had given him energy and hope. "It's this way."

Frankh followed him but refused to help him by carrying the dead grass-rat, which annoyed Nivvy, but he reminded himself that the man was going to take care of Zein, so it was worth the frustration every time the heavy body caught on a root or a stone. The man didn't seem disturbed by the slow pace, and in fact used the pauses to collect leaves from plants that as far as Nivvy could tell looked like all the other plants in the forest. The leaves low enough for him to smell did give off a faintly medicinal odor, though, even over the blood in his nose from the grass-rat. Might be that Frankh knew what he was doing and wasn't just a god-kissed hermit.

"Forgive me," Frankh said, "but though I converse often with the animals and with Aska, it's rarely that anyone responds in words. How come you to Lake Beatrice?"

"Nnnf." Nivvy tried to reply through his grip on the rat's tail. "Looking for...woman I work...for...worked for, I mean...she was...coming here...I think."

"It's a lovely lake, and the forest is quiet and usually undisturbed." Frankh waited while Nivvy wrestled the body around a root only to have it catch on another root he hadn't seen. "But the roads are not very good and there are bandits about. Did you have any trouble on the way here?"

"No," Nivvy said, but he wondered now if Bella would have had any trouble. "Except for the arrow."

"Thanks be to your goddess."

"She...brought me...to you," Nivvy grunted. "So...aye."

"A fair point." Frankh added to his handful of leaves. "All the pieces of the world play in harmony. Whatever god or goddess you follow has a part in it."

He kept talking about the harmony of the world and the teachings of Aska, while Nivvy wrestled the dead grass-rat over the forest floor. Somehow, Frankh's preaching made the journey seem even longer. Nivvy wasn't one to argue with someone else's beliefs unless those beliefs were being used to try to kill him, but in his childhood he'd seen

THE PRICE OF THORNS

his fair share of people who didn't want to push their beliefs on you, oh no, but they'd prate on about them at every opportunity and try to show you how your beliefs really fit into theirs if you'd only take a moment to see it. He'd discovered that the best course of action with those people was to nod politely and smile and then take your leave at the earliest chance.

Frankh felt like one of the more harmless sorts of fellows in that category, like he really loved the idea that the world was Aska's garden and he was one of the plants that could see the gardener (that was an actual thing he said). He certainly wasn't the priests of Apo outside the Great Sky Temple in Copper Port who got paid coin for every orphan they brought into the temple to work as an acolyte; Nivvy suspected that many of them didn't believe the sermons they spouted any more than he did. Frankh—naked, dirty, and alone—honestly seemed to take joy in the teachings of Aska. He felt more akin to Hajimo the old spice merchant, who would tell Nivvy stories many evenings simply because he loved the stories and wanted to share them. Oigal had been a bit like that too, though a little more mercenary; Nivvy supposed that if you sought out a profession where you told stories, you'd be best suited if you enjoyed that part of the job.

Not that the Aska stuff didn't sound like a lovely story. There was a comfort in thinking that someone was watching over all of Nivvy's path and perhaps pruning and tending to the world here and there. But if someone were watching over him, then that meant that being turned into a weasel and thrown in a cage was all part of their plan, and in that case Nivvy didn't think very much of the god or goddess who came up with it. Inira didn't pretend to know everything that was going to happen; she made it clear that if you wanted to laze about and have a goddess take care of your life for you, you'd best seek out some other goddess. But if you wanted to learn the way of thieves, to be stealthy and crafty and skilled, then Inira would reward your work as you made your way through the world. Getting caged by the Bouli priests hadn't been part of Inira's plan for him, but her teachings had given Nivvy the cunning and skill to get out of the cage, and, hopefully, to regain his human form again if he could only find Bella at the lake. Getting Zein shot wasn't part of Inira's plan, but putting Frankh where Nivvy might find him, that could be.

Then again, he would've laughed at anyone who said they were off to live alone in the woods naked and commune with the animals there, but here he stood with proof that someone could be happy doing that. So perhaps Aska tended a little garden in which Frankh and his fellows lived, while Inira and Nivvy ran about outside it and Zein and Apo soared above. Figuratively, anyway.

"Is that the bush up there?" Frankh asked, interrupting the middle of what felt like a poem about the elm trees they were walking through.

Nivvy put down the rat. He couldn't smell much else until he turned and tested the air. "Aye," he said, catching Zein's scent.

"I shall wait here while you make introductions." Frankh sat cross-legged and beamed up at the trees as drops from the leaves sprinkled his face.

Panting, Nivvy dragged the grass-rat into the bush. Zein lay there, unmoving. "Zein." Nivvy dropped the rat and hurried to the hawk's side. "Ey. Zein. I've got help."

The hawk didn't respond. He feared that they had died while he was gone, but a moment later, feathers stirred, and their head turned. An eye opened. "I don't know how hungry I am," they said.

"Not just that." Words spilled out of him in his relief that they were alive. "There's a man, a follower of Aska, I don't know her but she's a goddess of gardens, anyway, he lives out here in the woods by himself and he takes care of animals and he says he can help."

"Ah, that's nice. How do you know you can trust him?"

"I..." Nivvy paused. "I can't say exactly. But I do. He seems the gentle type and really devoted to Aska."

"Who's Aska?"

"Eat the rat." Nivvy pushed it toward them. "He doesn't like killing so you'd best do it in here and then we'll go out and meet him when you've got your strength back."

Zein tore at the rat weakly. "You didn't make as much a mess of it this time," they said. "I told you you'd get the hang of it."

They crunched bones and tore apart the ribcage, and Nivvy was heartened to see that Zein seemed to gain strength from those first bites. As they turned it over to get at the stomach, he said, "There were a whole lot of them there, all fat and grazing on the grass. You could've had ten of them in a minute."

Blood flowed sluggishly from the rat's wounds into the earth. Zein tore away flesh and organs and gulped them down. When Nivvy's stomach growled, they looked at him. "Did you get one for yourself?"

"Course I did."

"Good." They tore again, stronger now. "It's good. The meat is sweet. Who's this Aska person?"

Nivvy lowered his voice, aware of the shadow waiting outside humming to himself. "She's not a person, she's a god, as far as I can tell. She teaches that nature lives in harmony and all of us are part of it or something like that. I'm sure he'll tell you more about her."

"I only follow Apo because I'm a hawk, you know," Zein said as they pulled out more meat from the body and gulped it down. "It's comforting to think when I'm flying that I'm close to someone who's looking out for me."

"I know what you mean." Nivvy thought of the times he'd been alone needing to pick a lock, or even, most recently, the time he'd had to quietly sort through a chest of metal rings, and how he'd felt Inira there with him. And he thought about that time on the roof when he'd thought Zein was with him in this journey, and now he felt ashamed for thinking that they hadn't been with him just because they weren't sure about the outcome.

"Even if he's only looking out for me because I'm a hawk. We're kind of thrown together, although he's a god and I'm just a hawk, but it's nice to know that he'll look out for me anyway."

Nivvy didn't want to comment on a god looking out for someone who'd been shot out of the sky and who was currently trying awkwardly to eat without shifting the arrow in their wing, but Zein addressed that a moment later. "I know I got shot, but only through the wing, and I don't think it hit bone. It's touching bone and sometimes when it scrapes it makes me feel sick. I thought I was going to die but now I feel better, and that must be Apo, right? If I'd been shot on my own without you around then I'd be dead by now."

And if I hadn't paid you to bring me here, you'd never have been shot, Nivvy didn't say. Instead he said, "Maybe Apo was looking out for me, too. I didn't die when you dropped me."

"I dropped you?" Zein's head shot up with a piece of flesh dangling from their beak. They flipped their head back to gulp it down. "Oh, Apo must have been watching out for you. I'm so sorry. I tried to hang on, but I don't remember a lot about falling, and when I woke up, I was on the ground and you were yelling at someone."

"You remember that?"

"A little." They bent to eat another bite. "I was feeling very floaty, like when a draft of warm air catches me and I just have to keep my wings out and the air lifts me around. I heard you yelling, and someone was there and then they ran away, and I faded again and then you were trying to wake me up, and I came with you."

Nivvy exhaled. "I'm glad you survived," he said. "This man, Frankh, he's not a healer but he'll take care of you. Also, he's naked, just so you know."

Zein ripped up one of the rat's haunches. "You're going to go on to the lake, I expect."

"I expect." Nivvy avoided the golden eyes. He couldn't say why it made him feel bad to leave the hawk. They were going to be safe and looked after. "If Bella's there, I need to go on as soon as possible."

"I understand." Zein bent to take a large mouthful of the rat. Bones crunched. There wasn't much left of the carcass now. "I'm ready to go meet Frankh."

## 17

# THE STORY OF LAKE BEATRICE

Frankh greeted Zein gravely and asked permission to pick them up, which they gave. "Best leave this arrow in for now," he said, packing some herbs around the wound. "I can remove it back at my clearing, where I can tend to it better."

Zein didn't remark on Frankh's nakedness, only said, "It's very kind of you to look after us like this."

"We are all children of Aska. I can no more neglect my duty to you than to any other creature in misery." He placed some leaves near their beak. "Eat these. They will help with the pain."

"That's very kind." Zein took the leaves and then settled themself so their wounded wing hung down over Frankh's arm with the arrow still through it. "But we're not creatures, you know. We're former humans."

"We are all Aska's creatures."

"I don't mean to be contrary about it," Zein said, "but 'creature' is not a nice word, and many people use it to make us feel less than what we are."

"There's no reason you should." Frankh strode across the forest floor so that Nivvy had to run to keep up.

"Ay," he gasped out. "Which way is the lake?"

Frankh stopped and turned. "You're not going to the lake now, are you?"

"I thought I might, aye. I've still business there."

"What business might a weasel have at a lake?"

Zein cut in. "He's a former-human like me, and we may have whatever business we like."

"Zein," Nivvy said, "don't argue with the nice follower of Aska."

"Then he shouldn't think less of us—"

"My business is mine," Nivvy said. "Only tell me where the lake lies, and I shall leave you to your forest."

"But surely..." Frankh shifted the hawk, settling them into his arm. "Surely you don't mean to set out now? It would take the better part of a day for *me* to walk to the lake, so it will take you twice that long. The sun is already low. Why not come back with your friend, share a meal, rest, and you can go on at first light. I shall point you the way myself."

Night wasn't so much a challenge for a little weasel, but he did feel bad about leaving Zein to this strange fellow, even though Frankh seemed quite trustworthy. Besides, Nivvy was hungry, and he wouldn't feel right taking one of Frankh's pets for his meal. Anything that saved him from having to hunt would be welcome; he would expend enough energy getting to the lake. And if Bella were there at nightfall tonight, she'd likely be there at dawn tomorrow as well. "Yes," he said, "thank you."

"Splendid." Frankh's smile grew. His strides lengthened, so that Nivvy had to run even faster. "Zein, would you permit me to tell you about Aska?"

"Of course," the hawk said politely.

And so Nivvy heard much the same on the return trip as he had on the outgoing, about the Garden of Aska and the flowers of the garden and how Aska tended to all her flowers and how Frankh, as a follower of Aska, tended to flowers when he could.

Of the gods Nivvy knew, Aska seemed most similar to Liaji, the goddess of healers and mercy. Liaji, at least according to those followers Nivvy had met, didn't hold with taking life, instructing her followers to preserve life wherever possible. But Liaji also worked in concert with other gods, supporting them in their quarrels, making sure they survived; likewise, her followers hired out to armies and guilds—the Thieves' Guild kept a shrine to Liaji and at least one healer—and did not object to the necessary injuries that those fellows inflicted in the pursuit of their own duties. This Aska seemed to want everyone to be nice to each other all the time, which was a charming personal philosophy in the abstract but did not jibe at all with Nivvy's experience of the world. It did explain, though, why her follower was living alone in the woods naked. This was probably the only place where he could live a peaceful existence.

Far be it from Nivvy to question the lengths someone was willing to go to in order to live out their preferred life, especially when that person was going to help out him and his friend. So he kept his mouth shut and listened to the garden speech, and out of courtesy to their host, he tried to believe it at least a little bit. What made it easier to believe was that if it were true, and Aska looked after her "creatures," then Zein was going to pull through, and that, Nivvy desperately wanted to believe.

Squirrels and grass-rats chattered, and birds chirped and flitted alongside them the closer they got to Frankh's clearing. They kept their distance from Nivvy; sometimes the birds alit on Frankh's shoulders, only to spook at the sight of the hawk in his arms. Nivvy caught the scents of numerous animals but only saw a few, hurrying as he was to keep up with the man's long strides.

As they approached the clearing, the smell of grass-rat grew stronger, and there in front of them were a dozen, peacefully eating from the forest floor. At Frankh's approach, they looked up, but when Nivvy jumped into view, they scattered. Fine; he wasn't trying to be stealthy this time. He could've had any one of them if he'd wanted to.

Above him, the squirrels chittered their displeasure, and there was the wild cat, still asleep, with a squirrel not a foot from its closed mouth. That sense of something off prickled Nivvy's fur, now without the urgency of Zein's injury to temper it.

"It's so pretty here," Nivvy said. "I like seeing the animals all around. The little grass-rats. We'll have plenty to eat."

"Oh, you won't be eating other animals," Frankh said. "Aska would not like that."

Aska shouldn't have given us teeth and beaks and claws, Nivvy wanted to say, but it wasn't very polite to contradict a fellow who was going to tend to a serious injury, so he held his tongue. Besides, he wanted to see what Frankh was going to offer in place of meat, because if something didn't get offered soon, Nivvy might find out how much Frankh knew about what went on outside his precious clearing.

As if sensing his thoughts, the man turned and smiled down, and his smile wasn't particularly pretty (his teeth were yellowed and two were brown), but it was earnest. "Don't think I've forgotten you," he said. "Come around the rock here and we will share a dinner, the three of us."

Dinner turned out to be a fragrant cake of seeds and leaves, which Nivvy ate doubtfully, trying to sort through all the different flavors the plants brought to it. It wasn't objectionable, so he ate the whole thing, while Frankh fed Zein the same (they gulped it down gratefully) and then ate a larger cake himself.

"What are these made of?" Zein asked. "They're lovely."

Nivvy thought "lovely" a bit of an overstatement but was curious for the answer as well. Frankh beamed at the hawk. "Aska showed me where to gather seeds and nuts through the winter, and there are certain plants whose taste is most agreeable. I have lived out here for several years and have found a mixture that is palatable to me. I am glad you enjoy it as well."

"I do. I really do. I don't eat many plants, you know, but maybe I should try more of them. Are all of them like this?"

Frankh laughed. "Not in the slightest. There are many plants that would disagree with you."

"Then I won't try any other plants. But I like these. Do you have many of them? How long may we stay here?"

"Why, as long as you like. As long as you accept the guardianship of Aska." He set down the hawk and touched the arrow delicately. "Does this hurt?"

"Less than it did," Zein admitted.

"May I try to break it and remove it? I have some leaves here to serve as a poultice."

"Yes," Zein said. "Go ahead. Wait." They looked around and set their eyes on Nivvy. "Would you stay where I can see you?"

Nivvy nodded. "Course." He sat, but now that his stomach was full, his eyes kept drifting shut. He forced them open, meeting Zein's gaze as Frankh reached over and broke the arrow, then pulled the pieces out of the wing. The hawk flinched, but to their credit, didn't cry out, and soon enough Frankh had stuffed leaves around the wound.

"If you lie against this rock," he instructed, "it will hold the leaves there for the night. You needn't worry about any kind of hunter. Nothing will harm you in this circle here."

That sounded very pleasant indeed. Nearby the grass-rats foraged, making low squeaks to each other. A breeze brought smells of plants from the forest and hints of water from the lake. Nivvy watched Zein's eyes dart around and then slow, and he allowed his own eyes to droop. "So we can sleep?" he heard himself say.

"I insist on it," Frankh said, or maybe Nivvy dreamed that.

He woke to a silvery world, though when he blinked up at the sky, he could not see a moon, only stars. Hunger nibbled at his stomach, but not as strongly as he was used to feeling at this time of the night.

This place was peaceful. The breeze had died down and the forest was silent save for the high peeps of bats and mice. Even Frankh looked more noble in the silvery light, like a statue in a temple rather than a dirty, naked man. Nivvy rolled over and scratched his back against the ground and when he looked up, he was staring into the gold eyes of Zein, turned liquid silver by the night.

"Thank you for finding this place," they said quietly.

Nivvy flicked his eyes over to Frankh, but the man didn't wake. "Thank Apo," he said. "Someone put this man in our path."

"I have thanked Apo. But you know, you could have gone to the lake and left me. I thought you might."

He squirmed upright, but then he had to crane his neck to look up at them, so he lay on his side. "I wouldn't."

"I bet you thought about it. I would have thought about it. And you're angry with me, too."

He hadn't thought about that in hours, maybe more. He felt very happy in this moment. "Not really anymore."

They tilted their head, eyeing him. "Why *were* you angry with me?" Before he could answer, they went on. "I thought about it and it had to be something that happened at Oigal's place, but we got the story and the map and we're nearly here. It's what you wanted. So I can't figure out what it was. Did I do something wrong?"

Nivvy breathed in and let the breath go. The smells of the forest suffused him, and peace stilled his restless energy. "You told Oigal that this trip was a waste of time."

"I don't remember doing that."

"You said we'd both be back soon."

Zein shifted their weight. "I don't think this trip is a waste."

The feelings he hadn't wanted to put into words now tumbled out.

TIM SUSMAN

"It meant a lot when you said you'd take me, cause it meant you believed in me. I didn't really believe in myself, now I'm a former-human, and then Bella scarpered off an' left me in a cage, so she didn't believe in me. I made it back to Spire, but I needed help. And so... when you said we'd be coming back, it felt like you weren't really my friend. Like you was just doing this so I'd get it out of my system. Not cause it meant something."

Zein looked steadily at him. "You thought I wasn't your friend?"

Their tone was soft and casual, but the words threatened Nivvy's warm peace. "I..."

"I don't believe you'll see Bella again," Zein went on matter-of-factly. "But I knew you wanted to try, and so I wanted to help you try. That's what friends do."

The words should be making Nivvy feel miserable and guilty; he knew that. But what he felt instead was relief that they were talking it out, and relief that Zein was his friend. "I know," he said. "I don't think that now. I mean, that you ain't my friend. I know you are. I was scared."

"It's normal to be scared when you're first changed," Zein said. "That's also why I wanted to help you. There were other former-humans to help me ease into a new life, and there was nobody to help you. Except me."

"I didn't wanna need help," Nivvy said. "I've changed my life before. Ran away from home, joined the Thieves Guild, lived as a man..."

Zein's eyes traveled down Nivvy's body, and Nivvy almost flipped himself over to lie on his stomach, but the languid air of the forest slowed his movements. Zein had seen him before anyway; there was no point to hiding. "I was going to ask you about that," Zein said, "but I couldn't quite figure out how. I thought the fairy might have turned you female as well, but she didn't, did she?"

Normally whenever his secret was found out, Nivvy's throat closed up and he ran, but now the words came more easily. "No. I'm a man."

Zein looked at him out of one eye, then the other. "There's a merchant in Spire I know. She's nice to me. Last year I heard some people saying she was 'really a man,' and that didn't make any sense to me, because she was obviously a woman. But I never figured out how to ask her about it. So you're...born like that? But you're a man?"

"That's right." Nivvy had only ever explained this to two other

206

people, and not in many years. In neither case had it gone particularly well, both times ending with the other person saying, "I don't need to hear any more." But Zein wanted to hear more and at least had direct experience with changing into something different. So he chose his words carefully. "I wasn't just dressing as a man. I wanted to be a man. Always. Long ago as I could remember. I had a cousin—a girl—who wanted to marry and have a whole big family, but that was never for me. It was more'n that, though. I wanted to be looked at the way the boys were. I wanted to be one of them, and I wanted to be a thief, and my family all laughed at me and said I'd never be either, that I'd be a good little fisher-wife like all the rest of them. But I knew what was inside me. So when my folks died, I dressed as a boy and went to the Thieves' Guild an' asked them to teach me the trade. I became a boy then. They all knew me as a boy and treated me like a boy. Polu, and afterwards Vicho," it was nice to remember Vicho as his kind mentor, without the other stuff, "took me in like any other boy, and I was happy. I belonged like I never had before."

Zein said, "But it was just clothes."

"It wasn't just clothes. It was everything. I told my story the way I wanted it told, and everyone else listened."

"What happened when someone wanted to see you without clothes?"

"I had to be careful a little bit, but you get so you avoid that. Hajimo—he was an old merchant who was a man like me—he taught me how to make sure my story was told the way I wanted it. I'd go to the brothel with the others, and I'd pay for a girl but then tell her I wasn't feeling up to it, it was just a show. They thought I was one of those fellows who likes other fellows, an' they let me be. I'd teach them little tricks, with cards or coins, and they never gave away my secret. Still, I didn't do that too often."

"It seems like a lot of trouble to go to," Zein said, but then, before Nivvy could say anything, "so it must be very important to you. Thank you for telling me."

"Since you asked," Nivvy said, "ah, when Bella and I met you I made sure not to call you a boy or a girl, since it's not really obvious on you. What, ah, what should I call you?"

"Oh." Zein considered that. "That's kind of you but I don't think about myself in that way, to be honest. I was a girl when I was changed, but that was years ago, and it didn't really matter to me even then. Now, I'm not exactly going to go out and find a nice hawk to marry and settle down with, am I? Regular hawks are interested sometimes, but I don't really know how to behave around them, and even if I did work it all out, what would happen then? I'd be caring for a bunch of chicks who couldn't talk to me and would just grow up to be hawks and fly away, and that sounds depressing."

"They wouldn't be able to talk?"

"I don't know. That's what happened with Gregory. He was a rabbit and he went around after the girl rabbits and as far as he knew all they ever had were more rabbit-rabbits. I don't know any other former-humans who had families. Maybe if we were cursed by different objects it would come out different, but then there would be a lot of talking animals around. That's what Sessia says when we talk about it. She says she thinks about having a family, but it would be more like having pets who were your children, and that makes her feel uneasy. Also she doesn't think Aji would like it, but I don't think Apo would mind. He had all sorts of children."

"Not really lookin' for another weasel," Nivvy said, "but then, I didn't really look to bed humans either."

"You might want to find a way to cover yourself." Zein's attention shifted back to him. "There is someone in Spire who makes clothes for former-humans. I'll take you there when we return. I mean—if we return."

"If," Nivvy said, understanding now the sentiment behind the words.

"Clothes will stop people from trying to kill you. It doesn't work well for hawks, sadly. I can't very well put a shirt on. But he made the purse so that I could carry and work it with my talons."

Nivvy tried to imagine wearing clothes and the idea made him laugh. "I suppose that might be nice," he said.

"Keramin was turned into a ground-cat and he wears a little vest everywhere so that people know he can talk."

"I can't think how I would put on pants," Nivvy said.

"You'd figure it out. The tailor is quite cunning about it."

"Perhaps."

"You know, I feel much better about you now."

He blinked up into Zein's eyes. "As a friend?"

They laughed softly. "No. I know you're my friend. I mean, as a former-human. You didn't let the world make you into something you didn't want to be. That's the danger with former-humans, that you'll end up deciding 'well, I'm just an animal now.' Our little group in Spire doesn't do that, but that's because we all keep telling each other we're more. There's another rabbit, not Gregory, who doesn't come to our meetings because he just wants to be a rabbit. He talks to people sometimes but mostly he eats, he sleeps, he lets children pet him...he said there wasn't any use trying to be something he wasn't anymore. I was worried you might end up like that too, but now I know you won't. Or I'm pretty sure, at least, because nobody can really know anything. So I'm glad about that."

"Me too." Nivvy chuckled. "Though if there were going to be a place to just be a weasel, it might be here."

"It might be," Zein agreed. "It's so peaceful. It seems like we could live happily here."

"How long do former-humans live?"

Zein shook their head. "I'm not sure. Shanti is the oldest of us and she's been around twenty years, to hear her tell it, and that's longer than a fish should live, I'm pretty sure."

"So maybe we live our human lifespans. Lots of time to fill." Nivvy's mind stretched out to the lake, which seemed impossibly far away, and Spire little more than a memory.

Zein was quiet for a moment. "You're still going on to the lake?"

"Tomorrow." Nivvy looked over at Frankh, still asleep. "You'll be safe here."

"I suspect I will. Shall I wait for you to come back?"

Nivvy looked out into the silver-limned darkness of the forest. "Wait until your wing is healed. If I'm not back by then..." He trailed off. "Maybe I'll just wait until you're healed. Then we can go together."

"That sounds lovely." Zein leaned against the rock. "I feel so much better. My wing doesn't hurt anymore."

"Lovely," Nivvy agreed. He thought back over their talk. "How old were you when you were changed?"

"Fifteen." Zein answered without hesitation. "I'd run away from home because I didn't want to live there forever, and I found a stone tower outside our town that I didn't remember ever having seen before. I snuck inside and climbed to the top and found a chamber in which this old man was mixing elixirs. He yelled at me to get out, and a wind blew me out the window. When I was outside the tower, I was a hawk, and the tower was gone. I never saw it again. So I flew to Spire because I'd always wanted to go there and because my family wasn't there. I made some friends and stayed. That's all."

"You seem to have earned it even less than I did." It didn't seem strange to him then that Zein was so willing to talk about their past. "All I did was a job I was hired to do, and the person who hired me didn't even care, didn't even look out for me. If I had any other way to get turned back, I'd take it, believe me." They didn't answer. Nivvy stared off into the forest and breathed in, trying to catch the barest scent of the lake. "Maybe there's no chance she'll change me back, you know, not having any magic and all. But there's something else, something that I thought about on this trip and I can't stop wondering. She's killed before. She said so. An' I wasn't no more use to her after I got changed, so what kept the knife from me? She could've killed me in my sleep, and I'd never have known. No loose ends to trail after her."

He caught his breath, realizing he'd as good as told Zein that Bella wanted to kill them, but Zein didn't respond. The hawk's eyes had slid shut and their breathing stilled. Nivvy shook his head. It felt good that Zein acknowledged him as a man, or at least a male weasel, and he didn't want to ruin this feeling.

His gaze fell on Frankh, still in the moonlight. Maybe there was something to this Aska after all. If she could create this peaceful atmosphere in the middle of the forest, that was power that most gods couldn't show. He closed his eyes again, feeling safe.

Sunlight woke him, and instinct brought him to all fours quickly. Grass-rats skittered away and retreated to a safe distance, and then above him, a low chuckle sounded. "They remember," Frankh said.

The man stood near his rock, scattering little clumps of seeds and leaves around him for the rats. The odor of his urine came fresh and strong to Nivvy, but not nearby. He needed to relieve himself as well, so he said, "Feed them, I'll be right back," and hurried a little way into the forest.

With that urge sated, his stomach reminded him of another necessity. From the safety of the forest, he examined the fat grass-rats ambling about and the seed balls they were eating. One of those was more appetizing than the other, but the seed balls felt less strange than they had the previous day. Nivvy sighed; all in all, it was probably best that he didn't have to kill things with his mouth anymore, although he was a little proud of how good he was at it. You couldn't put that all down to instinct.

His gaze slid over to Zein, still asleep, and the memory of their conversation the night before filtered back to him. He hadn't met anyone since Marzin that he could talk to that way, and Marzin was currently eating flies in a swamp south of Copper Port, or else (more likely) had been reduced to a pile of shit slowly decomposing after being eaten by a bird or a lemur. Regardless, the closeness had been nice, although strange. Nivvy and Zein had both been very open about things they hadn't wanted to talk about, and Nivvy had also almost told Zein that Bella was going to kill them.

He didn't regret those conversations, but he didn't feel the need to reprise them. Something was strange about that. Zein had been possibly under the influence of the leaves—he'd known people to get very talkative around healers. But he himself hadn't taken any medicine...

A grass-rat scampered over toward a seed ball and took a big bite out of it. Nivvy's fur prickled as he watched. He had taken some leaves that Frankh had given him in his meal last night. And now that he was hungry again, the feeling of peace was fading.

He'd never been much on poisons as a thief, but there were some in the Guild who took to 'em. Some killed, but some just made you sleep, an' some made you not care that someone was robbin' you even if you did it in front of their sleepy smiling eyes. That felt a little like how he'd felt last night.

Frankh was creating this little sheltered world not through the magical influence of Aska, but by drugging all the animals. No wonder the grass-rats were so fat, no wonder that cat had been asleep on the branch. It was still impressive, but it lost some of its magic now that Nivvy knew how the trick was done. He had to get away from here and on to the lake.

Could he leave Zein here? They'd be safe, he didn't doubt that. Frankh wouldn't let any harm come to anyone under his care, or Aska's care, however you wanted to look at it. But if they stayed here too long, would they get fat and complacent like the grass-rats and squirrels?

"Nivvy," Frankh called. "Are you hungry?"

He walked slowly back from the edge of the forest. "No," he said. "I'd like to get to the lake. I'm very anxious to be there."

"Do you know the story of the lake?" Frankh's smile stayed wide, but now to Nivvy's eyes it seemed a little bit vacant. More than a bit, maybe. Or was he imagining that now he knew what the leaves were?

"Yes, we heard it. The kingdom angered Aji and she drowned it in revenge. That doesn't matter. I'm meeting someone there."

"Oh, that's not the story. Why don't you eat some breakfast, and I'll tell you and Zein the story while you eat? Then we can go."

Nivvy was tempted to just go, to run off through the forest. The breeze had picked up again and he was fairly sure he could follow it back to the lake. But the lure of another story tugged at him, and as long as he didn't eat any more of the leaves, he'd be fine. Right? "I'm not hungry," he said, and sat back to listen.

Zein, awake as well, also tilted their head up. Nivvy supposed he could call them "she" now, but he'd gotten used to saying "they," and they didn't seem to care one way or another. They seemed at peace, which was nice and made him feel better about maybe leaving them to the care of Frankh. He would worry about getting them away later (though, the thought itched, not that much later because it might get more difficult after they'd eaten a lot of those leaves—one of the thieves in Copper Port got so he couldn't go a day without some of that sleepy-smiling drug, and when the guild made him stop, he threw up and shit himself and screamed for days).

"The story is the whole reason I came to the lake," Frankh said. "But not too close. It's a cursed place, and I wanted to bring it some peace. The town here doesn't care about the curse. They know about the Drowned Kingdom, but they just live next to it. Would you live next to a house where thousands of people lost their lives? I hope that by bringing Aska here, I am shining the light of kindness into their lives and driving away the shadows.

"This place used to be kind. Over in Yamali, where I grew up, the order of Aska is older than the city; it is said that first there was a garden, then there was a town, then there was a city. One of the first stories of our temple there is of a man who came from the Drowned Kingdom. He said that his king was wise and just, that his kingdom was happy. All were well-fed and clothed, and sheltered by the mountains, they never felt storms nor invaders. They were a peaceful town.

"But one day an evil weather spirit drowned everyone in the space of a breath. He saw it happen and fled for his life. When he arrived in Yamali, he sought shelter and sanctuary from Aska, who granted it, and he wrote down his stories so that his kingdom would no longer be forgotten."

"Why did the spirit drown everyone?" Nivvy asked. "Did he record that?"

"Evil has no reason to exist save for evil," Frankh replied peaceably. "It is the duty of Aska to stand against evil."

Again, Nivvy held his tongue, but this story sounded even less plausible than the others he'd heard. As trivial as Bella's complaint was, about the king's son being inappropriately interested in her daughter, at least it was a reason. Evil people didn't do evil things for no reason, as a general rule (Nivvy did not consider himself "evil," but in his experience very few people did, so he allowed as how his perspective on this was as good as anyone's). Kids were spiteful sometimes, and people often did evil things to prove they had power over you, but you drowning a whole city was a massively difficult and cruel act. You wouldn't just wake up and say, "I should do something evil today. I know, let's drown that kingdom." That was something that'd been done with a purpose.

Also, and not to pick at small things, but Nivvy knew merchants who'd boasted that Copper Port was happy and prosperous, which was true of the merchants but not of everyone. He'd wager this survivor, if he'd even existed given this had happened ten centuries ago, had been one of the wealthy people in the city. Orphans and hungry people were invisible to that kind of person, even if they had to work hard to keep from seeing 'em. Lastly, what kind of story was that? It barely got started before it was over. Didn't the happy, prosperous city have any great accomplishments?

But he said, "It's very sad that the town ran afoul of evil that way. Your garden here keeps evil out, does it?"

"I do my best," Frankh said with a serene smile. "You must be very hungry. Are you sure you won't have breakfast?"

"Why don't we get started on our way to the lake," Nivvy countered, "an' I'll find a bite along the way?"

"I find it's much better to be fortified before a journey." Frankh smiled that same serene smile.

Zein blinked at Nivvy. "Just have something to eat," they said.

"You're hungry all the time."

"I'm not hungry right now," he said. "Why do I have to be hungry?" His stomach growled right then, and he hoped he was too far for them to hear it.

"You don't have to be hungry," Frankh said. "But there's food here if you want it." He gestured to the seed cakes he'd left on the ground. "I'm just going to check the clearing and see if anyone else is hungry, and then we'll go after that."

"Fine." Nivvy waited until Frankh had walked around the large rock and then he scampered over to Zein's side.

"Why are you being difficult?" they asked. "Frankh's trying to give you food. Isn't that easier than killing some grass-rat? Also, we shouldn't kill the grass-rats. They're cute. They're not harming us."

"If you could fly," Nivvy asked urgently, "would you take me to the lake right now?"

"I can't fly." Zein glanced toward their wing.

"But if you could. If I could heal your wing with magic right now, would you take me to the lake?"

"I..." They blinked at him. "I suppose I could, in a little while."

"Don't you want to see the lake? See the lovely underwater kingdom? It's so close now. It's one of the things you wanted to see."

"It is." They seemed reluctant to admit it. "But it's not going anywhere and it's so nice here. Why not stay?"

He nodded and took a step back. "You'll be safe here," he said. "But I'll come back for you if I can. I promise."

"I know you will. You're my friend. My best friend."

Frankh wasn't going to take Nivvy to the lake. He was going to wait until Nivvy was hungry enough to eat more of his leaves, and then Nivvy wouldn't want to go to the lake anymore. Zein, who had eaten more than he had, was already changing under the influence of the leaves, becoming complacent. Soon they would be as fat as the grass-rats. Nivvy couldn't get them away now, but maybe in a few days when their wing felt better—or a week? Or two weeks? He didn't know how long wings took to heal. It might be too late for them already.

But it wasn't too late for him. "Tell Frankh I had to go on my own," he said, and then he heard the man approaching, so he ran off into the forest before Zein could answer. It wasn't the good-bye he wanted, but it was the only one he could manage.

## ❧ 18 ❧

## GLÆDELIGDAL

**F**rankh might have called after him or might have not; Nivvy was more concerned with following the scent of the lake through the forest. He thought about killing one of the grass-rats to eat on his way out, but for one thing, that was too close to Frankh, and for another, he didn't want the man to have any reason to be ill-disposed to Zein. So Nivvy ran along the forest floor and didn't stop to eat until Frankh's clearing was far behind.

He followed a bird's scent to a nest full of eggs and cracked their fragile shells with his teeth, sucking out the warm fluid and meat in three of them before he was full enough to run from the bird's cries and mostly ineffectual flapping. The taste lingered around his lips, rich and sweet, as he kept to the shade under bushes and trees, avoiding brightly sunlit spots. Even though he wasn't sure there were any predatory birds interested in diving for a small, gamy weasel, keeping to the shadows was good sense. There were probably, at the very least, wild cats who hadn't been eating drugged seed cake.

This was the farthest he'd been from Copper Port in his life, he'd have known that even without the aid of a map. The grass-rats were familiar, but in addition to them there were smells of many animals he didn't know: More wild cats, as well as some other thing that smelled a little like a coney but different, and birds, so many new birds. They fluttered above him, flashes of blue, orange, pearl on black, brown and cream, some similar to birds he knew, others very different.

The trees, too, were thicker and more varied than he knew. He'd eaten walnuts and knew they came from trees, so although he'd never seen a walnut tree, he recognized them. Pine trees he knew from the mountains west of Copper Port, although these weren't quite the same. But elm trees were familiar and so were the aspen.

The great gnarled roots of the elm trees curved into natural weasel-sized shelters where Nivvy felt safe resting every couple of hours. In the afternoon, he hunted down one of those almost-coneys, which took a lot longer than any of the grass-rats. The almost-coney ran, and this was not one of Frankh's fat, complacent friends. Nivvy almost lost it twice, and he might've gone hungry if he hadn't guessed right when it switched direction, obviously desperate and tired.

The fight itself ended quickly. He knew where to bite, how to shift his grip, and when to wait patiently for his prey to die. It took him a minute or two to drag the body under a bush where he could eat it in relative peace, if you didn't count the birds screeching at him from the trees.

After the meal, his energy returned and he bounded through the forest, feeling more confident in this body than he had at any point since his transformation. He dodged around rocks and under tree roots, ran through bushes and across clearings, the smell of the lake strong in his nose. Mountains loomed ahead with the promise of meeting Bella and proving his worth.

More than once he thought about Zein, back in Frankh's clearing, reassuring himself that they'd be safe from outside harm even if they were being kept a drugged prisoner. He'd come back for them, either with Bella's help or someone else's, or (the flickering hope remained) as a human again.

After his meal of the almost-coney, he'd felt sure he would make it to the lake by sunset, but as the light around him grew dimmer and movements in the shadows sharper, he realized that he would either have to run through the night or sleep. For a while, he chose running, especially since the night was alive with small prey to keep his energy going. But the lake breeze died down around sunset, and without the sun to orient himself, he didn't trust that he was running in the right direction. So he climbed a tree and curled up in the crook of a branch. As he settled down to sleep, he looked along the rough bark of the tree and felt it strange that there was no hawk perched along there. He felt a little less safe as he closed his eyes.

In the early morning, with dawn just a hint of purple in the sky, Nivvy woke refreshed but still without a guiding scent from the lake. So he went for a hunt and caught a small mouse, and by the time he'd disemboweled it and eaten his fill, a wisp of a breeze had returned, and with it the songs of morning birds and a strong scent of the lake.

As light filled the forest, Nivvy ran toward the scent, and found that where he'd been running across level ground the previous day, today he was climbing. At one point he scampered up a tree to look back and saw spread out before him the forest he'd come through, and beyond that, smears of paler green that made up fields and the town.

Two hours after the bright pink and orange of dawn had given way to a hazy blue sky, Nivvy came to a pass through which the wind whistled, strong with the smell of water. To either side rose steep, forested slopes that melted into a haze of grey rock and grey clouds, and above him, some large birds wheeled in lazy circles. He hurried on ahead and climbed up another tree, and there he got his first look at Glædeligdal, or Lake Beatrice, several hundred feet below him.

With Zein's eyes, or even his own human ones, he might have appreciated the ring of mountains around the lake and their wobbling reflections, but the craggy peaks he suspected were there vanished against the cloudy sky. He could appreciate the deep azure of the lake at its center and the clear turquoise near the shore, and the size of the whole thing. It was immense, like an inland sea. If he could run straight across it, it would take him hours, if not the whole day, to do so. For a moment he just stared at it, at the little ruffles in the water made by the wind, at the dancing reflections of the clouds on the surface, at the stillness of it. Even without a drowned kingdom, Lake Beatrice was a sight worth seeing.

He'd grown up not too far from the sea, with the ever-present smell of fish coming out of it and the refuse of Copper Port sliding into it. There, the sea was vast but always in motion, waves breaking on the shore, whitecaps rolling as far out as one could see, swells rising and falling. Boats sailed on it, coming up to dock and sailing out again, men swarming over them, littler boats darting around them. Here there was none of that: there was only the lake. Birds flew about and swam on the water; their songs echoed, high-pitched and querulous as though seeking something. But even those distant songs couldn't mar the unnerving peace that emanated from the great body of water.

He searched the air with his nose: birds and fish, trees and loam, and over it all the watery smell of algae and water-flowers. No trace of humans came to him on the air. He didn't even smell Bella, much as he searched for her scent on the wind.

Maybe this wasn't where she was going after all. Maybe she'd remembered a different place and had gone there.

Down the tree and back into the world of shadow and scurry. Nivvy sniffed about for a path, but if there had ever been one, it was long gone now. No scent of human, fresh or old, reached his nose no matter where he ran, and finally he gave up the hunt and followed the slope of the hill down to the lake.

He reached the shore of the lake as the setting sun threw an almost human-sized shadow behind him across the pebbles. Here he could pick out the smell of fish from the air as well as the waterfowl and lake plants. Still no smell of Bella, no hint of smoke in the air that would come from a campfire, no smell of Rahila. It was possible that the wind was simply blowing the wrong way; the breezes around the lake's edge swirled and brought him different scents every minute or two.

And yet, none of those scents was Bella's. He paced around the small stones that covered the shore and argued with himself as the sun dropped below the mountains and the world darkened. How long would he wait here by the lake? A day, two days?

As long as it would take Zein's wing to heal, he decided. It was going to be difficult enough to get them away from Frankh, but with a functional wing, Nivvy might be able to manage it, and then, if Bella still hadn't shown up, well...he would figure out how to unpick that knot when it came to him.

So that would give him a few days. Maybe he'd just walk all the way around the lake. Might as well.

The moon came out from behind a cloud, not that he needed it to make his way. He headed first to his left, because that was the general direction of the town, and if Bella had stopped at the town first, she'd come from that way.

The lake had darkened when the sun went down, as most things did, and Nivvy hadn't really looked at it since then. Splinters of moon shimmered on it like they did on water; it was pretty, but not something to catch his attention. Until he'd been walking for a while and he took a break to catch one of the mice that ran around the lake shore, and then when he had eaten and happened to look out toward the lake, he stopped and stared.

The breeze had died down and the lake stilled, and in the light of the moon, silvery shapes appeared below the water. Even with his limited eyesight, Nivvy could tell that these were not fish, nor serpents, nor any other kind of water creature; they were too regular and too immobile. He'd often gone to the roof of the Thieves Guild and looked down on Copper Port and up at the taller towers; if he were now flying over Copper Port with Zein, the view might be similar to what he was seeing in the lake.

The shapes shone clearly through the water. A narrow tower stood above everything else, and below it, gleaming white roofs angled away. Beyond that, light and dark squares lay scattered as though someone had thrown a game board down at the lake bed. Those were roofs, houses. His imagination supplied streets and markets around what was probably the royal palace, stretching out farther than his eyes could see.

There was a whole city down there, perhaps as large as Copper Port. The reality struck him, the evidence of his eyes backing up the stories he'd heard. At one time this had been a valley, not a lake. There had been a city with marble towers and wooden houses, farmers and nobles and merchants and even thieves living in it, and Bella had—with the help of another fairy or djinn or what-have-you—drowned them all. The entire city, perhaps the entire kingdom.

He didn't know how long it had been that he'd stood there staring, building up the city around the glimmers of marble he could see, but when a breeze ruffled his fur, it broke the reflections into shards of silver on the water. Spell broken, Nivvy shook his head and resumed his walk around the lake. But thereafter, every time the breeze died down, he looked down into the depths of the lake to see that the city was still there.

His grandparents had told him about a row of houses built too close to the sea, down the shore from where they lived but still in the Shallows. In a violent storm, the sea had grabbed their foundations and destroyed them, crashed over the roofs and flooded the rooms, pulled all the houses down where they remained to this day. People had swum out to recover what they could, but if you dove down in a certain spot, you could still see rotting wood that if you squinted, might be in the shapes of houses.

This was different. The people of the Shallows knew that the sea was dangerous, that they lived at its sufferance. Sometimes it provided, sometimes it destroyed. You had to appreciate the one and live with the other, because the alternative for the residents of the Shallows was to move away from the sea and try to farm, and they didn't know how to do that.

But the people living here in this valley had been farmers, merchants, traders. Maybe they'd mined ore from the mountains around them or traded between the north and the east, where there were some port cities north of Copper Port. There were dangers here, but none that could destroy their city in a single night. None save for the vengeance of a powerful magic spell.

An uneasy thought came to him: if he were made human again and taken to stand at Queen Bella's side, would he have to watch another city drown, if it displeased her?

His fantasies of being her moral compass felt very distant. He shoved those thoughts away. Get your human form back first, then worry about the rest, he told himself.

Halfway through the night he grew tired and found a small space under a large rock where he could curl up and stare out at the lake. The buildings under the water shimmered like ghosts; sometimes he blinked and they'd be gone, only to reappear when the water settled. Shadows flitted among them, and even though he knew they must be fish, in his mind they were ghosts of the people who'd been killed. This drowned kingdom fascinated him, and he itched to explore it somehow. There must be all kinds of valuables there that nobody had found in a thousand years. What sorts of things? Nivvy couldn't imagine. None of the stories he'd heard had really told him anything about the people here. Oigal's had been about the warlike king, and sure, some of the people were warlike as well, but some of them probably joined the war because it paid well, or because they were a third son and weren't bound for anything great unless they made a name for themself. Nivvy'd had a friend who'd joined the Suzerain's army for exactly that reason. He'd been killed in the war with Tarisch. Nivvy, slighter of build and more sensible of mind, had opted for a different way to prove himself to the world, and one that had less of a chance of making him dead.

It had, however, made him a weasel, he was reminded as he curled his tail over his nose and closed his eyes. But that wasn't the end of his story, not yet.

The following day he continued to make his way around the lake. In the sunlight, the buildings were no longer visible under the water except at just the right angle, when the reflections of clouds and the bright sparkles of sunlight parted to show the shadows beneath, and then just as quickly closed again, allowing the ghosts to retreat from sight.

Still there was no sign of Bella, although on this day he did find a trail that he guessed led back to the town. It wasn't worth following; Bella wouldn't come to the town and then not go on to the lake, but it was perhaps worth keeping an eye on this spot, so when he stopped for the night, he made sure to have a view of the trail.

His walks were mostly undisturbed, although once a shadow crossed his path and his whiskers warned him of something diving at him from above. He jumped out of instinct and tumbled over the rocks as a small hawk, perhaps a kestrel, sent pebbles flying from the spot where he'd been a fraction of a second before. "Ha!" Nivvy yelled at it as it flew off. "Thought you could catch me off guard, did you? Got to be faster than that to catch me!" Then it occurred to him that perhaps there were faster predators around, and he kept his movements to quick darts after that, remembering the lessons of the rats in the streets of Spire.

Around mid-morning of his third day at the lake, as he was darting around near the base of the tallest mountain, he looked back at the trail and saw movement there: two horses, each with a rider. Excited, he reversed course and ran back along the shore of the lake, watching the figures as he did.

They didn't see him—of course they didn't—as they dismounted and walked down to the shore. One of the figures wore a plain shirt and trousers, but the other wore what Nivvy could tell even at this distance was a red dress with a wide skirt. It was Bella, he was sure of it. And that meant that one of the horses there was Rahila.

He didn't know if he was more excited to see Rahila again or at the slim chance that Bella would take him with her and eventually return him to his human form. How would Rahila react to him as a weasel? Would she recognize his scent? His voice?

It didn't matter; he'd see her again. And he'd prove himself to Bella.

He'd done all he could do, and after this it would be in the hands of Inira.

He wanted to run straight across the shore, but there were still kestrels, so he had to keep to his previous patterns, and in the meantime, he watched Bella and whoever that was with her. After only a few minutes, Bella walked down to the shore, hesitated, and then walked into the lake.

As anxious as he was to get back to her, Nivvy stopped to watch her slow, measured steps. She gave no indication that the cold water bothered her, walking along as though she were walking down a dry trail. Her legs disappeared under the water, then her chest, and then her head. A few ripples spread out from the place she'd been, and then the lake quieted again.

So she had a breathing spell, obviously. That must be what the other person was there to do. Nivvy knew families who made their living scavenging from the sea bed, sharing a breathing spell between them, but about once a year, one of them would get injured or killed while scavenging, and then the breathing spell was lost until someone else went and retrieved it from the dead body; they weren't cheap even in Copper Port. He himself had used such a spell once, when he was about seven, and that was the only time he'd really enjoyed being underwater. Without the fear of drowning, he'd been free to explore a weird new world, fish swimming around him and nibbling at his bare legs. He'd hoped to discover some treasure, but everywhere someone would let a seven-year-old go had already been picked as clean as the skeletons he found.

If Bella had a breathing spell, she could get whatever she needed from the lake. It was a pity he hadn't gotten here in time to help with her underwater exploration; he had at least a little experience in that, and you could get disoriented easily under the water. But maybe he could still ride north with her once she'd gotten whatever it was.

Easily an hour passed before Bella re-emerged from the water. Nivvy, still a way from the trail, could nonetheless read her body language as she stalked out of the lake, squeezed water from her hair and dress, and stomped over to the person she'd arrived with and the two horses. They had an animated conversation, loud enough that their voices carried across the water, though Nivvy couldn't make out the words. Bella pointed at the water and other person, in the shirt and trousers, folded their arms. Her tone was commanding and imperious, but as with the boys back in Plow, this town person was unmoved by her commands.

Nivvy sprinted back across the beach, keeping his eye on the pair. If they got on their horses and headed back to town, it would take him another several days to get there, and by then she'd be gone.

Fortunately for him, the townsperson was as stubborn as Bella. They argued for as long as it took him to get within shouting distance, which he promptly took advantage of. "Hey!" he yelled. "Bella!"

She and the townsperson stopped their argument and looked around. Nivvy jumped off the stones of the beach. "Ey! Down here!"

Bella cast her eyes down, and they widened when she saw him. "Nivvy?" she said faintly.

"What sorcery is this?" demanded the townsperson in a higher voice than he (Nivvy presumed from the loose shirt and trousers) had been using before.

"I'm a former-human," Nivvy announced, standing on his hind legs. "You never seen one?"

The townsperson backed away. Bella, her expression somewhere between annoyed and amused, stepped toward him and bent to one knee. Wet hair fell around her shoulders, but her eyes shone. Even with water dripping down her pale skin, she looked regal. "How did you come to be here?"

He had been running toward her with the thought that she would be his savior, but now he found himself angry with her all over again. "No great shakes," he said. "First I had to escape from the temple you left me a prisoner in. Then I had to make me own way back to Spire an' find a way to contact Zein. Remember? The hawk you were gonna kill? Then I had to steal money to pay Zein to take me here, since you stole my horse an' all our money. Nothin' a thief of my uncommon ability couldn't do." The difficulty of the past weeks came back to him until he was shaking.

Bella stood, her icy expression much easier to read now. "I meant, how do you come to be in this place? How did you know to seek me here? Did—" She stopped herself from saying whatever she was going to ask.

"Oh," Nivvy said, "are we tellin' secrets now? In front of this fellow? Cos I got some more questions for you, come to that."

"Do not presume to question me."

He couldn't tell how much of that was an act for the townsperson, who had stopped backing away and now stood at what he probably thought was a safe distance where he could easily reach his horse. Rahila stood next to the other horse, her ears perked up. Nivvy forced his attention away from her. "Then you shoulda just killed me back at the mountain," he said to Bella. "There's a question: why didn't you?"

Her face thawed and he saw that she hadn't been expecting this question. "Why didn't I? Why would I? You served me well."

"So did Zein. You think I wasn't a threat anymore, that it?"

"I underestimated you," she admitted. "But still."

The lake water lapped at his back. She'd done this, she'd created this lake and drowned a kingdom. He'd heard it from her own lips. "Still you wouldn't have killed me? Then why not take me?"

"I didn't foresee any use for you. I thought you'd be safer there than anywhere."

"You coulda told me you'd come back for me when you got your kingdom. That woulda helped."

Bella stared past him to the lake. "As it happens, though, you may be of great use here. Can you swim?"

"Course I can swim." He stood proudly. "Not sure about this body but I reckon it'll learn quick enough. You want me to go in there?" He jerked his head back toward the lake.

"The thing I came here to get is sealed behind a door that is open but a crack. I could not find a way in, but perhaps someone smaller than me..."

Nivvy sat back on his hind legs. He felt again the breeze from the lake tickling his whiskers. He could go back to Frankh's clearing, live with Zein in safe ignorant happiness. He could make his way back to Spire or even Copper Port and apply to be a thief; that at least felt more like his story. But none of those paths led him back to being human again. "If I do this, you keep me with you and find a way to turn me back human, ay?"

She pursed her lips and drew in a breath. "Yes."

"No contracts," Nivvy said. "How would I sign one anyway? Your word."

"My word," she agreed.

"All right," he said. "Tell me what you need me to do."

## 19

# THE DROWNED KINGDOM

The breathing charm, a copper fish the size of one of Nivvy's legs, hung from a leather strap meant to circle a human neck, so to make it work on Nivvy, Bella tried looping it around his neck three times (the townsman refused to come near Nivvy and retreated to his horse in sullen silence). He didn't like that so made her take it off and loop it behind his shoulders instead. It was awkward getting his legs through the leather strap the last time, but he felt much more confident that it wouldn't fall off and leave him without a way to breathe at the bottom of the lake.

Diving into the water had been a scary thing even after he'd recited, "The magical breath of Dobromir, who won it from the North Wind in a contest of skill," and felt his lungs chill. He dove below the surface and at first held his breath in the shock of cold water, then realized quickly that his head was surrounded by a small bubble of chilled air. Sounds vanished, muffled as they usually were underwater, but his whiskers worked just as they did in the air, sensitive to currents and movements.

After the first few seconds, his swimming exertions warmed him so that he did not mind the cold water anymore, and he could devote his attention to the world around him. He'd thought that the drowned city would be close, but he swam and swam, and the marble tower with the roofs below it remained stubbornly distant.

Fish approached him unafraid. Their bulbous eyes shone out of the water as they came up, scales gleaming in reflected light. Some grey and black ones faded into the water, others appeared as greenish streaks of sunlight in the cold blue, and a few looked like brightly colored jewels sparkling when the light hit them. They came in a variety of shapes and speeds: long and sleek, wide and slow, or tiny and quick, darting flashes of blue and silver around him. The daring ones nibbled at the fur of his hindquarters, which made him spin around in the water, but quick as he was, he was not fast enough to catch them.

He'd grown up eating fish, but always cooked; how would these taste raw? He'd grown accustomed to the taste of raw grass-rat, so surely these couldn't be much worse. If one came close enough, he resolved, he would try to catch one.

So he did, but the fish darted away from his grasping claws and then, rather than scurrying away to cover, hovered mockingly just out of his reach. Even the bigger, slower ones swam out of his way as easily as he, as a child, had dodged the guards in Copper Port.

But it was nice to be among the fish nevertheless. He'd never understood how some of his friends chose to spend all day diving without a breathing spell, looking for treasure below the surface, when you could find equally useful salvage in the back alleys of the Upper City. You had to evade guards, sure, but at least there wasn't any danger you'd get your foot stuck under a rock and drown.

With the pressure of the water against his mouth and nose gone, and a sleeker form that moved more easily through the water, Nivvy enjoyed the experience even more than when he'd used a breathing spell as a child. He experimented with a sinuous side to side motion that varied the flow of water through his fur, though he still couldn't match the speed some of the fish could summon with a flick of their fins.

A large shadow arrowed toward him. He tried clumsily to get out of its path, but without much success. Here was the other thing about water: it held all manner of things people didn't know about. If you kept to the shallows, you were pretty sure not to meet a giant squid, but there were still arrow-fish that would take a bite out of you as soon as look at you, and Nivvy now was not much more than bite-sized to the thing coming toward him. He took back all his kind thoughts about being underwater: it was terrible, and only desperate people would voluntarily go there.

The thing coming at him wasn't a fish, he saw a moment later. It was an otter—no, it was three otters, swimming in formation. Would otters eat him? He swam as fast as he could, but it soon became clear that his only choice would be to wait and find out.

They came at him with frightening speed, pushing water ahead of them that rushed past his whiskers and swamped his awareness of any other currents, and all he could do was keep swimming gamely forward as though he didn't notice them at all. His heart raced from more than just the exertion, but he kept his eyes fixed on the ghostly shapes of the city in front of him.

In a rush the three otters split apart and swam in a circle around him. They were taking his measure somehow, or maybe they were using the force of their swimming to disorient him; water swirled around him, and his view spun between the city, the depths, and the shining surface. His head spun similarly, and then in a rush they were gone.

"Shitbirds!" he yelled after the bubbles they left in their wake, and then struggled to find the city again. They'd carried him a little way back to the surface, which made him grumble as he regained lost ground and then swum doggedly down.

After some time, the light around him dimmed and the fish he'd previously seen disappeared. Down here, small, pale fish appeared out of the murk like spirits and then vanished again. Following them sometimes were long eels, mottled and dark on the back and lighter on the belly. Nivvy tried to give them a wide berth, but rarely saw them in time. Fortunately, they did not have more than a passing interest in him. The one time an eel approached him, he bared his teeth and thrashed at it, and thanks be to Inira, it drew back and went on its way. He hoped he wouldn't have to get close enough to bite one.

He swam deeper until the skeletal white of the tallest tower shone out before him. Here was where Bella had instructed him to start his quest: down through the tower, into the castle, and down into the keep was where he would find the thing he wanted. Or, more accurately, the thing she wanted, but he wanted it as well because that way lay his path to regaining his humanity.

He avoided one more eel and then swam up close to the tower. The marble seemed to glow softly, still impressively intact for its age—over a thousand years, if Bella was right—and it had become the home for tiny anemones and plants, wide green fronds waving lazily between little beds of bulbs and tentacles about the size of one of Nivvy's weasel teeth. The ones in Copper Port's shallows, much larger, could sting, though their little pricks would only persist for a few days of itching before they faded.

Regardless, he avoided the plants and bulbs that framed the tower window as he darted inside. Here he found a small chamber with fragments of wood that might, with a little imagination, have been parts of a chair, and a mass of debris that no amount of Nivvy's imagination could reconstruct. Nonetheless, he guessed this had been a sewing room. It would catch the morning or afternoon light, and one of the ladies of the castle would come up here to sew.

They must have climbed up through a hole in the floor that had perhaps once been covered by a trap door. Mussels now clustered around the edges amid wet moss and a few anemones. Nivvy swam down and into a dark spiral stair, filled with more mussels. There'd be enough good hunting here to keep a family of divers fed for a year or more, all untouched. If people from the town came diving into the lake for food, they avoided the buildings.

At the bottom of the stair, he found one possible reason why. At first, he thought the white branches were part of another sea creature, until he drew closer and made them out to be the bones of a human arm and hand. Nivvy swam past it out into the hall, and there he found the rest of the skeleton, in pieces. The fish, at least, had no reservations about coming into this place.

Whatever doors had separated the rooms in this castle had long since rotted away, as had much of the furniture (some worm-eaten wooden scraps remained here and there, in one place enough to approximate the outline of a large table) and the tapestries and banners (the metal rings they'd hung from had survived). Skeletons remained, and after that first one Nivvy grew accustomed to them so that they didn't shock him quite so much, except for one time when he came around a corner right at the height of a grinning skull, and really, wouldn't anyone squeal and turn as fast as they could if a great bony skull leered out of the darkness at them?

Fortunately, there was nobody but a curious eel to witness Nivvy's reaction, and he re-entered the room—closer to the floor—and proceeded on his way.

The number of skeletons and rooms in the castle spoke to a

bustling, lively place that had been taken by surprise by the catastrophe. Many of the skeletons huddled together, while others were curled up near the walls (perhaps they had been hiding under furniture). In some small rooms he found a heartbreaking jumble of skeletons, and turned away before he spent too much time imagining the people huddled together there as the water poured in.

Some of the skeletons lay next to what looked like jewelry, but with no direct light it was hard to tell, and Nivvy didn't want to swim close enough to the pieces to be sure. Down to the great banquet hall, he'd been told to go, so he swam down staircases to the largest room he'd entered so far. Some fish swam past him, and once he hid from a large eel, but nothing else disturbed his progress.

Here he found more scraps of wood but no skeletons. In fact, only a few skeletons remained on this lower level of the castle. People had had enough time to flee upwards, then; the valley had not filled in the blink of an eye, as in the stories he'd heard. Amid a few pieces of wood in an adjacent room Nivvy found a pile of heavily tarnished silver, next to ceramic plates and some glass, most of it broken but a few pieces intact. Each of the plates and glasses, and many of the fragments, looked to be painted in bright, happy patterns that persisted, ghostlike, through the murk of the water. One of the patterns he saw many times was three blue shapes set in a triangle, though he couldn't tell quite what the shapes were. Fruit or flowers, he guessed; that's what people usually put on their plates when they could afford to.

Hundreds of years ago, perhaps there would have been something here worth saving, but nobody was going to pay for a few plates. The blackened, crusted silver would take as much to clean as it would sell for, and what little jewelry was left might fetch a few coins, but all in all, with the cost of the breathing spell, you might only come out a little ahead for the effort you put into it.

And anyway, he wasn't here to make a few coins; he was here to get his human shape back. Through the banquet hall, two more rooms, left into the throne room. Down here, algae and mussels had covered the marble so that it did not glow, but fortunately Nivvy's eyes adjusted quickly to the murk. He repeated the instructions as he followed them and found the throne room, a large spacious chamber that let in a modicum of light through large broken windows. Pieces of colored glass on the floor left scant clue what the windows had shown, but they had clearly been elaborate stained glass. Little was left of the throne itself save for a mass of mussels on the stone dais that looked as though its four peaks might have been the legs of a great chair. The floor, though, still held a pattern crafted from small pieces of stone or glass, mostly blue and violet, still quite beautiful. Again Nivvy made out three blue shapes in a triangle, only now he could see the shapes clearly. The design reminded him of the ancient design he'd seen in Scarlet's cave; at least, they shared a similar style. At the top of the triangle was an open hand, and the two symbols that made up the base were a crudely-drawn wolf's head and a four-pointed star. Not flowers nor fruit at all.

He swam for a moment admiring the work and imagining the rest of the palace coming to life with the same meticulous beauty. It would've rivaled the Emperor's palace in Tarisch, and that was the shiniest and prettiest place Nivvy had ever been. But now, he reminded himself, it was nothing more than an obstacle for him to traverse, and he went on with that task.

Behind the throne there was a doorway, and through the doorway was a small set of apartments, as empty as any of the other rooms but darker. Nivvy swam through them, navigating by his whiskers and the faint shadows that his night vision could pick out of the murk around him. Movement spooked him even though he knew it was likely only the algae waving with the ripples of his passage. And then, two rooms in, a shape lunged out of the darkness at him, mouth open, gleaming white teeth showing.

Only the warning his whiskers had given him saved him, as he'd sensed the movement and hesitated, then dove so the great eel's momentum took it just by his ears. He swam frantically downward, knowing there was no way to outmaneuver the eel in the water, hoping only to find a place to hide from it.

His paws met stone floor, soft algae, and mussel shells. The water around him rippled unsettlingly and then he felt the same warning pressure on his whiskers and fur that he'd felt a moment before, only this time it was behind him. He used the mussels to pull himself along, but the eel was coming on faster, too fast, it was bigger than any of the other eels he'd seen and those teeth—

The next thing his fingers found weren't a mussel shell but a piece of wood half as big as his body. In one quick motion, or as quickly as the water allowed, Nivvy turned himself around and swung the piece of wood.

The eel, emerging quickly out of the darkness, grabbed his makeshift weapon away and bit down, carrying it off. Heart pounding, Nivvy kept pulling himself forward, trying to find a small place where he could hide, or—

Another piece of wood under his paws, around the same size. He used it to push himself along the ground, hoping that would help him go faster, but it didn't, not especially. And it wasn't even that strong; the third time he planted it in the floor and pushed, the wood twisted and splintered in his grasp.

He made it through a doorway, keeping to the wall, but the water rippled around him with the warning that the eel was coming back. Paddling as fast as he could, Nivvy probed at the algae and stone with the piece of wood left in his paw, but nothing opened up to him. All the hiding places had been eaten away by time and water, and there was nothing left but algae and mussels as big as his head.

And then his wood stick pushed something that moved: a broken mussel shell. Nivvy dropped the wood to seize the shell, thicker and solid and with a jagged point at one end. It didn't fit easily into his paw, but he found a place he could grip it. It served as a makeshift paddle, but more importantly, that point at the end drew his eye. Not much of a weapon, but he'd made do with worse.

Holding the shell steeled his nerves against the rippling of the water. Just let that eel come back, he'd show it who was prey and who could bite. In the meantime, he'd keep going...ah, forward? In his haste to get away from the eel, he'd lost his bearings. How had he left the previous room? Had he swum forward or had the doorway been to his left? He was supposed to swim forward, easy run all the way to the back of the suite of rooms, but now he couldn't say whether the eel had turned him around.

There was nothing for it but to keep going and hope he hadn't been diverted. So he swam on, and the rippling of the water died down the farther he got from that door. Maybe the eel had its own hunting grounds and he'd left it behind now. That made him feel better as long as he didn't think about whose hunting grounds he might be moving into now; what was fierce enough to scare the eel?

Whatever it was, he was fortunate enough not to encounter it, but not fortunate enough to have followed the correct route. He reached the last room along this path and looked for the open trapdoor Bella had told him about, but the floor remained smooth and unbroken—or at least unbroken; the algae were smooth, but the mussels and crumbled rocks definitely were not—all around the room.

He would have to go back and face the eel. Clutching the shell in his paw, he paddled back through the rooms to the place where he'd been diverted. How long did the breathing spell last? Thinking about being trapped down here with no air and no way to get back to the surface in time made his swimming more like thrashing as his heart pounded and panic jolted his muscles.

Quiet, calm, he told himself. If that happens, it happens, and there'll be no helping it. First fight the eel, then get to the trapdoor, get the crown, get out. Easy. Maybe the eel will still be chewing on that piece of wood.

Making his way back cautiously along the wall and near the floor, he tried to move slowly enough that the eel might not notice him, if indeed it was still there. The doorway loomed before him, a large space of open moving water, and the change confused his senses so that he couldn't tell if anything were moving toward him. He froze, letting ripples wash over him, and when he couldn't detect anything the size of an eel, he proceeded slowly forward.

If his mental map was correct, this must be the big room where he'd been attacked, so if he kept to the wall, he'd find the next doorway and hopefully that was the correct one. It wasn't too much different from making his way through a building at night—if you ignored the "moving in slow motion" and the "giant eel wanting to eat him" parts. And the slimy algae getting all over his paws. Fine; it was very different, but it was alike in the way that mattered, which was that he had to go by the map in his head and remember where he'd been.

He came to the corner, then a little while later to the next doorway. Here, emboldened by the quiet, he left the wall and pushed straight ahead, aiming for the doorway he hoped was on the other side of this room.

That's when the eel came at him.

As before, he had a moment's warning, but either it moved faster now or it had learned his movements, because even though he moved to evade it, its mouth seized his arm. Teeth sank into his flesh, although he had the reflexes to twist his arm so that its jaw couldn't completely close, his fingers pushing up against the roof of its slimy mouth. His other paw, the one holding the mussel shell, flailed against its head, a huge carp-like face with flat staring eyes and slit nostrils.

The eel thrashed, trying to get a better grip, while Nivvy kept swiping at its eye with the pointed shell. His paw slipped and the eel's mouth closed over it, but before it could bite down harder, Nivvy scratched at its soft palate and the pressure eased. He tried to bring up his hind legs and kick against it, but his claws slid across its slippery skin just as the shell was doing. *Inira, help me*, he cried out in his mind.

It clamped down again. Pain shot through his front leg and, desperate, he slashed across its face with the shell. One, two, three strokes and then, miraculously, the eel thrashed harder and let go of Nivvy, sending him floating off into the water. Looking back, he saw one of the flat eyes ruined, blood seeping out of it to join the stronger trail coming out of its mouth, but he didn't feel much satisfaction in that moment. His front leg throbbed painfully and was also leaking blood, and it didn't do one much good to stand and gloat over an enemy when you didn't know how many more were out there. Also, an eel with one good eye could still probably catch a weasel with only three good legs, especially if it wanted revenge for the lost eye, so he paddled as fast as he could. *Thanks be to Inira*, he prayed. *Knew you'd come through, good lady. Never a doubt.*

The eel's thrashing about muddled any sense he had of what the water around him was doing, until he passed through a doorway, where the water stilled somewhat. He stayed close to the floor, scanning for any dark patch or current that would indicate a trapdoor.

In the next chamber he found it, toward the back corner of the room. The stone door had been lifted and set to the side, and darkness yawned below him, giving him pause. You're already at the bottom of a bloody lake, he scolded himself, in a sunken castle inhabited by monsters, or at least very scary fish. What's going to be scarier down one more level?

That was exactly the question he didn't want the answer to. But whatever Bella wanted was down there, and what Nivvy wanted depended on getting Bella what she wanted, so down he would have to go.

His descent did not start auspiciously; forgetting his injury, he reached for the lip of the doorway with his bleeding foreleg, and pain shot through it. Cursing himself, he switched to the other and pulled himself down into the blackness below.

The room he swam into felt smaller to him, though he couldn't say what exactly made his whiskers tell him that (other than having swum through several different-sized rooms on the way to this point). Bella had told him there would be a door here, but she couldn't quite describe in which direction it lay, so he explored the walls, keeping a nervous eye to the slightly less dark square above him.

Soon enough he found the door, a large stone slab that had settled in the doorframe; there might have been wooden braces that had rotted away. He found an inch of clearance at the top and, with some distress to his injured foreleg, squeezed his way through.

This was the way the story went, the brave hero overcoming injury to bring the treasure back for the— "Zbells!" Nivvy shouted. "What are you?"

His words echoed around the small bubble of air surrounding his head, but the glowing figure in front of him turned as though it had heard him speak. That was bad, very bad. Eels he could wield a sharp shell against, but he had no protection against ghosts. He couldn't even remember the name of the god he was supposed to invoke to protect against them. "Inira," he said as he closed his eyes, "help me remember who to ask to get rid of ghosts. Or you could just get rid of it yourself, that'd be fine as well. I'm not picky."

When he opened his eyes, the ghost floated a foot in front of him. It was the spectre of a pale young man whose hair appeared dark against the simple golden circlet he wore. That wasn't the crown Nivvy was looking for, at least as Bella had described it to him, but then again Bella had not said one word about a cursed ghost. What was he supposed to do now?

The patterns on the prince's spectral doublet matched the patterns on the plates and the throne room floor: three blue triangles, wolf's head, open hand. "*Hwaz deser,*" the ghost said, or maybe it was a question. Nivvy didn't speak whatever language it was speaking, and who knew if it asked questions the same way he did.

"Look," he told it, and it recoiled in surprise from him. "I'm here for the crown, and I don't want trouble with no ghosts. If you need me to bring your bones to the surface, maybe I can come back for 'em later.

Just point me to where they are and I'll...I'll think about it." Even though he knew it couldn't understand him, he didn't feel like lying outright to it. If Bella's story was true, and he had no reason to doubt it, this ghost had been drowned a thousand years ago, poor blighter, and had spent all that time here with only eels to talk to.

It blathered at him some more in whatever language it was. Nivvy wished desperately for his language magic, even though that was only reading. At least if the ghost's story were written down somewhere, he might be able to read it then. The ghost did give off enough light to be able to see the rest of the room, if Nivvy looked behind it.

There was not much to see except for four well-preserved skeletons separated into pairs, each pair in a close embrace. They lay on couches, and though the cloth had rotted, a good portion of the wood remained intact here. Three small tables and several clay pots lay around the room as well. "So," Nivvy said to the ghost, gaining more confidence with every second it did not touch him and eat his soul, "which one of these unfortunates is you?"

The ghost said something at him. Nivvy pointed at the ghost and then at the nearest pair of skeletons.

It understood that. With a sorrowful expression, it floated down and touched one of the skulls on the couch. The gold circlet represented on the ghost's head did not encircle the skull, nor was it anywhere Nivvy could see it. Then its eyes went to the other one and its hand followed, as the other hand came to rest in the center of its chest.

"That one was your heart," Nivvy said. "Ah, poor fellow. Died here with your love and had to remain alone while she went on. Maybe you're guarding the crown?"

For he'd spotted the object of his quest now, clutched in the bony fingers of one of the skeletons on the other couch. The gold of the circlet, spun into whorls and flowers more ornate than the prince's simple circle, gleamed dully, but the crystals spaced an inch apart on the gold glittered in the ghost's ethereal light. A pendant lay around one of the skeleton's necks, and rings adorned both sets of hands (as they did on the nearer one), but the crown was what Nivvy was here for.

He swam toward it, and the ghost followed but did not interfere. Once it saw what his goal was, it spoke again in its ancient language.

"Right," Nivvy said, "I know what this is. If there's a curse on it, you'll have to find some other way to tell me."

With his paw a foot from the crown, the ghost interposed itself. Nivvy thought he could reach through it, but it was only polite to let the fellow have his moment. He'd waited years for this, after all. "Say your piece," Nivvy told him.

The ghost looked at the crown, mimed picking it up and placing it on Nivvy's head, and then shook his own head. Then he mimed picking it up, placing it on his own head for a moment, then holding it out to Nivvy. "What," Nivvy said, "I have to put it on you first? How's that meant to happen? Or do I have to pick it up and give it to you?"

Again the ghost mimed setting the crown on Nivvy's head and shook his own head from side to side. Who knew what shaking one's head meant, Nivvy asked himself. There were folk in the Thousand Kingdoms who shook their heads for yes and nodded for no; they occasionally came to Copper Port and the merchants knew to interpret them differently. "Look here," he said, "I'm not going to put it on my own head. How would a weasel wear that great thing? I'm just bringing it out the lake, and—and that's all." His mind, following that thought to its conclusion, shut his mouth before he could tell the ghost of the prince (probably) that he was bringing the crown to the person who'd murdered him and his family and his whole kingdom (probably).

That thought, more than the ghost, made him hesitate. Why was he making himself party to this horrendous act? By bringing Bella the crown, wasn't he making her destruction and murder worthwhile?

What's your alternative? he asked himself. You can turn around and swim up to the surface, tell her you failed, and live your life as a virtuous weasel. She'll have no use for you after this, and you might as well go live with Zein and Frankh in blissful stupor in the forest. That'll be the end of your story. "After many adventures, Nivvy the thief became a weasel and died in the forest."

Or, he told himself, you can take the crown. It's terrible what happened to these people, it is indeed, but it's done and has been done for a thousand years. If you want to rescue Zein, you probably have to be human, or at least it would help. And if you want to be human again, you need Bella. And Bella needs the crown. It's as simple as that.

"I get it," he said to the ghost. "You've been stuck here for a thousand years to give me a message, and then I get here and you can't tell me what you needed to. It's terrible. But I need to take that crown."

The ghost gesticulated again, and Nivvy tried to make sense of it, he really did, but his eyes kept being drawn to the gleaming gems in the crown. "I wish I could understand you, mate," he said with sincere regret, and swam forward toward the crown, through a spectral arm waving in front of him.

His uninjured paw closed over the metal, expecting some magical resistance, but it felt exactly like a piece of gold that had been at the bottom of a lake for a long time: cold, heavy, and a little slimy with algae. For a moment he worried that he wouldn't be able to carry it all the way to the surface, and then the skeletal fingers clasped around the crown came away and it lifted into the water. The ghost keened something Nivvy *still* couldn't understand—seriously, he hadn't magically learned Ancient Ghost in the last minute—and floated after him.

He'd half thought the ghost would dissipate when he touched the crown. Didn't matter; he had a crown to deliver, and the ghost was bound to look out for itself now. Maybe now it didn't have a crown to guard, it could find something else to do with its unlife. Nivvy'd reinvented himself several times in less than three decades, so surely a thousand-year-old ghost had to have some ideas.

There was a moment, wriggling through the gap at the stone door, when he worried the crown wouldn't fit through. He pushed it, turned it, and then, as he braced himself against the door's frame, it shifted, creating enough space for him to pull the crown through. Had Bella not tried to open the door, he wondered? It swung closed slowly after he'd pulled the crown through, returning to the position in which he'd found it.

Up through the trap door he went, back into rooms where his adjusted eyes could at least see where he was going. The first thing he did was stop and look for the eel, and then he got a little shock when he realized that he could see where he was going not only because the water was a shade lighter, but because of the shade behind him. The ghost had followed him up from the basement/crypt and hung behind him, not trying to communicate, just watching him and waiting to follow.

Let it follow him. Maybe it'd give Bella a good shock when she saw it.

Whether it was because he'd scared off the eel or because of the ghost trailing him, Nivvy saw no eels and precious few fish on his way back up, the swimming more painful from the eel bite. Every now and then he turned to see that the faint blue glow of the shade still followed him and to check its expression, but if it turned to mourn skeletons it had once known, it only did that when he wasn't looking at it. Otherwise, its expression stayed guarded, interested, close-mouthed.

Rather than wind his way back through the whole palace, Nivvy escaped through one of the windows near the roof of the banquet hall and headed straight up to the surface. When he turned back to the ghost, this time he caught it staring back at the palace and at the city beyond it.

Nivvy could hardly make out any details, not with these eyes and not underwater, but spots in the stretch beyond the castle shone reddish and white, and it wasn't hard for his imagination to once again turn that into the roofs of a sprawling city, perhaps a center of trade between the north and the west. A river must have run down out of the mountains here, and perhaps at one time had continued all the way to the sea.

And now all that was left was this prince and the crown. Too bad, but that's what happened. There were ships at the bottom of the Copper Port harbor, long since picked clean of valuables, and farther out, some older wrecks from battles Nivvy had heard stories about. More experienced divers went out to them and brought back strange coins, or knives with unfamiliar beautiful designs on the handles. "Who made these?" he'd asked when a friend showed him a knife her father had salvaged. "Someone dead," she'd said matter-of-factly.

If a ghost had followed the knife back, maybe that would've been a different matter, but none had, and once Nivvy gave the crown to Bella, the ghost would be her problem. In fact, maybe this was the fellow who'd been courting her daughter, which would be a little strange given that he'd died in someone else's arms. Oh well, people had mistresses when they could afford them, and most princes could. Or maybe that had been Bella's daughter, killed by accident.

It would have to have been an accident...wouldn't it?

He almost turned to ask the prince whose skeleton that was he'd been holding, and then remembered that he couldn't communicate with the ghost. Anyway, ghosts were unpredictable and unknowable in

THE PRICE OF THORNS

that Nivvy had never actually met one before. Was this ghost no more than a message to repeat over and over again? Or was it the spirit of the prince, with all of his memories and knowledge?

It wouldn't be his problem in just a few short minutes. He stared up to the glimmer at the surface of the lake and swam determinedly toward it.

## ❧ 20 ☙
# THE CROWN OF GLÆDELIGDAL

"**A**h," Nivvy gasped as he broke the surface of the lake, relief flooding through him. "I'd almost forgotten what sunlight feels like." Even the clouds that stood between himself and the sun couldn't weigh down his buoyant spirit. "Suppose I'll feel it again someday. At least there's no more eels, an' enough air to breathe, and I got—"

Behind him, more jabbering in Ghost and then, unmistakably, the sounds of crying. Nivvy turned, paddling to keep himself at the surface, and faced the sobbing spirit. No tears formed, and the ghost's attempts to wipe his spectral eyes made Nivvy smile for a second, but only a second, and then they became pitiable. "Well, you're still here," Nivvy said. "Ah, come on. Think about the good parts. You haven't seen the sun for a thousand years, and there it, well, there it is, sort of. Look at the mountains. Feel the air on you. Can you feel it?"

The ghost jabbered back at him and Nivvy realized that that was all that his words were to it, just incoherent babble. He tried to adopt a more soothing tone. "I know it must be hard. Imagine if I went back to Copper Port and it was all just underwater." Even though he didn't care for many people there save for his uncles and D'Alio, that thought sent a frisson down his spine.

The ghost seemed unmoved. Nivvy tried encouragement. "You're supposed to be guarding—accompanying—this crown, see? What's it going to look like if you show up on the shore with your face all twisted up like that? You've got to be regal and impressive."

Surprisingly, this tone seemed to work. The ghost looked directly at Nivvy, and his face relaxed from despair into a solemn kind of resolve. "Good," Nivvy said. "Now let's go get this crown business over with."

As he turned back toward the shore, maybe two hundred feet away, Bella's voice floated out across the water. "What are you playing at out there?" she shouted. "Did you get it?"

"I got it," he called, and tried to lift the crown out of the water to show her, but once it was in the air, it became much heavier and harder to manage, so he didn't quite get it out of the water.

"Answer me!" she yelled, so obviously she hadn't heard him nor seen the crown, and Nivvy gave it up and paddled determinedly toward the shore. She'd get her answer soon enough.

By the time he'd made it to shore and could make out Bella's features, she was staring beyond him at the ghost. "Ho," Nivvy said, trying to be cheery, "I'm done with being wet for a while, but I got your crown thing."

To Bella's right, the townsperson approached the lake slowly, staring out at the lake. He gestured at Nivvy. "Stay out!" he called. "Do not approach the shore!"

Bella ignored him, her eyes staring past Nivvy. "What is *that* doing here?"

"Oh." Nivvy hesitated at the townsperson's order, then kept paddling, continuing his cheery tone. "That's a ghost. I didn't bring him; he just came along. Seems attached to the crown."

Bella opened her mouth and then closed it again. "Fine," she said, stepping up to the shore. "Fine."

"Please!" the townsman called. "Stay back! Do not bring that to the shore."

Bella turned. "Be quiet," she said. "I've paid you for your breathing charm, not for your worthless thoughts on what I do with it."

Nivvy, mostly out of the water now, struggled with his injured paw dragging the crown over some pebbles and not keeping his eyes on the two people at the shore. Then motion blurred at the edge of his vision, and he snapped his head up to see Bella holding one hand up, palm flat, and a cloud of dust enveloping the townsperson. Before he could say anything, Bella seized the knife from the coughing man's belt in one hand and one of his fingers in the other. "Hey," Nivvy started to say, but scarcely had he gotten that word out before Bella had hacked off the finger—the man screamed—and thrown it into the lake very close to Nivvy. He only had time to see a lapis-stone ring on the bloody finger before it plunked into the water and sank.

"What was that about?" he yelled. The crown had half-emerged from the water, but Nivvy stopped dragging it, his eyes fixed on Bella. "Was that the ring I stole?"

Bella kept a tight grip on the wrist of the man's uninjured hand and pressed the point of the knife to his side. "Scarlet ensorcelled the ring before letting you have it," she said. "She used it to spy on me. Thought I wouldn't notice. But I remember the ways of fairies. I know how they can use magical tokens to possess the unwary. And I knew she wouldn't let me pursue the crown unhindered. When I traded the ring to this person, I only had to wait until the crown was within reach. When she knew I was close to possessing it, she made her move."

"I don't know what you're talking about," the man bleated, trying to twist away from Bella and failing. "You blow dust in my face and then cut off my finger! You're crazy!" He turned his attention to Nivvy. "You best get out of here, weasel or whatever you are, just go back in the lake and don't come out! She's crazy!"

"The dust is from my prison," Bella said coldly. "It dulls magical abilities. You might still have fled back through your ring, but," she gestured to the water with the hand holding the knife, "that now lies in the lake where its magic is inaccessible to you."

"Only magic I have is that breathing spell." The man pointed at Nivvy and the leather strap around his neck. "That one on the weasel. Go, weasel! Before she attacks you too!"

Bella jabbed the knife at his side, drawing blood. Nivvy took a step back, water splashing around his feet, almost up to his chin. He wasn't sure why Bella didn't just come take the crown. "Why'd you cut off his finger?"

"I told you," Bella said. "That's Scarlet possessing his body. I've trapped her in there for a few minutes and I need you to give me the crown before those few minutes are up." When he still hesitated, Bella snapped, "Now! If you want to be human again, give me the crown!"

That brought Nivvy half out of the water until the townsperson stopped him with a shout. "Listen to me," he said. "The fate of the world rests in your—with you. Do not give her the crown."

His tone was different now, authoritative enough to stop Nivvy where he stood. Blood ran down the man's arm, but he ignored it, his eyes blazing as if he were trying to push Nivvy back into the water with them.

"There you are," Bella purred. "I knew you'd reveal yourself when it came to the last moment. Thank you for coming to try to stop this. It saves me the trip back to your horrid volcano. Nivvy. Give me the crown right now."

"If you give her the crown," the man—Scarlet—said, "it will mean the end of the world."

"Ha!" Bella cackled.

"She has not changed as the world has," Scarlet persisted. "She will drag it back a thousand years."

"All I want," Bella said patiently, "is the kingdom that was stolen from me a thousand years ago. And all Nivvy wants is to be human again. We can both have what we want if he gives me the crown. You turned him into a weasel. You want him to keep the crown from me."

Bella was restraining Scarlet and couldn't come take the crown from him. Scarlet was—for the moment—powerless and could not force him back into the water. Nivvy shook his head and finally looked at Scarlet. "Right," he said. "She's not perfect, not by a long shot. But she's always done right by me—mostly. Worst thing she did was leave me at a temple. *You* turned me into a weasel."

"I didn't kill you," Scarlet said. "I very well might have."

"So might she have! You took everythin' away from me but left me to know it was all gone. Had to use every bit of wit an' a fair amount of luck to get here, where she's off'rin' it all back, every scrap of it, an' you got the nerve to tell me no?"

"There are larger considerations," Scarlet said. "The world is in danger."

Anger made Nivvy shake and say things he maybe wouldn't have meant in a more sober, considered moment; this was not that moment. "What's the world ever done for me? Shoved me aside, killed my friends, turned me away. Maybe it could do with a shaking up. Maybe I don't give two pieces of rat shit what happens to it as long as I get to be human again. Hah? What do you say to that?"

"I know that the words coming from me sound insincere, but you must—"

"The crown threatens her," Bella cut in. "She begs you so that she will not be cast down from the lofty perch she has grown so accustomed to."

"Oh," Nivvy said. "Why didn't you say that to begin with?" He dragged the crown out of the lake.

"No!" Scarlet wailed, but he ignored her. With some effort, he pulled the great heavy thing out of the water and dragged it along the lakeshore to the side of Bella opposite where she held Scarlet. The man's face contorted with the fairy/djinn's horror and continued to plead with him to stop. But when Nivvy reached Bella, the man quieted.

Nivvy lay the crown on the pebbles and stepped back. "There, and welcome to it," he said, already imagining how it would feel to be able to look people in the eye again instead of from the ground.

Bella lifted the knife to the man's throat. "Lie down, face to the earth," she said. "Do it now or we will see if you die when your host dies."

The djinn glared at her through the man's eyes, but when she pushed the point of the knife into his neck, lay down on the ground. Bella knelt on his back and stretched out her free hand. "Give it to me."

He almost grumbled that if she just leaned over another half foot, she could pick the thing up herself, but she had promised to make him human again, so he could spare her a few inches of reach. Besides, he realized, it would play better in her story to have him give her the key to getting her kingdom back, even if he didn't understand yet how this crown would do that, or why it would do that for her and not him. She understood that this moment required ceremony, and Nivvy had been so impatient to get his body back that he hadn't seen that. Well, it was part of his story, too, and bound to be an important one if she held to her promise.

He gripped the golden circlet and, with some effort, raised it to her fingers. "Here you go," he said, and then added, "Queen Bella. Delivered as promised: the Crown of Glædeligdal."

Something cold flashed through the crown as she grasped it. Nivvy tried to release it, but his fingers remained curled against the metal as though frozen to it. He only had a moment to panic before whatever had happened stopped and his paws came away from the crown, sending him tumbling back to the ground. Seemed the Crown had a sense of important moments too.

"Ahh," Bella breathed. "Yes." She held the crown reverently, staring at it.

"*Shawka*," Scarlet said, head lifted from the ground, "do not put it on. It can only lead to grief. Look at what happened to the last one to wear it."

"*I* happened to him," Bella said. "And if not for your sister, it could have remained at the bottom of the lake forever. But now..." She lifted it to her head.

"I beg you," Scarlet said quickly, "reconsider—"

She kept speaking, but Bella placed the crown on her head and then said, "Be quiet."

Scarlet trailed off and stopped speaking, but Bella shook her head. "That didn't feel right. Let's try your method." She stared at the lake, at the ghost still hovering over the water. "The Crown of Glædeligdal, forged by the fairy Carmine for King Bjorl and passed down to his son and his son's son, King Lars, who perished with it."

Nivvy couldn't tell whether that had worked—nets might move, but you don't know what's in 'em until you pull 'em up—but it sounded like a proper spell right enough. And Scarlet's head lowered to the ground, eyes closed. Though that might also have been from blood loss, because the puddle on the ground was thick and spreading.

"*Shawka*—"

"Don't call me that," Bella snapped.

"Rose," Scarlet said, "please stop. You have a chance to guide the world on its course here. One person cannot stand against the tides, but she may swim with them. You have been away for a thousand years. Let me teach you."

Bella stood, brushing down her dress. "A week ago, it was 'go before I kill you,' and now it's 'let me teach you.' I know you just as I knew your sisters. Power is the only thing you live for, the only thing you respect." Her fingers reached up and traced along the edge of the crown. "It is fitting, don't you think, that this crown which was the death of poor Cinnabar should now also be your death?"

The man struggled to his knees. "You needn't—"

"Be quiet," Bella said. "I'm tired of you, and that dust won't last forever. You know it's Cinnabar's body, don't you, the prison I was entombed in? Quite potent. I don't know what Carmine did to her, but her bones sapped my magic quite effectively, even ground to powder."

The man's mouth worked, but no sound came out. Then he ran for the water, a mad dash that crunched across pebbles, leaving bloody footprints in his wake.

"Stop," Bella said casually, and the man jerked to a halt as though pulled back by ropes. He teetered at the edge of the lake, and Nivvy couldn't see his face any longer, but his body twitched and strained.

"When I say, 'Proceed,' you will wash the dust off in the lake, but when you have recovered the use of your powers, you will only use them to give all your power to me." Bella showed teeth in a wide smile. "After that, I care not at all what you do."

The man shuddered and waited. With what seemed to be a good deal of effort he turned his head, but he did not look at Bella. He looked at Nivvy.

That was unsettling. The whole situation was unsettling, frankly: Nivvy as a weasel with his head three inches off the ground watching a woman who'd been born over a thousand years ago use magic to control a man possessed by an ancient djinn, who, to make the whole thing even more disturbing, had a missing finger and a hand dripping blood into the water of the lake that the woman had used to kill an entire kingdom. Not to mention that the whole scene was being watched by the ghost of one of the people that woman had killed, and one of the djinn's sisters had used the body of another to imprison the woman, somehow (had Bella been made small or the body made large?). But you couldn't always look at the big picture like that. Sometimes it was just too big to take in, and it would make you unable to do what you needed to. Best to look back on it afterwards when telling the story, and in the moment, pay attention to the thing you had to do.

Nivvy had done what he had to do; his part in this scene should have been played already. The problem was that he had the feeling, fur prickling all the way down his back to his tail, that the djinn wanted something from him, and for the life of him he had no idea what that could be. He had a good amount of confidence in his abilities, but also a fairly sober estimation of the limits of those abilities, and djinn and magic lay nearly entirely outside them. But he had to allow that Scarlet probably had an even lower estimation of his abilities, and if she thought he could do something, then he ought to pay attention.

But there were no further instructions, no indication of what the djinn wanted him to do. Bella said, "Proceed," and the man, looking as though he were being pulled against his will, lurched forward into the lake.

The ghost, looking alarmed, disappeared below the surface as the man approached, but the man gave no indication that he had even seen this. He kept going until all but his head was submerged, and then turned to stare back at the shore. Bella breathed, "Soon."

Ribbons of red trailed out from where Scarlet stood in the lake. The man's eyes glared at Bella with all the power of the djinn behind them, and then the eyes rolled back and the man's body fell backwards, disappearing into the lake.

Beside Nivvy, Bella gave a cry of triumph.

Her body flickered with what looked like dark flames, and even though Nivvy felt no heat from them, he jumped back. "Yesss," Bella hissed as the flames leapt and then subsided. "This is what I've needed. I thank you."

Nivvy turned back to the lake. The man had reappeared, walking or crawling back toward the lake, but now stopped, lifted the hand with the missing finger out of the water, and reached out to shore. The gesture was so innocuous it might simply be reaching out for some ethereal thing only the man, or djinn, could see. But for a split second the man's eyes were locked on Nivvy's, and the arm reached out almost as an extension of that gaze.

Then something changed. The man stared at his mutilated hand, screamed, and rose from the water to run laboriously back to the shore.

"Pity," Bella said. "I had wanted to send her to the prison I shared. I suppose without her power there was nothing left to keep her alive. She was only power, after all."

She did not pay any attention to the man currently charging out of the water toward her. "Er," Nivvy said, "Hadn't you—"

"I haven't forgotten you." She sounded mildly annoyed, like D'Alio back in Copper Port used to sound when he'd told a story about a daring theft and Nivvy responded by asking if he was going to finish his ale.

"I meant this fellow," Nivvy said. The man had reached the shore, gaining speed as his legs emerged from the water.

Bella watched coolly as the man splashed out of the lake, only a few yards from them. He took two more steps and then stopped and fell over as though he'd tripped, but he did not get up. He squirmed and writhed against invisible bonds, and now let out a series of curses that Nivvy partly understood. "You don't need to worry about him," Bella said. "Unless you want his body?"

"Ah," Nivvy said, "no, thank you much. Unless there's no other choice, in which case I can make do with nine fingers and I suppose I can cut that hair, but all in all I'd much rather have me own body back if that's possible."

"It's quite possible. I keep my promises." Bella stared down at him. "You shall be as you were before Scarlet transformed you."

"Thank," Nivvy said, and before he could say the next word, his body stretched. The cord holding the breathing charm snapped and fell to the ground as his point of view rose several feet and he gained a weight and solidity he hadn't felt in a couple weeks. His arms lengthened, his legs thickened, and in a moment, he stood looking eye to eye with Bella. "You," he finished, staring down at his human body, clothed in his old clothes. His dagger even hung at his belt, his charm bracelet around his wrist.

"There is your payment for stealing the ring," Bella said as casually as if she had handed him a few coins. "You have performed satisfactorily—nay, uncommonly well, I should say." She smiled at her own little joke. "Your horse is there. I will take this fellow's."

"Th-thank you." The sound of his human voice was familiar but still strange to him. He ran his hands down his sides and lifted his legs, his heart soaring. The simple movements of his body, balancing on two feet and raising his arms; the sharp clarity of vision from a man's height rather than a weasel's; all of it raised him up to human status again. He lifted his head and ran fingers through his hair. *Inira*, he prayed quickly and exultantly, *thank you for helping me find my way back.*

Bella's eyes fell on the townsman at their feet. "Did you encounter any of those eels in the palace?"

"I did." Nivvy swiped at the air, feeling invincible now. "Tried to eat me up but I did for 'em well enough."

"They did not bother me." She gestured at the man on the ground, and his body shrank and smoothed until it was an eel, flopping on the stones, its mouth and gills gaping. "There. You may save what is left of his life or leave him to expire on the rocks. Or make of him your first meal in your new life. I care not."

Nivvy's mouth was dry, his joy evaporated. The message was clear: what was given to him can be taken away again. Or maybe there was no message, just a casual cruelty. "I don't wanna eat him."

"As I said, I care not." She walked to where Rahila and the other horse stood placidly, and from her robes she took a simpler golden circlet than the one she wore. Nivvy's eyes, better now he was human again, thought he recognized the crown the prince's ghost had worn. But—if Bella had gotten into that room, why hadn't she taken the crown for herself?

The question fled from his mind as she set the crown on the other horse's head and stepped back. A moment later, in much the same way as the man had turned to an eel, the horse's body rippled unnaturally, making Rahila bolt for the forest in terror. As the horse grew to two times, three times, four times its size, its body thickened, and bright red scales sprouted all along its length; the mane hardened to a ridge of black spines, and the tail—now solid and scaly rather than a pretty shock of hair—stretched out until it was almost as long as the body. Wings sprouted and unfurled from its shoulders, and its head, now lizard-like, grew two black horns around which the crown, which had grown with the horse, settled. The creature—dragon, if Nivvy's stories told him true—shook itself, looking as uneasy as Nivvy had, and startled when its wings rattled.

"There," Bella said. "A mount much more suited to my station."

At some point, when Nivvy had been distracted with all the other terrifying magic being tossed about, Bella had clothed herself in a red velvet doublet and skirt. Over her shoulders lay a fine black cloak fastened at the throat with a jeweled rose that glittered in what little sunlight penetrated the clouds. Even her face looked smoother, younger somehow, the wrinkles gone, her eyes bright. Now she strode toward the dragon she'd made and crooned soothing noises at it. When it had calmed, Bella climbed up on its back. It curled its head around to her and she petted it on the nose. "I wonder if there are dragons anymore, or if everyone will be surprised," she mused.

Nivvy pushed words out past the dryness in his mouth. "There—

TIM SUSMAN

there are stories. Some say they still live in remote areas of the Thousand Kingdoms, or the far north."

"Well. I hope nobody has seen one in quite a while." Even from yards away and seated atop a ten foot tall dragon, the curve of her smile was clear to Nivvy's new (old) eyes.

"I don't suppose they have." He sought out Rahila and found her cowering just at the edge of the forest.

"That will have to do, then." She stared straight at Nivvy. "Would you like a dragon as well?"

"Ah, I, ah, do you," he stammered, and then closed his mouth and swallowed. "Do you mean to change Rahila? I don't believe she would like that."

"She's your horse. If you desire it, what does it matter?"

"Indeed." Even in the battle with the eel, his situation had not felt quite so perilous. "The thing of it is, you see, I rather like her the way she is."

"As you like. I can arrange for the dragon to carry her in her talons, or on her back."

"On her..."

She frowned. "You don't expect a mere horse to match a dragon's speed? She is a capable mount, for a horse, but that seems beyond her powers."

"No, I—" He looked at Rahila in the shadows of the trees. "I'm sorry, what's happening now?"

"You're coming along with me. You've proven yourself a capable assistant, and I know from experience how rare those are."

"Oh." He tried very hard not to look at the eel. "Y'see, not that I'm not terribly grateful for the invitation, and honored, you know, but I've got a friend in trouble, and I've promised to rescue—"

"When you are the Master Thief in service to the Queen, you may bring an army down here to rescue whomever you please." Bella stared down at him, but she leaned forward, and the dragon, sensing her impatience, sat back on its haunches and exhaled a large plume of smoke.

"Right. But y'see, time—that is, it's, ah—" Nivvy tried very hard not to look at the eel. A day ago, he'd have wanted nothing more than to accompany Bella to the northern kingdom, but the imaginary Bella was a considerably nicer and less dangerous companion than the woman who now had all the powers of a djinn and a short temper besides. If he told her about Zein, she would probably turn Frankh into a grass-rat or kill him outright, go charging into the clearing with the dragon, whatever she thought would work fastest, and as much as Nivvy didn't like what Frankh was doing to his friend, he didn't want to kill the fellow.

He'd hoped that Bella would change him back and he'd be happy to serve her, and they would rescue Zein together the way he wanted before going on to live a magnificent adventure. He'd expected there was a decent chance she wouldn't, and he'd be on his own as a weasel, which was not ideal but where he'd proven himself capable. He had not imagined that he would be human again *and* that his best chance of remaining so would be to stay as far from Bella as possible, but that was how he felt. Unfortunately, telling someone extremely powerful a thing they didn't want to hear was rarely the safest course of action, especially when they might consider it a personal betrayal.

Inira sent a thought into his head to remind him of a conversation they'd had back in the Bouli temple, back when he'd tried to convince Bella that she needed him, and she'd flared up at him. He said a silent thanks to his goddess. "Of course," he said, arranging his features into a more conciliatory expression, "if you *need* me, more'n what my friend does, why then of course I'd be right pleased to help you out." He was climbing the tallest tower without a line to secure him here, but it was the only way he could think of to get Bella to decide she didn't want him to come with her.

For a moment, as what little warmth had been in her expression set into icy indifference, he worried that he'd ventured too far. After all, her debt being paid and all didn't mean she didn't have the right to punish impertinence in whatever way she saw fit. And that, he understood with a clarity that could have changed his mind about what he'd said if he'd experienced it a few minutes ago, might well mean turning him back to a weasel. There would be a "fittingness" to it that would appeal to her.

The icy expression did not thaw, but nor did it turn cruel. After a long stare (during which Nivvy thought she was not seeing him for at least some of it), she turned away and caressed the dragon's scales. "Don't be ridiculous. I don't need you. Come in your own time. But mind you be quick."

Nivvy swallowed and tried to think of something pleasant to say.

"Aye. Good luck being queen again," was what he settled on, which seemed to satisfy her.

He thought he was clear of the situation, and had just been congratulating himself, when Bella turned and looked down from her mount. "Don't think I don't see what you are doing. I will not compel you to abandon your friend, but nor will I allow you to use that as an excuse to abandon me."

"I won't," Nivvy promised recklessly, but Bella had already turned away from him and tapped her mount on the shoulder. The dragon-horse, or horse-dragon, or just dragon at this point, spread its wings. Nivvy took a step back and then another as the wings beat for the first time, blowing up dust from the ground and sending ripples along the lake. Bella sat quite comfortably on its back (not, Nivvy couldn't help but think, clutched in its claws like prey) and did not move as it lifted off and hovered over the lake. It craned its neck, clearly getting used to this concept of flight, and then it lowered its shoulders, lifted its wings, and shot forward. Nivvy followed it until it was nothing but a speck in the sky over the mountain range, as much to enjoy the sight of his human eyes again as to say good-bye to Bella. For now.

## ❧ III ❧

# THE HAWK AND THE
# DJINN

## 21

# THE RING OF THE DJINN

**N**ivvy hurried to the eel, whose struggling had weakened. Today had given him a strong dislike of eels that he hadn't had before, but this one hadn't done anything to him and deserved to live as much as anything else.

After a moment of hesitation, he picked it up (in his hands! he had hands!). It tried to make noises, but all that came out was a hoarse gasp. "I'm putting you in the lake," he said. "I'm sorry about this. Go live your eel life. And if you see any weasels down there, don't eat them, right?"

He couldn't tell whether it understood him. It didn't matter; he didn't plan to be back in this lake, and certainly if he came back as a weasel and dove in again, he would have greater things to worry about than eels.

The lake water chilled his legs when he waded into it, colder on his skin even through clothes than it had been on his fur. When he dropped the eel into the lake, it hung there for a moment as though confused. "Don't blame you, mate," Nivvy muttered. "Welcome to the rest of yer life. Sorry about that, but...yer not dead, and that's something."

If it was really a former-human, it should've been able to understand him, but maybe it couldn't hear him properly under the water. It didn't react to his words, but at least it didn't try to bite him. It swam in a circle unsteadily, then gained more confidence and ventured out into deeper water. Nivvy dipped his hands in the lake and rubbed them together, waiting for a moment, but the eel didn't come back. That was that done. Now for Rahila—

The ghost floated in front of him. "Ay," he said. "Didn't you go with the crown? Crown?" He mimed a circlet around his head.

It shook its head and then pointed to a spot in the lake and cupped a hand to its ear. "What? You hear something in the lake? That's why you didn't go?" When it didn't respond, he tried miming the question, but the ghost shook its head and kept pointing at the same spot.

"I have to get my horse," Nivvy said. He pointed to Rahila. "I'll go get her and then I'll come back and...I'll look at whatever you're pointing at. Okay?" He pointed to himself, then to Rahila, and then back to the lake.

This seemed to satisfy the ghost. It floated in the water as Nivvy waded out of the lake and walked over to Rahila. "Hey, h'san," he said softly as he approached her. "Hey, hey, girl, I've missed you. You miss me?"

She huffed and stared as though she didn't recognize him. He shifted around to be upwind of her so she could catch his scent.

Her ears lifted and she stared, then walked out of the forest. "Hey, h'san," he said again. "Ready for more adventures?"

Now she hurried to him at a fast walk. He met her with a great hug around her neck and she pushed her soft nose into his chest and breathed hot horse breath against his shirt. He stroked her mane, joy bubbling up in his chest. "Never thought I'd hold you again," he said. "At best I figured I might get tangled in your mane. But here we are, hey girl? No thousand-year-old queen going to keep us apart. Here, let me look at you. How'd she treat you?"

Running his hands over her neck, he stepped back to examine her. He had to admit that Bella hadn't mistreated Rahila, at least not in an evident way. The mare looked well-fed and sleek, no crop marks on her shoulders or spur scars on her flanks. The bags at her side were gone, but those were just things, clothes and tools that could be replaced. They weren't important. "Good girl," he said. "Keep yourself safe and I'll always find you."

Rahila butted his stomach approvingly and a little demandingly. "Ah, h'san," he said, "I haven't anything nice to give you. I've barely any idea what I've got myself. But we've got each other now, and soon we'll have a hawk friend, and then we'll just see what the world has in store for us, right?"

She whuffed and allowed him to lead her back to the lake, though as they passed the spot where the other horse had been transformed into a dragon, she side-stepped away from it. "It's okay," Nivvy told her. "I won't let anyone change you. You're perfect the way you are."

Having her at his side, as much as being human again, grounded him and gave him confidence. Although, it must be said, he'd gotten the hang of being a weasel and had done as well at it as one might have expected. He'd killed his own food and had ridden a hawk—well, been carried—and had even stolen a precious magic item. He had, in effect, engineered his own salvation from that shape. And now he was human again, wiser and with his horse and a hawk friend—whom he could rescue, of course he could. Now that he was human it would be easy.

"Right." He turned to the lake. "Now what do you want, ghost?"

It pointed again at the lake. "All right, well, this is my day to get wet, I suppose," Nivvy said, and then squinted. "Hang on. Is that where that djinn was pointing?" It was hard to tell because his vantage point was several feet higher now, but it seemed about the same distance from the shore. "You trying to tell me what he—she—wanted?"

The ghost just gestured again, and Nivvy sighed. "Fine," he said, and waded out into the lake. The water felt warmer this time, maybe because the air had been cold on his wet trousers. He navigated over the lakebed to where the ghost was pointing and peered down into the water. Something was gleaming down there all right.

He'd gotten his hand all the way down in the water before he realized what it must be, and by that time his fingers had already closed around the ring and the severed finger inside it. "Eugh!" he cried, and dropped it, but in the split-second in which his fingers touched the metal of the ring, the djinn's voice had spoken a single word into his head.

*Please.*

The ghost gestured down at the water again, pleading. "No," Nivvy said. "Absolutely not. She turned me into a weasel! You saw that, right?" It didn't matter that the ghost couldn't understand him; he felt his tone should make his meaning plain. "And now she wants, what, for me to pick up the ring so she can possess me? No. Absolutely not."

The ghost's features contorted into a glare. It circled its head with its spectral hands, fixing Nivvy with its accusation. "Right," he said, "I nicked your crown, I know that. So go haunt Bella, or Rose, whatever her name is. Why bother me?"

He punctuated the question with a couple taps on his own chest, and the ghost seemed to understand. It pointed at him, then at the water, or at the severed finger in the water, or at the ring in the water, or the spirit still in the ring somehow. "No," Nivvy responded, and made that response as clear as he could, and then, to make it clearer, turned and walked back to the shore.

The ghost didn't appear in front of him, but he hadn't gotten back to shore before a keening arose right behind him, a loud high scream that raised the hairs on his arms. Nivvy jumped and then spun around to look right into the angry face of the ghost, mouth wide open. "Right," he said. "Stop that now."

Whether or not the ghost understood him, it kept making that wailing noise behind him. He kept walking, then ran toward Rahila, but at the sound and sight of the ghost, she bolted again. "Aw, h'san," he said, but not even the endearment could get her to approach closer.

All the while the ghost keened without even having to draw breath, which made sense, seeing as how it wasn't physically present and didn't have lungs or anything like them. Logically, it shouldn't have been able to make noise at all, but logic didn't seem to have much to do with ghosts. "You going to do that for long?" Nivvy asked acidly.

By way of answer, the ghost put its spectral face right up to his and notched up the keening even louder. Nivvy turned on his heel and made for the forest, hoping the ghost was tied to the lake in some way, but after some fifteen minutes of running around he had failed to find any limit to its range. "All right!" he snapped, losing his patience. "All right! Curse you to all ten of Inira's hells, fine, I'll pick up the damned ring and lose my mind to a bloody djinn, since I won't have a moment's peace otherwise."

As soon as he took a step back toward the lake, the prince's ghost stopped its unearthly scream, though it did not look away from him. "Fine," Nivvy muttered again. He waved to Rahila. "Hey, if I come back an' I'm not me, bite me, will you, girl?" He only half-believed that the djinn would possess him; if she could do that, she probably would have when he'd first touched the ring. But he was not at all anxious to talk to her again, especially if it was going to stick a needle in the guilt he already felt every time he looked at the ghost.

Rahila whickered. See, she understood him better than the ghost did. With a baleful look at the dead prince, Nivvy trudged back across the stones and mud of the lake shore, waded back into the chilly lake water, and followed the ghost to the ring and the severed finger. He stood there facing the ghost.

It pointed toward the water, no longer pleading, but angry, insistent. Nivvy reached down and felt around in the muddy lakebed until he found the ring again.

*Thank you for coming back.*

"You're not welcome at all." He pulled the finger out of the ring, dropped it, and then squeezed his eyes shut. "Least I got to say good-bye to my horse."

*Don't be an idiot. I'm not going to kill you.*

One eye flew open. The lake, the mountains, the sky, the ghost, all were still there, and Nivvy still controlled his body. "You're not?"

*I would, believe me. But I have no more power.*

Relief that he'd assessed the situation correctly suffused Nivvy and emboldened him. He stooped to rinse the ring in the lake, rubbing its surface between thumb and finger. "Then how are you in the ring?"

The ghost started babbling at this moment, excited and angry. "Quiet," Nivvy snapped at him. "I've picked up your cursed ring, leave me a moment."

*He's asking you why you did what you did. He wants to tell you about his family.*

"You understand his babble?"

*It is an ancient language. You understand that he is not merely speaking nonsense, don't you? That his words have meaning to him?*

"Yes, yes." Nivvy stared at the ghost and then back at the ring. The lapis stone caught the light of the sun and the shimmering reflections of the lake. It almost seemed alive. "Tell me about the ring, first, and then tell me what he's saying."

*The ring is an artifact. I ensorcelled it to allow anyone to put a small part of their being into it, enough to perceive, enough to report back to me when I needed to come take charge for myself. Think of it like putting one of your eyes into a thing, only the eye can think for itself. When I was stripped of my power and free from the crown's orders, I found the ring and used the spell I'd given it to put as much of myself in it as I could. But it does not allow me to possess you, more's the pity. I'd take your flawed vessel happily.*

"Might be flawed, but at least if I'm thrown in a lake, I can get up on me own," Nivvy said with not a little smugness. "What happens if I have you melted down?"

*It matters very little. I cannot survive for long without my power to sustain me. A decade or more perhaps.*

"Well, that's not nothing." He eyed the ghost. "What's he saying, then?"

*He is even more tiresome than you are, if you can believe that.*

"Is he more tiresome than you are, is the question."

The djinn paused before answering. *I can always let him scream at you again.*

"You heard that?"

*It was my idea.*

"So you can talk to him, too?"

*Obviously.*

"Tell him I'm sorry. But there was no other way to get my body back."

*You could have not stolen from me. Then you would have had no need to get your body back.*

Nivvy chose to ignore this truth. "Right, what'd he have to say about the family and all?"

The ghost came close and reached out his hand to Nivvy's, and Nivvy reflexively drew away, splashing back through the lake. *He only wants to talk to me*, Scarlet said.

"Do we have to be standing in the lake?"

*No.*

"Right." Nivvy slogged his way back to the shore. "Tell me what he said about his family."

*Ugh. His family was peaceful, they were kind, the crown is only meant to be used for good, why did you give it back to Rose who killed them all, that sort of thing.*

"Tell him I had to do it to get my human shape back."

*I know why you did it. I don't think I can make it sound reasonable to him.*

"I don't care if you think it's reasonable or if he thinks it's reasonable. I really don't. I just want to go rescue my friend and get my life back. Or...start a new one. Wherever Inira takes me." He tried not to think about Bella's parting threat.

*Sometimes it's cute how you humans base your lives around mysterious beings you've never seen while ignoring or hating the powerful beings you can see and touch. Sometimes it makes me want to grind all your temples to dust.*

"Well, you can't grind anything to dust now, can you?"

*No. So I'll say it's cute.*

Nivvy reached the mud and pebbles of the shore and turned to the ghost, who had floated on after him. He held out the ring. "All right, go ahead and talk to her," he said.

The ghost reached out a hand, through which Nivvy could see the water of the lake, and brushed the ring. Though the fingers passed through his own, Nivvy felt nothing at all. Weren't you supposed to feel cold when a ghost touched you? His hand was wet and cold anyway, so maybe the ghost's touch was lost on his already-icy skin.

*I've told him that you gave the crown to Rose because you didn't want to be a weasel for the rest of your life, and you didn't really care what happened to anyone else.*

"That's—" Nivvy composed himself. "I also want to go rescue my friend the hawk. She's being held captive by a naked man in the forest."

For a moment there was only silence. Then the djinn said, *We'll come back to that one.*

"And he's already dead anyway. Did he want me to use the crown to bring his city back?"

*No, he's disgustingly nice about it even though he's asked me if I could kill Rose, and I think he wouldn't mind if I could kill you as well. He didn't want me to tell you that. His whole family was like that, to be honest, all pretending they were worthy stewards of power and then doing the same things every other mortal ruler did. I didn't really mind that Rose drowned them all.*

This information give Nivvy a queasy feeling in his stomach, so he ignored it and voiced one of the other questions on his mind. "You called her 'Rose' but she told me her name was Bella."

*Her name is Rose. I don't know where 'Bella' came from. She's gone by many names over her life, but she was born Rose.*

A memory tickled at Nivvy's head. "Did she have a sister?"

*She did. Has she talked about her?*

"She told me a story about Primrose and Rose. No—Primrose and Just-Rose."

*Hah. That was a story that grew from her childhood.*

"That was real?"

*Probably not the way she told it. Rose always had a flair for dramatic self-pity. It makes for stories that people like to tell over and over, but not terribly accurate ones. She did hate her older sister, though.*

Nivvy had no siblings but had known siblings who didn't get along. "I got a little of that. Her sister got captured by a cursed prince and she rescued her and then the prince chose the sister. In the story."

*Which version did you hear? What was the prince cursed to be?*

"A bear."

*Ah, the forest version. That was a later one in her time. I believe that story became a tale to bind sisters together, to show that it is worth risking much to save your family, though for the life of me I don't know why people didn't just tell a true story about sisters who actually loved each other. Rose was the hero of the story, and her sister married the prince, and if people couldn't tell that would bring trouble, then they were idiots, which is to say, they were people.*

"She got to marry a prince, too, though."

*She did not have her choice. She told herself she was in love with her sister's prince even though her own was a perfectly fine man. I suppose he was, at any rate. I've lived for several millennia and still can't predict what makes people like each other.*

"Don't think I'll be much help there."

*I wasn't asking.*

"Right," Nivvy said. "Want to tell me the real story of her childhood?"

*Sometime perhaps, but not right now. You need to hear the prince's story of his kingdom and the crown.*

"Why do I need to hear that?" Nivvy stared at the ghost. "Tell him I'm sorry, I understand that what I did was selfish, but nothing was going to bring him back to life or get revenge on Bella—Rose, whatever. I'd like to get on with my life."

*He thinks you owe him this. As someone you helped Rose kill, I agree with him. I don't care whether or not you hear the story, but I promised him I would relay it to you, and I keep my promises.*

Nivvy held the ring and squinted at it. "You just want to get your powers back."

*The chances of that happening are vanishingly small. I hope to return to my home and end my days there, but I would be glad to see Rose dead before that happens.*

A dying djinn bent on revenge was enough to make Nivvy want to throw the ring back into the lake. "Don't you want to get revenge on me, too?" he asked. "Why should I trust you?"

The djinn's voice took on an amused tone. *You should not, of course. But Rose has now killed one of my sisters and stolen my powers, killing me as well, whereas all you have done is help her kill me. And as you are the only being in the world with a chance of stopping her now, it is in my interest to keep you alive until you can do that. If you die in the attempt, well, that's something.*

"Thanks." Nivvy started. "Wait, why am I the only person? I'm just a thief."

*If you would be quiet and listen to the prince's story, you'd find out.*

Nivvy sighed. "All right. I'm going to get my horse. Tell him not to scare her, and I'll listen to his story on the way to rescue my friend."

## 22

# THE TRUE STORY OF GLÆDELIGDAL

The ghost babbled behind him as he walked to Rahila, and Scarlet translated. *I don't have time to change his wording, so I'm just going to tell you what he's saying.*

"Fair enough. Why would you change his wording anyway?" Nivvy reached Rahila, who did not like the presence of the ghost but at least did not run away from them this time. He soothed her with strokes down her mane and muzzle.

*When you hear it, you'll understand. Here: "My family was the kindest known in all the world. My grandfather was known as Olaf the Beneficent, and his father was Lars the Just." You see? Not to mention that "just" isn't the same as "kind." I knew Lars the Just, and he wasn't all that kind to anyone he wasn't related to. "Our family land, the valley of Glædeligdal, had been blessed by the gods"—ugh—"but threatened by forces outside who craved the bounty and joy our kingdom enjoyed.*

*"So my grandfather entered into a bargain with a powerful mountain witch."—that was my sister, by the way—"He traveled to the top of the highest mountain to seek her help, and along the way he rendered services to many of the people living in her domain. When he arrived, twice she turned him away, but each time one of the people he had helped spoke on his behalf, and on the third time, impressed with his kindness, she allowed him an audience." That's almost certainly not—ah, he's still talking.*

*"He asked the witch how he could ensure that kindness would endure in the kingdom after his death. She told him that there would always be those who put*

*their petty concerns ahead of the welfare of others"—little dig at you there, if I'm not mistaken—"but that a ruler could only do so much. He asked if there was some way he himself could remain to guard the valley, offering any price to the witch if she would keep his kingdom and people safe.*

*"The witch offered him a way, but it would involve a great sacrifice."—that sounds right, at least—"He would have to give his life to watch over his kingdom. She would place his essence into a magical artifact that would allow his descendants to keep kindness the law. Because my grandfather was so kind, he gladly laid down his life for the kingdom, and the witch presented him with the Crown of Glædeligdal.*

*"When he had said his good-byes to his family, he gave the crown to his son, and as soon as it left his hands, he died. His spirit possessed the crown, and the witch's spell gave whoever wore the crown the power to compel others to do their bidding."—That sounds exactly like something a kind ruler who wanted to make his kingdom kind would do, doesn't it?—"His son vowed to rule in his name, as have I.*

*"But the evil queen put an end to our beautiful valley. And now you must—"* Wait a moment. Sorry. He was starting to give you a command, which was going to be to avenge him, but I wanted to ask him why Rose destroyed the valley. Ah. He said they "gave succor to her sister."

"Rose hated her sister that much?"

*I'll tell you about that later. It makes a lot more sense now. All right, here comes the important part.* "To preserve the power of the crown, it may only be given willingly. If someone takes the crown, its power will never work for him. That is why you are the only one who can stop the evil queen now."

The ghost stopped talking a moment before the djinn and looked expectantly at Nivvy. "I don't quite—" Nivvy said.

*Of course you don't. He's a fine storyteller but doesn't really know how to get to the point. The point is that you took the crown from his father. Therefore it will never work for you.*

"Right. I'm not planning to wear it."

*It will also never work* on *you.*

That hadn't occurred to him. "I can see why it wouldn't work if you take it, but why wouldn't it work on me either?"

*My sister wasn't stupid. She foresaw something exactly like what happened. I don't know quite how she managed it, but soon after it was created, she took it from the king and gave it back to him so that it wouldn't affect her. She told me I should do the same, but they were a long way from where I was, and I decided to wait. And then Cinnabar, the idiot, decided she didn't like that thing existing at all and she helped Rose drown everyone.*

"That's pretty horrible, if I'm being honest," Nivvy said.

*Only from your perspective. I've destroyed entire towns. Sometimes you need to make sure people know it's not worth it to make you angry. One big power demonstration can save you a lot of tedious battles.*

"Why make the crown in the first place, if it was so dangerous?"

*Not that I have to justify my family to you, but I haven't anything else to do. Carmine was like that. She wanted to know what little powerless humans would do when someone upset the power balance. She made so many magic artifacts...she loved to play around with humans. And this seemed like the ultimate toy, a crown of control. That's what she called it. It wasn't a crown of kindness, that's for sure.*

Nivvy leaned against Rahila. The mare whuffed, and her steady breathing comforted him. "So what can I do about it? Even if she can't control me, she still has all your magic. She can kill me with a thought."

*Rose values loyalty and you were loyal to her. She wants you to return to her, and she will let you get close enough that you may use a magic artifact on her. In that way you can defeat her.*

"You mean kill her."

*More than likely. But she has escaped death once before and could again. When I say "defeat her," I mean that you must render her incapable of using magic again.*

"How'm I meant to do that? And how did she cheat death?"

The djinn did not speak for several seconds. Finally, she said, *Tell the prince you will accept his charge.*

"He can't understand me."

*Tell him anyway and hold out the ring. I will translate.*

Nivvy looked at the earnest face of the ghost. "It'd be madness for me to try to kill, or defeat, or whatever, Bella—Rose—after she's got all a djinn's power."

The djinn managed to sigh without breathing, somehow. *Just tell him*, she said. *I've got a journey to convince you, and I'll wager you I succeed.*

"You're on," Nivvy said. "What's the stakes?"

*If I win, you take me back to my volcano and then go deal with Rose. If I lose, you can throw me wherever you like and go live your life, likely as one of Rose's pets.*

"That sounds like what would happen anyway."

*Good little human. You're not as thick as you look. Now tell the prince you'll do it, and he'll go back to his palace and never know if you do it or not.*

"Fine." Nivvy looked the prince in the eyes and said, "I promise I'll go deal with Rose and avenge your kingdom."

*The 'avenge your kingdom' is a nice touch. Hold me out to him.*

He held the ring out and the ghost touched it. His face went from hopeful to ecstatic in moments and he floated forward, trying to hug Nivvy with a predictable amount of success. "All right, all right," Nivvy said, trying to put meaning into his tone. "Go and, ah, be at peace. I'm sorry about what happened to you, I really am."

The ghost nodded as if he understood and bowed deeply, then retreated from Nivvy, back along the mud and the rocks, and when he reached the water, he disappeared under it.

"Poor fellow," Nivvy said. "All alone for a thousand years. Will he ever be released?"

*Hard to say. Maybe if someone goes down there and releases him. Maybe now the crown is gone, he'll fade. I don't know how that magic was worked.*

"Look here. I haven't even agreed to go do anything to Rose yet, and I'd appreciate it if you wouldn't add more tasks to my account before I've even done the ones I put on there."

*I don't care if he stays or goes. What does he matter? He's a little human soul, and in the balance of things, if he's not put to work powering a magical artifact, he's useless.*

"Lovely," Nivvy muttered, checking Rahila's tackle to make sure Rose hadn't done anything to it. It looked all in order, so he mounted and headed her toward the forest.

## ❧ 23 ❧

# FOREST RESCUE

Riding through the forest on Rahila was a good deal different from running through it as a weasel. Nothing looked familiar from this vantage point, and his sense of smell wasn't going to lead him anywhere. He appreciated being back in his regular body and his much better eyesight, but he had no idea what Frankh's clearing looked like from this perspective, and he couldn't rely on the scent memory of his weasel body. He'd have to pick his way through the forest and look for that big rock. Was it even that big, if he wasn't a half-foot-long animal? Would there be other big rocks?

"Any ideas about how to find a nature priest in a forest like this?" He'd put the ring on, his worries about being possessed diminished to the point that the annoyance of having to carry around a ring surpassed them.

*Do you know any more about him? What make-believe god does he worship?*

Nivvy told her about Aska the Gardener, and while he was at it mentioned Zein and the drugged animals. *This must be a new one*, Scarlet mused. *I'm not familiar with it. Not that it's unique. The whole gardener thing crops up every now and then, and then dies out. The 'just leave us alone' people always get trampled by the 'our god wants us to go to war' people. That's just how it is.*

"Does that—"

*Except that one religion, the church of, what was it, Goa? No. Xoa, that was it. They had this "walled garden" philosophy, so they built a city on a river and*

268

*called it Xoator, "Xoa's Castle," you know, and they held that city for a good two
hundred years.*

Nivvy was interested despite himself. "Where is it now?"

*Oh, it's gone. Every group of humans either gets trampled by another group
or corrupted from inside. It's just a matter of time. Their last High Priest took
extra shares of the harvest for himself and his friends, and when people started to
go hungry, he took more of the harvest. He could get away with it because he was
a leader, but after he died, his son tried to keep doing the same thing but nobody
liked him. They killed him and all his friends, and twenty years later Xoator was
conquered by the Villeans. They let it fall into disrepair, and then the Laliq built
another city ten miles down the river. Now, if you know where to look, you can
find the old guard tower of Xoator, but the rest of it is either underground or at
the bottom of the river.*

"You should meet this fellow I know, Oigal. He'd love to hear your
stories."

*I hate storytellers. They get everything wrong and then don't want to hear
about how it really happened. I used to try to talk to them, a long time ago. It
was always a waste of my time.*

"So this Frankh fellow, any ideas how to find him?"

*No. But when you find him, I have an idea of how to get your friend away
from him.*

Nivvy sighed. "Let's not spend the gold before we've got it back
home."

*Is that a common expression among thieves?*

"Was in my circles. It means if you're on a job and you got some
gold—"

*Yes, I puzzled out the meaning all by myself. Nevertheless, once you find this
Frankh man, I believe it will be easy to extract your friend.*

"All right," Nivvy said, and bent to Rahila, who didn't seem
disturbed that he was apparently talking to himself. "Come on, h'san,
let's go find a place where all the animals are sleeping."

They rode up the hill at the lakeside and down into the forest
proper, Nivvy in high spirits. After an hour of riding, he came up with
another problem: he needed to eat. As a weasel, he could catch his own
food, and while that was also a possibility as a human, he would have to
catch a lot more of it, and he wasn't fast enough to do it with his bare
hands. He'd fed himself in cities, but out here in the forest he had no
idea how to trap game, and all he had to make kills was his dagger.

In Frankh's clearing there would be plenty of prey, but killing Frankh's precious animals would likely make the man less inclined to give up Zein. The hungrier Nivvy got, though, the less he was going to care about that. He hoped they found Frankh soon.

After another hour, the path he was following inclined upward again. He stopped Rahila and squinted through the trees, and when he saw the grey shapes of mountains, he cursed. "We're headed back toward the lake. I need a better idea."

*If I could turn you into a weasel again so you could retrace your steps, I would.*

"Thank you for that." He scowled and stared at the path and the top of the hill. "Right, I came in around that oak tree—I think—so let's go back and start there. It took me a full day as a weasel, and Rahila probably goes three times as fast if she's walking, so maybe four hours, five hours? Got to keep going away from the lake. Oh, if I keep the sun on my right..."

*You weren't using the sun to navigate?*

"I didn't use it as a weasel," Nivvy said. "I just followed the smell of the lake."

*But you remember where the sun was. When you were running through the forest floor as a lowly weasel?*

There was an understood laugh behind that last statement. "If you like," Nivvy said, "I can toss you in the lake right here and you can keep company with that ghost."

*Do that and you won't have any chance against Rose,* came the cool reply. *You can either try to go stop her without my help or you can go back to your original plan of hiding out in a city and pretending she isn't going to come looking for you sooner rather than later.*

"Don't tempt me," he growled, but kept the ring on his finger as he turned Rahila back to the forest.

*You've got about four hours until nightfall, so let's hope you find him before then.*

"And I'll need to find something to eat," Nivvy said. "Any idea which of these plants won't make me sick?"

*You don't need to eat. You just want to eat. Humans can go for days without eating before they die.*

He started to ask how she knew that but decided he'd rather not know. "Fine," he said. "Fine." She was right; the growling insistence in his stomach would fade after hours. It was getting to that point that he wasn't going to enjoy.

The bit of the forest he guided Rahila through looked much like the part they'd wandered through already, but he kept going this time, past the growing hunger and past Rahila's uneasiness as the forest grew thicker and darker. This seemed somewhat familiar to Nivvy, but the middle of the forest anywhere would be just as dark, he suspected.

Scarlet remained quiet for most of the ride, quieter than Rahila, who huffed and did not keep secret her displeasure at the forest and the uneven footing. Nivvy calmed her, one thing he felt confident in his ability to do, and kept an eye around for anything that looked familiar.

Nothing did, not even when the light grew dim, but just as Nivvy was thinking he should find a place to sleep, he pulled Rahila to a stop and cocked his head.

*Recognize something?* Scarlet asked.

"Not a look, but a sound, sort of? There's a quiet, a stillness. I think it's near here somewhere. I'd better go on foot." He dismounted and patted the mare's neck. "You're just a little loud, h'san, and besides, if Frankh sees you he might feed you some of his drugged food and then how would we get out of the forest?"

*Wise choice.*

"You, as I recall," Nivvy said, "had an idea for how to deal with Frankh. I got to admit my best idea right now is waiting until he's asleep and then taking Zein." This was something a human could easily do that a weasel couldn't. "I don't think he'll be much trouble, and I do have some amount of thiefly talent." He touched the shadow charm on his wrist.

*Let's hope you don't take too long and get caught.*

"As long as nobody warns Frankh that there's a thief on his premises, it shouldn't be a problem," Nivvy shot back. "Why did you let me listen to your conversation? There at the volcano, I mean."

*Oh, Rose has always been excellent at telling stories. I didn't know what she'd told you, but I knew it wasn't what she would tell me in private. I wanted to cause trouble.*

"I don't think she told you the whole truth, either. What did she say about the king wanting to marry his son off to her daughter or something? The prince's skeleton was lying pretty close to another one there, the kind of close like he wasn't really looking for someone else to marry."

*Was there a ring on his finger?*

"I don't remember."

*It doesn't mean anything. She could've been his mistress, and the king wanted him to marry Rose's daughter for unity between the kingdoms. But I am inclined to believe you, because Rose rarely told the full truth where her daughter was concerned, and the prince already told me that Primrose was involved, which Rose did not. Still, if I didn't know that her daughter died a peaceful death later, I might believe that was her daughter in the prince's arms.*

"She wouldn't kill her own daughter."

*You really don't know Rose, do you?*

Nivvy swallowed. "Seemed like she'd be kind to those she loved."

*And she is. Until she stops loving them. She loved me, once.*

It was perhaps selfish of Nivvy to think about what this might bode for his relationship with Rose rather than feel sympathy for Scarlet, but that was where his mind went. "I'd better be quiet so I can listen for Frankh, and it'd be a help if you'd be quiet as well."

Scarlet didn't acknowledge his request, but also didn't say anything else. So Nivvy left Rahila sniffing at some ground plants and made his way quietly through the growing darkness in search of the stillness he'd sensed.

The last time he'd wandered through the trees, he'd been navigating by sound and scent more than vision, and now that he relied less on those senses than sight, the forest felt different. Not better or worse, just less familiar. Annoyance flickered at having lost some acuity of his senses, but with every step of his human feet, he pushed the annoyance away.

(It was like the annoyance of his packs being gone when he got Rahila back. He would have liked to have had his favorite lock picks, but the horse was the important thing.)

The sun had fully disappeared below the trees by the time Nivvy located the source of the stillness. His night vision, weak as it was, adjusted quickly to the darkness, and he was able to move quietly enough to avoid the rustling of snakes in the leaves the two times he heard them. Sometimes the clouds parted and allowed the light of the moon to guide him, and it was during one of these brighter periods that he spotted the rock.

There weren't many large rocks in the forest, and this was the first one that seemed the right size based on Nivvy's recollection of how big he'd been as a weasel. The sour, earthy smell of a long-unwashed person wasn't quite the same as he remembered, but it was definitely there too. When he crept around to get a better view of the other side of it, there lay Frankh, asleep. And there lay Zein with him, nestled right under the man's arm with their head under their wing.

Nivvy watched the two of them breathing peacefully. The shadow spell wouldn't do him any good if he had to touch Frankh to get Zein free. Truthfully, though, even if Frankh woke, there'd be little he could do to stop Nivvy. Might not even be able to get to his feet before Nivvy'd scarpered. But the peace of the clearing worked on him, especially after the turmoil of the day. Did he have a right to take Zein away from this peace?

Maybe not if they'd chosen it of their own free will. But Frankh had drugged them and had tried to drug Nivvy too. That languid torpor came back to him and made him angry all over again.

*Are you stealing your friend with just your thoughts? Maybe you are more accomplished than you were showing.*

"I'm thinking," he whispered.

*It doesn't seem to be working. Maybe you should try stealing with your hands.*

He hissed through his teeth. "What was your idea?"

*This ring. It allows the user to take on the guise of someone else if you know how to call on that magic in it.*

"So it does work?" Before Scarlet could answer, Nivvy hissed, "So if you'd just given this ring to Bella, to Rose, she'd have gone on happily up to her kingdom and wouldn't have bothered with this cursed crown thing? And you'd still have your powers and be happy in your smelly volcano?"

Scarlet was silent for long enough that Nivvy felt some small measure of satisfaction. Finally, she said, *Do you want to know how to cast the spell or not?*

"Who'm I meant to appear as?"

*Aska, of course. His goddess.*

"I can't do that!"

*It's very simple. I'll explain it all the way through.*

"I mean, that's...not right."

TIM SUSMAN

*Do you believe in his goddess?*

"No. But—"

*Then it's not blasphemy or heresy or whatever other word you want to call it. You're sparing him a fight he would almost certainly lose and giving him the gift of thinking his goddess is paying attention to him, which she certainly is not. Even if she were real, she wouldn't be. Everyone's happy.*

"What if..." Was he about to debate ethics with a djinn? Her morality, so far as he'd experienced it, was entirely rooted in power. She wouldn't have any conception of whether Zein might be happier and safer here. Or if she did, she would probably remind him that all the garden people ended up under the heels of warlike people. How long before hunters from the town found Frankh's enclave? They wouldn't even have the restraint that Nivvy'd had, and Nivvy had killed Frankh's animals for food. Not after he'd met Frankh, it was true. There was something about the peace here that he found seductive. Maybe that was why he was reluctant to remove Zein from it.

*Let me tell you another story,* Scarlet said. *A short one. This took place a few hundred years ago, far to the south beyond the Thousand Kingdoms. There was an island kingdom that was weak. They had enough to survive, but little more, and they often looked enviously at the grand ships passing by and wished for more. Many of their kings had in the past tried to conquer their neighbors, but the raids all came to nothing, and this little island wasn't even worth the effort for the neighbors to conquer back. So they existed for a few generations in this life of inadequacy, until one day a king ascended the throne and had an idea for ending their despondency. He called on a powerful djinn to create a magical artifact that would enable everyone in his kingdom to be perfectly happy with their lot.*

*The djinn granted his request, and there was a price involved but that's not important to the story. The king took the artifact throughout his kingdom, and it worked. Everyone who beheld the artifact became content and happy. And within two years the kingdom was gone, the people dead.*

"Why?" Nivvy whispered.

*When they were 'blessed' with a contentment they had not made for themselves, they stopped striving. Crops failed, food ran scarce, and nobody did anything about it because they were content.*

Nivvy had not taken his eyes from Frankh and Zein. At the naked man's feet slept two grass-rats. "The djinn was you, wasn't it?"

*Brilliant mind you have.*

274

"Why do you care about Zein? Why do you do things like give that prince a magical artifact?"

*I don't care about Zein. But you do, and I need you to get me back to the volcano, so the sooner this is over with the better.*

"And the other?"

There was a short silence before she responded. *Tell me, where you live normally, are there insects that build things?*

"Mud wasps? They make these little towers that they live in."

*Yes, exactly. So these wasps, they make their towers, and you are fascinated by them, yes? You allow them to build. Sometimes you maybe spill colors in the mud to see how they will build a tower with it. Their industry fascinates you. But if they try to build a tower in your home, you knock it down and kill them.*

"Aye?"

*You are a mud wasp,* Scarlet said. *Sometimes it is amusing to play with you.*

Nivvy scowled. "Fine," he said. "Teach me the spell."

The spell was a long one, but easy enough to memorize: six names anchoring the history of the ring. The harder part was what the goddess Aska would look like. Scarlet gave him a place to start. *Think of the tallest and most stately woman you have met. Hold her image in your mind. Now clothe her in green robes. Not all the same green. Try a darker outer robe and a lighter inner robe. Make her taller.*

"Stop talking," Nivvy said, trying to keep up. "Taller than what?"

*Taller than she was. Taller than you or Frankh are. Goddesses must be imposing. It wouldn't hurt to glow, if you can manage it.*

"How will I know if I'm doing it properly? Can I see myself?"

*No. But if you hold out your hand, I will be able to see you.*

"Right." He called to mind Hicala a'Stara, the former head of the Thieves Guild in Copper Port, someone Frankh was unlikely to have seen, who was also the tallest and scariest woman he knew. But she had a tender side for her thieves, and he pictured her with that smile, glowing and beneficent like a goddess. Then he held out his hand with the stone facing him and cast the spell.

*I told you green robes. Make the glow greener too.*

"Can I just change the image in my mind, or do I have to cast the spell again?"

*Cast it again.*

So he spoke the spell again with this new image in his mind. *Better,*

Scarlet said. *But make the robes filmier and gauzier and brighten the glow. Imagine the sun behind her.*

"Is this necessary? I'm a strange woman who knows his name appearing in the middle of the night. He's going to assume I'm a goddess."

*You need to get the details right. She has to look impressive and godly, but also she has to make him desire her.*

"Is he another mud wasp?"

*You all are.*

The "get the details right" order reminded him of his training at the Thieves' Guild enough that he cast the spell again without further complaint, and this time Scarlet judged his false Aska's appearance satisfactory. *Just remember to act like a goddess,* she told him. *I know you haven't known any personally, but imagine what I might say. That will work well enough.*

What he was about to do itched at him. "I still don't feel right about this," Nivvy said softly.

*You look fine. Just go be goddess-like.*

"I mean—"

*I know what you mean. Did you know that every single time someone has claimed a god or goddess appeared to them and told them to do something specific, it's been a trick much like this one? This is not the first time this exact ring has been used for that purpose.*

He didn't know what to think of that, so he didn't say anything. Scarlet continued. *That doesn't mean that gods don't exist or aren't real. It means that the chances of someone using magic to pretend they're a god are much greater than the chances that a god would take the time to appear to any individual person. Anyone who isn't smart enough to work that out for themselves deserves to be tricked.*

Nivvy wasn't sure he would be smart enough to work it out, but when he looked back at Frankh, his eyes lit on Zein and he remembered that he was here to rescue his friend, who had almost died for him.

He stepped closer to Frankh's sleeping form and looked down. "Frankh," he said.

*Make your voice higher.*

"Frankh," he said again, his voice high and delicate now.

The man turned his head and woke slowly. He gazed up at Nivvy and his eyes widened so much that they seemed to be mostly white with a dark, impenetrable center. "A-Aska?"

"I am Aska." Nivvy got the words out smoothly. "You have done well to build this garden in my name."

Frankh smiled beatifically. His face shone with the glow from Nivvy's disguise. "I knew it," he said.

"But there is one being here who does not belong in Aska's garden." Gods talked about themselves like that, right? This whole process itched at him.

Frankh's face fell. Nivvy went on. "The hawk is not from this forest. If you give them to me—"

*Not "if." Order him.*

"Give the hawk to me now and I will take them home." None of this was a lie. There was that, at least.

*Hold your hand out.*

He held his hand out. Frankh scrambled to his feet, holding Zein, who stirred sleepily. "Of course, great Aska," he said. "I'm so sorry. I didn't know. I only wanted it to be happy."

"You did well," Nivvy said. "The hawk is Aska's to care for now."

"Of course, of course." Frankh placed Zein in Nivvy's hand. He held them, marveling for a moment that they had once held him as easily as he now held them.

"Thank you, good Frankh," Nivvy said. "Be well, and keep your garden well tended."

"I shall," he breathed. "Oh, great Aska, I shall."

Before Nivvy could do anything else, Frankh fell to his knees and began reciting a prayer to Aska, a very long-winded one that roused the other animals around him.

*Back away, and when you can't see him, remove the spell.*

But as soon as Nivvy stepped back, Frankh stopped his prayer. "Great Aska," he cried, "please do not leave me!"

The anguish and adoration in his voice doubled Nivvy's guilt. "Ah, fear not, gentle Frankh," he said, "but continue my work here." Then he thought about Scarlet's story, and imagined townspeople coming and killing Frankh and all his animals, and said, "Peace and happiness are scarce indeed, and must be cherished," no, wait, use a gardening word, "and fertilized so they may grow fruitful."

At that, Frankh bowed his head. "Thank you, great Aska," he said, and resumed his prayer.

It took a very long time, Nivvy thought, to retreat through the forest until the trees hid Frankh from him, and even in the cool night his back was damp with sweat by the time he released the spell.

*Well,* Scarlet said with not a little smugness, *that worked as well as I thought it would.*

## ❧ 24 ❧

# FLIGHT FEATHERS

Zein stirred in his arms, and he brought another hand around to steady them. They blinked up. "Nivvy? But you're a weasel."

"Not anymore," he said. "Rose—that's Bella's real name—she turned me back."

*With stolen power.*

He focused on the hawk. "It's a long story. How are you?"

"Is this a dream? I feel lovely. Are you going to come live in the woods with us? Frankh would be glad to have you."

"No. I'm going to take you home to Spire."

Zein's eyes opened wider. "No. I don't want to go home. I'm content here."

"Frankh was drugging you. You only feel that way because of the food."

The hawk struggled weakly. "I know. It's the food of Aska that brings her peace."

"It doesn't really bring peace. It brings..." He kept walking, hoping he would find Rahila soon.

*The illusion of peace*, Scarlet supplied.

"The illusion of peace."

"What's the difference?" Zein asked, their struggles getting stronger.

Nivvy tightened his grip. "The illusion isn't true peace, is it?" he tried. "If you stop eating the food, you'll stop feeling it. True peace comes from...inside."

"That's where the food goes," Zein pointed out. "Let me go back."

"Scarlet, how would you explain it?"

"Who's Scarlet?" Zein asked, "and where are they?"

*Don't ask me. I'm not clear on the distinction or why we had to take this hawk away from its fake paradise.*

"You told me the story about the island of people dying!"

*I told you that story to make you stop thinking and do it so we could go. Would you like to hear a story about a land of happy people who lived long lives?*

"Forget it," Nivvy said.

"Who are you talking to?" Zein asked, sharper now.

"I'll tell you in the morning," Nivvy said. "Right now..." He had an idea. "I'm going to take you to see the lake. It's really beautiful. I just wanted to spend some time with you. Then if you still want to go back, I'll take you back to Frankh's." If he could just keep Zein away from the forest for a day, maybe the drugs would wear off. It had only taken him hours to shake free, but he'd eaten much less of the food, too.

"You made it to the lake?"

"I made it," he said. "You were right. It's worth seeing."

They turned their head, looking at him with one eye, then the other. "You were doing something else there, weren't you? How did... did you get to do that? I suppose if you're human again, you must have. Unless this is a dream."

"It's not a dream," Nivvy assured them.

"It's not a very nice dream. Taking me away without asking."

"I know." He called ahead of him. "H'san, h'san, Rahila, are you there?"

Something ahead of him responded with a low, eerie, "Hooooooo" call. "That's an owl," Zein said, their brief flurry of energy subsided. "Frankh had one in his garden. It was beautiful."

"Just wait until you see the lake," Nivvy promised.

"I know I wanted to go," Zein said. "But it doesn't seem important now. I'm glad for the chance, though. It's part of Aska's garden, you know."

"It is, that," Nivvy said.

He called ahead again, and this time heard Rahila's nicker in response. He changed his path to head toward the sound, and within a handful of steps he saw the horse's glossy flank. "Thank Inira," he murmured, and hurried to her side.

Zein couldn't hold on to the saddle, so Nivvy had to keep them in his arms as he guided Rahila back the way they'd come; this was fortunately easy, because they'd made something of a mess of the forest floor plants on their way here from the lake. He dozed off, but fortunately, reliable Rahila guessed where he wanted to go.

When he shook himself fully awake to a brightening dawn, Rahila had climbed the hill, and below them glimmered the bright silvery surface of Lake Beatrice, adorned with patches of drifting fog. Nivvy was not at all sure that he didn't see the old prince among the mist, but the ethereal forms stayed to the lake and did not approach them. Light played over the fog as it curled and roamed over the surface of the water, and below the shifting shapes, small ripples distorted the reflections. Across the lake, trees swathed the slopes of the mountains up to the snowy caps. The moist air carried a chill here that it hadn't in the protected depths of the forest.

Nivvy held Zein up so they could see over Rahila's ears. "Oh," they said. "It really is beautiful."

"And you know what else? There's a whole city down there." He pointed. "Under the water."

Their gaze drifted down. "I don't see it."

"It's there. I swam down and saw it myself. I met a ghost and stole a crown."

The hawk did not seem interested in Nivvy's adventures. They gazed around at the lake one more time and then said, "All right. I've seen it now. We can go back to Frankh's."

Nivvy rubbed fingers down Zein's neck, a touch the hawk leaned into. "We could, but I'm feeling quite hungry. I'd like to get some food in the nearby town first."

"You could take me to Frankh's. He has food."

"I'd rather get food from the town. It won't take long. I promise."

*A cunning deception*, Scarlet said drily.

Nivvy ignored her and turned Rahila along the path back to the town. As he did so, a glint caught his thief's eye. He stopped the horse and slid down, then walked over to pick up the breathing charm.

The leather cord had snapped, but the charm itself was intact. He could perhaps sell it, or trade it for food in the town, although the townspeople would probably recognize it. Still, a thief didn't let anything valuable lie about if he had room in his pocket. Maybe he could attach it to his bracelet once he got near a jeweler again.

A little farther away, what appeared to be a pile of cloth revealed itself to be, as Nivvy drew closer, saddlebags. Not his, no; he would've known those even at a distance of twenty paces. These must have been from the townsperson's horse.

The breathing charm might be recognizable, but probably there were many such. To ride into town with a vanished man's bags, well, he might as well tie the man's severed head to his saddle and parade it through the town. That's how it would have been regarded in any of the towns Nivvy was familiar with, anyway, and he had no desire to end up on a wheel again, or whatever punishment this town reserved for thieves or murderers. Especially since his only companions were a spirit in a ring and a sleepy hawk, neither of whom he would count on to release him from so much as a tangled vine, let alone a wheel or a stock.

There were, however, a length of finely-spun rope and two spare tunics in the bags, which Nivvy was happy enough to add to his store. He wrapped the rope around his waist, where his robe would hide it, and then laid the others over Rahila's neck in front of the saddle, where they provided a comfortable place for Zein to ride, their eyes still wide-pupiled and half-lidded.

They arrived outside the town in short order, and here Nivvy stopped. Daylight wasn't the best time to steal, but his stomach would not allow him to wait for sunset. So he tied up Rahila and arranged the tunics to mostly hide Zein on her back. "Don't let anything happen to them, h'san," he said.

*You trust the horse to look after the hawk?*

"I won't be gone long," he said, "and Rahila won't let anyone but me take her. Except for Rose, it seems."

*She always had a way with animals.*

"Not as much with people."

*People talk back.*

"Ha. That they do."

*You know, you could use the ring's magic to change yourself into that man and just walk into town.*

That hadn't occurred to him. He studied the lapis stone of the ring. "If I do that, there's people who'll know me and want a word or two or five and then I'll be lost. Much better chance of finding a loose door, especially in a town this small."

The town was not quite the six-buildings-around-a-square that Nivvy had seen in other places, but it wasn't far off. A well-traveled road ran north-south and another to the west, probably meaning this was a stop on a trade route between the northern and southern kingdoms, and judging from how busy it was, trade was not going well. In keeping with that, there were two public-houses, three stables, one shop selling wagon parts and riding gear, and a small trading post.

The public-houses were closed this early in the morning, so that's where Nivvy went first, and he got lucky on his first try, finding an open window into a storeroom that contained a pile of day-old bread next to a barrel of salted meat. He ate his fill of both, then picked up some salted meat for Zein and a small carving-knife and left the way he'd come in.

Zein, however, refused to eat the salted meat when Nivvy presented it to them. "I don't want to eat meat anymore," they said. "Get me something else."

"It's perfectly good," Nivvy insisted, "and you ate meat three or four days ago."

"I don't feel like it now." Zein turned their head away from him. "Take it away."

Nivvy returned the meat to a pocket. "I'll save it for later," he said. "You'll feel better by sunset."

"I feel fine now," the hawk snapped. "I want to go back to Frankh."

If the hawk could fly, they would have by now. He had to hope that by the time they felt able to fly, they would have gotten enough of the drug out of their system. "We're going that way," Nivvy said, getting up on Rahila and guiding the horse around the town toward the south-bound road, which skirted the edge of the forest.

He didn't think they would pass the whole day without realizing that he wasn't taking them back to Frankh, but it was mid-afternoon when Zein stirred from the dazed state they'd settled into. "We're not even at the forest yet," they said.

"Not yet." Nivvy shaded his eyes as though looking ahead.

Zein lifted their head to look around. "Wait—the forest is right there. Why aren't we riding into it?" Zein fluffed their feathers and stood up on the saddle, bouncing with Rahila's easy loping pace. "I'm a guide. You can't fool me like this."

Encouraged by their sharper tone and manner, Nivvy tried to stroke a finger down their neck, but Zein shook off the touch. "Hey," Nivvy said, "just trust me until sunset?"

"No." Zein spread their wings.

*You can stop it.*

"Stop what?"

"I'm not going to stop," Zein said. "I'm going to fly back."

*It's just a bird. You don't want it to leave, so grab its legs. I can tell you what feathers to pull out so it can't fly anymore.*

"I'm not going to do that!" Nivvy cried.

"You can't fly. I can." Zein wobbled and then regained their balance. "Good-bye, Nivvy." They spread their wings again. "Thank you for bringing me to the lake."

And then they launched themself from Rahila's back and were gone.

Nivvy watched them go. As they dwindled to a speck, Scarlet said, *So you went to all that trouble just to let them go? We could've been a day farther down the road.*

He urged Rahila forward without answering. But Scarlet, who had remained silent most of the day, had more to say. *I know what this is. You value the illusion of freedom.*

"They flew away." Nivvy couldn't help responding. "Seems pretty free to me."

*They're flying back to that prison you tried to rescue them from. What does it matter if they're in that prison or captive here? None, to them. To you, it makes all the difference.*

"I don't want to keep them here if they don't want to be here."

*You could've used the ring to make yourself look like Frankh.*

"And then what? Stayed in that disguise forever?"

*It wouldn't have taken forever. A day more at the most.*

"And in the meantime, I have to be a naked garden priest? No thank you."

*I see. I thought the hawk was important to you.*

"They are. But I don't want to keep them with a lie or by harming them."

*Pulling those feathers doesn't hurt. It just means they can't fly.*

"That's bad too. Flying is their life. I don't want them to be my prisoner. If they don't want to travel with me, that's fine. Maybe they really like being drugged all day." But that thought itched at him.

*If you can't even rescue them, how are you going to rescue an entire kingdom from Rose?*

"Maybe if Frankh killed an entire city of people, I'd be more insistent about it." Scarlet had managed to push her words into the crack of uncertainty Nivvy felt. Clearly Zein was still under the influence of Frankh's drugs. Shouldn't he have made more of an effort to keep them here until he was sure they'd worn off? Then again, they'd worn off enough that the hawk could fly. Maybe Zein really did want to go back to living in a stupor. In that case, they'd only be unhappy if Nivvy kept them from Frankh, and he really had done the right thing.

*Most people don't have the means to kill a whole city. That doesn't mean they're good people.*

He was about to mention Frankh's religious devotion, but knowing Scarlet's view of gods, he held his tongue. "Have you heard the story of the Suzerain and the Tayghid?"

*I have not heard you tell it.*

Nivvy took that as permission. "I'll keep it short. There was a great Suzerain who caused a garden to be planted outside his bedroom window. In the first spring that it blossomed, a tayghid came and perched on his window and sang the sweetest song for him some evenings. He desired to hear the song every evening, so, being the Suzerain, he appointed one of his servants to capture the tayghid and cage it so that it would sing for him every day. His servant caught the bird and kept it in a cage designed by the Suzerain's most gifted craftsman. They gave the tayghid the finest grass and seed, and for a little while, it sang. But after a week of being caged, it fell silent, and nothing the Suzerain did could coax a song out of it again. It remained silent for two more days and then it died."

*They probably didn't feed it properly.*

"The point is that the song came from the bird's freedom."

*I think the point is that the Suzerain thinks he has unlimited power, but he doesn't. And when he tries to use it, he ruins the thing he wants. Power is not what mortals think it is. But you had power, in this small case.*

Nivvy leaned into Rahila's gait. "I can see that. But a story can mean several different things, can't it?"

*They certainly did not know how to feed animals. Many people collected animals and they often died quickly.*

"Because they were caged."

*No, because people didn't know what to feed them. Sometimes they got better. Suzerain K'Leshi had a zoo of over a hundred exotic animals and only a few of them died every year.*

"It comes to the same thing."

*The fact of being in a cage wasn't what killed them. Many of them lived for quite a long time in cages.*

"The point is," Nivvy said, feeling that he was sliding down a conversational slope away from the point he was trying to make, "that I think they were able to make their own choice, so I let them do it."

Scarlet wasn't done, though. *What if you confront Rose and your feelings get in the way of what has to be done?*

"I'm of the mind that she'll have done something with that power of hers to remind me," Nivvy said. "Or that dragon will have burned something." He'd tried to put the sight out of his mind, but terror and fascination warred, keeping the horned head, scaled body, and great wide wings before his mind's eye.

*I'm certain it has. When people gain power, they tend to use it, and if I know Rose, she will at least want to have made a show of her power for the benefit of the people who won't be affected by the crown.*

"I thought I was the only one it didn't work on."

*The only one it won't work on if she tries. People who aren't present can't be ordered to follow her, but they can be intimidated by having their temples and palaces burned to the ground.*

That would make it easier, to be sure. Nivvy still wasn't sure he wanted to go confront the (probably) most powerful being in the world; he might be immune to the crown, but he certainly wasn't immune to fire, let alone the rest of her power. For the moment, he was committed to getting Scarlet to her volcano home, and after that, well, he'd see what he felt.

They did not encounter another town that day, but the salted meat he'd stolen kept Nivvy content; they did not encounter other travelers on the road, but spots of light appeared in the distance once the sun had set. So there were fires, and others on the road, and that meant there would be towns and people to steal from. As long as he had that, Nivvy felt certain that he could get back to Spire.

But why was he going to Spire without Zein? Shouldn't he turn around and head north to rejoin Rose? He didn't want to—and Scarlet would object, but he could throw the ring away if she got too annoying —but Rose was expecting him, and he didn't have another reason to delay his trip north. But he missed Zein for more than just an excuse. They were happy with Frankh, he told himself, even if it was false happiness. It wasn't that they were rejecting him. He couldn't give them the peace that drugs did.

Still, he did not sleep well that night. Staring toward the dawn sky the following morning, he wondered whether he should put the rising sun to his right and head north, and thought wearily of Scarlet's reaction. Would she scream into his mind as she'd told the ghost to scream at him? None of his options right now felt very worthwhile, so he continued to lie on the ground.

Against the clouds glowing pink, he picked out the silhouette of a bird flying toward him. As it resolved into a hawk, his heart leapt, and when it perched on Rahila's saddle, he stood up, remaining at a distance. "Zein?"

"I'm sorry," Zein said. They wouldn't meet his eye.

Nivvy walked over and put a hand on Rahila's neck, trying to catch Zein's eye, but they turned away from him. "Don't be sorry," he said. "Why did you come back?"

"I know you were being a friend. Even when I left, I was only a little muddled. I knew Frankh had been drugging me, but it was so peaceful that I was mad at you for taking me away from it. And then I flew back and saw the sunset over the lake, and I remembered how you took me to the lake even when I was drugged. You knew I wanted to see it. That meant something."

"It's a beautiful lake, even though..." Nivvy trailed off, not wanting to think about the dead below the water.

"Nobody's really done anything like that for me since—in a long time. So I didn't go back. I killed a grass-rat—not one of his—and I slept in the forest, and then I flew back here and found you."

"I'm glad you did." Nivvy smiled. "It's been a lonely ride."

*I beg your pardon?*

"With only a ghost of a djinn for company," he amended. "It feels like I'm talking to myself sometimes."

Scarlet did not respond to that at all, but Zein turned and now did look at him. "I want to hear this story," they said. "It sounds like a good one."

## ❧ 25 ❧

# THE NATURE OF STORIES

**W**ith renewed purpose, Nivvy headed for Spire. The excuse that he had to see Zein home would keep him from having to think about Rose for a week or more. Over the rest of that day, he spun out the story of his undersea adventure, Bella's transformation into Rose (that was how he now thought of it), and the prince's ghost and the djinn's ring. Zein couldn't hear Scarlet's acerbic commentary, but Nivvy could, and as a result, he was perhaps more honest in the telling than he would have been, though he did not repeat Scarlet's claim that he "squealed like a small child" when Rose turned the horse into a dragon. Truth doesn't always make for the best story, after all.

When he reached the part where Rose turned him human again, he hesitated. How would Zein react to that? They knew he was human again, obviously, but would they want to seek out Rose to get their human form back too? Would they feel jealous at how easily he'd been restored?

They did not. They listened to that part of the story as impassively as the rest—even if Nivvy thought he understood the back-and-forth tilts of their head or the fluffs of their feathers, they remained very still. But at the end of the story they said, sincerely as far as he could tell, "I'm so glad you got your body back."

"Thanks," he said, grateful that Scarlet did not comment on that part. "I went through a lot."

"It sounds like it. I don't think I could have lasted underwater for half that time even with a breathing spell."

"It was scary sometimes, but I was never worried. I knew I could get the job done."

Zein turned their head to scan the horizon in front of them, the great Merkhar Forest to their left, the Reiki Mountains to their right. "I'm glad you talked me into this adventure. It's sort of like that. I was afraid to leave Spire, but now I've done it, I know I can." They fluffed their feathers. "It was so wonderful to see the lake, but all the places we went along the way were fun too. You talked me into it, and you rescued me. Twice. You rescued me twice. And I didn't help you at all."

*That doesn't sound like you,* Scarlet broke her silence to say. *I assumed you were repaying a debt.*

Nivvy reached out to the hawk and rubbed their feathers lightly as best he could with Rahila's gait. "You rescued me in Spire and took me to Oigal and got me there in time. I could never have managed it on my own."

"You paid me to do that. I didn't ask you to rescue me, but you did anyway."

"You're my friend. Don't leave mates behind." He scratched below his ear. "Mate" didn't feel sufficient for someone who'd been through what they had together, nor for someone who'd accepted his secret so easily and shared their own with him, but it was more than just a friend, and close enough for now.

"That's what I need for adventures, is a mate, or at least a friend."

Nivvy nodded. "It helps, that's for sure. That's why there's a Thieves Guild."

"There's a guild for guides, but they won't let me join it. I offered to pay as a regular guide does, but...still."

Some time later, they passed a stone marker on the road that had a square on the top of it, and the number 50 underneath it. "50 miles to something," Zein said. "Whatever that square is."

"Some city." Nivvy thought about what he knew about the geography north of Spire, which was limited to the lake he'd just visited and the Merkhar Forest around it. He didn't even know the name of the town.

*It's Haggerin. The city was famous for its walls with a tower at each corner, so it was represented by a square.*

"Scarlet says it's a city called Haggerin." Nivvy rested the hand with the ring on Zein's shoulder so they could both hear the djinn.

"Is there anything interesting there?"

"Walls, it sounds like. Not sure what else."

*I last visited Haggerin two hundred and forty years ago to grant a wish to a merchant of cloth. He wished that he would be richer than anyone else in the city. So I struck the city with a plague that was carried through a delicacy he did not fancy. Everyone richer than he was grew sick and died, as did most of his family. But within three months, nobody in the city was richer than he was.*

"That's horrible," Zein said.

"People who wish from djinni should know what they're in for." Nivvy watched the road over Zein's head.

*As should people who steal from djinni.*

"Right, well, I ended up a weasel and you got your ring back so I'm going to say you came out ahead in that one, and maybe you don't need to keep bringing it up."

Zein ignored their remarks. "But the other people in the city, they didn't make a wish. They didn't deserve to be killed because of one foolish person."

*People die because of other foolish people all the time. The merchant at least had the industry to search for an artifact that could grant him a wish from a djinn, or a fairy, as he thought it. Nobody else in the city thought to do anything about the plague.*

"Why should they have to?" Zein asked. "Why couldn't they live their lives?"

*You always live your lives at the mercy of a higher power, if not the ones you think you do. Someone turned you into a hawk and you live your life. Someone might decide to kill you, and if you're not stronger than them, they'll succeed.*

"And yet," Nivvy said, "you insist that I must stop Rose because I'm the only one who can. What if I decide not to? According to your rules, I'm not obligated to do anything. Any of the people in that town might have found an artifact and summoned you, but they didn't. Any of the people in Rose's kingdom up there might find a way to defeat her, might have the, what did you say, 'industry' to solve their own problem. I don't live there, I've never laid eyes on any of 'em, and honestly, Rose might be a terrible person—seems like she is, on balance—but she was good to me."

"Except when she left you in the Bouli temple," Zein put in. "Or when she made you go get that crown from the bottom of the lake."

Nivvy ignored the itching. "The point is, I got my human form back, and so if I want to be done then I can be done. Story's over."

*Until she comes to get you, her loyal servant.*

"I'll worry about that when it happens. Maybe by that time she'll have what she wants an' I can be a good influence on her." If he told himself that story enough times, he might believe it.

*She's going to murder a lot of people up there. The royal family, at the very least.*

"Hold up. Doesn't the crown make people obey her?"

*I told you, only in her presence. She will have to find a more permanent solution to compel obedience, and fear is what she's used in the past. Besides that, she views the royal family as descendants of her sister, and she will wipe them out, possibly in very unpleasant ways.*

"You're an expert in those, I seem to recall," Nivvy said.

*And I saw well how it bothered you. She rode a dragon up to Heiterflus. You think she won't burn people to get the respect she wants?*

"That's likely done by now, I should think," Zein put in.

*She won't stop at Heiterflus. Maybe she will take a moment to settle there, but with the crown and my power, she will look to extend her reach. It may take a few years, but she will be in Spire before too long.*

"Or maybe," Nivvy said, "she just wants her sister's kingdom—that's Heiterflus, is it?—and she'll be happy once she's got it."

*If you're not going to listen to me, there's no point in me talking.*

"Lovely," he said, taking his hand from Zein's wing. "One more thing we agree on."

"You shouldn't dismiss her so quickly," Zein said. "She seems very passionate about it. When people care deeply about something, it's worth listening to them about it."

"She doesn't care about murdered people or Primrose's descendants. She wants revenge because Rose took all her magic away." Nivvy lifted his eyes to the road, a dusty beige stripe through green farmland, and looked across the seemingly endless forest toward where Spire might be. "I just got my life back. I don't need to be runnin' back out into a lightning storm just because..." His mind stopped his mouth then, because he'd been about to say, "just because Rose might murder a lot of people," and the moment before he spoke the words he heard how it would sound, and he did not want Zein to think him selfish in that way. So he took a breath and finished, "just because a djinn is mad that someone she double-crossed turned the tables on her."

"That does sound less important," Zein conceded. "She was making it sound very bad, what Rose is going to do. It was so strange hearing her talk in my head. Do you get used to it after a while?"

"Sommat. I can always take the ring off if she gets too sharp, can't I? So that's good."

Scarlet, if she was listening, did not dignify this with a reply, but Nivvy was under no illusion that she was afraid of his threat.

Rahila trotted along at a long-haul pace because Nivvy estimated that there were ten or eleven more days before they arrived in Spire. Every few hours he stopped to let her graze while he relieved himself and stretched his legs, and on those occasions Zein took flight in a broad circle, returning to tell him what lay ahead on the road. The small portions of meat he'd taken from the town did not last through the second day, but on the third day, they arrived at a small town where Nivvy was able to steal a flint.

"It was easier when you could eat the raw game," Zein said, tearing at the carcass of a tree-rat they'd caught, while Nivvy struck the flint over a small bed of dry grass. "And you were getting good at hunting, too."

"If I'd got much hungrier, I would have eaten it raw. Once you've done it, even in another body, you know it's not so bad." This flint was worn and Nivvy had to figure out how to strike it to get the best sparks. Finally, one caught in the grass, and a small tendril of smoke rose.

As Nivvy turned the tree-rat over his small fire, Scarlet said, *Would you like to hear a story?*

"Wouldn't say no." Nivvy called to Zein, "Scarlet's going to tell us a story."

He took the ring off as Zein flew over to land—carefully—on his bare leg below his trousers, then lifted one talon. Nivvy slid the ring over it and then returned his attention to the tree-rat, which was almost done.

*This story happened a long, long time ago. It's the story of two sisters who grew up in the house of a witch and how they came to hate each other.*

Her voice fell into a storytelling cadence as she continued on. *I do not know how they came to live in the house of the witch. Perhaps she took them*

TIM SUSMAN

as payment, perhaps she stole them. Perhaps they were her own children. However it came to happen, there they lived and there they grew, and there they learned magic, as children in a witch's house will do.

They differed in more ways than they resembled each other. They grew like two flowers in the same garden, one never more than an inch taller than the other. The fairer one, with golden hair and skin as fresh and clear as a new snowfall, found that her skills lay in healing magic, while the darker one, with hair black as charcoal and skin smooth as polished marble, surpassed even the witch in the art of curses.

Around this time, the king of a neighboring kingdom—there were many kingdoms in the north, some as small as a lake, others as large as a sea, and this one was perhaps the size of a very large lake—fell ill, and none of the healers in the kingdom could find a cure for his sickness, so they claimed it was a curse.

It wasn't, at least as far as I've been able to tell. I wasn't there, but I know everyone who would have cast a curse on him, and they all say they didn't.

The witch sisters were brought before the king and ordered to heal him. The darker sister with all her knowledge attempted to undo the curse on the king, but as I have said, it was not a curse, and therefore she failed. Then the fairer sister laid her hands on the king, and after mere seconds he rose to his feet and declared himself healed of his mysterious illness. So that he and his might never suffer illness in their lives, he bid his son marry the golden-haired sister, and welcomed her into his family.

The golden-haired sister, fair of temperament as well as features, begged that her sister be married into the family as well. The king had no other sons, but his sister, queen of a smaller lake-sized kingdom farther to the east, had a son, and so the darker-haired sister was married to this prince and became part of the royal family of that kingdom.

But while the fairer-haired sister lived quite happily with her prince, the darker-haired sister was not content with hers, who by all accounts was a very kind man, nor her kingdom, which was not the most prosperous in the region but did include enough rich farmland to keep all its people well fed. She believed that her sister had conspired to be married into the more prosperous kingdom and to send her away to this smaller one. This does not seem to be true, but who can tell? One may wear a fair face and conceal horrors within.

A year later, the fairer sister bore a child, a lovely daughter, and held a consecration, a pointless ritual meant to curry favor with the god that the kingdom supposed to be watching over them. The ritual was beloved by the royal families and by all of the poor people in the kingdom, or at least the poor people enjoyed *the free food they received when they attended. It was a great ceremony, three days of feasting and festivities, and of course the darker sister was invited. By now she, who had yet to conceive a child, felt that her sister only invited her to show off and throw her own life into miserable contrast.*

*So she prepared a curse that would, she felt, make their lives equal again. If you do not know about curses, it is helpful to think of them as a trap you might set in the forest. She could not, for example, use a curse to steal her sister's daughter outright. But she could curse the child so that when a particular event came to pass in the child's life, the curse would take effect. And she poured all the hatred and resentment she had into this curse, weaving a trap so complicated and thorough that even her equally skilled sister would not be able to unravel it.*

*Her sister's daughter, the pride of her life, would be taken from her at the point when her sister would be most proud of her, as her daughter flowered into womanhood on her fifteenth birthday. That was when they considered a girl to be a woman in those days. I don't know when it is now. I haven't kept up.*

"Still fifteen," Nivvy said. "At least in some places."

*On her fifteenth birthday, the curse went, should anyone comment upon the princess's beauty, she would faint on the spot. When she awoke, she would remember nothing of her life with her family but would believe herself to be the child of the darker-haired sister, all of her memories forever changed.*

"I've heard this story," Zein said. "Only not with the memories, it was that she would fall down dead. But the mother found out about the curse and got it changed so she would only sleep for a hundred years."

*How would the mother find out about the curse? Do you think her sister walked into the consecration and announced the curse to everyone in front of all the guests and royalty?*

"That's how I heard it."

*That's ridiculous. If they'd heard the curse, it would be easy to prevent it. No witch would announce the curse as they cast it.*

"I always thought that it was strange that she would be so clever as to create an elaborate curse but not clever enough to not tell people the curse to their faces."

*Do you want to hear my story or not?*

Zein fluffed their feathers. "Sorry," they said.

Nivvy kept quiet as he ate, but he too was familiar with the story, and shared Zein's memories and objections. But he was enjoying Scarlet's telling of the tale; when the djinn's acerbic tone wasn't directed at him, he enjoyed it. He suspected he knew who the darker-haired sister in the story was but didn't want to interrupt to confirm it.

*The darker-haired sister went to the consecration, smiled politely, and said all the right things. And she took a hair from the new princess's head when nobody was looking. That night she used the hair and a drop of her own blood to weave the curse. She spent an hour, and when she was done the curse was as strong as any she had ever cast. The festival ended and the queen embraced her sister and told her how lovely it was to see her again.*

*On the princess's fifteenth birthday, her father told her she looked more beautiful than the sun. She fell down into a dead faint, and when she awoke, she asked her mother and father why she was at their palace and when she would go home. Nothing they said could dissuade her from what she believed to be the truth, and the harder they tried, the angrier she got. Finally there was nothing they could do but let her go to the darker-haired sister's kingdom, where she was welcomed as a princess.*

Scarlet fell quiet. Both Nivvy and Zein waited, but the djinn didn't go on. Zein broke first. "Then what happened?"

*That's all. What do you want?*

"How did the fairer sister get her daughter back? How was the evil queen beaten?"

*She didn't. She wasn't.*

"What, ever?"

Here, Nivvy couldn't restrain himself. He put down the bones of the rat, stripped clean. "The evil queen is Rose. She's trying to tell us again how evil she is."

*I thought you should hear a truer story of her childhood than the one you had heard so far.*

Zein fluffed their wings again. "I didn't hear any stories of her childhood, unless you're talking about the Sleeping Princess story, but you just said this isn't that one."

*That is a version of this one.*

"But," Zein went on, "what happened to the princess? Did she become queen eventually?"

"I don't think so." Nivvy finished chewing the meat from the last bone. Having eaten raw meat the last few days, he wasn't entirely sure that the work of building a fire and waiting to cook the meat was worth it, but it reaffirmed his humanity, so he did it. "She told Scarlet something about protecting her daughter."

*That was the same daughter, yes*, Scarlet said.

"So she just got to keep her sister's daughter? What happened to the sister?" Zein shifted restlessly.

*She died of grief and a great statue was erected in her honor. Then people built many more statues, and now people think she was a goddess worshipped a thousand years ago. Rose has probably already destroyed the statues. She tried to destroy the original before she was imprisoned.*

"I want to hear that story," Nivvy said. "How was she imprisoned? Who did it? Why?"

*Another time*, Scarlet said.

"I don't like how that story ends," Zein declared. "The evil queen should be punished, or you should tell us how her curse didn't work, and the princess lived happily ever after."

*I don't know how happy the princess was.* Scarlet sounded bored. *I imagine she was happy because the memories she had were happy ones. She married and had a child and lived a boring life, which is as happy as one can expect, isn't it?*

The hawk fluttered their wings, brushing Nivvy's legs with air. "You shouldn't be telling that story if it doesn't have a good ending. That's what Oigal says. He won't tell a story that doesn't end properly. And he says stories should have a lesson."

*When does a story end?* Scarlet asked. *I could have gone on to tell you about how the fairer sister's kingdom went to war to get their princess back, and by the by, I believe Primrose visited Glædeligdal to ask them to use the Crown to restore her daughter's memories, but her sister got wind of it and decided the Crown would be better off underwater. It was one of the few magical artifacts at the time strong enough to break her curse. I could have described Rose negotiating alliances with honey and with nettles, how the war ultimately ended without a clear winner. I could have skipped forward years to the princess's wedding, which sparked another war, to the fairer sister's death, to the darker sister taking over the kingdoms, all the way up to the present day. Perhaps Rose's punishment is yet to come. Perhaps she will die without ever feeling it. And perhaps it has not been her story at all.*

"It doesn't have to be her story," Zein said. "But 'jealous person does something bad and gets away with it' isn't a good story."

*It is instructive*, Scarlet said. *The lesson, if you must have one, is that bad people will do things good people don't expect, and if you are not prepared then you may fall victim to them. That, too, I have seen over and over again in my life, and that is what I am trying to convince you to prevent. So it is a good story, just not of the sort you recognize. The fault is yours.*

Zein huffed and shook the ring free from their talon, then said to Nivvy, "I like Oigal better," and took flight.

Nivvy wiped his hands on the ground and then picked up the ring and slid it on. "You said Rose's kingdom was less prosperous," he said. "So the other sister—Primrose? Hers must have been glorious."

*Why do you say that?*

"Rose told me about her kingdom. White marble palace, gold trim, the envy of those around, but everyone came to ask her advice."

*Ha ha. She would have loved to have a kingdom like that, but no, she lived in a cold stone castle that was only called a castle because it was bigger than the other stone houses around it. Their people were mostly farmers and they sold meat and grain and animal pelts. As soon as Rose conquered another kingdom, she left that palace.*

"Maybe the new one was the one she was talking about?"

*No. That was a dream of hers that she has spoken to me about in the past. I suppose I understand why she wanted you to think it was real.*

"Why?"

*Because if someone else believed her story, that made it easier for her to believe it. It is how you humans treat stories. As your hawk tries to make my story not be true by disliking it.*

"Do you really not understand what makes a good story?" he asked. "Or are you doing this on purpose to be annoying to us poor stupid humans?"

*You all change around the events so that it isn't what really happened, and then you talk about how beautiful the story is, how marvelous, as though it was designed by one of these gods you place so much stock in.*

"We know the stories didn't really happen," Nivvy said. "That's not the point of them. They're like those tabards you had in your cave. People make designs out of 'em."

*I know how all of that happens. I know what you do to stories. It's different from drawing a wheat stalk as three golden triangles. If I tell you stories about how evil is always punished and good triumphs, it leads you to believe that that will always happen.*

"I see your point, but—"

*Just as you do with religion. Put yourselves in the hands of your gods, rather than figuring out what you can do to better yourselves.*

"Here now," Nivvy said. "Some of our gods encourage us to better ourselves."

*And some of them tell you to feed drugs to animals and live in the forest naked.*

"That's not my god." It was a feeble reply.

*No. But you worked against his god, if you believe in her, in a cause you believed in. You did not trust to a higher power; you acted. That is what I am asking you to do again.*

"The problem with that," Nivvy said, "is you ain't got me to believe in the cause yet. I think Rose will go conquer that kingdom, an' that'll take weeks or months, an' in the meantime maybe she'll think, oh, I don't really need that little thief when I got this whole kingdom. Then she can live her life an' I can live mine."

*She can do a devastating amount of damage before she turns her attention to you again.*

"I feel bad about that, truly, but..." Zein wasn't there. "I don't owe that kingdom a thing."

*I don't know why I expected more from you.* Scarlet did not deign to continue the conversation after that, no matter what Nivvy said.

## 26

# THE VELKI'S MIRROR

When Zein returned that night, they didn't say anything about the story, but told Nivvy that the walled city of Haggerin was two days' ride ahead of them. They didn't try to talk to Scarlet at all. Scarlet, perhaps marshaling future arguments, remained silent that night and most of the next two days, until they reached the city.

Nivvy's task in Haggerin was to steal some supplies for the rest of the journey or steal coin to buy them. Unlike at Spire, there were few other riders on the road and the guards did not seem particularly interested in Nivvy's business, waving him and all the others through while leaning back against the grey stones of the wall. Riding past the iron gates into congested streets hemmed in by thick wooden buildings, Nivvy looked ahead to the people walking and riding and felt as though he was coming back to a remembered life, even though it had only been two weeks or so since he'd been in Spire.

His instincts came back swiftly, if indeed they'd ever left. His fingers nimbly stole two purses in the first hour, enough to treat Rahila to a stabling and grooming, and himself to a bath. It was a pleasure to be able to run his hands over his skin in the water again, to be wet not at the mercy of the weather or in the depths of a lake, but in warm, rose-scented water from which he could emerge cleaner than he'd entered. At the bath, with the aid of his Shadow charm, he stole a little more money, and afterwards, he bought some dried meat for the journey, some raw meat for Zein, and a couple other basic things he'd been missing: blankets and a lock pick whose balance felt good in his hand. He didn't have enough for a whole set of tools, but a pick was a good start.

*They have not maintained this city*, Scarlet said. She had commented on his thievery, sardonically at first and then with what he fancied was a little bit of respect, but knowing her, might have been merely boredom. In either case, he hadn't responded to her because his experience of people who talked to unseen entities was that they were either clad in rags and living in muddy hovels outside the walls of the city, or they were in temples, and someone talking to an unseen entity in the streets would be likely hastened to one of those two places.

At this moment, though, there weren't many people around him, so he risked a low whisper. "It seems nice enough to me. Not many holes in roofs, most everyone has tunics, even the beggars." He spared a glance at the ragged-haired woman squatting in the alley, one twisted, withered foot stretched out in front of her.

She met his eye. "Spare a copper?" she said, well-spoken.

Nivvy made a quick sign of the goddess Liaji, who in addition to being the goddess of healing, was the patron of the destitute. "Blessings on you," he said quickly.

"Blessings." She turned her attention to the next person.

*The city had energy when I was here last. The people walked with purpose. They used to post wizards at the towers. There were grand displays of magic during festivals.* She sounded tired and peeved.

"Maybe they don't need wizards because nobody's using magic as much.," Nivvy said under his breath.

*Of course they don't. But why are all the people walking around so slowly? Where are the King's Guard to prod them on their way?*

"Been a while since you were in a city, I wager." Nivvy's image of Scarlet's memory changed from a bustling, lively city like Spire to a dark, crowded city where guards jabbed spears at any unlucky folk not moving quickly enough. "You should be glad—" He started to say, "that there's no guard," and then looked around and said instead, "that everyone's so calm and easy."

She took his meaning. *You should be glad, you mean. You've made out well enough today.*

"Aye." He arrived at the stable, where the old, bearded man in the black tunic greeted him and sent a boy to fetch Rahila.

"Didn't give you any trouble, did she?" Nivvy asked as his mare came back into view.

"Nar, nar, sweet she is as the dayflower." The old man took her reins and handed them to Nivvy. "Lovely mare, bring her anytime."

Nivvy bowed and rubbed Rahila's muzzle. She smelled of fresh hay. "Just passing through, but I'll remember you should I pass this way again."

"Ar," the man said. "Seems all anyone do these days, pass through." He tipped his cap as Nivvy mounted.

Zein found him a mile south of the city, as the shadows grew longer over the camp that Nivvy had made with his blanket. They alit on the ground nearby and walked over. "Did you get everything?"

He offered them a piece of the raw meat, which they gobbled down. "That's a nice change from tree-rat. How's the city? Is it like Spire? There wasn't anything I could see except the walls, and Spire has walls too. I didn't understand why those are so special."

Scarlet began to talk about how the walls had been built hundreds of years ago, as Nivvy also spoke. "From what I heard in the city, and from Scarlet," he lifted the ring, "they were the most impressive walls in the known world several hundred years ago. They're very thick and supposedly they were only breached once, through trickery. They claim that all the other walled cities borrowed their idea."

*Which is ridiculous*, Scarlet said.

"Which is ridiculous, because the idea of building a wall around your city is probably as old as cities."

*Slightly less old but yes.*

"But it was a nice quiet city, perfect for snatching a few purses. No guards like in Spire watching you all the time. Had a bath, gave Rahila one, and we're ready to go on our way. How was your flight?"

Zein groomed their feathers as they answered. "There are mostly farms around so there are plenty of rats and mice. I ate well. Not that I don't appreciate the meat."

"It won't keep long," Nivvy said. "I'll eat what you don't tonight."

They took a little more meat, and Nivvy ate the rest—raw, which felt appropriate after leaving the city for the wilderness again. He didn't want to build a fire, even though probably nobody was pursuing them out of the city (the roads were not heavily traveled).

When they'd eaten, Zein asked for the ring. They slipped it onto a talon again and stepped up onto Nivvy's leg. "Tell us the story of how Rose was captured," they said. "And how she lives for a thousand years."

*Those are different stories,* Scarlet said. *I don't know all the details of the second one. She made a bargain with some powerful being. There were more of them in those days, when magic was more abundant. It was likely the standard bargain, where she sacrificed other lives to prolong her own. There were other ways to go about it, such as killing one of those powerful beings, and since she later killed one of my sisters, it's not inconceivable that she could have succeeded in that. She's proud enough to have tried. At the same time, she had access to hundreds of lives she could have sacrificed. And now she has my power, so it matters not.*

Nivvy's ears warmed, but Scarlet didn't accuse him. She could have been talking about something that had happened hundreds of years ago.

*The story of how she was captured, that one I do know, because it cost me one sister at the hand of another. There were seven of us in the beginning, down to four a thousand years ago, and now just me. But at the time, it was my sisters Cinnabar and Karminrot, whom Rose called Carmine, and Cerise, and me.*

*Rose made many enemies over her life. She conquered a kingdom to the west and murdered the royal family, which was the way to do it, but one of the princes escaped. He spent years studying magic and collected all the stories of people who had tried to fight Rose—the true stories, the things that actually happened—and determined not to make the mistakes they had. His name was Prince Night and his studies brought him, eventually, to the great Wizard of the Mountains, one of the few humans to approach our level of power. This Wizard also hated Rose, because she killed some member of his family or chased him out of his city or something. She did a lot of things like that, hence the enemies.*

*They got the better of her after their first battle, so she called me to help her fight, but I was spending a lot of time down south around then, and besides, that thing about a lot of people hating you when you do things? I don't worry about it usually, any more than you worry about stepping on an anthill, but as I said, the Wizard of the Mountains was an unusually powerful human. Like an ant that could hurt you and remember things you'd done. Cinnabar, who was more reckless than I was, did answer, and together, she and Rose defeated the Prince of Night and the Wizard of the Mountains.*

"Prince Night," Zein said.

*What?*

"Was his name Prince Night or Prince of Night?"

*It doesn't matter,* Scarlet said irritably. *He's dead, he died, his body was turned into sand slowly and scattered out across a plain by the North Wind. There's a Desert of Night somewhere up north if you want to visit it. The Wizard of Winter's body was eaten from the inside out by thousands of insects. But before he died, he wounded my sister. She died in Rose's arms.*

*There are ways to kill our kind which I will not detail for you even though I'm one of the last of them. The Wizard was powerful for a human. But Carmine did not believe he was powerful enough to kill Cinnabar. She believed Rose killed Cinnabar to take her powers.*

Scarlet paused. *I did not think so. For one thing, Rose did not evince those powers afterwards. For another, I thought she knew better than to make enemies of the rest of us. In light of what happened at the lake, I now believe it was possible that Rose was attempting to take Cinnabar's powers. She was canny enough to recognize the opportunity presented.*

*Carmine was one of those who had disliked Rose for a long time. The incident with the Crown you know about, but that was only one of several. Rose was one of those humans Carmine felt we should kill because she was gaining too much power and might become another Wizard of Winter, but without his caution. Carmine was furious enough that rather than kill Rose, which would be over quickly, she wanted Rose to suffer for an entire age and, if she survived, to emerge into a world she would not understand.*

*From Cinnabar's body she made a system of caves, blank and white, all the same, with no other living being and only one small stream of warm water. Rose is a master of curses, but curses are only useful magic when there is someone to cast them on. Isolation was the most suitable prison for her. I am honestly surprised that Rose emerged from it with her senses intact.*

*Carmine lured Rose away from her kingdom by telling her that she'd found another temple to Rose's sister. Rose, infuriated, did not suspect as she should have, and she went inside expecting a statue of Primrose. Instead she found nothing. Carmine thought to make Rose suffer for centuries rather than release her with a quick death. She did not know Rose as well as I did; she gave no thought to how determined Rose would be should she survive. And now I have paid the price.*

*But that punishment also tells me the best way to defeat her.*

"What," Nivvy asked, startled, "that she survived a thousand years without losing her mind?"

*Yes.*

Zein shivered. "I don't like the part about the prison made from a body."

*Rose has a very strong will and sense of self. The idea that she has been wronged throughout her life, though false, sustains her through many trials, more than I would have thought possible. But the core of this idea is wrong. The truth is that her powerful sense of self-righteousness is not the walls of Haggerin, but rather a mirage. Shatter that mirage and her confidence and her powers will crumble.*

"All right, that's a fine theory, and I suppose you have a way to do that."

*Back in my cave there is a small mirror that you could carry in your hand. It was crafted by one of the Velki, a race of creatures skilled at metalworking.*

"A selkie? The seal-people?"

*Velki. They live in pools of molten rock and eat earth. They fashion silver and gold and other metals into intricate designs and decorate caverns with them, then throw them back into the molten rock when they grow bored.*

"I've never heard of them," Zein said.

"Nor I," Nivvy added.

*I'm not surprised. When would you have? No-one has traveled to their realm in over one hundred years.*

"So what does this mirror do?" Nivvy asked. "Tell you the truth?"

*Yes. Anyone who looks into it sees themself as they truly are, with all the artifice stripped away. I enjoyed looking into it because it reminded me how powerful I am. Now I don't want it anymore.*

"Isn't there a more certain way to kill her? Your sister thought that being trapped in corpse caves would destroy her, and it didn't."

*I've known Rose almost since her childhood. I have forgotten more magical artifacts than either of you will ever know in your lifetimes. There are artifacts that might kill her, but she could also have protected herself against blades or fire.*

"Or insects that eat you up from the inside out?"

*Yes, any of that. Now that she has the Crown and my power, she can defend herself against nearly any artifact. But there is no defense against the Velki's Mirror. Once you see it, it works its magic on you.*

"Like the mirror that turned people to stone," Zein said. "In that story about Javian's adventures. Nobody could figure out how to get past it."

*The Mirror of Csravic turned everyone to stone, no matter how deluded they were. The Velki's Mirror has sometimes destroyed humans who built their lives on self-deception, but fewer than I would have hoped. None of those it destroyed have been as devoted to their self-deception as Rose is.*

"Do you have the mirror that turned people to stone, too?" Zein asked. "Or anything that turns people to stone?"

"She likes turning people to animals," Nivvy said. "Not stone."

*The Mirror of Csravic lay a thousand leagues to the south, the last time I heard of it, which was two hundred years ago. I had a pendant that could turn people to stone. It was boring. I might still have it. But I know where this mirror is.*

"So hang on." Nivvy stared at the ring. "Got to make sure I got this right. Your idea for me to destroy Rose is for me to walk up to her with this mirror and say 'here, old friend, would you mind taking a look into this'? That's it?"

*I'm sure we can come up with better wording, but yes, that is the idea.*

"Right. Perfect. Puts me in mind of the time I walked up to the fire and told it to put itself out. Like as it'll be just as successful."

*I knew you wouldn't think you could get close enough to use it.*

"Oh, an' you do? Got such faith in me, fair warms my heart."

*She trusts you. You can do it.*

Nivvy leaned back on his elbows. "Ah, let's say there's a one in two chance it works. Let's say there's a two in three chance it works, even. That leaves me a one in three chance of standing in front of the most powerful person or being or whatever in the world, whom I've just betrayed. Now if I choose not to undertake this very necessary adventure, yes, of course, there's always the chance of getting my throat cut sometime in the next few months. I might very well fall into the river and drown. But I don't think I'd put those at one chance in three."

*What about when she summons you back to her side? How long before you make one mistake big enough for her to punish you?*

"If that happens," he said, "I'll take good care to walk proper. But there's lots can happen between now and then. Besides, what if she really was wronged? I know she's hurt people, present company included, and she's not a nice person, no argument there, but she did turn me back human, and she could've killed me as easy as she killed that other fellow. She didn't even kill him, just turned him into an eel."

"She might harm a lot of people up north," Zein said. Nivvy opened his mouth to respond, but Zein clacked their beak, going on. "But that kind of thing goes on all the time. Nivvy's right about that part of it. Just because the crown won't affect him doesn't mean he's the only one who can do it."

*Under other circumstances, that would be a compelling argument. Certainly neither of you would be my first choice for a hero.*

"Hey," Nivvy said.

*But Nivvy is immune to the crown, and I can no longer scour the world for another champion worthy of the fight. I must make do with what I have, and what I have is you."*

"To do your revenge job."

*To do what needs to be done in the world.*

"Right." This was a moment when Nivvy really wanted to look Scarlet in the eyes, but the best he could do was look Zein in the eyes, trying to be their ally in this argument. "What's the world got to do with it? Why don't you try explaining to me exactly what's so bad about Rose having all those powers while it was perfectly fine for you to have them. Didn't you kill people, too?"

Scarlet was quiet for so long that Zein said, "I think you made her mad. Maybe she won't talk to us anymore."

"That's fine too." Nivvy was about to get up when the djinn spoke again.

*I have no wish to rule human kingdoms. I have killed people, yes, but not out of any human ambition. I am—I was power, and when lesser power encounters greater, sometimes it does not survive. But my killings were not motivated by passion. Rose, as you have heard from the stories, is quite passionate.*

"The stories you told us," Nivvy said.

*And that you have witnessed.*

"I didn't really witness anything." Zein looked around alertly and then locked eyes with Nivvy again.

*She turned a horse into a dragon,* Scarlet said. *She has even now flown into the kingdom of Heiterflus on the back of a dragon to reclaim her throne, when there were countless subtler and less destructive ways to do that. She will not hesitate to continue to use magic to destroy whatever she can of the world before someone inevitably destroys her.*

"So...you want me to destroy her before someone else does."

*In a quieter, safer way.*

"You're worried about the potential damage to humans and their cities. Right? 'Scuse me if that concern don't quite ring true. Based on what I witnessed."

*You can believe whatever you want. What I have seen in the world dwarfs your experiences combined. I can assure you that when I tell you an act is necessary, it is necessary.*

"Why didn't you kill her when you had the chance? You knew she was dangerous. Why didn't you kill her and me when we stole the ring from you?"

*I should have. I wish I had. But I was being cautious. I thought Rose had enough power that she might have cursed me, and...she was a relic of the past.*

To Zein, Nivvy said, "She has a whole hall full of artifacts she's collected through the years. It's interesting to walk through."

*Yes. Rose was like an artifact I wanted to keep in my hall. But she might have been able to cast a curse that would cause me great harm. Remember that she might have helped kill my sister.*

"And you're careful."

"Bad things can happen even to careful people," Zein said, shifting the talon the ring was circling.

*Yes, they can,* Scarlet said wearily.

## 27

# THE FATE OF THE DJINN

The days grew warmer and warmer. They left the Merkhar Forest behind, and the northern mountains gave way to shallow hills. Scarlet knew stories about some of the towns they passed and told them, in between continuing to pressure them to go after Rose.

Most of the time, Nivvy reassured himself that he didn't have to make the decision until after returning Scarlet to her volcano, and put it out of his mind. But in some moments, usually as he lay trying to sleep or after waking in the morning, he told himself that the decision was going to have to be made sometime. He could keep putting it off, but not forever.

Nivvy did not want to confess it to Scarlet, but her words were working on him. He would have talked to Zein, but there was no chance to hide any conversation from Scarlet without removing the ring from his finger. So he turned over the arguments in his mind, lying on his blanket or sometimes while riding Rahila along the southbound road.

Rose was pretty clearly not going to be a good queen, at least from the perspective of the people she was ruling over, and as one of those non-royal people, Nivvy sympathized. It put him in mind of the time when the jellyfish would come into the harbor. They were dangerous, and something needed to be done about them, but not everyone was suited to that. His people put on a feast for the brave jellyfish trappers who waded into the water with nets and scoops, and they also held a funeral for those who did not survive their heroism.

Rose was much more dangerous than a cluster of jellyfish. Nivvy had an idea of how many more people she could harm, but that made the smell of the funeral meats in his nose sharper. He wanted to be a good person, but Inira taught that the first step to being a good person was to make sure you were alive to keep being a good person. You should take care of yourself first, and help others when they needed it, especially other followers of Inira.

For all Scarlet's angry rhetoric about gods, Inira had rarely led Nivvy astray. Yes, one might argue that being tied to a wooden wheel in the baking sun in a town that smelled of dirt and manure qualified as "astray," or maybe being blamed for Vicho's death and kicked out of the Thieves Guild in the first place, or even being turned into a weasel, but Nivvy believed that Inira had also led him back here, to a place where he had escaped from all that (or the first and third, anyway) and had a chance to build a life.

What would Inira say about going against Rose? She would not be in favor of it unless there were some way Nivvy would benefit from it. In the Thieves Guild there was a game they played called What Price, in which you had to tell all your friends how much reward it would take for you to rob them. Vila, who always seemed inclined to take things too far, had a habit of adding, "and if they want me to kill ya, it'll be three times that," and then laughing.

Nivvy couldn't think of a price that would be right for him to go after Rose with the intention of probably killing her. He could set aside any question of loyalty—she had abandoned him before saving him, after all—but not the very real peril. Weighing against the peril was Scarlet's fear that Rose could literally take over the world, which Nivvy found himself more and more inclined to believe. This was not jellyfish in a harbor; this was a tidal wave heading for his home. Maybe it was years away, but if there'd been a tidal wave heading toward Copper Port, wouldn't everyone there have done their best to stop it?

The only time he'd done anything like that had been that business with the ruby crown, and he had to admit that more than once in his year of exile from the Thieves Guild, he'd thought, *Well, if I did nothing else in my life, I spared a lot of people from becoming slaves.* It had been and was still a comfort. Putting aside his conflicted personal feelings about

Rose, if she really was a world-threatening danger, defeating her would be something he could be proud of no matter what happened after.

Course, there seemed a fair chance that if he tried it, there wouldn't be an after for him. But it would still be something to be proud of, even if he wouldn't be around to enjoy that.

He did talk with Zein about his dilemma, one morning when Scarlet was being quiet and Rahila trotted through tendrils of mist in the cool air. The sun warmed his left side, and Zein, perched on the pommel of the saddle, had just turned from watching the road ahead to watching Nivvy. "My left is too warm and my right is chilly," they complained.

"Wish I could turn around," Nivvy said. After a pause, he added, "You could fly back to Spire, you know."

Zein cocked their head. "I'm enjoying the adventure. I can feed myself and I'm helping get food for you, too. And Scarlet tells good stories. Also, I want to see her cave now and all those artifacts. It sounds so interesting."

"Right," Nivvy said. "And after that?"

"I don't know." The hawk studied him. "Are you going to stay in Spire?" Before he could answer, they went on. "I think you should. It's a lovely city, big enough for people to do whatever they want. You could be a thief there. I know you had some trouble with the Thieves Guild but you can figure that out."

There was something: if he went after Rose, he wouldn't have to deal with the Thieves Guild. "Are you going to stay in Spire?"

"Where else would I go? I suppose if you wanted to go to another city, and you wanted a hawk to go with you, I could go along. If I do get shot again, you'll have a much easier time fighting off the hunters."

Nivvy laughed shortly and then stopped, remembering the dread he'd felt at how close Zein had come to death, how it had been his fault. "You're welcome anytime. Few enough people I can rely on in this world that I don't want to turn my back on one of them."

"I feel the same way!" Zein said. "The other former-humans mostly just complain about how they're treated, which I understand, because in general it's terrible, but some of them are really well looked after. But we don't really do anything except sit and talk to each other, and that means something, it really does, to have someone else who understands what you're going through. You understand too, though, and you still want to go adventure."

"Course I do. Though I might want to keep the adventures small for a little."

Zein spread their wings, stretching. "Then you don't think you'll go to fight Rose?"

"I haven't decided yet. I'm not an assassin, you know." They both looked at the ring, but Scarlet remained quiet. "What do you think I should do?"

"Oh, I can't tell you that. The hero can't have someone tell him to go on his adventure."

"Sure he can." Nivvy laughed. "Happens all the time."

"What if I told you to go and then you got killed? What if I told you not to and then Rose destroyed Spire? I'm just glad it's not my decision to make."

"Well," Nivvy said, "Right, I see that, an' I wish it weren't my decision either. Do you really think I'm a hero?"

"I think you could be. But you don't have to be. The heroes in the stories, they don't always have it easy. And what if you're part of another story and you're not the hero at all?"

Nivvy nodded. "I know just what you mean."

They rode on in silence until Zein turned again to look at the road ahead. Then Nivvy asked, "If I do go, will you come with me?"

They half-turned their head. "Of course I will. I want to see how the story ends. Even if it's not yours."

Later in the day, when Zein had left to scout ahead of them, Scarlet spoke to him. *You still have not made your decision, I see.*

So she had been listening. "Try to see it from my perspective, eh?"

*I have tried. It is difficult to cut myself off from so much knowledge and experience, but I have managed it. Somewhat.*

"I could put a glove on over the ring if that would help."

*If you mean to restrict my perception of the world around me, a glove would make no difference.*

"Good to know." He kept riding.

ONE NIGHT, NIVVY DREAMED THAT HE WAS BACK IN THE SHALLOWS where he'd grown up, wading out into the tide to scavenge. Usually, the waves threw up little of value, which was why Nivvy preferred to skulk around the alleys of Copper Port proper, but in this dream, detritus floated thickly on the surface of the waves, and he had to push it aside to wade through it. He was dimly aware that he should just pick through what was floating against his legs, but the certainty that something better was out deeper in the water drove him past floating timbers (which might be used for home repairs) and lengths of cloth (which might be a new robe) until he was up to his chest in the water.

Something glimmered white, floating ahead of him. A swell brought it closer, and he made it out to be a small porcelain doll with black hair. Excited, he strode toward it and picked it out of the water; a prize like this came along once a year. Dried out and cleaned, it might feed his family for a month.

He turned the doll over. Its face had a couple cracks in it, but there were miraculously no serious chips out of it. It looked as though it had fallen out of a child's hands into the water just an hour before. The eyes were made of grey glass, but when he turned it over, they glimmered green.

And then the eyes fixed on his and the lips moved.

"Are you on your way here?" the doll said in Rose's voice.

Nivvy startled and almost dropped it. His blood chilled, and the entire dream seemed to become colder. "I'm takin' Zein back to Spire," he said.

"I'm Queen of Heiterflus now," it said with some satisfaction.

"It's been, what, a week?"

"It took a little longer than I expected," the doll said. "But the dragon was perfect, and Scarlet's power did the rest."

"Did you burn the castle down?"

"It's stone, and where would I live if I burned it down? No." The doll chuckled. "But some of the people, yes. Don't worry, I let many of them live. And I have you to thank for that."

Nivvy's dread mounted. He did not feel like being thanked for anything involved in this, so he didn't pursue it. "Well, good, so you've got what you want an' I don't see as you need me no more, right?"

"I simply wish to reward you for your service. Head of the Thieves Guild, is that not what you wanted? You have shown me how much you know and are capable of."

He wanted to throw the doll back in the water, but he couldn't make his hands obey him. "Aye, that's me all right," he said. "All capable and whatnot. But listen, we're not nearly at Spire yet so it might be another week or more, then I gotta come north and find you."

"Tell me where you are, and I will send the dragon for you. The hawk can make its own way to Spire, or the dragon can go there."

"Right. Course. Listen, the dragon, I just worry it might alarm folks, y'understand? Just be patient. I'll make my way back."

The doll laughed, as sharp and brittle as its porcelain lips. "You needn't be afraid. Sigurd won't hurt you unless I tell her to. Where are you?"

"No, sure she won't," Nivvy said. "I just, I don't know if I can—"

Though the porcelain features of the doll remained fixed, Rose's tone grew colder. "Don't think that I can't have you brought to me. For the last time, where are you?"

"I don't really know." Nivvy's heart pounded. "I don't, honest."

He waited for a response, but the doll was lifeless in his hands again. Shaking, he threw it back into the ocean and a moment later sat up on his blanket, panting.

Clouds covered the moon. Rahila stood nearby, Zein on her saddle, both motionless. A long moment of staring revealed the slow rise and fall of the horse's chest. Bella was nowhere in sight.

"Scarlet?" he whispered, closing the hand on whose finger the ring sat.

*I don't want to hear about your dream*, the djinn said tiredly.

"Rose spoke to me in my dream."

Scarlet's voice sharpened. *What did she say?*

He told her briefly, though the conversation was running out of his mind like sand through his fingers. "She said she's queen and she wants to bring me back."

*She told you she wanted you to come to her. We talked about you taking the mirror when you go.*

"Yes, but—" Nivvy laced his fingers together. "If I go to fight her, it's my choice. If I go back to serve her, it's my choice. If she drags me back...it ain't my life then. Not my story anymore."

*If you choose not to fight her, then you will serve her and get a taste of her power, which is more power than you will ever come by naturally. In either case, you are going back to her, so I don't see what the problem is.*

"The problem is..." Nivvy took a breath. "I don't think I want a taste of that power. After seein' what she did with it."

*I don't think "not going back to her" is a choice you have, now. The choice you have is whether you go back as a friend or a foe.*

"She's already suspicious," he said. "What if it's already too late? What if she don't trust me now? I won't be able to get close enough to use the mirror or to serve her. I'm doomed."

*Now we have at least one thing in common. If you're asking me whether I think Rose could kill you, I think you already know the answer. But I do not think she is seeking you out in order to kill you. She values your company; that much was clear even when you came to steal the ring.*

"Clear? How?"

*Because she sent you away when she wanted to tell me about Glædeligdal. She cared what you thought of her. Now you are the one who has been with her and helped her to her triumph and listened to her dreams. She wants you there to witness her reign.*

Nivvy took in a deep breath. This made him feel like a pet who'd wandered away from its master, and he did not like that feeling. "She's using your powers. Why doesn't she just come down and get me?"

*I never cared much for finding specific people. Carmine could do that. I've no doubt if Rose wanted to find you, she could, but it would take a lot of effort and she'd likely have to come down here herself to do it, or send a part of herself in something, maybe the dragon, as I did with this ring. But that's complicated magic and she might not know how to do it.*

"You underestimated her before."

A pause. *You are right. But if she could easily come find you, she would have, therefore you can assume that she can't. I rarely went into dreams, but I did for her, which is probably why she knows she can do it. Creating dreams is easier than going out and finding people in the real world. I often had to try for hours to catch someone in a dream, but it was better than going out and searching for months.*

"So she wanted me badly enough to spend hours to send a message."

*Maybe hours over several nights.*

Nivvy's hands shook. He pressed them under his arms. "I hoped she would forget about me, leave me alone."

*If you like, when we get home, I have a charm that will keep your dreams private.*

"Yes," he said quickly.

*But if Rose thinks you're hiding from her...*

"I don't care," he said. "I don't want to dream about her again."

*I don't blame you.*

"Thank you." Nivvy lay back down so he could see Rahila and Zein. Every time he closed his eyes, he saw the doll's face again. It took him a long time to get back to sleep.

৩৺৵

THE IRIDI MOUNTAINS APPEARED AS SMUDGES ON THE HORIZON THE next day, and two days after that, Zein returned with the news that they had spotted the spire of Spire and the Mountain of Fire.

Nivvy had just been thinking that he dearly wanted to wash his clothes. Rose would have insisted on it long ago, but he did not want to think of her. Since Haggerin's perfumed bath, they had crossed two rivers that carried some mineral scent down from the mountains, so he smelled like his own odor plus some mix of those rivers.

Unfortunately, his only bathing options at the volcano were Scarlet's cave and the Bouli temple, and he was not anxious to see the priests at the temple again. As a human, they'd been proper nice to him, but now he'd know that niceness was a façade. Maybe the cage they'd kept him in was still there and he could steal it as a souvenir.

No; he didn't want a souvenir. He wanted to cram one of the priests into it and make them swing from the roof the way they'd done to him. But that wasn't why he was here. He was here to return Scarlet to her cave and get the mirror from her, and then...and then figure out what came next.

But the urge to run into the temple and steal something, or scream at the priests, or stab someone, returned when the three red triangles shone in the late afternoon sunlight out of the dark grey stone building. "If any of them are outside," he told Zein, riding on the pommel again, "maybe you could shit on them for me?"

They laughed shortly. "I appreciate that you think I can aim that well. I've been very careful not to do that in places where it might hit people. Although I did get blamed for it once and I told the person that it wasn't me, but I don't think they believed me."

"It was worth a shot." He sighed and eyed the trail up the volcano, then patted Rahila's neck as the mare slowed, trying to turn away. "Come on, h'san," he said. "I don't want to leave you at the temple, so you gotta come up the mountain with us."

She allowed him to guide her to the temple and a short way beyond, but when the path became steep and rocky, she shied and wouldn't go on no matter how much Nivvy coaxed her. When he dismounted and tried to lead her up the slope, she went a short way, but the first time rocks slid out from under her feet, she backed up and wouldn't go forward again.

*Can't you leave the nag?* Scarlet asked.

"She's not a nag," Nivvy growled, wrestling with the mare and being dragged backwards. "She knows what she wants and doesn't want."

"She doesn't want to go up the mountain, that's for sure," Zein observed from the pommel.

Nivvy stopped, hands on hips, and stared down at the temple. "If I leave her here, I don't trust that those priests won't come and take her," he said.

*Didn't you tell Rose that she wouldn't go with anyone but you? Then she went with Rose. Ah, I see the worry.*

Nivvy stared at the horse, who stared back at him defiantly. "Why you gotta be so stubborn?" he asked her. "We can't walk up there before dark without you."

*The bird could carry me up.*

"If they carry you up," Nivvy said aloud, looking at Zein, "could you bring that dream-charm down as well?"

"Not that and a mirror. Let's wait and all go together," Zein said. "We can camp here and maybe Rahila will feel different in the morning. I know I sometimes feel better after a good night's sleep. And there's plenty of mice around here I can eat."

"There's not much for her to eat." Nivvy looked down the path and all the rocks to the scant patches of grass a couple hundred feet downs-lope. He was hungry but could wait until morning, and still had some dried meat in his bags. But every night his sleep had been tense and fitful. He'd had dreams, and in every one he'd thrummed with an undercurrent of tension waiting for Rose to appear again. So far she hadn't.

*Fine. I've waited this long. I can wait one more day.*

One more night. It had been less than a week since his dream. Rose should grant him at least that much time.

They retreated down the slope, where Rahila grazed on grass and Zein hunted mice. Nivvy ate a little dried meat and brushed down

Rahila to soothe her. "How did you end up living in a volcano?" he asked Scarlet.

*I live where I please. I wanted to live somewhere remote, where people who wanted to find me would have trouble finding me and might die trying. Many did. Eventually stories of my work faded into nothing but words, and people stopped trying to find me, even though they built a city and that ridiculous tower three days away. The idiots at the temple sometimes come up, but they are mostly smart enough not to die.*

Nivvy looked up at the dark sky and the smattering of stars across it. "Do you like all the stories about you?"

*All the ones I've heard. Even if they get the facts wrong—and they almost always do—people are still talking about me.*

"You want to be talked about, but you don't want to be found." Nivvy rubbed his hand over Rahila's flank and patted it. She whickered and tossed her head.

*Doesn't everyone?*

"I like being around people." He stroked down Rahila's back and caught sight of Zein circling nearby. "When I'm around people, we end up telling stories about each other, so that takes care of that. I'd like for people to tell stories about me when I'm not around, but...comes in time, don't it?"

*It comes faster if you make it happen.*

"Been trying, but not the kind of thing you can force, eh? Got to take opportunities where you can and do the best you can with 'em. Like—you know the Tarisch Empire, across the eastern ocean?"

*Don't bother telling me. I don't care at all.*

"What good is it to have stories if people don't want to listen to 'em? I'd love to hear any of your stories."

*Of course you would. My stories are better than yours.*

"You won't even listen to mine."

*When you've defeated Rose, come back and tell me about it. That I would be glad to listen to.*

With a pat on Rahila's flank, Nivvy finished his grooming and walked a little way away to sit on the ground. "If I survive it."

*If you don't, I'll go north and hear it from her. Or I'll wait until she is destroyed and listen to that story.*

"You said you only had a decade."

*True. She might well last several decades before she exhausts magic.*

Zein soared back over and alit next to him, a dead mouse in their beak. Nivvy held out the hand with the ring on it and Zein allowed him to put it on their back while they ate. "What do you mean, *exhausts* magic?"

Scarlet didn't say anything. Nivvy stared at the ring, dread creeping over him. "You mean exhausts for everyone? Not just for her?"

*What do you think is happening in the world?* Scarlet asked. *Why are there no more miracles, no more floating cities, no more dragons? Why do you think Rose escaped her prison? Do you think it was somehow cursed to last exactly a thousand years? It has been one thousand twenty-six years and three months since my sister imprisoned her in the body of my other sister. The spell was a powerful one and required a great deal of magic to work, and to continue to work. There is no longer enough magic in the world to sustain it.*

"Hold up," Nivvy said. "She said she cast a counterspell. Didn't she? Am I remembering that wrong?"

*A ruse to deceive me into thinking she might still have magic. Which worked. Just as I pretended not to know the length of her imprisonment so she might not know how much I was involved.*

"Wait, you didn't tell us that part," Nivvy said. "You were involved?"

*That isn't important. What's important is that the magic has faded.*

Zein stopped eating and turned their head to look at Nivvy. "Magic is going away anyway? Even without Rose?"

*Are you having trouble understanding my words? Magic is weaker now than it was a thousand years ago, and weaker then than it was three thousand years before that, when my sisters and I were born. I believe—though I do not know for sure—that this is why artifacts now require stories to activate, why wizards can no longer draw directly on magic, why the great palace at Vali'ala fell fifty years ago.*

"I heard about that," Nivvy said. "They said it was the work of evil djinn."

*I am not the only djinn left, but I seriously doubt that. The palace was built with magic. Its floating chambers could not stay aloft by other means.*

"How have people not noticed this, if it's true?" Nivvy asked. "Seems like big magic things going away would get some notice."

*At least one person has noticed. The Suzerain of the Thousand Kingdoms summoned me to his court eighty-six years ago to answer this very question. He wanted to build a magical palace and was told it was impossible. Many of his advisors, in the course of their research throughout the land far and wide, found that a century had passed since the last great magical work was created, but in that time, three magical works had ceased to exist.*

"What did you tell him?"

*What I am telling you. Magic is weaker now than it was. I cannot say why.*

Zein swallowed a bit of mouse. "Could you have built the palace for him?"

*He also asked that. I told him that if he wished it to fall apart in a hundred years, I could do it, but I did not wish to.*

"What kind of person had that much power over you?" Nivvy asked. "I can't even get you to answer a question properly."

*I am bound by rules. The world has many more rules than you can possibly know.*

"See? That's what I'm talking about."

Zein gulped the last bit of the mouse. "I always thought it was just that the old stories were exaggerated. People get turned into animals, but I've never seen anyone cast a curse. Or build a magical palace. There's the Spire, but when you get to the top of that it's just bricks and mortar. Maybe they were put there by magic, but they stay on their own. So...I thought people made up stories about things that happened, then made them sound fancy so they would be better stories. Oigal says that's how stories work. Like the Lake Beatrice story where he said it was mostly there to be a lesson to people. But then that turned out to be real. So I don't know."

"So," Nivvy said, putting things together, "is that why you want me to stop Rose? You worry she'll use up magic?"

*I don't "worry." I know she will.*

"Because of the dragon."

*And because of how long I've known her and the power she longed for, but more importantly, the acclaim she craves. If respect does not come to her, she will force it.*

"That sounds like her," Nivvy said.

*How grateful I am that your two weeks of her acquaintance agrees with my fifty years.*

"You've an awful sharp manner for someone asking someone else a favor."

Zein gave a short laugh. "I don't think she can help it, honestly. Some people have to be the way they are and they can't change. And those people have only been around for thirty years, not thousands. I can't imagine how hard it would be to pretend like people actually matter to you if you've lived a hundred times their lifetime."

*Wise bird.*

"Doesn't mean I have to listen to her." Nivvy rubbed Zein's feathers. "Best thing to do with folk like that is leave 'em to themselves. They want pleasant company, they can learn to be pleasant."

Scarlet said, *This is not about company—*

Zein interrupted. "I do wonder, though, what will happen to you if magic gets all used up. Scarlet, I mean, not you, Nivvy. I don't expect you or I would be much affected by it."

"Fewer former-humans about," Nivvy said. "I guess that's good for them but maybe bad for you? Less company?"

"I'm quite happy with my life as it is now. I'd like to be accepted by people, but also I get to fly. But not all of my former-human group are happy. Shanti hates living in the water. She says it's like a moving prison. And all of that is magic. Of course, I suppose there are unhappy people who haven't had anything to do with magic, but none of them are stuck in a pond they don't like."

*Magic has also built. That spire that your precious city is named for was built with magic. The Thousand Kingdoms were founded after the Great War of Jalaic and Tacca, which was fought with magic. Magic has been a part of the foundation of this land since I was born, and it is being used up. Rose will use it up even faster.*

"She couldn't use up all the magic," Nivvy said, and then stared down at the ring. "Could she?"

*I don't know. There's no lake of magic I can travel to that shows a draining of it. But by the feel of it, I think a Rose determined to make a show of her power and conquer other nations could very easily use a great deal of magic in a short period of time.*

"And then," Zein persisted. "What would happen to you? Oigal says djinni are made of magic, so would you...die?"

"She's going to die anyway," Nivvy said. "She's told us. In a decade or so."

"But this could happen faster."

Nivvy returned his gaze to the ring. "That would explain why she's so bound and determined to knock down Rose." When Scarlet didn't say anything, Nivvy asked, "Why didn't you tell us this from the start?

Magic goin' out of the world seems a lot bigger than people from some country I never been to getting murdered."

There was a moment of hesitation, and then Scarlet said, *I thought that you would care more about people than magic. And...it is true. Rose's use of magic could end my days sooner than I will naturally die without my power to sustain me.*

"Didn't you just come back here to die?" Nivvy asked, and then immediately regretted his flippancy. "Sorry. I know what it's like to not want to tell people things."

*I did want to die*, Scarlet said. *But I will confess that remembering the stories of my life and others has made me reluctant to embrace death more quickly than I need to.*

"I get that too," Nivvy said. "It's the big reason I don't want to fight Rose."

"There's other magical creatures too, aren't there?" Zein asked.

"Wait." Nivvy sat up in alarm, his hand slipping off the hawk for a moment. "Could all the former-humans also die?"

Scarlet waited until he had returned his hand to the hawk before replying. *I'm so tired of telling you that I don't know. But I don't think so. They exist in non-magical forms. You don't need to keep striking a flint to keep a fire going.*

Nivvy relaxed. "Well, all right then."

*It should be astonishing to me that you measure the scale of a world-wide catastrophe based on how it will affect the tiny portion of the world you know directly, but I have known enough humans to have given up being astonished at your idiocy centuries ago.*

"Sorry we idiots are all you have left to extend your life another paltry few years," Nivvy said, and, peeved, told a little lie. "Yer not making me more inclined to help, if that's what you were trying to do."

*I've never had to ask one of you to do something for me, so I'm not surprised I'm bad at it.* Scarlet paused and then said, *I'm done. Just take me to my cave tomorrow.*

## ❧ 28 ❧

# THE FIRE OF THE MOUNTAIN

In the morning, Nivvy had more success coaxing Rahila up the rocky slope. She didn't like the loose rocks, but in the diffuse light from the cloud-covered sky, Nivvy could guide her away from the worst patches, and she responded to his confidence. At the disguised cave entrance, though, she backed away from the heat and smell of sulfur and nearly skidded back onto the path before Nivvy stopped her.

So Nivvy left her, as she did not seem very inclined to walk back down the rocky path alone, and he went on with Zein on his shoulder and Scarlet's ring on his finger, through the illusion and past the dead bat onto the path that skirted the scorching lava-filled pit at the center of the volcano. The hellish red glow cast shadows through heat-rippled air onto the walls, which made them seem to move of themselves.

"I don't like this." Zein fluttered on Nivvy's right shoulder, which happened to be the one nearer the lava. "Move me to the other side, if you please."

*Don't stop*, Scarlet said. *I'm almost there.*

Probably another hundred feet remained, and it wasn't like Nivvy was going to jog them. "You can wait a moment," he said.

"All right," Zein said meekly, and then, "Oh!" as he lifted his hands to the folded cloth their claws were dug into.

"Sorry." Nivvy moved them carefully to the other shoulder and waited until he felt their talons secure around his shoulder. "Scarlet didn't want to stop even for a moment."

"I understand how nice it is to come home," Zein said. "I'm sorry to delay you."

*At least the hawk has manners*, Scarlet sniffed.

"More than you do." Nivvy continued edging along the wall, and then added, "Manners, I mean," to clarify for Zein. "Who wouldn't wait for a minute or two if a friend wasn't feeling well?"

*All of my friends are dead.*

"Well, that's cheery." Nivvy turned to Zein. "She says all her friends are dead."

"Oh, that's terrible." Zein kept their eyes turned toward the wall. "I suppose if I lived forever, all my friends would die eventually too. But then the nice thing is that you get to make new ones. And now she has us."

Nivvy did not think Scarlet would respond to this, and she did not. "She's being dramatic," he said. "She said there were other djinn still alive."

*And do you consider every other thief in the world your friend, little weasel?*

"Thief is a profession, not something yer born as." Nivvy placed his feet carefully. "Where's the door?"

*I'll tell you when we get there.*

"She doesn't have to be friends with all the other djinn." Zein stared at the wall and away from the lava. "I'm not friends with all the former-humans in Spire."

"But you meet with them all the time."

"I know, but I'm not friends with all of them. I like Terria a lot because she's very cheerful, and Kelli is nice because he can fly too. Not just because he can fly. He's nice too. And Vilan, I don't get to see him very much but he always has the funniest stories. He was turned into a rat, so he can sneak into anywhere and he has a knack for finding people doing strange things."

If Zein was back to their talkative ways, it meant they were less scared of the volcano, so Nivvy let them go on about the former-humans in Spire while he concentrated on keeping his feet well away from the edge.

"Is it here?" Nivvy asked, stopping at what looked like a likely spot.

*I said I would tell you. It's farther along*, Scarlet snapped.

"All right, all right. Don't pretend I'm not in a hurry to be quit of you either."

Nivvy came up to another spot that looked familiar, and here Scarlet spoke before he could. *Here*, she said. *But wait.*

"Wait? You been pushin' me to run along this ledge and now you want to wait?"

*One word of caution. Let me talk to the hawk as well.*

Nivvy lifted the hand with the ring to rest on Zein's talons, and Scarlet went on. *I was always able to sense when someone entered my home. It is possible that Rose now has that ability.*

"What?" Nivvy exclaimed, just as Zein said, "That doesn't sound very safe."

*I will lead you to the mirror, and then you should leave as quickly as possible with it. If Rose appears, we may be able to use the mirror right here, but I suspect she will not be that foolhardy.*

"And the dream-charm," Nivvy said.

*Yes, that as well. I think we will have time. Rose may not even have the sense, and if she does, may not understand immediately what it is.*

"Good, as long as we're relying on someone else to not understand how easy they can kill us, I feel loads better," Nivvy said. He cast a glance back along the ledge, but even if he wasn't going to use the mirror—which he still hadn't decided—the dream-charm was in there, and he did want that, very badly. "Let's go get this over with."

The illusory wall and the step up were just as Nivvy remembered, and as he stepped into the cool air of Scarlet's cave, Zein fluttered in alarm and then said, "Oh! This is magnificent."

*Take me to the menagerie*, Scarlet ordered.

"You can fly on ahead," Nivvy said. "Don't know as I'd touch anything that looks like it might be magic, because it probably is."

"I'll stay with you. I don't feel right flying around someone else's home when they're not here."

Nivvy didn't bother pointing out that Scarlet was in fact here, because the menagerie was the next room. He crossed into the creepy still tableau of animals, and at that point Zein said, "I think I will fly ahead. Just call me when you're ready to leave."

They took off from his shoulder, sending the cloth to the ground, and flew on through the still life animals into the long corridor where weapons and armor hung. Nivvy looked around at all the animals, trying not to meet any of the frozen, glassy eyes.

*Take the ring to that one, the eagle*, Scarlet said.

To his left, a tree protruded from what looked like the natural wall of the cave, its trunk starting about fifteen feet from the ground. On the tree perched a variety of birds, from sparrows to crows to one great eagle dominating the crown, hooked yellow beak haughtily raised to survey the motley assemblage of animals below. "It's all the way up there," Nivvy said. "Can I throw you at it? Will that work?"

*In my day, thieves could climb,* Scarlet replied.

He sighed and walked between a large cat he didn't recognize and what looked like a relative of a sand fox, trying not to touch any of the animals. When he got to the wall, he found enough handholds for purchase anywhere he started. "When I climbed the tallest tower of the royal palace of the Tarisch Empire, in Tarischi, I had a rope anchored at the top and a harness to help."

*If you can't do it, call the hawk back and have them take the ring.*

He reached for a handhold and pushed himself up. "I can do it."

He hadn't climbed anything like this in over a year, but the memory came back to his fingers and feet well enough. When he got to the tree, he stared at a large bird with a red crest clinging to the bark. "Are the animals alive?"

*Enough to serve my purpose.*

Nivvy swallowed and looked away from the bird. "Right," he said. "On we go, then."

Climbing the tree was easier than climbing the wall because there were so many branches to hold onto, and harder because on many of the branches, birds perched, frozen in the act of turning their head or staring down at the ground. Nivvy avoided them as best he could, but halfway up he put his foot on a branch that he thought was clear and kicked something that came loose.

He yanked his foot back, almost unbalancing himself, and watched as a small bird fell from the tree to the ground, where it lay on its side. "Sorry," he said.

*It doesn't matter at all, but if it would make you feel better, you may replace it after you reach the eagle.*

"Don't know what part of this is going to make me feel better," Nivvy muttered, but he kept climbing, more slowly now so that he could check every spot of the brown, jagged bark before he rested his hand or foot on it. Just like a thief ought to do, he reminded himself, and thanked Inira for the calm focus he was able to bring to it, even with the threat of Rose discovering them at any moment.

*Finally*, Scarlet remarked as he reached the top branch. It barely bent under his weight, and not for the first time, he wondered what manner of tree this was that could grow out of the side of a mountain and thrive without sunlight or water. Its small oval leaves and hard bark felt real enough, but clearly it fed on something Nivvy couldn't see.

But here he was at the top of it, and there within reach was the eagle's talon, gripping the branch. *Slide the ring over the claw*, Scarlet ordered.

Nivvy obliged and then let go. He leaned back against the tree, keeping his eye on the ring and the large body of the eagle above it.

For a moment, nothing happened. Then the talon flexed, letting the ring drop to the ground, and the great body shifted, feathers sliding over one another. A noise came from the beak, and then the head shook, and a raspy voice, barely comprehensible, issued from it. "Need...water."

"Um." Nivvy stared around. "Where is there water?"

"Other cave. Where we talked." The eagle's wings lifted briefly and then fell back.

From here, it was a forty-foot drop to the ground, Nivvy estimated. So he climbed back down the tree, careful not to dislodge any other birds, and then dropped from the trunk to the ground into a clear space.

The hallway beyond felt twice as long as he remembered. He passed the curved blade from which a face had screamed at him, the suits of armor and bracers and wands. Zein, perched on the shoulder of a standing suit of armor, said, "Hallo. Have you ever seen so many swords?"

"I have to get water," Nivvy said, pointing ahead. "Scarlet's an eagle now." That was as much explanation as he felt he could deliver while still hurrying to get water. The sight of the many swords sparked the thought that he could, while Scarlet was in a weakened state, return with a sword and kill her, but that didn't feel like a very heroic thing to do, and anyway she was going to give him a dream-charm and this mirror that would let him defeat Rose if he were inclined to do so. Now that the djinn wasn't powerful anymore, and moreover had been reduced to the body of an animal, she was a former-human as much as Zein, as much as Nivvy had been, and so the thought of killing her retreated from whence it had come without leaving so much as an itch behind.

He avoided the whispering room of smoky ideas and the other still dark archway and entered the middle door at the end of the hall, still brightly lit. There in the small salon where Scarlet and Rose had sat and discussed the murder of the kingdom of Glædeligdal, Nivvy checked every likely-looking vessel and found one that held water, a clay jug with a narrow mouth. Mindful that the eagle's beak couldn't reach into it, he brought along a shallow dish from the cabinet nearby and hurried back to the menagerie.

Zein followed him, taking off from the armor and gliding down the hallway behind him, where there was enough room for them to bank from side to side under the high arched ceiling. When they reached the menagerie, Zein landed on the floor just outside. "I don't want to go back in," they said. "It's creepy. All those dead animals."

"Not quite dead." Nivvy didn't tell them about the provenance of the animals. One thing at a time, and he had to get water up to—no, the eagle was on the floor now, walking about.

"That's worse," Zein called to him as he picked his way through all the animals, trying not to touch any of them.

Nivvy placed the bowl in front of the eagle, who stopped walking and tried again to stretch her wings, with a little more success. He emptied the water jug into the bowl and stepped back.

The eagle drank thirstily, lifted her head, then drank again. After four drinks, she fixed Nivvy with an eye. "Thank you," she said, more clearly.

A small feather floated in the water, smaller than would have come from the eagle. Nivvy looked for the bird he'd knocked out of the tree and couldn't see it anywhere. He knew with the certainty of a some-what experienced thief that the two were related. "Ah," he said, "thought you didn't have enough magic left to possess a body."

"Not your body," the eagle said, "but this one was little more than a vessel anyway. Now, I suppose you'll be wanting that mirror."

"I suppose," Nivvy said. "But the dream charm first, and let's hurry about it."

Scarlet stepped toward him, and Nivvy took a startled step back. The beak was sharp enough to do some damage, not to mention the angry talons that scraped at the rock floor. "Listen, you little creature," Scarlet said.

The incongruity of being called "little" by a bird that didn't come up to his waist emboldened Nivvy. "No, listen, you," he said. "Don't call me little. You want me to save magic or save your life again or whatever, how about you treat me with the respect due to someone you think might be able to do it? How about that?"

"When you've done something worthy of my respect, then you'll receive it," the eagle snapped back.

"Saving your life once doesn't count?"

"I saved my own life, and you followed my instructions well enough to get me back to this body where at least I can speak aloud and perhaps in a day or a week I'll be able to fly. But don't think that's worthy of respect. You want respect? You want to be in one of those stories I see you drinking in so greedily? Then do something worthwhile."

What if a story about him did, somehow, make its way back to Copper Port, to his uncles and aunt and cousins, to the Thieves Guild there? That would vindicate him more than anything else could. And more, it was a chance to do something good for the world. Maybe not saving magic, which seemed as often used to cause hurt as to cause joy, but delivering the northern kingdom and the rest of the world from Rose—saving people, real people, from a dragon-riding fairy-powered woman, that was a story for sure.

Scarlet didn't think much of him, that was clear, but she must have thought him capable of defeating Rose, or she wouldn't be giving him the only weapon that would work—if she were telling the truth about that, which he couldn't judge. If he turned his back on this chance, what would he say to himself in years to come? The job in Tarisch had been scary and dangerous as well, but there had been the brooch to claim, and he'd been handsomely paid for the danger he'd risked. Only in coin, though. His heroic performance in a foreign land had not become a story the way he'd hoped.

He could also become part of a story people told their children if he went north to serve Rose. Or, with the dream-charm, he could run from her long enough to live out his life, his part in her story written and done. But he did not think he would like either of those stories. "All right," he said. "Where's this mirror?"

While he'd been pondering, the eagle had turned away from him, staring down at the ground (or so it seemed), and now the air in front of him shimmered and then Scarlet as he'd known her appeared in front of him. "There," she said. "That seemed to work. Come, I'll show you."

When she walked toward him, her footsteps clicked even though she appeared to be wearing soft slippers. "Oh," Nivvy said. "The ring."

The withering expression she turned on him shouldn't have been a surprise, really; who better to know her face and expressions than she who'd worn them for thousands of years. But it took him aback regardless. "Yes." She walked past him and past Zein, shuffling slowly down the hallway.

"She's really an eagle," he told Zein, who watched them pass bemusedly. "She's just using the ring to look like her former self."

"Oh. I didn't think it was really her, but you never know, do you? May I ride on your shoulder? I can't fly that slowly."

Scarlet turned to look balefully at the hawk as Nivvy picked up Zein's cloth and placed it on his shoulder. Zein alit there and kept talking. "Whatever you need to do, you should do, but speaking from experience, and not just mine but all the other former-humans, the best thing is to think about the good things about your new shape. If you're an eagle, you can fly, and that's a good feeling. You have to watch out for people trying to shoot you down, which isn't as good, but most of them have terrible aim, so there is that. Also you should keep a friend around in case you do get shot. I know that's not easy but it did save my life."

Nivvy's cheeks warmed. Scarlet, however, seemed unimpressed. "This is the best I could do with what I had left. Flying is indeed why I chose this shape, but I assure you I do not intend to fly anywhere someone with an arrow might even spot me. I will live here, surrounded by my trophies, until my life ebbs away—or until Rose kills me—and then I will die among them."

"That sounds terribly grim," Zein said. "Why not go see a sunrise from the top of the mountain? Or see how far south you can fly? Or go to the top of the spire in Spire? There's mostly birds there and most of them don't talk, which seems just right for you, if you don't mind me saying."

"Ha," Nivvy said. "If she still had magic, we'd have been silenced the whole trip back, I shouldn't wonder."

"If I still had magic, we would have used it to come back here, or I would've left you two and dealt with Rose myself as I should have done when you brought her here. Oh, this is maddening."

This last seemed to be aimed at her short steps and slow progress, so Nivvy ignored that part. "Brought her here? She brought me, or have you forgotten?"

"It's not that I forgot," Scarlet said. "It's that I don't care. She wouldn't have come without you, and you did try to steal this ring."

This didn't feel like a winnable argument, or even one worth trying to win. "Speaking of, shouldn't we be hurrying? Do you want me to carry you?" Nivvy asked.

"Certainly not," Scarlet snapped. "If Rose knew we were here, she'd have acted by now. She's still figuring it out, or she's busy and she ignored the feeling, or she didn't sense us at all. I had enough of being a ring on your finger. I'd much rather spend an extra few minutes walking under my own power than have to be carried again."

Nivvy wasn't sure he believed that, but he didn't know what exactly Rose would do if she knew they were here. Send the dragon? It would take at least a day to get here. And he didn't want to keep talking to the ungrateful djinn. "Right, then, you won't mind if I walk Zein around and show them some of my favorite things here? Just call when you've reached it, ay?"

Without waiting for an answer, he strode by Scarlet and took Zein down to the chest of rings. "That was a little rude," Zein said.

"She started it."

"Ay, but that doesn't mean you need to reply in kind. You don't act nice to people because you want them to act nice back to you; you do it because it's the best way to be."

Nivvy sighed, stopping some twenty feet short of the chest. He pointed. "That's the chest I stole the ring from, where she turned me into a weasel."

"There are a lot of rings there," Zein said.

"Aye."

"You must be a good thief to have found the right one."

Nivvy smiled. "All right," he said. "Let's go back to the eagle-djinn and keep her company."

"I don't need your company," Scarlet said as they returned.

"No, of course you don't," Nivvy said. "But Zein here feels some kinship to you now you're a flying former-human—or former-djinn, I suppose—and pointed out that just because you're rude doesn't mean we shouldn't give you comfort."

"I told you, I don't need your company."

"Maybe," Nivvy said to Zein, "Former-djinn are different from you and me. Maybe they prefer to be alone. She did live alone here for a long time."

"But she had visitors. And she kept mementoes of them. A big room like this, this feels like someone who wants to remember things."

"Doesn't mean she appreciates the company of people while they're here."

"True." Zein lifted a wing to preen it. "I just know that if I had a big room like this, I'd love to show it off to people."

"Enough!" Scarlet snapped. "Would you derive pleasure from the company of ants? That is what you are to me."

"I think she likes arguing with us, too," Nivvy said.

"Not ants." Zein responded to Scarlet. "But some people I know keep rats as pets, or cats, and falcons. They get pleasure from their company, and those animals don't even talk to them. We can at least talk."

Scarlet didn't reply, so Nivvy said, "They make a good point, they do. I have to say that I think we make passably good conversation."

"You're at least as good a conversationalist as you are a thief," Scarlet said.

Nivvy laughed. The weight of his decision to pursue Rose had eased with his decision to take the mirror. "I can see you meant that to be insulting but I'll take it as a compliment, and many thanks."

"You may take it however you like," Scarlet said without looking at him.

He mulled over that conciliatory statement as Zein asked about some of the trophies they were passing. Scarlet told stories about them, short at first: "That one was a raider from Fort of Sand—that's what Spire was before it was Spire—and I imprisoned him in his sword." But as Zein kept asking and expressing admiration, the stories grew longer: "That armor is a style that is no longer worn, probably because people discovered that there was a weakness where the arms were joined where a sword could slip through, but for a hundred years, all the knights from the western lands wore it. That design, the five-petaled flower, is from a kingdom a hundred miles from here whose enemy sought my help in destroying them. I could have turned all their soldiers to ash, but the king wanted them kept as slaves, so I merely tore apart their generals on the field in front of them, and they surrendered in moments."

She paused to look at the armor. "Possibly nobody remembers that kingdom now save for me."

"Sounds like a lovely anthill," Nivvy said.

"It was. It passed into dust like everything else."

"What happened to the kingdom that enslaved them?" Zein asked, their voice a little duller.

"They also passed into dust," Scarlet said. "Their emperor La-Oh ruled over more land than anyone else I have known, and she tried to pass the kingdom on to her eldest daughter, but her two younger sons conspired to assassinate the daughter, and when La-Oh found out, she banished them both. One went north and one went south, and after her death they returned with armies to take pieces of her empire that they felt belonged to them. Within a generation the empire had fallen into squabbling factions." She turned to Nivvy. "The anthill had been kicked over."

"I never heard of an emperor La-Oh," Nivvy said.

"Nor I," Zein said.

"I'm not surprised you don't get many stories from the west," Scarlet told them. "There were trade routes across the desert and mountains in La-Oh's time, but no longer. You may have seen that type of armor, or delicate glass that seems beyond your abilities to make, but such things were given to wealthy and powerful people, so I wouldn't be surprised to learn you'd never seen them."

"I've been in the rooms of wealthy and powerful people," Nivvy said. "Granted, they didn't know I was there, and I didn't have time to stop and look round, but I was there. What might this glass look like?"

"There's some of it in the room with the mirror." Scarlet gestured ahead of them. "The glass room. We are nearly there. But first, that dream-charm? It's a ring in that chest. Give me a moment."

She appeared to bend over the chest, but rather than her hands picking through the rings, she bent and shoved her face into the chest.

Nivvy clapped a hand to his mouth to stop himself laughing; the eagle was no doubt looking through with her beak and the magic of the ring only went so far.

A ring came clattering out of the chest, skittering across the floor past Nivvy's feet. He bent to pick it up: a silver ring with a trio of garnet-red stones in it. It looked to be too big, but when he slipped it onto his finger, the ring settled and then shrank to fit, which was somewhat unnerving.

Scarlet straightened. "There. Nobody can get to your dreams now." If she knew they had been watching her root around in the chest with her face, she gave no sign. "The mirror is just up here."

Fifteen feet ahead of them was an alcove he hadn't paid much attention to previously; it seemed to contain only a tapestry depicting three horned, blue-skinned djinn playing some kind of game, tossing a ball amid the clouds. As Scarlet led them closer, Nivvy saw that the ball was actually the head of a bearded man, tinted green in death and dripping blood from his neck. "Whose head is that?" he asked, wiping a trickle of sweat from his brow as Scarlet pushed the tapestry aside.

She stopped and craned her head back to look. "This was my sister's. I don't remember exactly who that was meant to be. She did help kill the wizard Covazza with another djinn...no, this must be the great general Tannogammon. He had djinn assisting him as well, and it took Carmine and two other djinn to best him."

Nivvy's head was already spinning with stories, so he didn't ask any further; besides, as soon as he pushed behind the tapestry, he entered a room full of glittering, sparkling glass that put the tapestry out of his mind.

Myriad gems fixed into the ceiling shone down on shelves that lined this circular room, twenty feet from one wall to the other. On the shelves sat vases, cups, and intricate sculptures he could not divine a use for, all made of glass in different thicknesses and colors. There were delicate glass animals and thick sturdy goblets, plain clear glass and swirled colors so bright they almost hurt to look at. All of them seemed to come from different creators: a squat, wide goblet swirled with blue sat next to a shimmering slender glass so delicate it looked like a soap bubble, and behind a sphere the size of Nivvy's fist filled with midnight blue stood a wavy glass screen the size of his chest, green at the bottom and silver-specked blue at the top. But one shelf held no fewer than four glass animals that seemed to come from the same hand: a coiled snake, a rearing jungle cat, a bright red fox, and a colorful bird that Nivvy recognized as a parrot: some had come to Copper Port on ships from the Thousand Kingdoms.

Scarlet said, "Those are five hundred years old. I don't wonder they catch your eye; the glassmaker lived in Copper Port. Perhaps you've seen the like."

"I don't think so." Nivvy leaned closer, keeping his hands back. The detail on the pieces was amazing: the serpent had scales, the jungle cat spots. "But they are wonderful."

"Copper Port was known for its glass at one time. Sadly, the school lost many of its students to Bannarong, to the west, and eventually it closed. That was after the time of Salzi, the maker of those animals, but his student was the one who led the exodus when the government of Copper Port did something that showed they did not value the glass trade. It was some petty mortal thing, taxing glass or not taxing foreign glass enough or not inviting the right person to the festival. It was too boring to make a story of. Conditions changed and people left over the span of some decades and then one day all the old people sat around and said, 'Didn't the glass work here used to be lovelier?' and they all agreed that it had. That is the way of things most often. Now come over here and take the mirror."

When Nivvy turned, Scarlet had shed her human fairy guise and stood as the eagle, looking up at a shelf upon which stood several mirrors of different sizes. "The one on the end," she said. "The velvet covered one."

This was a rectangular mirror that looked as though if Nivvy held it in front of him it might contain the reflection of his face quite nicely. He reached for the velvet cloth that hid the silver face of the mirror, but as he did, Scarlet jabbed her hooked beak at his leg. "Don't look into it, you fool," she said. "Haven't you been listening to me tell you what it will do to those who gaze into it?"

"You told me what it would do to Rose," Nivvy said, "who built her whole life on a lie, but I haven't done that, so what harm would it do?"

"All humans build their lives on lies of one sort or another. Yours might not be the kind that will destroy you, but I did show one visitor his face and he promptly decided to jump off the causeway into the lava, so you'll excuse me if I prefer not to take chances, especially since

I haven't any other weapon that will be nearly as effective against Rose nor any other agent with as good a chance of succeeding."

"Fine," Nivvy said. He removed the mirror from the shelf without lifting the cloth, using both hands because his fingers had a sheen of sweat on them and because Zein balancing on his shoulder made him move with more consideration. When he held the mirror against his chest, it pressed against the small breathing charm he'd taken from Glædeligdal.

He took the small copper fish out and held it up to the light. "Look," he said. "I know this don't belong with glass, but would you mind if I left this here in place of the mirror?"

"It's hardly a substitute," Scarlet said.

"I know, but...it's something to remember me with. In case things go bad, or maybe even if they don't...you can have something of me and Zein in here."

"I think that's a lovely idea," Zein said.

Scarlet stood silently, looking at the small copper fish, and then said, in a softer tone than Nivvy was accustomed to hearing, "Put it on the shelf."

The fish clinked softly as he placed it there, and it did look poor and shabby and out of place among all the lovely glass. Nevertheless, it made Nivvy smile, and the three of them stood in silence for a moment.

Practical thoughts about the upcoming adventure intruded quickly. "So, ah, you haven't any magical things that would get me back there faster than riding, would you?" he asked. "Flying carpet big enough for a horse, tame roc, anything of that nature?"

"Why do you need your horse if you have something else to get you there?" Scarlet asked, the edge returning to her voice. "I've got seven-league boots, that's all. Flying carpets are terribly unpredictable and difficult to keep in one place."

"Not leaving Rahila," Nivvy said. "We been everywhere together."

"I assure you she will not mind and might even thank you for excluding her from this mission...if she had the awareness to understand what was happening to her, which she does not."

"Rahila's special," Nivvy insisted.

"Then find her a nice stable and keep her there." Scarlet turned and spread her wings experimentally. "I'll go get the boots."

Zein and Nivvy followed her back out into the main corridor and watched as she launched herself and then, with wobbling wings, continued on down toward the salon. "There's so much here," Zein said. "So much magic."

"An' people turned into things and animals," Nivvy said. He wiped his head again, keeping a secure grip on the mirror with the other hand. "Don't forget that part. That eagle body she's wearing was once a person she turned into an eagle and then she just took that body away from them as well."

"Maybe it was just an eagle," Zein said faintly.

"Maybe." Nivvy looked around. "But you seen her trophies. You think she'd keep an ordinary eagle?"

Zein turned their head slowly from side to side. "They keep so many things."

"Out of thousands of years. Besides, I picked up a sword the other time an' it had a human face in it."

Zein sighed. "She does seem to like to keep people."

"Best make sure she don't keep us," Nivvy said. He looked down at the mirror. Seeing that it was real nudged him along a path toward a decision, the right thing, the noble thing. Scary, but deciding to do it felt good. Zein would be proud of him, Vicho would've been proud. "Say...you know you're free to go back to Spire, and I got no call to ask you to come along to fight Rose, but—"

"Of course I'll come," Zein said. "You've rescued me twice, and besides, if there's a chance to save the world, or at least some of it, then I'll help as best I can. Is it warmer in here than it used to be?"

"We're inside a volcano," Nivvy said, but a trickle of sweat was making its way down his back. Even when he'd been stealing the ring, he hadn't sweated this much. "I wonder if Rose is doing this."

"Maybe it's just her magic weakening. We'll be out of here soon." Zein made a soft chirp. "You don't think she left us here in a trap or anything like that, do you? I don't think she would, but..." they looked back at the tapestry and the bloody head, "I don't know her terribly well."

"She might, but she could have killed us in any other way, don't you think? She wouldn't do something that might risk her precious trophies." The trickle down his back grew more noticeable and more maddening. "But it is warmer in here than it was." He glanced toward the entrance and then back toward the salon room. "You reckon maybe she got a back door?"

"Stay here." Zein took off from his shoulder and flew toward the entrance down that long hallway. Nivvy cradled the mirror in one hand and rubbed the sweat on his back into his tunic with the other. At least that stopped the tickling.

Zein soared back to him but didn't alight on his shoulder. "It's definitely warmer at that end."

"Then we're going this way." Nivvy marched toward the three archways and Zein flew on ahead calling for Scarlet.

The eagle appeared out of the rightmost archway, tendrils of smoke clinging to her wings. Her words echoed down the hallway. "Can't you wait for two minutes without bothering me?"

"It's getting warmer in here," Zein, who was closer, said. "Especially back there. We thought your magic might be weakening."

"It shouldn't be, not this quickly." Scarlet tilted her head and then swore. "Curse that Rose. I can't feel my spell at all."

"See for yourself," Zein said. "We're not lying."

Scarlet responded by pushing herself off the ground with uneven flaps of her wings. "Go through that far door, the dark one," she croaked as she labored to fly, "and wait there."

"What's in there?" Nivvy asked as she approached him, but she flew past without answering.

Zein flew back to him and landed on his shoulder, matching his pace so he didn't have to break stride. "She seemed worried."

"I'm worried about what's in that hallway and what she was doing in that smoky room."

"There are people in Spire who breathe in flavored smoke," Zein said.

"She told me that smoke was ideas she'd stolen from people."

"How would she steal ideas? Why would they look like smoke? If you go in there, can you hear them?"

"I don't know," Nivvy said. "It's hardly the creepiest thing in here, if you ask me." He arrived at the three archways. "Though I don't know as I wouldn't say this dead quiet room isn't creepier."

"She told us to go in there, and nothing else in here is really unsafe, is it?"

"Not if we don't touch it, I suppose." Nivvy sighed and took a tentative step toward the archway, then looked back down the hall. "Does it look like the hall is...rippling?"

"It does rather," Zein said, and then the blast of hot air hit them, as if Nivvy were standing right next to a raging fire that also smelled of sulfur. He uttered a short cry and leapt into the dark archway.

Light disappeared, even from the hallway behind them. The ground sloped down and Nivvy followed it, smacking into a wall and stumbling to his right, following the downward slope for a dozen beats of his pounding heart until he realized the heat was lessening. "It's better here, yeah?" he asked Zein, slowing with one arm in front of him.

"I think so. I can't see anything, Nivvy."

"I know. Me neither." His feet bumped what felt like a large wooden chest. He stopped and reached down to find that the chest, if that's what it was, was half his height and very large. He turned and sat on it. "If she don't show in a minute, we'll try to find our way, but I'd rather have a guide to stumble through the dark."

"That's fine with me," Zein said.

They probably waited two minutes, as it happened, sweat trickling down Nivvy's back and the air growing warmer, before a rush of wings and a hot breeze signaled Scarlet's return. "We haven't much time," she said tersely. "The boots are in one of the coffins here."

"Coffins!" Nivvy jumped up.

"Sometimes people were buried with powerful magic things. Not often, and not at all these days, but—just listen." Her voice got closer. "Rose is pushing the lava up to destroy us. We need to get out and those boots are the only thing that will do it. They're in one of the coffins and I think..." Her voice moved to Nivvy's left. "I think it's this one."

"Surprised you didn't just fly out," he muttered. His knees suffered most from the darkness, colliding often with what he was trying very hard to think of as only big wooden trunks.

"It's very warm. I don't trust these wings yet. And how would you have gotten out?"

She's only concerned because she wants you to kill Rose, he reminded himself because there seemed to be an actual note of worry there. He followed her voice to her side. "Why do you have coffins?"

"That's what they tend to bury people in. Hurry and open this one."

Nivvy's experienced hand searched for the latch. "I mean, why do you still have coffins? Why not take the magical items out and put them on shelves or something?"

"These are powerful ones," Scarlet said as Nivvy's fingers found a metal catch and worked out how to open it. They slipped twice from the sweat on them, and then the ground trembled, which did not help his concentration. "I'd put extra magic protections on this chamber, and I always said someday I would come in here and get all the magic items out, but there's always something better to do than mess around with disgusting old corpses. Can you go any slower at that?"

"I've only got one hand to work with because the other's holding your precious mirror. Can you make some light?"

"With what?"

"One of those things you've got stored back in the hallway. Surely one of them must make light."

Zein piped up. "I think maybe a lot of them would now because they might be on fire."

"As will we be in a moment," Scarlet retorted.

"Never mind," Nivvy said as his fingers slid the catch free. "I've got it."

He lifted the coffin lid with a sense of accomplishment that quickly faded in the smell that came up to him of decayed, ancient flesh. "Really wish you'd found the time to put these on a shelf," he said. "You going to grab the boots or what? Starting to get a mite uncomfortable in here." In fact, his fingers were so sweaty he worried he might drop the coffin lid, which did not want to stay open without his support. The ground was vibrating now, trembling with what Nivvy thought of as anticipation for the explosion that was coming. He forced himself to take deep breaths, even though the sulfurous tang in the air had sharpened.

"I'm not going in there," Scarlet said. "You get them."

"I'm holding up this bloody heavy lid and having some trouble breathing because there's lava coming toward us!"

"That's why I told you to hurry!" Scarlet croaked.

"I'll get them." Zein jumped into the coffin before Nivvy could stop them. They shuffled around for a moment. "Boots, right?"

"Yes," Scarlet said.

"I don't understand how you can have a tapestry of a bloody head and that creepy room of frozen living animals and think a dead body is disgusting."

"It is disgusting," Scarlet said. "Blood is wonderful, blood is life. When the blood is gone, it's just decaying skin and organs."

"You have a dead bat strung up outside your cave!" Nivvy wiped sweat from his forehead with his sleeve. Was he imagining the ground under his feet growing hotter?

"Yes. It's disgusting. I wanted to keep people away."

"Found them." Some scuffling noises and then a pause. "I can't seem to jump out though. Not with the boots. They're heavy."

"Oh, for—" How was it harder to get a pair of boots out of a coffin than to steal a ring out of hundreds? "Here, I'm putting the mirror down. Don't worry, I'm not shutting you in there—oh."

Zein had flown up to the lip of the coffin. "It's okay, I'm out now. But they're there, down this end. I think they should come up easily."

Nivvy bent down and placed the mirror on the ground, still holding the coffin lid up. "Don't move, either of you," he said. With his now-free hand, he reached down near where Zein had spoken, and his fingers encountered—thank Inira—leather. He gripped the boots and pulled, and they came easily, as Zein had predicted, at least until he got them to the lip of the coffin. Then a weight pulled them back down into the coffin.

At the same time, the floor slid and tilted below him, and the coffin scraped slowly away to his right. Desperate, Nivvy pulled harder, trying to keep his balance, and with dusty cracking sounds the boots came free. "Jump down, Zein," he said. "I'm closing the coffin."

"Hurry!" Scarlet cried. "The mountain is coming apart!"

The hawk fluttered to the ground. Nivvy made sure of the mirror and then dropped the coffin lid and let the coffin slide away. Rumbles came stronger now and the heat was terrible. He imagined the lava oozing through the menagerie, all the petrified animals' suffering ended in a quick burst of flame, and then put that image out of his mind.

Scarlet let out a squawk at the thump of the coffin lid. "I warned you," he said.

"I didn't expect the noise," she retorted. "Get the boots on!"

He tried, but—"There's something in them," he said, and upon reaching in found crumbling bone and skin. It stuck to his sweaty fingers, and he dropped the boots with a cry of disgust.

The floor shuddered again. A scraping sound warned Nivvy to skip to one side as another coffin slid by. "What are you waiting for?" Scarlet snapped.

"There's feet in the boots!" The lava couldn't be close because if it were, they'd see the glow and feel the heat. Nivvy stuck his hand in again, driven by necessity, and pulled out bone and parchment-dry skin, throwing it from him.

"Careful!" Scarlet's wings beat next to him.

"I don't like it any more than you do." Nivvy switched to the other boot, clawing out the desiccated foot in it. "Sorry, mate, whoever you are or were, but we need the boots. How do I use these once I've got them on? What's their story?"

"'The Seven-League Boots made by Viridian for Phrah Leka Kimmad, that carried him to his death,' that should work. Pick me up and hold the mirror and walk downslope."

"Won't I hit the mountain around us?"

"Not while you're walking. When you land, careful where you place your feet."

"Zein!" Nivvy called as he shoved one foot into a boot, then the other, the boots accommodating enough to fit his shoes. "Get back on my shoulder!"

"Make sure to hold them!" Scarlet yelled over the rumbling.

The ground lurched, and a blast of scorching air hissed past them, not from the archway they'd come through, but from Nivvy's right, where they finally had light: the floor had cracked, and a hellish red glow suffused the cave. Zein's talons scrabbled at his neck and shoulder and gripped there, one of them missing the cloth and piercing his skin but he didn't care. He found the mirror and reached out for Scarlet while holding Zein with his other hand.

The eagle crashed into his chest as she flew up and into him, her head pressing up under his chin. He wrapped the arm holding the mirror around her as best he could, recited the spell Scarlet had told him, and then lifted his leg and took a step forward. The floor fell away from under him—

—and he was propelled forward through dark mists and then emerged into the sunlight outside the mountain, air whistling by him but not against his skin, his stride carrying him ten feet above the ground, the rocky slope far below—

"Aim down!" the eagle in his arms screeched. Talons dug into his shoulder and Zein pressed against him.

He angled his body downward, the ground rushing up impossibly fast to meet him, and he couldn't do anything to slow himself. He braced for an impact, but when his foot met the rocky ground, they kissed as softly as if he'd taken but a single step.

Ash drifted through the air. Even here, the ground trembled and the air felt unnaturally warm, tense like the air before a storm but magnified a hundredfold. "We need to get farther away," Scarlet said. "Keep going."

That seemed an odd thing to say for someone who'd a few minutes ago said she'd be willing to die in her home, but Nivvy lifted his foot and then remembered Rahila, waiting for him all alone in the middle of the eruption. He spun to face the white smoke spewing from the mountain's crater, the air around it thick with ash. "Rahila!" he cried. "I have to go back for her!"

"There's no time—" Scarlet's protest ended in a squawk as Nivvy dumped her onto the ground.

"Fly toward Spire!" he called, pulling his robe over his nose and mouth. "I'll meet you on the road!"

Zein took off from his shoulder. "I'll stay with her," they said, and perhaps they said more, but whatever words followed were lost as Nivvy stretched out his foot and the ground sped away below him.

Smoke obscured his vision, but while he was traveling with the boots, he did not feel it on his skin. In a moment, though, the mountain rose up before him and he had to stretch out his foot to meet it. He landed awkwardly and fell, and then fine dust coated his skin, filled his nose as he breathed even through the tunic. Heat radiated from the mountain like a malevolent force. "Rahila!" he cried, getting to his feet, and smoke filled his mouth. He coughed and called again.

Through the cloud, as he looked around wildly, he spotted the Bouli temple below him, and that let him judge about how far up the mountain he was. He looked up the slope toward where Rahila probably stood, terrified, and then over the rumbling and groaning of the mountain he heard the loose scree of stones along the side of the mountain and what sounded like a horse trying to make her way down an unstable path.

"H'san!" he called, getting another mouthful of smoke for his trouble, and took a step forward, which sent him twenty feet and tumbling to the ground again when he landed. But now the frantic clatter of rocks was closer. With short steps he stuttered through suffocating ash and rising heat, and once the mountain shook and sent him to the ground again.

But then, thank Inira, there was Rahila, her eyes wide and terrified, skidding down the path of loose stones. Nivvy leapt for her bridle. "It's me, h'san," he said, "it's me, I've got you now, don't worry." Already he was finding it hard to breathe and his strength was failing.

She didn't stop, too overwhelmed to listen to him, but that was fine. His fingers closed around the leather of the reins. He spit dust out of his mouth and lifted his foot to take a giant step.

The smoke and heat melted away from him. And so did the leather in his fingers, leaving Nivvy with nothing in his hands as the mountain receded behind him.

# ❧ 29 ☙

# REFLECTION

**N**ivvy landed in the middle of a stiff, prickly bush and lost his balance, falling halfway to the ground while the bush both supported him and stabbed his legs and midsection. He wrestled free of it and jumped up to stare back at the mountain, now completely hidden by smoke and ash. Even as he lifted a foot to go back to it, a loud explosion sounded, and the plume of smoke tripled in size. A massive, baleful cloud raced down the sides of the mountain, and above it came creeping the telltale red glow of lava. The Bouli temple, appearing as small as a child's plaything, vanished in an instant.

Nivvy dropped his foot and sat down hard on the ground. "Rahila!" he cried out, scraping his throat. The sight of her terrified eyes danced before him, an image he knew he would never forget. She hadn't wanted to go up the volcano at all, but he'd coaxed her, told her he would keep her safe. And she'd waited for him even as the mountain had started to shake, and then he'd found her and promised to rescue her, but he hadn't thought to simply throw his arm around her. If he'd only done that, she'd be alive right now and he'd be stroking her flanks to calm her down.

In stories, people wailed and rent their garments, and Nivvy had never understood that, but now he stared up at the sky and let out his anguish and guilt and heartbreak in a scream, and seemed for a moment to be carried away and out of his body on that tide of emotion. His fingers seized his robe over his heart, twisting and tearing the cloth.

A wave of hot air knocked him onto the ground next to the bush. He got to his feet, ready to run, but that had simply been the advance guard; the cloud of ash continued to struggle toward him but had lost much of its speed, and the lava remained a foreboding glow around the remnants of the volcano. The skies darkened as smoke thickened and covered the sun, and Nivvy sat heavily on the ground, drained and hollow.

He'd lost mates before, but they'd by and large been adults like him who'd made decisions that could at least partly be blamed for how they'd ended up. Marzin knew that when you stole from a wizard you risked getting magicked for it, and though the wizard definitely deserved part of the blame, you couldn't say Marzin was innocent. Nor was Vicho, whose appetites had done him in, whom Nivvy maybe could've saved if he'd tried a little harder. No thief was innocent, least not if they got hurt while thieving.

But Rahila, she'd stuck with him even when everyone else had abandoned him. She'd carried him down the coast from Copper Port to Tagrabul, across the western mountains to Vuamma, and almost all the way back to Copper Port before they'd met Rose. She'd guided him to a merchant with dates outside of Tagrabul (she loved dates, and when he gave her one she would snuffle him looking for the next before she'd even swallowed the first), had faced down a boar to protect him along the road to Penuca, and had bitten Vila once, maybe the thing he was proudest of her for. Every beloved memory stuck another needle in his heart. She'd been with him for most of his life as a thief, and that dedication had killed her.

No; that plus Rose had killed her. If only he'd turned Rose down back in Plow. That would've been the sensible thing to do. She was clearly not of sound mind, or else she was extremely dangerous, and either way it wasn't the kind of company a good thief would choose.

Ah, but he hadn't been a good thief, had he? He'd been a desperate one, looking for glory, and, in the very short term, to get off that cursed wheel. Stealing trinkets from inconsequential people was a waste of his time, so even the small chance of something important, something that mattered—no, no, be honest with yourself, something that would get you back into a Thieves Guild, if not First Thief in one, that would show them all that you belonged—even that small chance was worthwhile.

He had stories to tell, yes, and he'd seen incredible things and lived. He might be the only person in the world who'd been an animal and been changed back. And he'd give it all up now if he could be back in that nothing farm town with the chance to say no to Rose, to get back on Rahila and seek out their destiny together. He'd even give up his human form if it meant Rahila would be alive again.

He'd been right there, and she'd trusted him, and now she was ash. If he couldn't even save her, how could he save anyone? He sat and stared at the erupting mountain of fire, at the rolling cloud of ash, at the fiery inexorable tongues of lava. Even if the lava hadn't reached the Bouli temple yet, everyone within was surely dead. That they had died thinking it was at the hands of their god was perhaps their only consolation. Nivvy knew better. It was Rose who'd killed them, Rose who'd killed Rahila, Rose who had almost killed him and Scarlet and Zein.

When Vicho had been killed, D'Alio had sat with Nivvy all that night, both of them mourning him, and D'Alio had told him that there was no bringing him back. Nivvy'd wanted to go kill that merchant, the one who'd sent the body back, and steady D'Alio had told him that wouldn't do any good, that it wouldn't fill the hole of Vicho's loss. He'd been right; Nivvy had seen that over the last year.

But Vicho, dear as he'd been, hadn't been Rahila, and D'Alio wasn't here now, and Nivvy thought his heart was going to split in half every time he thought about going on without his dear horse. The pain pulsing through him demanded that if he couldn't get Rahila back, he could at least avenge her. He could make sure that Rose didn't come after any of his other friends, few of them as there were: D'Alio and his uncles in Copper Port; maybe he could count Scarlet now, although he doubted Scarlet would, and Zein. Zein, with whom he'd shared secrets and adventures that he wouldn't have dreamed possible before meeting them. They had a good heart and they believed in him. He wanted to be the person they believed him to be.

When he'd decided to take the mirror a scant half hour (a lifetime) ago, he'd been looking forward to being the hero in a story. That no longer mattered to him. He wanted to defeat Rose because justice demanded it.

Sweat trickled through the grit on his forehead, and as Nivvy lifted a hand to wipe it away, the mirror shifted against his side. He took it out and held it before him, staring at the now-dirty purple velvet cloth.

Around the edges showed fine silver crafting, patterns of what looked like the edges of faces, but constructed out of silver threads as delicate as spiderwebs. Work this finely detailed never appeared in the markets he shopped in, only the ones he stole from. Nivvy brushed a thumb along them and they resisted his touch, solid in a way that spun silver was not. So there was some other craft at work here. He lifted his eyes to the volcano and wondered whether any of the Velki traveled to the surface through the lava spewing onto the ground.

He ran his thumb along the other edge of the mirror. Supposedly it showed you who you truly were, that's what Scarlet claimed, that was the key to defeating Rose. She'd warned him not to look into it, but if it wasn't magic, then he needed to know that, and if it was, then it would tell him whether he was really the kind of hero who could confront Rose and defeat her.

So he picked up one corner of the velvet cloth and lifted it away, and gazed down into the Velki's mirror.

The spiderweb tracings around the side were revealed to be faces, each the size of his thumb: women with flowing hair, men with square jaws, strange faces with flat noses, tiny ears, and thick brows, whom Nivvy assumed to be Velki. There were more of those faces than of humans, and, at the top, one wild monstrous face that was more than likely a djinn.

And then his eyes dropped down to the reflection of his own face. The surface of the mirror gleamed, clean of scratches or dust, unlike his skin—glass, perhaps, but ethereally perfect. He turned the mirror one way and then another, marveling at the sharpness of his brown complexion against the hazy, smoky sky. Maybe there was a story he was supposed to say that he didn't know, and this was simply an exceptionally clear mirror.

On his reflected cheek, he noticed a thin red cut that he hadn't felt. It reminded him about getting a cut as a child. His mother had tried to attend to him and he'd pushed her away, running to his father instead.

A month later, they'd been dead. His uncles had wanted him to help bury them; they had laid out a funeral dress for him to wear at the consecration. After that, he'd be engaged, and the bride price would help pay for the funeral. But Nivvy had run away rather than honor his parents while wearing a dress, because boys didn't wear dresses.

He'd joined the Thieves Guild and had taken on risky jobs right away to prove himself. He'd been sent across the sea to Tarisch, but he hadn't been honoring Inira, not properly. He hadn't taken the job thinking about a wrong he was righting, nor about the challenge of the work itself, nor yet about how the job would credit the Guild. He'd been thinking only about his own reputation, putting himself ahead of other thieves.

When he'd succeeded, which he did a lot in those early years, those things could be forgiven, and he saw now how his first teacher at the Guild, Polu, had tried to steer him in the right direction. "If the job needs to be done, and I do it," Nivvy had said, "why does Inira care what I'm thinking as I do it?"

"Different paths may on occasion pass in the same direction," Polu had told him. "When they diverge, the proper attitude toward Inira and thieving will ensure you remain on the correct one."

"I know the correct one," Nivvy had said, an arrogant youth of nineteen at the time, and over the next ten years of his work with the Guild he had not changed his attitude at all. Hicala a'Stara, the first First Thief Nivvy had known at the Guild, had praised him while also cautioning him with veiled words, and Nivvy had ignored those as well.

Polu and Hicala were both dead now, and the First Thief as of a year ago had been (and perhaps still was) Vila Viladu, a vain thief who believed in the gospel of burnishing his own reputation at the cost of everyone else. Where Hicala had reprimanded Nivvy the time Nivvy had impulsively pushed through a window he believed to be safe, bringing the guards around and endangering his fellow thief on the job, Vila had taken him aside after that and told him it was a bold move, and that Nivvy's quick action to distract the guard, which had given his companion time to reach safety, had been the real act of heroism.

But now Nivvy could see the folly, how his self-involvement had endangered a fellow thief even before poor Vicho.

Vicho had succeeded Polu as his teacher, but now Nivvy was a journeyman thief, no longer an apprentice. Vicho was amiable, genial, making a point to be on good terms with everyone. He gave away too much, Nivvy thought, even though he'd been as fond of Vicho as everyone else was. Looking back now, he could see that he would've been impatient with any master around that time; the fault hadn't been with good-natured Vicho. Even when Vicho kept dragging Nivvy to brothels to indulge his main vice, he was only trying to be kind. He couldn't have known Nivvy's secret or how knotted up inside those brothel trips made the young thief feel.

D'Alio became his best friend around then, and the two of them dreamed of the day they would be running the Guild. Not by being everyone's friend, but by doing the most daring jobs, bringing the most acclaim to the Guild. Vicho was kind but unambitious, Vila ambitious but not that smart. They were the future of the Guild, the two of them believed with all the arrogance of the young.

Nivvy and Vicho had been assigned to steal from a merchant who had hired cutpurses—non-Guild thieves—to steal a case of valuable jewels from his rival as a gift for his wife, or one of his wives, or his concubine, Nivvy did not quite care about the details. Nivvy was the "hands," the one who would actually grab the jewels; Vicho was the "eyes," meant to keep lookout while Nivvy was inside. The theft went well enough to start with: there were two guards outside the woman's quarters, but nobody thought to guard the room with the large bath and only one window. The window didn't open; what was the danger?

Thieves have ways of separating glass from wood, and after pulling the window free, Nivvy and Vicho had slipped inside. Vicho went first, and when he surprised the woman in her parlor, rather than putting her to sleep, he decided he fancied her and so tried to seduce her into coming along with him. She didn't even notice Nivvy as he slipped behind her back into her bedroom, found the case, and returned. She wouldn't have noticed him at all if he hadn't desperately thrown a candied nut from one of the many little tables around the parlor in an attempt to get Vicho's attention, because the man was so absorbed in pressing his lips to hers that he didn't even notice Nivvy coming out.

Nivvy had always maintained that that was the real crime right there, getting distracted, but it didn't change what came next: his aim was bad, the woman looked up, she shrieked for the guards. There were only two. Had Nivvy stayed, he and Vicho might have prevailed, and he had a dagger ready to throw. But he called, "Flee!" and ran for the bathroom, hoping Vicho would follow.

He did not. Nivvy climbed out, hauled himself up to the roof, and lay there while the guards looked down to the ground and marveled at the spider he must be. And in that moment, he remembered, he had felt more warmth at their praise for his skills than he did worry for Vicho. Vicho was a big fellow and could take care of himself, or he could talk his way out of the situation with his round, pleasant face and that smile that worked on everyone. Nivvy hadn't even thought that he could drop down on one of the guards' heads as they looked out the window, incapacitate him, and take the other by surprise.

No, that wasn't true. He had thought it, how heroic it would be. But it was extremely dangerous, he'd reasoned, and did he really want to take that risk to rescue Vicho, who had always preached caution to him?

He could have stayed to see where they took Vicho, to plan a rescue. But he made his way back to the Guild, showed off the case of gems, and told Vila scornfully that Vicho had gotten infatuated with a woman and had been captured. To his surprise, the First Thief ordered a full meeting of the Guild, at which Nivvy eventually had to confess his acts of cowardice.

He hadn't seen them that way at the time, of course. He'd done the job; that was the important thing. But the next day, Vicho had been returned to the Guild with a note from the merchant explaining how sorry he was to convey this information but alas, thieves who prance around on roofs sometimes do fall fifty feet to the cobblestones directly on their heads, especially when climbing after their friends. What is there for a merchant to do but collect the remains?

The story became that Vicho had attempted to climb out the window and Nivvy, rather than helping him, had left him behind. Nivvy protested that this was not true, but it didn't matter; he was expelled from the Guild and stripped of all his possessions, which should have included Rahila, except that D'Alio had helped him escape.

At the core of the matter, though, he had abandoned Vicho. Whether the man had fallen to his death while climbing or been captured and beaten to death, Nivvy had abandoned him. He had focused on the particulars, had built that story up that Vicho's proclivities had led the man to his own demise, but he could no longer escape the truth that he could have helped him and had not.

He hadn't helped Rose because he pitied her; he'd helped her because he wanted to regain his stature as a thief. He hadn't rescued Zein because he feared for their life; he'd rescued them because he needed them to get him to the lake, because he felt guilty at having caused their injury and didn't want to feel guilty over their death. He had rescued them the second time perhaps because he cared for them, that was true. But he had also been searching for an excuse not to follow Rose, because she'd scared him. If he'd still trusted her, been enticed by her offer, he would have left Zein behind.

This was the truth of who the man in the mirror was: no hero, just a man who valued himself above all others. That didn't mean he wouldn't help a friend, just that he wouldn't take a great risk to do it. And if he wouldn't even risk his life for a friend, how could he expect to do it for the world? If Rose offered him the post of Master Thief, he couldn't be sure he wouldn't take it, world be damned.

That thought itched at him (*she killed Rahila!*) beneath the self-loathing burying him like volcanic ash. He'd always thought of himself as a piece of jewelry found in salvage: if you bothered to look past the dirt, there was something of real value underneath. With the facts of his life spread out before him in sharp relief, every myth he'd constructed around them stripped away, he no longer felt like a hidden jewel. He was a piece of glass being sold as jewelry to fools.

He tilted the mirror. It showed the scrub behind him and then the dirt and then the sky with the sun beginning the descent from its zenith, each thing solid and real. Slowly, he let the velvet cover fall over it again. He felt worthless and shaken, and the thought crossed his mind that if he simply sat here and let the volcano's ash cloud roll over him, the world would be better off.

He could walk into it with a moment's thought, and that impulse felt attractive to him. But he saw a hawk's eyes behind that thought, dark and grieving, and he felt in that the echo of his own unbearable pain. Foolish, maybe, to think that he meant as much to Zein as Rahila had meant to him, but Zein was one break in the clouds that surrounded him, a lifeline he clung to desperately. If he did kill himself, there'd be nobody to protect Zein from Rose, who knew the hawk and knew that Nivvy had spurned her for them.

Rejoining Scarlet and Zein wasn't the answer, either. Bringing them along to fight Rose would only put both of them in danger. He wanted badly to see Zein again, for the falcon to tell him he was worthy, but the mirror had shown that to be a comfort he didn't deserve.

But he wasn't ready to fight Rose yet. He couldn't be sure that he would fight her when the moment came, that he wouldn't give in to the same kind of selfish weakness that he had so many times before. He wanted justice for her? What right did he have to mete that out when he was running from it himself? The only way to ease the burden of guilt, to show that he was a different, worthy person, was atonement. Vicho had told him that, and Nivvy had scoffed at the time, but now he saw his old mentor's bearded face and that scratchy, friendly voice saying, "You'll make mistakes, my boy; it's what you do after that's how people judge you."

The man reflected in the mirror had to atone in order to be worthy of anyone's respect, especially Zein. And there was only one place that would punish him properly now: the place where it had really started, before he'd met Rose on that wheel. If he'd accepted responsibility for Vicho's death and taken his punishment then, he would never have been on that wheel and the world would be safe. Going back to submit to that judgment felt right to him (though that feeling too itched, just a little). Once he'd done that, maybe he would be able to look Zein in the eye again. Maybe he could trust himself to fight Rose.

With the mirror tucked securely under his arm, Nivvy stood, faced the volcano, and then turned. His shadow stretched out before him, but it was faint, and even as he watched, the smoke thickened in the sky and the ground darkened until he could no longer see his outline. He drew in a breath and took a step, not toward the needle-like spire to the east, but south of there, and the land sped by under his feet as he left the volcano behind.

# 30
# COPPER PORT

The desert blurred into a golden tan carpet below him, dotted with shadows that passed by as flashes. The oasis where they'd stopped, or one much like it, rose around him and vanished, a ghost on his journey. The desert gave way to drab farms, spiky olive trees and date palms that seemed to erupt from the ground, and then the first signs of green grass. From Nivvy's perspective, speeding through, it was almost as if the land were changing below his feet, plants pushing through the desert sand to take hold, bringing water with them, letting more and more greenery transform the land until he arrived at the swamps of the Copper Port triangle. There he angled his foot, seeking out a particular spot.

The boots seemed to know his intentions. At the swamp, his progress slowed, and when he spotted the bow of the rotting ship sticking out of the water, he slowed even further. The ghostly wood became substantial, and as he set his foot down on the wood of the sloping deck, the world slowed and stabilized, and there he was, standing on the Horizon once more.

The smells came back to him first: aging wood, mold, and then the thick green smell of the swamp all around. And then, in patches of soft breeze, the salt of the sea. Here at Copper Port the sea had its own unique smell, darker and older than farther south at Tagrabul, where the light turquoise water smelled of the nearby islands of the Thousand Kingdoms, the port teeming with fragrant spices. In

Copper Port it was fish, and in the Shallows it was refuse and mussels.

But in the swamp, it was just the sea, the sea and the brackish water around him. He'd liked the Horizon as a child because it didn't smell like garbage, and also because he had painstakingly found his way through the swamp to the Horizon (parents told their children to stay out of the swamp because there were monsters that would pull children under and eat them, but Nivvy had never encountered them; as a thief he suspected that the monsters weren't real, but quicksand and swamp fever definitely were).

The Horizon lay deepest in the swamp, and its boards dripped with moss and lichen, so when children wanted to play on old ships against the warnings of their parents, they went to the Sun Dog or the Great Lady, both of which lay on their sides in cleaner water closer to the Shallows, their boards bleached dry rather than rotting.

Nivvy, never content with the spaces other children could get to, had ventured farther than any others were willing to, and his prize had been the Horizon—at least, he'd never encountered anyone else there. In his days with the Guild, he'd often thought it would make a useful hiding place, but he'd never needed one badly enough to negotiate the swamp. Now he removed the boots, then entered the captain's cabin and made his way up the angled floor, avoiding the slimy patches of moss, to the small cabinet built into the side wall near the bow.

At one time, the beautifully crafted cabinet doors had been bright and new, the sea serpents that coiled on their faces painted, maybe detailed in gold leaf. Now only their ghostly shapes were visible on the door that hung from one rusted hinge. The other door had fallen off or been stolen a long time ago, and the cabinet emptied of anything valuable.

Inside, though, the wood remained dry, and the surviving door provided at least a small amount of protection. Nivvy set the boots and the mirror in the cabinet and then pushed the door closed as best he could. From the entrance to the cabin, it would look empty, and nothing about the cabin suggested that anything valuable would be concealed there. And that was if anyone could be bothered to navigate the swamp to come out to an old wreck that had been here for decades, picked clean long ago.

Lighter and slower, he left the cabin and made his way down the deck. The notch he'd made on the railing was still there, looking like any other piece of damage to the wood, except that he remembered the precise location and shape of it. He had stood right there on the deck, looking down to the tuft of grass, sawing away at the soft wood with his knife.

Over the railing, the footholds he remembered were there as well, spaced for a ten-year-old. The grass tuft below him still held his weight, which was a relief, because he knew that the swamp could change its ground very easily with no sign on the surface.

Indeed, there were several places on the long way back where either he misremembered the step or missed it in the lengthening shadows, but his skill guided him when the route he'd memorized failed. He sprang lightly from grass to grass, the late afternoon sun giving him just enough light to tell firm ground from swamp. It would be nice, he thought, to feel ten years old again, that aura of invincibility surrounding him in this place that (he felt) belonged to him. The swamp, and later, the Horizon, had been places where he'd been able to call himself a boy out loud and feel the warm confidence of that truth.

But that truth was maybe the only one he took comfort in anymore. He saw now that while he thought he'd been leaping agilely from tuft to tuft through the world, he had been simply sloshing through the swamp, pretending the muck wasn't there and wasn't clinging to him. He couldn't pretend anymore. He could smell it and feel it all over him.

Before the light faded completely, he made it to the great trees at the edge of the swamp. Jungle cats and other predators sometimes stalked these woods, but tonight nothing threatened Nivvy. He emerged from the trees and paused to look over the towers of Copper Port and, nearer, the fires of The Shallows.

The Shallows brought back more memories, but even from afar against the purpling sky, he saw unfamiliar silhouettes: a house missing, another roof a different shape. Well, things changed, didn't they? Nivvy had changed too, and more than any of those people or houses in The Shallows, he'd wager. Likely none of them would recognize him if he strolled in there now, except for his uncles and maybe his cousin.

It took him another half hour to reach the south gate of Copper Port, where the smells of ocean and fish rolled over him. This was a "gate" only in the sense that it was the place where the city of Copper Port met the road into Copper Port; there was no wall, no gate, and only one desultory guard snoozing against the post. There was something reassuring in seeing his familiar darker skin and the livery of the Copper Port city-state, the linked copper rings with the fish swimming through them.

Nivvy shook the guard awake so that he wouldn't lose his job if his captain checked on him. He received his gruff thanks and then walked into the town. This too was familiar, though it had only been a year and so little had changed. He walked by his favorite bakery, closed with the moon halfway up the evening sky, and felt only a twinge of happiness that they were still there. The inns farther down the street would normally be tempting, and he might have been able to steal a few silver from one of the stables, but that wasn't what had driven him back here.

Like the rest of the city, the tall stone of the Thieves Guild building stood just as Nivvy remembered it: three stories tall, with windows in the front that he knew only let onto unused, locked rooms. Across the top of the building, carved lettering read, "Goods Exchange," both a way to conceal the true nature of the building and a joke to the thieves who lived there: they did indeed help goods exchange hands. On the building's left, a shorter brick building housed a smithy who was friendly to the thieves, and on the right, a dirt lot showed scrapes and debris where merchants set up stalls during the day.

Nivvy walked up to the plain wooden door and rapped sharply on it. Even at this time of night, there should be an attendant there, and though he had to rap a second time, the door did eventually open and a sleepy dark-complexioned face peered out. "Wossat?"

"You must be new," Nivvy said. "Is D'Alio still here?"

The face blinked at him. "Been here a year, I have. Who're you?"

Nivvy stood his ground. "Is D'Alio here?"

"Ain't going to tell him 'til I know who you," the young man jabbed a finger at Nivvy's chest, "are."

"Tell him Nivali al Tamsin is here to see him." Nivvy had worked the door before, and he knew what instructions this young man probably had. "I'll wait in the front room and you can lock the door behind you when you go up to the second floor to the second room after the stairs."

The young man reached up to scratch behind his ear. He'd probably been napping on the chairs there. "Right," Nivvy said, "I've told you my name, and you know I used to be a thief here because I know where D'Alio sleeps, so off you go."

"He don't sleep there no more," the young man said, but he opened the door. "Moved up."

Nivvy stepped inside. The room was just as he remembered it, from the uncomfortable wooden chair that was supposed to keep the attendant from sleeping to the even less comfortable wicker chairs for guests to wait, down to the smell of the men and women who passed through it and the soap they used on their robes. "Go get him," he said tiredly, and sat down on the nearer wicker chair. "I'll wait here."

The young man closed the door and then stared at him, shifting his weight uncertainly. "Go," Nivvy said, closing his eyes. "I've no interest in picking your lock, and if you hurry, you'll be back before I'd have time to, even if I had my tools here."

"If you were a good thief, it wouldn't take you that long," the man retorted.

Nivvy cracked one eye open. "If you were a good thief, you'd be gone already."

"Inira's seven silver bells," the young man swore. "Fine, I'm going."

He kept an eye on Nivvy as he opened the inside door, slid through, and shut it quickly, and then the thunk of the lock signaled that it had been thrown from the other side. Nivvy exhaled and settled back in the chair.

His skin prickled with the thief's sense of danger, the memory of the last time he'd been in the room, D'Alio hurrying him out the door —about this time of night, too, as he recalled—telling him that Rahila was saddled and waiting. Nivvy had been caught between facing indentured servitude to the Guild until Vicho's blood price had been worked off and fleeing the Guild, becoming a fugitive thief. He and D'Alio alone thought the latter course wiser. "At least then," D'Alio had told him, "you got a chance to get back in Inira's favor on your terms."

Here, Nivvy thought, was where his paths diverged, as Polu had taught him, and he chose to put his fate in his own hands rather than follow the course of a bunch of ignorant thieves who, after all, couldn't even trust him to tell the truth of the night. Now, still under the influence of the mirror, that decision felt corrupt and selfish. Had he accepted his responsibility for Vicho's death, an evil queen out of children's stories wouldn't at this moment be setting a great horrible dragon on a kingdom that hadn't thought of her in fifty generations. Wouldn't have reached out from the north to cause a volcano to erupt and kill Rahila.

Again he felt the impulse to do away with himself, spare the world any further harm he might cause, but it was weaker now, more easily set aside. He rested his head back against the wall and told himself not to be silly. Rose wasn't setting the dragon on the kingdom now; she'd already done that. They were probably sleeping in the burned ruins of the castle. If Rose slept, which he was now inclined to believe she did not.

The image of her sitting on a sleeping dragon gazing out at the smoking ruins of a castle grew strong in his mind. He could see her faint smile, the contentment at the destruction she'd wrought, but also the dissatisfaction behind her eyes. She wanted her kingdom back, but that wasn't enough. What she wanted was more complicated than that, something Nivvy could relate to. He'd wanted to prove that he belonged in the Thieves Guild, that they'd been wrong about him. Rose wanted to prove to the world that it had been wrong about her.

The problem was, the Guild and the world hadn't been wrong. That was the rough thing when you gambled on yourself: you might lose. Rose wasn't a good person. From the stories Scarlet told, her sister had seemed like a good-hearted person. She got Rose a kingdom, invited her to the christening of her daughter, all the things you're supposed to do. Rose was the one who'd resented all of it.

In his imagination, Rose was staring out past the dragon and thinking of her sister, wishing Primrose could see what Rose had done.

Funny what power did to you, he thought. But no, Rose had tried to kill Zein even when she was powerless. That should've been it right there, Nivvy thought, only he hadn't quite known then how bad Rose could be. The intensity of his anger at that memory surprised him. He had to make his atonement here and then take the mirror up to Rose. And if he failed, maybe Scarlet would find another way. Not likely, though, not with all her magic gone and melted.

"Nivvy."

A hand seized his shoulder. He blinked up into a lined face, ochre skin under white-streaked black hair. "You came back to us?"

"D'Alio." He smiled and reached up to clasp his friend's hand. "I've learned a lot."

His friend didn't smile back. "You must have done. And yet, not enough. Why you back here?"

"Back to make amends. I got Vicho killed and I ran away rather'n own up to it, so I'm here to pay the price." He squared his shoulders.

D'Alio shook his head. "Nivvy, idiot. When you ran, the price went up. They want your life now. You prepared to pay that?"

Nivvy's eyes widened. D'Alio nodded. "Yah. And you just told Kilan your name, like an idiot. He gone to get Vila, I bet. Come on, where's Rahila?"

"Gone." Nivvy wiped his face as he stood, his legs shaky for a moment. "I lost her."

"How did you—never mind. I'll take you to my brother's and you can hide there a moment while we get you another horse."

"No." He resisted. "Whatever—whatever the price—" But if he were dead, who would fight Rose? Was there no middle ground between selfish-alive and worthy-dead?

"Come *on*!" D'Alio grabbed his arm and pulled.

Dazed, Nivvy stumbled back out the door of the Guild into the streets of Copper Port. "They would really take my life?" he asked.

D'Alio kept a firm grip on his arm, hurrying down the deserted street. "Vila said that you runnin' away meant you were for sure guilty an' that if you didn't want to work off your debt, you'd pay it in blood."

"Never heard of that happening before," Nivvy said.

"Nobody ever got a fellow killed and then skipped."

"I didn't—"

"I know." They stopped at a corner where D'Alio checked cautiously around it, then pulled Nivvy forward again. "He got himself killed. We all knew he would. Couldn't resist a lady."

"I could've helped him, though," Nivvy said. "More'n I did."

"What's Inira say about that?" D'Alio demanded, striding faster. "Says those who make their beds need to lie down in 'em."

"Right, but," Nivvy stumbled, then ran to catch up. "But that don't mean if we're right there, I mean, *right* there, that we shouldn't help, right?"

"Maybe," D'Alio said, now a little short of breath. "Can't be your responsibility, though."

Nivvy thought it could, but he was tired and short of breath too, and the grim certainty of his path that had brought him to Copper Port no longer felt so certain. He'd come for justice, but was it justice to give up his life? So he followed D'Alio another three blocks until his friend stopped and rapped sharply on a door.

The brass trim on the door gleamed even in the moonlight, and the white limestone of the building, like most of the buildings in this area, fairly shone. No refuse or beggars littered the paving stones here. Along the street, three small stands remained out in front of their buildings where during the day the merchants must show their wares; the others either stowed theirs for the night or invited customers into the shop proper. The shops, in the lower stories of the buildings along the street, all sat dark and still, and even in the apartments above them only one lamp burned. Nivvy knew that D'Alio's brother sold rugs, but had not known that he was successful enough to own a shop on Brin Ala Street.

D'Alio rapped again. Now a noise came from inside, a scuffling, and someone approached the door. "Who's there, this time of night?" a voice came, a low male voice.

"Anzo, it's me, Taja," D'Alio said. "Open up, hurry!"

The door cracked open and a shadowy face peered out, eyes glinting below a mop of jet-black hair. But Anzo had the same long nose as his brother and the same jutting chin, though his was cloaked in a long beard. He pulled a loose robe tighter around himself. "Taj? It's the middle of the night. Who's this?"

Behind Anzo, a sleepy female voice called, "Who's at the door?"

"This is Nivvy, he needs a place to hide. Just a short time, until we find a horse for him."

Anzo measured the two of them and then nodded sharply and opened the door.

Nivvy stepped into a warm room that smelled of carpets, and that plus the large rolls leaning against the wall confirmed his memory of what Anzo sold. "Thank you," he said.

"What's he done?" Anzo kept his eye on Nivvy while addressing his brother.

"I'll tell you the story later. Trust me for now." D'Alio scanned the room. "Can he stay in the back? Is there room? He could hide behind the carpets."

"Maybe." Anzo stroked his beard. "Who's likely to come looking?"

"Nobody, nobody." D'Alio raised his hands. "But there's plenty on this street what don't mind their business, and there was a light on. Could've been seen. Best not to take chances."

"I'll just sleep," Nivvy promised. "Won't be no trouble." His Copper Port accent was coming back thickly.

"Anzo, who is it?" The woman's voice came from the stairs at the back of the store just over the door that D'Alio had indicated Nivvy would go through. Now the woman herself stepped down to become visible, wearing a white nightdress. She was attractive even when not dressed for company, with long black hair, a rounded nose and soft chin, and green eyes that appraised Nivvy sharply.

"It's just Taja and a friend," Anzo said. "They won't be staying long."

"Not long at all," D'Alio assured her. "In an' out before you know it."

"Just like you always do, ay?" Anzo elbowed him. "That why you can't keep a girl?"

"Ha!" D'Alio let out a laugh. "There's no girl can keep up with me." He beckoned Nivvy toward the back door under the stairs. "Let's get you hid."

The back room, piled with rolls of carpet, had a small window through which silver moonlight spilled, and a space behind a stack of carpet that was long enough for a tired thief to lay his bones down and close his eyes, which was what Nivvy did. "Thank you," he told D'Alio.

"You can pay me back later," his friend said, and left the room, closing the door behind him.

Voices continued outside for a moment in a low murmur, and then Nivvy caught Anzo's wife saying, "Traitor?" He sighed. That's what they must think of him now. If he weren't so tired, he would be a good deal sadder about it. He'd come here to make amends, and now he was fleeing again. How did this make him a better person?

That was a question for morning-Nivvy. He didn't have the energy to ponder it now.

## ✿ 31 ✿

# THE SHALLOWS

H e had no idea how long he'd been asleep when he was woken by a thin hand shaking his foot. "Get up, get up," a woman's voice called in a soft hiss.

"Uh," he said, and propped himself up on his elbows. The thick smell of carpet surrounded him, and a cloud had dimmed the moon's light. "Right, I'm up. Horse is here?"

Anzo's wife shook her head. "Taja just left. I said I'd come to see if you needed water or tea, but you gotta go, before Taja gets back."

"No." Nivvy shook the sleep from his head. "D'Alio—Taja is my friend. He's going to help me get away."

"Some friend," she said sharply. "He gon' sell you, he said. Told Anzo he'd get a hundred gold for you so probably it's really two hundred, that's Taja."

"He wouldn't," Nivvy said. "Who'd pay two hundred gold for me? The Thieves Guild wants me dead, that's what he told me." But wheels turned in his head. D'Alio was his friend, sure, but what friendship was worth two hundred gold crowns? If that were true, that kind of money could change a life.

"All I know is he told Anzo he could sell you, but he had to go north for a long while. I called him 'traitor,' an' he said you'd do the same if you could sell him, an' then he an' Anzo talked a bit more an' then Taja left. You need to go."

"Maybe he en't wrong." Nivvy sat up. "I just wanted to come back, pay for what I did at the Guild. But first he said they wanted to kill me, now someone's offering gold for me? All I did was scarper when I should've helped, got a friend killed. Just want to make it right."

The woman reached for his hand and, when he grasped it, pulled. "Don't know what Inira got to say about takin' your own measure, but Massi tells us the wise merchant is the one what knows the value of his own goods. Don't take someone else's measure. Okay? Feel better?"

Nivvy allowed her to pull him forward, off the carpet rolls. The black cloud the mirror had brought over him had not dissipated, but perhaps it had thinned. In any case, if D'Alio was going to bring him north, he wasn't going to be atoning for Vicho's death. "Nah," he said, "but s'pose I'd best scarper again. It's what I'm good at." He eyed the window. "Not sure I can fit there."

"Nah," she said. "Have to go out front. I'll leave the door open a bit an' then I'll keep Anzo's attention. Get to the front door an' out, and I 'spect you can run faster than my husband. I love him but," she looked Nivvy up and down, "if he can catch you at a run, I'll eat one of them carpets."

"You'll get in trouble." Nivvy held her hand for a moment even after standing. "For letting the door open."

"Maybe. But if yer as good a thief as they say, mebbe you just opened it all on yer own." She winked at him. "I won't say if you don't."

"Thank you," he said. "Massi bless you."

"Already has. You spare your life an' that's payment enough." Her brow darkened. "Y'don't sell friends an' family, that's what he says. 'Gain a customer, lose a friend.' What Taja does, that's 'tween him and Inira, but we don't show a fella hospitality an' then turn around and betray him. Massi'd be displeased an' he'd show it, sure as sun."

"All right." Nivvy released her hand. "Go on. I'll give you a minute or two."

"Won't need more'n one." She smoothed down her nightdress with some pride.

He rubbed sleep from his eyes as she slipped out the door, pushing it almost all the way closed. Lamplight shone through the sliver that remained open. Nivvy put his ear to it and listened.

"Tell me again what we're gonna buy with our share of the gold," Anzo's wife purred to him.

His reply was indistinct, but she cooed at him. "Would he really sell it to us? Barrua'd love that, to be next door to his father. I wouldn't have to walk two blocks to bring him cakes and tea."

Again the soft reply, and then her voice. "So clever. And your brother thought to bring him here. Your family is blessed indeed. Ah!"

Her soft moan felt like the signal for Nivvy to ease open the door. He did so as quietly as he could—he could likely have opened it even had she not left it ajar—and slid out.

There was Anzo, seated against one of the rolls of carpet with a good view of the door; at least, he would have had a good view had his face not been buried in his wife's chest. His hands showed dark against her white nightdress, right where she was seated on one of his knees. "Ah!" she cried again, and her own hands disappeared between the two of them. Anzo gave a grunt, and Nivvy made for the door.

Here he had to navigate the latch, which fortunately did not have a great deal of rust on it, and he lifted it without a sound. When the door opened, it did so on silent oiled hinges, allowing him to slip out silently. But when he closed it, the latch caught with a thunk.

He didn't wait to hear whether Anzo had heard that but ran down the street as fast as he could.

Two blocks away, he thought he heard a horse's hooves, and he ducked down a street in the opposite direction, out of the merchant district and along the fringe of the great serpentine government buildings of Copper Port: The Port Control, the Heart of the City, the Conclave. Their stately bulks loomed dark over him as he kept to their shadows amid the stiff smells of parchment and ink. Here one public-house remained open, spilling boisterous chatter and light out onto the street, but Nivvy avoided that as well. The trees lining either side of Port Avenue, which ran from the Heart down to the docks, afforded some cover for him, past stately wooden houses and the shops he'd often stolen from but never patronized, until the down-sloping street curved around to his right and the masts of ships appeared before him like great reeds in the water.

Men idled on the boats keeping watch, some with lanterns, others little more than shadows. The closest swung his lantern around, though it was too far away to cast any light on where Nivvy was walking. He slowed his pace, matching the quiet lapping of the water at the docks, the gentle swaying of ships with the creaking of wood. No sound of pursuit disturbed the stillness.

D'Alio's betrayal, though, followed him even if the man himself wasn't. It was true what he'd said, that Inira taught that everyone was responsible for their own destiny, but that couldn't be the only teaching one followed, or the Thieves Guild wouldn't have held him responsible for Vicho. In fact, there wouldn't be a Guild if all thieves truly believed in everyone for themself. He'd thought he had friends here, or at least colleagues whose judgment he could trust, but D'Alio had proven as selfish as he'd thought himself to be. His dream of being First Thief at this guild, or any guild, felt foolish now, not only because he wasn't worthy, but because none of them were either.

His eyes slid up to the crows' nests at the top of the mainmasts on the nearby ships. He missed Zein. At least he'd saved them, with Scarlet's help. At least he'd done that good deed. If only they were here right now, and not only to fly to the wreck and bring back the seven-league boots; just for him to sit down and talk to. They would be horrified that D'Alio had betrayed him and would tell him something like, "then he wasn't really your friend." Just imagining Zein saying that made him smile. He hoped they were safe in Spire with Scarlet. He hoped one day he would see them again.

His eyes had drifted shut while remembering his friend, but the clink of a chain snapped them open. There were hours yet until daylight, and he needed the boots to flee but would not risk the swamp at night, not as tired as he was. He couldn't sleep here on the streets; the Watch would be along presently and D'Alio—and maybe much of the Guild—would be looking for him.

So he walked along the water, past the docks where the great galleons moored, down to the smaller docks where the fishing boats rocked gently against short wooden piers and the smell of fish drowned out everything except the salt of the ocean, and even that sometimes. These boats weren't guarded; they belonged to the families that lived in the wooden houses squatting to the right of the heavily rutted dirt road that separated the houses from the beach.

When the smell of refuse tickled his nose, he knew he was close, and indeed a few moments later the wall rose up before him.

Only four feet high on this side, the drop on the other side would be ten to fifteen depending on where along the length you were. The mortar between the large stones crumbled, but it had held for as long as Nivvy had been alive, as long as his parents had been alive. It stretched from the top of the hill, fifty feet short of the south gate, down into the ocean. There had perhaps been a time a few hundred years ago when Copper Port had been these small docks and The Shallows next to them, when the wall had been a real barrier and not just an inconvenience you could walk round if you really wanted to.

(Well, a barrier from the Shallows side. From this side it was just high enough to fling your refuse over and forget about it.)

He clambered up to the top of the wall. Looking back toward Copper Port proper, he saw a figure in the grey and orange uniform of the Watch staring at him, but someone climbing over into The Shallows wasn't anything they needed to be concerned about, so they weren't. It was barely even interesting, in that most people would just go up to where it ended and walk around if they wanted to.

Nivvy dropped down the ten feet to the other side, soft muck and sand and probably some rotting cloth, judging from the smell, but at least no sharp metal. No officers from the Watch on this side, no ships down in the water because the shelf here extended too far out to make a good port. Instead, it wrecked ships, and the favorable currents held the remains greedily, along with anything else people dumped into the sea.

The canvas-and-wood shelters here changed often, but the main paths between them tended to remain the same. Nivvy trod carefully through them, recognizing a house here and there, and once even recognizing a particular tunic that a friend of his father's had owned, a lovingly patched cotton garment with part of an embroidered crest on the sleeve. It hung drying half out of the window of their home, and the sight, like many here in Copper Port, reminded him of the good times and bad times when he was growing up here and still figuring out who he was.

Even some fifteen years later, his steps took him unerringly to the sturdy house with three wooden sides and thick sail canvas on the fourth side. The canvas had been painted with a design, three starfish in a triangle and two waves underneath them, his uncle's joke at having a family crest. The joke was common throughout The Shallows; Nivvy could see two or three more from where he was standing.

He drew in a breath of the fishy, rotty smell of The Shallows, then walked up to scratch gently on the door, another thick piece of canvas hung rather than stretched over a doorway.

Rustling came from inside and then whispers: "Someone's here?" "I heard it too." "I'll go see." A moment later, a brown hand grasped the canvas, and Nivvy's Uncle Foli looked out at him.

"Uncle Foli," Nivvy said. "It's me, Nivvy."

"Nivala?" Foli gasped. "Not joking, are you?"

"Nivali, now," Nivvy corrected. "Can I?" He gestured toward the inside.

"Aye, aye, come in!" Foli pulled the canvas aside and turned to the low bed on which another figure sat up. "Moru, look what the current's brought in!"

Nivvy's Uncle Moru, shorter and plumper than skinny Foli, lit a candle and stood, holding it up. His jet-black hair and beard gleamed as he came to stand next to Foli, whose grey streaks stood out in the dim light. "Who's this handsome fellow?"

"It's Nove's—child." Foli studied Nivvy carefully before the next word. "They go by Nivali now."

Moru smiled easily. "Welcome, Nivali."

"'He' is fine," Nivvy said to Foli's questioning look.

"Then come in, young man," Foli said, stepping back.

Nivvy bowed his head in respect and entered the small room. It had changed very little, from the bed taking up a third of the space to the old trunk at the foot of it, a trunk Foli had found and painstakingly repaired before Nivvy was born. Even the two wooden stools were the same. One had a mended leg where Nivvy had broken it trying to climb to the roof, and the other one's patterns he would always remember because he'd collected the driftwood and fashioned it himself, a present for his uncle Foli on the occasion of his marriage to Moru.

Shells still hung on the wooden walls, but Nivvy only recognized some of them. His eye lit on a circular design made up of the small cowry shells that were common along the beach.

"Moru did that," Foli said proudly, following Nivvy's gaze.

"They're all unbroken," Nivvy marveled. "This must have taken a long time."

"Not so long." Moru smiled, pleased.

"He has a talent for spotting the best quality shells."

Moru set the candle down on a stool. "The lad didn't come here to look at shells," he said.

Nivvy turned. "Well," he said. "Got in a spot of trouble with the Guild."

"We heard," Foli said, and at Nivvy's surprise, he nodded toward his husband. "Moru sells shells in the city and keeps an ear. Sounded as maybe someone got killed and they blamed you even though wasn't your hand on the knife."

"About right." Nivvy nodded. "So I set out to make my own name, nothin' but Inira and my horse." He couldn't bring himself to say her name aloud. "An' fell in with a magic woman, ah, met a djinn, got turned into a weasel and back again, an' now there's a fight I should be fightin' but..." He sighed.

His uncles stared at him. Foli spoke first. "You were turned...back?"

Nivvy nodded. Moru put a hand on Foli's arm. "Maybe he was under a spell to think he was a weasel."

"No." Nivvy sighed. "A djinn has the power to change someone. I did a service to—it's complicated." The memory and what he'd done itched badly in the back of his head. "And now there's a price on my head." There wasn't much question who was offering hundreds of gold pieces as a reward, somewhere in the north. Rose had told him she would get him back, and he'd imagined her sending the dragon, but queens also had very ordinary ways of enforcing their will. Did she know he'd helped Scarlet, that they'd escaped the volcano? Or was she summoning him to sit by her side, thinking she'd killed Scarlet? In either case, it was clear that Nivvy could no longer return to a Thieves Guild and that Rose would never let him go. "The magic woman—she wants me to come back to work for her again. She's a queen now."

"Work for a queen?" Moru's eyes brightened.

Nivvy shook his head. "Not nice work. She's—she's done terrible things. And I've helped her. Wish I hadn't, but I did."

"What's out to sea is lost and there's no use staring after it," Foli said.

"Is this fight with her or 'gainst her?" Moru asked.

Nivvy stared down at the wooden floor. "'Gainst."

"So you've a chance to make up for it."

"Hush," Foli said. "Lad said he don't want to fight."

"You always understood me better than they did," Nivvy said.

"Ah." Foli waved a hand. "Yer dad weren't bad. Just wanted best for you an' couldn't see any way but the way he knew."

"I know that well."

"We was raised with a strict hand on the rudder, and it made me wonder what could be outside the path, but it made your dad strict himself."

Nivvy smiled slightly. "I know. You told me."

"Why couldn't you stay with us?" Moru asked. "When they died?"

"Ah." Nivvy looked down again. "Jus' couldn't see myself here."

"We would've understood, you know. Whatever you wanted to do."

"Could you've stopped me marrying Oorin?"

Moru's face fell. "Maybe."

Foli patted Moru on the shoulder. "It's love behind that question, not blame."

Nivvy nodded agreement. "Figured you'd not want to be stuck with me, but sorry I left you holding the burial an' all. I shoulda said that years ago."

Foli shook his head. "Always knew you'd not be long for this place. Figured you for a thief, the way you always had a good haul, but didn't figure you for a man. You make a fine one though, an' that's not just the moon on the water."

Warmth rushed to Nivvy's cheeks. Perhaps it was the aftermath of looking into the mirror, but the selfishness of his leaving echoed back to him. If he'd stayed with his uncles—no, he reminded himself, even his uncles' love could not have solved the many problems he'd been fleeing. But he should have come to visit them. That, he regretted. "Thank you, uncle," he said. "Can I sleep here? Just until morning, and then I'll be gone."

"Soon as that, eh?" Moru asked.

Foli put an arm around his husband's shoulders. "That's Nivvy. Rushin' forward an' then gone before you know it."

Nivvy smiled tiredly. "It's been a day, it has. Did I tell you I escaped an exploding mountain this morning?" He sagged to the floor and leaned against a patch of wall without any decoration.

Hands grasped his wrists and lifted him to his feet. "You'll use the bed," Foli said firmly. "And in the morning we'll feed you and see you on yer way."

"No," Nivvy protested, but he didn't have the strength to back up his words, and so a moment later he sank down into the cloth and smell of fresh reeds, and just as it had throughout his childhood, the smell lulled him to calm and pulled him down into sleep.

He woke to a brighter, empty house. Foli and Moru had no doubt woken with the sun to do their diving as soon as light permitted. Above him, the thick canvas that made up the roof was broken up by square holes that had been cut into it and overlaid with thinner cloth, so the sun lit the house without allowing any rain in.

Nivvy stared up at the pattern in the ceiling and thought about what he would do next. The spell of the mirror was clearer to him now that it had faded overnight; though he still felt the guilt around Rahila's and Vicho's deaths, he no longer felt compelled to suffer punishment for them. Which left him the options of running from Rose or fighting Rose.

With the dream-charm, he could run and hide; south to Tagrabul where he wasn't so well known, and from there perhaps a ship to the Thousand Kingdoms. Rose might not give up looking for him, true, but it was a big wide world, and Nivvy didn't have to hide from her forever, only as long as he lived, and that would be what, another twenty years, thirty if he was lucky and didn't keep living the life he was living now? Even if he visited a different kingdom every month, he wouldn't get through half of the Thousand Kingdoms, and he'd always wanted to see the southern seas.

If he did that, he would have to find Zein and bring them along. The hawk had wanted to see other lands, and Nivvy would much rather go in their company than alone. And if he asked, they would go. They wouldn't be mad at him for running from Rose rather than fighting. "The hero can't have someone tell him to go on his adventure," they'd said.

But that hadn't been the end of the conversation, had it? "Do you really think I'm a hero?" he'd asked.

"I think you could be," they'd replied.

He sighed and rolled over onto his side, and from there he saw two small bean-cakes on a folded cloth. Now that he saw them, the smell he'd been aware of registered in his brain, and he reached out and devoured them. They were plain, but rich, and they were delicious.

Eating them reminded him of who he'd been as a child, and how different he was now. He'd stolen things as a child, but he hadn't known what it meant to be a thief; he'd dressed as a girl even though he knew that wasn't who he was. If he'd looked into the mirror the day his parents died, what would he have seen?

He lay back on the bed. Scarlet had said that the mirror showed you the truth of who you are, and that he couldn't deny. All the things it showed him were true, all those things he'd done.

But.

Inira's first lesson, the very first principle new thieves and acolytes were taught, was that when you couldn't find a way, you looked for another one. When the door is locked, try a window. When you can't get to the roof, dig to the cellar.

So if he wasn't a hero now...

*I think you could be.*

A hero, a real hero, didn't chase adventure looking to put themself in stories. A hero didn't dispense justice or revenge; well, maybe they did sometimes, but that wasn't what made them a hero. A hero was someone who saw a chance to make the world better and took that chance, no matter the risk, no matter the reward. Rose had hurt many people and would hurt many more, unless Nivvy stopped her. He'd tried to make the situation more complicated, but it wasn't.

He'd faced his old friend and the Thieves Guild, the things that, like heroic stories, past Nivvy had believed in and aspired to, and had seen the truth in them as clearly as if they'd been reflected in the Velki's mirror. His uncles and Zein saw good in him, and he now saw the possibility of it in himself. The belief was shaky, but it was there. He could be a Nivvy worthy of their confidence.

He drew in a deep breath and closed his eyes. When he opened them again, he swung his legs out of bed, stood, and stretched. The mirror might mean death to Rose—it quite definitely worked—but to Nivvy it showed a single path through the darkness to salvation. He couldn't remedy most of the things he'd done, but this one, this biggest one, he could.

It was easy when he put it together in a few steps. Go through the swamp, get the boots and mirror, go north, find Rose, tell her he'd come to join her, show her the mirror. And if it worked, it worked; if it didn't, well, maybe there was a Thousand Kingdoms in the next life. He couldn't properly enjoy it if he felt he'd left something undone here anyway.

Easy. He laughed. Just put on some magic shoes, go confront the most powerful being in the world, and try not to die. Whyever had he had doubts about that?

When Foli and Moru came back, he'd tell them a little, enough so they would know what was going on in the world. And then he'd leave before Rose could stretch her fingers down here, although if he was being honest with himself, he wouldn't care what she did to most of The Shallows. But he didn't want to put his uncles in danger.

When the canvas door was pulled aside to let in sunlight, Nivvy stood from the stool and stepped toward the tall, thin silhouette of his uncle Foli. "Uncle, I have to go, but I need to tell you something first."

He stopped at the tears on his uncle's cheeks. "I'm sorry," Foli said. "He threatened Moru."

A lean man pushed Foli out of the way and stopped with arms folded. "Now, Nivvy, I know you like a good scarper, but wasn't polite to run out on a friend."

"Well, Taja," Nivvy said to D'Alio, "when I heard you talk about sellin' me, I figured you weren't no friend, so scarpering seemed best."

D'Alio lifted the coil of rope he held in his right hand. "You going to make a fuss?"

"Depends," Nivvy said. "You're taking me north?"

"Why, is there a bigger ransom on you elsewhere?" D'Alio cracked a smile. "Tell me an' I'll share it with your uncles here."

"Not so's anyone's told me about it." Nivvy reached out to clasp Foli's hand; the old man shook. "I'll go with you. But I need to stop and pick up something first."

"Ha!" D'Alio tossed a loop of rope around Nivvy's shoulders and pulled it tight before Nivvy could slip out of it. "What's Inira say 'bout runnin' the same trick twice?"

"But—"

"Quiet or I'll leave orders for your other uncle to be drowned."

Nivvy met Foli's eyes. "I'll be all right," he said. "Sorry for bringin' this down on you."

The old man embraced him. "Inira keep you," he whispered, and then D'Alio yanked on the rope and Nivvy left his uncle behind.

&#x273f; IV &#x273f;

# THE ROSE

# ❧ 32 ❧

# THE ROAD TO DESTINY

D'Alio had got himself a small, covered cart, "so nobody recognizes you an' tries to fight me." Nivvy clambered into the back, which was empty save for a birdcage hanging near the front with a small swallow inside. "Guess we'll get food on the way?" he asked, but if D'Alio heard, he didn't answer. He lashed Nivvy to a steel ring inside the cart, then cut off Nivvy's charm bracelet and took the dream-charm ring as well (though Nivvy refused to tell him what it was). Its loss didn't bother Nivvy. If Rose wanted to check in on his dreams now then he could tell her truthfully that he was on his way.

The cart rattled out of The Shallows and out of the city. Nivvy hoped Foli and Moru would be safe now, making their life the best they could. Better without him involved, at least for now. He said a short prayer to Inira for them and then added, "My lady, I was going to do the right thing. Didn't need to send D'Alio to drag me there, did you?" He didn't expect an answer and received none, but he tried to find amusement rather than exasperation in his predicament. Perhaps Inira thought the boots would make the whole thing too easy, and Nivvy was meant to feel every step of the journey. Or perhaps she favored D'Alio more than him and wanted his friend to get his however many hundred gold.

Tied up though he was, Nivvy could move around and put his head near a gap in the covering so he could see out of it. The main road that ran north and south through Copper Port followed the shore about half a mile inland, so he could watch the buildings go by and smell the sea on the cool air.

The bean cakes did not sustain him for long, but outside of Copper Port the cart stopped and D'Alio called back, "Not a word, unnerstand?"

"I'll be quiet," Nivvy promised, "but I'll need some kind of necessary back here or yer cart won't smell too good."

D'Alio grumbled, but when he returned with two sacks of biscuits, dried meat, and several large skins of water (Nivvy guessed), he pointed at one of the skins. "When that's emptied, use that. Anything else, hold it 'til we make camp. I know how long you can hold it, remember. We both had to."

It would be hard for Nivvy to use the skin, especially with the cart moving, but it was better than nothing. D'Alio took some seed from a pouch and scattered it into the bottom of the birdcage, where the swallow glanced at it and then ignored it. And then they were on the road again.

That night, when they stopped, D'Alio came back to the cart and sat across from Nivvy, cross-legged. Nivvy wasn't inclined to talk, but his former friend seemed to want to justify his actions. "Weren't nothin' we'd seen before," he said. "These birds showed up bringin' posters, had a good likeness of you on't, said there was a gold reward for you up north. Lots of gold."

"More than a hundred, I wager," Nivvy said.

D'Alio held up two fingers and grinned wide enough to show the one rotten tooth he'd had as long as Nivvy had known him. "Imagine! Could go start my own guild if I wanted. Could finally be First Thief in Copper Port."

Nivvy nodded; First Thief was voted on, and if you had enough gold to spread around, you could buy the votes easily enough. "I get why you're doin' this," he said.

"You'd be doin' the same," D'Alio said. "For two hundred?"

Nivvy shook his head. "Maybe was a time I would've. 'Zbells, I took a chance for a promise of one hundred, but never betrayed a friend. Things're different now—"

"Wouldn't betray a friend, eh?" D'Alio's brow lowered. "You know what it cost me when you scarpered?"

That brought Nivvy's head up. "You helped me escape," he said.

"I helped you! You were fair cryin' about can't pay off blood prices, don't wanna be indentured, so I took pity. Got yer horse an' all, figured you'd go off for a month, steal some money, come back an' try to bargain. But no! You just vanished. They figured out who helped you. Yer only friend." D'Alio grimaced as though the words tasted bitter.

"Since Marzin got turned into a toad," Nivvy said. "What's happened to him, then?"

"Let 'im loose in the swamp." D'Alio gestured dismissively. "Seemed t'be where he'd be happiest."

He'd also abandoned Marzin by running away. The mirror's cloud gathered shadows around his thoughts. "You helped me," he repeated. "I was grateful. I never thought that it'd hurt you. What did they do? Did they make you pay the blood price?"

D'Alio looked away. "No," he said. "But I didn't get good jobs. Not fer months. An' when that poster came to us," he jabbed a finger in Nivvy's direction, "they tried t'hide it from me."

All thieves went through stretches of not getting good jobs. Nivvy saw that D'Alio was trying to justify to himself what he was doing to a friend. "I'm right sorry," he said. "I only thought well of you for helpin' me."

His former friend frowned, and then smiled again, thin-lipped. "Think of it like yer payin' me back for it now, and more."

Nivvy nodded. "Reckon that's fair."

After a moment, D'Alio tilted his head. "What'd you do that's got someone two hundred crowns mad at you?"

"Not sure it's 'mad' she is." Nivvy leaned his head back and closed his eyes. He thought about the volcano. "But maybe."

"Oh ho. Some skirt finally trapped the shark, did she?"

"I s'pose that's more or less what happened."

D'Alio cackled. "Shoulda known! Shoulda known. Always respected you for keepin' yer distance. Lots of thieves get trapped by love. Thing is, it gets you all eventually. An' she got you when you weren't even a real thief!"

"We sort of took a chance on each other," Nivvy said. "She got what she wanted; I didn't. So I left. But I guess she wants me back."

"That Nivali charm." D'Alio chuckled.

"Shouldn't laugh at it. It's earnin' you two hundred crowns. If she pays."

D'Alio looked at Nivvy sharply. "Got an offer. She wouldn't welch."

"She could. She's a queen; she can do what she wants."

That made D'Alio think, rubbing his chin so that his fingers scraped the slight unshaven roughness. "Nah," he said finally. "I see what yer doin'. Try to talk me out of it, someone else gets the two stacks. Maybe you keep it."

"I'm telling you true," Nivvy said. "I'm not the one what betrayed a friend."

At that, D'Alio got up and left the cart without a response or a look back. He did not speak to Nivvy again that night, nor the next morning when they set out, not until the afternoon when they passed a caravan and he warned Nivvy again to be quiet. Nivvy spent much of this time thinking about all the years he'd spent with D'Alio on jobs, drinking, practicing, talking about their futures, and wondering if it had always been a friendship that could be knocked down with enough gold.

He also wondered what he could do to Rose without the mirror. Perhaps being able to resist the Crown would help. If he could get it away from her, then give it to someone else who could order her to never use magic again...before she noticed and killed him with a thought...provided he could find someone he trusted with the power of the Crown...

There were a lot of "ifs" there, and Polu had taught him that ifs were like fleas: you might never get rid of all of them, but you should get rid of as many as you could. Problem was, the only person he would have a chance to plan with was D'Alio, and even if his former friend had not recently betrayed him, he wasn't sure he would trust D'Alio with the power of the Crown.

Maybe Rose would want to keep him around. Maybe he would have a chance to earn her trust, and identify someone else nearby who could be trusted with the Crown. He sighed and leaned his head back against the canvas of the cart's sides. Without a better plan, he would have to wait for Inira to show him a surer path. If she didn't, that meant that he would have to deal with all those fleas.

After several days the road grew busier. Nivvy saw near them both the colorful attire of Copper Port and the southern cities and the drab cotton and leather of the north, along with some who looked like soldiers with unfamiliar crests. That night, D'Alio pulled the cart well off the road as he'd done before, but this time when he opened the cart, for the first time since that first night, he spoke to Nivvy. "We're coming up on Sul'Aji," he said, "and it's getting more crowded. I don't want to be among people. If I go west along one of these roads, can I still get to Heiterflus?"

"I don't know," Nivvy said. "Never been there."

But partway through those words, the swallow answered. "There are many roads north," it said in a deep voice with a strange accent and a harshly staccato rhythm of speech. "You will have to return to this one, but you may avoid Sul'Aji."

"Good," D'Alio said, and did not address the swallow again.

But Nivvy sat next to the cage. The past few nights, D'Alio had let the swallow out of its cage to catch insects and it had always come back, so he'd suspected it was a former-human, but it could also simply have been tame. He didn't want to assume. Now it'd talked in front of him, there wasn't much point in pretending he hadn't heard or wasn't interested. "Are you from there?" he asked. "Heiterflus?"

Before the swallow could answer, D'Alio said, "This is the messenger. He brought the news of the price on your head and he's our guide. Had to get him out the Guild without anyone else noticing."

"How long you been a swallow?" Nivvy asked.

"A short time," the bird said. "Queen Bella transformed us and ordered us to fly to every city in the land to seek out Nivali al Tamsin with greatest haste. Six of us went to Copper Port."

"Good gamble." Nivvy wondered how many had gone to Spire. "How many were changed?"

"Dozens."

"Always wanted to be a bird, did you?"

The swallow didn't answer for a moment, and then said, "I wanted to be a maker of maps. There is a school in Heiterflus for that. I was a journeyman map-maker. But Queen Bella summoned the entire school and when she said we should all submit to be turned into birds, the idea was right. I don't know why. It felt as though Reik himself spoke to us through her, and who could deny the king of the Gods?"

"It's that crown," Nivvy told him. "When she wears it, people have to do what she says. Even djinn."

"I don't know what a djinn is," the swallow said.

"You might know her as a fairy."

"There aren't fairies anymore."

"Maybe not now," Nivvy said, "but that's on account of how this one got her powers taken. The point is that it's the crown. How do you like being a swallow? Closer to Apo? Or, what'd you call him, Reik?"

"Catching insects is hard work but I don't like any other food," the swallow complained.

"You'll get better at it," Nivvy assured him.

He fluffed his feathers out. "Shan't have to. Now I'm returning with you, I'll be human again. Queen Bella promised."

"Very nice for you. What about all your fellows?"

"They didn't find you, did they? Only I did."

Nivvy nodded. "Bad time to need a map in Heiterflus, I suppose."

"What?"

"Not many left to make them, I mean. Sorry."

The swallow looked down. "Queen Bella is going to rewrite all the maps."

"Don't doubt it."

"Aren't you worried?"

Nivvy looked up at the bird, whose beady dark eyes stared down. "You'd think I should be, wouldn't you?" He stretched his legs out. "Long way between here and there."

"Don't doubt I'll get you there," D'Alio told him through the covering.

"I don't," Nivvy called forward. "Just saying, never know what might change."

"I know what won't change, an' that's you in the cart and me here pulling into Heiterflus."

Nivvy looked up at the swallow and tried rolling his eyes, but if the bird sympathized, he wasn't able to return the gesture. More likely he thought Nivvy a fool.

Regardless, Nivvy had an opportunity to talk to him alone that night when D'Alio walked off to relieve himself. The swallow's cage was open, so Nivvy hissed at him, "Pss! Here." He nodded over to his shoulder.

The bird flew down, checking the bushes in the direction D'Alio had gone, from which some loud grunts issued. "Don't worry 'bout him," Nivvy whispered. "From the noises he's makin', he'll be a few minutes. What's your name?"

"Friedich."

"Friedich, you know where Spire is from here?"

"Several days' journey west and a little south. It is not on our road."

"You think you could fly there? See, I've got a friend, a hawk, might be in the company of an eagle, and I'd just love to get a message to 'em. Tell 'em I'm alive."

The swallow's small feet shifted on his shoulder. "This sounds like you are asking me to fly into the beak of a hawk. Or an eagle."

"No, no. They're perfectly friendly. They're former-humans as well."

"Is that what you call me? 'Former-human'?"

"It's, ah," Nivvy stumbled. "It's what they call themselves."

"And you want me to fly to Spire and find this hawk and eagle and tell them you are well."

A loud flatulent sound came from the bushes. "Yes," Nivvy said quickly, "only tell them in a certain way. There's a particular message I need to get to them." He wasn't about to tell the swallow about the mirror unless he was sure he was going to go. "Will you do it, Friedich?"

For a moment the swallow didn't move, and then the silence was interrupted by D'Alio's relieved groan. "I don't think I ought," Friedich said. "Queen Bella promised to make me human again when we return. If you escape or if I get eaten, I will not see my parents again. So I will stay with the cart."

Nivvy exhaled. "But," he started, and then Friedich flew off, not back to the cage, but away and quickly out of sight.

D'Alio came back to the camp shaking his head. "I miss fish. That dried meat don't do me no good," he said, and then spied the empty cage. "Where's the bird?"

"Still hungry," Nivvy said.

D'Alio sat down across from him. "What'd you do, anyhow, that this queen wants you so bad?"

Nivvy was glad for a chance to tell his story, after so many silent nights. "I made myself useful," he said. "I stole a ring from a djinn for her."

D'Alio scoffed. "You never. You made Marzin do the wizard job an' you turned down any other magic jobs."

"I did that thing in Tagrabul with the wizard's coins. You just weren't with me on that'n. After the ring, I got a magic crown from the bottom of a lake."

"Then what? You just walked away?"

"Aye. Job got too difficult. She's scary an' powerful, an' just because I stepped right six times don't mean I'll step right the seventh."

"Hmm." D'Alio rubbed his chin, where his beard had thickened after not having shaved for nearly a week. "How much she pay you? You got all that gold somewhere?"

Nivvy laughed. "Why? You gonna offer me freedom for it? Seems you woulda done that right away if you'd had a mind."

"Maybe I been thinkin'," D'Alio said.

"Ah, now that explains the constipation."

The other man scowled. "You'd do best to remember who holds the rope."

Nivvy glanced down at his bound wrists. "She didn't pay me in gold. I got turned into a weasel after stealing from the djinn, and when I got the crown for her, she stole the djinn's power with it an' turned me back, an' that was my payment."

"Hoo hoo," D'Alio crowed. "Now I know yer havin' me on. If yer gonna make up a story, don't use one I already know. You got turned into an animal like Marzin but then turned back? How come you got turned back but nobody else can be?"

"I told you, she has a djinn's power."

Uncertainty flickered in D'Alio's eyes but didn't touch his smile. "Yer tryin' to scare me. Well, I'm not the Quartermaster's husband. I don't believe in tales like that."

"Believe or don't, but it happened that way."

D'Alio leaned back. "If she's powerful as a djinn, then I'm of a mind to put her in my debt and see what may come of it."

"Probably nothing," Nivvy said. "Ask Friedich."

"Who?"

"The swallow. Think he asked to be changed? She got a crown will make you agree to whatever she says. Like as not she gets me an' then tells you you don't need the reward and you'll nod as nice as anything."

D'Alio snorted and closed his eyes. "Last time she wouldn't pay me, now she's got magic what'll make me not want to be paid. Ring the other one, why don't you."

"Don't say I didn't warn you." Nivvy continued to watch the bushes for Friedich, but when the swallow reappeared, he flew right to his cage and stayed there without a word.

## ❧ 33 ☙

## FEATHER DREAM

Friedich said the journey would take definitely at least three weeks, but probably not a month. Just over one week into it, Nivvy's wrists were chafed and his back sore from trying to find a comfortable position in the cart with bound arms, so he asked D'Alio to free him. As they had just left the trade city of Sulimas behind, and Friedich informed them there would not be another city for several days, D'Alio complied, and the ride was more comfortable from then on.

The frequency of D'Alio's complaints about the dried meat and biscuits he himself had purchased only grew the longer they traveled. Nivvy found the diet boring but tolerable, especially when compared to the lean times over the last year or so; when his priority was to keep Rahila fed, he sometimes ate rotten food he had to pick maggots out of. Dried meat and even stale biscuits were fine for a while.

The concession D'Alio made to his stomach was to stop at a public-house for an ale every third or fourth day, and sometimes he brought back enough for Nivvy to have a swallow. It was a nice change from the musty water, though afterwards Nivvy's mouth tasted sour, and he needed water to clean it out.

It was after one of the nights when he'd had a few swallows of ale that his thoughts turned, as they often did, to Zein. Riding in the cart over a very poorly maintained road, Nivvy was grateful for his freed hands in bracing himself. He looked up at Freidich's cage, which brought back memories of his own time in a cage, as it often did. Then he thought of his escape and of Caphram, and that brought thoughts of Zein, very strongly. He could almost see the hawk in front of him, questing about as though looking for a grass-rat they'd spotted just a moment before.

Then their eyes met his and they said, *Nivvy!*

He startled upright. "Zein?"

"What?" Friedich said.

*I'm talking in your head the way we talked to Scarlet in the ring*, the hawk said. *You're alive!*

He'd always talked aloud to Scarlet, but he didn't want to do that with the swallow and D'Alio sitting right there. *Can you hear me?* he thought carefully at Zein.

*Yes! Where are you?*

*I'm in a cart on the way north to Heiterflus. Where Rose is. Where are you? How are you talking to me? I'm so happy to see you!*

*I found him!* Zein called to the side, and then turned back to Nivvy. *We found a wizard with a spell, and we traded him Scarlet's ring. She still had it. What happened to you?*

*I lost Rahila.*

*Oh, Nivvy, I'm so sorry*, Zein said. *In the volcano?*

*Aye. And then...I went back to Copper Port to pay an old debt.*

*Did you pay it off with the boots? Is that why you're in a cart? What city did you pass? We can come find you.*

*No*, he said. *I hid the boots and the mirror.*

Zein was silent, and then something to their side took their attention. *He's in a cart on the way to Rose*, they said.

*You need to get the mirror*, he said urgently. *It's in the cabin of a wrecked ship in the swamp. South of Copper Port.*

*Why did you leave it behind?*

His lips were dry, his mouth too. *I—I didn't think I could do it. Fight Rose, I mean.*

*But you're heading north toward her.*

*I'm a prisoner. She sent out dozens of messengers with a price on my head.*

*Oh.* Zein's head lowered.

Their disappointment stung deep in his chest. *I looked in the mirror*, he said, trying to explain. *It said I wasn't a hero, but when I remembered what you—*

Zein's head snapped around to the side and then they jumped. *Scarlet's just clawed out the wizard's eyes,* they said. *Now she's tearing out his throat. Eagles have very powerful beaks. Did you know that? I knew they were sharp, because mine is too, but—*

And then they were gone. *Zein?* Nivvy called, and then called aloud, "Zein!"

"What?" Friedich asked again. "Why do you say that word?"

The spell must have died when the wizard did. Nivvy sagged back against the side of the cart. He hoped Zein had enough information to get the mirror. He wished he'd been able to tell them that he was going to fight Rose anyway, after he'd decided he was too weak.

"What's goin' on back there?" D'Alio demanded through the canvas.

"Nivvy's saying a strange word. Maybe it's a spell."

"Ha!" D'Alio barked. "He don't know magic, an' I got his charms." He paused. "Does he? Is anything happening?"

"I was sleeping!" Nivvy yelled. "I had a dream about my friend and then I woke up and called their name, that's all."

"It sounded like a spell," Friedich said.

"It wasn't a spell." Nivvy drew up his knees and rested his arms on them.

"If something happens back there," D'Alio called, "tell me."

"Nothing's going to happen," Nivvy muttered.

And nothing did, not that day nor the next, nor the day after that. The cart moved up—literally, as the road most often inclined upward— into country Nivvy had never visited. "That road leads to Vir'Aji," Friedich said as they approached one intersection, and Nivvy remembered that name from Oigal's story, but otherwise he had no bearings. In the distance, in the opposite direction from Vir'Aji, mountains jutted along the horizon, but he didn't know if any of those were the ones around Glædeligdal, and he didn't want to ask Friedich, who had been pretty poor company on the ride, what with not talking and refusing to carry Nivvy's message. The air, chillier and drier than in Copper Port, carried a smell of pine that he rather enjoyed; that and the memory of Zein were bright spots he held onto.

About a week after Zein's contact, or maybe more (the days blurred together), the cart slowed. Nivvy peeked through the gap in the canvas to see what was happening. On the right side, there was nothing but pine forest, wisps of fog clinging to the trees. On the left, a great statue lay on its side facing the road. The lady of stone looked old and worn, but her beatific face beamed out at the road as if she were merely resting and supremely content with her lot. Her arms had once been outstretched, perhaps, but they had both broken at the elbows and lay askew in front of her. She wore a crown of flowers and long robes from which a small stone cat peered out. Behind her, a dirt road or perhaps a wide path stretched away across fields broken up by low walls of stone.

"Friedich," Nivvy said, "what's that statue?"

He pulled the canvas aside, but the swallow barely looked. "Many towns had statues of Prula. She is a goddess of the harvest, and her statues are good luck. But Queen Bella has decreed that she will provide for the kingdom and so all the statues of Prula must be torn down. Many towns brought the statues to the road so that all travelers see their dedication to the Queen."

This must be Rose's sister; who else's statues would Rose demand destroyed? Though the stone was worn, Nivvy could see the likeness in her features and imagined her, a fairer mirror of Rose. "She looks like a good goddess," he said.

"The Queen is our goddess now," Friedich intoned, and then looked around as though afraid Rose might manifest in a corner from where she'd been listening to him.

"Strange place," D'Alio said, and the cart sped up again. "Nivvy, you remember that town outside Tagrabul? With all the statues?"

"Ay," Nivvy said, not wanting to give D'Alio any acknowledgment of their friendship, not in these situations. If the man was feeling guilty, good.

"Those weren't the same as these, but—"

"Say," Nivvy interrupted, "Friedich. I bet you have a story of Prula, eh? Goddess of the harvest? How'd she come to that? I never heard of her. Come on," he went on when the swallow ignored him. "I'm curious now we've seen the statue."

"I am not a storyteller," the swallow said stiffly.

"I got nothin' to pay you with in any case. I bet you know the story, though, ay? Come on, you tell me one, I'll tell you one."

"I have no interest in your stories."

"What," Nivvy said, "all that time makin' maps of faraway places and you never wondered what stories they had? I bet you'll like the one

THE PRICE OF THORNS

about the Honest Merchant. I heard this from a merchant of the Thousand Kingdoms."

Friedich looked down at him and then tilted his head. "Tell me your story first."

"Fine." So Nivvy told the Tale of the Honest Merchant as well as he remembered it, which he fancied was reasonably well, and he was pleased when D'Alio interrupted to ask him to repeat a part, because he had hoped the other thief would be listening as well.

When he'd concluded the tale, Friedich was silent for a moment and then admitted grudgingly, "That was a good story."

"So? Tell me about Prula."

"All right." The swallow shifted on his perch, looked around nervously (or maybe that was just how swallows moved), and then spoke in a low voice. "The Sky and the Sea had five children, did you know this?" Nivvy shook his head. "There was Reik, the king of the gods, and his brothers Kak and Vik, gods of war and industry, and his sisters Sij, goddess of love, and Tig, goddess of wisdom. But there were also other gods and goddesses and I do not know where they came from. Prula was one such. She could make the harvests grow and she saw to it that all men received the bounty of the land. Vik took her to wife because he also loved the land, and they had a daughter, whose name was Decia.

"But his brother Kak desired Prula for himself and was so jealous that he determined to steal her. He could not kidnap her himself, because she was always with her husband. But her daughter was curious and so he lured her with trinkets into his palace, a dark place devoid of joy.

"When Prula learned of Decia's disappearance she wept for an entire month. Rain fell everywhere without stopping. And then she withdrew, and all warmth went from the land. Crops died, people died.

"Then Tig worried that her brother's rash action would mean the end of people. So she went to Kak and told him that if he did not release Decia, there would be no more people and no more wars. Kak said that he would release Decia if he could spend three months out of the year with Prula. Vik did not like this, but Tig pointed out that if he did not agree, Kak would keep Decia and Prula would likely die.

"Vik agreed to the bargain on the condition that he could take something of Kak's while Kak had his wife. Kak, who had no wife nor children, agreed to this. So Vik took Kak's manhood."

"Smart," Nivvy said, and D'Alio cursed from the front of the cart.

"And that is why there are three months during which the land is cold and nothing will grow, and why it is so hard to wage a war during that time."

Nivvy gave an approving nod. "You're a better storyteller than you give yourself credit for," he said.

"I don't think I am," Friedich replied.

"Why'd you have to talk about his manhood?" D'Alio shouted back.

"It's how the story goes," Friedich said mildly. "That's why there's winter."

Nivvy couldn't help but notice that Prula's daughter had been kidnapped in the story, just as in the story Scarlet had told them. The rest of it didn't seem to match as well, but he'd heard three different versions of the story of Glædeligdal, so there you were.

That evening when D'Alio pulled the cart off the road, the air was cool enough that he made a small fire. Sitting next to Nivvy, whom he'd left unbound, perhaps thinking they were far enough from Copper Port that Nivvy wouldn't run away, D'Alio asked him, "Changed, en't ya?"

The question surprised Nivvy enough that he forgot his desire not to talk to his captor. "What d'you mean?"

D'Alio waved at the cart. "I know yer coulda got out of them knots. Told the bird to yell if you jumped out back. But you didn't even try, not once. Nivvy I knew, he'da done a scarper first chance, first couple days outta Copper Port."

"You threatened my uncles," Nivvy said mildly.

D'Alio squinted at him. "Can't just be that. You coulda got back to warn 'em. 'Zbells, you coulda attacked me."

Nivvy hid a smile. He hadn't realized that his peaceful behavior had unnerved D'Alio so much. "Maybe I want to go north," he said.

"Nobody wants to go somewhere there's a gold reward on 'em."

"I didn't know about the reward until you kidnapped me."

"Yer different," D'Alio said. "Y'always were a little different, an' I liked that, but this? Seems like yer not a thief at all."

"Did you not hear the Tale of the Honest Merchant?" Nivvy countered. "His charity, honesty, faith, and industry were rewarded. I returned to Copper Port to face my crime honestly. I'm allowin' you to get two hundred crowns; that sounds like charity." D'Alio sneered at that. "An' maybe now I'm restin' on faith."

"So yer a follower of Massi now, is it?" D'Alio jeered.

"Inira also rewards honesty, charity, faith, and industry," Nivvy said. "But some of us who mightn'ta got all the virtues, we need friends to get us there. The right kind, not the kind that lets us be selfish liars." He grinned at D'Alio, humorless. "We always had faith in Inira an' ourselves, but it was the wrong kind, the kind that said things'd come to us because we deserved them. There's another kind, the kind what accepts what Inira gives you an' works to get what you want." He thought for a moment. "I wish I coulda saved Marzin, but could be he's happier in the swamp now. If he wanted to not be there, I s'pose he coulda told you, eh?"

D'Alio frowned, and then laughed shortly. "Ha. That kinda faith? That's for them too weak t'make the world fit them. You an' me, we coulda made whatever world we wanted. But now I'm makin' the world an' you're lettin' it happen t'you. Maybe you shoulda stayed my friend, hah?"

"Maybe so," Nivvy said. "Wasn't all bad. We did some good. But I feel good now. I think Inira wants me t'be here."

"Maybe she wants you t'be here so she can favor me with gold." D'Alio winked. "Think of that, did you?"

Torn between a desire to talk to D'Alio as though he were talking to himself a year ago and the desire to shake his captor's smug confidence, Nivvy threaded the needle. "Was a time I thought gold or bein' First Thief would make me happy too," he said. "Friends told me it would, wanted all the same things, so I went along. But there's other things can make us happy. I don't think I was ever really happy with you. With you it was more about hunger, about gettin' what we thought we deserved. We didn't think about bein' who we were an' what life we might want if we let go the things everyone else expected from us."

"So you're happy now?" D'Alio leaned forward. "On yer way to someone who wants yer so bad they set aside two stacks of gold?"

"I'm happy now," Nivvy said, and was surprised to find it was true. "I've got friends—one, at least—who think I can do some good. Maybe I'll die, but at least I'll have tried. That'll feel a lot better than runnin' away my whole life."

D'Alio snorted and got up. "Long as you don't die before I get my gold," he said, and walked off to relieve himself.

Nivvy leaned back on the ground and stared up at the darkening sky. It was very possible that these were the last days of his life. This company wouldn't have been his choice, but the crisp air and the fresh buds on the trees around them, the quiet of the grass and bushes a good way from the road, these were new, and Nivvy was glad he had a chance to see them before he died. The tree-rats here looked different from the ones even as far north as Lake Beatrice; they were a drab charcoal grey, but with bushier tails, and they chattered like a saw blade cutting through a piece of knotted wood. Nivvy spotted a bird he didn't recognize, a brilliant blue with a soft trilling call, and an orange-and-black bird he did know.

Zein would like these woods, he thought. He hoped they would get to see them.

## ❦ 34 ❧

# THE ROSE PALACE

Two days later, the cart stopped in the middle of the day. Nivvy checked to either side and saw no more statues of interest (they had passed two more the previous day). A moment later, a gruff voice said, "What is your business in the Kingdom of Heiterflus?"

D'Alio hesitated and then said, "Bringing a prisoner to Queen Bella."

"You have business with the Queen? Then you must have been given an instruction—"

"The Queen is aware of them, Deisser," said a light voice atop the cart. "They are to pass freely." Then there was a flutter. Nivvy pushed around the gap in the canvas in time to see a crow land on the shoulder of a great brown bear, which was standing on its hind feet and dressed in a white tabard with a rose on the front, and nothing else. The crow put its beak to the bear's ear and spoke quietly.

The bear nodded and looked up toward D'Alio. "Pass," it said in the gruff voice, and the crow fluttered back up to the roof of the cart.

Friedich looked up and then at Nivvy as the cart moved on. "What's happening?" he said in a hoarse whisper.

"There's a crow on top of the cart. They spoke to the bear guard and the guard let us pass," Nivvy whispered back.

"How long has it been there?" Again, Friedich looked up at the top of the cart, pacing on his perch.

"First I seen of them," Nivvy said. "Maybe D'Alio knows." He turned to the front of the cart.

"No no!" Friedich said. "If you ask, that will be suspicious." He hunched his wings and huddled into a small feathery ball.

"Did you not know what to say to the guard?" Nivvy asked.

"I did not know there *was* a pass sign. I am a simple maker of maps." Friedich hid his head under his wing and would not speak again, not when Nivvy asked whether all the guards had been turned into bears, not when Nivvy tried to flatter him into telling another story.

"Hey," Nivvy called up to the top of the cart. "You! Crow!"

After a moment, the light voice replied, "My name is Remelstaub."

Friedich removed his head to stare in horror at Nivvy, and then hid again when Nivvy responded. "Good day to you. I'm Nivvy and that fellow driving the cart is D'Alio."

"I know who you are, and I care not for the others," Remelstaub responded.

"You may not, but it's my pleasure to meet you." Nivvy leaned back. "I thought we were in Heiterflus already? Have we only just entered it?"

"We have entered Heiterflus proper. We have just been in the kingdom of Skanlapp," he pronounced both a's very long, as "ahhh," "which has traditionally been allied with Heiterflus and is currently under the rule of Queen Bella."

None of those names meant anything to Nivvy, except for the last one, and none of that information changed anything. "Will you ride the rest of the way with us?"

"I will."

"Is the Queen looking forward to seeing me, you think?"

There was a moment's pause, and then Remelstaub said, "The Queen has made it clear to us that she wishes your presence."

"Puttin' an awful lot of effort to it," Nivvy said. "Will there be a banquet for us when we arrive? Perhaps some fish? It's been dried meat and biscuits the whole way and I know D'Alio up there has a delicate constitution."

"Mind your business," D'Alio growled. Remelstaub didn't respond, and after a moment D'Alio asked, "She mean to harm Nivvy?"

"You'll get your payment," Remelstaub said.

D'Alio absorbed that and then said, "Sorry, mate."

"I'm not worried," Nivvy lied. "She wants me there alive, ay? So either she likes me or wants to kill me in person, an' while that last is a real thing that's not unlikely, I also might be able to talk her out of it."

"Might could," D'Alio said, "but yer history don't exactly suggest that."

"Nobody threatened to kill me to my face before." This also wasn't quite true, but as far as D'Alio knew, it was.

"Ah well, it's a poor life if your first threat of death is your last." D'Alio laughed.

"Wasn't my first," Nivvy said. "Guild was gonna put me to death, eh?"

"Ah," D'Alio said, "I mighta exaggerated that just a bit. T'get you away, you know?"

That figured. "Well," Nivvy said. "Didn't know it at the time, so I thought it was a real death threat. So it counts."

Did the eel's attack count as a death threat? It should, shouldn't it? Even if it couldn't talk, the eel was definitely threatening him with death. And where did Rose fall on that? Nivvy felt like Jalil in the story of Inira's figurine, facing a choice that was being made for him. Would he face death or reward? In this case, he doubted there would be a third option. This wasn't an adventure he would simply walk away from—but that adventure happened to everyone sooner or later, and there was some peace in knowing that this was the one. "Thanks, Inira," he said.

Friedich called back to D'Alio, "He's saying strange names again!"

AFTER TWO MORE DAYS OF TRAVEL, THEY STOPPED AT ANOTHER guard post. This time, peering out, Nivvy spied ancient grey stone walls stretching to either side, but with gaps along the top here and there. Rather than just one bear, three occupied this post that Nivvy could see, all wearing the rose tabard he'd seen previously. Two of the bears, a black and a brown, ambled about on all fours, while the third had risen to a standing position to challenge the cart. "What business have you in the city of Heiterflus?" they asked.

Again, Remelstaub flew down to the bear's shoulder and whispered in their ear, and the bear allowed the cart to move on, this time through streets lined with small stone buildings huddled together in groups. Nivvy spotted some thatched roofs, patchy and dry, but the farther in they traveled, the more the houses pressed together under sturdy slate roofs. Nivvy hadn't seen this style of squat, solid building in such abundance before; they resembled some of the buildings in the center of Haggerin, perhaps the oldest ones. As the cart rolled on over stone-paved streets, a white banner with a single rose on it showed more and more often. They hung from windows and roofs, sometimes over doors, looking quite foreign to the rest of the city, like petals from some giant flower that had been blown down and were yet to be swept away.

But the most unnerving thing was that Nivvy saw almost no people. Not in windows, not walking along the street, not standing in doorways calling passers-by into their shops. At one shop, a gaunt woman appeared at the door to watch the cart go by, and then retreated silently. A young boy gawked from a second-story window. A pair of men rode horses in the opposite direction. But that was all.

With every empty street they passed, Nivvy's neck prickled more strongly. If there were no people, though, there were hundreds of birds: mockingbirds, jays, swallows, crows, and more he didn't recognize. They crowded the roofs and watched the streets silently, sometimes fidgeting or preening. Then he spotted a rat running along the street with a rose flag on its back, and on the next street, a pair of foxes sauntered alongside the cart for a short time talking about a job they'd been ordered to carry out. That was when he realized that many, if not all, of the birds must be former-humans, that Rose had not only transformed guards and map-makers. As Scarlet had said, she wanted to show off her power, and the city streets nearly empty of anyone but former-humans for certain accomplished that.

He would have asked Friedich about it, but Remelstaub's presence had dulled conversation in the cart, which was not exactly knife-sharp to begin with. Even in the evenings, when the crow either remained perched atop the cart or flew off to feed the way Friedich did, his absence only reminded Nivvy (though Friedich was the one who remarked on it most loudly) that they had no idea how long the crow had been traveling with them. Nivvy tried to reassure the swallow that the crow's mission was only to guide them through the guard posts, so it wouldn't have been there for the telling of the story of Prula (which seemed to be the primary worry). This quieted Friedich but did not appear to reassure him.

That night, D'Alio asked directions to a stable where, for a small fee, he was allowed to park the cart behind it. "No point paying for a room when we can sleep in the cart," he told Nivvy as he opened the back of the cart and climbed in. Nivvy stood to stretch his legs and walked to the end to breathe in the air of the city, which here smelled of hay and horses and a nearby river.

Friedich flew past them, off to feed himself. D'Alio watched him go. "Wouldn't be at all surprised if that's the last we see of 'im," he said. "Been twitchy ever since the crow."

"You haven't been turned into an animal," Nivvy said. "If he's got so much as a scrap of hope he'll be turned human again, he'll come back."

D'Alio chewed over this. "You think that's why she's turned so many people into animals? They got to be loyal to her now or they're animals forever?"

"I...um. Might could be." Nivvy looked up at the birds roosting on the roofs and felt a sinking feeling. Where might Rose have recently learned the lesson that former-humans would be loyal servants if she were the only one who could change them back? Was that what she'd meant in the dream when she'd said, "Thanks to you"?

"Those bear guards and the swallow there and the crow—"

"Remelstaub," a shadow croaked from the top of the cart.

"—and besides that, all these birds been talkin' to each other, an' I saw a pair of foxes trotting down the road talkin' on how best to steal sommat or other."

"I suppose," Nivvy said. "Nobody else can change 'em back."

"Zbells, think of that." D'Alio shook his head. "Livin' as an animal. Wait, now, you did that a'ready." He laughed.

Nivvy chuckled, but his mind was on Remelstaub and Friedich and all of the others, changed to animals perhaps because of him. Course, it was fair odds if Rose hadn't changed 'em, she'd have done something else—made rings with eyes in them maybe, like Scarlet's ring, or else something else out of the old stories like magical spiked collars.

What would happen when Rose didn't turn enough people back? Would the former-humans revolt or flee? Would she turn enough people back to keep everyone's loyalty, but only that many? How quickly would that use up the magic in the world?

And if Nivvy and Zein did somehow manage to defeat her, what would happen to all those former-humans?

He couldn't worry about that. What the former-humans showed him was that Rose needed to be defeated one way or another. He already knew she wouldn't leave him alone, and that was reason enough for him to go, but he'd been thinking that if he died, that would also solve the problem. Now he saw quite clearly that there was more than just his peace at stake, more clearly than when Scarlet had given him a formless worry about magic leaving the world. So this mission became more important and heroic, like the time when he and D'Alio had been sent to steal the ruby crown that the merchant Tolungamon was going to use to finance his new slave trade.

If it wasn't him, then maybe Zein and Scarlet could somehow bring the mirror here and get around the crown and all Rose's powers. But the thought of Zein having to risk their life because he, Nivvy, had failed, itched like no other thought he'd ever had.

D'Alio did not tie him up that night before falling asleep in the cart. Friedich did return, but remained silent, flying directly to the perch in his cage and putting his head under his wing, ignoring D'Alio's snoring. Nivvy felt alert and awake, and the idea came to him to go to the palace himself. Zein and Scarlet might have reached the city by now and be looking for him, and they wouldn't spot him in the covered cart.

He hopped lightly down, landed without a sound, and looked up to the top of the cart for the crow. Nothing stirred amid the shadows, so Nivvy walked quietly around the corner of the stable.

If his friends had arrived, they would likely be near the palace. He'd hoped that he would be able to see it from here; in Copper Port, the Heart of the City's bell tower rose above all the other buildings. In Tarisch, the Emperor's palace had been atop a large hill, visible from anywhere in the city. But now, as he scanned the moonlit horizon, he saw only rooftops and a great dark wall in the middle of the city.

In the other direction, very near, he heard water, which accounted for the riverine smell in the air. The palace would want to overlook the river, so it must be near, and that dark wall was in just the right place for it. So he lifted his eyes to it and walked forward.

Every city was different, but he could not remember ever having visited a city where the activity at night was so quiet, so furtive. He passed the stable and the inn in front of it, walked past a temple to a god he didn't recognize, though from the crossed hammer and scythe out front, he suspected it might be the god of industry that Friedich had told him about. Birds roosted along the roof of the temple, as well as on the shorter roof over the entrance, and unusually, large birds roosted next to small, sparrows next to thrushes next to crows. No hawks nor eagles were among them, though.

Foxes, weasels, rats, and other quick animals darted out of sight when he rounded corners, and it wasn't until he'd passed the temple and emerged into a large open square that he saw another human being. A woman, wearing the now-familiar white rose tabard over a black cloak, strode away from the dark wall across the square. She glanced at Nivvy and then looked again, but didn't break stride nor say anything to him, and a moment later she was gone.

"Inira guide me," Nivvy muttered. Rats scurried around his feet now, unafraid in a way he'd never seen, so that it was impossible for him to look only at the roofs. Some rats wore a small white tabard and some not, but in either case they managed to stay out from under his feet, if only by inches.

Why had Rose turned so many people into rats and birds, and in such a short time? Rats and birds couldn't be soldiers to conquer a world. But, he realized, they could be everywhere without anyone knowing, and if your power lay all in magic, then you needed eyes more than swords. If he'd had any urge to use his newfound freedom to run away, the idea that he would never again be able to trust any rat or bird —or indeed any animal—that crossed his path would have put that urge to rest faster than a merchant pounced on a loose coin.

On one side of this open square, a great stone bridge crossed a wide flowing river. Directly across from the bridge, a spacious boulevard led directly to the dark wall. This had to be the palace. Once he'd drawn closer, the darkness of the wall resolved into patches of deeper dark between small ovals of grey, with occasional lighter patches dotted around it. Nivvy had to get even closer before realizing that the darkness was an enormous wall of plants rendered silvery in the faint moonlight; the grey ovals were the outermost leaves and the lighter patches flowers. It was a rosebush, of course it was, a rosebush the size of a palace, with a small bright archway at street level and two dark silhouettes in front. It was hard to tell at this distance, but Nivvy suspected they were bears guarding the castle entrance.

He stopped in the shadow of another temple (likely the goddess of Wisdom, to go by the austere woman sculpted on the building over the door, one hand to her head, the other holding a suspended balance). If the eagle and hawk were here, they'd probably be watching this street. He scanned all the rooftops but found no shapes large enough to be either.

"The bears can smell you if you get much closer," a light voice croaked over his head.

Nivvy jumped and looked above him. On the goddess's foot perched a crow, staring down at him. "Remelstaub?" he said.

"And you haven't the password," the crow continued. Now that he could see the voice issuing from the beak, he recognized it.

"You followed me?"

"My task is to watch over the prisoner and ensure he arrives at the palace."

Nivvy nodded. "An' as I was headed there anyway, you just watched." He rubbed his face. "Can you get me past the gate?"

"I have the pass sign."

The ancient granite cold against his back, Nivvy kept his eyes on the crow. "Will you get me past the gate?"

"If that is what you wish."

Nivvy considered this. "What were you, before you were a crow?"

"I was a soldier. I served this country for fifteen years. My father had been a soldier before me, and I wanted to make him proud."

"And Queen Bella said you should be a crow to better serve the country, and you thought that sounded like the best idea anyone had ever had."

Remelstaub tilted their head. "You know much."

"I talked to Friedich. He did the same thing. How many of your fellows are animals now?"

"All of them. We became crows and ravens and mockingbirds and jays. That was how we could best serve Heiterflus." The declaration came somewhat mechanically, and the crow lifted their head to the palace as they said it, as though staring back into the past at that younger self standing before the queen.

"Still seem like a good idea?" Nivvy asked softly.

"My only chance to regain my human form is to complete my mission." Remelstaub focused on him again.

"What if," Nivvy chose his words carefully, tiptoeing along this very dangerous path, "you had to remain a crow, but the kingdom would be the better for it?"

As soon as he said it, he was struck by his own foolishness, despite the care he'd taken. This crow worked for Rose and owed him nothing. But Remelstaub did not seem to understand that there was a question behind his question. "Of course I would give up my life for Heiterflus. That is why I became a soldier."

"Of course you would," Nivvy said. "It's noble to give up your life for your land, even if you don't go to the trouble of becoming a soldier, ey?"

"That is what I believe," Remelstaub said.

"So if I had a magic spell that could get rid of that queen," Nivvy said, "would you still bring me into her presence?"

The crow stared down at him. Nivvy could almost feel the thoughts turning one over the other. Finally, Remelstaub said, "My orders are to bring you before the Queen."

"Right then," Nivvy said. "Glad we've got that sorted."

He stared at the rosebush surrounding the palace. Zein and Scarlet weren't here yet. It had been many days since he'd told them where to go, enough—he hoped—for them to find the mirror and fly north. And yet they weren't here. Maybe they weren't coming after all, or maybe they'd given up on him and decided to try themselves. Maybe they'd already succeeded. Or failed.

With a sigh, Nivvy started back toward the cart, but he'd only gone a few steps before the crow fluttered in front of him. "Where are you going?" Remelstaub demanded, their words strained through the exertion of flying.

"Back to the cart. Might as well see D'Alio get his gold, or whatever Rose has planned for him."

Remelstaub alit on a window above. "You are to come before the Queen."

"Aye," Nivvy said, "an' if you were a human soldier, you might could force the question, but since yer not, I'm goin' back to get some sleep."

He walked back down the boulevard, scanning the roofs but no longer hopeful that he would see a familiar shape there. No sound came from behind him, but when he arrived back at the cart, there was the crow, perched on the roof, watching him as he climbed back in.

# ❧ 35 ❧

## PROMISES KEPT

"What business have you in the Palace of Heiterflus?" the bear rumbled as the cart stopped.

Again, Remelstaub flew down and delivered the pass sign, and again the cart rumbled forward. But this time Nivvy, at the back of the cart, pushed the canvas aside and thrust his head and shoulders out, looking along all the rooftops for anything larger than a crow.

No eagle, no hawk. His heart sank as the cart rolled on and the thick rosebush hid everything else from his sight.

The fragrance of the roses was not as strong as he would have thought; the bush smelled more of the green of the leaves, and behind that green was a sharp, sour smell, as of old mushrooms. Thorns bristled out of the stems wherever he looked, and even the leaves seemed to have sharp edges.

But the flowers, however rarely they appeared, drew his attention. In blossoms nearly as large as his head, pristine petals of a uniform deep red color shone out even in the shadows of the bush. Nivvy had never been a flower fancier, but he felt that even Pala the flower merchant would describe each of these blooms as perfect. He was sorry when the cart came out the other side of the thicket and onto the palace grounds.

The palace, it turned out, was more like a castle, a squat stone thing with a pair of turrets at the front overlooking a great archway and drawbridge that, from the look of the rust on the chains as Nivvy passed them, had not been raised in quite a while. A peaceful kingdom, then, or at least one that hadn't had to worry about nasty people storming its castle. Until very recently.

Nivvy hadn't been in a castle before, but he supposed they weren't usually funereally silent and still. The large courtyard paved with worn flagstones stood empty; birds perched on the ledges of windows that overlooked it, in the same unsettlingly different groups that Nivvy had seen the previous night.

Only when the cart came to a halt did a human emerge from a door, but he came directly to the horse. When D'Alio came around to bind Nivvy's wrists and lead him out of the cart, he waved to the skinny youth with untidy blond hair stroking the horse's nose. "Ho," he called. "You in charge of welcoming us to the castle?"

The young man looked at him blankly, then went back to tending to the horse. Ah, one of those fellows that got on better with horses than people. Nivvy appreciated them when it came to tending Rahila, because he knew they'd take good care of her even if they couldn't bear to say more than a word to him.

Ignoring the stab in his heart at the memory, he held his chin up and turned to D'Alio. "Right, then, let's do this, ay?"

"Right." But D'Alio, too, seemed puzzled by the lack of any welcoming official. He pointed to the largest door apart from the gate they'd driven in by. "There, I reckon. You think?"

"Why would I know?"

"You said you'd done work for her."

"Aye, but she wasn't queen here then. First time I seen this place." Nivvy let his gaze roam up to the top of the rosebush wall, and there, with a thrill, he saw the silhouette of an eagle. But the next moment, it was gone, and doubt crept in. Had it been an eagle? It was hard to judge the distance to the top of the wall. He turned to the cart. "Remelstaub?" he called.

The crow hopped to the edge of the canvas roof and peered down. "Yes?"

"Where should we go? Nobody's here."

Remelstaub looked up, and Nivvy followed their gaze to a balcony overlooking the courtyard. "Her Majesty holds court there," they said. "I will fly up."

They took wing and disappeared over the balcony railing. D'Alio watched them go. "Don't like this," he muttered.

"How'd you think I feel?" Nivvy asked.

"Friedich," Nivvy called softly, for the swallow hadn't left his cage. "You coming to join us?"

The swallow's voice came back just as softly. "Perhaps. I have not decided."

More birds flew into the courtyard, and now Nivvy noticed some rats around the edges of the inside walls as well. D'Alio looked around and said, "Right creepy this is."

"Don't worry," Nivvy said. "They won't hurt you. Unless they've been ordered to."

D'Alio glared at him, and then his expression softened. "Didn't know this was what I was bringin' you to."

Nivvy smiled thinly back. "Wouldn't have changed yer mind if you did, not for two stacks."

"Probably not," the other thief conceded. "'Specially if I knew you'd already been a weasel. Reckon you're back to four feet now?"

"I've no idea what's in store for me any more'n you."

"Huh." D'Alio looked around again and then snapped his head back. "Wait. You mean any more'n I know what's in store for you, or for me?"

"Either, mate."

D'Alio paced, holding the rope. "Thought I'd drive in, hand you over, gold in the cart, done. This..." He waved around at the assembled animals. "This makes me wonder if I won't be flyin' back home on me own wings."

"Might could happen," Nivvy allowed. "Sure seems like she's taken to that. Plus she could pay you and turn you an' wouldn't be breakin' her word."

That might have been enough to send D'Alio back to the cart, wrenching control of the horse from the stable boy who was even now undoing the harness, except that at that moment, Rose's voice rang out over the courtyard. "Guests! How lovely. Do attend me on the balcony and excuse my lack of a proper staff."

D'Alio stared up for a full three seconds after she'd finished talking and then turned to Nivvy. "Aye," he said, as calmly and reasonably as if he hadn't been about to flee a moment ago. "C'mon, up we go."

"Now you're okay with it?" Nivvy asked, following D'Alio to the door Rose was pointing at, the large one he'd been heading for initially.

"Weren't her fault her staff's occupied." D'Alio seemed completely at ease, which was as unnerving a display of the crown's power as Rose's command of Scarlet at the lakeside. Nivvy kept his mouth shut and followed.

They entered a large hall that at one time might have been welcoming. Candelabras stood empty and cold all around, the stark stone walls showed discolored patches where tapestries must have recently hung, and only one window of plain glass remained intact; the others had been smashed. Small pieces of colored glass in the frame and around the floor nearby told Nivvy they'd been picture windows. There were still cushioned benches, but many of them had been fouled with bird droppings. Jays and thrushes stood on the cushions and stared at Nivvy and D'Alio, unmoving, unspeaking.

"There." D'Alio pointed, unnecessarily, to the large staircase opposite the door, the same grey stone as the rest of the room but with newer-looking polished wooden banisters. At the top of the stairs, looking down over the hall, a picture window larger than any of the others had also been smashed, allowing a chill breeze to run down the stairs and past them as they climbed.

From the landing, a set of stairs on either side doubled back up to the next floor and presumably the balcony. Without hesitating, D'Alio chose the left-hand stair and led Nivvy up to a hallway stretching to the left and right, lined with empty pedestals and mysterious shadows. Normally Nivvy appreciated a good shadowy hallway with lots of places to hide, but that was when he was more in control of his own movements and not being pulled by his bound wrists. D'Alio tugged him toward the open double doors and through them, out onto the balcony.

Nivvy blinked in the light and quickly got his bearings. He and D'Alio stood in a semicircular space about fifteen feet across, bounded by a wide stone railing on which perched Remelstaub. The only other person on the balcony was Rose.

The Queen wore the Crown of Glædeligdal and a lovely dress, a deep red that Nivvy bet would match the colors of the roses in the rosebush. In the center of her chest, a jeweled rose glittered in the light; a purple robe lined with white fur hung around her shoulders. Her complexion still shone white, but she no longer looked like an aged porcelain figure. Rather, with her red lips and smooth white skin, she looked every inch a brand-new porcelain figure, an austere and dangerous one who knew every bit of the power she possessed. And yet she was also still Bella, the worn and faded queen who had approached a thief on a wheel. Nivvy felt far distant from that wretched thief, but Rose had not changed, merely been restored.

She looked past D'Alio to Nivvy and those lips curved into a smile. "At last, my master thief," she purred.

"Ah," D'Alio said. "Not yet, but with yer grace's—" He stopped as she walked past him to take Nivvy's bound hands. At her touch, the rope unwound its knots, and she removed it with one snow-white hand, her dark eyes fixed on his.

"Good to see you again." Nivvy had been thinking of her as Rose but now didn't know what name to use, so he used his old trick when he didn't know someone's name and just addressed her directly. He didn't dare look past her to see if the eagle was visible anywhere.

"Is it?" The rope fell to the stone. "It seems you didn't want to come back here after all."

"I, uh." Nivvy's throat was dry. He worked his fingers, rubbing life back into them. His whole body tingled like he was on a precipice. "Had some business back in Copper Port."

"Is that where you were? Where Friedich found you?"

He nodded. "Ah, well, D'Alio there found me, in truth. But I was planning to come on my own."

"Were you now? I wonder." She stared at him as though trying to read his thoughts. "Tell me the truth: Were you?"

"Yes," he said immediately.

"Hm." She searched his face again.

D'Alio stood just beyond the queen, mouth opening and closing, trying to work up the courage to break in. "But, ah, as it happens," Nivvy said, "Taja D'Alio was the one who brought me so he should get the reward, don't you think?"

The smile returned to her face, and she spun around. "Of course, of course. It's important for my people to see that I keep my promises. And I have three promises to keep before we can get to you, my dear thief. First..." She feigned distress. "Where is Friedich? Where is the little swallow who found my thief, of all the mapmakers and explorers I sent out?"

"He remains in the cart, your Majesty," Remelstaub said.

"Indeed." Rose leaned over the railing. "Friedich, come up here this instant."

As far back on the balcony as he was, Nivvy couldn't see the cart nor most of the animals except the highest-perched birds. But a definite rustle of movement and whispering came up from the courtyard, and seconds later Friedich alit on the railing next to Rose. "Your Majesty," he said, his voice trembling.

"Why so scared?" Rose asked in a honey-sweet voice. "Have you not done exactly as I requested?"

"Y-yes, your Majesty." The swallow had shrunken in on himself, a small ball of feathers with a terrified head protruding.

"You found the thief and brought him back. And for that you shall have your human form restored, just as I promised."

The head rose cautiously. "Th-thank you, your Majesty."

"I always keep my promises," Rose said.

Nivvy's hackles prickled with dread. Rose was acting too nice, and she could've restored him to human form by now if she wanted to.

Friedich waited for a moment while Rose watched, giving him enough time to let his hope fade. "But," she said, and the swallow shrank back. "I believe I heard something about a story that you told? Of the goddess Prula?"

"No," he squeaked.

She lowered her head to him, a smile on her lips but nowhere near her eyes. "Tell me the truth: did you tell that story?"

"Yes." He seemed horrified at his answer, his little legs carrying him backwards, and then he launched himself from the railing and flew over the courtyard.

He had only made it halfway to the outer wall when Rose glanced in his direction and the swallow was replaced by a short, plump pale-skinned man dressed in a green jerkin and leggings. The man hung in the air for a moment and then fell to the courtyard stones.

Nivvy heard the impact of his body very clearly. In the silence that followed, a low, broken groan came from below, and after that nothing. The bustle and murmur of the assembled birds stilled just as quickly.

"There's one promise kept." Rose turned to Remelstaub. "Soldier."

The crow stood at attention as best a crow can. "Your Majesty."

"You have brought the thief safely to me, and you reported on Friedich's treachery."

"What treachery?" Nivvy cried. "He told a story, that's all!"

Rose ignored him, continuing to address the crow. "Tell the truth: is there any other treachery you wish to report?"

Nivvy's heart sank. The crow spoke promptly. "I believe the thief may have a magic spell that could harm you."

Now Rose did turn to Nivvy with a smile. "Is that so? We will come to that presently. Thank you for your service." She stepped back, and a moment later a young man, tall and lean and as pale as Rose herself, with blond hair and a beard, stood on the railing.

Remelstaub felt down the white rose tabard that covered his grey shirt, then looked at his hands, jumped down to the balcony, and bowed deeply. "Thank you, my Queen," he said.

"Remain here a moment. I will require one more service of you." She glanced at Nivvy before turning her attention to D'Alio.

Relief that she hadn't killed Remelstaub warred with anger that she'd made the crow—soldier—betray him, and with self-congratulation that he hadn't confided further in the crow. But when he took in D'Alio, he saw a man clearly too terrified even to speak. It reminded Nivvy of how he'd first felt when Marzin had been turned to a toad. He'd hopped into Nivvy's path, and even when he'd croaked in Marzin's voice, Nivvy had had trouble believing that this was his friend. If he hadn't known that they'd been assigned to steal from a wizard, he might have thought it all a trick. This was likely the first time D'Alio had seen magic tossed about as casually as fish at a market.

"It is a long journey from Copper Port," Rose said, and leaned in close to D'Alio. "Now tell the truth: what do you think fair compensation for bringing this thief back to me?"

D'Alio's terror changed in an instant to thoughtful calculation. "Well, yer Majesty, it was two silver for our food all the way here. I bought the cheapest I could. An' another half-silver for a bag of oats. Salla—that's the horse there—she can eat grass but needs oats now an' again. So it's two and a half silver for the ride up, and I'd say one and a half for the ride back since I won't have no prisoner. So that's four silver for the food. As for fair, well, your swallow..." He glanced over the railing. "He did say you promised two hundred gold coin, and if that's what you promised then that's what's fair. That's the truth."

The words spilled out of him and then he stared as though surprised at what he'd said. But Rose nodded with a smile. "Well and truly said. Then two hundred gold coins and four silver you shall have."

D'Alio's gape turned into a smile. Rose shot Nivvy a look over her shoulder, a kind of "didn't expect that, did you?" smug look, and then addressed Remelstaub. "Soldier, do you know where the treasury room is?"

"Yes, your Majesty."

"Please escort this gentleman there and count out two hundred of our gold coins, plus four of our silver, then help him carry them out to the cart. Don't worry about Sigurd. She will know that I sent you."

When the two men had left the balcony, Nivvy said, "Sigurd?"

"My dragon. You remember." Rose turned her full attention on him again. "Now that I am queen, I no longer need her to enforce my desires. She likes it there among the gold of the treasury, which has grown substantially in the last month. Two hundred coins is a pittance."

"Glad to hear it. It'll be a nice boon for that Copper Port crew. I don't bear all of them ill will." He searched the skies again but there was no sign of the eagle.

"You resolved whatever you went there to accomplish, then?"

She hadn't ordered him to tell the truth. Was she uninterested in the answer, or did she know the crown didn't work on him? "Aye, more or less."

"Good. Then there's no impediment to you remaining here in my service. Is there?"

He shook his head. "I suppose not."

Her eyes flashed, and she said, "Kneel."

It took him a second to process that and another half-second to react, and even though he knelt, she smiled down at him and said, "Just as I thought."

"What?" He touched the top of his head, trying to conceal his nervousness. "Losing my hair?"

She laughed. "You're immune to the Crown. By rights I should kill you. That's very dangerous, you know."

He had never felt more acutely how close his story was to ending. Good stories didn't end with "and then the evil queen killed the hero," but as Scarlet had pointed out to him, life wasn't always like stories. If Rose wanted to kill him...but no, she continued to smile, those bright red lips curving up as she looked down at him. That didn't mean anything; she'd smiled as she killed Friedich, too. And then she kept talking.

"But...there's also something quite enticing about knowing that you're bound to me by your will rather than magic. You were an excellent servant to me. At least, back when you were a weasel." She rubbed her chin. "You may rise. I have one concern before I accept you back into my service."

Nivvy stood. "What's that?"

She looked him right in the eye. "Did you take Scarlet back to the volcano?"

How long could he play along with this? Was Scarlet here with the mirror or had he been imagining things? "She wanted to die there," he said.

Rose studied his face, and then her intensity dropped, and she laughed. "I'm glad I could grant that last wish of hers. How did you get out before it erupted?"

"You did do that, then," Nivvy said. "I barely escaped. Lost my horse."

"If you hadn't helped Scarlet, your horse would still be alive," Rose said. "Consider that your punishment."

Nivvy focused on calming breaths, in and out. She had lots of power besides the crown, and jumping her wouldn't do him any good. He'd be dead before he could touch her. "She was a good horse," he said roughly. "She didn't deserve to die terrified." Don't forget that you failed her, he reminded himself.

"Very few get what they deserve," Rose said. "I'm surprised you haven't learned that lesson already. The question is who has the power to enforce their desire, that is all."

"You've done pretty well for yourself, no doubt," Nivvy said. "So it's just power that lets you come in here and decide all these people get turned into animals and," he gestured to the courtyard, "sometimes killed?"

"Power is all that gives kings and queens their titles. How many kings do you think Scarlet has installed on thrones in her lifetime?"

Above the rosebush wall, a large bird soared toward the castle. Perhaps an eagle. Knowing how keen Zein's eyes were, he raised a hand

and hoped Scarlet's were as keen. "And what's this great thicket for, then?" he asked, to explain the hand gesture.

"Do you like it?" Rose smiled indulgently as though she knew he was playing for time. "It keeps out undesirables. My birds can fly over it; my rats can creep through it. Weasels can get through it too." She looked significantly at him. "Yes, I think you might be more useful as a weasel. I have not made many other weasels here, you know. That form is special to me now."

The eagle angled toward him. Nivvy tried to buy himself a few more seconds without begging for his human form, which was clearly what she wanted him to do. "Tell me, were all those windows downstairs of your sister or did you just object to the art?"

The change in subject took Rose aback. Her smile twisted slightly and then straightened. "All of those honored in the windows belong to the past of Heiterflus, and I am the future. There will be new windows."

"Can't you just make 'em?"

"I..." She paused again. "I have not decided what to put in them. Myself and Sigurd, of course, but..."

"I'm sure it'll come to you," Nivvy said.

At that moment, a shadow passed over the balcony. He looked up, as Rose did, and saw the eagle hovering overhead. Its eyes met his, and an object fell from its talons. Rose jumped back, startled, but Nivvy caught the velvet-covered mirror, its face toward him. "What is that?" Rose demanded. "Put it down!"

The command had no effect on Nivvy. He turned the mirror around and grasped the velvet to draw it back, but it slipped from his fingers as he shrank, falling into a pile of his clothes which cushioned his fall onto the stone. His robe covered him, darkening his world. He was a weasel again.

The shock of this was followed by the crash of glass on the stone near him. The Velki's mirror had shattered.

## ❧ 36 ❧

# THE PRICE OF THORNS

"Traitor!" Rose screeched.

Nivvy's struggles ceased. He stood frozen in the middle of his crumpled robe, hidden for the moment but aware of how vulnerable he was. She could pick him up and fling him off the balcony. She could step on him. She could take him down and feed him to her dragon.

But then Rose screamed again, a different note, and something small and heavy struck Nivvy through his robe as he regained control of his limbs. He jumped out of the cloth pile to see Scarlet clawing at Rose's face, her great wings beating around the queen's head.

Nivvy turned to run for the door. Next to him on the sleeve of his robe lay Scarlet's ring with the rectangular lapis stone; it must have flown off her talon when she attacked Rose, or else she'd thrown it to him. He grabbed it in his teeth and ran for the hallway.

Inside the doors, he paused to think and to listen. The sounds of scuffling and Rose's cries stopped, and a moment later came the soft thump of an eagle-sized body hitting the balcony stone.

"Now," Rose said, her voice dripping malevolence, "when I release you, claw your own eyes out as you tried to do to me. Then stand here until I bring you the weasel, and then eat it."

Nivvy's heart pounded. What could he do with just the ring? He couldn't hide anywhere in the castle, and Rose would see through any disguise. She would never look in the mirror now, never be confronted with her past sins—

Her past sins. The broken window at the base of the landing caught his eye. It was a slim chance, but the only one he could see. He gulped and climbed up one of the nearby empty pedestals, little claws giving him purchase on the rough stone. Atop it, one paw on the ring, he spoke the spell Scarlet had taught him, holding in his mind the face of the statue he'd seen, imagining it living, like Rose, but fair. He imagined Rose's voice with a lilt of kindness and laughter rather than sharp edges of hurt and rage; a gown of soft blue and green, and golden hair like the stable-boy.

Outside, the eagle screamed in pain. Nivvy stared fixedly ahead at the door, trying not to imagine Scarlet's talons raking her eyes. Granted, she'd caused worse pain to probably thousands of people over the years, and granted, Nivvy was a weasel again largely because of her, but did she deserve to claw her own eyes out? If he thought about it too much, the answer started to lean toward 'yes,' which made him feel bad because she'd attacked Rose to help him and give him time to get away. So he focused on casting the spell.

He couldn't see the image around himself, but when Rose stepped into the hallway and turned in his direction, she stopped dead in her tracks. "Hello, sister," Nivvy said.

Rose stared at him. Her face bore no marks from the eagle's claws. "Why did you have to erase me from the kingdom?" he asked. "Couldn't we live here together?"

The shock wore off, and Rose's face regained that confident smile. "So this was the magic spell you thought would destroy me? A simulacrum of my sister? And not a very good one."

"Ghosts can change, dear sister." Primrose had loved her sister, Nivvy reminded himself. Also she probably talked all fancy like Rose did. And he had felt a bond with Rose, too, not to the level of love, but in her bitterness and despair he saw the person he had perhaps been becoming, and here was his chance to reach out and pull her back with her sister's arm. "And it has been over a thousand years. You've changed as well, but perhaps you cannot see that."

"All right." Rose's lips curved into a smile. "Very well, ghost of my sister. You wish to live here with me? I will allow it. You may stay at my side always, attending my every move as I rule the kingdom that should by rights have been mine."

Rose needed to tell her sister that she'd won, Nivvy realized. He thought back to his uncles and how his victory at leaving home had been undercut by their love when he'd returned. "By rights?" he said. "By whose rights?"

"The prince came to see *me*!" Rose cried. "And you stole him, and the kingdom!"

"He chose me." Nivvy caught himself. "He chose my gift. But I never meant it to cause you pain, my dear. I loved you. I still do."

"So you always said." Rose stalked along the hallway, and Nivvy turned to face her. "And then you took my prince and came here to live with him, and exiled me to," she flung her arm out, "a kingdom of goats!"

"I wanted us to be queens together," Nivvy said. "Together we could have been so happy."

"You were happy, here in your perfect castle with your perfect king and your perfect kingdom. You never came to see me."

"Didn't I?" Nivvy blurted that out in surprise.

Rose stopped and stared at him. "You did," she said. "You're right. But only to gloat, only to see your sister in such shabby surroundings and then to return here." Her arm swept out so violently that her fur-lined cloak nearly fell from her shoulders. She clutched at it, pulling it more tightly around her. "To sit in your throne and laugh at your poor sister."

Outside, on the patio, something scrabbled around. Rose hadn't noticed, and so Nivvy turned to draw her farther from the doorway. "I never laughed at you. I tried my best to help you."

Rose walked along the hallway, following Nivvy's turn, until his pedestal was between her and the open door. He hoped that Primrose's image blocked the view of the door; just to be sure, he kept turning until he was facing down the hallway, and Rose moved to remain in front of him. "Help," she scoffed as she walked. "With those gifts?"

"I meant them out of love."

"Love? Or pity?" Rose's eyes flashed in the dim hallway. "Gifts that reminded me of your rich kingdom?"

"They were meant to remind you of me, and our love."

"You keep saying you loved me," Rose said. "But what use was it to me to get gifts in a poor dirt kingdom?"

"You're right." Nivvy heard again his uncles. "I shouldn't have left you. I was being selfish, and I'm sorry I didn't stay with you. I'm sorry I didn't do more."

Rose's anger felt suspended for a moment, and her voice lost its ferocity. "You should be sorry."

More noises and then a light hopping sound behind him. Too soft for an eagle, but maybe a hawk? Hope soared. If Zein could carry him away, they could at least escape this day.

For now, though, while Rose was talking to her sister's ghost, he needed to press farther into her past. Scarlet had told him about the worst thing Rose had done. He put a plaintive note into his voice, remembering how his mother had talked about him, how his aunt had talked about his cousins. "Why did you steal my darling, my light?"

Rose's eyes narrowed and her brow lowered. "Because I could."

"You could have had children of your own. Why take mine?"

"I tried to have children." Rose's voice darkened.

"Did you not see a healer?" Zbells, that's right, Primrose's gift had been healing. "I know you wouldn't have wanted to come to me."

"Of course I wouldn't have come to you," Rose sneered. "Give you one more chance to show off your gift?"

"I never wanted to show off. I only wanted to help people."

"So they would love you."

"No—well, yes, perhaps. Can you fault me there? We got little enough of it at home." Whoops, there was a little of his own childhood slipping in.

He held his breath, but it worked. "So we did. But it was always the two of us against the world." Rose paced back and forth. "It was easy for you, the sweet flower. You healed the world and they loved you for it. Who loves a curse-witch? I was well named: beautiful but covered in thorns." She pressed a hand to her red dress.

"Seems to me, ah." Nivvy stopped and started over. "It seems that you took pleasure in wielding those thorns."

"What would you know of thorns, sweet simple flower? It amuses me to watch people stick their fingers on them when they think they've had the best of me. Many have tried over the years and yet here I still stand and there are you, a shade, a memory, no more than that."

A flutter of air, and then Zein landed on the pedestal beside Nivvy. His heart jumped with joy and then fear, because it looked like Rose was staring right at them. But no; Zein kept their head down, and Rose did not react. Nivvy wanted to wrap his arms around the hawk's leg, but didn't know whether that would make ghost-Primrose hug empty air, so he restrained himself. What had Rose just said? Never mind, he'd go back to the daughter. "Why did you steal my daughter?"

"Why do you think?" Rose snapped. "I wanted to take away your happiness."

"But you stole her," Nivvy pressed. "You could have simply killed her."

"Yes, I stole her!" Rose glared at him and stepped closer. "I stole her because I wanted her for my own. I wanted her more than I wanted a child of my own because she was yours, and I wanted to take her. And I did. And do you know what the worst part is? The cruel joke the gods who do not exist played on us? I changed her memories so she would think I was her mother, so she would love me as she had loved you. I saw the way she laughed with you, the way you doted on her, the way she clung to you, and I wanted all that. So I gave her memories of laughing with me, clinging to me."

Rose laughed bitterly. "I still failed. She loved me, yes. Dutifully, because her memories told her to. Not unreservedly. She never again laughed the way she had with you. Even at the height of my power, with the chance to write an entire childhood from whole cloth, I could not be as good, as loving," she spat the word, "a mother as you were."

Nivvy stood stunned and saddened. "Does that make you happy?" Rose demanded. "To know that I failed, that your daughter was never happier than she was with you?"

"No," Nivvy said without thinking. "I think it's the saddest thing I've ever heard. I wish she could have loved you."

Rose stood for a long moment, enough time for Nivvy's racing heart to count to twenty, and then she said, "Whatever spell this is, you've played Prim's part well. But this is over now."

Nivvy edged closer to Zein. The hawk leaned on him, and as Rose swept her fingers across the air between them, her eyes searched beyond the ghost of her sister, and met the fragment of mirror that Zein held up in one talon.

Nivvy held his breath. Zein, leaning on him so they could keep one talon raised, also froze. Rose stared into the depths of the mirror, her eyes widening slowly. "No," she breathed, so softly that a moment later Nivvy wasn't sure he'd heard the word.

He had no idea how much time had passed when he'd looked into the mirror, but Rose was looking back on a longer lifetime, even if you didn't count the thousand-year imprisonment when she probably hadn't done much but think evil thoughts. He remembered the stark recitation of his crimes that had paraded through his memory, and the bleak despair that had accompanied them. He had had less to look back on and Zein to cling to; how much worse would it be to look back on her life when she had only moments before rejected the only person who might still have loved her—who had, albeit with Nivvy's voice, said that she did? Despite all that Rose had done, he felt sorry for her.

"No," she said again, louder. "I—I tried—I wanted—"

Her eyes closed and her mouth contorted, and then she let out a long, agonized wail. Nivvy's fur stood on end; he huddled closer to Zein, unable to look away. Rose threw her head back so violently that the crown tumbled off it, but she made no move to retrieve it. Her skin darkened wood-brown, and leaves and branches sprouted from it as her features were lost in the bark of the bush. The fur-lined cloak fell from her shoulders; the other clothes tore into fragments. Thorny stems filled out the bush, and then blooms of deep red, the color of blood, appeared on the rosebush. They blossomed and then stopped, everything stopped, the world was still.

Zein broke the silence by dropping the mirror shard with a clatter. "I think she's gone," they said. "It worked."

Nivvy startled and then threw his arms around one feathered leg, happy to not have to look at the rosebush. "It worked, it did work. I can't believe it." His heart still pounded, and he half-expected the rosebush to start talking behind him, but the room remained silent. Even the people and former-humans outside seemed to be holding their breath.

"Is she going to stay like that forever?" Zein said in a hushed voice.

"Don't think she can do anything else, now," Nivvy said, though he wouldn't put it past Rose. "Never heard of a person turned into a plant what could still talk, even in the old stories."

"There's Mother Willow," Zein reminded him. "But I think she was always a tree." They both waited, but the rosebush made no noise other than a gentle rustling of its leaves.

The finality sunk in. "She's gone," Nivvy whispered, and breathed in the comforting smell of the feathers. "Oh, Zein. I'm so happy to see you, I can't tell you. An' not just because you were so clever to bring the mirror in."

Zein curved a wing gently around his back. "And I you. But you're a weasel again."

"I don't care. Rather be a weasel with you than a human alone."

"But," Zein said, "that's very sweet of you and I love you too, even if you are very confusing sometimes, but you had been a human with me."

"Aye." Nivvy laughed, and then all the tension of the moment drained out of him and he couldn't stop laughing, or crying, or something in between. His small body shook, and he buried his face in the hawk's feathers. "You're so sensible. I do think you could look in that mirror and have it tell you nothing but how lovely and right you are. But don't," he added hurriedly.

"You said you looked into it?"

"Yes." He sat back and looked up into their concerned eyes. "I shouldn't have, I suppose. Mighta been here sooner and spared you two all this. But I lost Rahila, and it was my fault. I grabbed at her reins instead of her mane, and the boots didn't bring her with me. So I wasn't feeling good about myself and then the mirror told me how selfish I'd been and I thought I couldn't be a proper hero."

"You'll have to tell me the whole story sometime," Zein said. "Scarlet isn't in too good a way, and we should look after her."

"Right," Nivvy said, aware that after Scarlet there would be a lot of people to talk to and things to take care of and he might not get a moment with Zein again for a while. "Just one thing. I'm sorry for leaving you, and for almost getting you killed, and for Frankh, and all of that."

Zein's wing pulled him against them. "You also rescued me and helped me go on two wonderful adventures. Three, if you count the ride back from the lake as a different one, which it really was, because you were human and we had a captive djinn."

"Thank you for believing in me," Nivvy said. "That too. I'll tell you sometime how it made all the difference in the world."

"It was easy," Zein said, "because you'd already done so much, I knew you could do more. But there will be time for all that." Voices on the balcony signaled the need for them to go back out.

"Yes." Nivvy couldn't keep the smile from his face. "I can't wait for all of it."

## ❧ 37 ❧

# THE ROSE BUSH

They went back out to the balcony, Zein flying and Nivvy scampering down the pedestal and out the door. Scarlet, alone on the flagstones, faced an array of birds who had alit on the railing, with bloody sockets where her eyes had been and wings half-spread, threatening enough to keep them at a distance. The half-dozen jays and mockingbirds squawked at her in a chaotic chorus: "You attacked the Queen!" "How dare you?" "Where is she?" One mockingbird seemed genuinely angry, but the others felt to Nivvy as though they were putting on a performance in case Rose was right outside watching them.

Zein reached Scarlet first, landing at her side. "Scarlet! Oh, your eyes, I'm so sorry."

"I'm fine," the eagle snapped. "Where's Rose?"

"Back there," Nivvy said, dancing around fragments of the mirror. "Zein swooped in with a piece of the mirror and she looked right in it and turned herself into a rosebush. Is that it, then? She can't turn herself back, can she? What happened to her magic?"

The birds on the railing quieted to listen to them. "A rosebush?" Scarlet coughed. "Clung to that even at the end. That's what stories will do to you. No, I think she's gone for good, and my magic with her. People used to get turned back from animals, but when you turned a human into a tree or something, you might as well chop them up and build yourself a nice chair. Nobody ever came back from that." She turned her bloody eye sockets between them. "I'm impressed that you managed it."

"It was brilliant. Zein was, I mean. I didn't even think to pick up the mirror pieces."

"Nivvy distracted her long enough for me to get into the right spot," Zein said. "You should've seen him play her sister. He was fantastic. When I dropped the ring for you," they said to him, "I thought you could just turn into someone else long enough to escape. I never thought about playing her sister. That thing you said about wishing her lost daughter could have loved Rose...I would never have said that."

"Might be that came from Primrose's stories," Nivvy said, though part of him felt there had been some spiritual influence on him. "I felt like she, Primrose I mean, was rather like the little dough-boy,[1] if you know that story, giving and giving 'til there weren't nothing left. It felt like what she woulda said. But anyway none o'that woulda mattered if you hadn't given me time by attacking Rose." Nivvy looked up at the eagle's eye sockets and winced. "That was..."

"Yes, yes, we were all terribly brave. Where's the crown?" Scarlet bobbed her head toward the two of them.

"Back there," Nivvy said. "It fell off."

"Fell off?" The eagle turned and tottered toward the door. "Get it before some simpleton puts it on."

"There's nobody else in the castle," Nivvy said. "Ah, to your left, the door is. No, a little more...there, you've got it."

"There's your captor and that soldier," Scarlet pointed out, but Zein had already taken off and flown ahead of them to guide Scarlet to the crown and stand guard over it.

"Hallo!" one of the jays called to Nivvy. "What does this mean, the queen is a rosebush?"

He turned, near the door, and looked back at the array of birds. More had joined the initial few and now they all stared at him, waiting for an answer.

"Oh." He gulped. On the one hand, they were free of a tyrant. On the other, they were likely going to be birds forever. How did one break that kind of news? Well, he was going to be a weasel forever, probably, so at least he was in the same boat, though he knew that didn't always make bad news easier to take. "She, ah, she repented of her sins and decided to spend the rest of her days as a rosebush. Like the one outside the castle. But, ah, smaller, right?"

They stared unblinking at him. He paced and then went on, "So, if there's any of the previous royal family still around, and, ideally, um…" Their silence told him how unlikely that was. "Distant cousin? Someone in another kingdom maybe?"

"Queen Rose killed all the previous royal family," one of the jays said. They all looked alike and three of them were standing together so Nivvy couldn't tell whether it was the one who'd spoken before.

"Maybe not," one of the mockingbirds chirped. "Where's old Cormundsgrasse? He knows everything about the royal family."

"And what about the dragon?" another mockingbird chirped.

Nivvy'd forgotten about the dragon. "Ah, I don't really know any of that," he said.

"Cormundsgrasse lives over on Clocktower Square." One of the jays took wing. "I'll fetch him."

"What about the dragon?" the mockingbird chirped again.

"I'll, er, just go see about that." Nivvy turned to go back inside.

As he passed through the doors, one of the birds said, "What's that on the ground? It looks shiny!"

Nivvy skidded to a halt and ran back out to see the birds eying the shattered mirror. "Don't look at that!" he cried. "It's magic and it's bad, it'll show you the worst of yourself. Just stay away. We need to clean it up."

He ignored the bewildered comments following that remark and ran back inside, where he found Scarlet with the crown around her neck and Zein guiding her back to the outside. "We need to clean up the mirror," he said, "and deal with the dragon. What's going on?"

"I'm taking the crown back to Glædeligdal to dump it in the lake," Scarlet said. "Zein's going to fly me there and be my eyes. We'll be back in a few days. Maybe a week. You can handle things here."

"I—what? No! Let me go with you."

"Nivvy." Zein turned to him. "Someone has to stay and help these people."

"Why? They can figure it out as well as I can."

"Because you know the story and they don't. Scarlet's right, the crown is dangerous and needs to be dealt with first."

He sat back on his haunches. "All right. Fine. But what about the dragon? I've never dealt with a dragon."

"Don't antagonize it," Scarlet advised. "And stay away from the mouth end. It gets very hot."

"Thank you," Nivvy said. "Never woulda figured that out on me own."

Zein curled a wing around him as Scarlet wobbled through the door. "We'll be back soon, I promise. You can do this."

He took in the smell of their breath, the feel of their feathers, the warmth of their belief. "All right," he said. "I'll do my best."

Scarlet was met with a flurry of questions when she emerged into the light. "Out of my way," she ordered, and took off into the air.

"Hurry back," Nivvy told Zein, and hugged their leg.

"We will. I'd better go." They lifted their head to watch Scarlet's irregular flight and then took off after her.

The birds on the railing turned to Nivvy. "What now?" one of the jays said.

"First, tell me who all of you are," he said. "Then get someone up here to clean up this mirror."

࿇

OF THE CHORUS OF NAMES AND RANKS THAT FLEW AT NIVVY AFTER that question, the two remaining jays of the group of three proved most useful. One was Jorgenstern, who had been the second senior advisor to the old queen, and the other was Rimmauld, who had been the junior steward. The senior advisor and steward had been killed with the royal family, but the two of them were smart and observant enough to step into those jobs as needed. They were also good friends and had been lovers; at least, Nivvy got that impression later, after spending the better part of two days in their company.

Rimmauld, who knew the castle inside and out, correctly identified the stable boy as the solution to two of the most pressing problems. "He hasn't a mean bone in his body," he said, when recommending him to clean up the mirror, "and so if he accidentally looks, all he will see is that he perhaps did not brush a horse as often as he ought." Indeed, the straw-haired boy swept up the mirror shards without wailing or rending his garments and placed them into a small chest that Rimmauld led him to, which he then stored in a shelf in the treasury when he went to see about the dragon.

The boy also had a gift with horses, so as he was cleaning up the mirror, Nivvy asked him how he felt about dragons. The boy's face creased in terror and he shook his head violently. But when Nivvy told him that the dragon had once been a horse, the boy looked up and smiled, and then it was all they could do to make him finish his task before he set off to the treasury.

From a safe distance, the two jays and Nivvy watched as the boy approached the dragon, making soothing sounds. The dragon lifted her head curiously, watched the boy, and allowed him to touch her face. In moments, it was clear that they were going to be great friends, and Nivvy breathed a sigh of relief.

"Say," he said as they were leaving the cavernous treasury for the more comfortable stone-walled corridors of the palace, "what happened to old D'Alio and that soldier?"

The jays looked at each other and then Jorgenstern flew on ahead to see. He reported back in moments. "The cart is gone from the yard, and Remelstaub has been asking what his duties are now. I told him to meet old Cormundsgrasse when he arrives, but that is only a temporary solution."

"Better see to that," Nivvy muttered as they made their way along the ancient stone floors, the jays walking because Nivvy couldn't run as fast as they could fly. He was glad D'Alio had gone; that chapter of his life was closed forever.

"And," Jorgenstern said delicately, "Friedich's body still lies there."

"Right." Nivvy sighed. "I presume he's got family?"

Neither of the jays knew, but Rimmauld knew who to ask and promised he would find them. They were at this point outside a room that looked to be a small salon. The jays stopped walking, and so Nivvy did too. "We need to ask you something," Jorgenstern said.

"Let's go in here," Rimmauld said, obviously knowing what Jorgenstern was about to ask.

Nivvy could guess too, and it was a conversation he wasn't going to enjoy. But he followed them into the fancy room and took a moment to survey the lovely chairs, chaise longue, credenzas, and large piano before settling down on the plush carpet. The jays arrayed themselves to face him. "What we were wondering," Jorgenstern said.

"Is whether we are to be jays forever," Rimmauld finished.

"And likewise for the whole city, and kingdom."

Nivvy nodded. Before he could answer, Rimmauld went on. "We understand that you are in the same situation."

"Yes," Nivvy said. "To get it out of the way, short answer, yes, we're all as we are. Rose was the only one with the power to change that an' I don't know that there's anyone who can do it now. I don't know where her power went, but Scarlet says it's gone, an' if anyone knows, she would. I'm sorry about that, but there wasn't really time to make her change everyone back even if I'd a way to do that."

The jays looked at each other. "We feared as much," Jorgenstern said. "Rimmauld, you have a way with the people. Can you break the news?"

"We should wait for Cormundsgrasse," Rimmauld said. "When he arrives, we may learn who will be our next king, and he should issue that proclamation. Until then we must say that we do not know but we are investigating. Some people will figure it out, but...there's little else we can do."

"If that's what you think, I'll say the same," Nivvy said. "It's your kingdom, not mine." He remembered Scarlet's ring and wondered where it was; he'd lost it near the pedestal. "Ah, if you don't mind, can we go back to the balcony? I lost a ring there that I should keep track of."

"Of course," Rimmauld said. "We simply wanted to have this word in private."

"We know," Jorgenstern added, "that this is as strange to you as it is to us. You are bearing it quite well. It took us days to learn to fly properly and even now I do not trust myself at it."

"Ah, well." Nivvy followed them out into the hallway. "Not my first time, actually. Rose—Queen Bella, she changed me back before she changed me again."

"Ah." Rimmauld hopped alongside him. "You fell from her favor but then were restored?"

"Sort of." The hallways seemed to stretch on forever to small weasel legs, but the motion of four-legged walking felt familiar and fluid, and he took some joy from that. "Scarlet actually turned me first, on account of I stole a thing from her, but then Rose stole her powers and turned me back. Then I got convinced that maybe she wasn't such a nice person—I mean, you all learned that quick but I knew her when she didn't have anything, and she wasn't—well, it was harder to see then. Or—no, it wasn't. I just wasn't as good at seeing, or I didn't want to."

"Scarlet is...another queen?" Jorgenstern said faintly.

"She was a djinn—a fairy, maybe you'd call her. But then she took on the form of an eagle—she was the one what attacked the queen at the end there and gave me time to get away."

The jays fluttered along silently beside him until they reached the great entrance hall and started up the stairs, and then Rimmauld—their voices were different and by this time Nivvy could tell them apart—said, "Truly, Sir Nivvy, you have lived a wondrous story. I should like to hear the whole tale sometime."

Nivvy grunted, pulling himself up the stairs. "En't over yet," he said.

When they finally reached the upper balcony hallway, they found a crowd around the rose bush: mostly birds, but a few squirrels and rats as well. And, Nivvy discovered, one weasel, who bounded over to him excitedly asking who he was and if he wanted to join the Brotherhood of Weasels. He got as far as telling Nivvy that they were the only members and that their meeting place was secret before Jorgenstern herded him away with clipped orders.

The ring had fallen next to the balcony doors and lay there partly in shadow. Nivvy scooped it up and slid it up his forearm until it stuck. It wasn't easy to walk with it, but he didn't have anywhere else to keep it.

At that moment, two pairs of human footsteps sounded on the stair. Nivvy climbed up the empty pedestal and stood there to welcome Remelstaub, escorting an old man dressed in a brown robe who walked with a gnarled wooden stick.

When they reached the top, Remelstaub looked around. "Er," he said, "This is Cormundsgrasse. To whom should I present him?"

Rimmauld flew up to perch beside Nivvy, but Nivvy spoke first. "Hallo, Remelstaub," he said. "Remember me? I was the thief in the cart. We talked in that street outside the castle when you was a crow. Tide's shifted on us a bit, ay?"

Remelstaub blinked and stared at Nivvy. "I am sorry to see that," he said.

"I am Rimmauld, steward of the castle," Rimmauld said. "You may present Cormundsgrasse to me."

"Yes, sir." Remelstaub saluted smartly. "Sir, this is Cormundsgrasse, a scholar of the royal family."

"Please approach." Rimmauld had adopted the formal tone of a court official, and the old man responded, tottering forward. "Do you know why you have been summoned here?"

"The bird said something about the queen being dead," Cormundsgrasse said. "And good riddance to her."

This provoked a small murmur, but nobody objected aloud. "That rose bush you see yonder is what remains of the queen, thanks to Sir Nivvy here," Rimmauld confirmed, and went on without giving Nivvy time to object. "We need you to tell us if any of the royal family survive, either here or in another kingdom. The throne sits empty and must be filled posthaste."

"Oh, aye," Cormundsgrasse said. "Two survive, or had as of a month ago, one with better claim than the other. The queen's nephew Kelivin was sent to Vir'Aji, where the Heiter empties out. And the King Consort's first son remains in his father's homeland of Fruktfelt, far to the north of here. Kelivin would be the nearest in line to the throne, but there is precedent for the issue of a consort to assume the throne if there are no other claimants. Following the reign of Günter the Third, during the Three Years' War, the royal family—yes, yes, let me finish." He brushed off Rimmauld's attempt to stop him. "The royal family had lost two sons to the war, and then their daughter took sick at the same time as her father, who was an only child. So the queen's brother's child was deemed next in line to the throne and ascended to it." He nodded his head forcefully.

"So this royal family," Nivvy said, "they weren't even properly descended from Primrose." He wondered whether that would have made a difference if Rose had known it.

"I remember Kelivin," Rimmauld said. "He is a good man. One of us shall fly to Vir'Aji and summon him to return. Jorgenstern, can you find a suitable messenger and have Cormundsgrasse tell all he knows about where to find the youth?"

"Of course." Jorgenstern flew up to the pedestal and addressed the old man. "May I alight on your shoulder?"

Cormundsgrasse's eyes widened. "Never has a bird asked so politely," he said. "Is that Jorgenstern the junior advisor to the royal family?"

"The second senior advisor." Jorgenstern executed a bow that was reasonably formal for a bird, spreading his wings and lowering his head.

"Then I would be honored." The old man offered his shoulder, and Jorgenstern flew across to it. Cormundsgrasse walked to the rosebush, where he stared at the flowers and conversed with the jay in low tones.

"Sir Nivvy," Rimmauld said, "it will likely take several days to reach and recall Kelivin, and there is much to prepare in that time. I would be glad of your help if you have no other pressing work."

Nivvy almost laughed. "No need for the 'sir' there, but aye, if there's more I can do, I'm happy to. I have to stay until Zein and Scarlet come back anyway an' that's likely to be a week as well."

"We will be in your debt." Rimmauld spread his wings and bowed. "The first thing I would ask is what you know of this Remelstaub: is he of good character? Does he owe allegiance to the rose queen?"

Nivvy glanced at the soldier, standing at attention and probably able to hear everything they were saying. "I believe his first allegiance is to his kingdom. He served the queen because he hoped to regain his human form. That's all from one little chat we had at night when he was a crow, but I think it's a fair measure of him."

"Remelstaub," Rimmauld called.

The soldier snapped to attention. "Yes, sir?" It was entirely possible, Nivvy mused, that the soldier had specifically not listened to any of the talk until it was directed at him.

"Will you serve the new king of Heiterflus as you served the old king and queen?"

"To my last breath, sir."

"The castle will need a new leader of the Guard. Will you take that post?"

"Me, sir?" Remelstaub's eyes widened, and his formal demeanor dropped for a moment. "I—there must be others more suited. I have only fifteen years of service."

"Your fellows are all rats and birds as far as I am aware," Rimmauld said. "Sometimes, my boy, history pushes us to take on tasks before our time, and then we must stand and answer the call. Will you serve your kingdom in this way?"

Remelstaub stiffened and then saluted, his eyes bright. "Yes, sir, I will, sir."

"I am glad to hear it. We will administer the oath when the new king is crowned, but for now, you will act with my authority. The first thing we must do is find those who worked willingly with Queen Bella, capture them, and take them to prison to await trial. I know some of them, and my friend Greta knows them as well. Greta!"

He called sharply to the group of birds around the bush. A mockingbird startled and then flew up to the pedestal, where Nivvy moved aside to make room. "Hallo, Rimmauld," she said in a high, papery voice.

"Remelstaub, this is Greta, who was the Chamberlain to the household. Greta, Remelstaub has agreed to serve as the leader of the Guard, and to help us find and imprison the traitors who helped Queen Bella. Will you help guide him in this task?"

"Ah, with pleasure, dear boy." Greta laughed and flew to Remelstaub's shoulder. The soldier flinched but stayed at attention. "Come, let us mete out Heiterflus justice. I know where old Keil has hidden himself away."

"We will not find all of them," Rimmauld said to Nivvy as the soldier descended the stairs. "Those who were changed to animals will be indistinguishable from other animals. But many curried her favor to remain human, and those we will be able to recognize."

"Right." Nivvy looked around. "I don't know the kingdom, or anyone in it save you and Jorgen and Remelstaub there. Don't quite know what good I'm to be to you. Anyway, when Zein gets back we'll probably leave."

Rimmauld ignored that last bit. "You mean Jorgenstern? Jorgen is one of the kitchen staff. I believe he was allowed to remain human to prepare meals."

"Yes." Nivvy gave a moment's gratitude to Inira that he hadn't told Rimmauld his full proper name. He was certain the steward would be using it constantly.

"What is your training? Are you a soldier? A diplomat?"

"Ah." Nivvy ducked his head. "My specialty is, ah, takin' things and scarpering before I get caught."

"Oh, a thief." Nivvy hadn't thought jays could smile, but Rimmauld did a credible job of it. "I'm afraid I haven't any jobs that require thieving, but if you would, I would put you in charge of the rose bush. I fear people may not understand it or try to destroy it, and it should be left here."

"Oh, aye," Nivvy said. "I can do that. And—listen, Rimmauld, you seem like a decent sort and you've a lot of work ahead of you, so..." He pulled the ring off his arm and lowered his voice. "Listen, this thing, it —it lets you take on the appearance of other people. Might be useful if you want to seem human while yer goin' about getting things back in order?"

Rimmauld stared at the ring but did not reach for it. Finally, he said, "I thank you, Sir Nivvy, for the generous offer. It is tempting. But if, as you said, our situation is not to be helped, then pretending it does not exist will not benefit any of us. There may be a use for it in the future, but for now..." He shook out his wings. "This is my form, and there is no shame in it."

"That's—that's wise," Nivvy said. He slipped the ring back on his arm. "I feel the same 'bout it, to be honest with you. Helps that everyone else here's got the same problems to deal with."

"Indeed." Rimmauld walked to the edge of the pedestal. "And I will not say that the joy of flight is but a meager gift to accompany this curse. I enjoy it far more than I would have thought. But not all feel the same." He called down to the assembled birds and the three rats and one weasel. "Attention, all of you. Sir Nivvy here is Heiterflus's first Knight of the Rose, and his duty is to stand guard over the rose bush and tell its story to any who want to listen. Attend him and help him and affirm his title to others as they arrive."

"I told you," Nivvy said, ears flushing warm, "no need to bother with that 'sir' stuff."

Rimmauld spread his wings. "We will see about that," he said, and flew off.

## ❦ 38 ❦
## HEITERS

The humans who remained in the city had mostly been in hiding for fear of being turned into animals, and as news of Queen Bella's transformation spread, they emerged into the streets again, reaching out to each other in wonder and hope. Many former-humans came to stare at the rose bush, and eventually, since he could not keep out the winged and four-footed people of Heiterflus, Rimmauld opened the castle gates and balcony hallway to all.

By and large, the humans Nivvy saw behaved respectfully toward the former-humans, with a few exceptions. In Spire, there were hardly any former-humans, so he understood why they got treated poorly, as Zein had told him. But here in Heiterflus, Bella had changed hundreds of soldiers and students and priests (the temples and college had very few humans left). Merchants and tradespeople, especially those who needed their hands for a trade (farmers, tailors, carpenters, sailors, and so on) had been spared, though some had been changed as punishment. The point was, every human knew a former-human, so they were kinder to them.

Two of the humans were kind enough to move the pedestal over to stand next to the rose bush, and that was where Nivvy remained for the next few days, watching over the bush and talking to the people who came to see it. He told a little of Bella's story, leaving himself generally out of it unless they asked, and then he confessed to his part in it, both the beginning, where he'd helped her, and the end, where he'd destroyed her.

Everyone was awed by the bush enough to keep their distance, with the exception of one crow that perched on the back side of the bush and ripped out two petals from a flower before Nivvy heard the noise. The next day, the crow came back and laid the petals down on the pedestal. "I felt strange when I took them," he confessed, "and overnight I dreamed I was being judged for everything I did in my life. It was very real. I didn't like it, so I am returning the petals. I am sorry."

The crowd assembled to stare at the bush heard this apology, and thereafter, people who came to look at it asked Nivvy if the bush were cursed or blessed. He said, "I dunno, but I wouldn't touch it if my life depended on gettin' a rose."

Jorgenstern appointed himself to fly to Vir'Aji and return with Kelivin, leaving Rimmauld in charge of the castle. The jay took to spending his evenings with Nivvy on the pedestal by the rose bush, gazing at it in silence if the day had been a tiring one. Other evenings, he returned with energy and engaged Nivvy in plans for the future of the kingdom. The third day, for example: "What trades must we encourage for the former-humans? There will be less food needed; that is a boon. What will we need to make them feel comfortable and welcome here? This is their city too."

"Zein mentioned clothes," Nivvy said. "There's tailors, or one, I suppose, that makes clothes for former-humans in Spire."

Rimmauld bobbed his head. "Like the tabards Queen Bella created. But different, of course."

"Course." Nivvy smiled. "Dunno how that'd work for birds, though."

Rimmauld lifted one skinny leg and claw. "Charot—she was the assistant to the late seneschal—thought that we birds might wear precious metal bands on our legs so that we might know each other from a distance. You may perhaps not have noticed that all birds of a type look exactly the same. Whereas a jay in the wild might be a brighter blue on his wing, or have a different pattern on his head, we are all identical. Queen Bella did not have a very good imagination."

"She was pretty focused on the one thing," Nivvy agreed. "Rings sounds like a splendid plan t'me. Only not as big as this one." He gestured to the magic ring with the lapis stone, which he now kept beside him on the pedestal and only put on his arm to sleep.

"Very well," Rimmauld said. "I shall convene the tailors and jewelers and instruct them to learn to clothe our new forms."

Another day, they talked about keeping windows open for the birds and providing access to the four-footed residents, while also finding ways to keep rooms and buildings secure against unwanted intruders. Here Nivvy could be of more help, having learned many of the ways one could enter a building without being noticed, and while he felt a touch guilty betraying some of his thiefly secrets, he reasoned that Inira wouldn't want a bunch of amateur thieves running around who thought they could steal just because they were now a mockingbird or a rat. The true thieves would find a way regardless.

On the sixth day since Jorgenstern's departure, and the seventh since Zein and Scarlet's, Nivvy asked Rimmauld if there were wizards in the city. "There were two employed by the royal family," Rimmauld said, "and I think you can guess what has happened to them. I knew of one other wizard who lived twenty miles up the river and discouraged visitors."

"I'd be lookin' for someone with a reputation for healing," Nivvy said.

"That is more difficult." The jay had picked up a habit of clicking his beak when he was thinking, which he did now.

"I confess," Nivvy said, "I only heard of healin' wizards as a story, like what kings and queens might have, and that's why I thought you might know."

"Are you injured?" Rimmauld examined him, tilting his head this way and that.

"Not me, but my—my friend the eagle. Bella made her claw her own eyes out and I'd like to give her her eyes back."

"Ah. Ever the noble."

"Not 'ever'," Nivvy said. "But I'm tryin' to get there."

"You are correct to think of kings and queens," Rimmauld said. "Our closest allies who have not been harmed by Queen Bella are in Fruktfelt at present, and while they are a poorer kingdom than Heiter-flus, I do believe that they might have a healing wizard there. They are not likely to offer service for free, though."

"No," Nivvy said. "I 'spect not, but I got some trade for 'em."

Rimmauld eyed the ring. "I cannot gainsay your use of your magical ring, but I had been thinking that it might be useful for our envoys to other lands, to allow them to assume a human seeming at first. If you decide to trade it—"

"It's yours if you want it." Nivvy pushed the ring toward the jay. "Glad to be rid of it. No, I had sommat else in mind."

"Thank you," Rimmauld said.

They stood quietly for a moment and then Nivvy, feeling awkward, said, "It looks like you're doing a brilliant job here. I seen a few squabbles, but people have jobs an' things to do. They talk about how relieved they feel t'be able to go around and not worry 'bout being turned into animals, or bein' eaten or killed or whatever she did with former-humans she didn't like."

"Thank you." Rimmauld bowed his head. "It is not difficult to be a more calming presence than Queen Bella, but I and my staff are doing our best. There are many scared people. One soldier who had been made a rat turned on his fellows and tried to harm them. We attempted to restrain him, but he died from the exertion. Many others have simply left, to seek their fortune elsewhere or to live as animals. But many have stayed, and many of the unchanged have helped. We have a tradition of helping here in Heiterflus. The land is forbidding and the winters harsh, but we hold together."

"Very nice," Nivvy said. "Where d'your poor live?"

"On the heights on the other side of the river." Rimmauld spoke matter-of-factly. "There is a temple to Vik there and they minister to the ill and infirm and those who do not wish to work. The rag-men and tinkers and charcoal-burners live there with trappers and hunters as well."

"There's a Shallows everywhere, I s'pose," Nivvy said.

"What?"

"Never mind. But all the former-humans, they're doing well? The ones that don't go bad, that is."

"I believe we are creating a kingdom where they will thrive," Rimmauld said. "Where we will thrive. And there is another matter, one I hoped to discuss with you. The last few days, we have been calling ourselves former-humans, as you have, but many people are unhappy with that name. They feel it reminds us too much of who we were and not who we are."

"Never thought of that," Nivvy said, guessing that modest Rimmauld might be one of the main people unhappy with the name. "Reckon you're right. Got another idea?"

"I thought," the jay ducked his head modestly, "that we might call ourselves 'Heiters' after our kingdom."

Nivvy hid his smile. "What about them of us from other parts?"

"We hope that in time, Heiterflus may become a place where all those changed into animals may live freely, and that they will come join us here."

The weasel nodded his head. "It's attractive indeed. Well, I like it better than 'former-humans,' an' I for one would be proud to call myself a Heiter."

"That was my hope," Rimmauld said.

❧

JORGENSTERN RETURNED TWO DAYS LATER WITH THE NEWS THAT Kelivin was riding close behind and would be arriving by sunset. The castle swarmed with activity during that time, and when cries echoed of "He's here, he's here!" Nivvy ran out to the balcony to stand among foxes and rats and the one weasel (a palace clockmaker named Brint who now held Nivvy in reverence and had given up on his Brotherhood of Weasels talk), while birds perched atop and several human servants stood looking down.

Kelivin rode in on a chestnut-brown horse glossy with sweat, bundled up in a riding cloak and a green cap. Nivvy couldn't quite make out his face from the balcony, but he could tell when the king-to-be stopped and stared up at the people and Heiters watching him from all around the courtyard. A bird on his shoulder—Jorgenstern, likely—said something that he tilted his head to, and then he spoke in a youthful voice.

"Citizens of Heiterflus," he said. "I am so sorry to hear of the tragedy that befell my family. We will mourn them properly in the coming weeks. I promise to serve you well as your next king, whether you walk on two legs or four or fly on wings. All of you will be my subjects and equal in my eyes."

"Pretty words," said a rat softly next to Nivvy in a lady's voice.

"Hush," said the rat on his other side, sounding like a young man if Nivvy had to guess. "He's our king now."

Kelivin went on with a flowery speech about a new age dawning in Heiterflus, but the rats either ignored him or were good at listening to one thing while talking about another. "Easy enough to slip away if he won't do right," the first said. "Who cares where rats go?"

"Give us a chance," Nivvy said. "There's lots being done here for us types. He's been made well aware."

"Us," the rat nearer Nivvy said. "Who's 'us'? Where do you work?"

"He's the Knight of the Rose," the other said before Nivvy could answer. "Have you not seen him guarding the rose bush?"

"Oh, a knight?" The rat looked Nivvy back to front. "So you mean the king will take care of his knights and nobles. We never doubt that."

"No," Nivvy protested. "I meant us, Heiters, the animals changed by the Queen."

"We were kitchen workers," the first rat said. "We stood in the kitchen and minded our business and when the Queen came down to demand some dreadful soup she wanted, the chef said he could not make it. So she killed him and turned us all into rats."

"I'm sorry," Nivvy said.

"You got changed too. Least now we can feed ourselves better." The rat scratched behind his ear. "I went to sleep full the last week."

The other rat spoke up. "I would still like to cook. I was learning how to do it."

"We're working to help everyone," Nivvy said. "Not just nobles. I promise you, Rimmauld is looking out for the whole kingdom."

"Why should he start now?" the first rat asked. "Did you hear what this king just said about how important nobles are?"

"This is Rimmauld, not Coike," the other rat said. "Of course he must say that. He must win support of the nobles. But he may also help us."

"See?" Nivvy said. "Listen to your friend."

"What is it to you?"

"I just want all us Heiters to stick together," Nivvy said. "More of us there are, more they have to take account of us, ey?"

"Nobody has taken account of us," the first rat grumbled.

"Well, I'm going to," Nivvy said.

The king had ridden into the castle, and now Rimmauld flew to the balcony—or maybe he'd been there all along; he was right that all the jays looked alike—and called down to Nivvy, who was distinguishable from Brint by the ring he wore on his arm. "Sir Nivvy, your presence is required."

"Oh, Sir Nivvy, best go attend the king," the rat said.

"Hush," her companion said.

Two dozen nobles attended the audience with the king, only two of them human. Nivvy was asked to tell the story of the Queen, after which one of the nobles told the story of her arrival in Heiterflus on the back of a dragon ("where is the dragon now?" Kelivin asked nervously, and was assured it was being tended to and was very placid) and the murder of the royal family (which sounded horrifying and made Nivvy's fur stand on end, and also made him selfishly glad that he'd never gotten on Bella's bad side until the very end there). And then it was Nivvy's turn again to relate the Battle of the Balcony, as people had come to call it, in which he endeavored to tell Zein's and Scarlet's parts before his.

Rimmauld allowed him to finish, then told Kelivin that Nivvy had been the bravest and had also remained behind to provide a great service to the kingdom in guarding the rose bush. He told Kelivin that he had promised Nivvy to be made a knight of a new order, and to Nivvy's surprise, Kelivin agreed wholeheartedly.

He was not at all what Nivvy had expected of someone who was to be made King. He felt the deaths of his family deeply and wore those feelings on his young face for all to see. He listened carefully to everyone who spoke and weighed their words. And when Nivvy hesitantly asked him for the favor—the boon—he and Rimmauld had discussed, Kelivin asked Jorgenstern whether such a thing was possible. Upon being told that it was, he nodded gravely and granted Nivvy the boon.

Maybe, Nivvy thought, just maybe, they were building something that was worth being a part of.

## ❧ 39 ❧

# THE ORDER OF THE ROSE

Nivvy had asked Greta, the mockingbird, to keep an eye out for an eagle and a hawk flying together, but Greta had other things to do, so he was caught by surprise when Zein swooped into the hallway two days after Kelivin's return. Literally by surprise: they flew in through the window and alit on his pedestal, and before he had time to register their calling his name, he'd jumped to the floor in a flash of panic.

The hawk craned their head down over the edge. "Nivvy! I'm sorry, I should've warned you. Are you hurt? Do you want me to come down?"

"I'm fine," Nivvy said. "Been practicing me jumping actually, want to see what I can do since I'm likely to be a weasel 'til I die now." He swarmed easily up the pedestal and leapt to Zein's feathers. "When did you get back?"

"Just now!" They curled a wing over him. "Scarlet's on the balcony outside. She's getting used to flying blind, but the landings are always hard."

He rubbed his face against the soft feathers of their belly. "Crown's gone?"

"Well, it's in the lake. I asked why she didn't want to destroy it and she said it's a relic of her sister, and only you and she know how to use it, and you can't and she won't. You know how she is with her relics. She said she talked to the prince's ghost, but I didn't see him. I didn't get close, though. It was a lot of flying and I had to do all the hunting but I

438

did it, I brought her there and back safely." They leaned down. "And the lake reminded me of when you took me to see it, and I missed you, and I'm glad to be back."

"I missed you too." Nivvy sat back and beamed up at them.

"I am worried about Scarlet, though. She didn't want to come back, and I had to tell her that we would miss her if she didn't come back, and then I had to tell her that we needed her to deal with the magic Rose left behind, because she didn't seem to care that we would miss her. So be nice to her."

"I was going to be." Nivvy couldn't stop smiling. "You did a fantastic job getting Scarlet there and back."

Zein butted his head affectionately. "I did, didn't I?"

"Remember when you didn't want to go on adventures?"

"Alone," they reminded him. "I wasn't alone. But you're right. I have learned a lot." They peered at the grey cloth band around his arm. "What's that? Why is there a rose on it?"

"Oh! They, uh, made me a knight. There's a new order called Order of the Rose, and right now it's me and this fox Eyos who told Rose the royal family were somewhere else. With the dragon in his face, too, very brave fellow. But they want you and Scarlet to be knighted too, if you want." He paused for a breath. "Actually, I said you were as brave as me and deserved it an' they agreed."

Zein tilted their head. "What do you have to do? What would I have to do?"

He gulped. "The big thing, I s'pose, is...we'd live here. I didn't think I'd want to, but...there's lots of Heiters—'Heiters' is what we call former-humans here now—an' it actually feels like..."

"Like home?" Zein asked when Nivvy hesitated.

Nivvy nodded. "It en't Copper Port, nor Spire, but...it might be better than that. If you don't want to stay, though, I'll leave with you."

Zein laughed and curled a wing around him. "If you want to stay, I'll stay. What does the Order of the Rose do?"

"Me, I look after the rose bush here an' tell people about it. Eyos helps people get used to bein' Heiters. I dunno if you'd have to do anything, it's just a mark of respect."

Zein eyed his armband again. "Would I have to wear a band on my wing?"

"Nah, they're makin' metal rings for birds to wear on their legs. Rimmauld has one, he says he can barely feel it."

"I suppose that would be all right," Zein said. "You and me, knights. Who would have thought?"

"Yeah." Nivvy grinned wide. "Oh, but that ain't even the best news."

A thump from the doorway made them both turn their heads. An outstretched eagle wing showed through the door, followed by the rest of the eagle. "You left me outside alone," Scarlet complained. "I can hear you being all happy in here."

"Sorry! We're over here," Zein called.

A mockingbird flew in and landed on the ground in front of the eagle. "I'm sorry, Sir Nivvy," Greta called up. "The eagle and hawk are here!"

"'Sir' Nivvy?" Zein murmured.

"Part of the whole 'knight' thing," he said, and then called down to Greta, "Can you lead Scarlet over here? I've got something for her."

"Just drop it on the floor and I'll find it," Scarlet grumbled.

"This way, ma'am," Greta said, hopping in front of the eagle and keeping an eye on the large sharp beak.

"I can follow the voices." Scarlet stepped in a dignified manner toward the pedestal.

"I can't drop it," Nivvy called down. "It's a visit to a wizard. He says he can fix your eyes."

Scarlet stood still for a moment, blind face looking up at Nivvy and Zein. Then she said, "Don't bother."

"What? Why not? I thought you'd be happy!"

"I told you," Zein murmured.

The eagle turned her head from side to side. "I got rid of Rose. That's all I wanted to do. Then I was going to go back and die in my cave with all my lovely things around me, but I can't do that, thanks to her, so I'll just find somewhere to die. I was going to go to that naked man in the woods and eat his drugs, but that one wouldn't let me."

"Don't you want to be able to see again?" Nivvy asked.

"I don't care."

"I've tried," Zein said. "You see?"

Nivvy thought for a moment. "Thing is," he said, "I already made the deal with the wizard what can do it, an' he accepted the deal, so if I back out now, he might be angry, an' I'd rather not have a wizard angry with me."

Scarlet fluffed her feathers. "I don't see that that's my problem. I didn't ask you to make any deal."

Zein had been looking around and interrupted Nivvy's indignant response. "What happened to the mirror? The pieces of it?"

"Oh," Nivvy said. "They're in a box somewhere."

"Scarlet," Zein said, "just as we disposed of that crown, we should dispose of the mirror, don't you think?"

The eagle cocked her head but didn't answer. Zein went on. "And none of us know how to reach the Velki. But you do."

"Impossible without magic," Scarlet snapped.

"Wouldn't some of them have come near the surface when the volcano erupted?" Zein asked. "Remember, I asked if I could see one and you said 'maybe'? Could they still be around? It's only been a couple weeks."

"They...might be," Scarlet said grudgingly.

"So what if you were to take the mirror back to them? They could fix it or keep it or do whatever they like. And while you're talking to them, you could ask them to look for anything you had that might have survived. You had other things from the Velki, didn't you? They might have survived the lava."

The eagle stood very still. Zein and Nivvy watched as she considered this idea. "Do you really think something might have survived?" she asked finally.

"You'd need the Velki to help you look," Nivvy said.

"And wouldn't that be easier with eyes?" Zein asked.

"I think it would," Greta the mockingbird chipped in.

"Fine," Scarlet snapped. "You see, this is why nobody wants to give you mortals power. You're so intolerable when you get even a little bit of it."

"I know," Nivvy said. "Doin' nice things for our friends, what a scandal."

"So tell me about this deal," Scarlet said. "What did you promise?"

TIM SUSMAN

The item Nivvy had promised was all the way down in Copper Port, but he'd taken advantage of that to include his uncles in the plan. The palace tailor crafted a sling that Nivvy could ride in and Zein could carry, and so the two of them flew along the river to the coast.

Together they shared their first sight of the great port of Vir'Aji with its hundreds of trading ships; they turned south from there and skirted the edge of a thunderstorm while rain hissed into the ocean and lightning crackled through dark stormclouds. Zein had never had ocean fish, so Nivvy snuck into one of Vir'Aji's markets at night and made off with a small flounder that was twice as big as his body, dragging it over the ground until Zein could pick it up. They feasted on the fish and thereafter Zein insisted on fish whenever they were near a port.

The wild coastline was lovely, too. One night they stopped at a rocky promontory where the waves crashed against the rocks in beautiful explosions of spray. "You grew up near the sea," Zein said.

"Not like this." Nivvy leaned against them. "We'd get waves, but it was all flat. Rocks was all under the water, not above. Shipwrecks there too, stuff would wash up. This is all clean. If it was like this, I might not have left."

"I can see why." They draped a wing over him.

"Did you grow up near water at all?"

Zein went rather still. "There was a river," they said, but nothing else.

"I just asked..." Nivvy paused as another wave hit the rocks with a loud crash. "On accounta we're goin' to my home an' maybe meeting my uncles, an' I just wondered if you wanted...I know you said you argued with your family..." When Zein still didn't answer, Nivvy said, "I'm sorry."

"No, no, it's all right." The hawk heaved a sigh. "I don't think about that life. You understand, when I was changed, it was like—well, Gregory said for him it was being born again, and I like that. So I was born five years ago and before that there was a girl who lived somewhere and then died. I remember a few of the things that happened to her, but I'm not her. I'm me. My family is..." They watched the spray explode from another wave but didn't speak again immediately when it subsided. "I thought it was the other former-humans in Spire, but...I think my family is right here."

442

Their wing tightened a little bit over Nivvy. "Ah," he said, "I feel that too."

"I was thinking about the Order of the Rose," Zein went on.

"Oh?"

"I'd like to join it," they said. "But I want us as Knights of the Order of the Rose to travel around the world, like we're doing now. There's so much of it to see. So I thought that maybe we could go around the world to other former-humans—Heiters—and maybe offer to bring them back to Heiterflus or else try to make their lives better."

It felt for a moment as though Nivvy's heart were in his throat, and words couldn't quite push past. Zein leaned down. "What do you think of that?" they said anxiously.

"Us," Nivvy croaked, and then cleared his throat of the congestion, if not the emotion. "You mean us, you and me, together?"

"The only other one in the Order is Eyos and I don't think I can carry a fox." They laughed softly. "Of course I meant you and me. Maybe Scarlet if she wants to fly along."

"It sounds beautiful," Nivvy said thickly. "I dunno if Scarlet will go for it though."

"I don't care so much if she does as long as you do," Zein said.

Nivvy slipped an arm around their leg. "I do," he said. "Absolutely."

⚜

THEY ARRIVED IN COPPER PORT LATE IN THE AFTERNOON ON A DAY when a light drizzle coated Zein's feathers with droplets of water and painted the world with a misty grey through which town and sea blurred together. But the wall was obvious, and beyond it The Shallows, where a few people took advantage of the coolness of the rain to scavenge along the beach or sit outside to make crafts.

Nivvy found his uncles' house by the design on the canvas. Neither of them sat out in the street with their neighbors, so he directed Zein to the wood part of the roof, where they set Nivvy's sling down and deftly landed just to the side. "They live in here?" they said. "Two of them?"

"Aye. My father and mother and I lived in one of these too." Nivvy extracted himself from the sling and ran to the edge of the roof over the canvas doorway to call down. "Uncle Foli? It's Nivvy!"

After a moment, the canvas was thrust aside, and his uncle's silver-and-black hair appeared below him. "Nivvy!" He looked around and his voice grew puzzled. "Nivvy?"

"Up here," Nivvy called.

Foli turned and looked up, squinting into the rain, and his eyes widened at the sharp furry face looking back at him. "What happened?"

Nivvy winked. "Thought that'd be obvious, no?"

"Are you...all right?"

"Put your hands up, please," Nivvy said, and when Foli did, he shook his wet fur and then jumped down into them. "Can my friend the hawk come in as well?"

Foli looked up toward the roof, but Zein was still back out of sight, so Nivvy called to them. "Come on down," he said.

Zein walked over to the edge, and Foli took a step back. "That's a large hawk," he said. "Never been so close to one."

"They're a lovely person," Nivvy said. "They've done wonders for me."

"Well, it's a pleasure to meet you," Foli said. "I'm Nivvy's Uncle Foli."

"I'm Zein," said the hawk. "Nivvy has spoken well of you."

"Come in out of the wet, won't you?" And Foli carried Nivvy in, holding the canvas so Zein could fly though.

Moru jumped up from the bed when the hawk swooped in, but once the situation was explained and introductions made, he sat down again, though he kept eyeing Zein's beak. They offered Zein and Nivvy bean paste and grouper, and Nivvy explained that he preferred meat and fish these days, but tried the bean paste to see if it tasted the same (not really). The grouper, however, was excellent.

"So," Foli said after they'd eaten, "might I guess the fight against this magic woman didn't go well?"

"We won," Nivvy said. "But it took all three of us. One of us, the friend who isn't here, she lost her eyes. I got turned back to a weasel."

"I'm glad you came back to tell us," Foli said. "We would have wondered what happened to you if you hadn't."

Under that statement was light reproach for all the years Nivvy hadn't come back, the decade or more. He accepted that. "We came back to ask a favor for our friend who lost her eyes. We need to trade with a wizard to have her eyes restored, but the thing we want to trade, we need a human to use. I guess Zein could carry it, but it'll be a lot faster if someone uses it."

"What thing?" Moru asked.

"Hold on," Nivvy said. "I'll tell you in a moment here. But we also, because we won and freed the kingdom, they like us rather a lot." He touched his armband with a nose. "Made a whole knightly order for us an' all. So I asked if they would mind much if I brought my uncles to live with us up north. There's not much wading around for garbage in the ocean, but there's much to be done an' I'd like it not to be another however many years before we see each other again. An' I want to offer you more comforts than here."

"We're very comfortable here," Foli said.

"But it is a generous offer." Moru looked at his husband. "I have thought about seeing another part of the world. And if we could live better…"

"We don't need more than we have."

"No, but…should we turn it down if it's offered?"

"Besides," Nivvy said, "you'd get to see your favorite nephew more often."

"Oh!" Foli's eyes brightened. "You're going to bring Cavali as well? You shoulda said!"

"Maybe I changed my mind," Nivvy said to Zein. "C'mon, we should go."

Foli laughed, and Zein did too. "It's a generous offer, dear boy. Let us discuss it."

"You can come back here anytime."

"I don't know about that." Foli gestured around. "If we leave here for too long, someone else'll take it."

"I think we should go with him," Moru said. "But what is this thing you want us to help you with?"

⊙⊰⊙

"They're seven-league boots," Nivvy said, perched on Foli's shoulder as his uncle removed the boots from the cupboard in the captain's cabin. The two men were damp from the drizzle, which had continued on from the previous day, and their legs were filthy with muck and swamp water up to the knees. "You put 'em on an' then you can walk anywhere as fast as you can think it."

Foli eyed the shabby leather boots. "They don't seem magic."

"Nothing seems magic until it is," Nivvy said. "Put 'em on, and then keep hold of Moru and Zein."

Foli wanted to clean his feet first before putting on the magic boots, so Moru ended up taking off his shirt to help, and then wrapped the shirt around his arm so Zein could perch on it. Nivvy kept hold of Foli's shoulder, and then instructed Moru to take one hand. "And you have to put the other on Zein directly or they might be left behind."

"But they're touching Moru," Foli said, obliging anyway.

"Aye, but...to be sure," Nivvy said, and Zein gave him a look that said they understood.

Being transported by the boots was more disorienting than wearing them. Land rushed past them, shapes flitting around while the ocean remained constant on their right, shades of blue deepening and lightening as they sped past it.

"This is marvelous," Foli breathed.

"Look for Vir'Aji," Nivvy told him, watching the blurs of scrubby trees and jagged rocks. "You can slow down by putting your foot down but don't put it all the way down until you want to stop."

"I know, you told me," Foli said.

Vir'Aji came up quickly upon them, a mass of buildings and ships sprawling out at the river mouth. "Follow the river," Nivvy told his uncle.

"How do I..." Foli leaned to one side and the little group veered to the left.

"Urk," Moru said, reaching up to steady Zein.

"You got it," Nivvy said encouragingly. "Follow the river here and Heiterflus will be comin' up any moment now."

There was the city rising up along the river, the castle still hidden behind the giant thicket of roses that nobody could figure out how to take down short of chopping. "Where should I go?" Foli asked.

"Right for the big bush," Nivvy said, "but slow down, we'll be landin' right inside."

The thicket came at them and then they were through it in a blur of roses and leaves, and the castle wall flashed at them. "Now!" Nivvy cried, and Foli put his foot down and Zein took wing as the others all went tumbling to the ground in the middle of the courtyard.

"This is Heiterflus," Nivvy said as Foli picked him up.

"It's colder," Foli observed, and then he noticed the collection of animals in the courtyard staring at them: a few rats on the ground, mockingbirds and jays and crows all around. A few people in plain tunics stood and stared as well.

And then a man in a grey and white uniform with three gold stars on his shoulder ran into the courtyard from the main gate, sword drawn. "Intruders!" he called. "Stand and identify yourself."

"Ho, Remelstaub," Nivvy said from Foli's hand, and turned to show his armband. "It's just me an' Zein, the Order of the Rose, back from our first mission."

## ❧ 40 ❧

# FRESH EYES

T he wizard lived in the middle of the kingdom of Fruktfelt, in a cave halfway up a mountain that overlooked a small town. To avoid frightening him, Scarlet suggested taking the boots to the town rather than directly to the cave, and Foli was happy to oblige, especially since he hadn't quite got the trick of going up a mountain on his own, let alone with two large birds in his arms.

The people of the town first thought that Foli was a rival wizard and were fearful. When told that they were merely visiting the resident wizard, everyone in the town grew even more fearful, and warned them against going to him even when told that an agreement had already been negotiated. "He will do good," they said, "if the mood strikes him. But it does not often strike him." None of the villagers would prevent them from going on, but none would guide them. So Foli carried Scarlet up the mountain while Zein flew up with Nivvy.

Zein spotted the cave first and guided the others to it. As with Scarlet's lair, it looked quite nondescript from the outside, but as they stepped into it, the grey snow-dusted stone melted away, replaced by polished wooden beams; bright pink, green, and yellow silks; a cheery fire; and warm air scented with something similar to pine but not quite the same. A lush carpet with a design in it that Nivvy could just make out as a phoenix, rendered in the striking reds and yellows of a flame, covered most of the floor. (Nivvy thought it felt like a lot of colors had been thrown together without much consideration for how they looked next to each other, but they were here for healing magic, not decorating lessons, and anyway, this was this fellow's home, so he could put up whatever he liked.) Opposite the fireplace stood a long low table. There was nowhere to sit.

A deep red curtain hung across the back of the room, and just as Foli was depositing Nivvy and Scarlet on the table, a tall, lanky man strode out from behind the curtain, pulling a thin cotton robe around himself. "Ah," he said in a harsh northern accent, "you are the ones who came about the eyes."

"Yes," Nivvy said, standing on his hind legs for a moment to show off the new pants the castle tailor had made for him. "I'm Nivvy, an' this is Scarlet—"

The wizard ignored him, walking over to Scarlet and examining her empty eye sockets. "This is the eagle that needs the eyes?"

Like most of the people in the town, his complexion was as white as snow. It appeared he didn't make use of magic to wash his silvery hair or beard, nor water for that matter, nor to make himself smell better than a piece of meat that had been lying in the sun for a week. Nivvy wasn't one to judge people by their appearances, but he had taken pains to rub a pleasant scent into his fur before visiting someone for the first time. Scented powders had become quite popular in Heiterflus, at least among the keen-nosed mammals.

"Yes," Scarlet said. "Unless we've brought another blind person with us."

"Very good. You have the boots?" He looked shrewdly at Foli, who waved to the boots he'd set next to the table. "They don't look like much. I'm going to try them before we start, to make sure they work."

"Ah, we were hoping you might be able to try them after," Nivvy said, "by carrying us back to the castle since my uncle there has no other way to get back."

"I'll try them now." The wizard suited action to words. "And when it's done, I will send you back with a spell of my own."

Having secured the boots on his feet, he took a step forward and vanished.

"What if he don't come back?" Nivvy asked when several seconds had elapsed.

"Then we help ourselves to his artifacts," Scarlet said. "I'm sure I will recognize some of them."

"I'm hungry." Zein flew to the mouth of the cave. "I saw some tree-rats moving around outside. Nivvy, Scarlet, do you want any?"

They both declined, and Zein flew off to hunt. They had only just returned with their prey when the wizard reappeared, sweating and panting slightly. "Very well," he said, taking the boots off. "The bargain is good. You! Whose hawk is that? Don't eat that on my carpet."

"I wasn't," Zein said, taking their meal from the stone next to the carpet and moving it farther away.

"Right." The wizard turned back to Foli. "Now, is this the one giving up his eyes?"

"No!" Nivvy said.

"Oh." The wizard looked over to Zein. "Hawk eyes will be better." He flipped a small copper coin in his hand.

"None of us are giving up our eyes," Nivvy said.

The wizard looked rather put out. "Then whose eyes are you using? Go find someone from the town if you need to."

"We're not using any other eyes," Scarlet said. "Heal my eyes. Don't take eyes from anyone else to restore my sight."

"Is that so?" The wizard palmed his coin and stuck both fists to his hips, glaring at Scarlet, the only one who couldn't glare back. "That's much harder, I'll have you know. When we made this agreement, we did not specify a method, so—"

"Fine," Scarlet said, and spread her wings. "Then we will find another wizard who can heal rather than steal, and we will give that wizard this priceless magical artifact."

The thin man's mouth snapped shut, and he looked to Nivvy and Foli, who both stared back resolutely. Nivvy tried to hide how proud he was of Scarlet, who just a month ago would not have hesitated to take someone else's eyes. Her feeling might be less a concern for others' welfare and more a peevish refusal to let others pay a price for what she was no longer able to do, but it was progress all the same.

In the face of their resolve, the wizard half-turned toward the red curtain at the back of the cave, where Nivvy presumed he had other artifacts hidden. "I wouldn't do that," Zein called from the front of the cave. "She might not be able to see, but she's still faster than you. And you don't seem to want blood on your carpet."

"I didn't say I couldn't," the man said peevishly. "I just said it was harder, that's all." He stared at Scarlet and swallowed nervously.

"Best get started then, hadn't you?" Scarlet stood regally. "Foli, take the boots back until he's done. If he isn't doing exactly what we asked, take Nivvy and Zein and go."

Nivvy coughed. "I'll just give you space," he said, jumping down from the table to the carpet.

"Fine. Fine!" The wizard removed the boots and stalked back behind his curtain. A moment later, he emerged holding a long silver branch, complete with leaves. He called out, "I need the hawk."

Nobody moved. "Not to take its eyes," the man said impatiently. "I need to create eagle eyes and I believe that eagle eyes are much like hawk eyes, only larger."

"Close enough," Scarlet agreed.

"Fine. Then I need the hawk here to study its eyes—only looking, no changing or harming."

Finally, Zein flew over to the table, and the wizard bent to his work. Nivvy couldn't see what he was doing, but he heard the murmurs of the spell and then Scarlet's soft cries. "Stop moving," the wizard said. There were more soft cries, going on for several minutes. "It's going to hurt a little. How is that? Can you see out of that one?"

"Yes," Scarlet said. "Not very well."

He made a dissatisfied noise. After a bit he said, "Is that better?"

"A little." And then, "Aah!"

"I told you it would hurt." Seconds passed, feathers rustled. Finally: "How about now?"

"That is excellent," Scarlet said. "Thank you."

"Good. I'll do the other one now." More cries, more rustling of feathers, and at last an exhalation from the wizard.

"That's satisfactory," Scarlet said. "They work quite well."

"Excellent." The wizard sounded bored. "Now collect here, all of you. Where is that weasel?"

"Here." Nivvy ran out from under the table.

"Heiterflus castle, was it?" The man took a black feather out of the inside of his robe.

"Yes, if you please," Foli said.

The wizard muttered under his breath and then touched each one of them in turn with the feather. The two birds and Foli vanished as he touched them, and then he knelt down. For a moment Nivvy worried that the wizard would try to keep him, but the wizard only reached out the feather and—

—in the blink of his eye, Nivvy stood in front of the main gate to Heiterflus castle with the others.

By this time, they were known to the guards. Foli scooped Nivvy up to his shoulder and walked in while Zein and Scarlet flew up to the quarters they'd all been assigned. "Magic is terrible," was the first thing Foli said. "He was set to take my eyes to give to Scarlet!"

"Aye," Nivvy said, "magic can be cruel. It's power, eh? But he won't be takin' from others to heal, not for a while." He reached down into his pants where they pressed against his hips and pulled out a copper coin.

"Nivvy!" Foli said. "You stole from a wizard? What if he notices?"

"Doubt he will. He's got a whole apothecary back there, but his scent was strongest on the drawer with this coin in it, the one he was gonna use to take someone else's eyes. Found it quick enough, nicked it, an' closed the drawer again." Nivvy's little tail swished. "He likely won't check it again for a while, an' even if he remembers an' comes here to the castle, it'll be long melted by then."

"You went while he was healing Scarlet." Foli climbed the great stairs up to the balcony, and then turned away from the rose bush— Eyos the fox was watching it—and walked down the hallway.

"Nobody was watchin' for a li'l weasel," Nivvy said with some satisfaction. "An' when Inira puts an opportunity in front of a thief, you know…"

"Why melt it?" Foli took the coin and turned it over.

"Stealin' ain't healing," Nivvy said. "I should know. It's just movin' pain around. Some magic shouldn't be used."

His uncle smiled at him and opened the door to their quarters where Moru, Zein, and Scarlet were waiting for them. "Always a thief at heart, even when you're a knight," he said.

Scarlet wanted to leave that night with the chest containing the shards of the Velki's Mirror, but they prevailed on her to stay with them one more night. "We might not see you again," Zein said.

"You two are going to stay here?" the eagle asked, avoiding the question. She was perched on a large branch that Moru had brought in for that purpose. He had already begun to decorate the chamber with pine and holly, some of the clay found near the river, and pointedly no roses.

"Much of the time," Nivvy said. "I've a feeling we'll be traveling around. There's a lot of world to see."

Zein put a wing over him, and he leaned into them. "Good," Scarlet said unexpectedly. "Of all the mortals I've encountered in my thousands of years, you two are—well, not the best. There were smarter and braver ones. But I haven't known—I mean, I haven't felt—"

"We're the Order of the Rose together," Zein said. "That means something."

"We stuck by you when you had nothin'," Nivvy added. "Even when you were so sour you'd've curdled milk."

Foli, his arm around Moru, looked on from the bed. "I think the word you're looking for is 'friends.'"

"Hmph." Scarlet tossed her head.

"Privileged an' honored," Nivvy said.

"As you should be." Scarlet lowered her head and looked up at the weasel and hawk, up in the little nest on their shelf. "As...as am I."

"'Zbells," Nivvy said to Zein. "Maybe she really is gonna leave us forever."

"Forever." Scarlet turned to stare out the window. "You have no concept of forever, but let me tell you, forever can also end."

"No it can't," Nivvy said. "That's what it means. It don't end."

"Tell me, Zein." The eagle turned deliberately to the hawk. "How would you end this story?"

"What?" The hawk perked up. "What story?"

"This story, of you and Nivvy and Rose."

"And you," Zein said.

"And me, I suppose. You told me once that you didn't like the ending to a story I told. So tell me, how would you end this one, if you were to tell it?"

Zein tilted their head. "What's got you thinking about stories?"

"The end of forever," Scarlet said. "Perhaps I am looking at things in a different way now. I knew that death comes to all, but it came to my sisters swiftly and unexpectedly. Maybe that is what I mean: I did not expect to have time to contemplate it. I believed I would live forever until I stopped living, and what use is there in thinking about something when it might happen tomorrow or not for five hundred or five thousand years?"

Foli and Moru sat together, raptly listening. "Death's never that far away for us," Nivvy said.

"Obviously. That is why I am asking Zein about stories. My cave is gone, and when I pass away, there will be nothing except, perhaps, some stories."

"I suppose," Zein mused, "that I would end it with Rose dying. 'And the evil queen, faced with the truth of her deeds, collapsed in on herself and her body thickened and hardened into a bush from which roses sprouted.' Something like that."

"It's good," Nivvy said.

"So you wouldn't tell about how we disposed of the crown, or about how Nivvy is working with the people here, or about how I got new eyes?"

"Perhaps." Zein considered. "There's always something about what happened after, but just a little part. Something like, 'Nivvy and Zein remained in Heiterflus to help the transformed Heiters live happily, and flew around the world to help others, while Scarlet returned to her lair —or no, maybe went to live near the Drowned Kingdom?—and still visited them sometimes when they were able.'"

"Mmm." Scarlet drew her beak through the feathers on one wing.

"But," Zein added hastily, "that doesn't mean that's the end of all stories. This could be the beginning of another story. Oigal says that often, and he knows many stories he calls 'tapestries' which features the same people at different parts of their lives. It's only that, well, Rose was really what brought us all together, and then defeating her kept us together, and now she's gone. So that's a story."

"And what would be the point of the story?" Scarlet asked. When Zein didn't respond, she said, "What would Oigal say about it?"

"I don't know," Zein said slowly. "Live a life you can be proud of, maybe? If faced with the truth of your life, it shouldn't make you so sad that you turn into a plant?"

"It's never too late to start living that life," Nivvy said. "If you really want to." He leaned against Zein.

"Hmph," Scarlet said. "I don't think I'm going to enjoy being mortal."

"It's not so bad." Foli spoke for the first time, leaning against Moru. "The gifts the tide brings you mean more when you can count the number of tides left to you. How do you feel about your new eyes?"

Scarlet fixed him with a look and then said, "I'm tired," and put her head under her wing.

Foli looked up at Nivvy, and Nivvy smiled down as his uncle reached for the lantern and closed it. Though the room went dark, Nivvy's weasel eyes could make out much more than his human eyes could have: the shapes of his uncles getting comfortable on the bed, the huge eagle perched on a branch as thick as a human leg, the lines of the stonework surrounding them, the stars outside the window, and, most importantly, the patterns and grain of the feathers next to and around him.

"Good night," Zein murmured to him.

"Good night," he whispered back, and as the room fell silent around him, Nivvy offered a short prayer. *Ah, Inira, thank you for this path, and thank you for sending the people to walk it with me. I'll do my best to remain worthy of them.*

Scarlet might insist that the gods weren't real, but as Nivvy closed his eyes, he felt sure that he had been heard.

## ❧ 41 ❧

# HAPPILY THEREAFTER

## (ABOUT ONE YEAR LATER)

"Then the evil queen gazed into the magic mirror, and there she saw her true self laid bare. All the stories she'd told, all the deals she'd made, all of the lies she'd spoken to others and herself, all of them were rent and scattered like leaves before a storm. You know, of course, that every one of us believes that he or she is good, and the more one does evil, the greater the lies and stories one must tell oneself in order to survive. For when you are that evil, deep down inside, as I am sure none of you are," here Oigal looked around at his audience of a dozen men and women and almost as many children, "you cannot bear to look upon your own face. And the queen was so evil that upon confronting the truth of her evil nature, she crumbled into dust, and the Knights of the Order of the Rose were victorious.

"On the place where the queen fell, the Knights planted a great Rose Bush, which instantly grew taller than the tallest man. All around the castle, roses sprang up as well, circling the stone walls to make the castle even stronger. No man can scale those thorny thickets, and yet they are lovelier than walls, for they produce roses whose scent fills the city.

"Thus is the victory remembered. The Great Rose Bush stands still as a monument to the battle, and it is said that the thicket of roses which surrounds the castle will stand while one Knight of the Order of the Rose yet lives."

His audience snapped their fingers appreciatively; the sound echoed and multiplied within the small plaza. A few people leaning out of windows above the others joined in, as did the baker and weaver whose shops opened onto the plaza (the tailor was too busy or was not interested in hearing this story again). Oigal bowed and modestly indicated the child at his side, who made her way through the audience with a small pouch into which the people showed their respect with coin.

One of the children at the front of the crowd asked, "Mister Oigal? Is that eagle the Knight of the Order of the Rose in the story?"

"No," the eagle said before Oigal could answer. She spread her wings and opened her beak. "I'm just an eagle who's here to eat little children who ask too many questions."

The child screamed, but delightedly, and hid behind the boy next to her, who said, "Don't be stupid, Delia. The real Knights of the Order of the Rose wouldn't be here in Spire. They're off doing bold deeds."

"That's right." Oigal's gaze rose above the heads of his audience. "And remember that the Knights of the Order of the Rose may be human, or they may be Heiter. You'll know them by the rose they wear, but sometimes," he put a finger aside his nose and winked, "sometimes they may not wear the rose, so as to truly test your worth when they meet you. So be kind and respectful to all humans and Heiters alike."

"What's a Heiter?" the little girl asked, and the boy turned to explain it to her.

Another boy took his father's arm as they walked beneath a window ledge out of the plaza and said, "Did that really happen?"

"No," his father laughed. "Or if it did, it was hundreds of years ago. There isn't that much magic in the world anymore."

They did not look up and so did not see the hawk and weasel on the window ledge watching as they walked away, the weasel with a white cloth band on one forearm, the hawk with a silver ring around one leg, both bearing a red rose emblem. "That last part wasn't wrong," Nivvy said.

"He should have more faith in stories." Zein smiled and watched Oigal. "It looks like he's almost done now."

Indeed, Oigal's apprentice had returned to him with a fat pouch full of coins. He weighed it and then said to those who remained behind, "Thank you all for your generosity. You can hear my stories here every day, and I'll tell the story of the Order of the Rose again every week."

As the people filtered out, he caught the eye of the hawk and weasel and, with a smile, nodded up at the roof of the building upon whose steps he stood. His apprentice lowered her heavily padded arm for the eagle to climb onto, and then the three of them entered the building.

Nivvy got back in his pouch and Zein carried him up to the roof, where they waited until Oigal came up a wooden stair from one of his windows. The apprentice followed behind with the eagle, who hopped off as soon as they reached the roof. "Shantri," Scarlet said, "that hawk is Zein, and the weasel is Nivvy."

"Pleased to meet you." Zein performed a hawk-bow, wings outstretched, head down.

"It's an honor," Shantri said in a faint voice, bowing back so deeply that Scarlet had to spread her wings to keep her balance.

"Honor's all ours," Nivvy said, "to meet the young lady tasked with carrying the great Scarlet, too important to fly herself about now."

"You're one to talk," the eagle retorted, but she did jump down from Shantri's arm. "Getting carried around everywhere."

"If I had wings, you couldn't stop me." Nivvy pranced back and forth on the roof. "Flyin' here, flyin' there."

"I just got back from the volcano and I'm tired. And hungry." Scarlet approached him, fixing him with one eye.

Nivvy grinned, leapt up onto the eagle's back, and hugged her neck. "Good to see you again. Looks like yer keepin' well."

"I'm alive. Still."

Zein flew to Oigal's padded shoulder and rubbed their head against his cheek. "You tell it very well."

"It's a joy to see my friends again." Oigal's lined face beamed brightly. "I'm sorry about causing problems with the other ending. Thank you for sending a message to tell me. It's often hard to know what happens to stories when you release them."

"Made for a good story," Nivvy said. "But once we got people comin' up tryin' to pull all the roses off the bush so they could end 'the curse,' see, that wasn't gonna be any good."

"One of them got so many petals that he jumped off the balcony," Zein said. "It was very sad."

Shantri's eyes widened, but Oigal merely nodded. "I'm surprised you've allowed the bush to remain in the palace."

"For one, we thought it the least we could do to let Rose stay in the castle she wanted so bad. For another, anytime someone tries to move it, they come over all sad an' stop working. So we let it be." Nivvy rubbed Scarlet's head. "Anyway, I'm surprised this one didn't correct you every step of the way."

"I am developing an appreciation for stories," Scarlet said with dignity, "and I have agreed that it is more constructive for me to talk to Oigal after the story is told, in private, rather than interrupt him in the telling."

"That took a while," Oigal said, "but it is worth it to hear all the stories she shares with me."

"I don't share stories," Scarlet corrected.

"No, no." Oigal laughed. "You share history and I make them into stories. My apologies."

"It's so lovely to see you both here," the hawk said from Oigal's shoulder. "When you wrote and said that Scarlet had taken up residence..."

Nivvy finished the thought when Zein hesitated. "We didn't believe it. An' we've seen all kinds of things we might not have believed."

"He is good company." Scarlet tossed her head, but not so violently as to shake Nivvy off. "Much better than the Velki. They only want to talk about how one of their tribes is taking over all the best magma or how the rocks at the surface taste. Sometimes they try to tell me stories, but their stories are terrible."

"You hate stories," Nivvy reminded her.

"I told one of their stories to Oigal and he said it was terrible." Scarlet turned her head so that Nivvy could see one great golden eye. "So it isn't just me."

"It had a different flow to it," Oigal said. "They don't seem concerned about lessons in their stories, or beginnings or ends. I feel their stories probably continue on for generations and we only hear parts of them."

"How is it going with the Velki?" Zein asked. "Have they recovered anything more from your lair?"

"Shantri," Scarlet said. "Fetch the bag." And then, a moment later, "if you please."

The apprentice nodded. "Yes'm," she said, and ran down the stairs.

"I have a few things for you," Scarlet said. "But while she's fetching them, tell me where you've been and what brings you down to Spire? I thought you'd brought all the Heiters from here who wanted to leave."

"To see our dear friends," Nivvy said, "what else?"

Zein laughed. "That, of course, but we are also looking for wizards now. The wizard who changed me lives somewhere to the southeast of here, and the one who changed Nivvy's friend lives south of there."

Oigal frowned. "You're looking for wizards who can turn people to animals?"

"See," Nivvy broke in, "this wonderful thing just happened last month. Everyone'd been scared to have babies, but 'course, you can't stop people from doin' what people do, an' after a few months, there were some rat babies an' some nests of eggs."

"People were worried," Zein continued. "We didn't know what the babies would be like. I was told that some couples destroyed their babies because they didn't want to have wild rats or birds as children."

"Sad," Nivvy said, "but you understand maybe what they was thinkin'."

"But a few of them hatched and were born. At first we didn't really know how it would turn out."

"You're giving away the end of the story." Oigal smiled. "You already told us it was something wonderful, so I know that the babies are Heiters."

"They are, when both parents are." Zein rubbed their head against his cheek. "But we didn't know they were going to be. Even when one of the rats started making sounds, we weren't sure. Then a fledgling jay said some words."

"It took a year." Nivvy cocked his head to the tread of the apprentice on the stair. "For them to grow up enough that they're sayin' real words, actin' like real children. Human children, I mean. Heiter children."

"So," Zein said, "there are a few dozen people whose husbands and wives have been changed but they haven't, and since everyone has accepted that Heiters are Heiters—"

"Not quite everyone," Nivvy put in.

"—and won't be human again, some of those spouses—"

"Not all," he broke in again. "Not by a long shot."

"Not all," Zein repeated, "and let me finish, Niv, but some of them want to be turned into whatever their spouse is so they can be with them."

"That's either very sweet or very stupid," Scarlet said.

"People are often both." Oigal spread his hands. "That is what stories are about."

"So you're looking for wizards. I suppose that makes sense. Thank you, Shantri." The apprentice came over to Scarlet and sat next to her, opening the pouch in her lap.

Nivvy craned his neck to look at the items the girl brought out. The first was an oblong black rock the size of his head, polished and glossy, with spatters of white through it. "This one," Scarlet said, "they tell me contains some of my favorite glass sculptures. They can taste the glass in the lava rock. I don't know how they know that these were my favorites, but they might be. That one stays," she told Shantri.

The girl nodded and placed it to one side and then drew out what looked like a handful of glittering finely wrought chain mail. She spread it out on the roof before her, where the handful became three small gloves, the largest the length of Nivvy's body, the smallest nearly the size of his own paw. "These," Scarlet said, "were the Velki's idea, much as I would like to take credit. There was much magic stored in metal in weapons and armor in my cave, and they have managed to extract some of it to make new items. Here are three gloves that, when worn on paws or talons, will function as hands. I know that you two make do well enough with your natural forms, but—"

"The foxes will love these," Zein said.

"An' the mockingbirds," Nivvy added. "Maybe the jays as well. Hard for them to get their claws around things."

"Good," Scarlet said. "I had to tell them some of their ideas were not good, but I thought that one might be."

"How much do they want to make more of them?" Zein asked. "I think we will take as many as they can make."

"They don't take payment in the way you would think of it," Scarlet said. "They are grateful that I pointed them to my cave, and they love all the tastes there. They don't need food—they eat molten rock—so mostly they want to not be bored. Making these will be its own payment. Until they get bored of it."

The next thing Shantri pulled out of the pouch, a square mirror with a familiar-looking frame, flooded Nivvy with panic. "Don't look in that!" he cried.

The girl stopped with the mirror halfway down to the roof, eyes wide and fearful. "Don't worry," Scarlet said. "You're safe. Yes, that is the fragments of the mirror remade, but they have imbued it with a different property. Rather than showing you the truth of your nature—"

"I think it showed you the worst of yourself," Nivvy said. "Not the truth. There was good in my life that I never saw when I looked in it."

"But I looked into it many times..." Scarlet regarded the mirror thoughtfully.

"Forgive me," Zein said, "but you probably didn't think the worst things you did were bad. At the time, I mean."

Scarlet considered that, and then noticed Shantri's hand trembling. "Go ahead and put it down," the eagle told her, and the girl did, pulling her hand back quickly. "Whatever it did before, now it merely shows you the form you were born with. I thought it might be useful if you were seeking someone and wanted to know who they had been as a human."

Nivvy exchanged a look with Zein, who said, "Yes, thank you, I think that will be useful. Rimmauld has been wondering if something like that exists."

"Do you want to try it?" Scarlet asked. "I did. It works."

"No," Zein said.

"No, thank you." Nivvy stayed on the eagle's neck and wondered what the mirror showed Scarlet when she looked into it. The fairy? The blue warrior? Formless power? He stored away the question to ask another time.

"There is one more thing," Scarlet said as Shantri fished around in the bottom of the pouch. The girl drew out what looked like a copper coin on a small leather cord. "That one to Nivvy, please."

Nivvy took the coin from the girl's fingers. The copper was not a smooth circle, but radiated wavy points, as if it were an artistic rendering of the sun. An elaborate spiral decorated one side, and several lines ending in a cloud-shape marked the other. The leather cord was the right size to slip over his neck. "What's this?"

"A breathing-charm," Scarlet said. "Remade from another one I believe you are familiar with."

He turned the coin over again. The radiating points could also be the tentacles of an anemone. "Oh."

"It doesn't have the same spell, though." The eagle cleared her throat. "Do you want to know its spell?"

"Not much use otherwise, is it?"

"It's pretty," Zein contributed, peering at it from Oigal's shoulder.

"The spell is: 'The breath of the North Wind, worn by Nivali al Tamsin to fulfill a quest for Queen Rose.'"

Several seconds of silence followed this revelation. "Well," Nivvy said, pulling the cord over his neck, "that's fair, I suppose. An' this'll be useful."

"You know," Zein said, "you could just add, 'which he later put right' to the end of it every time you say it. Maybe that won't make a difference as long as you say the first part."

"From what I have learned of spells and stories," Scarlet said, "I believe that is true. And what's more, if you say that enough times, it may become part of the spell."

The coin hung from his neck, not heavy, but noticeable. "I'll do that, then," Nivvy said.

The eagle nodded. "That's all I have. But the Velki say there is at least a little more magic consumed by the volcano that they can retrieve. I will ask for more of the gloves. Anything else?"

Nivvy and Zein checked with each other before Zein said, "Thank you, and thank them, but we are all learning our new lives and doing rather well. The humans are helping."

"The rats and mockingbirds sometimes get attacked by wild animals," Nivvy said, "but we're makin' them little light armor that seems t'help, an' pairing them up with bigger Heiters, and we hadn't lost anyone in months last we were there."

"There was Currit," Zein reminded him.

"Right, but I don't count him cause he just wandered off an' got actually lost, not killed. I mean, probably killed, but maybe not. Rats can make their way. He just didn't like bein' a rat."

"I would love to come visit," Oigal said, "when summer comes around again. But I don't know if these old bones will make such a long trip."

"You're always welcome," Zein said, "but we are happy to see you here."

"Quite, an' we'll see you again on our way back." Nivvy grinned and ran his claws down Scarlet's feathers. "Can't shake us that easy."

"There was a time you'd have never dared do that," Scarlet said.

"True enough." He didn't stop. "Don't you prefer this time?"

"I have not yet decided."

Nivvy laughed. "Sour old bird. I've some complaints with the way the wheel turned, but I'd not trade out the bad if it meant losing the good, so I'll be a little weasel happily enough."

"Speaking of wheels," Scarlet said, "did you have the chance to visit the glass castle in the Western desert?"

"Not yet." Zein perked up. "We do want to go. Maybe when we've finished this. Why did wheels make you think of that?"

"Oh, the people who lived there believed that life is a wheel, always turning. Sometimes you're on top, sometimes on bottom, but never in one place all the time. I thought it silly at the time because I was on top, but...I could not see that I was on a very large wheel."

"A merchant from Akkar told me a story about a god whose symbol was a wheel," Oigal mused. "Perhaps they are related."

"Tell me and I'll try to recall the myths I've heard," Scarlet said.

"There was a time," Nivvy said teasingly, "when you'd have told him gods don't exist and not to be foolish."

"All right." Scarlet shook her head, and Nivvy let go to jump to the ground. "Somehow you are even more annoying as a weasel than you were as a human."

"I work at it." Nivvy shook himself and smiled. "Anyway, if I am, it's your fault."

"Don't think I don't know that." Scarlet sighed. "Think of the trouble I could have saved the world if I'd simply killed you."

"And Rose with me," Nivvy reminded her cheerfully. "But you did what you did, and I did what I did, and the wheel turns ever on."

"So it does." Oigal gestured toward the stair. "Will you stay for supper?"

"We would be delighted," Zein said. "We'll leave early in the morning. There's so much to do."

"An' so much to see. A whole world! But we'll be back." Nivvy followed Shantri to the stairs. "There's always more stories to share, an' who better to share them with?"

At the stair, the apprentice offered her hand to Nivvy, and he jumped up onto it, with Oigal, Zein, and Scarlet close behind. Shantri touched Nivvy's arm on the embroidered rose and said, "So the Knights of the Order of the Rose did live happily thereafter."

Nivvy peered up over her shoulder at Zein. "I dunno about 'thereafter,'" he said. "That's a long time."

"But we're living happily," Zein said.

"An' truthfully," Nivvy dropped his eyes to Shantri's smile, "who can ask for more than that?"

# ❧ V ❧
# APPENDIX: STORIES

# THE TALE OF PRIMROSE AND
## JUST-ROSE

L ong ago, but not so long as you might think, a simple
woodcutter lived with his wife beside the woods. They were
most desirous of children, yet had lived many years without
one. So the wife set out to seek counsel from an old witch who lived in
the nearby lake.

To speak to the witch, she brought a loaf of freshly-baked bread, a
freshly-killed chicken, and a stoppered jug of good wine or ale, and
threw each one into the lake, saying before each, "O Adalinda," (that
was the witch's name), "I bring this gift and I ask you nothing in
return." And after the third gift, she cut her finger and let three drops
of blood drip into the water of the lake.

Then Adalinda rose from the lake, an old crone with green weeds in
her hair and blue robes that rippled in the water. The wife asked her
how she and her husband might have children, and Adalinda told her:
"On the other side of the lake there is a tree that stands above all the
others. Climb to the top of that tree and you will find a nest with eggs
in it like smooth stones. Take as many eggs as you want children and
sleep with them under your pillow. In the morning you will have your
children."

So the woman did as she was told. She climbed the tallest tree on
the far side of the lake, and found a nest that contained two eggs, as
white and smooth as stones from the bottom of the lake. Carefully she

bundled the eggs into her dress and made her way home. That night she placed the eggs under her pillow as she slept.

She dreamed that she was standing by the lake and that two young girls walked out of it, one with golden hair and the other with bright red locks. And the girl with golden hair held out her hand and said, "I will be the first to arrive." And the girl with red hair, a step behind her, said, "I will be the first to leave."

When she woke, the eggs beneath her pillow had vanished, and one babe lay in her arms, and another lay on the bed beside her. So she named the one in her arms Primrose, because she had been first to arrive, and she named the other Rose, because of the red hair she'd seen in her dream.

So she and her husband lived happily with Primrose and Rose in that cottage beside the woods. Many who passed by the cottage became enchanted with the golden-haired Primrose and the red-haired Rose, and often it happened that upon meeting them, a stranger would say, "So this one is Primrose and this one is just Rose?" And after a time, Rose became known as "Just-Rose."

On the other side of the woods lay a forest, and as sunny and light as the woods were, the forest was sinister and dark. Primrose and Just-Rose had been warned many times not to stray beyond the stream that separated the wood from the forest, and though they often sat on its bank because they loved the sound the water made, they never even set foot in the stream.

Then one day when they had brought their lunch to eat by the water, a large bear appeared on the opposite bank. He held up one of his front paws as though it were injured and called out, "Girls, girls, please help me!"

Primrose said, "We cannot go into the forest; but come to this bank and we will help you."

"I cannot cross the stream," the bear said. "You must come over here."

"We are not allowed," Just-Rose called.

"Then alas, I must suffer all of my days," the bear called mournfully.

His cries tore at Primrose's soft heart. "We cannot allow an innocent creature to suffer," she cried, and heedless of her sister's warning, she forded the stream and made her way to the bear's side.

Immediately he snatched her up and ran back into the forest with her, leaving Just-Rose alone.

Now, Just-Rose was afraid to go back to her parents without her sister lest they blame her for Primrose's disappearance. So she forded the stream and made her way cautiously into the forest.

The thick trees crowded around her as she entered, and though the bear had been quite large, there was no sign of his passage. As Just-Rose pushed through the trees she heard a high cry of "Help, help!" that was quite close. Thinking it might be her sister, she ran to it and found a dove on her nest in the low branches of a tree, below which paced a fox. As Just-Rose drew nearer, the fox leapt to the branch and caught it.

"Oh kind girl!" cried the dove. "Please beat this cruel fox and save me and my family!"

But Just-Rose had a kind heart as well. "Sir Fox," she said, "I know you must be hungry. If I give you this cheese from my lunch, will you let Madame Dove and her family live?"

The fox demanded to see the cheese, and when Just-Rose drew it from her pocket, he let go the branch and agreed. So she fed him the cheese, and he said, "Because you showed kindness, I will help you in turn. If you wish to escape the forest, I can show you the way out."

"Dear Fox," Just-Rose said, "I seek my sister, who was captured by a bear."

"Ah," the fox said, "then he will have taken her to his lair. Pluck a hair from the very tip of my tail and it will point you true no matter where in the forest you are."

Just-Rose plucked one of the soft white hairs and held it upright, upon which it bent over as though blown by a wind. She walked on through the forest, following the direction it pointed, and after a space she heard again a cry of, "Help, help!"

Thinking that it must be her sister, she hurried toward the cry, only to find a serpent crushed under a rock. "Oh kind girl," the serpent cried, "Please move this rock and save me. I promise I will not bite you."

"I believe you," Just-Rose said, and pushed the rock so that the serpent could escape.

"Because you have helped me," the serpent said, "I will help you. If you are hungry, I can show you where to find food in the forest."

Just-Rose told her that she was going to the bear's lair to rescue her sister, and the serpent said, "As you approach the lair, you must bring the bear a gift of food or he will eat you straight away. Twenty paces in that direction you will find an apple tree: pick three apples and throw them to the bear and you will enter safely."

So Just-Rose found the apple tree and she picked the three reddest apples and put them in her pocket. And when she had walked a little farther following the fox's hair, she heard again a cry of "Help, help!"

Thinking that surely this time, it must be her sister, she hurried to the source of the cry and found a hawk trapped in a thorn bush. "Oh kind girl," the hawk said, "please free me from this bush!"

The hawk's beak and claws were sharp, but Just-Rose's kind heart won the day. She carefully disentangled the wings from the thorns, and presently pulled the hawk free from the bush.

"Thank you for your kindness, my dear," the hawk said. "Since you have helped me, I will help you. There are many treasures hidden in this forest; simply ask and I can tell you a spell to find one of them to bring home, and you may live like a queen for the rest of your days."

"I seek only my sister, who has been captured by a bear," Just-Rose replied.

"Then as I see you have the fox's hair and apples to offer the bear, I will give you this bit of advice: when you have fed the bear, you must utter the following words: *Thrice around the old oak tree, Show your truest self to me.* Then you may see what will happen."

"Thank you," Just-Rose said, and went on her way.

After a time, she could not say how long, she came upon a large mound of earth, taller than she was. No matter where she set her feet, to the north or south or east or west, the fox's hair pointed at the mound of earth. So she inspected it closely, but she could not find a way in.

Just-Rose settled down to watch the mound, and stayed there for a good long time, until presently a great hole opened in the earth, and out from it walked the bear. She would have confronted him then and there, but she had eaten two of the apples while waiting and did not have time to gather more. So when the bear had turned his back, she bravely ran into the hole before it closed up.

Inside she found no mound of earth but a tidy little home, with a large bed for the bear and a smaller bed next to it, a table set with dishes, a cupboard full of turnips and apples and plums and honeycomb and bread, and a warm stove in which a cheerful fire burned. And in front of the stove was Just-Rose's sister Primrose.

The two sisters fell into each other's arms. "Are you harmed?" Just-Rose asked.

"Not at all," Primrose told her. "He has told me that I must cook and clean and tend to his bed and I may never leave this place until his curse is broken. However did you find me?"

Just-Rose told her the story of her adventure, and recited the lines that she must say to the bear. "Oh thank you," Primrose said. "For he has told me that I may break his curse but that I must discover how to do it, and now I have."

She fed her sister bread with honey, and they passed a pleasant hour together. By and by, the ground trembled, and Primrose said, "The bear returns! Quick, sister, hide yourself in my bed and make no sound!"

Even though Just-Rose had braved the dangers of the forest herself, she saw that it was the wisest course for her, whom the bear did not know, to hide. So she ran to the small bed and threw the covers over herself and there lay very still.

The door parted and the fresh air of the forest blew in as the bear's heavy feet fell like tree trunks on the soft ground. "Hello, young Primrose," he said. "I have brought more grain to make bread, as you asked." Then he stopped, and Just-Rose heard him snuffling around the room. "What's this? There has been another here?"

"Never mind that," Primrose said.

"Have you betrayed me?" the bear roared.

Just-Rose almost threw back the covers then, fearing for her sister's life, but lifted just one corner so she could see. Her sister, brave Primrose, stood her ground and spoke the words the hawk had told Just-Rose, and she had passed on:

*Thrice around the old oak tree*
*Show your truest self to me*

To her surprise, the bear reared up on his hind legs and then spun three times in a circle. When he had completed the third time, a handsome dark-haired prince stood in his place. "Ah!" he cried. "You have released me from the spell!"

Primrose and the prince were married, and Just-Rose married the prince's brother, and so they were happy to the end of their days.

# THE TALE OF THE HONEST
# MERCHANT

O n the Isle of Ivory there dwelt a King who was renowned far
and wide for his fairness and justice, so much so that on the
longest day of every year he sent his servants out into his city
to find the person whose circumstances had fallen the lowest, that he
might hear their story and raise them up if there were cause.

One year it so happened that three of his servants each returned
with a person, and after discussing their misfortunes, they could not
decide which of them should be presented to the King, and so they
decided they must let the King hear each of their stories and decide for
himself.

The first servant was the second-oldest in the King's service. He
brought before the King a woman dressed in rags, her hair as grey as
ash. She knelt before the King and touched her forehead to the ground.
"Rise," said the King, "and pray you tell me your story, and leave
nothing out."

"Sire," she said, "I thank you for your indulgence in hearing my
tale. I was born not on this Isle, but on the Isle of the Crescent
Moon, the third daughter of the chief gardener to the Suzerain of the
Isle. When it came time for me to marry, I was courted by a sailor
whose father owned a fleet of ships and whose prospects were
excellent.

"We were married and had every hope for a fruitful life. My father
gave us a small cottage on the Isle of the Crescent Moon and my

husband carefully saved his sequins so that we might purchase a larger home here on the Isle of Ivory, where he had always dreamed of living.

"But only a year had passed before his father's fleet of ships were destroyed in a cyclone that passed between the Isles of the Crescent Moon and of the Wandering Star. By the grace of Aji, goddess of the sea, my husband was washed ashore on the Isle of the Wandering Star. There, with no money, he was forced to work for seven long years to make his way back to me. When he did, he had saved enough money to buy a single ship, and with that ship he worked for seven more years until he owned a fleet, and with that fleet he worked for seven more years until he had made enough money to purchase a house on the Isle of Ivory.

"We set sail from the Isle of the Crescent Moon, my husband and myself and our two children, and just as had happened three times seven years previous, a cyclone struck the fleet. Again, all the vessels were lost, and this time Aji claimed the lives of all except for me. I washed up on the shore of the Isle of Ivory with nothing but a board and a purse of twenty sequins to my name, my beautiful black hair turned grey, and since then I have wandered the streets searching for Aji's forgiveness, for I must have done her a terrible wrong to lose my family thus."

With that she bowed her head and touched the floor again, and on her knees retreated from the King's presence.

He signaled to his second servant to bring forward the second supplicant. The second servant, a young man whose father had served the King for seven times seven years, brought forward a man dressed in the plain robes of an acolyte, a fair-skinned man. The man knelt before the King and touched his forehead to the floor. "Rise," said the King, "and tell us your story."

The man rose and clasped his hands together. "Sire, I thank you for your indulgence in hearing my tale," he said. "I hope that this tale does not cause you distress, so sad is it.

"I also was not born on the Isle of Ivory, but in a land far to the north, as you can no doubt tell from my complexion. My parents owned several cattle and supplied milk and meat to many wealthy nobles in a prosperous city ruled by a just and wise king.

"One day, a month past my tenth year, my mother sent me to the hills to gather frostberries for my younger sister's birthday, for they were her favorite fruit and frostberries did not grow near us, but only up where Old Man Winter's feet touch the tops of the hills.

"I had gathered many berries and had stopped for a moment to lie down in a patch of sunlight. It seemed I had barely closed my eyes when I felt a deep rumble, as though a giant had set his foot down very close to me. When I got up, I did not perceive anything different, and so I thought it had been merely a clap of thunder, though the skies were clear and bright.

"But when I came to the edge of the forest and looked down upon where my city should be, it was gone as though it had never been. I cried out and ran along the path, but the path ended and there was nothing in front of me left of the place where I had lived, the family I had known, and the wise and just king who had ruled us. The earth had swallowed up the entire kingdom in a moment.

"For seven days and nights I waited and wept, but the kingdom did not return. At last, a caravan bound for my home arrived and, most perplexed, the drivers asked me whether they were lost. I told them that their destination had been lost.

"They took pity on me and took me south to their next destination, a thriving city on the sea, where a family took me in and fed me and clothed me and treated me as one of their own. I lived with them for many years, and when I was grown I fished with their boats.

"One day as I was fishing, I felt a strike upon my line. As I was accustomed to doing by then, I pulled on the line, but to my surprise the fish pulled back with great force and nearly spilled me out of the boat. It pulled so hard that it led my boat out into the ocean before I could think to cut my line, and once I was there I knew that my only chance was to wait for the fish to return to shallow water and then make my way to land.

"During this journey I had the chance to see the shadow of the fish that was pulling my boat, and I saw that it was no fish at all, but a great serpent ten times the length of my boat. It came to the surface once every day and regarded me with its great eye, and then set off again.

"We traveled for a day and a night before I saw land, and even then the serpent did not approach land until the following day. When I was close enough, I cut the line free and the serpent vanished, and I have never seen its like again. I made my way to the land, which proved to be the Isle of Ivory, and since then I have spent my life in contemplation to discover how it can be that I could lose two families in one lifetime."

He knelt, touched his head to the ground, and retreated.

The third servant, a man who had entered the King's service as a gift from a neighboring King, brought forward a man whose black beard was streaked with grey, whose turban was made of plain cloth yet impeccably arranged, whose robes were of the crudest material yet kept clean. This man knelt before the King and bowed so that his head touched the marble floor. "Rise," said the King, "and tell us your story."

The man bowed again. "Sire," he said, "thank you for your indulgence in hearing my tale. I hope it does not bring you undue distress."

"I was born on the Isle of Ivory, and with the help of my father and my own industry I began a trade as a merchant of fine cloth. I sailed to many different islands to gather the finest and brightest cloths, so that everyone might wear robes most pleasing to them. I married a wife, and we had a daughter who brought much joy to our home.

"For many years I sold my wares in the marketplaces of a dozen islands, and I knew my fellow merchants well. One day, many years ago, it happened that I was leaving crumbs for the mice in the marketplace, for I had learned that if the mice are fed crumbs, they would not destroy my wares. Two mice arrived and fed on the crumbs, and to my surprise I heard them speak. 'What fine food this is!' the first said to the other. 'Yes,' replied the second, 'it is a pity that that djinn has determined to destroy this market tomorrow to punish the greedy oil merchant who cheated him.' The first replied that they should eat all they could manage before that happened.

"Astonished, I left an entire honey-cake for the mice in gratitude and immediately set about taking down my wares and packing them carefully away. My fellow merchants were curious indeed, for the market had only just begun. I told them what I had heard and bade them also remove their wares. At first they did not believe me, but then the story reached the ears of the oil merchant. 'I did do business with a djinn,' he said, 'and though the bargain was fair, he was most displeased by it.' Then they believed my story and all the merchants took their wares to a secure warehouse. But we all concealed ourselves around the market, for none of us had seen a djinn and we were most desirous to, all except the oil merchant, who took a ship and departed that night.

"When the djinn arrived the next day, he appeared as a giant man with skin of lapis riding on a cloud that descended slowly into the empty marketplace. It was a fearsome sight, and the anger on his face was terrible to behold. We merchants all perceived at once that we had made a mistake in remaining to await his arrival, but we hoped that in finding an empty market, he would leave to seek the oil merchant elsewhere.

"Instead, his face grew even angrier and the cloud he rode upon roiled black, and he shouted, 'Why is there no market here?'

"Understanding at once that without a target, he might do great damage to the city, I stepped forward from my concealment and bowed before him. 'Great Djinn,' I said, 'I heard of your plans and, wishing to spare my own life and that of my fellows, I warned the market of your destruction. I pray you show me mercy, for my intentions were honorable; but if you cannot, then make me alone the recipient of your rage.'

"He reached down and picked me up in one hand. 'I shall do both,' he roared. 'You will bear my rage, but in mercy I will not end your life.' And saying thus, he threw me through the air so quickly that ocean and islands blurred below me and ships on the water appeared frozen in place.

"I landed so roughly that both my legs broke instantly. Fortunately, or perhaps by design of the djinn, the island upon which I landed was inhabited by two tribes, who, perceiving my need, took me in and fed me and allowed my legs to heal. This island lay far to the south, so far that the stars were unfamiliar to me and I despaired of ever seeing my home and family again.

"And yet this island was not unknown to ships. Once every year a ship would arrive from some foreign nation to gather the fruit and nuts that grew in abundance on the island, and sometimes trade with the natives. I approached these ships and asked for passage to the Empire of the Isles, and in every case the answer was the same: 'Will you forsake your god and follow ours? If only you will do so, we will take you with us when we depart, but we are under orders to bring nobody onto our ship who does not follow our god.' 'Alas,' I replied, 'I cannot forswear my faith to Massi, the patron of merchants.' 'Then we must leave you behind,' they said, 'for this Massi is unknown to us.'

"On the seventh year, a ship arrived, and when I spoke the name of Massi they cried out in delight. 'Then you are a fellow of ours, for we follow Aji who lives below the waves!' Then we embraced and they welcomed me aboard with good hearts.

"For seven months we sailed back to the Empire of the Isles, so far did the djinn throw me, and finally I returned to the Isle of Ivory. But my wife had married another and thought me dead, and my daughter had grown and forgotten me, and neither of them would speak to me nor believe that I was returned, no matter how many petitions I made to them. Since then I have taken work cutting cloth for other merchants in the hope that I may one day rebuild my trade. And still my wife and daughter come to buy cloth, and do not recognize me, and will not speak to me."

Having concluded his story, he knelt, touched his head to the ground, and retreated from the King.

Then the King addressed the gathered crowd, many of whom were weeping at the misery of the tales they had heard. "My heart is heavy," he said, "for never have I heard three stories so tragic told in the same place. In any other year, I am certain that any one of these supplicants would receive my mercy, but this year my custom forces me to choose one. Therefore I have come to the following decision."

He extended his hand to the third supplicant, the merchant. "You have suffered misfortune," he said, "but at every turn of your story you displayed virtue. You showed charity in warning your fellow merchants; you showed honesty in confronting the djinn; you showed faith in remaining true to Massi; you have shown industry in accepting even menial labor to rebuild your trade. Therefore I judge you to be a man worthy beyond your station, and I shall offer you my daughter's hand in marriage, that you might rule the kingdom in my place when I am gone with all the justice to which my people have become accustomed."

Then the merchant bowed again, weeping so greatly that his tears collected on the floor below him. "Great King," he said, "your mercy is wise and kind. I will happily accept your daughter's hand. May I ask a boon of you, as your future son?"

The King could not refuse anything, so he bade the man continue. "I ask," said the former merchant, "that I may be allowed to take seven hundred sequins from the royal treasury, and that I might speak to the High Priest of the Great Temple here on the Isle of Ivory."

"Of course you may," the King said with some surprise. "But pray, reveal the reasons behind these requests, that I may understand them better."

The former merchant indicated his fellow supplicants. "The seven hundred sequins are for this poor woman, that she may finally have her home and live in comfort for the rest of her days. And the audience with the High Priest is to ask him to take this man into his employ, for surely if any answers to his plight may be found, it will be at the Great Temple."

The King granted his wishes, and all three of the supplicants lived well after that. And when that King passed, his son ruled with the same fairness and justice, and so the Isle of Ivory has been known since that day.

# THE STORY OF TALI'A MA

Once long ago on the island of Kotala, there was a prosperous merchant named Tali'a Ma. He bought spices from surrounding islands and sold spice and perfume to the nobility of Kotala. Thanks to his charming and canny nature, he built his trade up to surpass all others on Kotala, and even became known as far as The Sun Kingdom. He was known to be shrewd but fair, funny yet honest, and in general a remarkable man as well as a skilled merchant.

As is the way of human nature, the other merchants on Kotala became jealous of him, and his greatest rival, a powerful man named Bodrin Da, paid a steep price to engage the services of a djinn. It is very difficult to find a djinn, and more difficult still to survive an encounter, but Bodrin Da was a man of significant will.

When he had paid his price (it was a terrible price and let that be all that is said of it), he asked the djinn to remove his enemy, "the infernal Tali'a Ma," as he called him. But the djinn cautioned him that his price had not bought unlimited favors.

A better merchant, you may think, would have negotiated the service before paying the price, but so great was Bodrin Da's jealousy and hatred that he had failed to do this. So he had no choice but to listen to the djinn's pronouncement: "I may turn him into an animal. Thus will his business fall to his second, the less intelligent Algiri, as if he were dead."

"Very well," said Bodrin Da. "Then turn him into a cat, for cats are despised on Kotala. If he were to be a mouse, he might escape into my storehouses and do mischief; if he became a dog or a horse he might win favor with some lord and thus rescue his business. But if he is a cat, no lord will take him in, and I may drown him and be rid of him forever."

"So it shall be done," spoke the djinn. "He will be transformed in the moment the sun next rises. But mind you attend and catch him just after the transformation, when he will be most confused, else you may never be sure which cat is him."

"I shall," Bodrin Da promised. And he intended to do that very thing, wicked man that he was. He waited outside Tali'a Ma's chambers all night with eyes on the sunrise. But he fell asleep and so when Tali'a Ma woke as a cat and jumped out the window in his fright, he ran past his enemy, neither of them aware of the other.

Now Tali'a Ma was clever and soon understood his predicament. The djinn's magic had given him the form of a cat, but he retained his human voice. However, he soon found that nobody would listen to a talking cat: he was chased away from homes with brooms and sticks.

But Tali'a Ma was resourceful even when he had nothing. He had started his trade from nothing and so now he started over again. The other cats mistrusted him, but Tali'a Ma knew the ways of the market-place and could open doors that were closed to cats, and so he went into the market in the dead of night when there were only mice there and he ate his fill of fish heads and offal. Then he brought a fish head back to the other cats and said, "If you follow me, there will be this and more every night, and you will never feel the tightness of your ribs around empty bellies."

The cats murmured among themselves that he had only brought one fish head, but they observed that he had a full belly and therefore must know where there were more. So they agreed to follow him, and he led them to the marketplace and the tables where fish were cleaned and gutted, and there all the cats fed as they never had before.

Now, it was also the custom of the cats to fight with the sea-birds for a share of what the humans had left behind. But now that the cats were eating the offal at the marketplace before it was thrown to the garbage heap, there was no more fighting between bird and cat. So

Tali'a Ma went to the birds and said, "Birds, now you may eat in peace. In return I ask only a small favor, that if I sit here as you eat, you tell me of the ships you see arriving from distant lands."

The birds, who liked to talk anyway, agreed that this was fair, and from then on the sea-birds brought him information about ships that came and went, and the cats brought him information about how people moved through the city.

By now, Bodrin Da had become the foremost merchant in Kotala and he had declared that all cats must be put to death. But Tali'a Ma, who could read the proclamations posted on the streets, warned the cats to keep to the shadows and not to trust any humans, and thus kept his faithful alive.

Tali'a Ma had greater plans than merely remaining alive. He and his cats began to steal from Bodrin Da's warehouses. A bag of spice here, a bottle of oil there, things they stored in an empty house that the cats told Tali'a Ma of. At this time, Tali'a Ma befriended a monkey who could use a pen, and with the monkey's help he crafted letters to Bodrin Da's rivals. He told them when Bodrin Da's ships were near and what they were carrying, and he signed the letters, "The Shadow of Kotala."

He gave the best information to his old friend Algiri and began to send him separate letters about how to manage the trade. And soon, Algiri had recovered many of his losses and began to again rival Bodrin Da for supremacy in Kotala.

All the while Tali'a Ma observed and used his information to great effect, so much so that Bodrin Da became furious with this "Shadow of Kotala" who evaded all his informants and slaves. He grew so desperate at the loss of his trade that he summoned the djinn once again. "Find the Shadow of Kotala and bring him to me!" he commanded.

He had once again brought the djinn's terrible price, which cost him not in gold but in his soul, and so the djinn obliged. He brought every cat in Kotala to Bodrin Da's chamber and said, "There; I have brought the Shadow of Kotala to you."

Bodrin Da was lost in the sea of cats. "Tell me which one he is!" he shrieked. "I will kill him myself!"

But the djinn said, "You no longer have the power to command me, and I find your insolence less entertaining than it was." And with that, he turned the wicked merchant into a mouse.

The cats set upon Bodrin Da immediately and devoured him so thoroughly that there was not a scrap of hide left. And thus assured of the death of his greatest enemy, Tali'a Ma revealed himself to Algiri, and became known as the Cat Merchant of Kotala. And if you visit Kotala today you will find cats on every street, for they are held in high regard by the Kotalans.

# THE TALE OF THE LITTLE
## DOUGH-BOY

Once in a small town far from here, there lived two bakers, Ada and Oda, who lived together and baked together and were well loved by all the town. But one day Oda fell sick and then perished, leaving Ada by herself.

Ada wept for many days, but the town needed bread, and so on the eighth day she returned to the kitchen. First, she decided, she would make some crescent rolls, because they had been Oda's favorite. Even as she kneaded the dough, she wept, and into one of the rolls eight of her tears fell.

At once that roll sprang to life in the shape of a little dough-boy. "Hello, Mother," he said. "Why do you cry?"

Ada was afraid at first, but the dough-boy's warm manner and cheerful smile won her over quickly. "I am crying for my dear Oda," she said, "who has left me eight days ago."

The little dough-boy put a small hand on her finger and said, "Tell me about her."

And so Ada told him about Oda while she made the rolls, and by the time they had finished baking, she had decided to name him Ludo, which meant the crescent moon.

Ludo and Ada baked for many more years, and all the town came to know and love the little dough-boy, for his mother raised him to be generous of spirit. He had a smile for the old and a kind word for the young, questions for the scholars and sympathy for the laborers.

Though the town missed Oda, they said that Ludo had added joy to Ada's bread and cakes, and people came from neighboring towns to sample them.

Eventually, as must happen to us all, Ada died, and when Ludo and the town had mourned her, the little dough-boy decided that it was time he make his way in the world. "The king is said to be the most just person in the world, and I would like to meet him," he said, "so that way I shall go." So the tailor made him a smart little outfit and the weaver sewed him a bundle to keep his possessions in, and the blacksmith made him a little knife to protect himself, and off he went into the world.

At the first village he stopped in, he was greeted with wonder and made many friends, but there was one person who seemed sad despite the dough-boy's good cheer. "Pray tell, my friend, what troubles you?" the dough-boy asked.

"I am a wood-carver," said the man, "and much celebrated for my fine detail work. But my smallest knife broke, and I haven't time to travel to the nearest blacksmith for a new one before this very important piece is to be done!"

"Why, I have a small knife right here," said Ludo, and with his dough-hand he held it out. "You may take it if you like."

"I could not take your only knife," the carver said.

"Nonsense!" The dough-boy smiled. "I have little need of it. Do I look like a fighter?"

"Then thank you," the carver said. "If you stay but a month, I will return it to you."

"A month! No, I am off to see the king. But perhaps I will return this way."

And Ludo said his farewells and went on his way.

He passed through several more villages, spreading good cheer and kindness, and eventually came upon a road that led to a castle. Wanting to see the King, he followed it to a bridge where he found a young woman weeping. "Pray tell, my dear, what troubles you?" he said.

She showed him a doll covered in mud. "This doll belongs to the princess," she said. "I am her servant, and I was meant to bring it to her as a gift, but I have soiled all its clothes. If I bring it to her in this state, I'll be whipped!"

"Why, I have just the solution for you," said the dough-boy, and he removed his clothes. "I wager these clothes will fit your doll. Now there's no need for you to be whipped."

"I can't take your clothes," protested the servant girl.

"Of course you can! I have little need of them. Do I look like a noble?" And he insisted until she dressed the doll in his clothes, and it looked as good as new.

"How can I ever thank you?" she asked him, overcome with delight.

"I would like to meet the king," he said. "Can you bring me to him?"

"Of course I may," the girl said, and gathered him up in her arms. "He will be delighted to meet you."

She carried him into the castle where he met the other servants and charmed all of them, and met the princess and charmed her as well. She brought him to meet her father the king, and before this great man the dough-boy was humbled. "Your Majesty," he said, "I would provide you any service it is in my power to."

The king looked at the dough-boy, and without his clothes and without his knife he looked just like a crescent roll. "I'm hungry," said the king, "and supper is an hour away still." And he reached for the dough-boy.

"Well," said the dough-boy, "if the king is hungry, then I must fill his belly for him." And he allowed the king to eat him all up, and that was the end of the kind little dough-boy.

# NOTES

## 4. THE STORIES AT THE OASIS

1. See Appendix for full story.
2. See Appendix for full story.

## 12. BREAKING THE CURSE

1. See Appendix for full story.

## 37. THE ROSE BUSH

1. See Appendix for the full story.

# ACKNOWLEDGMENTS

This novel was serialized on my Patreon page at http://www.patreon.com/timsusman, and has been supported by the following members, to whom I owe great thanks: Furiia, John Hawley, Kanashio Koroshi, Kario Tojima, Marcwolf, Mevolas, Philip Ribbs, Shader, Stephan Harman, and tav fox.

❧

In the decade-plus that I've been working on this story, a number of people have been instrumental in helping shape it:

Kij Johnson and Barbara Webb's Novel Architects workshop provided structure and helpful discussion in the early outlining stages. In addition to Kij and Barb, Luke Tolvaj and Jerry Seeger from that workshop also contributed above and beyond (the idea that spells could be stories came initially from Jerry).

Alisa Alering, Dayna Smith, Brooke Wonders, Becky Wright, Ryan Campbell, David Cowan, Watts Martin, and Malcolm Cross all read the novel in various stages. Their feedback is represented in large and small ways throughout the story.

I am indebted to Mark Harrison at Argyll Productions, whose enthusiasm and trust allows me to drop a whopping great fantasy novel in his lap, and whose dedication to recognizing underrepresented voices inspires me every day.

And none of this would be possible without Mark and Jack, my co-authors in the story we continue to tell, and the best companions any little forest creature could possibly hope for. Not to mention our faithful dog Kobalt, whose story we only know part of, but who has become integral to ours. Wherever you find your family, I hope you are as lucky as I have been.

# ABOUT THE AUTHOR

Tim Susman started a novel in college and didn't finish one until almost twenty years later. In that time, he earned a degree in Zoology, worked with Jane Goodall, co-founded Sofawolf Press, and moved to California. He has attended Clarion in 2011 (arooo to my Narwolves!) and published short stories in *Apex*, *Lightspeed*, and *ROAR*, among others. He also publishes under the name Kyell Gold, and has won several awards for his furry fiction. In 2016 he helped found RAWR, the writing workshop for furry writers, and has taught there since its founding. You can find out more about his stories at *timsusman.word press.com* and *www.kyellgold.com* and follow him on Twitter (for now) at @WriterFox or @Kyellgold, and on Mastodon at @KyellGold@furries.club.

𝕏 x.com/writerfox

❘● patreon.com/timsusman

ⓜ furries.club/@kyellgold

# ALSO BY TIM SUSMAN

If you would like to get monthly updates on upcoming publications, excerpts of works in progress, and writing tips, sign up for his mailing list (your e-mail address will not be sold or used for anything else).

## New Tibet

***Breaking The Ice: Stories from New Tibet*** (editor) - On a hostile ice planet, survival is guaranteed to nobody.

***Shadows in Snow*** (editor) - More stories from the unforgiving ice world of New Tibet.

***Common and Precious*** - A kidnapped heiress comes to sympathize with her desperate captors, while her father discovers the limits of his power in trying to rescue her.

***Patterns in Frost*** - Return to the world of New Tibet with six more stories.

## The Calatians

***Book 1: The Tower and the Fox*** - Kip and his friends encounter prejudice and mysteries in their first few months at Prince George's College of Sorcery.

***Book 2: The Demon and the Fox*** - The forces of revolution grow in Massachusetts as Kip and his friends rush to solve the mystery of the attack on the College of Sorcery.

***Book 3: The War and the Fox*** - Kip and his friends are drafted into the fight for independence from Britain, but there is more at stake.

***Book 4: The Revolution and the Fox*** - Two years after the war, Kip and his friends face their greatest threat yet.

## Other books

***Unfinished Business*** — A detective uncovers a plot against him and must turn to his werewolf ex-boyfriend for help.

***The Price of Thorns*** - A down-on-his-luck thief meets the actual evil queen from many fairy tales when she offers him the job of a lifetime. (Coming 2022)

## WRITING AS KYELL GOLD:

### Love Match

***Love Match (vol. 1, 2008-2010)*** — Rocky arrives in the States from Africa and navigates the treacherous worlds of professional tennis and high school.

***Love Match (vol. 2, 2010-2012)*** — Rocky begins his professional career, at the cost of his family and romantic relationships.

***Love Match (vol. 3, 2013-2015)*** — As his career trends upward, Rocky's romantic life becomes less stable.

### Out of Position (Dev and Lee)

***Out of Position*** – Dev the football player and Lee the gay activist discover how to navigate their relationship. *(mature readers)*

***Isolation Play*** – The continuing story of Dev and Lee, as they contend with family and friends in their search for acceptance. *(mature readers)*

***Divisions*** – As Dev's team fights to make the playoffs, Lee fights to keep his sense of self. *(mature readers)*

***Uncovered*** – The playoffs are here, and Dev needs his focus more than ever. So when Lee becomes too distracting, something has to give. *(mature readers)*

***Over Time*** – Dev and Lee try to plan their future while dealing with crises all around them. *(mature readers)*

***Ty Game*** — Dev's teammate Ty navigates an arranged marriage while also falling in love. *(mature readers)*

***Tales of the Firebirds*** — A collection of stories exploring the lives of some of the other characters from the Out of Position series. *(mature readers)*

***Titles*** – In the two weeks leading up to Dev's third try at a championship, Dev and Lee face new challenges and changes in their lives. *(mature readers)*

### Dangerous Spirits

***Green Fairy*** – A gay high school senior struggling through his final year finds a strange old book that changes his dreams and his life.

***Red Devil*** – A gay fox who fled his abusive family in Siberia seeks help from a ghost who demands he give up his gay lifestyle.

***Black Angel*** – A young otter struggles to understand her sexuality as her friends prepare for post-high school life and dreams of women in other times plague her.

## Argaea

***Volle*** – The story of how Volle came to Tephos, a spy masquerading as a noble, and the first adventure he had there. *(mature readers)*

***The Prisoner's Release and Other Stories*** – The story of how Volle escaped from prison, and the story of what happened after, plus two other stories following characters from "Volle." *(mature readers)*

***Pendant of Fortune*** – Volle returns to Tephos to defend his honor, but soon finds himself fighting for much more. *(mature readers)*

***Shadow of the Father*** – Volle's son, Yilon, must travel to the far-off land he is meant to rule, but he will have to fight treachery to take the lordship. *(mature readers)*

***Weasel Presents*** – Five short stories from the land of Argaea, including "Helfer's Busy Day" and "Yilon's Journal." *(mature readers)*

***Return From Divalia*** — Years after a night of adventure ruined his life, a young wolf gets a chance at redemption. *(mature readers, coming 2022)*

## Forester Universe

***Waterways*** – The full story of Kory's journey to understand himself and what it means to be gay. *(mature readers)*

***Bridges*** – Hayward seems content to set up pairs of his friends. But what does he really need for himself? *(mature readers)*

***Science Friction*** – Vaxy never took sex seriously, until he found out the professor he was sleeping with was married... *(mature readers)*

***Winter Games*** – Sierra Snowpaw was an unsure high school student when someone he thought was a friend changed his life. Now he's fifteen years older and still looking for answers. *(mature readers)*

***The Mysterious Affair of Giles*** – A servant in a British manor house tries to solve a murder.

***Dude, Where's My Fox?*** – Lonnie chases down a fox he hooked up with at a party as a way to get over his breakup. *(mature readers)*

***Dude, Where's My Pack?*** — Lonnie tries to navigate relationships old and new. *(mature readers)*

***Losing My Religion*** – On tour with his R.E.M. cover band, Jackson mentors the new guy in the band as his own life falls apart. *(mature readers)*

***The Time He Desires*** — A Muslim immigrant struggles with the betrayal of his son and the dissolution of his marriage, as well as his own long-past trauma.

***Camouflage*** — When Danilo is sent 500 years into the past, he must choose between safety in an unfamiliar world and his own sense of what is right. *(mature readers)*

## Other Books

***The Silver Circle*** – Valerie thought the old hunter was crazy when he warned her about werewolves—until she met one.

***In the Doghouse of Justice*** – Seven stories of superheroes and their not-so-super relationships. *(mature readers)*

***Twelve Sides*** — Twelve short stories about side characters from the above books. *(mature readers)*

***Do You Need Help?*** — Writing advice for furry (and non-furry) writers.

Printed in the USA
CPSIA information can be obtained
at www.ICGtesting.com
LVHW022139061123
763206LV00050B/626